Brenna Higham.

The Green Gables Collection

THE ANNE OF GREEN GABLES NOVELS

Anne of Green Gables
Anne of Avonlea
Anne of the Island
Anne of Windy Poplars
Anne's House of Dreams
Anne of Ingleside
Rainbow Valley
Rilla of Ingleside

THE EMILY BOOKS

Emily of New Moon
Emily Climbs
Emily's Quest

L. M. MONTGOMERY

The GREEN GABLES COLLECTION

Anne of Green Gables

Anne of Avonlea

Anne of the Island

DOUBLEDAY CANADA

To the memory of my Father and Mother

This edition contains the complete texts of the original hardcover editions.

Anne of Green Gables copyright © 1908 L.C. Page & Company, Inc.
Copyright renewed 1935 by L.C. Page & Company, Inc.
Anne of Avonlea copyright © 1909 L.C. Page & Company, Inc.
Copyright renewed 1936 by L.C. Page & Company, Inc.
Anne of the Island copyright © 1915 L.C. Page & Company, Inc.
Copyright renewed 1943 by Ewan Macdonald

Doubleday Canada edition published 2008

All rights reserved. The use of any part of this publication, reproduced,
 transmitted in any form or by any means electronic, mechanical, photocopying,
recording or otherwise, or stored in a retrieval system without the prior written
consent of the publisher—or in the case of photocopying or other reprographic
copying, license from the Canadian Copyright Licensing agency—is an
infringement of the copyright law.

Anne of Green Gables and other images of "Anne" are trademarks and
Canadian official marks of the Anne of Green Gables Licensing Authority Inc.,
which is owned by the heirs of L.M. Montgomery and the Province of
Prince Edward Island and located in Charlottetown, Prince Edward Island.

Doubleday Canada and colophon are trademarks

Library and Archives of Canada Cataloguing in Publication has been
applied for

ISBN: 978-0-385-66599-5

This book is a work of fiction. Names, characters, places and incidents are
products of the author's imagination or are used fictitiously. Any resemblance
to actual events or locales or persons, living or dead, is entirely coincidental.

Printed and bound in the USA

Published in Canada by Doubleday Canada,
a division of Random House of Canada Limited

Visit Random House of Canada Limited's website: www.randomhouse.ca

RRD 10 9 8 7 6 5 4 3 2 1

ONTENTS

ANNE of GREEN GABLES

The good stars met in your horoscope,
Made you of spirit and fire and dew.

BROWNING

CONTENTS

1

Mrs. Rachel Lynde is Surprised

Mrs. Rachel Lynde lived just where the Avonlea main road dipped down into a little hollow, fringed with alders and ladies' eardrops and traversed by a brook that had its source away back in the woods of the old Cuthbert place; it was reputed to be an intricate, headlong brook in its earlier course through those woods, with dark secrets of pool and cascade; but by the time it reached Lynde's Hollow it was a quiet, well-conducted little stream, for not even a brook could run past Mrs. Rachel Lynde's door without due regard for decency and decorum; it probably was conscious that Mrs. Rachel was sitting at her window, keeping a sharp eye on everything that passed, from brooks and children up, and that if she noticed anything odd or out of place she would never rest until she had ferreted out the whys and wherefores thereof.

There are plenty of people, in Avonlea and out of it, who can attend closely to their neighbor's business by dint of neglecting their own; but Mrs. Rachel Lynde was one of those capable creatures who can manage their own concerns and those of other folks into the bargain. She was a notable housewife; her work was always done and well done; she "ran" the Sewing Circle, helped run the Sunday-school, and was the strongest prop of the Church Aid Society and Foreign Missions Auxiliary. Yet with all this Mrs. Rachel found abundant time to sit for hours at her kitchen window, knitting "cotton warp" quilts—she had knitted sixteen of them, as Avonlea housekeepers were wont to tell in awed voices—and keeping a sharp eye on the main road that crossed the hollow and wound up the steep red hill beyond. Since Avonlea occupied a little triangular peninsula jutting out into the Gulf of St. Lawrence, with water on two sides of it, anybody who went out of it or into it had to pass over that hill road and so run the unseen gauntlet of Mrs. Rachel's all-seeing eye.

She was sitting there one afternoon in early June. The sun was coming in at the window warm and bright; the orchard on the slope below the house was in a bridal flush of pinky-white bloom, hummed over by a myriad of bees. Thomas Lynde—a meek little man whom Avonlea people called "Rachel Lynde's husband"—was sowing his late turnip seed on the hill field beyond the barn; and Matthew Cuthbert ought to have been sowing his on the big red brook field away over by Green Gables. Mrs. Rachel knew that he ought because she had heard him tell Peter Morrison the evening before in William J. Blair's store over at Carmody that he meant to sow his turnip seed the next afternoon. Peter had asked him, of course, for Matthew Cuthbert had never been known to volunteer information about anything in his whole life.

And yet here was Matthew Cuthbert, at half-past three on the afternoon of a busy day, placidly driving over the hollow and up the hill; moreover, he wore a white collar and his best suit of clothes, which was plain proof that he was going out of Avonlea; and he had the buggy and the sorrel mare, which betokened that he was going a considerable distance. Now, where was Matthew Cuthbert going and why was he going there?

Had it been any other man in Avonlea Mrs. Rachel, deftly putting this and that together, might have given a pretty good guess as to both questions. But Matthew so rarely went from home that it must be something pressing and unusual which was taking him; he was the shyest man alive and hated to have to go among strangers or to any place where he might have to talk. Matthew, dressed up with a white collar and driving in a buggy, was something that didn't happen often. Mrs. Rachel, ponder as she might, could make nothing of it and her afternoon's enjoyment was spoiled.

"I'll just step over to Green Gables after tea and find out from Marilla where he's gone and why," the worthy woman finally concluded. "He doesn't generally go to town this time of year and he *never* visits; if he'd run out of turnip seed he wouldn't dress up and take the buggy to go for more; he wasn't driving fast enough to be going for the doctor. Yet something must have happened since last night to start him off. I'm clean puzzled, that's what, and I won't know a minute's peace of mind or conscience until I know what has taken Matthew Cuthbert out of Avonlea today."

Accordingly after tea Mrs. Rachel set out; she had not far to go; the big, rambling, orchard-embowered house where the Cuthberts lived was a scant quarter of a mile up the road from Lynde's Hollow. To be sure, the long lane made it a good deal further. Matthew Cuthbert's father, as shy and silent as his son after him, had got as far away as he possibly could from his fellow men without actually retreating into the woods when he founded his homestead. Green Gables was built at the furthest edge of his cleared land and there it was to this day, barely visible from the main road along which all the other Avonlea houses were so sociably situated. Mrs. Rachel Lynde did not call living in such a place *living* at all.

"It's just *staying*, that's what," she said as she stepped along the deep-rutted, grassy lane bordered with wild rose bushes. "It's no wonder Matthew and Marilla are both a little odd, living away back here by themselves. Trees aren't much company, though dear knows if they were there'd be enough of them. I'd ruther look at people. To be sure, they seem contented enough; but then, I suppose, they're used to it. A body can get used to anything, even to being hanged, as the Irishman said."

With this Mrs. Rachel stepped out of the lane into the backyard of Green Gables. Very green and neat and precise was that yard, set about on one side with great patriarchal willows and on the other with prim Lombardies. Not a stray stick nor stone was to be seen, for Mrs. Rachel would have seen it if there had been. Privately she was of the opinion that Marilla Cuthbert swept that yard over as often as she swept her house. One could have eaten a meal off the ground without overbrimming the proverbial peck of dirt.

Mrs. Rachel rapped smartly at the kitchen door and stepped in when bidden to do so. The kitchen at Green Gables was a cheerful apartment—or would have been cheerful if it had not been so painfully clean as to give it something of the appearance of an unused parlor. Its windows looked east and west; through the west one, looking out on the back yard, came a flood of mellow June sunlight; but the east one, whence you got a glimpse of the bloom white cherry trees in the left orchard and nodding, slender birches down in the hollow by the brook, was greened over by a tangle of vines. Here sat Marilla Cuthbert, when she sat at all, always slightly distrustful of sunshine, which seemed to her too dancing and irresponsible a thing for a world which was meant to be taken seriously; and here she sat now, knitting, and the table behind her was laid for supper.

Mrs. Rachel, before she had fairly closed the door, had taken mental note of everything that was on that table. There were three plates laid, so that Marilla must be expecting some one home with Matthew to tea; but the dishes were every-day dishes and there was only crab apple preserves and one kind of cake, so that the expected company could not be any particular company. Yet what of Matthew's white collar and the sorrel mare? Mrs. Rachel was getting fairly dizzy with this unusual mystery about quiet, unmysterious Green Gables.

"Good evening, Rachel," Marilla said briskly. "This is a real fine evening, isn't it? Won't you sit down? How are all your folks?"

Something that for lack of any other name might be called friendship existed and always had existed between Marilla Cuthbert and Mrs. Rachel, in spite of—or perhaps because of—their dissimilarity.

Marilla was a tall, thin woman, with angles and without curves; her dark hair showed some gray streaks and was always twisted up in a hard little knot behind with two wire hairpins stuck aggressively through it. She looked like a woman of narrow experience and rigid conscience, which she was; but there was a saving something about her mouth which, if it had been ever so slightly developed, might have been considered indicative of a sense of humor.

"We're all pretty well," said Mrs. Rachel. "I was kind of afraid you weren't, though, when I saw Matthew starting off today. I thought maybe he was going to the doctor's."

Marilla's lips twitched understandingly. She had expected Mrs. Rachel up; she had known that the sight of Matthew jaunting off so unaccountably would be too much for her neighbor's curiosity.

"Oh, no, I'm quite well although I had a bad headache yesterday," she said. "Matthew went to Bright River. We're getting a little boy from an orphan asylum in Nova Scotia and he's coming on the train tonight."

If Marilla had said that Matthew had gone to Bright River to meet a kangaroo from Australia Mrs. Rachel could not have been more astonished. She was actually stricken dumb for five seconds. It was unsupposable that Marilla was making fun of her, but Mrs. Rachel was almost forced to suppose it.

"Are you in earnest, Marilla?" she demanded when voice returned to her.

"Yes, of course," said Marilla, as if getting boys from orphan asylums in Nova Scotia were part of the usual spring work on any well-regulated Avonlea farm instead of being an unheard of innovation.

Mrs. Rachel felt that she had received a severe mental jolt. She thought in exclamation points. A boy! Marilla and Matthew Cuthbert of all people adopting a boy! From an orphan asylum! Well, the world was certainly turning upside down! She would be surprised at nothing after this! Nothing!

"What on earth put such a notion into your head?" she demanded disapprovingly.

This had been done without her advice being asked, and must perforce be disapproved.

"Well, we've been thinking about it for some time—all winter in fact," returned Marilla. "Mrs. Alexander Spencer was up here one day before Christmas and she said she was going to get a little girl from the asylum over in Hopetown in the spring. Her cousin lives there and Mrs. Spencer has visited her and knows all about it. So Matthew and I have talked it over off and on ever since. We thought we'd get a boy. Matthew is getting up in years, you know—he's sixty—and he isn't so spry as he once was. His heart troubles him a good deal. And you know how desperate hard it's got to be to get hired help. There's never anybody to be had but those stupid, half-grown little French boys; and as soon as you do get one broke into your ways and taught something he's up and off to the lobster canneries or the States. At first Matthew suggested getting a

Barnado boy. But I said 'no' flat to that. 'They may be all right—I'm not saying they're not—but no London street Arabs for me,' I said. 'Give me a native born at least. There'll be a risk, no matter who we get. But I'll feel easier in my mind and sleep sounder at nights if we get a born Canadian.' So in the end we decided to ask Mrs. Spencer to pick us out one when she went over to get her little girl. We heard last week she was going, so we sent her word by Richard Spencer's folks at Carmody to bring us a smart, likely boy of about ten or eleven. We decided that would be the best age—old enough to be of some use in doing chores right off and young enough to be trained up proper. We mean to give him a good home and schooling. We had a telegram from Mrs. Alexander Spencer today—the mail man brought it from the station—saying they were coming on the five-thirty train tonight. So Matthew went to Bright River to meet him. Mrs. Spencer will drop him off there. Of course she goes on to White Sands station herself."

Mrs. Rachel prided herself on always speaking her mind; she proceeded to speak it now, having adjusted her mental attitude to this amazing piece of news.

"Well, Marilla, I'll just tell you plain that I think you're doing a mighty foolish thing—a risky thing, that's what. You don't know what you're getting. You're bringing a strange child into your house and home and you don't know a single thing about him nor what his disposition is like nor what sort of parents he had nor how he's likely to turn out. Why, it was only last week I read in the paper how a man and his wife up west of the Island took a boy out of an orphan asylum and he set fire to the house at night—set it *on purpose,* Marilla—and nearly burnt them to a crisp in their beds. And I know another case where an adopted boy used to suck the eggs—they couldn't break him of it. If you had asked my advise in the matter—which you didn't do, Marilla—I'd have said for mercy's sake not to think of such a thing, that's what."

This Job's comforting seemed neither to offend nor alarm Marilla. She knitted steadily on.

"I don't deny there's something in what you say, Rachel. I've had some qualms myself. But Matthew was terrible set on it. I could see that, so I gave in. It's so seldom Matthew sets his mind on anything that when he does I always feel it's my duty to give in. And as for the risk, there's risks in pretty near everything a body does in this world. There's risks in people's having children of their own if it comes to that—they don't always turn out well. And then Nova Scotia is right close to the Island. It isn't as if we were getting him from England or the States. He can't be much different from ourselves."

"Well, I hope it will turn out all right," said Mrs. Rachel in a tone that plainly indicated her painful doubts. "Only don't say I didn't warn you if he burns Green Gables down or puts strychnine in the well—I heard of a case over in New Brunswick where an orphan asylum child did that and the whole family died in fearful agonies. Only, it was a girl in that instance."

"Well, we're not getting a girl," said Marilla, as if poisoning wells were a purely feminine accomplishment and not to be dreaded in the case of a boy. "I'd never dream of taking a girl to bring up. I wonder at Mrs. Alexander Spencer for doing it. But there, *she* wouldn't shrink from adopting a whole orphan asylum if she took it into her head."

Mrs. Rachel would have liked to stay until Matthew came home with his imported orphan. But reflecting that it would be a good two hours at least before his arrival she concluded to go up the road to Robert Bell's and tell them the news. It would certainly make a sensa-tion second to none, and Mrs. Rachel dearly loved to make a sensation. So she took herself away, somewhat to Marilla's relief, for the latter felt her doubts and fears reviving under the influence of Mrs. Rachel's pessimism.

"Well, of all things that ever were or will be!" ejaculated Mrs. Rachel when she was safely out in the lane. "It does really seem as if I must be dreaming. Well, I'm sorry for that poor young one and no mis-take. Matthew and Marilla don't know anything about children and they'll expect him to be wiser and steadier than his own grandfather, if so be's he ever had a grandfather, which is doubtful. It seems uncanny to think of a child at Green Gables somehow; there's never been one there, for Matthew and Marilla were grown up when the new house was built—if they ever *were* children, which is hard to believe when one looks at them. I wouldn't be in that orphan's shoes for anything. My, but I pity him, that's what."

So said Mrs. Rachel to the wild rose bushes out of the fulness of her heart; but if she could have seen the child who was waiting patiently at the Bright River station at that very moment her pity would have been still deeper and more profound.

2
Matthew Cuthbert
is Surprised

Matthew Cuthbert and the sorrel mare jogged comfortably over the eight miles to Bright River. It was a pretty road, running along between snug farmsteads, with now and again a bit of balsamy fir wood to drive through or a hollow where wild plums hung out their filmy bloom. The air was sweet with the breath of many apple orchards and the meadows sloped away in the distance to horizon mists of pearl and purple; while

> "The little birds sang as if it were
> The one day of summer in all the year."

Matthew enjoyed the drive after his own fashion, except during the moments when he met women and had to nod to them—for in Prince Edward Island you are supposed to nod to all and sundry you meet on the road whether you know them or not.

Matthew dreaded all women except Marilla and Mrs. Rachel; he had an uncomfortable feeling that the mysterious creatures were secretly laughing at him. He may have been quite right in thinking so, for he was an odd-looking personage, with an ungainly figure and long iron-gray hair that touched his stooping shoulders, and a full, soft brown beard which he had worn ever since he was twenty. In fact, he had looked at twenty very much as he looked at sixty, lacking a little of the grayness.

When he reached Bright River there was no sign of any train; he thought he was too early, so he tied his horse in the yard of the small Bright River hotel and went over to the station house. The long platform was almost deserted; the only living creature in sight being a girl who was sitting on a pile of shingles at the extreme end. Matthew, barely noting that it *was* a girl, sidled past her as quickly as possible without looking at her. Had he looked he could hardly have failed to notice the tense rigidity and expectation of her attitude and expression. She was sitting there waiting for something or somebody and, since sitting and waiting was the only thing to do just then, she sat and waited with all her might and main.

Matthew encountered the stationmaster locking up the ticket office preparatory to going home for supper, and asked him if the five-thirty train would soon be along.

"The five-thirty train has been in and gone half an hour ago," answered that brisk official. "But there was a passenger dropped off for you—a little girl. She's sitting out there on the shingles. I asked her to go into the ladies' waiting room, but she informed me gravely that she preferred to stay outside. 'There was more scope for imagination,' she said. She's a case, I should say."

"I'm not expecting a girl," said Matthew blankly. "It's a boy I've come for. He should be here. Mrs. Alexander Spencer was to bring him over from Nova Scotia for me."

The stationmaster whistled.

"Guess there's some mistake," he said. "Mrs. Spencer came off the train with that girl and gave her into my charge. Said you and your sister were adopting her from an orphan asylum and that you would be along for her presently. That's all *I* know about it—and I haven't got any more orphans concealed hereabouts."

"I don't understand," said Matthew helplessly, wishing that Marilla was at hand to cope with the situation.

"Well, you'd better question the girl," said the stationmaster carelessly. "I dare say she'll be able to explain—she's got a tongue of her own, that's certain. Maybe they were out of boys of the brand you wanted."

He walked jauntily away, being hungry, and the unfortunate Matthew was left to do that which was harder for him than bearding a lion in its den—walk up to a girl—a strange girl—an orphan girl—and demand of her why she wasn't a boy. Matthew groaned in spirit as he turned about and shuffled gently down the platform towards her.

She had been watching him ever since he had passed her and she had her eyes on him now. Matthew was not looking at her and would not have seen what she was really like if he had been, but an ordinary observer would have seen this:

A child of about eleven, garbed in a very short, very tight, very ugly dress of yellowish gray wincey. She wore a faded brown sailor hat and beneath the hat, extending down her back, were two brands of very thick, decidedly red hair. Her face was small, white and thin, also much freckled; her mouth was large and so were her eyes, that looked green in some lights and moods and gray in others.

So far, the ordinary observer; an extraordinary observer might have seen that the chin was very pointed and pronounced; that the big eyes were full of spirit and vivacity; that the mouth was sweet-lipped and expressive; that the forehead was broad and full; in short, our discerning extraordinary observer might have concluded that no commonplace soul inhabited the body of this stray woman-child of whom shy Matthew Cuthbert was so ludicrously afraid.

Matthew, however, was spared the ordeal of speaking first, for as soon as she concluded that he was coming to her she stood up, grasping with one thin brown hand the handle of a shabby, old-fashioned carpetbag; the other she held out to him.

"I suppose you are Mr. Matthew Cuthbert of Green Gables?" she said in a peculiarly clear, sweet voice. "I'm very glad to see you. I was beginning to be afraid you weren't coming for me and I was imagining all the things that might have happened to prevent you. I had made up my mind that if you didn't come for me tonight I'd go down the track to that big wild cherry tree at the bend, and climb up into it to stay all night. I wouldn't be a bit afraid, and it would be lovely to sleep in a wild cherry tree all white with bloom in the moonshine, don't you think? You could imagine you were dwelling in marble halls, couldn't you? And I was quite sure you would come for me in the morning, if you didn't tonight."

Matthew had taken the scrawny little hand awkwardly in his;

then and there he decided what to do. He could not tell this child with the glowing eyes that there had been a mistake; he would take her home and let Marilla do that. She couldn't be left at Bright River anyhow, no matter what mistake had been made, so all questions and explanations might as well be deferred until he was safely back at Green Gables.

"I'm sorry I was late," he said shyly. "Come along. The horse is over in the yard. Give me your bag."

"Oh, I can carry it," the child responded cheerfully. "It isn't heavy. I've got all my worldly goods in it, but it isn't heavy. And if it isn't carried in just a certain way the handle pulls out—so I'd better keep it because I know the exact knack of it. It's an extremely old carpetbag. Oh, I'm very glad you've come, even if it would have been nice to sleep in a wild cherry tree. We've got to drive a long piece, haven't we? Mrs. Spencer said it was eight miles. I'm glad because I love driving. Oh, it seems so wonderful that I'm going to live with you and belong to you. I've never belonged to anybody—not really. But the asylum was the worst. I've only been in four months, but that was enough. I don't suppose you ever were an orphan in an asylum, so you can't possibly understand what it is like. It's worse than anything you could imagine. Mrs. Spencer said it was wicked of me to talk like that, but I didn't mean to be wicked. It's so easy to be wicked without knowing it, isn't it? They were good, you know—the asylum people. But there is so little scope for the imagination in an asylum—only just in the other orphans. It *was* pretty interesting to imagine things about them—to imagine that perhaps the girl who sat next to you was really the daughter of a belted earl, who had been stolen away from her parents in her infancy by a cruel nurse who died before she could confess. I used to lie awake at nights and imagine things like that, because I didn't have time in the day. I guess that's why I'm so thin—I *am* dreadful thin, ain't I? There isn't a pick on my bones. I do love to imagine I'm nice and plump, with dimples in my elbows."

With this Matthew's companion stopped talking, partly because she was out of breath and partly because they had reached the buggy. Not another word did she say until they had left the village and were driving down a steep little hill, the road part of which had been cut so deeply into the soft soil that the banks, fringed with blooming wild cherry-trees and slim white birches, were several feet above their heads.

The child put out her hand and broke off a branch of wild plum that brushed against the side of the buggy.

"Isn't that beautiful? What did that tree, leaning out from the bank all white and lacy, make you think of?" she asked.

"Well now, I dunno," said Matthew.

"Why, a bride, of course—a bride all in white with a lovely misty veil. I've never seen one, but I can imagine what she would look like. I don't ever expect to be a bride myself. I'm so homely nobody will ever want to marry me—unless it might be a foreign missionary. I suppose a foreign missionary mightn't be very particular. But I do hope that some day I shall have a white dress. That is my highest ideal of earthly bliss. I just love pretty clothes. And I've never had a pretty dress in my life that I can remember—but of course it's all the more to look forward to, isn't it? And then I can imagine that I'm dressed gorgeously. This morning when I left the asylum I felt so ashamed because I had to wear this horrid old wincey dress. All the orphans had to wear them, you know. A merchant in Hopeton last winter donated three hundred yards of wincey to the asylum. Some people said it was because he couldn't sell it, but I'd rather believe that it was out of the kindness of his heart, wouldn't you? When we got on the train I felt as if everybody must be looking at me and pitying me. But I just went to work and imagined that I had on the most beautiful pale blue silk dress—because when you *are* imagining you might as well imagine something worth while—and a big hat all flowers and nodding plumes, and a gold watch, and kid gloves and boots. I felt cheered up right away and I enjoyed my trip to the island with all my might. I wasn't a bit sick coming over in the boat. Neither was Mrs. Spencer, although she generally is. She said she hadn't time to get sick, watching to see that I didn't fall overboard. She said she never saw the beat of me for prowling about. But if it kept her from being sea-sick it's a mercy I did prowl, isn't it? And I wanted to see everything that was to be seen on that boat, because I didn't know whether I'd ever have another opportunity. Oh, there are a lot more cherry trees all in bloom!

This Island is the bloomiest place. I just love it already, and I'm so glad I'm going to live here. I've always heard that Prince Edward Island was the prettiest place in the world, and I used to imagine I was living here, but I never really expected I would. It's delightful when your imaginations come true, isn't it? But those red roads are so funny. When we got into the train at Charlottetown and the red roads began to flash past I asked Mrs. Spencer what made them red and she said she didn't know and for pity's sake not to ask her any more questions. She said I must have asked her a thousand already. I suppose I had, too, but how are you going to find out about things if you don't ask questions? And what *does* make the roads red?"

"Well now, I dunno," said Matthew.

"Well, that is one of the things to find out sometime. Isn't it splendid to think of all the things there are to find out about? It just makes me feel glad to be alive—it's such an interesting world. It wouldn't be half so interesting if we knew all about everything, would it? There'd be no scope for imagination then, would there? But am I talking too much? People are always telling me I do. Would you rather I didn't talk? If you say so I'll stop. I *can* stop when I make up my mind to it, although it's difficult."

Matthew, much to his own surprise, was enjoying himself. Like most quiet folks he liked talkative people when they were willing to do the talking themselves and did not expect him to keep up his end of it. But he had never expected to enjoy the society of a little girl. Women were bad enough in all conscience, but little girls were worse. He detested the way they had of sidling past him timidly, with sidewise glances, as if they expected him to gobble them up at a mouthful if they ventured to say a word. This was the Avonlea type of well-bred little girl. But this freckled witch was very different, and although he found it rather difficult for his slower intelligence to keep up with her brisk mental processes he thought that he "kind of liked her chatter." So he said as shyly as usual:

"Oh, you can talk as much as you like. I don't mind."

"Oh, I'm so glad. I know you and I are going to get along together fine. It's such a relief to talk when one wants to and not be told that children should be seen and not heard. I've had that said to me a million times if I have once. And people laugh at me because I use big words. But if you have big ideas you have to use big words to express them, haven't you?"

"Well now, that seems reasonable," said Matthew.

"Mrs. Spencer said that my tongue must be hung in the middle. But it isn't—it's firmly fastened at one end. Mrs. Spencer said your place was named Green Gables. I asked her all about it. And she said there were trees all around it. I was gladder than ever. I just love trees. And there weren't any at all about the asylum, only a few poor weeny-teeny things out in front with little whitewashed cagey things about them. They just looked like orphans themselves, those trees did. It used to make me want to cry to look at them. I used to say to them, 'Oh, you *poor* little things! If you were out in a great big woods with other trees all around you and little mosses and Junebells growing over your roots and a brook not far away and birds singing in your branches, you could grow, couldn't you? But you can't where you are. I know just exactly how you feel, little trees.' I felt sorry to leave them behind this morning. You do get so attached to things like that, don't you? Is there a brook anywhere near Green Gables? I forgot to ask Mrs. Spencer that."

"Well now, yes, there's one right below the house."

"Fancy! it's always been one of my dreams to live near a brook. I never expected I would, though. Dreams don't often come true, do they? Wouldn't it be nice if they did? But just now I feel pretty nearly perfectly happy. I can't feel exactly perfectly happy because—well, what color would you call this?"

She twitched one of her long glossy braids over her thin shoulder and held it up before Matthew's eyes. Matthew was not used to deciding on the tints of ladies' tresses, but in this case there couldn't be much doubt.

"It's red, ain't it?" he said.

The girl let the braid drop back with a sigh that seemed to come from her very toes and to exhale forth all the sorrows of the ages.

"Yes, it's red," she said resignedly. "Now you see why I can't be perfectly happy. Nobody could who had red hair. I don't mind the other things so much—the freckles and the green eyes and my skinniness. I can imagine them away. I can imagine that I have a beautiful rose leaf complexion and lovely starry violet eyes. But I *cannot* imagine that red hair away. I do my best. I think to myself, 'Now my hair is a glorious black, black as the raven's wing.' But all the time I *know* it is just plain red, and it breaks my heart. It will be my lifelong sorrow. I read of a girl once in a novel who had a lifelong sorrow, but it wasn't red hair. Her hair was pure gold rippling back from her alabaster brow. What is an alabaster brow? I never could find out. Can you tell me?"

"Well now, I'm afraid I can't," said Matthew, who was getting a little dizzy. He felt as he had once felt in his rash youth when another boy had enticed him on the merry-go-round at a picnic.

"Well, whatever it was it must have been something nice because she was divinely beautiful. Have you ever imagined what it must feel like to be divinely beautiful?"

"Well now, no, I haven't," confessed Matthew ingenuously.

"I have, often. Which would you rather be if you had the choice—divinely beautiful or dazzlingly clever or angelically good?"

"Well now, I—I don't know exactly."

"Neither do I. I can never decide. But it doesn't make much real difference for it isn't likely I'll ever be either. It's certain I'll never be angelically good. Mrs. Spencer says—oh, Mr. Cuthbert! Oh, Mr. Cuthbert! Oh, Mr. Cuthbert!!!"

That was not what Mrs. Spencer had said; neither had the child tumbled out of the buggy nor had Matthew done anything astonishing. They had simply rounded a curve in the road and found themselves in the "Avenue."

The "Avenue," so called by the Newbridge people, was a stretch of road four or five hundred yards long, completely arched over with huge, wide-spreading apple-trees, planted years ago by an eccentric old farmer. Overhead was one long canopy of snowy fragrant bloom. Below the boughs the air was full of a purple twilight and far ahead a glimpse of painted sunset sky shone like a great rose window at the end of a cathedral aisle.

Its beauty seemed to strike the child dumb. She leaned back in the buggy, her thin hands clasped before her, her face lifted rapturously to the white splendor above. Even when they had passed out and were driving down the long slope to Newbridge she never moved or spoke. Still with rapt face she gazed afar into the sunset west, with eyes that saw visions trooping splendidly across that glowing background. Through Newbridge, a bustling little village where dogs barked at them and small boys hooted and curious faces peered from the windows, they drove, still in silence. When three more miles had dropped away behind them the child had not spoken. She could keep silence, it was evident, as energetically as she could talk.

"I guess you're feeling pretty tired and hungry," Matthew ventured at last, accounting for her long visitation of dumbness with the only reason he could think of. "But we haven't very far to go now—only another mile."

She came out of her reverie with a deep sigh and looked at him with the dreamy gaze of a soul that had been wondering afar, star-led.

"Oh, Mr. Cuthbert," she whispered, "that place we came through—that white place—what was it?"

"Well now, you must mean the Avenue," said Matthew after a few moments' profound reflection. "It is a kind of pretty place."

"Pretty? Oh, *pretty* doesn't seem the right word to use. Nor beautiful, either. They don't go far enough. Oh, it was wonderful—wonderful. It's the first thing I ever saw that couldn't be improved upon by imagination. It just satisfied me here"—she put one hand on her breast—"it made a queer funny ache and yet it was a pleasant ache. Did you ever have an ache like that, Mr. Cuthbert?"

"Well now, I just can't recollect that I ever had."

"I have it lots of times—whenever I see anything royally beautiful. But they shouldn't call that lovely place the Avenue. There is no meaning in a name like that. They should call it—let me see—the White Way of Delight. Isn't that a nice imaginative name? When I don't like the name of a place or a person I always imagine a new one and always think of them so. There was a girl at the asylum whose name was Hepzibah Jenkins, but I always imagined her as Rosalia DeVere.

Other people may call that place the Avenue, but I shall always call it the White Way of Delight. Have we really only another mile to go before we get home? I'm glad and I'm sorry. I'm sorry because this drive has been so pleasant and I'm always sorry when pleasant things end. Something still pleasanter may come after, but you can never be sure. And it's so often the case that it isn't pleasanter. That has been my experience anyhow. But I'm glad to think of getting home. You see, I've never had a real home since I can remember. It gives me that pleasant ache again just to think of coming to a really truly home. Oh, isn't that pretty!"

They had driven over the crest of a hill. Below them was a pond, looking almost like a river so long and winding was it. A bridge spanned it midway and from there to its lower end, where an amber-hued belt of sand hills shut it in from the dark blue gulf beyond, the water was a glory of many shifting hues—the most spiritual shadings of crocus and rose and ethereal green, with other elusive tintings for which no name has ever been found. Above the bridge the pond ran up into fringing groves of fir and maple and lay all darkly translucent in their wavering shadows. Here and there a wild plum leaned out from the bank like a white-clad girl tiptoeing to her own reflection. From the marsh at the head of the pond came the clear, mournfully-sweet chorus of the frogs. There was a little gray house peering around a white apple orchard on a slope beyond and, although it was not yet quite dark a light was shining from one of its windows.

"That's Barry's pond," said Matthew.

"Oh, I don't like that name, either. I shall call it—let me see—the Lake of Shining Waters. Yes, that is the right name for it. I know because of the thrill. When I hit on a name that suits exactly it gives me a thrill. Do things ever give you a thrill?"

Matthew ruminated.

"Well now, yes. It always kind of gives me a thrill to see them ugly white grubs that spade up in the cucumber beds. I hate the look of them."

"Oh, I don't think that can be exactly the same kind of a thrill. Do you think it can? There doesn't seem to be much connection between grubs and lakes of shining waters, does there? But why do other people call it Barry's pond?"

"I reckon because Mr. Barry lives up there in that house. Orchard Slope's the name of his place. If it wasn't for that big bush behind it you could see Green Gables from here. But we have to go over the bridge and round by the road, so it's near half a mile further."

"Has Mr. Barry any little girls? Well, not so very little either—about my size."

"He's got one about eleven. Her name is Diana."

"Oh!" with a long indrawing of breath. "What a perfectly lovely name!"

"Well now, I dunno. There's something dreadful heathenish about it, seems to me. I'd ruther Jane or Mary or some sensible name like that. But when Diana was born there was a schoolmaster boarding there and they gave him the naming of her and he called her Diana."

"I wish there had been a schoolmaster like that around when _I_ was born, then. Oh, here we are at the bridge. I'm going to shut my eyes tight. I'm always afraid going over bridges. I can't help imagining that perhaps, just as we get to the middle, they'll crumple up like a jackknife and nip us. So I shut my eyes. But I always have to open them for all when I think we're getting near the middle. Because, you see, if the bridge _did_ crumple up I'd want to _see_ it crumple. What a jolly rumble it makes! I always like the rumble part of it. Isn't it splendid there are so many things to like in this world? There, we're over. Now I'll look back. Good night, dear Lake of Shining Waters. I always say good night to the things I love, just as I would to people. I think they like it. That water looks as if it was smiling at me."

When they had driven up the further hill and around a corner Matthew said:

"We're pretty near home now. That's Green Gables over—"

"Oh, don't tell me," she interrupted breathlessly, catching at his partially raised arm and shutting her eyes that she might not see his gesture. "Let me guess. I'm sure I'll guess right."

She opened her eyes and looked about her. They were on the crest of a hill. The sun had set some time since, but the landscape was still clear in the mellow afterlight. To the west a dark church spire rose up against a marigold sky. Below was a little valley and beyond a long, gently-rising slope with snug farmsteads scattered along it. From one to another the child's eyes darted, eager and wistful. At last they lingered on one away to the left, far back from the road, dimly white with blossoming trees in the twilight of the surrounding woods. Over it, in the stainless southwest sky, a great crystal-white star was shining like a lamp of guidance and promise.

"That's it, isn't it?" she said, pointing.

Matthew slapped the reins on the sorrel's back delightedly.

"Well now, you've guessed it! But I reckon Mrs. Spencer described it so's you could tell."

"No, she didn't—really she didn't. All she said might just as well have been about most of those other places. I hadn't any real idea what it looked like. But just as soon as I saw it I felt it was home. Oh, it seems as if I must be in a dream. Do you know, my arm must be black and blue from the elbow up, for I've pinched myself so many times today. Every little while a horrible sickening feeling would come over me and I'd be so afraid it was all a dream. Then I'd pinch myself to see if it was real—until suddenly I remembered that even supposing it was only a dream I'd better go on dreaming as long as I could; so I stopped pinching. But it *is* real and we're nearly home."

With a sigh of rapture she relapsed into silence. Matthew stirred uneasily. He felt glad that it would be Marilla and not he who would have to tell this waif of the world that the home she longed for was not to be hers after all. They drove over Lynde's Hollow, where it was already quite dark, but not so dark that Mrs. Rachel could not see them from her window vantage, and up the hill and into the long lane of Green Gables. By the time they arrived at the house Matthew was shrinking from the approaching revelation with an energy he did not understand. It was not of Marilla or himself he was thinking or of the trouble this mistake was probably going to make for them, but of the child's disappointment. When he thought of that rapt light being quenched in her eyes he had an uncomfortable feeling that he was going to assist at murdering something—much the same feeling that came over him when he had to kill a lamb or calf or any other innocent little creature.

The yard was quite dark as they turned into it and the poplar leaves were rustling silkily all round it.

"Listen to the trees talking in their sleep," she whispered, as he lifted her to the ground. "What nice dreams they must have!"

Then, holding tightly to the carpetbag which contained "all her worldly goods," she followed him into the house.

3

Marilla Cuthbert is Surprised

arilla came briskly forward as Matthew opened the door. But when her eyes fell on the odd little figure in the stiff, ugly dress, with the long braids of red hair and the eager, luminous eyes, she stopped short in amazement.

"Matthew Cuthbert, who's that?" she ejaculated. "Where is the boy?"

"There wasn't any boy," said Matthew wretchedly. "There was only *her*."

He nodded at the child, remembering that he had never even asked her name.

"No boy! But there *must* have been a boy," insisted Marilla. "We sent word to Mrs. Spencer to bring a boy."

"Well, she didn't. She brought *her*. I asked the stationmaster. And I had to bring her home. She couldn't be left there, no matter where the mistake had come in."

"Well, this is a pretty piece of business!" ejaculated Marilla.

During this dialogue the child had remained silent, her eyes roving from one to the other, all the animation fading out of her face. Suddenly she seemed to grasp the full meaning of what had been said. Dropping her precious carpetbag she sprang forward a step and clasped her hands.

"You don't want me!" she cried. "You don't want me because I'm not a boy! I might have expected it. Nobody ever did want me. I might have known it was all too beautiful to last. I might have known nobody really did want me. Oh, what shall I do? I'm going to burst into tears!"

Burst into tears she did. Sitting down on a chair by the table, flinging her arms out upon it, and burying her face in them, she proceeded to cry stormily. Marilla and Matthew looked at each other deprecatingly across the stove. Neither of them knew what to say or do. Finally Marilla stepped lamely into the breach.

"Well, well, there's no need to cry so about it."

"Yes, there *is* need!" The child raised her head quickly, revealing a tear-stained face and trembling lips. "*You* would cry, too, if you were an orphan and had come to a place you thought was going to be home and found that they didn't want you because you weren't a boy. Oh, this is the most *tragical* thing that ever happened to me!"

Something like a reluctant smile, rather rusty from long disuse, mellowed Marilla's grim expression.

"Well, don't cry any more. We're not going to turn you out-of-doors tonight. You'll have to stay here until we investigate this affair. What's your name?"

The child hesitated for a moment.

"Will you please call me Cordelia?" she said eagerly.

"*Call* you Cordelia! Is that your name?"

"No-o-o, it's not exactly my name, but I would love to be called Cordelia. It's such a perfectly elegant name."

"I don't know what on earth you mean. If Cordelia isn't your name, what is?"

"Anne Shirley," reluctantly faltered forth the owner of that name, "but oh, please do call me Cordelia. It can't matter much to you what you call me if I'm only going to be here a little while, can it? And Anne is such an unromantic name."

"Unromantic fiddlesticks!" said the unsympathetic Marilla. "Anne is a real good plain sensible name. You've no need to be ashamed of it."

"Oh, I'm not ashamed of it," explained Anne, "only I like Cordelia better. I've always imagined that my name was Cordelia—at least, I always have of late years. When I was young I used to imagine it was Geraldine, but I like Cordelia better now. But if you call me Anne please call me Anne spelled with an *e*."

"What difference does it make how it's spelled?" asked Marilla with another rusty smile as she picked up the teapot.

"Oh, it makes *such* a difference. It *looks* so much nicer. When you hear a name pronounced can't you always see it in your mind, just as if it was printed out? I can; and A-n-n looks dreadful, but A-n-n-e looks so much more distinguished. If you'll only call me Anne spelled with an *e* I shall try to reconcile myself to not being called Cordelia."

"Very well, then, Anne spelled with an *e,* can you tell us how this mistake came to be made? We sent word to Mrs. Spencer to bring us a boy. Were there no boys at the asylum?"

"Oh, yes, there was an abundance of them. But Mrs. Spencer said *distinctly* that you wanted a girl about eleven years old. And the matron said she thought I would do. You don't know how delighted I was. I couldn't sleep all last night for joy. Oh," she added reproachfully, turning to Matthew, "why didn't you tell me at the station that you didn't want me and leave me there? If I hadn't seen the White Way of Delight and the Lake of Shining Waters it wouldn't be so hard."

"What on earth does she mean?" demanded Marilla, staring at Matthew.

"She—she's just referring to some conversation we had on the road," said Matthew hastily. "I'm going out to put the mare in, Marilla. Have tea ready when I come back."

"Did Mrs. Spencer bring anybody over besides you?" continued Marilla when Matthew had gone out.

"She brought Lily Jones for herself. Lily is only five years old and she is very beautiful. She has nut-brown hair. If I was very beautiful and had nut-brown hair would you keep me?"

"No. We want a boy to help Matthew on the farm. A girl would be of no use to us. Take off your hat. I'll lay it and your bag on the hall table."

Anne took off her hat meekly. Matthew came back presently and they sat down to supper. But Anne could not eat. In vain she nibbled at the bread and butter and pecked at the crab apple preserve out of the little scalloped glass dish by her plate. She did not really make any headway at all.

"You're not eating anything," said Marilla sharply, eying her as if it were a serious shortcoming.

Anne sighed.

"I can't. I'm in the depths of despair. Can you eat when you are in the depths of despair?"

"I've never been in the depths of despair, so I can't say," responded Marilla.

"Weren't you? Well, did you ever try to *imagine* you were in the depths of despair?"

"No, I didn't."

"Then I don't think you can understand what it's like. It's a very uncomfortable feeling indeed. When you try to eat a lump comes right up in your throat and you can't swallow anything, not even if it was a chocolate caramel. I had one chocolate caramel once two years ago and it was simply delicious. I've often dreamed since then that I had a lot of chocolate caramels, but I always wake up just when I'm going to eat them. I do hope you won't be offended because I can't eat. Everything is extremely nice, but still I cannot eat."

"I guess she's tired," said Matthew, who hadn't spoken since his return from the barn. "Best put her to bed, Marilla."

Marilla had been wondering where Anne should be put to bed. She had prepared a couch in the kitchen chamber for the desired and expected boy. But, although it was neat and clean, it did not seem quite the thing to put a girl there somehow. But the spare room was out of the question for such a stray waif, so there remained only the east gable room. Marilla lighted a candle and told Anne to follow her, which Anne spiritlessly did, taking her hat and carpetbag from the hall table as she passed. The hall was fearsomely clean; the little gable chamber in which she presently found herself seemed still cleaner.

Marilla set the candle on a three-legged, three-cornered table and turned down the bedclothes.

"I suppose you have a nightgown?" she questioned.

Anne nodded.

"Yes, I have two. The matron of the asylum made them for me. They're fearfully skimpy. There is never enough to go around in an asylum, so things are always skimpy—at least in a poor asylum like ours. I hate skimpy night dresses. But one can dream just as well in them as in lovely trailing ones, with frills around the neck, that's one consolation."

"Well, undress as quick as you can and go to bed. I'll come back

in a few minutes for the candle. I daren't trust you to put it out yourself. You'd likely set the place on fire."

When Marilla had gone Anne looked around her wistfully. The
whitewashed walls were so painfully bare and staring that she thought they
must ache over their own bareness. The floor was bare, too, except for a
round braided mat in the middle such as Anne had never seen before. In
one corner was the bed, a high, old-fashioned one, with four dark, low-
turned posts. In the other corner was the aforesaid three-cornered table
adorned with a fat, red velvet pincushion hard enough to turn the point
of the most adventurous pin. Above it hung a little six by eight mirror.
Midway between table and bed was the window, with an icy white muslin
frill over it, and opposite it was the washstand. The whole apartment was
of a rigidity not to be described in words, but which sent a shiver to the very
marrow of Anne's bones. With a sob she hastily discarded her garments,
put on the skimpy nightgown and sprang into bed where she burrowed
face downward into the pillow and pulled the clothes over her head.
When Marilla came up for the light various skimpy articles of raiment scattered most untidily over the floor and a certain tempestuous appearance
of the bed were the only indications of any presence save her own.

She deliberately picked up Anne's clothes, placed them neatly on
a prim yellow chair, and then, taking up the candle, went over to the bed.

"Good night," she said, a little awkwardly, but not unkindly.

Anne's white face and big eyes appeared over the bedclothes with
a startling suddenness.

"How can you call it a *good* night when you know it must be the
very worst night I've ever had?" she said reproachfully.

Then she dived down into invisibility again.

Marilla went slowly down to the kitchen and proceeded to wash
the supper dishes. Matthew was smoking—a sure sign of perturbation
of mind. He seldom smoked, for Marilla set her face against it as a filthy
habit; but at certain times and seasons he felt driven to it and then
Marilla winked at the practice, realizing that a mere man must have
some vent for his emotions.

"Well, this is a pretty kettle of fish," she said wrathfully. "This is
what comes of sending word instead of going ourselves. Robert

Spencer's folks have twisted that message somehow. One of us will have to drive over and see Mrs. Spencer tomorrow, that's certain. This girl will have to be sent back to the asylum."

"Yes, I suppose so," said Matthew reluctantly.

"You *suppose* so! Don't you know it?"

"Well now, she's a real nice little thing, Marilla. It's kind of a pity to send her back when she's so set on staying here."

"Matthew Cuthbert, you don't mean to say you think we ought to keep her!"

Marilla's astonishment could not have been greater if Matthew had expressed a predilection for standing on his head.

"Well now, no, I suppose not—not exactly," stammered Matthew, uncomfortably driven into a corner for his precise meaning. "I suppose—we could hardly be expected to keep her."

"I should say not. What good would she be to us?"

"We might be some good to her," said Matthew suddenly and unexpectedly.

"Matthew Cuthbert, I believe that child has bewitched you! I can see as plain as plain that you want to keep her."

"Well now, she's a real interesting little thing," persisted Matthew. "You should have heard her talk coming from the station."

"Oh, she can talk fast enough. I saw that at once. It's nothing in her favor, either. I don't like children who have so much to say. I don't want an orphan girl and if I did she isn't the style I'd pick out. There's something I don't understand about her. No, she's got to be dispatched straightway back to where she came from."

"I could hire a French boy to help me," said Matthew, "and she'd be company for you."

"I'm not suffering for company," said Marilla shortly. "And I'm not going to keep her."

"Well now, it's just as you say, of course, Marilla," said Matthew rising and putting his pipe away. "I'm going to bed."

To bed went Matthew. And to bed, when she had put her dishes away, went Marilla, frowning most resolutely. And upstairs, in the east gable, a lonely, heart-hungry, friendless child cried herself to sleep.

4

Morning at Green Gables

It was broad daylight when Anne awoke and sat up in bed, staring confusedly at the window through which a flood of cheery sunshine was pouring and outside of which something white and feathery waved across glimpses of blue sky.

For a moment she could not remember where she was. First came a delightful thrill, as of something very pleasant; then a horrible remembrance. This was Green Gables and they didn't want her because she wasn't a boy!

But it was morning and, yes, it was a cherry-tree in full bloom outside of her window. With a bound she was out of bed and across the floor. She pushed up the sash—it went up stiffly and creakily, as if it hadn't been opened for a long time, which was the case; and it stuck so tight that nothing was needed to hold it up.

Anne dropped on her knees and gazed out into the June morning, her eyes glistening with delight. Oh, wasn't it beautiful? Wasn't it a lovely place? Suppose she wasn't really going to stay here! She would imagine she was. There was scope for imagination here.

A huge cherry-tree grew outside, so close that its boughs tapped against the house, and it was so thickset with blossoms that hardly a leaf was to be seen. On both sides of the house was a big orchard, one of apple trees and one of cherry trees, also showered over with blossoms; and their grass was all sprinkled with dandelions. In the garden below were lilac trees purple with flowers, and their dizzily sweet fragrance drifted up to the window on the morning wind.

Below the garden a green field lush with clover sloped down to the hollow where the brook ran and where scores of white birches grew, upspringing airily out of an undergrowth suggestive of delightful possibilities in ferns and mosses and woodsy things generally. Beyond it was a hill, green and feathery with spruce and fir; there was a gap in it where the gray gable end of the little house she had seen from the other side of the Lake of Shining Waters was visible.

Off to the left were the big barns and beyond them, away down over green, low-sloping fields, was a sparkling blue glimpse of sea.

Anne's beauty-loving eyes lingered on it all, taking everything greedily in; she had looked on so many unlovely places in her life, poor child; but this was as lovely as anything she had ever dreamed.

She knelt there, lost to everything but the loveliness around her, until she was startled by a hand on her shoulder. Marilla had come in unheard by the small dreamer.

"It's time you were dressed," she said curtly.

Marilla really did not know how to talk to the child, and her uncomfortable ignorance made her crisp and curt when she did not mean to be.

Anne stood up and drew a long breath.

"Oh, isn't it wonderful?" she said, waving her hand comprehensively at the good world outside.

"It's a big tree," said Marilla, "and it blooms great, but the fruit don't amount to much never—small and wormy."

"Oh, I don't mean just the tree; of course it's lovely—yes, it's *radiantly* lovely—it blooms as if it meant it—but I meant everything, the garden and the orchard and the brook and the woods, the whole big dear world. Don't you feel as if you just loved the world on a morning like this? And I can hear the brook laughing all the way up here. Have you ever noticed what cheerful things brooks are? They're always laughing. Even in wintertime I've heard them under the ice. I'm so glad there's a brook near Green Gables. Perhaps you think it doesn't make any difference to me when you're not going to keep me, but it does. I shall always like to remember that there is a brook at Green Gables even if I never see it again. If there wasn't a brook I'd be *haunted* by the uncomfortable feeling that there ought to be one. I'm not in the depths of despair this morning. I never can be in the morning. Isn't it a splendid thing that there are mornings? But I feel very sad. I've just been imagining that it was really me you wanted after all and that I was to stay here for ever and ever. It was a great comfort while it lasted. But the worst of imagining things is that the time comes when you have to stop and that hurts."

"You'd better get dressed and come downstairs and never mind your imaginings," said Marilla as soon as she could get a word in edgewise. "Breakfast is waiting. Wash your face and comb your hair. Leave the window up and turn your bedclothes back over the foot of the bed. Be as smart as you can."

Anne could evidently be smart to some purpose for she was downstairs in ten minutes' time, with her clothes neatly on, her hair brushed and braided, her face washed, and a comfortable consciousness pervading her soul that she had fulfilled all Marilla's requirements. As a matter of fact, however, she had forgotten to turn back the bedclothes.

"I'm pretty hungry this morning," she announced, as she slipped into the chair Marilla placed for her. "The world doesn't seem such a howling wilderness as it did last night. I'm so glad it's a sunshiny morning. But I like rainy mornings real well, too. All sorts of mornings are interesting, don't you think? You don't know what's going to happen through the day, and there's so much scope for imagination. But I'm glad it's not rainy today because it's easier to be cheerful and bear up under affliction on a sunshiny day. I feel that I have a good deal to bear up under. It's all very well to read about sorrows and imagine yourself living through them heroically, but it's not so nice when you really come to have them, is it?"

"For pity's sake hold your tongue," said Marilla. "You talk entirely too much for a little girl."

Thereupon Anne held her tongue so obediently and thoroughly that her continued silence made Marilla rather nervous, as if in the presence of something not exactly natural. Matthew also held his tongue—but this at least was natural—so that the meal was a very silent one.

As it progressed Anne became more and more abstracted, eating mechanically, with her big eyes fixed unswervingly and unseeingly on the sky outside the window. This made Marilla more nervous than ever; she had an uncomfortable feeling that while this odd child's body might be there at the table her spirit was far away in some remote airy cloudland, borne aloft on the wings of imagination. Who would want such a child about the place?

Yet Matthew wished to keep her, of all unaccountable things! Marilla felt that he wanted it just as much this morning as he had the night before, and that he would go on wanting it. That was Matthew's way—take a whim into his head and cling to it with the most amazing silent persistency—a persistency ten times more potent and effectual in its very silence than if he had talked it out.

When the meal was ended Anne came out of her reverie and offered to wash the dishes.

"Can you wash dishes right?" asked Marilla distrustfully.

"Pretty well. I'm better at looking after children, though. I've had so much experience at that. It's such a pity you haven't any here for me to look after."

"I don't feel as if I wanted any more children to look after than I've got at present. *You're* problem enough in all conscience. What's to be done with you I don't know. Matthew is a most ridiculous man."

"I think he's lovely," said Anne reproachfully. "He is so very sympathetic. He didn't mind how much I talked—he seemed to like it. I felt that he was a kindred spirit as soon as ever I saw him."

"You're both queer enough, if that's what you mean by kindred spirits," said Marilla with a sniff. "Yes, you may wash the dishes. Take plenty of hot water, and be sure you dry them well. I've got enough to attend to this morning for I'll have to drive over to White Sands in the afternoon and see Mrs. Spencer. You'll come with me and we'll settle what's to be done with you. After you've finished the dishes go upstairs and make your bed."

Anne washed the dishes deftly enough, as Marilla, who kept a sharp eye on the process, discerned. Later on she made her bed less successfully, for she had never learned the art of wrestling with a feather tick. But it was done somehow and smoothed down; and then Marilla, to get rid of her, told her she might go out-of-doors and amuse herself until dinner time.

Anne flew to the door, face alight, eyes glowing. On the very threshold she stopped short, wheeled about, came back and sat down by the table, light and glow as effectually blotted out as if some one had clapped an extinguisher on her.

"What's the matter now?" demanded Marilla.

"I don't dare go out," said Anne, in the tone of a martyr relinquishing all earthly joys. "If I can't stay here there is no use in my loving Green Gables. And if I go out there and get acquainted with all those trees and flowers and the orchard and the brook I'll not be able to help loving it. It's hard enough now, so I won't make it any harder. I want to go out so much—everything seems to he calling to me, 'Anne, Anne, come out to us. Anne, Anne, we want a playmate'—but it's better not. There is no use in loving things if you have to be torn from them, is there? And it's so hard to keep from loving things, isn't it? That was why I was so glad when I thought I was going to live here. I thought I'd have so many things to love and nothing to hinder me. But that brief dream is over. I am resigned to my fate now, so I don't think I'll go out for fear I'll get unresigned again. What is the name of that geranium on the windowsill, please?"

"That's the apple-scented geranium."

"Oh, I don't mean that sort of a name. I mean just a name you gave it yourself. Didn't you give it a name? May I give it one then? May I call it—let me see—Bonny would do—may I call it Bonny while I'm here? Oh, do let me!"

"Goodness, I don't care. But where on earth is the sense of naming a geranium?"

"Oh, I like things to have handles even if they are only geraniums. It makes them seem more like people. How do you know but that it hurts a geranium's feelings just to be called a geranium and nothing else? You wouldn't like to be called nothing but a woman all the time. Yes, I shall call it Bonny. I named that cherry tree outside my bedroom window this morning. I called it Snow Queen because it was so white. Of course, it won't always be in blossom, but one can imagine that it is, can't one?"

"I never in all my life saw or heard anything to equal her," muttered Marilla, beating a retreat down cellar after potatoes. "She *is* kind of interesting, as Matthew says. I can feel already that I'm wondering what on earth she'll say next. She'll be casting a spell over me, too. She's cast it over Matthew. That look he gave me when he went out said everything he said or hinted last night over again. I wish he was like other men and would talk things out. A body could answer back then and argue him into reason. But what's to be done with a man who just *looks?*"

Anne had relapsed into reverie, with her chin in her hands and her eyes on the sky, when Marilla returned from her cellar pilgrimage. There Marilla left her until the early dinner was on the table.

"I suppose I can have the mare and buggy this afternoon, Matthew?" said Marilla.

Matthew nodded and looked wistfully at Anne. Marilla intercepted the look and said grimly:

"I'm going to drive over to White Sands and settle this thing. I'll take Anne with me and Mrs. Spencer will probably make arrangements to send her back to Nova Scotia at once. I'll set your tea out for you and I'll be home in time to milk the cows."

Still Matthew said nothing and Marilla had a sense of having wasted words and breath. There is nothing more aggravating than a man who won't talk back—unless it is a woman who won't.

Matthew hitched the sorrel into the buggy in due time and Marilla and Anne set off. Matthew opened the yard gate for them, and as they drove slowly through, he said, to nobody in particular as it seemed:

"Little Jerry Buote from the Creek was here this morning, and I told him I guessed I'd hire him for the summer."

Marilla made no reply, but she hit the unlucky sorrel such a vicious clip with the whip that the fat mare, unused to such treatment, whizzed indignantly down the lane at an alarming pace. Marilla looked back once as the buggy bounced along and saw that aggravating Matthew leaning over the gate, looking wistfully after them.

5

Anne's History

"Do you know," said Anne confidentially, "I've made up my mind to enjoy this drive. It's been my experience that you can nearly always enjoy things if you make up your mind firmly that you will. Of course, you must make it up *firmly*. I am not going to think about going back to the asylum while we're having our drive. I'm just going to think about the drive. Oh, look, there's one little early wild rose out! Isn't it lovely? Don't you think it must be glad to be a rose? Wouldn't it be nice if roses could talk? I'm sure they could tell us such lovely things. And isn't pink the most bewitching color in the world? I love it, but I can't wear it. Redheaded people can't wear pink, not even in imagination. Did you ever know of anybody whose hair was red when she was young, but got to be another color when she grew up?"

"No, I don't know as I ever did," said Marilla mercilessly, "and I shouldn't think it likely to happen in your case, either."

Anne sighed.

"Well, that is another hope gone. My life is a perfect graveyard of buried hopes. That's a sentence I read in a book once, and I say it over to comfort myself whenever I'm disappointed in anything."

"I don't see where the comforting comes in myself," said Marilla.

"Why, because it sounds so nice and romantic, just as if I were a heroine in a book, you know. I am so fond of romantic things, and a graveyard full of buried hopes is about as romantic a thing as one can imagine, isn't it? I'm rather glad I have one. Are we going across the Lake of Shining Waters today?"

"We're not going over Barry's pond, if that's what you mean by your Lake of Shining Waters. We're going by the shore road."

"Shore road sounds nice," said Anne dreamily. "Is it as nice as it sounds? Just when you said 'shore road' I saw it in a picture in my mind, as quick as that! And White Sands is a pretty name, too; but I don't like it as well as Avonlea. Avonlea is a lovely name. It just sounds like music. How far is it to White Sands?"

"It's five miles; and as you're evidently bent on talking you might as well talk to some purpose by telling me what you know about yourself."

"Oh, what I *know* about myself isn't really worth telling," said Anne eagerly. "If you'll only let me tell you what I *imagine* about myself you'll think it ever so much more interesting."

"No, I don't want any of your imaginings. Just you stick to bald facts. Begin at the beginning. Where were you born and how old are you?"

"I was eleven last March," said Anne, resigning herself to bald facts with a little sigh. "And I was born in Bolingbroke, Nova Scotia. My father's name was Walter Shirley, and he was a teacher in the Bolingbroke High School. My mother's name was Bertha Shirley. Aren't Walter and Bertha lovely names? I'm so glad my parents had nice names. It would be a real disgrace to have a father named—well, say Jedediah, wouldn't it?"

"I guess it doesn't matter what a person's name is as long as he behaves himself," said Marilla, feeling herself called upon to inculcate a good and useful moral.

"Well, I don't know." Anne looked thoughtful. "I read in a book once that a rose by any other name would smell as sweet, but I've never been able to believe it. I don't believe a rose *would* be as nice if it was called a thistle or a skunk cabbage. I suppose my father could have been a good man even if he had been called Jedediah; but I'm sure it would have been a cross. Well, my mother was a teacher in the High School, too, but when she married father she gave up teaching, of course. A husband was enough responsibility. Mrs. Thomas said that they were a pair of babies and as poor as church mice. They went to live in a weeny-teeny little yellow house in Bolingbroke. I've never seen that house, but I've imagined it thousands

of times. I think it must have had honeysuckle over the parlor window and lilacs in the front yard and lilies of the valley just inside the
gate. Yes, and muslin curtains in all the windows. Muslin curtains give
a house such an air. I was born in that house. Mrs. Thomas said I was
the homeliest baby she ever saw, I was so scrawny and tiny and nothing but eyes, but that mother thought I was perfectly beautiful. I
should think a mother would be a better judge than a poor woman
who came in to scrub, wouldn't you? I'm glad she was satisfied with
me anyhow; I would feel so sad if I thought I was a disappointment
to her—because she didn't live very long after that, you see. She died
of fever when I was just three months old. I do wish she'd lived long
enough for me to remember calling her mother. I think it would be so
sweet to say 'mother,' don't you? And father died four days afterwards
from fever, too. That left me an orphan and folks were at their wits'
end, so Mrs. Thomas said, what to do with me. You see, nobody wanted
me even then. It seems to be my fate. Father and mother had both come
from places far away and it was well known they hadn't any relatives living. Finally Mrs. Thomas said she'd take me, though she was poor and
had a drunken husband. She brought me up by hand. Do you know if
there is anything in being brought up by hand that ought to make people who are brought up that way better than other people? Because
whenever I was naughty Mrs. Thomas would ask me how I could be
such a bad girl when she had brought me up by hand—reproachful-like.

"Mr. and Mrs. Thomas moved away from Bolingbroke to
Marysville, and I lived with them until I was eight years old. I helped look
after the Thomas children—there were four of them younger than me—
and I can tell you they took a lot of looking after. Then Mr. Thomas was
killed falling under a train and his mother offered to take Mrs. Thomas
and the children, but she didn't want me. Mrs. Thomas was at *her* wits'
end, so she said, what to do with me. Then Mrs. Hammond from up the
river came down and said she'd take me, seeing I was handy with children,
and I went up the river to live with her in a little clearing among the
stumps. It was a very lonesome place. I'm sure I could never have lived
there if I hadn't had an imagination. Mr. Hammond worked a little
sawmill up there, and Mrs. Hammond had eight children. She had twins

three times. I like babies in moderation, but twins three times in succession is *too much.* I told Mrs. Hammond so firmly, when the last pair came. I used to get so dreadfully tired carrying them about.

"I lived up river with Mrs. Hammond over two years, and then Mr. Hammond died and Mrs. Hammond broke up housekeeping. She divided her children among her relatives and went to the States. I had to go to the asylum at Hopeton, because nobody would take me. They didn't want me at the asylum, either; they said they were overcrowded as it was. But they had to take me and I was there four months until Mrs. Spencer came."

Anne finished up with another sigh, of relief this time. Evidently she did not like talking about her experiences in a world that had not wanted her.

"Did you ever go to school?" demanded Marilla, turning the sorrel mare down the shore road.

"Not a great deal. I went a little the last year I stayed with Mrs. Thomas. When I went up river we were so far from a school that I couldn't walk it in winter and there was vacation in summer, so I could only go in the spring and fall. But of course I went while I was at the asylum. I can read pretty well and I know ever so many pieces of poetry off by heart—'The Battle of Hohenlinden' and 'Edinburgh after Flodden,' and 'Bingen on the Rhine,' and lots of the 'Lady of the Lake' and most of 'The Seasons,' by James Thompson. Don't you just love poetry that gives you a crinkly feeling up and down your back? There is a piece in the Fifth Reader—'The Downfall of Poland'—that is just full of thrills. Of course, I wasn't in the Fifth Reader—I was only in the Fourth—but the big girls used to lend me theirs to read."

"Were those women—Mrs. Thomas and Mrs. Hammond—good to you?" asked Marilla, looking at Anne out of the corner of her eye.

"O-o-o-h," faltered Anne. Her sensitive little face suddenly flushed scarlet and embarrassment sat on her brow. "Oh, they *meant* to be—I know they meant to be just as good and kind as possible. And when people mean to be good to you, you don't mind very much when they're not quite—always. They had a good deal to worry them, you know. It's very trying to have a drunken husband, you see; and it must be very trying to have twins three times in succession, don't you think? But I feel sure they meant to be good to me."

Marilla asked no more questions. Anne gave herself up to a silent rapture over the shore road and Marilla guided the sorrel abstractedly while she pondered deeply. Pity was suddenly stirring in her heart for the child. What a starved, unloved life she had had—a life of drudgery and poverty and neglect, for Marilla was shrewd enough to read between the lines of Anne's history and divine the truth. No wonder she had been so delighted at the prospect of a real home. It was a pity she had to be sent back. What if she, Marilla, should indulge Matthew's unaccountable whim and let her stay? He was set on it; and the child seemed a nice, teachable little thing.

"She's got too much to say," thought Marilla, "but she might be trained out of that. And there's nothing rude or slangy in what she does say. She's ladylike. It's likely her people were nice folks."

The shore road was "woodsy and wild and lonesome." On the right hand, scrub firs, their spirits quite unbroken by long years of tussle with the gulf winds, grew thickly. On the left were the steep red sandstone cliffs, so near the track in places that a mare of less steadiness than the sorrel might have tried the nerves of the people behind her. Down at the base of the cliffs were heaps of surf-worn rocks or little sandy coves inlaid with pebbles as with ocean jewels; beyond lay the sea, shimmering and blue, and over it soared the gulls, their pinions flashing silvery in the sunlight.

"Isn't the sea wonderful?" said Anne, rousing from a long, wide-eyed silence. "Once, when I lived in Marysville, Mr. Thomas hired an express wagon and took us all to spend the day at the shore ten miles away. I enjoyed every moment of that day, even if I had to look after the children all the time. I lived it over in happy dreams for years. But this shore is nicer than the Marysville shore. Aren't those gulls splendid? Would you like to be a gull? I think I would—that is, if I couldn't be a human girl. Don't you think it would be nice to wake up at sunrise and swoop down over the water and away out over that lovely blue all day; and then at night to fly back to one's nest? Oh, I can just imagine myself doing it. What big house is that just ahead, please?"

"That's the White Sands Hotel. Mr. Kirke runs it, but the season hasn't begun yet. There are heaps of Americans come there for the summer. They think this shore is just about right."

"I was afraid it might be Mrs. Spencer's place," said Anne mournfully. "I don't want to get there. Somehow, it will seem like the end of everything."

6

Marilla Makes Up Her Mind

et there they did, however, in due season. Mrs. Spencer lived in a big yellow house at White Sands Cove, and she came to the door with surprise and welcome mingled on her benevolent face.

"Dear, dear," she exclaimed, "you're the last folks I was looking for today, but I'm real glad to see you. You'll put your horse in? And how are you, Anne?"

"I'm as well as can be expected, thank you," said Anne smilelessly. A blight seemed to have descended on her.

"I suppose we'll stay a little while to rest the mare," said Marilla, "but I promised Matthew I'd be home early. The fact is, Mrs. Spencer, there's been a queer mistake somewhere, and I've come over to see where it is. We sent word, Matthew and I, for you to bring us a boy from the asylum. We told your brother Robert to tell you we wanted a boy ten or eleven years old."

"Marilla Cuthbert, you don't say so!" said Mrs. Spencer in distress. "Why, Robert sent the word down by his daughter Nancy and she said you wanted a girl—didn't she, Flora Jane?" appealing to her daughter who had come out to the steps.

"She certainly did, Miss Cuthbert," corroborated Flora Jane earnestly.

"I'm dreadful sorry," said Mrs. Spencer. "It is too bad; but it certainly wasn't my fault, you see, Miss Cuthbert. I did the best I could and I thought I was following your instructions. Nancy is a terrible flighty thing. I've often had to scold her well for her heedlessness."

"It was our own fault," said Marilla resignedly. "We should have come to you ourselves and not left an important message to be passed along by word of mouth in that fashion. Anyhow, the mistake has been made and the only thing to do now is to set it right. Can we send the child back to the asylum? I suppose they'll take her back, won't they?"

"I suppose so," said Mrs. Spencer thoughtfully, "but I don't think it will be necessary to send her back. Mrs. Peter Blewett was up here yesterday, and she was saying to me how much she wished she'd sent by me for a little girl to help her. Mrs. Peter has a large family, you know, and she finds it hard to get help. Anne will be the very girl for her. I call it positively providential."

Marilla did not look as if she thought Providence had much to do with the matter. Here was an unexpectedly good chance to get this unwelcome orphan off her hands, and she did not even feel grateful for it.

She knew Mrs. Peter Blewett only by sight as a small, shrewish-faced woman without an ounce of superfluous flesh on her bones. But she had heard of her. "A terrible worker and driver," Mrs. Peter was said to be; and discharged servant girls told fearsome tales of her temper and stinginess, and her family of pert, quarrelsome children. Marilla felt a qualm of conscience at the thought of handing Anne over to her tender mercies.

"Well, I'll go in and we'll talk the matter over," she said.

"And if there isn't Mrs. Peter coming up the lane this blessed minute!" exclaimed Mrs. Spencer, bustling her guests through the hall into the parlor, where a deadly chill struck on them as if the air had been strained so long through dark green, closely drawn blinds that it had lost every particle of warmth it had ever possessed. "That is real lucky, for we can settle the matter right away. Take the armchair, Miss Cuthbert. Anne, you sit here on the ottoman and don't wriggle. Let me take your hats. Flora Jane, go out and put the kettle on. Good afternoon, Mrs. Blewett. We were just saying how fortunate it was you happened along. Let me introduce you two ladies. Mrs. Blewett, Miss Cuthbert. Please excuse me for just a moment. I forgot to tell Flora Jane to take the buns out of the oven."

Mrs. Spencer whisked away, after pulling up the blinds. Anne, sitting mutely on the ottoman, with her hands clasped tightly in her lap, stared at Mrs. Blewett as one fascinated. Was she to be given into the keeping of this sharp-faced, sharp-eyed woman? She felt a lump coming up in her throat and her eyes smarted painfully. She was beginning to be afraid she couldn't keep the tears back when Mrs. Spencer returned, flushed and beaming, quite capable of taking any and every difficulty, physical, mental or spiritual, into consideration and settling it out of hand.

"It seems there's been a mistake about this little girl, Mrs. Blewett," she said. "I was under the impression that Mr. and Miss Cuthbert wanted a little girl to adopt. I was certainly told so. But it seems it was a boy they wanted. So if you're still of the same mind you were yesterday, I think she'll be just the thing for you."

Mrs. Blewett darted her eyes over Anne from head to foot.

"How old are you and what's your name?" she demanded.

"Anne Shirley," faltered the shrinking child, not daring to make any stipulations regarding the spelling thereof, "and I'm eleven years old."

"Humph! You don't look as if there was much to you. But you're wiry. I don't know but the wiry ones are the best after all. Well, if I take you you'll have to be a good girl, you know—good and smart and respectful. I'll expect you to earn your keep, and no mistake about that. Yes, I suppose I might as well take her off your hands, Miss Cuthbert. The baby's awful fractious, and I'm clean worn out attending to him. If you like I can take her right home now."

Marilla looked at Anne and softened at sight of the child's pale face with its look of mute misery—the misery of a helpless little creature who finds itself once more caught in the trap from which it had escaped. Marilla felt an uncomfortable conviction that, if she denied the appeal of that look, it would haunt her to her dying day. Moreover, she did not fancy Mrs. Blewett. To hand a sensitive, "highstrung" child over to such a woman! No, she could not take the responsibility of doing that!

"Well, I don't know," she said slowly. "I didn't say that Matthew and I had absolutely decided that we wouldn't keep her. In fact, I may say that Matthew is disposed to keep her. I just came over to find out how the mistake had occurred. I think I'd better take her home again and talk it over with Matthew. I feel that I oughtn't to decide on any-thing without consulting him. If we make up our mind not to keep her we'll bring or send her over to you tomorrow night. If we don't you may know that she is going to stay with us. Will that suit you, Mrs. Blewett?"

"I suppose it'll have to," said Mrs. Blewett ungraciously.

During Marilla's speech a sunrise had been dawning on Anne's face. First the look of despair faded out; then came a faint flush of hope; her eyes grew deep and bright as morning stars. The child was quite transfigured; and, a moment later, when Mrs. Spencer and Mrs. Blewett went out in quest of a recipe the latter had come to borrow she sprang up and flew across the room to Marilla.

"Oh, Miss Cuthbert, did you really say that perhaps you would let me stay at Green Gables?" she said, in a breathless whisper, as if speak-ing aloud might shatter the glorious possibility. "Did you really say it? Or did I only imagine that you did?"

"I think you'd better learn to control that imagination of yours, Anne, if you can't distinguish between what is real and what isn't," said Marilla crossly. "Yes, you did hear me say just that and no more. It isn't decided yet and perhaps we will conclude to let Mrs. Blewett take you after all. She certainly needs you much more I do."

"I'd rather go back to the asylum than go to live with her," said Anne passionately. "She looks exactly like a—like a gimlet."

Marilla smothered a smile under the conviction that Anne must be reproved for such a speech.

"A little girl like you should be ashamed of talking so about a lady and a stranger," she said severely. "Go back and sit down quietly and hold your tongue and behave as a good girl should."

"I'll try to do and be anything you want me, if you'll only keep me," said Anne, returning meekly to her ottoman.

When they arrived back at Green Gables that evening Matthew met them in the lane. Marilla from afar had noted him prowling along it and guessed his motive. She was prepared for the relief she read in his face when he saw that she had at least brought Anne back with her. But she said nothing to him, relative to the affair, until they were both out in the yard behind the barn milking the cows. Then she briefly told him Anne's history and the result of the interview with Mrs. Spencer.

"I wouldn't give a dog I liked to that Blewett woman," said Matthew with unusual vim.

"I don't fancy her style myself," admitted Marilla, "but it's that or keeping her ourselves, Matthew. And, since you seem to want her, I suppose I'm willing—or have to be. I've been thinking over the idea until I've got kind of used to it. It seems a sort of duty. I've never brought up a child, especially a girl, and I dare say I'll make a terrible mess of it. But I'll do my best. So far as I'm concerned, Matthew, she may stay."

Matthew's shy face was a glow of delight.

"Well now, I reckoned you'd come to see it in that light, Marilla," he said. "She's such an interesting little thing."

"It'd be more to the point if you could say she was a useful little thing," retorted Marilla, "but I'll make it my business to see she's trained to be that. And mind, Matthew, you're not to go interfering with my methods. Perhaps an old maid doesn't know much about bringing up a child, but I guess she knows more than an old bachelor. So you just leave me to manage her. When I fail it'll be time enough to put your oar in."

"There, there, Marilla, you can have your own way," said Matthew reassuringly. "Only be as good and kind to her as you can be without spoiling her. I kind of think she's one of the sort you can do anything with if you only get her to love you."

Marilla sniffed, to express her contempt for Matthew's opinions concerning anything feminine, and walked off to the dairy with the pails.

"I won't tell her tonight that she can stay," she reflected, as she strained the milk into the creamers. "She'd be so excited that she wouldn't sleep a wink. Marilla Cuthbert, you're fairly in for it. Did you ever suppose you'd see the day when you'd be adopting an orphan girl? It's surprising enough; but not so surprising as that Matthew should be at the bottom of it, him that always seemed to have such a mortal dread of little girls. Anyhow, we've decided on the experiment and goodness only knows what will come of it."

7

Anne Says Her Prayers

When Marilla took Anne up to bed that night she said stiffly:

"Now, Anne, I noticed last night that you threw your clothes all about the floor when you took them off. That is a very untidy habit, and I can't allow it at all. As soon as you take off any article of clothing fold it neatly and place it on the chair. I haven't any use at all for little girls who aren't neat."

"I was so harrowed up in my mind last night that I didn't think about my clothes at all," said Anne. "I'll fold them nicely tonight. They always made us do that at the asylum. Half the time, though, I'd forget, I'd be in such a hurry to get into bed nice and quiet and imagine things."

"You'll have to remember a little better if you stay here," admonished Marilla. "There, that looks something like. Say your prayers now and get into bed."

"I never say any prayers," announced Anne.

Marilla looked horrified astonishment.

"Why, Anne, what do you mean? Were you never taught to say your prayers? God always wants little girls to say their prayers. Don't you know who God is, Anne?"

"'God is a spirit, infinite, eternal and unchangeable, in His being, wisdom, power, holiness, justice, goodness, and truth,'" responded Anne promptly and glibly.

Marilla looked rather relieved.

"So you do know something then, thank goodness! You're not quite a heathen. Where did you learn that?"

"Oh, at the asylum Sunday-school. They made us learn the whole catechism. I liked it pretty well. There's something splendid about some of the words. 'Infinite, eternal and unchangeable.' Isn't that grand? It has such a roll to it—just like a big organ playing. You couldn't quite call it poetry, I suppose, but it sounds a lot like it, doesn't it?"

"We're not talking about poetry, Anne—we are talking about saying your prayers. Don't you know it's a terrible wicked thing not to say your prayers every night? I'm afraid you are a very bad little girl."

"You'd find it easier to be bad than good if you had red hair," said Anne reproachfully. "People who haven't red hair don't know what trouble is. Mrs. Thomas told me that God made my hair red *on purpose,* and I've never cared about Him since. And anyhow I'd always be too tired at night to bother saying prayers. People who have to look after twins can't be expected to say their prayers. Now, do you honestly think they can?"

Marilla decided that Anne's religious training must be begun at once. Plainly there was no time to be lost.

"You must say your prayers while you are under my roof, Anne."

"Why, of course, if you want me to," assented Anne cheerfully. "I'd do anything to oblige you. But you'll have to tell me what to say for this once. After I get into bed I'll imagine out a real nice prayer to say always. I believe that it will be quite interesting, now that I come to think of it."

"You must kneel down," said Marilla in embarrassment.

Anne knelt at Marilla's knee and looked up gravely.

"Why must people kneel down to pray? If I really wanted to pray I'll tell you what I'd do. I'd go out into a great big field all alone or into the deep, deep woods, and I'd look up into the sky—up—up—up—into that lovely blue sky that looks as if there was no end to its blueness. And then I'd just *feel* a prayer. Well, I'm ready. What am I to say?"

Marilla felt more embarrassed than ever. She had intended to teach Anne the childish classic, "Now I lay me down to sleep." But she had, as I have told you, the glimmerings of a sense of humor—which is simply another name for a sense of the fitness of things; and it suddenly occurred to her that that simple little prayer, sacred to white-robed childhood lisping at motherly knees, was entirely unsuited to this freckled witch of a girl who knew and cared nothing about God's love, since she had never had it translated to her through the medium of human love.

"You're old enough to pray for yourself, Anne," she said finally. "Just thank God for your blessings and ask Him humbly for the things you want."

"Well, I'll do my best," promised Anne, burying her face in Marilla's lap. "Gracious heavenly Father—that's the way the ministers say it in church, so I suppose it's all right in a private prayer, isn't it?" she interjected, lifting her head for a moment.

"Gracious heavenly Father, I thank Thee for the White Way of Delight and the Lake of Shining Waters and Bonny and the Snow Queen. I'm really extremely grateful for them. And that's all the blessings I can think of just now to thank Thee for. As for the things I want, they're so numerous that it would take a great deal of time to name them all, so I will only mention the two most important. Please let me stay at Green Gables; and please let me be good-looking when I grow up. I remain,

"Yours respectfully,

"Anne Shirley.

"There, did I do it all right?" she asked eagerly, getting up. "I could have made it much more flowery if I'd had a little more time to think it over."

Poor Marilla was only preserved from complete collapse by remembering that it was not irreverence, but simply spiritual ignorance on the part of Anne that was responsible for this extraordinary petition. She tucked the child up in bed, mentally vowing that she should be taught a prayer the very next day, and was leaving the room with the light when Anne called her back.

"I've just thought of it now. I should have said 'Amen' in place of 'yours respectfully,' shouldn't I?—the way the ministers do. I'd forgotten it, but I felt a prayer should be finished off in some way, so I put in the other. Do you suppose it will make any difference?"

"I—I don't suppose it will," said Marilla. "Go to sleep now like a good child. Good night."

"I can say good night tonight with a clear conscience," said Anne, cuddling luxuriously down among her pillows.

Marilla retreated to the kitchen, set the candle firmly on the table, and glared at Matthew.

"Matthew Cuthbert, it's about time somebody adopted that child and taught her something. She's next door to a perfect heathen. Will you believe that she never said a prayer in her life till to-night? I'll send to the manse tomorrow and borrow the Peep of Day series, that's what I'll do. And she shall go to Sunday-school just as soon as I can get some suitable clothes made for her. I foresee that I shall have my hands full. Well, well, we can't get through this world without our share of trouble. I've had a pretty easy life of it so far, but my time has come at last and I suppose I'll just have to make the best of it."

8

Anne's Bringing-up is Begun

or reasons best known to herself, Marilla did not tell Anne that she was to stay at Green Gables until the next afternoon. During the forenoon she kept the child busy with various tasks and watched over her with a keen eye while she did them. By noon she had concluded that Anne was smart and obedient, willing to work and quick to learn; her most serious shortcoming seemed to be a tendency to fall into daydreams in the middle of a task and forget all about it until such time as she was sharply recalled to earth by a reprimand or a catastrophe.

When Anne had finished washing the dinner dishes she suddenly confronted Marilla with the air and expression of one desperately determined to learn the worst. Her thin little body trembled from head to foot; her face flushed and her eyes dilated until they were almost black; she clasped her hands tightly and said in an imploring voice:

"Oh, please, Miss Cuthbert, won't you tell me if you are going to send me away or not? I've tried to be patient all the morning, but I really feel that I cannot bear not knowing any longer. It's a dreadful feeling. Please tell me."

"You haven't scalded the dishcloth in clean hot water as I told you to do," said Marilla immovably. "Just go and do it before you ask any more questions, Anne."

Anne went and attended to the dishcloth. Then she returned to Marilla and fastened imploring eyes on the latter's face.

"Well," said Marilla, unable to find any excuse for deferring her explanation longer, "I suppose I might as well tell you. Matthew and I have decided to keep you—that is, if you will try to be a good little girl and show yourself grateful. Why, child, whatever is the matter?"

"I'm crying," said Anne in a tone of bewilderment. "I can't think why. I'm glad as glad can be. Oh, *glad* doesn't seem the right word at all. I was glad about the White Way and the cherry blossoms—but this! Oh, it's something more than glad. I'm so happy. I'll try to be so good. It will be uphill work, I expect, for Mrs. Thomas often told me I was desperately wicked. However, I'll do my very best. But can you tell me why I'm crying?"

"I suppose it's because you're all excited and worked up," said Marilla disapprovingly. "Sit down on that chair and try to calm yourself. I'm afraid you both cry and laugh far too easily. Yes, you can stay here and we will try to do right by you. You must go to school; but it's only a fortnight till vacation so it isn't worth while for you to start before it opens again in September."

"What am I to call you?" asked Anne. "Shall I always say Miss Cuthbert? Can I call you Aunt Marilla?"

"No; you'll call me just plain Marilla. I'm not used to being called Miss Cuthbert and it would make me nervous."

"It sounds awfully disrespectful to say just Marilla," protested Anne.

"I guess there'll be nothing disrespectful in it if you're careful to speak respectfully. Everybody, young and old, in Avonlea calls me Marilla except the minister. He says Miss Cuthbert—when he thinks of it."

"I'd love to call you Aunt Marilla," said Anne wistfully. "I've never had an aunt or any relation at all—not even a grandmother. It would make me feel as if I really belonged to you. Can't I call you Aunt Marilla?"

"No. I'm not your aunt and I don't believe in calling people names that don't belong to them."

"But we could imagine you were my aunt."

"I couldn't," said Marilla grimly.

"Do you never imagine things different from what they really are?" asked Anne wide-eyed.

"No."

"Oh!" Anne drew a long breath. "Oh, Miss—Marilla, how much you miss!"

"I don't believe in imagining things different from what they really are," retorted Marilla. "When the Lord puts us in certain circumstances He doesn't mean for us to imagine them away. And that reminds me. Go into the sitting room, Anne—be sure your feet are clean and don't let any flies in—and bring me out the illustrated card that's on the mantelpiece. The Lord's Prayer is on it and you'll devote your spare time this afternoon to learning it off by heart. There's to be no more of such praying as I heard last night."

"I suppose I was very awkward," said Anne apologetically, "but then, you see, I'd never had any practice. You couldn't really expect a person to pray very well the first time she tried, could you? I thought out a splendid prayer after I went to bed, just as I promised you I would. It was nearly as long as a minister's and so poetical. But would you believe it? I couldn't remember one word when I woke up this morning. And I'm afraid I'll never be able to think out another one as good. Somehow, things never are so good when they're thought out a second time. Have you ever noticed that?"

"Here is something for you to notice, Anne. When I tell you to do a thing I want you to obey me at once and not stand stock-still and discourse about it. Just you go and do as I bid you."

Anne promptly departed for the sitting-room across the hall; she failed to return; after waiting ten minutes Marilla laid down her knitting and marched after her with a grim expression. She found Anne standing motionless before a picture hanging on the wall between the two windows, with her hands clasped behind her, her face uplifted, and her eyes astar with dreams. The white and green light strained through apple trees and clustering vines outside fell over the rapt little figure with a half-unearthly radiance.

"Anne, whatever are you thinking of?" demanded Marilla sharply.

Anne came back to earth with a start.

"That," she said, pointing to the picture—a rather vivid chromo entitled, "Christ Blessing little Children"—"and I was just imagining I was one of them—that I was the little girl in the blue dress, standing off by herself in the corner as if she didn't belong to anybody, like me. She looks lonely and sad, don't you think? I guess she hadn't any father or mother of her own. But she wanted to be blessed, too, so she just crept shyly up on the outside of the crowd, hoping nobody would notice her—except Him. I'm sure I know just how she felt. Her heart must have beat and her hands must have got cold, like mine did when I asked you if I could stay. She was afraid He mightn't notice her. But it's likely He did, don't you think? I've been trying to imagine it all out—her edging a little nearer all the time until she was quite close to Him; and then He would look at her and put His hand on her hair and oh, such a thrill of joy as would run over her! But I wish the artist hadn't painted Him so sorrowful looking. All His pictures are like that, if you've noticed. But I don't believe He could really have looked so sad or the children would have been afraid of Him."

"Anne," said Marilla, wondering why she had not broken into this speech long before, "you shouldn't talk that way. It's irreverent—positively irreverent."

Anne's eyes marveled.

"Why, I felt just as reverent as could be. I'm sure I didn't mean to be irreverent."

"Well, I don't suppose you did—but it doesn't sound right to talk so familiarly about such things. And another thing, Anne, when I send you after something you're to bring it at once and not fall into mooning and imagining before pictures. Remember that. Take that card and come right to the kitchen. Now, sit down in the corner and learn that prayer off by heart."

Anne set the card up against the jugful of apple blossoms she had brought in to decorate the dinner-table—Marilla had eyed that decoration askance, but had said nothing—propped her chin on her hands, and fell to studying it intently for several silent minutes.

"I like this," she announced at length. "It's beautiful. I've heard it before—I heard the superintendent of the asylum Sunday school say it over once. But I didn't like it then. He had such a cracked voice and he prayed it so mournfully. I really felt sure he thought praying was a disagreeable duty. This isn't poetry, but it makes me feel just the same way poetry does. 'Our Father who art in heaven, hallowed be Thy name.' That is just like a line of music. Oh, I'm so glad you thought of making me learn this, Miss—Marilla."

"Well, learn it and hold your tongue," said Marilla shortly.

Anne tipped the vase of apple blossoms near enough to bestow a soft kiss on a pink-cupped bud, and then studied diligently for some moments longer.

"Marilla," she demanded presently, "do you think that I shall ever have a bosom friend in Avonlea?"

"A—a what kind of a friend?"

"A bosom friend—an intimate friend, you know—a really kindred spirit to whom I can confide my inmost soul. I've dreamed of meeting her all my life. I never really supposed I would, but so many of my loveliest dreams have come true all at once that perhaps this one will, too. Do you think it's possible?"

"Diana Barry lives over at Orchard Slope and she's about your age. She's a very nice little girl, and perhaps she will be a playmate for you when she comes home. She's visiting her aunt over at Carmody just now. You'll have to be careful how you behave yourself, though. Mrs. Barry is a very particular woman. She won't let Diana play with any little girl who isn't nice and good."

Anne looked at Marilla through the apple blossoms, her eyes aglow with interest.

"What is Diana like? Her hair isn't red, is it? Oh, I hope not. It's bad enough to have red hair myself, but I positively couldn't endure it in a bosom friend."

"Diana is a very pretty little girl. She has black eyes and hair and rosy cheeks. And she is good and smart, which is better than being pretty."

Marilla was as fond of morals as the Duchess in Wonderland, and was firmly convinced that one should be tacked on to every remark made to a child who was being brought up.

But Anne waved the moral inconsequently aside and seized only on the delightful possibilities before it.

"Oh, I'm so glad she's pretty. Next to being beautiful oneself—and that's impossible in my case—it would be best to have a beautiful

n I lived with Mrs. Thomas she had a bookcase in
glass doors. There weren't any books in it; Mrs.
best china and her preserves there—when she had any
to keep. One of the doors was broken. Mr. Thomas smashed
one night when he was slightly intoxicated. But the other was whole
and I used to pretend that my reflection in it was another little girl who
lived in it. I called her Katie Maurice, and we were very intimate. I used
to talk to her by the hour, especially on Sunday, and tell her everything.
Katie was the comfort and consolation of my life. We used to pretend
that the bookcase was enchanted and that if I only knew the spell I
could open the door and step right into the room where Katie Maurice
lived, instead of into Mrs. Thomas' shelves of preserves and china.
And then Katie Maurice would have taken me by the hand and led me
out into a wonderful place, all flowers and sunshine and fairies, and we
would have lived there happy for ever after. When I went to live with
Mrs. Hammond it just broke my heart to leave Katie Maurice. She felt
it dreadfully, too, I know she did, for she was crying when she kissed me
good-bye through the bookcase door. There was no bookcase at Mrs.
Hammond's. But just up the river a little way from the house there was
a long green little valley, and the loveliest echo lived there. It echoed
back every word you said, even if you didn't talk a bit loud. So I imagined that it was a little girl called Violetta and we were great friends and
I loved her almost as well as I loved Katie Maurice—not quite, but
almost, you know. The night before I went to the asylum I said good-
bye to Violetta, and oh, her good-bye came back to me in such sad, sad
tones. I had become so attached to her that I hadn't the heart to imagine a bosom friend at the asylum, even if there had been any scope for
imagination there."

"I think it's just as well there wasn't," said Marilla drily. "I don't
approve of such goings-on. You seem to half believe your own imaginations. It will be well for you to have a real live friend to put such nonsense out of your head. But don't let Mrs. Barry hear you talking about
your Katie Maurices and your Violettas or she'll think you tell stories."

"Oh, I won't. I couldn't talk of them to everybody—their memories are too sacred for that. But I thought I'd like to have you know

about them. Oh, look, here's a big bee just tumbled out of an apple blossom. Just think what a lovely place to live—in an apple blossom! Fancy going to sleep in it when the wind was rocking it. If I wasn't a human girl I think I'd like to be a bee and live among the flowers."

"Yesterday you wanted to be a sea gull," sniffed Marilla. "I think you are very fickle minded. I told you to learn that prayer and not talk. But it seems impossible for you to stop talking if you've got anybody that will listen to you. So go up to your room and learn it."

"Oh, I know it pretty nearly all now—all but just the last line."

"Well, never mind, do as I tell you. Go to your room and finish learning it well, and stay there until I call you down to help me get tea."

"Can I take the apple blossoms with me for company?" pleaded Anne.

"No; you don't want your room cluttered up with flowers. You should have left them on the tree in the first place."

"I did feel a little that way, too," said Anne. "I kind of felt I shouldn't shorten their lovely lives by picking them—I wouldn't want to be picked if I were an apple blossom. But the temptation was *irresistible*. What do you do when you meet with an irresistible temptation?"

"Anne, did you hear me tell you to go to your room?"

Anne sighed, retreated to the east gable, and sat down in a chair by the window.

"There—I know this prayer. I learned that last sentence coming upstairs. Now I'm going to imagine things into this room so that they'll always stay imagined. The floor is covered with a white velvet carpet with pink roses all over it and there are pink silk curtains at the windows. The walls are hung with gold and silver brocade tapestry. The furniture is mahogany. I never saw any mahogany, but it does sound so luxurious. This is a couch all heaped with gorgeous silken cushions, pink and blue and crimson and gold, and I am reclining gracefully on it. I can see my reflection in that splendid big mirror hanging on the wall. I am tall and regal, clad in a gown of trailing white lace, with a pearl cross on my breast and pearls in my hair. My hair is of midnight darkness and my skin is a clear ivory pallor. My name is the Lady Cordelia Fitzgerald. No, it isn't—I can't make *that* seem real."

She danced up to the little looking-glass and peered into it. Her pointed freckled face and solemn gray eyes peered back at her.

"You're only Anne of Green Gables," she said earnestly, "and I see you, just as you are looking now, whenever I try to imagine I'm the Lady Cordelia. But it's a million times nicer to be Anne of Green Gables than Anne of nowhere in particular, isn't it?"

She bent forward, kissed her reflection affectionately, and betook herself to the open window.

"Dear Snow Queen, good afternoon. And good afternoon, dear birches down in the hollow. And good afternoon, dear gray house up on the hill. I wonder if Diana is to be my bosom friend. I hope she will, and I shall love her very much. But I must never quite forget Katie Maurice and Violetta. They would feel so hurt if I did and I'd hate to hurt anybody's feelings, even a little bookcase girl's or a little echo girl's. I must be careful to remember them and send them a kiss every day."

Anne blew a couple of airy kisses from her fingertips past the cherry blossoms and then, with her chin in her hands, drifted luxuriously out on a sea of daydreams.

9

Mrs. Rachel Lynde is Properly Horrified

Anne had been a fortnight at Green Gables before Mrs. Lynde arrived to inspect her. Mrs. Rachel, to do her justice, was not to blame for this. A severe and unseasonable attack of grippe had confined that good lady to her house ever since the occasion of her last visit to Green Gables. Mrs. Rachel was not often sick and had a well-defined contempt for people who were; but grippe, she asserted, was like no other illness on earth and could only be interpreted as one of the special visitations of Providence. As soon as her doctor allowed her to put her foot out-of-doors she hurried up to Green Gables, bursting with curiosity to see Matthew's and Marilla's orphan, concerning whom all sorts of stories and suppositions had gone abroad in Avonlea.

Anne had made good use of every waking moment of that fortnight. Already she was acquainted with every tree and shrub about the place. She had discovered that a lane opened out below the apple orchard and ran up through a belt of woodland; and she had explored it to its furthest end in all its delicious vagaries of brook and bridge, fir coppice and wild cherry arch, corners thick with fern, and branching byways of maple and mountain ash.

She had made friends with the spring down in the hollow—that wonderful deep, clear icy-cold spring; it was set about with smooth red sandstones and rimmed in by great palm-like clumps of water fern; and beyond it was a log bridge over the brook.

That bridge led Anne's dancing feet up over a wooded hill beyond, where perpetual twilight reigned under the straight, thick-growing firs and spruces; the only flowers there were myriads of delicate "June bells," those shyest and sweetest of woodland blooms, and a few pale, aerial starflowers, like the spirits of last year's blossoms. Gossamers glimmered like threads of silver among the trees and the fir boughs and tassels seemed to utter friendly speech.

All these raptured voyages of exploration were made in the odd half hours which she was allowed for play, and Anne talked Matthew and Marilla half-deaf over her discoveries. Not that Matthew complained, to be sure; he listened to it all with a wordless smile of enjoyment on his face; Marilla permitted the "chatter" until she found herself becoming too interested in it, whereupon she always promptly quenched Anne by a curt command to hold her tongue.

Anne was out in the orchard when Mrs. Rachel came, wandering at her own sweet will through the lush, tremulous grasses splashed with ruddy evening sunshine; so that good lady had an excellent chance to talk her illness fully over, describing every ache and pulse beat with such evident enjoyment that Marilla thought even grippe must bring its compensations. When details were exhausted Mrs. Rachel introduced the real reason of her call.

"I've been hearing some surprising things about you and Matthew."

"I don't suppose you are any more surprised than I am myself," said Marilla. "I'm getting over my surprise now."

"It was too bad there was such a mistake," said Mrs. Rachel sympathetically. "Couldn't you have sent her back?"

"I suppose we could, but we decided not to. Matthew took a fancy to her. And I must say I like her myself—although I admit she has her faults. The house seems a different place already. She's a real bright little thing."

Marilla said more than she had intended to say when she began, for she read disapproval in Mrs. Rachel's expression.

"It's a great responsibility you've taken on yourself," said that lady gloomily, "especially when you've never had any experience with children. You don't know much about her or her real disposition, I suppose, and there's no guessing how a child like that will turn out. But I don't want to discourage you I'm sure, Marilla."

"I'm not feeling discouraged," was Marilla's dry response. "When

I make up my mind to do a thing it stays made up. I suppose you'd like to see Anne. I'll call her in."

Anne came running in presently, her face sparkling with the delight of her orchard rovings; but, abashed at finding herself in the unexpected presence of a stranger, she halted confusedly inside the door. She certainly was an odd-looking little creature in the short tight wincey dress she had worn from the asylum, below which her thin legs seemed ungracefully long. Her freckles were more numerous and obtrusive than ever; the wind had ruffled her hatless hair into over-brilliant disorder; it had never looked redder than at that moment.

"Well, they didn't pick you for your looks, that's sure and certain," was Mrs. Rachel Lynde's emphatic comment. Mrs. Rachel was one of those delightful and popular people who pride themselves on speaking their mind without fear or favor. "She's terrible skinny and homely, Marilla. Come here, child, and let me have a look at you. Lawful heart, did any one ever see such freckles? And hair as red as carrots! Come here, child, I say."

Anne "came there," but not exactly as Mrs. Rachel expected. With one bound she crossed the kitchen floor and stood before Mrs. Rachel, her face scarlet with anger, her lips quivering, and her whole slender form trembling from head to foot.

"I hate you," she cried in a choked voice, stamping her foot on the floor. "I hate you—I hate you—I hate you—" a louder stamp with each assertion of hatred. "How dare you call me skinny and ugly? How dare you say I'm freckled and redheaded? You are a rude, impolite, unfeeling woman!"

"Anne!" exclaimed Marilla in consternation.

But Anne continued to face Mrs. Rachel undauntedly, head up, eyes blazing, hands clenched, passionate indignation exhaling from her like an atmosphere.

"How dare you say such things about me?" she repeated vehemently. "How would you like to have such things said about you? How would you like to be told that you are fat and clumsy and probably hadn't a spark of imagination in you? I don't care if I do hurt your feelings by saying so! I hope I hurt them. You have hurt mine worse than

they were ever hurt before even by Mrs. Thomas' intoxicated husband. And I'll *never* forgive you for it, never, never!"

Stamp! Stamp!

"Did anybody ever see such a temper!" exclaimed the horrified
Mrs. Rachel.

"Anne, go to your room and stay there until I come up," said
Marilla, recovering her powers of speech with difficulty.

Anne, bursting into tears, rushed to the hall door, slammed it until
the tins on the porch wall outside raffled in sympathy, and fled through
the hall and up the stairs like a whirlwind. A subdued slam above told
that the door of the east gable had been shut with equal vehemence.

"Well, I don't envy you your job bringing *that* up, Marilla," said
Mrs. Rachel with unspeakable solemnity.

Marilla opened her lips to say she knew not what of apology or
deprecation. What she did say was a surprise to herself then and ever
afterwards.

"You shouldn't have twitted her about her looks, Rachel."

"Marilla Cuthbert, you don't mean to say that you are upholding
her in such a terrible display of temper as we've just seen?" demanded
Mrs. Rachel indignantly.

"No," said Marilla slowly, "I'm not trying to excuse her. She's been
very naughty and I'll have to give her a talking to about it. But we
must make allowances for her. She's never been taught what is right.
And you *were* too hard on her, Rachel."

Marilla could not help tacking on that last sentence, although
she was again surprised at herself for doing it. Mrs. Rachel got up with
an air of offended dignity.

"Well, I see that I'll have to be very careful what I say after this,
Marilla, since the fine feelings of orphans, brought from goodness
knows where, have to be considered before anything else. Oh, no, I'm
not vexed—don't worry yourself. I'm too sorry for you to leave any
room for anger in my mind. You'll have your own troubles with that
child. But if you'll take my advice—which I suppose you won't do,
although I've brought up ten children and buried two—you'll do that
'talking to' you mention with a fair-sized birch switch. I should think

that would be the most effective language for that kind of a child. Her temper matches her hair I guess. Well, good evening, Marilla. I hope you'll come down to see me often as usual. But you can't expect me to visit here again in a hurry, if I'm liable to be flown at and insulted in such a fashion. It's something new in *my* experience."

Whereat Mrs. Rachel swept out and away—if a fat woman who always waddled *could* be said to sweep away—and Marilla with a very solemn face betook herself to the east gable.

On the way upstairs she pondered uneasily as to what she ought to do. She felt no little dismay over the scene that had just been enacted. How unfortunate that Anne should have displayed such temper before Mrs. Rachel Lynde, of all people! Then Marilla suddenly became aware of an uncomfortable and rebuking consciousness that she felt more humiliation over this than sorrow over the discovery of such a serious defect in Anne's disposition. And how was she to punish her? The amiable suggestion of the birch switch—to the efficiency of which all of Mrs. Rachel's own children could have borne smarting testimony— did not appeal to Marilla. She did not believe she could whip a child. No, some other method of punishment must be found to bring Anne to a proper realization of the enormity of her offense.

Marilla found Anne face downward on her bed, crying bitterly, quite oblivious of muddy boots on a clean counterpane.

"Anne," she said, not ungently.

No answer.

"Anne," with greater severity, "get off that bed this minute and listen to what I have to say to you."

Anne squirmed off the bed and sat rigidly on a chair beside it, her face swollen and tear-stained and her eyes fixed stubbornly on the floor.

"This is a nice way for you to behave, Anne! Aren't you ashamed of yourself?"

"She hadn't any right to call me ugly and redheaded," retorted Anne, evasive and defiant.

"You hadn't any right to fly into such a fury and talk the way you did to her, Anne. I was ashamed of you—thoroughly ashamed of you.

I wanted you to behave nicely to Mrs. Lynde, and instead of that you have disgraced me. I'm sure I don't know why you should lose your temper like that just because Mrs. Lynde said you were redhaired and homely. You say it yourself often enough."

"Oh, but there's such a difference between saying a thing yourself and hearing other people say it," wailed Anne. "You may know a thing is so, but you can't help hoping other people don't quite think it is. I suppose you think I have an awful temper, but I couldn't help it. When she said those things something just rose right up in me and choked me. I *had* to fly out at her."

"Well, you made a fine exhibition of yourself I must say. Mrs. Lynde will have a nice story to tell about you everywhere—and she'll tell it, too. It was a dreadful thing for you to lose your temper like that, Anne."

"Just imagine how you would feel if somebody told you to your face that you were skinny and ugly," pleaded Anne tearfully.

An old remembrance suddenly rose up before Marilla. She had been a very small child when she had heard one aunt say of her to another, "What a pity she is such a dark, homely little thing." Marilla was every day of fifty before the sting had gone out of that memory.

"I don't say that I think Mrs. Lynde was exactly right in saying what she did to you, Anne," she admitted in a softer tone. "Rachel is too outspoken. But that is no excuse for such behavior on your part. She was a stranger and an elderly person and my visitor—all three very good reasons why you should have been respectful to her. You were rude and saucy and"—Marilla had a saving inspiration of punishment—"you must go to her and tell her you are very sorry for your bad temper and ask her to forgive you."

"I can never do that," said Anne determinedly and darkly. "You can punish me in any way you like, Marilla. You can shut me up in a dark, damp dungeon inhabited by snakes and toads and feed me only on bread and water and I shall not complain. But I cannot ask Mrs. Lynde to forgive me."

"We're not in the habit of shutting people up in dark, damp dungeons," said Marilla drily, "especially as they're rather scarce in Avonlea.

But apologize to Mrs. Lynde you must and shall and you'll stay here in your room until you can tell me you're willing to do it."

"I shall have to stay here for ever then," said Anne mournfully, "because I can't tell Mrs. Lynde I'm sorry I said those things to her. How can I? I'm *not* sorry. I'm sorry I've vexed you; but I'm *glad* I told her just what I did. It was a great satisfaction. I can't say I'm sorry when I'm not, can I? I can't even *imagine* I'm sorry."

"Perhaps your imagination will be in better working order by the morning," said Marilla, rising to depart. "You'll have the night to think over your conduct in and come to a better frame of mind. You said you would try to be a very good girl if we kept you at Green Gables, but I must say it hasn't seemed very much like it this evening."

Leaving this Parthian shaft to rankle in Anne's stormy bosom, Marilla descended to the kitchen, grievously troubled in mind and vexed in soul. She was as angry with herself as with Anne, because, whenever she recalled Mrs. Rachel's dumfounded countenance her lips twitched with amusement and she felt a most reprehensible desire to laugh.

10

Anne's Apology

arilla said nothing to Matthew about the affair that evening; but when Anne proved still refractory the next morning an explanation had to be made to account for her absence from the breakfast table. Marilla told Matthew the whole story, taking pains to impress him with a due sense of the enormity of Anne's behavior.

"It's a good thing Rachel Lynde got a calling down; she's a meddlesome old gossip," was Matthew's consolatory rejoinder.

"Matthew Cuthbert, I'm astonished at you. You know that Anne's behavior was dreadful, and yet you take her part! I suppose you'll be saying next thing that she oughtn't to be punished at all."

"Well now—no—not exactly," said Matthew uneasily. "I reckon she ought to be punished a little. But don't be too hard on her, Marilla. Recollect she hasn't ever had any one to teach her right. You're—you're going to give her something to eat, aren't you?"

"When did you ever hear of me starving people into good behavior?" demanded Marilla indignantly. "She'll have her meals regular, and I'll carry them up to her myself. But she'll stay up there until she's willing to apologize to Mrs. Lynde, and that's final, Matthew."

Breakfast, dinner, and supper were very silent meals—for Anne still remained obdurate. After each meal Marilla carried a well-filled tray to the east gable and brought it down later on not noticeably depleted. Matthew eyed its last descent with a troubled eye. Had Anne eaten anything at all?

When Marilla went out that evening to bring the cows from the back pasture, Matthew, who had been hanging about the barns and watching, slipped into the house with the air of a burglar and crept upstairs. As a general thing Matthew gravitated between the kitchen and the little bedroom off the hall where he slept; once in a while he ventured uncomfortably into the parlor or sitting room when the minister came to tea. But he had never been upstairs in his own house since the spring he helped Marilla paper the spare bedroom, and that was four years ago.

He tiptoed along the hall and stood for several minutes outside the door of the east gable before he summoned courage to tap on it with his fingers and then open the door to peep in.

Anne was sitting on the yellow chair by the window, gazing mournfully out into the garden. Very small and unhappy she looked, and Matthew's heart smote him. He softly closed the door and tiptoed over to her.

"Anne," he whispered, as if afraid of being overheard, "how are you making it, Anne?"

Anne smiled wanly.

"Pretty well. I imagine a good deal, and that helps to pass the time. Of course, it's rather lonesome. But then, I may as well get used to that."

Anne smiled again, bravely facing the long years of solitary imprisonment before her.

Matthew recollected that he must say what he had come to say without loss of time, lest Marilla return prematurely.

"Well now, Anne, don't you think you'd better do it and have it over with?" he whispered. "It'll have to be done sooner or later, you know, for Marilla's a dreadful determined woman—dreadful determined, Anne. Do it right off, I say, and have it over."

"Do you mean apologize to Mrs. Lynde?"

"Yes—apologize—that's the very word," said Matthew eagerly. "Just smooth it over so to speak. That's what I was trying to get at."

"I suppose I could do it to oblige you," said Anne thoughtfully. "It would be true enough to say I am sorry, because I *am* sorry now. I wasn't a bit sorry last night. I was mad clear through, and I stayed mad all night. I know I did because I woke up three times and I was just furious every time. But this morning it was all over. I wasn't in

a temper any more—and it left a dreadful sort of goneness, too. I felt
so ashamed of myself. But I just couldn't think of going and telling Mrs.
Lynde so. It would be so humiliating. I made up my mind I'd stay shut
up here for ever rather than do that. But still—I'd do anything for
you—if you really want me to—"

"Well now, of course I do. It's terrible lonesome downstairs without you. Just go and smooth it over—that's a good girl."

"Very well," said Anne resignedly. "I'll tell Marilla as soon as she
comes in that I've repented."

"That's right—that's right, Anne. But don't tell Marilla I said
anything about it. She might think I was putting my oar in and I promised not to do that."

"Wild horses won't drag the secret from me," promised Anne
solemnly. "How would wild horses drag a secret from a person anyhow?"

But Matthew was gone, scared at his own success. He fled hastily
to the remotest corner of the horse pasture lest Marilla should suspect
what he had been up to. Marilla herself, upon her return to the house,
was agreeably surprised to hear a plaintive voice calling, "Marilla," over
the banisters.

"Well?" she said, going into the hall.

"I'm sorry I lost my temper and said rude things, and I'm willing
to go and tell Mrs. Lynde so."

"Very well." Marilla's crispness gave no sign of her relief. She had
been wondering what under the canopy she should do if Anne did not
give in. "I'll take you down after milking."

Accordingly, after milking, behold Marilla and Anne walking
down the lane, the former erect and triumphant, the latter drooping
and dejected. But halfway down Anne's dejection vanished as if by
enchantment. She lifted her head and stepped lightly along, her eyes
fixed on the sunset sky and an air of subdued exhilaration about her.
Marilla beheld the change disapprovingly. This was no meek penitent
such as it behooved her to take into the presence of the offended Mrs.
Lynde.

"What are you thinking of, Anne?" she asked sharply.

"I'm imagining out what I must say to Mrs. Lynde," answered Anne dreamily.

This was satisfactory—or should have been so. But Marilla could not rid herself of the notion that something in her scheme of punishment was going askew. Anne had no business to look so rapt and radiant.

Rapt and radiant Anne continued until they were in the very presence of Mrs. Lynde, who was sitting knitting by her kitchen window. Then the radiance vanished. Mournful penitence appeared on every feature. Before a word was spoken Anne suddenly went down on her knees before the astonished Mrs. Rachel and held out her hands beseechingly.

"Oh, Mrs. Lynde, I am so extremely sorry," she said with a quiver in her voice. "I could never express all my sorrow, no, not if I used up a whole dictionary. You must just imagine it. I behaved terribly to you—and I've disgraced the dear friends, Matthew and Marilla, who have let me stay at Green Gables although I'm not a boy. I'm a dreadfully wicked and ungrateful girl, and I deserve to be punished and cast out by respectable people for ever. It was very wicked of me to fly into a temper because you told me the truth. It *was* the truth; every word you said was true. My hair is red and I'm freckled and skinny and ugly. What I said to you was true, too, but I shouldn't have said it. Oh, Mrs. Lynde, please, please, forgive me. If you refuse it will be a lifelong sorrow to me. You wouldn't like to inflict a lifelong sorrow on a poor little orphan girl, would you, even if she had a dreadful temper? Oh, I am sure you wouldn't. Please say you forgive me, Mrs. Lynde."

Anne clasped her hands together, bowed her head, and waited for the word of judgment.

There was no mistaking her sincerity—it breathed in every tone of her voice. Both Marilla and Mrs. Lynde recognized its unmistakable ring. But the former understood in dismay that Anne was actually enjoying her valley of humiliation—was reveling in the thoroughness of her abasement. Where was the wholesome punishment upon which she, Marilla, had plumed herself? Anne had turned it into a species of positive pleasure.

Good Mrs. Lynde, not being overburdened with perception, did not see this. She only perceived that Anne had made a very thorough apology and all resentment vanished from her kindly, if somewhat officious, heart.

"There, there, get up, child," she said heartily. "Of course I forgive you. I guess I was a little too hard on you, anyway. But I'm such an outspoken person. You just mustn't mind me, that's what. It can't be denied your hair is terrible red; but I knew a girl once—went to school with her, in fact—whose hair was every mite as red as yours when she was young, but when she grew up it darkened to a real handsome auburn. I wouldn't be a mite surprised if yours did, too—not a mite."

"Oh, Mrs. Lynde!" Anne drew a long breath as she rose to her feet. "You have given me a hope. I shall always feel that you are a benefactor. Oh, I could endure anything if I only thought my hair would be a handsome auburn when I grew up. It would be so much easier to be good if one's hair was a handsome auburn, don't you think? And now may I go out into your garden and sit on that bench under the appletrees while you and Marilla are talking? There is so much more scope for imagination out there."

"Laws, yes, run along, child. And you can pick a bouquet of them white June lilies over in the corner if you like."

As the door closed behind Anne Mrs. Lynde got briskly up to light a lamp.

"She's a real odd little thing. Take this chair, Marilla; it's easier than the one you've got; I just keep that for the hired boy to sit on. Yes, she certainly is an odd child, but there is something kind of taking about her after all. I don't feel so surprised at you and Matthew keeping her as I did—nor so sorry for you, either. She may turn out all right. Of course, she has a queer way of expressing herself—a little too—well, too kind of forcible, you know; but she'll likely get over that now that she's come to live among civilized folks. And then, her temper's pretty quick, I guess; but there's one comfort a child that has a quick temper, just blaze up and cool down, ain't never likely to be sly or deceitful. Preserve me from a sly child, that's what. On the whole, Marilla, I kind of like her."

When Marilla went home Anne came out of the fragrant twilight of the orchard with a sheaf of white narcissi in her hands.

"I apologized pretty well, didn't I?" she said proudly as they went down the lane. "I thought since I had to do it I might as well do it thoroughly."

"You did it thoroughly, all right enough," was Marilla's comment. Marilla was dismayed at finding herself inclined to laugh over the recollection. She had also an uneasy feeling that she ought to scold Anne for apologizing so well; but then, that was ridiculous! She compromised with her conscience by saying severely:

"I hope you won't have occasion to make many more such apologies. I hope you'll try to control your temper now, Anne."

"That wouldn't be so hard if people wouldn't twit me about my looks," said Anne with a sigh. "I don't get cross about other things; but I'm *so* tired of being twitted about my hair and it just makes me boil right over. Do you suppose my hair will really be a handsome auburn when I grow up?"

"You shouldn't think so much about your looks, Anne. I'm afraid you are a very vain little girl."

"How can I be vain when I know I'm homely?" protested Anne. "I love pretty things; and I hate to look in the glass and see something that isn't pretty. It makes me feel so sorrowful—just as I feel when I look at any ugly thing. I pity it because it isn't beautiful."

"Handsome is as handsome does," quoted Marilla.

"I've had that said to me before, but I have my doubts about it," remarked skeptical Anne, sniffing at her narcissi. "Oh, aren't these flowers sweet! It was lovely of Mrs. Lynde to give them to me. I have no hard feelings against Mrs. Lynde now. It gives you a lovely, comfortable feeling to apologize and be forgiven, doesn't it? Aren't the stars bright tonight? If you could live in a star, which one would you pick? I'd like that lovely clear big one away over there above that dark hill."

"Anne, do hold your tongue," said Marilla, thoroughly worn out trying to follow the gyrations of Anne's thoughts.

Anne said no more until they turned into their own lane. A little gypsy wind came down it to meet them, laden with the spicy perfume of young dew-wet ferns. Far up in the shadows a cheerful light gleamed out through the trees from the kitchen at Green Gables. Anne suddenly came close to Marilla and slipped her hand into the older woman's hard palm.

"It's lovely to be going home and know it's home," she said. "I love Green Gables already, and I never loved any place before. No place ever seemed like home. Oh, Marilla, I'm so happy. I could pray right now and not find it a bit hard."

Something warm and pleasant welled up in Marilla's heart at touch of that thin little hand in her own—a throb of the maternity she had missed, perhaps. Its very unaccustomedness and sweetness disturbed her. She hastened to restore her sensations to their normal calm by inculcating a moral.

"If you'll be a good girl you'll always be happy, Anne. And you should never find it hard to say your prayers."

"Saying one's prayers isn't exactly the same thing as praying," said Anne meditatively. "But I'm going to imagine that I'm the wind that is blowing up there in those tree tops. When I get tired of the trees I'll imagine I'm gently waving down here in the ferns—and then I'll fly over to Mrs. Lynde's garden and set the flowers dancing—and then I'll go with one great swoop over the clover field—and then I'll blow over the Like of Shining Waters and ripple it all up into little sparkling waves. Oh, there's so much scope for imagination in a wind! So I'll not talk any more just now, Marilla."

"Thanks be to goodness for that," breathed Marilla in devout relief.

11

Anne's Impressions of Sunday-School

"Well, how do you like them?" said Marilla.

Anne was standing in the gable room, looking solemnly at three new dresses spread out on the bed. One was of snuffy colored gingham which Marilla had been tempted to buy from a peddler the preceding summer because it looked so serviceable; one was of black-and-white checked sateen which she had picked up at a bargain counter in the winter; and one was a stiff print of an ugly blue shade which she had purchased that week at a Carmody store.

She had made them up herself, and they were all made alike— plain skirts fulled tightly to plain waists, with sleeves as plain as waist and skirt and tight as sleeves could be.

"I'll imagine that I like them," said Anne soberly.

"I don't want you to imagine it," said Marilla, offended. "Oh, I can see you don't like the dresses! What is the matter with them? Aren't they neat and clean and new?"

"Yes."

"Then why don't you like them?"

"They're—they're not—pretty," said Anne reluctantly.

"Pretty!" Marilla sniffed. "I didn't trouble my head about getting pretty dresses for you. I don't believe in pampering vanity, Anne, I'll tell you that right off. Those dresses are good, sensible, serviceable dresses, without any frills or furbelows about them, and they're all you'll get this summer. The brown gingham and the blue print will do you for school when you begin to go. The sateen is for church and Sunday school. I'll expect you to keep them neat and clean and not to tear them. I should think you'd be grateful to get most anything after those skimpy wincey things you've been wearing."

"Oh, I *am* grateful," protested Anne. "But I'd be ever so much gratefuller if—if you'd made just one of them with puffed sleeves. Puffed sleeves are so fashionable now. It would give me such a thrill, Marilla, just to wear a dress with puffed sleeves."

"Well, you'll have to do without your thrill. I hadn't any material to waste on puffed sleeves. I think they are ridiculous-looking things anyhow. I prefer the plain, sensible ones."

"But I'd rather look ridiculous when everybody else does than plain and sensible all by myself," persisted Anne mournfully.

"Trust you for that! Well, hang those dresses carefully up in your closet, and then sit down and learn the Sunday school lesson. I got a quarterly from Mr. Bell for you and you'll go to Sunday school tomorrow," said Marilla, disappearing downstairs in high dudgeon.

Anne clasped her hands and looked at the dresses.

"I did hope there would be a white one with puffed sleeves," she whispered disconsolately. "I prayed for one, but I didn't much expect it on that account. I didn't suppose God would have time to bother about a little orphan girl's dress. I knew I'd just have to depend on Marilla for it. Well, fortunately I can imagine that one of them is of snow-white muslin with lovely lace frills and three-puffed sleeves."

The next morning warnings of a sick headache prevented Marilla from going to Sunday-school with Anne.

"You'll have to go down and call for Mrs. Lynde, Anne," she said. "She'll see that you get into the right class. Now, mind you behave yourself properly. Stay to preaching afterwards and ask Mrs. Lynde to show you our pew. Here's a cent for collection. Don't stare at people and don't fidget. I shall expect you to tell me the text when you come home."

Anne started off irreproachably, arrayed in the stiff black-and-white sateen, which, while decent as regards length and certainly not open to the charge of skimpiness, contrived to emphasize every corner and angle of her thin figure. Her hat was a little, flat, glossy, new sailor, the extreme plainness of which had likewise much disappointed Anne, who had permitted herself secret visions of ribbon and flowers. The latter, however, were supplied before Anne reached the main road, for being confronted halfway down the lane with a golden frenzy of wind-stirred buttercups and a glory of wild roses, Anne promptly and liberally garlanded her hat with a heavy wreath of them. Whatever other people might have thought of the result it satisfied Anne, and she tripped gaily down the road, holding her ruddy head with its decoration of pink and yellow very proudly.

When she reached Mrs. Lynde's house she found that lady gone. Nothing daunted Anne proceeded onward to the church alone. In the porch she found a crowd of little girls, all more or less gaily attired in whites and blues and pinks, and all staring with curious eyes at this stranger in their midst, with her extraordinary head adornment. Avonlea little girls had already heard queer stories about Anne; Mrs. Lynde said she had an awful temper; Jerry Buote, the hired boy at Green Gables, said she talked all the time to herself or to the trees and flowers like a crazy girl. They looked at her and whispered to each other behind their quarterlies. Nobody made any friendly advances, then or later on when the opening exercises were over and Anne found herself in Miss Rogerson's class.

Miss Rogerson was a middle-aged lady who had taught a Sunday school class for twenty years. Her method of teaching was to ask the printed questions from the quarterly and look sternly over its edge at the particular little girl she thought ought to answer the question. She looked very often at Anne, and Anne, thanks to Marilla's drilling, answered promptly; but it may be questioned if she understood very much about either question or answer.

She did not think she liked Miss Rogerson, and she felt very miserable; every other little girl in the class had puffed sleeves. Anne felt that life was really not worth living without puffed sleeves.

"Well, how did you like Sunday school?" Marilla wanted to know when Anne came home. Her wreath having faded, Anne had discarded it in the lane, so Marilla was spared the knowledge of that for a time.

"I didn't like it a bit. It was horrid."

"Anne Shirley!" said Marilla rebukingly.

Anne sat down on the rocker with a long sigh, kissed one of Bonny's leaves, and waved her hand to a blossoming fuchsia.

"They might have been lonesome while I was away," she explained. "And now about the Sunday-school. I behaved well, just as you told me. Mrs. Lynde was gone, but I went right on myself. I went into the church, with a lot of other little girls, and I sat in the corner of a pew by the window while the opening exercises went on. Mr. Bell made an awfully long prayer. I would have been dreadfully tired before he got through if I hadn't been sitting by that window. But it looked right out on the Lake of Shining Waters, so I just gazed at that and imagined all sorts of splendid things."

"You shouldn't have done anything of the sort. You should have listened to Mr. Bell."

"But he wasn't talking to me," protested Anne. "He was talking to God and he didn't seem to be very much interested in it, either. I think he thought God was too far off to make it worth while. I said a little prayer myself, though. There was a long row of white birches hanging over the lake and the sunshine fell down through them, 'way, 'way down, deep into the water. Oh, Marilla, it was like a beautiful dream! It gave me a thrill and I just said, 'Thank you for it, God,' two or three times."

"Not out loud, I hope," said Marilla anxiously.

"Oh, no, just under my breath. Well, Mr. Bell did get through at last and they told me to go into the classroom with Miss Rogerson's class. There were nine other girls in it. They all had puffed sleeves. I tried to imagine mine were puffed, too, but I couldn't. Why couldn't I? It was as easy as could be to imagine they were puffed when I was alone in the east gable, but it was awfully hard there among the others who had really truly puffs."

"You shouldn't have been thinking about your sleeves in Sunday school. You should have been attending to the lesson. I hope you knew it."

"Oh, yes; and I answered a lot of questions. Miss Rogerson asked ever so many. I don't think it was fair for her to do all the asking. There were lots I wanted to ask her, but I didn't like to because I didn't think she was a kindred spirit. Then all the other little girls recited a paraphrase. She asked me if I knew any. I told her I didn't, but I could recite, 'The Dog at His Master's Grave' if she liked. That's in the Third Royal Reader. It isn't a really truly religious piece of poetry, but it's so sad and melancholy that it might as well be. She said it wouldn't do and she told me to learn the nineteenth paraphrase for next Sunday. I read it over in church afterwards and it's splendid. There are two lines in particular that just thrill me.

> *"Quick as the slaughtered squadrons fell*
> *In Midian's evil day.'*

I don't know what 'squadrons' means nor 'Midian,' either, but it sounds so tragical. I can hardly wait until next Sunday to recite it. I'll practice it all the week. After Sunday school I asked Miss Rogerson— because Mrs. Lynde was too far away—to show me your pew. I sat just as still as I could and the text was Revelations, third chapter, second and third verses. It was a very long text. If I was a minister I'd pick the short, snappy ones. The sermon was awfully long, too. I suppose the minister had to match it to the text. I didn't think he was a bit interesting. The trouble with him seems to be that he hasn't enough imagination. I didn't listen to him very much. I just let my thoughts run and I thought of the most surprising things."

Marilla felt helplessly that all this should be sternly reproved, but she was hampered by the undeniable fact that some of the things Anne had said, especially about the minister's sermons and Mr. Bell's prayers, were what she herself had really thought deep down in her heart for years, but had never given expression to. It almost seemed to her that those secret, unuttered, critical thoughts had suddenly taken visible and accusing shape and form in the person of this outspoken morsel of neglected humanity.

12

A Solemn Vow and Promise

It was not until the next Friday that Marilla heard the story of the flower-wreathed hat. She came home from Mrs. Lynde's and called Anne to account.

"Anne, Mrs. Rachel says you went to church last Sunday with your hat rigged out ridiculous with roses and buttercups. What on earth put you up to such a caper? A pretty-looking object you must have been!"

"Oh. I know pink and yellow aren't becoming to me," began Anne.

"Becoming fiddlesticks! It was putting flowers on your hat at all, no matter what color they were, that was ridiculous. You are the most aggravating child!"

"I don't see why it's any more ridiculous to wear flowers on your hat than on your dress," protested Anne. "Lots of little girls there had bouquets pinned on their dresses. What was the difference?"

Marilla was not to be drawn from the safe concrete into dubious paths of the abstract.

"Don't answer me back like that, Anne. It was very silly of you to do such a thing. Never let me catch you at such a trick again. Mrs. Rachel says she thought she would sink through the floor when she saw you come in all rigged out like that. She couldn't get near enough to tell you to take them off till it was too late. She says people talked about it something dreadful. Of course they would think I had no better sense than to let you go decked out like that."

"Oh, I'm so sorry," said Anne, tears welling into her eyes. "I never thought you'd mind. The roses and buttercups were so sweet and pretty I thought they'd look lovely on my hat. Lots of the little girls had artificial flowers on their hats. I'm afraid I'm going to be a dreadful trial to you. Maybe you'd better send me back to the asylum. That would be terrible; I don't think I could endure it; most likely I would go into consumption; I'm so thin as it is, you see. But that would be better than being a trial to you."

"Nonsense," said Marilla, vexed at herself for having made the child cry. "I don't want to send you back to the asylum, I'm sure. All I want is that you should behave like other little girls and not make yourself ridiculous. Don't cry any more. I've got some news for you. Diana Barry came home this afternoon. I'm going up to see if I can borrow a skirt pattern from Mrs. Barry, and if you like you can come with me and get acquainted with Diana."

Anne rose to her feet, with clasped hands, the tears still glistening on her cheeks; the dish towel she had been hemming slipped unheeded to the floor.

"Oh, Marilla, I'm frightened—now that it has come I'm actually frightened. What if she shouldn't like me! It would be the most tragical disappointment of my life."

"Now, don't get into a fluster. And I do wish you wouldn't use such long words. It sounds so funny in a little girl. I guess Diana'll like you well enough. It's her mother you've got to reckon with. If she doesn't like you it won't matter how much Diana does. If she has heard about your outburst to Mrs. Lynde and going to church with buttercups round your hat I don't know what she'll think of you. You must be polite and well behaved, and don't make any of your startling speeches. For pity's sake, if the child isn't actually trembling!"

Anne *was* trembling. Her face was pale and tense.

"Oh, Marilla, you'd be excited, too, if you were going to meet a little girl you hoped to be your bosom friend and whose mother mightn't like you," she said as she hastened to get her hat.

They went over to Orchard Slope by the short cut across the brook and up the firry hill grove. Mrs. Barry came to the kitchen door in answer to Marilla's knock. She was a tall, black-eyed, black-haired woman, with a very resolute mouth. She had the reputation of being very strict with her children.

"How do you do, Marilla?" she said cordially. "Come in. And this is the little girl you have adopted, I suppose?"

"Yes, this is Anne Shirley," said Marilla.

"Spelled with an *e,*" gasped Anne, who, tremulous and excited as she was, was determined there should be no misunderstanding on that important point.

Mrs. Barry, not hearing or not comprehending, merely shook hands and said kindly:

"How are you?"

"I am well in body although considerably rumpled up in spirit, thank you, ma'am," said Anne gravely. Then aside to Marilla in an audible whisper, "There wasn't anything startling in that, was there, Marilla?"

Diana was sitting on the sofa, reading a book which she dropped when the callers entered. She was a very pretty little girl, with her mother's black eyes and hair, and rosy cheeks, and the merry expression which was her inheritance from her father.

"This is my little girl, Diana," said Mrs. Barry. "Diana, you might take Anne out into the garden and show her your flowers. It will be better for you than straining your eyes over that book. She reads entirely too much—" this to Marilla as the little girls went out—"and I can't prevent her, for her father aids and abets her. She's always poring over a book. I'm glad she has the prospect of a playmate—perhaps it will take her more out-of-doors."

Outside in the garden, which was full of mellow sunset light streaming through the dark old firs to the west of it, stood Anne and Diana, gazing bashfully at one another over a clump of gorgeous tiger lilies.

The Barry garden was a bowery wilderness of flowers which would have delighted Anne's heart at any time less fraught with destiny. It was encircled by huge old willows and tall firs, beneath which flourished flowers that loved the shade. Prim, right-angled paths, neatly bordered with clamshells, intersected it like moist red ribbons and in the beds between old-fashioned flowers ran riot. There were rosy bleeding-hearts and great splendid crimson peonies; white, fragrant narcissi and thorny, sweet Scotch roses; pink and blue and white columbines and lilac-tinted Bouncing Bets; clumps of southernwood and ribbon grass and mint; purple Adam-and-Eve, daffodils, and masses of sweet clover white with its delicate, fragrant, feathery sprays; scarlet lightning that shot its fiery lances over prim white musk-flowers; a garden it was where sunshine lingered and bees hummed, and winds, beguiled into loitering, purred and rustled.

"Oh, Diana," said Anne at last, clasping her hands and speaking almost in a whisper, "do you think—oh, do you think you can like me a little—enough to be my bosom friend?"

Diana laughed. Diana always laughed before she spoke.

"Why, I guess so," she said frankly. "I'm awfully glad you've come to live at Green Gables. It will be jolly to have somebody to play with. There isn't any other girl who lives near enough to play with, and I've no sisters big enough."

"Will you swear to be my friend for ever and ever?" demanded Anne eagerly.

Diana looked shocked.

"Why, it's dreadfully wicked to swear," she said rebukingly.

"Oh no, not my kind of swearing. There are two kinds, you know."

"I never heard of but one kind," said Diana doubtfully.

"There really is another. Oh, it isn't wicked at all. It just means vowing and promising solemnly."

"Well, I don't mind doing that," agreed Diana, relieved. "How do you do it?"

"We must join hands—so," said Anne gravely. "It ought to be over running water. We'll just imagine this path is running water. I'll repeat the oath first. I solemnly swear to be faithful to my bosom friend, Diana Barry, as long as the sun and moon shall endure. Now you say it and put my name in."

Diana repeated the "oath" with a laugh fore and aft. Then she said:

"You're a queer girl, Anne. I heard before that you were queer. But I believe I'm going to like you real well."

When Marilla and Anne went home Diana went with them as far as the log bridge. The two little girls walked with their arms about each other. At the brook they parted with many promises to spend the next afternoon together.

"Well, did you find Diana a kindred spirit?" asked Marilla as they went up through the garden of Green Gables.

"Oh, yes," sighed Anne, blissfully unconscious of any sarcasm on Marilla's part. "Oh, Marilla, I'm the happiest girl on Prince Edward Island this very moment. I assure you I'll say my prayers with a right good-will to-night. Diana and I are going to build a playhouse in Mr. William Bell's birch grove tomorrow. Can I have those broken pieces of china that are out in the woodshed? Diana's birthday is in February and mine is in March. Don't you think that is a very strange coincidence? Diana is going to lend me a book to read. She says it's perfectly splendid and tremenjusly exciting. She's going to show me a place back in the woods where rice lilies grow. Don't you think Diana has got very soulful eyes? I wish I had soulful eyes. Diana is going to teach me to sing a song called 'Nelly in the Hazel Dell.' She's going to give me a picture to put up in my room; it's a perfectly beautiful picture, she says— a lovely lady in a pale blue silk dress. A sewing machine agent gave it to her. I wish I had something to give Diana. I'm an inch taller than Diana, but she is ever so much fatter; she says she'd like to be thin because it's so much more graceful, but I'm afraid she only said it to soothe my feelings. We're going to the shore some day to gather shells. We have agreed to call the spring down by the log bridge the Dryad's Bubble. Isn't that a perfectly elegant name? I read a story once about a spring called that. A dryad is a sort of grown-up fairy, I think."

"Well, all I hope is you won't talk Diana to death," said Marilla. "But remember this in all your planning, Anne. You're not going to play all the time nor most of it. You'll have your work to do and it'll have to be done first."

Anne's cup of happiness was full, and Matthew caused it to overflow. He had just got home from a trip to the store at Carmody, and he sheepishly produced a small parcel from his pocket and handed it to Anne, with a deprecatory look at Marilla.

"I heard you say you liked chocolate sweeties, so I got you some," he said.

"Humph," sniffed Marilla. "It'll ruin her teeth and stomach. There, there, child, don't look so dismal. You can eat those, since Matthew has gone and got them. He'd better have brought you peppermints. They're wholesomer. Don't sicken yourself eating them all at once now."

"Oh, no, indeed, I won't," said Anne eagerly. "I'll just eat one tonight, Marilla. And I can give Diana half of them, can't I? The other half will taste twice as sweet to me if I give some to her. It's delightful to think I have something to give her."

"I will say it for the child," said Marilla when Anne had gone to her gable, "she isn't stingy. I'm glad, for of all faults I detest stinginess in a child. Dear me, it's only three weeks since she came, and it seems as if she'd been here always. I can't imagine the place without her. Now, don't be looking I-told-you-so, Matthew. That's bad enough in a woman, but it isn't to be endured in a man. I'm perfectly willing to own up that I'm glad I consented to keep the child and that I'm getting fond of her, but don't you rub it in, Matthew Cuthbert."

13

The Delights of Anticipation

"It's time Anne was in to do her sewing," said Marilla, glancing at the clock and then out into the yellow August afternoon where everything drowsed in the heat. "She stayed playing with Diana more than half an hour more'n I gave her leave to; and now she's perched out there on the woodpile talking to Matthew, nineteen to the dozen, when she knows perfectly well that she ought to be at her work. And of course he's listening to her like a perfect ninny. I never saw such an infatuated man. The more she talks and the odder the things she says, the more he's delighted evidently. Anne Shirley, you come right in here this minute, do you hear me!"

A series of staccato taps on the west window brought Anne flying in from the yard, eyes shining, cheeks faintly flushed with pink, unbraided hair streaming behind her in a torrent of brightness.

"Oh, Marilla," she exclaimed breathlessly, "there's going to be a Sunday school picnic next week—in Mr. Harmon Andrews' field, right near the Lake of Shining Waters. And Mrs. Superintendent Bell and Mrs. Rachel Lynde are going to make ice cream—think of it, Marilla—*ice cream!* And oh, Marilla, can I go to it?"

"Just look at the clock, if you please, Anne. What time did I tell you to come in?"

"Two o'clock—but isn't it splendid about the picnic, Marilla? Please can I go? Oh, I've never been to a picnic—I've dreamed of picnics, but I've never—"

"Yes, I told you to come at two o'clock. And it's a quarter to three. I'd like to know why you didn't obey me, Anne."

"Why, I meant to, Marilla, as much as could be. But you have no idea how fascinating Idlewild is. And then, of course, I had to tell

Matthew about the picnic. Matthew is such a sympathetic listener. Please can I go?"

"You'll have to learn to resist the fascination of Idle-whatever-you-call-it. When I tell you to come in at a certain time I mean that time and not half an hour later. And you needn't stop to discourse with sympathetic listeners on your way, either. As for the picnic, of course you can go. You're a Sunday-school scholar, and it's not likely I'd refuse to let you go when all the other little girls are going."

"But—but," faltered Anne, "Diana says that everybody must take a basket of things to eat. I can't cook, as you know, Marilla, and—and—I don't mind going to a picnic without puffed sleeves so much, but I'd feel terribly humiliated if I had to go without a basket. It's been preying on my mind ever since Diana told me."

"Well, it needn't prey any longer. I'll bake you a basket."

"Oh, you dear good Marilla. Oh, you are so kind to me. Oh, I'm so much obliged to you."

Getting through with her "ohs" Anne cast herself into Marilla's arms and rapturously kissed her sallow cheek. It was the first time in her whole life that childish lips had voluntarily touched Marilla's face. Again that sudden sensation of startling sweetness thrilled her. She was secretly vastly pleased at Anne's impulsive caress, which was probably the reason why she said brusquely:

"There, there, never mind your kissing nonsense. I'd sooner see you doing strictly as you're told. As for cooking, I mean to begin giving you lessons in that some of these days. But you're so feather-brained, Anne, I've been waiting to see if you'd sober down a little and learn to be steady before I begin. You've got to keep your wits about you in cooking and not stop in the middle of things to let your thoughts rove over all creation. Now, get out your patchwork and have your square done before teatime."

"I do *not* like patchwork," said Anne dolefully, hunting out her workbasket and sitting down before a little heap of red and white diamonds with a sigh. "I think some kinds of sewing would be nice; but there's no scope for imagination in patchwork. It's just one little seam after another and you never seem to be getting anywhere. But of course

I'd rather be Anne of Green Gables sewing patchwork than Anne of any other place with nothing to do but play. I wish time went as quick sewing patches as it does when I'm playing with Diana, though. Oh, we do have such elegant times, Marilla. I have to furnish most of the imagination, but I'm well able to do that. Diana is simply perfect in every other way. You know that little piece of land across the brook that runs up between our farm and Mr. Barry's. It belongs to Mr. William Bell, and right in the corner there is a little ring of white birch trees— the most romantic spot, Marilla. Diana and I have our playhouse there. We call it Idlewild. Isn't that a poetical name? I assure you it took me some time to think it out. I stayed awake nearly a whole night before I invented it. Then, just as I was dropping off to sleep, it came like an inspiration. Diana was *enraptured* when she heard it. We have got our house fixed up elegantly. You must come and see it, Marilla—won't you? We have great big stones, all covered with moss, for seats, and boards from tree to tree for shelves. And we have all our dishes on them. Of course, they're all broken but it's the easiest thing in the world to imagine that they are whole. There's a piece of a plate with a spray of red and yellow ivy on it that is especially beautiful. We keep it in the parlor and we have the fairy glass there, too. The fairy glass is as lovely as a dream. Diana found it out in the woods behind their chicken house. It's all full of rainbows—just little young rainbows that haven't grown big yet— and Diana's mother told her it was broken off a hanging lamp they once had. But it's nicer to imagine the fairies lost it one night when they had a ball, so we call it the fairy glass. Matthew is going to make us a table. Oh, we have named that little round pool over in Mr. Barry's field Willowmere. I got that name out of the book Diana lent me. That was a thrilling book, Marilla. The heroine had five lovers. I'd be satisfied with one, wouldn't you? She was very handsome and she went through great tribulations. She could faint as easy as anything. I'd love to be able to faint, wouldn't you, Marilla? It's so romantic. But I'm really very healthy for all I'm so thin. I believe I'm getting fatter, though. Don't you think I am? I look at my elbows every morning when I get up to see if any dimples are coming. Diana is having a new dress made with elbow sleeves. She is going to wear it to the picnic. Oh, I do hope it will be fine next Wednesday. I don't feel that I could endure the disappointment if anything happened to prevent me from getting to the picnic. I suppose I'd live through it, but I'm certain it would be a lifelong sorrow. It wouldn't matter if I got to a hundred picnics in after years; they wouldn't make up for missing this one. They're going to have boats on the Lake of Shining Waters—and ice cream as I told you. I have never tasted ice cream. Diana tried to explain what it was like, but I guess ice cream is one of those things that are beyond imagination."

"Anne, you have talked even on for ten minutes by the clock," said Marilla. "Now, just for curiosity's sake, see if you can hold your tongue for the same length of time."

Anne held her tongue as desired. But for the rest of the week she talked picnic and thought picnic and dreamed picnic. On Saturday it rained and she worked herself up into such a frantic state lest it should keep on raining until and over Wednesday, that Marilla made her sew an extra patchwork square by way of steadying her nerves.

On Sunday Anne confided to Marilla on the way home from church that she grew actually cold all over with excitement when the minister announced the picnic from the pulpit.

"Such a thrill as went up and down my back, Marilla! I don't think I'd ever really believed until then that there was honestly going to be a picnic. I couldn't help fearing I'd only imagined it. But when a minister says a thing in the pulpit you just have to believe it."

"You set your heart too much on things, Anne," said Marilla with a sigh. "I'm afraid there'll be a great many disappointments in store for you through life."

"Oh, Marilla, looking forward to things is half the pleasure of them," exclaimed Anne. "You mayn't get the things themselves; but nothing can prevent you from having the fun of looking forward to them. Mrs. Lynde says, 'Blessed are they who expect nothing for they shall not be disappointed.' But I think it would be worse to expect nothing than to be disappointed."

Marilla wore her amethyst brooch to church that day as usual. Marilla always wore her amethyst brooch to church. She would have thought it rather sacrilegious to leave it off—as bad as forgetting her

Bible or her collection dime. That amethyst brooch was Marilla's most treasured possession. A seafaring uncle had given it to her mother who in turn had bequeathed it to Marilla. It was an old-fashioned oval, containing a braid of her mother's hair, surrounded by a border of very fine amethysts. Marilla knew too little about precious stones to realize how fine the amethysts actually were; but she thought them very beautiful and was always pleasantly conscious of their violet shimmer at her throat, above her good brown satin dress, even although she could not see it.

Anne had been smitten with delighted admiration when she first saw that brooch.

"Oh, Marilla, it's a perfectly elegant brooch. I don't know how you can pay attention to the sermon or the prayers when you have it on. I couldn't, I know. I think amethysts are just sweet. They are what I used to think diamonds were like. Long ago, before I had ever seen a diamond, I read about them and I tried to imagine what they would be like. I thought they would be lovely glimmering purple stones. When I saw a real diamond in a lady's ring one day I was so disappointed I cried. Of course, it was very lovely but it wasn't my idea of a diamond. Will you let me hold the brooch for one minute, Marilla? Do you think amethysts can be the souls of good violets?"

14

Anne's Confession

n the Monday evening before the picnic Marilla came down from her room with a troubled face.

"Anne," she said to that small personage, who was shelling peas by the spotless table and singing "Nelly of the Hazel Dell" with a vigor and expression that did credit to Diana's teaching, "did you see anything of my amethyst brooch? I thought I stuck it in my pincushion when I came home from church yesterday evening, but I can't find it anywhere."

"I—I saw it this afternoon when you were away at the Aid Society," said Anne, a little slowly. "I was passing your door when I saw it on the cushion, so I went in to look at it."

"Did you touch it?" said Marilla sternly.

"Y-e-e-s," admitted Anne, "I took it up and I pinned it on my breast just to see how it would look."

"You had no business to do anything of the sort. It's very wrong in a little girl to meddle. You shouldn't have gone into my room in the first place and you shouldn't have touched a brooch that didn't belong to you in the second. Where did you put it?"

"Oh, I put it back on the bureau. I hadn't it on a minute. Truly, I didn't mean to meddle, Marilla. I didn't think about its being wrong to go in and try on the brooch; but I see now that it was and I'll never do it again. That's one good thing about me. I never do the same naughty thing twice."

"You didn't put it back," said Marilla. "That brooch isn't anywhere on the bureau. You've taken it out or something, Anne."

"I *did* put it back," said Anne quickly—pertly, Marilla thought. "I don't just remember whether I stuck it on the pincushion or laid it in the china tray. But I'm perfectly certain I put it back."

"I'll go and have another look," said Marilla, determining to be just. "If you put that brooch back it's there still. If it isn't I'll know you didn't, that's all!"

Marilla went to her room and made a thorough search, not only over the bureau but in every other place she thought the brooch might possibly be. It was not to be found and she returned to the kitchen.

"Anne, the brooch is gone. By your own admission you were the last person to handle it. Now, what have you done with it? Tell me the truth at once. Did you take it out and lose it?"

"No, I didn't," said Anne solemnly, meeting Marilla's angry gaze squarely. "I never took the brooch out of your room and that is the truth, if I was to be led to the block for it—although I'm not very certain what a block is. So there, Marilla."

Anne's "so there" was only intended to emphasize her assertion, but Marilla took it as a display of defiance.

"I believe you are telling me a falsehood, Anne," she said sharply. "I know you are. There now, don't say anything more unless you are prepared to tell the whole truth. Go to your room and stay there until you are ready to confess."

"Will I take the peas with me?" said Anne meekly.

"No, I'll finish shelling them myself. Do as I bid you."

When Anne had gone Marilla went about her evening tasks in a very disturbed state of mind. She was worried about her valuable brooch. What if Anne had lost it? And how wicked of the child to deny having taken it, when anybody could see she must have! With such an innocent face, too!

"I don't know what I wouldn't sooner have had happen," thought Marilla, as she nervously shelled the peas. "Of course, I don't suppose she meant to steal it or anything like that. She's just taken it to play with or help along that imagination of hers. She must have taken it, that's clear, for there hasn't been a soul in that room since she was in it, by her own story, until I went up tonight. And the brooch is gone, there's nothing surer. I suppose she has lost it and is afraid to own up for fear she'll be punished. It's a dreadful thing to think she tells falsehoods. It's a far worse thing than her fit of temper. It's a fearful responsibility to have a child in your house you can't trust. Slyness and untruthfulness— that's what she has displayed. I declare I feel worse about that than about the brooch. If she'd only have told the truth about it I wouldn't mind so much."

Marilla went to her room at intervals all through the evening and searched for the brooch, without finding it. A bedtime visit to the east gable produced no result. Anne persisted in denying that she knew anything about the brooch but Marilla was only the more firmly convinced that she did.

She told Matthew the story the next morning. Matthew was confounded and puzzled; he could not so quickly lose faith in Anne but he had to admit that circumstances were against her.

"You're sure it hasn't fell down behind the bureau?" was the only suggestion he could offer.

"I've moved the bureau and I've taken out the drawers and I've looked in every crack and cranny," was Marilla's positive answer. "The brooch is gone and that child has taken it and lied about it. That's the plain, ugly truth, Matthew Cuthbert and we might as well look it in the face."

"Well now, what are you going to do about it?" Matthew asked forlornly, feeling secretly thankful that Marilla and not he had to deal with the situation. He felt no desire to put his oar in this time.

"She'll stay in her room until she confesses," said Marilla grimly, remembering the success of this method in the former case. "Then we'll see. Perhaps we'll be able to find the brooch if she'll only tell where she took it; but in any case she'll have to be severely punished, Matthew."

"Well now, you'll have to punish her," said Matthew, reaching for his hat. "I've nothing to do with it, remember. You warned me off yourself."

Marilla felt deserted by every one. She could not even go to Mrs. Lynde for advice. She went up to the east gable with a very serious face and left it with a face more serious still. Anne steadfastly refused to confess. She persisted in asserting that she had not taken the brooch. The child had evidently been crying and Marilla felt a pang of pity which she sternly repressed. By night she was, as she expressed it, "beat out."

"You'll stay in this room until you confess, Anne. You can make up your mind to that," she said firmly.

"But the picnic is tomorrow, Marilla," cried Anne. "You won't keep me from going to that, will you? You'll just let me out for the afternoon, won't you? Then I'll stay here as long as you like afterwards *cheerfully*. But I *must* go to the picnic."

"You'll not go to picnics nor anywhere else until you've confessed, Anne."

"Oh, Marilla," gasped Anne.

But Marilla had gone out and shut the door.

Wednesday morning dawned as bright and fair as if expressly made to order for the picnic. Birds sang around Green Gables; the Madonna lilies in the garden sent out whiffs of perfume that entered in on viewless winds at every door and window, and wandered through halls and rooms like spirits of benediction. The birches in the hollow waved joyful hands as if watching for Anne's usual morning greeting from the east gable. But Anne was not at her window. When Marilla took her breakfast up to her she found the child sitting primly on her bed, pale and resolute, with tight shut lips and gleaming eyes.

"Marilla, I'm ready to confess."

"Ah!" Marilla laid down her tray. Once again her method had succeeded; but her success was very bitter to her. "Let me hear what you have to say then, Anne."

"I took the amethyst brooch," said Anne, as if repeating a lesson she had learned. "I took it just as you said. I didn't mean to take it when I went in. But it did look so beautiful, Marilla, when I pinned it on my breast that I was overcome by an irresistible temptation. I imagined how perfectly thrilling it would be to take it to Idlewild and play I was the Lady Cordelia Fitzgerald. It would be so much easier to imagine I was the Lady Cordelia if I had a real amethyst brooch on. Diana and I made necklaces of roseberries but what are roseberries compared to amethysts? So I took the brooch. I thought I could put it back before you came home. I went all the way around by the road to lengthen out the time. When I was going over the bridge across the lake of Shining Waters I took the brooch off to have another look at it. Oh, how it did shine in the sunlight! And then, when I was leaning over the bridge, it just slipped through my fingers—so—and went down—down—down, all purply-sparkling, and sank forevermore beneath the Lake of Shining Waters. And that's the best I can do at confessing, Marilla."

Marilla felt hot anger surge up into her heart again. This child had taken and lost her treasured amethyst brooch and now sat there calmly reciting the details thereof without the least apparent compunction or repentance.

"Anne, this is terrible," she said, trying to speak calmly. "You are the very wickedest girl I ever heard of."

"Yes, I suppose I am," agreed Anne tranquilly. "And I know I'll have to be punished. It'll be your duty to punish me, Marilla. Won't you please get it over right off because I'd like to go to the picnic with nothing on my mind."

"Picnic, indeed! You'll go to no picnic today, Anne Shirley. That shall be your punishment. And it isn't half severe enough either for what you've done!"

"Not go to the picnic!" Anne sprang to her feet and clutched Marilla's hand. "But you *promised* me I might! Oh, Marilla, I must go to the picnic. That was why I confessed. Punish me any way you like but that. Oh, Marilla, please, please, let me go to the picnic. Think of the ice cream! For anything you know I may never have a chance to taste ice cream again."

Marilla disengaged Anne's clinging hand stonily.

"You needn't plead, Anne. You are not going to the picnic and that's final. No, not a word."

Anne realized that Marilla was not to be moved. She clasped her hands together, gave a piercing shriek, and then flung herself face downwards on the bed, crying and writhing in an utter abandonment of disappointment and despair.

"For the land's sake!" gasped Marilla, hastening from the room. "I believe the child is crazy. No child in her senses would behave as she does.

If she isn't she's utterly bad. Oh dear, I'm afraid Rachel was right from the first. But I've put my hand to the plough and I won't look back."

That was a dismal morning. Marilla worked fiercely and scrubbed the porch floor and the dairy shelves when she could find nothing else to do. Neither the shelves nor the porch needed it—but Marilla did. Then she went out and raked the yard.

When dinner was ready she went to the stairs and called Anne. A tear-stained face appeared, looking tragically over the banisters.

"Come down to your dinner, Anne."

"I don't want any dinner, Marilla," said Anne sobbingly. "I couldn't eat anything. My heart is broken. You'll feel remorse of conscience some day, I expect, for breaking it, Marilla, but I forgive you. Remember when the time comes that I forgive you. But please don't ask me to eat anything, especially boiled pork and greens. Boiled pork and greens are so unromantic when one is in affliction."

Exasperated Marilla returned to the kitchen and poured out her tale of woe to Matthew, who, between his sense of justice and his unlawful sympathy with Anne, was a miserable man.

"Well now, she shouldn't have taken the brooch, Marilla, or told stories about it," he admitted, mournfully surveying his plateful of unromantic pork and greens as if he, like Anne, thought it a food unsuited to crises of feeling, "but she's such a little thing—such an interesting little thing. Don't you think it's pretty rough not to let her go to the picnic when she's so set on it?"

"Matthew Cuthbert, I'm amazed at you. I think I've let her off entirely too easy. And she doesn't appear to realize how wicked she's been at all—that's what worries me most. If she'd really felt sorry it wouldn't be so bad. And you don't seem to realize it, neither; you're making excuses for her all the time to yourself—I can see that."

"Well now, she's such a little thing," feebly reiterated Matthew. "And there should be allowances made, Marilla. You know she's never had any bringing up."

"Well, she's having it now," retorted Marilla.

The retort silenced Matthew if it did not convince him. That dinner was a very dismal meal. The only cheerful thing about it was Jerry

Buote, the hired boy, and Marilla resented his cheerfulness as a personal insult.

When her dishes were washed and her bread sponge set and her hens fed Marilla remembered that she had noticed a small rent in her best black lace shawl when she had taken it off on Monday afternoon on returning from the Ladies' Aid. She would go and mend it.

The shawl was in a box in her trunk. As Marilla lifted it out, the sunlight, falling through the vines that clustered thickly about the window, struck upon something caught in the shawl—something that glittered and sparkled in facets of violet light. Marilla snatched at it with a gasp. It was the amethyst brooch, hanging to a thread of the lace by its catch!

"Dear life and heart," said Marilla blankly, "what does that mean? Here's my brooch safe and sound that I thought was at the bottom of Barry's pond. Whatever did that girl mean by saying she took it and lost it? I declare I believe Green Gables is bewitched. I remember now that when I took off my shawl Monday afternoon I laid it on the bureau for a minute. I suppose the brooch got caught in it somehow. Well!"

Marilla betook herself to the east gable, brooch in hand. Anne had cried herself out and was sitting dejectedly by the window.

"Anne Shirley," said Marilla solemnly, "I've just found my brooch hanging to my black lace shawl. Now I want to know what that rigmarole you told me this morning meant."

"Why, you said you'd keep me here until I confessed," returned Anne wearily, "and so I decided to confess because I was bound to get to the picnic. I thought out a confession last night after I went to bed and made it as interesting as I could. And I said it over and over so that I wouldn't forget it. But you wouldn't let me go to the picnic after all, so all my trouble was wasted."

Marilla had to laugh in spite of herself. But her conscience pricked her.

"Anne, you do beat all! But I was wrong—I see that now. I shouldn't have doubted your word when I'd never known you to tell a story. Of course, it wasn't right for you to confess to a thing you hadn't done—it was very wrong to do so. But I drove you to it. So if you'll forgive me, Anne, I'll forgive you and we'll start square again. And now get yourself ready for the picnic."

Anne flew up like a rocket.

"Oh, Marilla, isn't it too late?"

"No, it's only two o'clock. They won't be more than well gathered yet and it'll be an hour before they have tea. Wash your face and comb your hair and put on your gingham. I'll fill a basket for you. There's plenty of stuff baked in the house. And I'll get Jerry to hitch up the sorrel and drive you down to the picnic ground."

"Oh, Marilla," exclaimed Anne, flying to the washstand. "Five minutes ago I was so miserable I was wishing I'd never been born and now I wouldn't change places with an angel!"

That night a thoroughly happy, completely tired out Anne returned to Green Gables in a state of beatification impossible to describe.

"Oh, Marilla, I've had a perfectly scrumptious time. Scrumptious is a new word I learned today. I heard Mary Alice Bell use it. Isn't it very expressive? Everything was lovely. We had a splendid tea and then Mr. Harmon Andrews took us all for a row on the Lake of Shining Waters—six of us at a time. And Jane Andrews nearly fell overboard. She was leaning out to pick water lilies and if Mr. Andrews hadn't caught her by her sash just in the nick of time she'd have fallen in and prob'ly been drowned. I wish it had been me. It would have been such a romantic experience to have been nearly drowned. It would be such a thrilling tale to tell. And we had the ice cream. Words fail me to describe that ice cream. Marilla, I assure you it was sublime."

That evening Marilla told the whole story to Matthew over her stocking basket.

"I'm willing to own up that I made a mistake," she concluded candidly, "but I've learned a lesson. I have to laugh when I think of Anne's 'confession,' although I suppose I shouldn't for it really was a falsehood. But it doesn't seem as bad as the other would have been, somehow, and anyhow I'm responsible for it. That child is hard to understand in some respects. But I believe she'll turn out all right yet. And there's one thing certain, no house will ever be dull that she's in."

15

A Tempest in the School Teapot

"hat a splendid day!" said Anne, drawing a long breath. "Isn't it good just to be alive on a day like this? I pity the people who aren't born yet for missing it. They may have good days, of course, but they can never have this one. And it's splendider still to have such a lovely way to go to school by, isn't it?"

"It's a lot nicer than going round by the road; that is so dusty and hot," said Diana practically, peeping into her dinner basket and mentally calculating if the three juicy, toothsome, raspberry tarts reposing there were divided among ten girls how many bites each girl would have.

The little girls of Avonlea school always pooled their lunches, and to eat three raspberry tarts all alone or even to share them only with one's best chum would have forever and ever branded as "awful mean" the girl who did it. And yet, when the tarts were divided among ten girls you just got enough to tantalize you.

The way Anne and Diana went to school was a pretty one. Anne thought those walks to and from school with Diana couldn't be improved upon even by imagination. Going around by the main road would have been so unromantic; but to go by Lover's Lane and Willowmere and Violet Vale and the Birch Path was romantic, if ever anything was.

Lover's Lane opened out below the orchard at Green Gables and stretched far up into the woods to the end of the Cuthbert farm. It was the way by which the cows were taken to the back pasture and the wood hauled home in winter. Anne had named it Lover's Lane before she had been a month at Green Gables.

"Not that lovers ever really walk there," she explained to Marilla, "but Diana and I are reading a perfectly magnificent book and there's a Lover's Lane in it. So we want to have one, too. And it's a very pretty name, don't you think? So romantic! We can imagine the lovers into it, you know. I like that lane because you can think out loud there without people calling you crazy."

Anne, starting out alone in the morning, went down Lover's Lane as far as the brook. Here Diana met her, and the two little girls went on up the lane under the leafy arch of maples—"maples are such sociable trees," said Anne; "they're always rustling and whispering to you,"—until they came to a rustic bridge. Then they left the lane and walked through Mr. Barry's back field and past Willowmere. Beyond Willowmere came Violet Vale—a little green dimple in the shadow of Mr. Andrew Bell's big woods. "Of course there are no violets there now," Anne told Marilla, "but Diana says there are millions of them in spring. Oh, Marilla, can't you just imagine you see them? It actually takes away my breath. I named it Violet Vale. Diana says she never saw the beat of me for hitting on fancy names for places. It's nice to be clever at something, isn't it? But Diana named the Birch Path. She wanted to, so I let her; but I'm sure I could have found something more poetical than plain Birch Path. Anybody can think of a name like that. But the Birch Path is one of the prettiest places in the world, Marilla."

It was. Other people besides Anne thought so when they stumbled on it. It was a little narrow, twisting path, winding down over a long hill straight through Mr. Bell's woods, where the light came down sifted through so many emerald screens that it was as flawless as the heart of a diamond. It was fringed in all its length with slim young birches, white-stemmed and lissom boughed; ferns and starflowers and wild lilies-of-the-valley and scarlet tufts of pigeon berries grew thickly along it; and always there was a delightful spiciness in the air and music of bird calls and the murmur and laugh of wood winds in the trees overhead. Now and then you might see a rabbit skipping across the road if you were quiet—which, with Anne and Diana, happened about once in a blue moon. Down in the valley the path came out to the main road and then it was just up the spruce hill to the school.

The Avonlea school was a whitewashed building low in the eaves and wide in the windows, furnished inside with comfortable substantial old-fashioned desks that opened and shut, and were carved all over their lids with the initials and hieroglyphics of three generations of schoolchildren. The schoolhouse was set back from the road and behind it was a dusky fir wood and a brook where all the children put their bottles of milk in the morning to keep cool and sweet until dinner hour.

Marilla had seen Anne start off to school on the first day of September with many secret misgivings. Anne was such an odd girl. How would she get on with the other children? And how on earth would she ever manage to hold her tongue during school hours?

Things went better than Marilla feared, however. Anne came home that evening in high spirits.

"I think I'm going to like school here," she announced. "I don't think much of the master, though. He's all the time curling his moustache and making eyes at Prissy Andrews. Prissy is grown-up, you know. She's sixteen and she's studying for the entrance examination into Queen's Academy at Charlottetown next year. Tillie Boulter says the master is *dead gone* on her. She's got a beautiful complexion and curly brown hair and she does it up so elegantly. She sits in the long seat at the back and he sits there, too, most of the time—to explain her lessons, he says. But Ruby Gillis says she saw him writing something on her slate and when Prissy read it she blushed as red as a beet and giggled; and Ruby Gillis says she doesn't believe it had anything to do with the lesson."

"Anne Shirley, don't let me hear you talking about your teacher in that way again," said Marilla sharply. "You don't go to school to criticize the master. I guess he can teach *you* something and it's your business to learn. And I want you to understand right off that you are not to come home telling tales about him. That is something I won't encourage. I hope you were a good girl."

"Indeed I was," said Anne comfortably. "It wasn't so hard as you might imagine, either. I sit with Diana. Our seat is right by the window and we can look down to the Lake of Shining Waters. There are a lot of nice girls in school and we had scrumptious fun playing at dinner time. It's so nice to have a lot of little girls to play with. But of course I like Diana best and always will. I *adore* Diana. I'm dreadfully far behind the others. They're all in the fifth book and I'm only in the fourth. I feel that it's kind of a disgrace. But there's not one of them has such an imagination as I have and I soon found that out. We had reading and geography and Canadian History and dictation today. Mr. Phillips said my spelling was disgraceful and he held up my slate so that everybody could see it, all marked over. I felt so mortified, Marilla; he might have been politer to a stranger, I think. Ruby Gillis gave me an apple and Sophia Sloane lent me a lovely pink card with 'May I see you home?' on it. I'm to give it back to her tomorrow. And Tillie Boulter let me wear her bead ring all the afternoon. Can I have some of those pearl beads off the old pincushion in the garret to make myself a ring? And oh Marilla, Jane Andrews told me that Minnie MacPherson told her that she heard Prissy Andrews tell Sara Gillis that I had a very pretty nose. Marilla, that is the first compliment I have ever had in my life and you can't imagine what a strange feeling it gave me. Marilla, have I really a pretty nose? I know you'll tell me the truth."

"Your nose is well enough," said Marilla shortly. Secretly she thought Anne's nose was a remarkably pretty one; but she had no intention of telling her so.

That was three weeks ago and all had gone smoothly so far. And now, this crisp September morning, Anne and Diana were tripping blithely down the Birch Path, two of the happiest little girls in Avonlea.

"I guess Gilbert Blythe will be in school today," said Diana. "He's been visiting his cousins over in New Brunswick all summer and he only came home Saturday night. He's *aw'fly* handsome, Anne. And he teases the girls something terrible. He just torments our lives out."

Diana's voice indicated that she rather liked having her life tormented out than not.

"Gilbert Blythe?" said Anne. "Isn't it his name that's written up on the porch wall with Julia Bell's and a big 'Take Notice' over them?"

"Yes," said Diana, tossing her head, "but I'm sure he doesn't like Julia Bell so very much. I've heard him say he studied the multiplication table by her freckles."

"Oh, don't speak about freckles to me," implored Anne. "It isn't delicate when I've got so many. But I do think that writing take-notices up on the wall about the boys and girls is the silliest ever. I should just like to see anybody dare to write my name up with a boy's. Not, of course," she hastened to add, "that anybody would."

Anne sighed. She didn't want her name written up. But it was a little humiliating to know that there was no danger of it.

"Nonsense," said Diana, whose black eyes and glossy tresses had played such havoc with the hearts of Avonlea schoolboys that her name figured on the porch walls in half a dozen take-notices. "It's only meant as a joke. And don't you be too sure your name won't ever be written up. Charlie Sloane is *dead gone* on you. He told his mother—his *mother*, mind you—that you were the smartest girl in school. That's better than being good-looking."

"No, it isn't," said Anne, feminine to the core. "I'd rather be pretty than clever. And I hate Charlie Sloane. I can't bear a boy with goggle eyes. If any one wrote my name up with his I'd *never* get over it, Diana Barry. But it *is* nice to keep head of your class."

"You'll have Gilbert in your class after this," said Diana, "and he's used to being head of his class, I can tell you. He's only in the fourth book although he's nearly fourteen. Four years ago his father was sick and had to go out to Alberta for his health and Gilbert went with him. They were there three years and Gil didn't go to school hardly any until they came back. You won't find it so easy to keep head after this, Anne."

"I'm glad," said Anne quickly. "I couldn't really feel proud of keeping head of little boys and girls of just nine or ten. I got up yesterday spelling 'ebullition.' Josie Pye was head and, mind you, she peeped in her book. Mr. Phillips didn't see her—he was looking at Prissy Andrews—but I did. I just swept her a look of freezing scorn and she got as red as a beet and spelled it wrong after all."

"Those Pye girls are cheats all round," said Diana indignantly, as they climbed the fence of the main road. "Gertie Pye actually went and put her milk bottle in my place in the brook yesterday. Did you ever? I don't speak to her now."

When Mr. Phillips was in the back of the room hearing Prissy Andrews' Latin Diana whispered to Anne, "That's Gilbert Blythe sitting right across the aisle from you, Anne. Just look at him and see if you don't think he's handsome."

Anne looked accordingly. She had a good chance to do so, for the said Gilbert Blythe was absorbed in stealthily pinning the long yellow braid of Ruby Gillis, who sat in front of him, to the back of her seat. He was a tall boy, with curly brown hair, roguish hazel eyes and a mouth twisted into a teasing smile. Presently Ruby Gillis started up to take a sum to the master; she fell back into her seat with a little shriek, believing that her hair was pulled out by the roots. Everybody looked at her and Mr. Phillips glared so sternly that Ruby began to cry. Gilbert had whisked the pin out of sight and was studying his history with the soberest face in the world; but when the commotion subsided he looked at Anne and winked with inexpressible drollery.

"I think your Gilbert Blythe *is* handsome," confided Anne to Diana, "but I think he's very bold. It isn't good manners to wink at a strange girl."

But it was not until the afternoon that things really began to happen.

Mr. Phillips was back in the corner explaining a problem in algebra to Prissy Andrews and the rest of the scholars were doing pretty much as they pleased, eating green apples, whispering, drawing pictures on their slates, and driving crickets, harnessed to strings, up and down the aisle. Gilbert Blythe was trying to make Anne Shirley look at him and failing utterly, because Anne was at that moment totally oblivious, not only of the very existence of Gilbert Blythe, but of every other scholar in Avonlea school and of Avonlea school itself. With her chin propped on her hands and her eyes fixed on the blue glimpse of the Lake of Shining Waters that the west window afforded, she was far away in a gorgeous dreamland, hearing and seeing nothing save her own wonderful visions.

Gilbert Blythe wasn't used to putting himself out to make a girl look at him and meeting with failure. She *should* look at him, that red-haired Shirley girl with the little pointed chin and the big eyes that weren't like the eyes of any other girl in Avonlea school.

Gilbert reached across the aisle, picked up the end of Anne's long red braid, held it out at arm's length and said in a piercing whisper, "Carrots! Carrots!"

Then Anne looked at him with a vengeance!

She did more than look. She sprang to her feet, her bright fancies fallen into cureless ruin. She flashed one indignant glance at Gilbert from eyes whose angry sparkle was swiftly quenched in equally angry tears.

"You mean, hateful boy!" she exclaimed passionately. "How dare you!"

And then—Thwack! Anne had brought her slate down on Gilbert's head and cracked it—slate, not head—clear across.

Avonlea school always enjoyed a scene. This was an especially enjoyable one. Everybody said, "Oh" in horrified delight. Diana gasped. Ruby Gillis, who was inclined to be hysterical, began to cry. Tommy Sloane let his team of crickets escape him altogether while he stared openmouthed at the tableau.

Mr. Phillips stalked down the aisle and laid his hand heavily on Anne's shoulder.

"Anne Shirley, what does this mean?" he said angrily.

Anne returned no answer. It was asking too much of flesh and blood to expect her to tell before the whole school that she had been called "carrots." Gilbert it was who spoke up stoutly.

"It was my fault, Mr. Phillips. I teased her."

Mr. Phillips paid no heed to Gilbert.

"I am sorry to see a pupil of mine displaying such a temper and such a vindictive spirit," he said in a solemn tone, as if the mere fact of being a pupil of his ought to root out all evil passions from the hearts of small imperfect mortals. "Anne, go and stand on the platform in front of the blackboard for the rest of the afternoon."

Anne would have infinitely preferred a whipping to this punishment, under which her sensitive spirit quivered as from a whiplash. With a white, set face she obeyed. Mr. Phillips took a chalk crayon and wrote on the blackboard above her head.

"Ann Shirley has a very bad temper. Ann Shirley must learn to control her temper," and then read it out loud so that even the primer class, who couldn't read writing, should understand it.

Anne stood there the rest of the afternoon with that legend above her. She did not cry or hang her head. Anger was still too hot in her heart for that and it sustained her amid all her agony of humiliation. With resentful eyes and passion-red cheeks she confronted alike Diana's sympathetic gaze and Charlie Sloane's indignant nods and Josie Pye's malicious smiles. As for Gilbert Blythe, she would not even look at him. She would *never* look at him again! She would never speak to him!!

When school was dismissed Anne marched out with her red head held high. Gilbert Blythe tried to intercept her at the porch door.

"I'm awful sorry I made fun of your hair, Anne," he whispered contritely. "Honest I am. Don't be mad for keeps, now."

Anne swept by disdainfully, without look or sign of hearing. "Oh, how could you, Anne?" breathed Diana as they went down the road, half reproachfully, half admiringly. Diana felt that *she* could never have resisted Gilbert's plea.

"I shall never forgive Gilbert Blythe," said Anne firmly. "And Mr. Phillips spelled my name without an *e,* too. The iron has entered into my soul, Diana."

Diana hadn't the least idea what Anne meant but she understood it was something terrible.

"You mustn't mind Gilbert making fun of your hair," she said soothingly. "Why, he makes fun of all the girls. He laughs at mine because it's so black. He's called me a crow a dozen times; and I never heard him apologize for anything before, either."

"There's a great deal of difference between being called a crow and being called carrots," said Anne with dignity. "Gilbert Blythe has hurt my feelings *excruciatingly,* Diana."

It is possible the matter might have blown over without more excruciation if nothing else had happened. But when things begin to happen they are apt to keep on.

Avonlea scholars often spent noon hour picking gum in Mr. Bell's spruce grove over the hill and across his big pasture field. From there they could keep an eye on Eben Wright's house, where the master boarded. When they saw Mr. Phillips emerging therefrom they ran for the schoolhouse; but the distance being about three times longer than

Mr. Wright's lane they were very apt to arrive there, breathless and gasping, some three minutes too late.

On the following day Mr. Phillips was seized with one of his spasmodic fits of reform and announced, before going home to dinner, that he should expect to find all the scholars in their seats when he returned. Any one who came in late would be punished.

All the boys and some of the girls went to Mr. Bell's spruce grove as usual, fully intending to stay only long enough to "pick a chew." But spruce groves are seductive and yellow nuts of gum beguiling; they picked and loitered and strayed; and as usual the first thing that recalled them to a sense of the flight of time was Jimmy Glover shouting from the top of a patriarchal old spruce, "Master's coming."

The girls, who were on the ground, started first and managed to reach the schoolhouse in time but without a second to spare. The boys, who had to wriggle hastily down from the trees, were later; and Anne, who had not been picking gum at all but was wandering happily in the far end of the grove, waist deep among the bracken, singing softly to herself, with a wreath of rice lilies on her hair as if she were some wild divinity of the shadowy places, was latest of all. Anne could run like a deer, however; run she did with the impish result that she overtook the boys at the door and was swept into the schoolhouse among them just as Mr. Phillips was in the act of hanging up his hat.

Mr. Phillips' brief reforming energy was over; he didn't want the bother of punishing a dozen pupils; but it was necessary to do some-thing to save his word, so he looked about for a scapegoat and found it in Anne, who had dropped into her seat, gasping for breath, with her forgotten lily wreath hanging askew over one ear and giving her a par-ticularly rakish and dishevelled appearance.

"Anne Shirley, since you seem to be so fond of the boys' company we shall indulge your taste for it this afternoon," he said sarcastically. "Take those flowers out of your hair and sit with Gilbert Blythe."

The other boys snickered. Diana, turning pale with pity, plucked the wreath from Anne's hair and squeezed her hand. Anne stared at the master as if turned to stone.

"Did you hear what I said, Anne?" queried Mr. Phillips sternly.

"Yes, sir," said Anne slowly, "but I didn't suppose you really meant it."

"I assure you I did,"—still the sarcastic inflection which all the children, and Anne especially, hated. It flicked on the raw. "Obey me at once."

For a moment Anne looked as if she meant to disobey. Then, realizing that there was no help for it, she rose haughtily, stepped across the aisle, sat down beside Gilbert Blythe, and buried her face in her arms on the desk. Ruby Gillis, who got a glimpse of it as it went down, told the others going home from school that she'd "acksually never seen anything like it—it was so white, with awful little red spots in it."

To Anne, this was as the end of all things. It was bad enough to be singled out for punishment from among a dozen equally guilty ones; it was worse still to be sent to sit with a boy; but that that boy should be Gilbert Blythe was heaping insult on injury to a degree utterly unbearable. Anne felt that she could *not* bear it and it would be of no use to try. Her whole being seethed with shame and anger and humiliation.

At first the other scholars looked and whispered and giggled and nudged. But as Anne never lifted her head and as Gilbert worked fractions as if his whole soul was absorbed in them and them only, they soon returned to their own tasks and Anne was forgotten. When Mr. Phillips called the history class out Anne should have gone; but Anne did not move, and Mr. Phillips, who had been writing some verses "To Priscilla" before he called the class, was thinking about an obstinate rhyme still and never missed her. Once, when nobody was looking, Gilbert took from his desk a little pink candy heart with a gold motto on it, "You are sweet," and slipped it under the curve of Anne's arm. Whereupon Anne arose, took the pink heart gingerly between the tips of her fingers, dropped it on the floor, ground it to powder beneath her heel, and resumed her position without deigning to bestow a glance on Gilbert.

When school went out Anne marched to her desk, ostentatiously took out everything therein, books and writing tablet, pen and ink, testament and arithmetic, and piled them neatly on her cracked slate.

"What are you taking all those things home for, Anne?" Diana wanted to know, as soon as they were out on the road. She had not dared to ask the question before.

"I am not coming back to school any more," said Anne.

Diana gasped and stared at Anne to see if she meant it.

"Will Marilla let you stay home?" she asked.

"She'll have to," said Anne. "I'll *never* go to school to that man again."

"Oh, Anne!" Diana looked as if she were ready to cry. "I do think you're mean. What shall I do? Mr. Phillips will make me sit with that horrid Gertie Pye—I know he will because she is sitting alone. Do come back, Anne."

"I'd do almost anything in the world for you, Diana," said Anne sadly. "I'd let myself be torn limb from limb if it would do you any good. But I can't do this, so please don't ask it. You harrow up my very soul."

"Just think of all the fun you will miss," mourned Diana. "We are going to build the loveliest new house down by the brook; and we'll be playing ball next week and you've never played ball, Anne. It's tremenjusly exciting. And we're going to learn a new song—Jane Andrews is practising it up now; and Alice Andrews is going to bring a new Pansy book next week and we're all going to read it out loud, chapter about, down by the brook. And you know you are so fond of reading out loud, Anne."

Nothing moved Anne in the least. Her mind was made up. She would not go to school to Mr. Phillips again; she told Marilla so when she got home.

"Nonsense," said Marilla.

"It isn't nonsense at all," said Anne, gazing at Marilla with solemn, reproachful eyes. "Don't you understand, Marilla? I've been insulted."

"Insulted fiddlesticks! You'll go to school tomorrow as usual."

"Oh, no." Anne shook her head gently. "I'm not going back, Marilla. I'll learn my lessons at home and I'll be as good as I can be and hold my tongue all the time if it's possible at all. But I will not go back to school I assure you."

Marilla saw something remarkably like unyielding stubbornness looking out of Anne's small face. She understood that she would have trouble in overcoming it; but she resolved wisely to say nothing more just then.

"I'll run down and see Rachel about it this evening," she thought. "There's no use reasoning with Anne now. She's too worked up and I've an idea she can be awful stubborn if she takes the notion. Far as I can make out from her story, Mr. Phillips has been carrying matters with a rather high hand. But it would never do to say so to her. I'll just talk it over with Rachel. She's sent ten children to school and she ought to know something about it. She'll have heard the whole story, too, by this time."

Marilla found Mrs. Lynde knitting quilts as industriously and cheerfully as usual.

"I suppose you know what I've come about," she said, a little shamefacedly.

Mrs. Rachel nodded.

"About Anne's fuss in school, I reckon," she said. "Tillie Boulter was in on her way home from school and told me about it."

"I don't know what to do with her," said Marilla. "She declares she won't go back to school. I never saw a child so worked up. I've been expecting trouble ever since she started to school. I knew things were going too smooth to last. She's so highstrung. What would you advise, Rachel?"

"Well, since you've asked my advice, Marilla," said Mrs. Lynde amiably—Mrs. Lynde dearly loved to be asked for advice—"I'd just humor her a little at first, that's what I'd do. It's my belief that Mr. Phillips was in the wrong. Of course, it doesn't do to say so to the children, you know. And of course he did right to punish her yesterday for giving way to temper. But today it was different. The others who were late should have been punished as well as Anne, that's what. And I don't believe in making the girls sit with the boys for punishment. It isn't modest. Tillie Boulter was real indignant. She took Anne's part right through and said all the scholars did, too. Anne seems real popular among them, somehow. I never thought she'd take with them so well."

"Then you really think I'd better let her stay home," said Marilla in amazement.

"Yes. That is, I wouldn't say school to her again until she said it herself. Depend upon it, Marilla, she'll cool off in a week or so and be ready enough to go back of her own accord, that's what, while, if you were to make her go back right off, dear knows what freak or tantrum she'd take next and make more trouble than ever. The less fuss made the better, in my opinion. She won't miss much by not going to school, as far as *that* goes. Mr. Phillips isn't any good at all as a teacher. The order he keeps is scandalous, that's what, and he neglects the young fry and puts all his time on those big scholars he's getting ready for Queens. He'd never have got the school for another year if his uncle hadn't been a trustee—*the* trustee, for he just leads the other two around by the nose, that's what. I declare, I don't know what education in this Island is coming to."

Mrs. Rachel shook her head, as much as to say if she were only at the head of the educational system of the Province things would be much better managed.

Marilla took Mrs. Rachel's advice and not another word was said to Anne about going back to school. She learned her lessons at home, did her chores, and played with Diana in the chilly purple autumn twilights; but when she met Gilbert Blythe on the road or encountered him in Sunday school she passed him by with an icy contempt that was no whit thawed by his evident desire to appease her. Even Diana's efforts as a peacemaker were of no avail. Anne had evidently made up her mind to hate Gilbert Blythe to the end of life.

As much as she hated Gilbert, however, did she love Diana, with all the love of her passionate little heart, equally intense in its likes and dislikes. One evening Marilla, coming in from the orchard with a basket of apples, found Anne sitting alone by the east window in the twilight, crying bitterly.

"Whatever's the matter now, Anne?" she asked.

"It's about Diana," sobbed Anne luxuriously. "I love Diana so, Marilla. I cannot ever live without her. But I know very well when we grow up that Diana will get married and go away and leave me. And oh, what shall I do? I hate her husband—I just hate him furiously. I've been imagining it all out—the wedding and everything—Diana dressed in snowy garments, with a veil, and looking as beautiful and regal as a queen; and me the bridesmaid, with a lovely dress, too, and puffed sleeves, but with a breaking heart hid beneath my smiling face. And then bidding Diana good-bye-e-e—" Here Anne broke down entirely and wept with increasing bitterness.

Marilla turned quickly away to hide her twitching face, but it was no use; she collapsed on the nearest chair and burst into such a hearty and unusual peal of laughter that Matthew, crossing the yard outside, halted in amazement. When had he heard Marilla laugh like that before?

"Well, Anne Shirley," said Marilla as soon as she could speak, "if you must borrow trouble, for pity's sake borrow it handier home. I should think you had an imagination, sure enough."

16

Diana is Invited to Tea
With Tragic Results

ctober was a beautiful month at Green Gables, when the birches in the hollow turned as golden as sunshine and the maples behind the orchard were royal crimson and the wild cherry trees along the lane put on the loveliest shades of dark red and bronzy green, while the fields sunned themselves in aftermaths.

Anne revelled in the world of color about her.

"Oh, Marilla," she exclaimed one Saturday morning, coming dancing in with her arms full of gorgeous boughs, "I'm so glad I live in a world where there are Octobers. It would be terrible if we just skipped from September to November, wouldn't it? Look at these maple branches. Don't they give you a thrill—several thrills? I'm going to decorate my room with them."

"Messy things," said Marilla, whose aesthetic sense was not noticeably developed. "You clutter up your room entirely too much with out-of-doors stuff, Anne. Bedrooms were made to sleep in."

"Oh, and dream in too, Marilla. And you know one can dream so much better in a room where there are pretty things. I'm going to put these boughs in the old blue jug and set them on my table."

"Mind you don't drop leaves all over the stairs then. I'm going to a meeting of the Aid Society at Carmody this afternoon, Anne, and I won't likely be home before dark. You'll have to get Matthew and Jerry their supper, so mind you don't forget to put the tea to draw until you sit down at the table as you did last time."

"It was dreadful of me to forget," said Anne apologetically, "but that was the afternoon I was trying to think of a name for Violet Vale and it crowded other things out. Matthew was so good. He never scolded a bit. He put the tea down himself and said we could wait awhile as well as not. And I told him a lovely fairy story while we were waiting, so he didn't find the time long at all. It was a beautiful fairy story, Marilla. I forgot the end of it, so I made up an end for it myself and Matthew said he couldn't tell where the join came in."

"Matthew would think it all right, Anne, if you took a notion to get up and have dinner in the middle of the night. But you keep your wits about you this time. And—I don't really know if I'm doing right— it may make you more addlepated than ever—but you can ask Diana to come over and spend the afternoon with you and have tea here."

"Oh, Marilla!" Anne clasped her hands. "How perfectly lovely! You *are* able to imagine things after all or else you'd never have understood how I've longed for that very thing. It will seem so nice and grown-uppish. No fear of my forgetting to put the tea to draw when I have company. Oh, Marilla, can I use the rosebud spray tea set?"

"No, indeed! The rosebud tea set! Well, what next? You know I never use that except for the minister or the Aids. You'll put down the old brown tea set. But you can open the little yellow crock of cherry preserves. It's time it was being used anyhow—I believe it's beginning to work. And you can cut some fruitcake and have some of the cookies and snaps."

"I can just imagine myself sitting down at the head of the table and pouring out the tea," said Anne, shutting her eyes ecstatically. "And asking Diana if she takes sugar! I know she doesn't but of course I'll ask her just as if I didn't know. And then pressing her to take another piece of fruitcake and another helping of preserves. Oh, Marilla, it's a wonderful sensation just to think of it. Can I take her into the spare room to lay off her hat when she comes? And then into the parlor to sit?"

"No. The sitting-room will do for you and your company. But there's a bottle half full of raspberry cordial that was left over from the church social the other night. It's on the second shelf of the sitting room closet and you and Diana can have it if you like, and a cooky to eat with it along in the afternoon, for I daresay Matthew'll be late coming in to tea since he's hauling potatoes to the vessel."

Anne flew down to the hollow, past the Dryad's Bubble and up the spruce path to Orchard Slope, to ask Diana to tea. As a result, just after Marilla had driven off to Carmody, Diana came over, dressed in her second best dress and looking exactly as it is proper to look when asked out to tea. At other times she was wont to run into the kitchen without knocking; but now she knocked primly at the front door. And when Anne, dressed in *her* second best, as primly opened it, both little girls shook hands as gravely as if they had never met before. This unnatural solemnity lasted until after Diana had been taken to the east gable to lay off her hat and then had sat for ten minutes in the sitting room, toes in position.

"How is your mother?" inquired Anne politely, just as if she had not seen Mrs. Barry picking apples that morning in excellent health and spirits.

"She is very well, thank you. I suppose Mr. Cuthbert is hauling potatoes to the *Lily Sands* this afternoon, is he?" said Diana, who had ridden down to Mr. Harmon Andrews' that morning in Matthew's cart.

"Yes. Our potato crop is very good this year. I hope your father's potato crop is good, too."

"It is fairly good, thank you. Have you picked many of your apples yet?"

"Oh, ever so many," said Anne, forgetting to be dignified and jumping up quickly. "Let's go out to the orchard and get some of the Red Sweetings, Diana. Marilla says we can have all that are left on the tree. Marilla is a very generous woman. She said we could have fruitcake and cherry preserves for tea. But it isn't good manners to tell your company what you are going to give them to eat, so I won't tell you what she said we could have to drink. Only it begins with an *r* and a *c* and it's a bright red color. I love bright red drinks, don't you? They taste twice as good as any other color."

The orchard, with its great sweeping boughs that bent to the ground with fruit, proved so delightful that the little girls spent most of the afternoon in it, sitting in a grassy corner where the frost had spared the green and the mellow autumn sunshine lingered warmly, eating apples and talking as hard as they could. Diana had much to tell Anne of what went on in school. She had to sit with Gertie Pye and she hated it; Gertie squeaked her pencil all the time and it just made her—Diana's—blood run cold; Ruby Gillis had charmed all her warts away, true's you live, with a magic pebble that old Mary Joe from the Creek gave her. You had to rub the warts with the pebble and then throw it away over your left shoulder at the time of the new moon and the warts would all go. Charlie Sloane's name was written up with Em White's on the porch wall and Em White was *awful* mad about it; Sam Boulter had "sassed" Mr. Phillips in class and Mr. Phillips whipped him and Sam's father came down to the school and dared Mr. Phillips to lay a hand on one of his children again; and Mattie Andrews had a new red hood and a blue crossover with tassels on it and the airs she put on about it were perfectly sickening; and Lizzie Wright didn't speak to Mamie Wilson because Mamie Wilson's grown-up sister had cut out Lizzie Wright's grown-up sister with her beau; and everybody missed Anne so and wished she'd come to school again; and Gilbert Blythe—

But Anne didn't want to hear about Gilbert Blythe. She jumped up hurriedly and said suppose they go in and have some raspberry cordial.

Anne looked on the second shelf of the sitting room pantry but there was no bottle of raspberry cordial there. Search revealed it away back on the top shelf. Anne put it on a tray and set it on the table with a tumbler.

"Now, please help yourself, Diana," she said politely. "I don't believe I'll have any just now. I don't feel as if I wanted any after all those apples."

Diana poured herself out a tumblerful, looked at its bright red hue admiringly, and then sipped it daintily.

"That's awfully nice raspberry cordial, Anne," she said. "I didn't know raspberry cordial was so nice."

"I'm real glad you like it. Take as much as you want. I'm going to run out and stir the fire up. There are so many responsibilities on a person's mind when they're keeping house, isn't there?"

When Anne came back from the kitchen Diana was drinking her second glassful of cordial; and, being entreated thereto by Anne, she offered no particular objection to the drinking of a third. The tumblerfuls were generous ones and the raspberry cordial was certainly very nice.

"The nicest I ever drank," said Diana. "It's ever so much nicer than Mrs. Lynde's although she brags of hers so much. It doesn't taste a bit like hers."

"I should think Marilla's raspberry cordial would prob'ly be much nicer than Mrs. Lynde's," said Anne loyally. "Marilla is a famous cook. She is trying to teach me to cook but I assure you, Diana, it is uphill work. There's so little scope for imagination in cookery. You just have to go by rules. The last time I made a cake I forgot to put the flour in. I was thinking the loveliest story about you and me, Diana. I thought you were desperately ill with smallpox and everybody deserted you, but I went boldly to your bedside and nursed you back to life; and then I took the smallpox and died and I was buried under those poplar trees in the graveyard and you planted a rosebush by my grave and watered it with your tears; and you never, never forgot the friend of your youth who sacrificed her life for you. Oh, it was such a pathetic tale, Diana. The tears just rained down over my cheeks while I mixed the cake. But I forgot the flour and the cake was a dismal failure. Flour is so essential to cakes, you know. Marilla was very cross and I don't wonder. I'm a great trial to her. She was terribly mortified about the pudding sauce last week. We had a plum pudding for dinner on Tuesday and there was half the pudding and a pitcherful of sauce left over. Marilla said there was enough for another dinner and told me to set it on the pantry shelf and cover it. I meant to cover it just as much as could be, Diana, but when I carried it in I was imagining I was a nun—of course I'm a Protestant but I imagined I was a Catholic—taking the veil to bury a broken heart in cloistered seclusion; and I forgot all about covering the pudding sauce. I thought of it next morning and ran to the pantry. Diana, fancy if you can my extreme horror at finding a mouse drowned in that pudding sauce! I lifted the mouse out with a spoon and threw it out in the yard and then I washed the spoon in three waters. Marilla was out milking and I fully intended to ask her when she came in if I'd give the sauce to the pigs; but when she did come in I was imagining that I was a frost fairy going through the woods turning the trees red and yellow, whichever they wanted to be, so I never thought about the pudding sauce again and Marilla sent me out to pick apples. Well, Mr. and Mrs. Chester Ross from Spencervale came here that morning. You know they are very stylish people, especially Mrs. Chester Ross. When Marilla called me in dinner was all ready and everybody was at the table. I tried to be as polite and dignified as I could be, for I wanted Mrs. Chester Ross to think I was a ladylike little girl even if I wasn't pretty. Everything went right until I saw Marilla coming with the plum pudding in one hand and the pitcher of pudding sauce, *warmed up,* in the other. Diana, that was a terrible moment. I remembered everything and I just stood up in my place and shrieked out, 'Marilla, you mustn't use that pudding sauce. There was a mouse drowned in it. I forgot to tell you before.' Oh, Diana, I shall never forget that awful moment if I live to be a hundred. Mrs. Chester Ross just *looked* at me and I thought I would sink through the floor with mortification. She is such a perfect housekeeper and fancy what she must have thought of us. Marilla turned red as fire but she never said a word—then. She just carried that sauce and pudding out and brought in some strawberry preserves. She even offered me some, but I couldn't swallow a mouthful. It was like heaping coals of fire on my head. After Mrs. Chester Ross went away Marilla gave me a dreadful scolding. Why, Diana, what is the matter?"

Diana had stood up very unsteadily; then she sat down again, putting her hands to her head.

"I'm—I'm awful sick," she said, a little thickly. "I—I—must go right home."

"Oh, you mustn't dream of going home without your tea," cried Anne in distress. "I'll get it right off—I'll go and put the tea down this very minute."

"I must go home," repeated Diana, stupidly but determinedly.

"Let me get you a lunch anyhow," implored Anne. "Let me give you a bit of fruitcake and some of the cherry preserves. Lie down on the sofa for a little while and you'll be better. Where do you feel bad?"

"I must go home," said Diana, and that was all she would say. In vain Anne pleaded.

"I never heard of company going home without tea," she mourned. "Oh, Diana, do you suppose that it's possible you're really taking the smallpox? If you are I'll go and nurse you, you can depend on that. I'll never forsake you. But I do wish you'd stay till after tea. Where do you feel bad?"

"I'm awful dizzy," said Diana.

And indeed, she walked very dizzily. Anne, with tears of disappointment in her eyes, got Diana's hat and went with her as far as the Barry yard fence. Then she wept all the way back to Green Gables, where she sorrowfully put the remainder of the raspberry cordial back into the pantry and got tea ready for Matthew and Jerry, with all the zest gone out of the performance.

The next day was Sunday and as the rain poured down in torrents from dawn till dusk Anne did not stir abroad from Green Gables. Monday afternoon Marilla sent her down to Mrs. Lynde's on an errand. In a very short space of time Anne came flying back up the lane, with tears rolling down her cheeks. Into the kitchen she dashed and flung herself face downward on the sofa in an agony.

"Whatever has gone wrong now, Anne?" queried Marilla in doubt and dismay. "I do hope you haven't gone and been saucy to Mrs. Lynde again."

No answer from Anne save more tears and stormier sobs!

"Anne Shirley, when I ask you a question I want to be answered. Sit right up this very minute and tell me what you are crying about."

Anne sat up, tragedy personified.

"Mrs. Lynde was up to see Mrs. Barry today and Mrs. Barry was in an awful state," she wailed. "She says that I set Diana *drunk* Saturday and sent her home in a disgraceful condition. And she says I must be a thoroughly bad, wicked little girl and she's never, never going to let Diana play with me again. Oh, Marilla, I'm just overcome with woe."

Marilla stared in blank amazement.

"Set Diana drunk!" she said when she found her voice. "Anne, are you or Mrs. Barry crazy? What on earth did you give her?"

"Not a thing but raspberry cordial," sobbed Anne. "I never thought raspberry cordial would set people drunk, Marilla—not even if they drank three big tumblerfuls as Diana did. Oh, it sounds so—so—like Mrs. Thomas' husband! But I didn't mean to set her drunk."

"Drunk fiddlesticks!" said Marilla, marching to the sitting room pantry. There on the shelf was a bottle which she at once recognized as one containing some of her three year old homemade currant wine for which she was celebrated in Avonlea, although certain of the stricter sort, Mrs. Barry among them, disapproved strongly of it. And at the same time Marilla recollected that she had put the bottle of raspberry cordial down in the cellar instead of in the pantry as she had told Anne.

She went back to the kitchen with the wine bottle in her hand. Her face was twitching in spite of herself.

"Anne, you certainly have a genius for getting into trouble. You went and gave Diana currant wine instead of raspberry cordial. Didn't you know the difference yourself?"

"I never tasted it," said Anne. "I thought it was the cordial. I meant to be so—so—hospitable. Diana got awfully sick and had to go home. Mrs. Barry told Mrs. Lynde she was simply dead drunk. She just laughed silly like when her mother asked her what was the matter and went to sleep and slept for hours. Her mother smelled her breath and knew she was drunk. She had a fearful headache all day yesterday. Mrs. Barry is so indignant. She will never believe but what I did it on purpose."

"I should think she would better punish Diana for being so greedy as to drink three glassfuls of anything," said Marilla shortly. "Why, three of those big glasses would have made her sick even if it had only been cordial. Well, this story will be a nice handle for those folks who are so down on me for making currant wine, although I haven't made any for three years ever since I found out that the minister didn't approve. I just kept that bottle for sickness. There, there, child, don't cry. I can't see as you were to blame although I'm sorry it happened so."

"I must cry," said Anne. "My heart is broken. The stars in their courses fight against me, Marilla. Diana and I are parted forever. Oh, Marilla, I little dreamed of this when first we swore our vows of friendship."

"Don't be foolish, Anne. Mrs. Barry will think better of it when she finds you're not really to blame. I suppose she thinks you've done it for a silly joke or something of that sort. You'd best go up this evening and tell her how it was."

"My courage fails me at the thought of facing Diana's injured mother," sighed Anne. "I wish you'd go, Marilla. You're so much more dignified than I am. Likely she'd listen to you quicker than to me."

"Well, I will," said Marilla, reflecting that it would probably be the wiser course. "Don't cry any more, Anne. It will be all right."

Marilla had changed her mind about its being all right by the time she got back from Orchard Slope. Anne was watching for her coming and flew to the porch door to meet her.

"Oh, Marilla, I know by your face that it's been no use," she said sorrowfully. "Mrs. Barry won't forgive me?"

"Mrs. Barry, indeed!" snapped Marilla. "Of all the unreasonable women I ever saw she's the worst. I told her it was all a mistake and you weren't to blame, but she just simply didn't believe me. And she rubbed it well in about my currant wine and how I'd always said it couldn't have the least effect on anybody. I just told her plainly that currant wine wasn't meant to be drunk three tumblerfuls at a time and that if a child I had to do with was so greedy I'd sober her up with a right good spanking."

Marilla whisked into the kitchen, grievously disturbed, leaving a very much distracted little soul in the porch behind her. Presently Anne stepped out bareheaded into the chill autumn dusk; very determinedly and steadily she took her way down through the sere clover field over the log bridge and up through the spruce grove, lighted by a pale little moon hanging low over the western woods. Mrs. Barry, coming to the door in answer to the timid knock, found a white-lipped, eager-eyed suppliant on the doorstep.

Her face hardened. Mrs. Barry was a woman of strong prejudices and dislikes, and her anger was of the cold, sullen sort which is always hardest to overcome. To do her justice, she really believed Anne had made Diana drunk out of sheer malice prepense, and she was honestly anxious to preserve her little daughter from the contamination of further intimacy with such a child.

"What do you want?" she said stiffly.

Anne clasped her hands.

"Oh, Mrs. Barry, please forgive me. I did not mean to—to—

intoxicate Diana. How could I? Just imagine if you were a poor little orphan girl that kind people had adopted and you had just one bosom friend in all the world. Do you think you would intoxicate her on purpose? I thought it was only raspberry cordial. Oh, please don't say that you won't let Diana play with me any more. If you do you will cover my life with a dark cloud of woe."

This speech, which would have softened good Mrs. Lynde's heart in a twinkling, had no effect on Mrs. Barry except to irritate her still more. She was suspicious of Anne's big words and dramatic gestures and imagined that the child was making fun of her. So she said, coldly and cruelly:

"I don't think you are a fit little girl for Diana to associate with. You'd better go home and behave yourself."

Anne's lip quivered.

"Won't you let me see Diana just once to say farewell?" she implored.

"Diana has gone over to Carmody with her father," said Mrs. Barry, going in and shutting the door.

Anne went back to Green Gables calm with despair.

"My last hope is gone," she told Marilla. "I went up and saw Mrs. Barry myself and she treated me very insultingly. Marilla, I do *not* think she is a well-bred woman. There is nothing more to do except to pray and I haven't much hope that that'll do much good because, Marilla, I do not believe that God Himself can do very much with such an obstinate person as Mrs. Barry."

"Anne, you shouldn't say such things," rebuked Marilla, striving to overcome that unholy tendency to laughter which she was dismayed to find growing upon her. And indeed, when she told the whole story to Matthew that night, she did laugh heartily over Anne's tribulations.

But when she slipped into the east gable before going to bed and found that Anne had cried herself to sleep an unaccustomed softness crept into her face.

"Poor little soul," she murmured, lifting a loose curl of hair from the child's tearstained face. Then she bent down and kissed the flushed cheek on the pillow.

17

A New Interest in Life

he next afternoon Anne, bending over her patchwork at the kitchen window, happened to glance out and beheld Diana down by the Dryad's Bubble beckoning mysteriously. In a trice Anne was out of the house and flying down to the hollow, astonishment and hope struggling in her expressive eyes. But the hope faded when she saw Diana's dejected countenance.

"Your mother hasn't relented?" she gasped.

Diana shook her head mournfully.

"No; and oh, Anne, she says I'm never to play with you again. I've cried and cried and I told her it wasn't your fault, but it wasn't any use. I had ever such a time coaxing her to let me come down and say goodbye to you. She said I was only to stay ten minutes and she's timing me by the clock."

"Ten minutes isn't very long to say an eternal farewell in," said Anne tearfully. "Oh, Diana, will you promise faithfully never to forget me, the friend of your youth, no matter what dearer friends may caress thee?"

"Indeed I will," sobbed Diana, "and I'll never have another bosom friend—I don't want to have. I couldn't love anybody as I love you."

"Oh, Diana," cried Anne, clasping her hands, "do you *love* me?"

"Why, of course I do. Didn't you know that?"

"No." Anne drew a long breath. "I thought you *liked* me of course, but I never hoped you *loved* me. Why, Diana, I didn't think anybody could love me. Nobody ever has loved me since I can remember. Oh, this is wonderful! It's a ray of light which will forever shine on the darkness of a path severed from thee, Diana. Oh, just say it once again."

"I love you devotedly, Anne," said Diana stanchly, "and I always will, you may be sure of that."

"And I will always love thee, Diana," said Anne, solemnly extending her hand. "In the years to come thy memory will shine like a star over my lonely life, as that last story we read together says. Diana, wilt thou give me a lock of thy jet-black tresses in parting to treasure forevermore?"

"Have you got anything to cut it with?" queried Diana, wiping away the tears which Anne's affecting accents had caused to flow afresh, and returning to practicalities.

"Yes. I've got my patchwork scissors in my apron pocket fortunately," said Anne. She solemnly clipped one of Diana's curls. "Fare thee well, my beloved friend. Henceforth we must be as strangers though living side by side. But my heart will ever be faithful to thee."

Anne stood and watched Diana out of sight, mournfully waving her hand to the latter whenever she turned to look back. Then she returned to the house, not a little consoled for the time being by this romantic parting.

"It is all over," she informed Marilla. "I shall never have another friend. I'm really worse off than ever before, for I haven't Katie Maurice and Violetta now. And even if I had it wouldn't be the same. Somehow, little dream girls are not satisfying after a real friend. Diana and I had such an affecting farewell down by the spring. It will be sacred in my memory forever. I used the most pathetic language I could think of and said 'thou' and 'thee.' 'Thou' and 'thee' seem so much more romantic than 'you.' Diana gave me a lock of her hair and I'm going to sew it up in a little bag and wear it around my neck all my life. Please see that it is buried with me, for I don't believe I'll live very long. Perhaps when she sees me lying cold and dead before her Mrs. Barry may feel remorse for what she has done and will let Diana come to my funeral."

"I don't think there is much fear of your dying of grief as long as you can talk, Anne," said Marilla unsympathetically.

The following Monday Anne surprised Marilla by coming down from her room with her basket of books on her arm and her lips primmed up into a line of determination.

"I'm going back to school," she announced. "That is all there is left in life for me, now that my friend has been ruthlessly torn from me. In school I can look at her and muse over days departed."

"You'd better muse over your lessons and sums," said Marilla, concealing her delight at this development of the situation. "If you're going back to school I hope we'll hear no more of breaking slates over people's heads and such carryings-on. Behave yourself and do just what your teacher tells you."

"I'll try to be a model pupil," agreed Anne dolefully. "There won't be much fun in it, I expect. Mr. Phillips said Minnie Andrews was a model pupil and there isn't a spark of imagination or life in her. She is just dull and poky and never seems to have a good time. But I feel so depressed that perhaps it will come easy to me now. I'm going round by the road. I couldn't bear to go by the Birch Path all alone. I should weep bitter tears if I did."

Anne was welcomed back to school with open arms. Her imagination had been sorely missed in games, her voice in the singing, and her dramatic ability in the perusal aloud of books at dinner hour. Ruby Gillis smuggled three blue plums over to her during testament reading; Ella May MacPherson gave her an enormous yellow pansy cut from the covers of a floral catalogue—a species of desk decoration much prized in Avonlea school. Sophia Sloane offered to teach her a perfectly elegant new pattern of knit lace, so nice for trimming aprons. Katie Boulter gave her a perfume bottle to keep slate-water in and Julia Bell copied carefully on a piece of pale pink paper, scalloped on the edges, the following effusion:

"TO ANNE
"When twilight drops her curtain down
And pins it with a star
Remember that you have a friend
Though she may wander far."

"It's so nice to be appreciated," sighed Anne rapturously to Marilla that night.

The girls were not the only scholars who "appreciated" her. When Anne went to her seat after dinner hour—she had been told by Mr. Phillips to sit with the model Minnie Andrews—she found on her desk a big luscious "strawberry apple." Anne caught it up all ready to take a bite, when she remembered that the only place in Avonlea where strawberry apples grew was in the old Blythe orchard on the other side of the Lake of Shining Waters. Anne dropped the apple as if it were a red-hot coal and ostentatiously wiped her fingers on her handkerchief. The apple lay untouched on her desk until the next morning, when little Timothy Andrews, who swept the school and kindled the fire, annexed it as one of his perquisites. Charlie Sloane's slate pencil, gorgeously bedizened with striped red and yellow paper, costing two cents where ordinary pencils cost only one, which he sent up to her after dinner hour, met with a more favorable reception. Anne was graciously pleased to accept it and rewarded the donor with a smile which exalted that infatuated youth straightway into the seventh heaven of delight and caused him to make such fearful errors in his dictation that Mr. Phillips kept him in after school to rewrite it.

But as,

> "The Caesar's pageant shorn of Brutus' bust
> Did but of Rome's best son remind her more,"

so the marked absence of any tribute or recognition from Diana Barry, who was sitting with Gertie Pye, embittered Anne's little triumph.

"Diana might just have smiled at me once, I think," she mourned to Marilla that night. But the next morning a note, most fearfully and wonderfully twisted and folded, and a small parcel, were passed across to Anne.

"Dear Anne," ran the former, "Mother says I'm not to play with you or talk to you even in school. It isn't my fault and don't be cross at me, because I love you as much as ever. I miss you awfully to tell all my secrets to and I don't like Gertie Pye one bit. I made you one of the new bookmarkers out of red tissue paper. They are awfully fashionable now and only three girls in school know how to make them. When you look at it remember

"Your true friend,

"DIANA BARRY."

Anne read the note, kissed the bookmark, and dispatched a prompt reply back to the other side of the school.

"MY OWN DARLING DIANA:—

"Of course I am not cross at you because you have to obey your mother. Our spirits can commune. I shall keep your lovely present forever. Minnie Andrews is a very nice little girl—although she has no imagination—but after having been Diana's busum friend I cannot be Minnie's. Please excuse mistakes because my spelling isn't very good yet, although much improved.

"Yours until death us do part,

"ANNE OR CORDELIA SHIRLEY."

"P. S.. I shall sleep with your letter under my pillow tonight.

"A. or C. S."

Marilla pessimistically expected more trouble since Anne had again begun to go to school. But none developed. Perhaps Anne caught something of the "model" spirit from Minnie Andrews; at least she got on very well with Mr. Phillips thenceforth. She flung herself into her studies heart and soul, determined not to be outdone in any class by Gilbert Blythe. The rivalry between them was soon apparent; it was entirely good-natured on Gilbert's side; but it is much to be feared that the same thing cannot be said of Anne, who had certainly an unpraise-worthy tenacity for holding grudges. She was as intense in her hatreds as in her loves. She would not stoop to admit that she meant to rival Gilbert in school work, because that would have been to acknowledge his existence which Anne persistently ignored; but the rivalry was there and honors fluctuated between them. Now Gilbert was head of the spelling class; now Anne, with a toss of her long red braids, spelled him down. One morning Gilbert had all his sums done correctly and had his name written on the blackboard on the roll of honor; the next morning Anne, having wrestled wildly with decimals the entire evening before, would be first. One awful day they were ties and their names were written up together. It was almost as bad as a "take-notice" and Anne's mortification was as evident as Gilbert's satisfaction. When the written examinations at the end of each month were held the suspense was terrible. The first month Gilbert came out three marks ahead. The second Anne beat him by five. But her triumph was marred by the fact that Gilbert congratulated her heartily before the whole school. It would have been ever so much sweeter to her if he had felt the sting of his defeat.

Mr. Phillips might not be a very good teacher; but a pupil so inflexibly determined on learning as Anne was could hardly escape making progress under any kind of a teacher. By the end of the term Anne and Gilbert were both promoted into the fifth class and allowed to begin studying the elements of "the branches"—by which Latin, geometry, French and algebra were meant. In geometry Anne met her Waterloo.

"It's perfectly awful stuff, Marilla," she groaned. "I'm sure I'll never be able to make head or tail of it. There is no scope for imagination in it at all. Mr. Phillips says I'm the worst dunce he ever saw at it. And Gil—I mean some of the others are so smart at it. It is extremely mortifying, Marilla. Even Diana gets along better than I do. But I don't mind being beaten by Diana. Even although we meet as strangers now I still love her with an *inextinguishable* love. It makes me very sad at times to think about her. But really, Marilla, one can't stay sad very long in such an interesting world, can one?"

18

Anne to the Rescue

All things great are wound up with all things little. At first glance it might not seem that the decision of a certain Canadian Premier to include Prince Edward Island in a political tour could have much or anything to do with the fortunes of little Anne Shirley at Green Gables. But it had.

It was in January the Premier came, to address his loyal supporters and such of his non-supporters as chose to be present at the monster mass meeting held in Charlottetown. Most of the Avonlea people were on the Premier's side of politics; hence, on the night of the meeting nearly all the men and a goodly proportion of the women had gone to town, thirty miles away. Mrs. Rachel Lynde had gone too. Mrs. Rachel Lynde was a red-hot politician and couldn't have believed that the political rally could be carried through without her, although she was on the opposite side of politics. So she went to town and took her husband—Thomas would be useful in looking after the horse—and Marilla Cuthbert with her. Marilla had a sneaking interest in politics herself, and as she thought it might be her only chance to see a real live Premier, she promptly took it, leaving Anne and Matthew to keep house until her return the following day.

Hence, while Marilla and Mrs. Rachel were enjoying themselves hugely at the mass meeting, Anne and Matthew had the cheerful kitchen at Green Gables all to themselves. A bright fire was glowing in the old-fashioned Waterloo stove and blue-white frost crystals were shining on the windowpanes. Matthew nodded over a *Farmer's Advocate* on the sofa and Anne at the table studied her lessons with grim determination, despite sundry wistful glances at the clock shelf, where lay a new book that Jane Andrews had lent her that day. Jane had assured her that it was warranted to produce any number of thrills, or words to that effect, and Anne's fingers tingled to reach out for. it. But that would mean Gilbert Blythe's triumph on the morrow. Anne turned her back on the clock shelf and tried to imagine it wasn't there.

"Matthew, did you ever study geometry when you went to school?"

"Well now, no, I didn't," said Matthew, coming out of his doze with a start.

"I wish you had," sighed Anne, "because then you'd be able to sympathize with me. You can't sympathize properly if you've never studied it. It is casting a cloud over my whole life. I'm such a dunce at it, Matthew."

"Well now, I dunno," said Matthew soothingly. "I guess you're all right at anything. Mr. Phillips told me last week in Blair's store at Carmody that you was the smartest scholar in school and was making rapid progress. 'Rapid progress' was his very words. There's them as runs down Teddy Phillips and says he ain't much of a teacher; but I guess he's all right."

Matthew would have thought any one who praised Anne was "all right."

"I'm sure I'd get on better with geometry if only he wouldn't change the letters," complained Anne. "I learn the proposition off by heart, and then he draws it on the blackboard and puts different letters from what are in the book and I get all mixed up. I don't think a teacher should take such a mean advantage, do you? We're studying agriculture now and I've found out at last what makes the roads red. It's a great comfort. I wonder how Marilla and Mrs. Lynde are enjoying themselves. Mrs. Lynde says Canada is going to the dogs the way things are being run at Ottawa, and that it's an awful warning to the electors. She says if women were allowed to vote we would soon see a blessed change. What way do you vote, Matthew?"

"Conservative," said Matthew promptly. To vote Conservative was part of Matthew's religion.

"Then I'm Conservative too," said Anne decidedly. "I'm glad, because Gil—because some of the boys in school are Grits. I guess

Mr. Phillips is a Grit too, because Prissy Andrews' father is one, and Ruby Gillis says that when a man is courting he always has to agree with the girl's mother in religion and her father in politics. Is that true, Matthew?"

"Well now, I dunno," said Matthew.

"Did you ever go courting, Matthew?"

"Well now, no, I dunno's I ever did," said Matthew, who had certainly never thought of such a thing in his whole existence.

Anne reflected with her chin in her hands.

"It must be rather interesting, don't you think, Matthew? Ruby Gillis says when she grows up she's going to have ever so many beaus on the string and have them all crazy about her; but I think that would be too exciting. I'd rather have just one in his right mind. But Ruby Gillis knows a great deal about such matters because she has so many big sisters, and Mrs. Lynde says the Gillis girls have gone off like hot cakes. Mr. Phillips goes up to see Prissy Andrews nearly every evening. He says it is to help her with her lessons, but Miranda Sloane is studying for Queen's, too, and I should think she needed help a lot more than Prissy because she's ever so much stupider, but he never goes to help her in the evenings at all. There are a great many things in this world that I can't understand very well, Matthew."

"Well now, I dunno as I comprehend them all myself," acknowledged Matthew.

"Well, I suppose I must finish up my lessons. I won't allow myself to open that new book Jane lent me until I'm through. But it's a terrible temptation, Matthew. Even when I turn my back on it I can see it there just as plain. Jane said she cried herself sick over it. I love a book that makes me cry. But I think I'll carry that book into the sitting room and lock it in the jam closet and give you the key. And you must *not* give it to me, Matthew, until my lessons are done, not even if I implore you on my bended knees. It's all very well to say resist temptation, but it's ever so much easier to resist it if you can't get the key. And then shall I run down the cellar and get some russets, Matthew? Wouldn't you like some russets?"

"Well now, I dunno but what I would," said Matthew, who never ate russets but knew Anne's weakness for them.

Just as Anne emerged triumphantly from the cellar with her plateful of russets came the sound of flying footsteps on the icy board walk outside and the next moment the kitchen door was flung open and in rushed Diana Barry, white-faced and breathless, with a shawl wrapped hastily around her head. Anne promptly let go of her candle and plate in her surprise, and plate, candle, and apples crashed together down the cellar ladder and were found at the bottom embedded in melted grease, the next day, by Marilla, who gathered them up and thanked mercy the house hadn't been set on fire.

"Whatever is the matter, Diana?" cried Anne. "Has your mother relented at last?"

"Oh, Anne, do come quick," implored Diana nervously. "Minnie May is awful sick—she's got croup, Young Mary Joe says—and father and mother are away to town and there's nobody to go for the doctor. Minnie May is awful bad and Young Mary Joe doesn't know what to do—and oh, Anne, I'm so scared!"

Matthew, without a word, reached out for cap and coat, slipped past Diana and away into the darkness of the yard.

"He's gone to harness the sorrel mare to go to Carmody for the doctor," said Anne, who was hurrying on hood and jacket. "I know it as well as if he'd said so. Matthew and I are such kindred spirits I can read his thoughts without words at all."

"I don't believe he'll find the doctor at Carmody," sobbed Diana. "I know that Doctor Blair went to town and I guess Doctor Spencer would go too, Young Mary Joe never saw anybody with croup and Mrs. Lynde is away. Oh, Anne!"

"Don't cry, Di," said Anne cheerily. "I know exactly what to do for croup. You forget that Mrs. Hammond had twins three times. When you look after three pairs of twins you naturally get a lot of experience. They all had croup regularly. Just wait till I get the ipecac bottle—you mayn't have any at your house. Come on now."

The two little girls hastened out hand in hand and hurried through Lovers' Lane and across the crusted field beyond, for the snow was too deep to go by the shorter wood way. Anne, although sincerely sorry for Minnie May, was far from being insensible to the romance of the situation and to the sweetness of once more sharing that romance with a kindred spirit.

The night was clear and frosty, all ebony of shadow and silver of snowy slope; big stars were shining over the silent fields; here and there the dark pointed firs stood up with snow powdering their branches and the wind whistling through them. Anne thought it was truly delightful to go skimming through all this mystery and loveliness with your bosom friend who had been so long estranged.

Minnie May, aged three, was really very sick. She lay on the kitchen sofa, feverish and restless, while her hoarse breathing could be heard all over the house. Young Mary Joe, a buxom, broad-faced French girl from the Creek, whom Mrs. Barry had engaged to stay with the children during her absence, was helpless and bewildered, quite incapable of thinking what to do, or doing it if she thought of it.

Anne went to work with skill and promptness.

"Minnie May has croup all right; she's pretty bad, but I've seen them worse. First we must have lots of hot water. I declare, Diana, there isn't more than a cupful in the kettle! There, I've filled it up, and, Mary Joe, you may put some wood in the stove. I don't want to hurt your feelings, but it seems to me you might have thought of this before if you'd any imagination. Now, I'll undress Minnie May and put her to bed, and you try to find some soft flannel cloths, Diana; I'm going to give her a dose of ipecac first of all."

Minnie May did not take kindly to the ipecac, but Anne had not brought up three pairs of twins for nothing. Down that ipecac went, not only once, but many times during the long, anxious night when the two little girls worked patiently over the suffering Minnie May, and Young Mary Joe, honestly anxious to do all she could, kept on a roaring fire and heated more water than would have been needed for a hospital of croupy babies.

It was three o'clock when Matthew came with the doctor, for he had been obliged to go all the way to Spencervale for one. But the pressing need for assistance was past. Minnie May was much better and was sleeping soundly.

"I was awfully near giving up in despair," explained Anne. "She got worse and worse until she was sicker than ever the Hammond twins were, even the last pair. I actually thought she was going to choke to death. I gave her every drop of ipecac in that bottle, and when the last dose went down I said to myself—not to Diana or Young Mary Joe, because I didn't want to worry them any more than they were worried, but I had to say it to myself just to relieve my feelings—'this is the last lingering hope and I fear 'tis a vain one.' But in about three minutes she coughed up the phlegm and began to get better right away. You must just imagine my relief, doctor, because I can't express it in words. You know there are some things that cannot be expressed in words."

"Yes, I know," nodded the doctor. He looked at Anne as if he were thinking some things about her that couldn't be expressed in words. Later on, however, he expressed them to Mr. and Mrs. Barry.

"That little redheaded girl they have over at Cuthbert's is as smart as they make 'em. I tell you she saved that baby's life, for it would have been too late by the time I got here. She seems to have a skill and presence of mind perfectly wonderful in a child of her age. I never saw anything like the eyes of her when she was explaining the case out to me."

Anne had gone home in the wonderful, white-frosted winter morning, heavy-eyed from loss of sleep, but still talking unweariedly to Matthew as they crossed the long white field and walked under the glittering fairy arch of the Lovers' Lane maples.

"Oh, Matthew, isn't it a wonderful morning? The world looks like something God had just imagined for His own pleasure, doesn't it? Those trees look as if I could blow them away with a breath—pouf! I'm so glad I live in a world where there are white frosts, aren't you? And I'm so glad Mrs. Hammond had three pairs of twins after all. If she hadn't I mightn't have known what to do for Minnie May. I'm real sorry I was ever cross with Mrs. Hammond for having twins. But, oh, Matthew, I'm so sleepy. I can't go to school. I just know I couldn't keep my eyes open and I'd be so stupid. But I hate to stay home for Gil—some of the others will get head of the class, and it's so hard to get up again—although of course the harder it is the more satisfaction you have when you do get up, haven't you?"

"Well now, I guess you'll manage all right," said Matthew, looking at Anne's white little face and the dark shadows under her eyes. "You just go right to bed and have a good sleep. I'll do all the chores."

Anne accordingly went to bed and slept so long and soundly that it was well on in the white and rosy winter afternoon when she awoke and descended to the kitchen where Marilla who had arrived home in the meantime, was sitting knitting.

"Oh, did you see the Premier?" exclaimed Anne at once. "What did he look like, Marilla?"

"Well, he never got to be Premier on account of his looks," said Marilla. "Such a nose as that man had! But he can speak. I was proud of being a Conservative. Rachel Lynde, of course, being a Liberal, had no use for him. Your dinner is in the oven, Anne; and you can get yourself some blue plum preserve out of the pantry. I guess you're hungry. Matthew has been telling me about last night. I must say it was fortunate you knew what to do. I wouldn't have had any idea myself, for I never saw a case of croup. There now, never mind talking till you've had your dinner. I can tell by the look of you that you're just full up with speeches, but they'll keep."

Marilla had something to tell Anne, but she did not tell it just then, for she knew if she did Anne's consequent excitement would lift her clear out of the region of such material matters as appetite or dinner. Not until Anne had finished her saucer of blue plums did Marilla say:

"Mrs. Barry was here this afternoon, Anne. She wanted to see you, but I wouldn't wake you up. She says you saved Minnie May's life, and she is very sorry she acted as she did in that affair of the currant wine. She says she knows now you didn't mean to set Diana drunk, and she hopes you'll forgive her and be good friends with Diana again. You're to go over this evening if you like, for Diana can't stir outside the door on account of a bad cold she caught last night. Now, Anne Shirley, for pity's sake don't fly clean up into the air."

The warning seemed not unnecessary, so uplifted and aerial was Anne's expression and attitude as she sprang to her feet, her face irradiated with the flame of her spirit.

"Oh, Marilla, can I go right now—without washing my dishes? I'll wash them when I come back, but I cannot tie myself down to anything so unromantic as dishwashing at this thrilling moment."

"Yes, yes, run along," said Marilla indulgently. "Anne Shirley—are you crazy? Come back this instant and put something on you. I might as well call to the wind. She's gone without a cap or wrap. Look at her tearing through the orchard with her hair streaming. It'll be a mercy if she doesn't catch her death of cold."

Anne came dancing home in the purple winter twilight across the snowy places. Afar in the southwest was the great shimmering, pearl-like sparkle of an evening star in a sky that was pale golden and ethe-real rose over gleaming white spaces and dark glens of spruce. The tinkles of sleigh bells among the snowy hills came like elfin chimes through the frosty air, but their music was not sweeter than the song in Anne's heart and on her lips.

"You see before you a perfectly happy person, Marilla," she announced. "I'm perfectly happy—yes, in spite of my red hair. Just at present I have a soul above red hair. Mrs. Barry kissed me and cried and said she was so sorry and she could never repay me. I felt fearfully embarrassed, Marilla, but I just said as politely as I could, 'I have no hard feelings for you, Mrs. Barry. I assure you once for all that I did not mean to intoxicate Diana and henceforth I shall cover the past with the mantle of oblivion.' That was a pretty dignified way of speaking, wasn't it, Marilla? I felt that I was heaping coals of fire on Mrs. Barry's head. And Diana and I had a lovely afternoon. Diana showed me a new fancy crochet stitch her aunt over at Carmody taught her. Not a soul in Avonlea knows it but us, and we pledged a solemn vow never to reveal it to any one else. Diana gave me a beautiful card with a wreath of roses on it and a verse of poetry:

"'If you love me as I love you
Nothing but death can part us two.'

And that is true, Marilla. We're going to ask Mr. Phillips to let us sit together in school again, and Gertie Pye can go with Minnie

Andrews. We had an elegant tea. Mrs. Barry had the very best china set out, Marilla, just as if I was real company. I can't tell you what a thrill it gave me. Nobody ever used their very best china on my account before. And we had fruitcake and pound cake and doughnuts and two kinds of preserves, Marilla. And Mrs. Barry asked me if I took tea and said, 'Pa, why don't you pass the biscuits to Anne?' It must be lovely to be grown up, Marilla, when just being treated as if you were is so nice."

"I don't know about that," said Marilla with a brief sigh.

"Well, anyway, when I am grown up," said Anne decidedly, "I'm always going to talk to little girls as if they were, too, and I'll never laugh when they use big words. I know from sorrowful experience how that hurts one's feelings. After tea Diana and I made taffy. The taffy wasn't very good, I suppose because neither Diana nor I had ever made any before. Diana left me to stir it while she buttered the plates and I forgot and let it burn; and then when we set it out on the platform to cool the cat walked over one plate and that had to be thrown away. But the making of it was splendid fun. Then when I came home Mrs. Barry asked me to come over as often as I could and Diana stood at the window and threw kisses to me all the way down to Lovers' Lane. I assure you, Marilla, that I feel like praying tonight and I'm going to think out a special brand-new prayer in honor of the occasion."

19

A Concert, a Catastrophe,
and a Confession

"Marilla, can I go over to see Diana just for a minute?" asked Anne, running breathlessly down from the east gable one February evening.

"I don't see what you want to be traipsing about after dark for," said Marilla shortly. "You and Diana walked home from school together and then stood down there in the snow for half an hour more, your tongues going the whole blessed time, clickety-clack. So I don't think you're very badly off to see her again."

"But she wants to see me," pleaded Anne. "She has something very important to tell me."

"How do you know she has?"

"Because she just signalled to me from her window. We have arranged a way to signal with our candles and cardboard. We set the candle on the windowsill and make flashes by passing the cardboard back and forth. So many flashes mean a certain thing. It was my idea, Marilla."

"I'll warrant you it was," said Marilla emphatically. "And the next thing you'll be setting fire to the curtains with your signaling nonsense."

"Oh, we're very careful, Marilla. And it's so interesting. Two flashes mean, 'Are you there?' Three mean 'yes' and four 'no.' Five mean, 'Come over as soon as possible, because I have something important to reveal.' Diana has just signalled five flashes, and I'm really suffering to know what it is."

"Well, you needn't suffer any longer," said Marilla sarcastically. "You can go, but you're to be back here in just ten minutes, remember that."

Anne did remember it and was back in the stipulated time, although probably no mortal will ever know just what it cost her to confine the discussion of Diana's important communication within the limits of ten minutes. But at least she had made good use of them.

"Oh, Marilla, what do you think? You know tomorrow is Diana's birthday. Well, her mother told her she could ask me to go home with her from school and stay all night with her. And her cousins are coming over from Newbridge in a big pung sleigh to go to the Debating Club concert at the hall tomorrow night. And they are going to take Diana and me to the concert—if you'll let me go, that is. You will, won't you, Marilla? Oh, I feel so excited."

"You can calm down then, because you're not going. You're better at home in your own bed, and as for that Club concert, it's all nonsense, and little girls should not be allowed to go out to such places at all."

"I'm sure the Debating Club is a most respectable affair," pleaded Anne.

"I'm not saying it isn't. But you're not going to begin gadding about to concerts and staying out all hours of the night. Pretty doings for children. I'm surprised at Mrs. Barry's letting Diana go."

"But it's such a very special occasion," mourned Anne, on the verge of tears. "Diana has only one birthday in a year. It isn't as if birthdays were common things, Marilla. Prissy Andrews is going to recite 'Curfew Must Not Ring Tonight.' That is such a good moral piece, Marilla. I'm sure it would do me lots of good to hear it. And the choir are going to sing four lovely pathetic songs that are pretty near as good as hymns. And oh, Marilla, the minister is going to take part; yes, indeed, he is; he's going to give an address. That will be just about the same thing as a sermon. Please, mayn't I go, Marilla?"

"You heard what I said, Anne, didn't you? Take off your boots now and go to bed. It's past eight."

"There's just one more thing, Marilla," said Anne, with the air of producing the last shot in her locker. "Mrs. Barry told Diana that we might sleep in the spare room bed. Think of the honor of your little Anne being put in the spare room bed."

"It's an honor you'll have to get along without. Go to bed, Anne, and don't let me hear another word out of you."

When Anne, with tears rolling over her cheeks, had gone sorrow-fully upstairs, Matthew, who had been apparently sound asleep on the lounge during the whole dialogue, opened his eyes and said decidedly:

"Well now, Marilla, I think you ought to let Anne go."

"I don't then," retorted Marilla. "Who's bringing this child up, Matthew, you or me?"

"Well now, you," admitted Matthew.

"Don't interfere then."

"Well now, I ain't interfering. It ain't interfering to have your own opinion. And my opinion is that you ought to let Anne go."

"You'd think I ought to let Anne go to the moon if she took the notion, I've no doubt," was Marilla's amiable rejoinder. "I might have let her spend the night with Diana, if that was all. But I don't approve of this concert plan. She'd go there and catch cold like as not, and have her head filled up with nonsense and excitement. It would unsettle her for a week. I understand that child's disposition and what's good for it better than you, Matthew."

"I think you ought to let Anne go," repeated Matthew firmly. Argument was not his strong point, but holding fast to his opinion cer-tainly was. Marilla gave a gasp of helplessness and took refuge in silence. The next morning, when Anne was washing the breakfast dishes in the pantry, Matthew paused on his way out to the barn to say to Marilla again:

"I think you ought to let Anne go, Marilla."

For a moment Marilla looked things not lawful to be uttered. Then she yielded to the inevitable and said tartly:

"Very well, she can go, since nothing else'll please you."

Anne flew out of the pantry, dripping dish-cloth in hand.

"Oh, Marilla, Marilla, say those blessed words again."

"I guess once is enough to say them. This is Matthew's doings and I wash my hands of it. If you catch pneumonia sleeping in a strange bed or coming out of that hot hall in the middle of the night, don't blame me, blame Matthew. Anne Shirley, you're dripping greasy water all over the floor. I never saw such a careless child."

"Oh, I know I'm a great trial to you, Marilla," said Anne repen-tantly. "I make so many mistakes. But then just think of all the mistakes

I don't make, although I might. I'll get some sand and scrub up the spots before I go to school. Oh, Marilla, my heart was just set on going to that concert. I never was to a concert in my life, and when the other girls talk about them in school I feel so out of it. You didn't know just how I felt about it, but you see Matthew did. Matthew understands me, and it's so nice to be understood, Marilla."

Anne was too excited to do herself justice as to lessons that morning in school. Gilbert Blythe spelled her down in class and left her clear out of sight in mental arithmetic. Anne's consequent humiliation was less than it might have been, however, in view of the concert and the spare room bed. She and Diana talked so constantly about it all day that with a stricter teacher than Mr. Phillips dire disgrace must inevitably have been their portion.

Anne felt that she could not have borne it if she had not been going to the concert, for nothing else was discussed that day in school. The Avonlea Debating Club, which met fortnightly all winter, had had several smaller free entertainments; but this was to be a big affair, admission ten cents, in aid of the library. The Avonlea young people had been practicing for weeks, and all the scholars were especially interested in it by reason of older brothers and sisters who were going to take part. Everybody in school over nine years of age expected to go, except Carrie Sloane, whose father shared Marilla's opinions about small girls going out to night concerts. Carrie Sloane cried into her grammar all the afternoon and felt that life was not worth living.

For Anne the real excitement began with the dismissal of school and increased therefrom in crescendo until it reached to a crash of positive ecstasy in the concert itself. They had a "perfectly elegant tea;" and then came the delicious occupation of dressing in Diana's little room upstairs. Diana did Anne's front hair in the new pompadour style and Anne tied Diana's bows with the especial knack she possessed; and they experimented with at least half a dozen different ways of arranging their back hair. At last they were ready, cheeks scarlet and eyes glowing with excitement.

True, Anne could not help a little pang when she contrasted her plain black tam and shapeless, tight-sleeved, home-made gray cloth coat with Diana's jaunty fur cap and smart little jacket. But she remembered in time that she had an imagination and could use it.

Then Diana's cousins, the Murrays from Newbridge, came; they all crowded into the big pung sleigh, among straw and furry robes. Anne reveled in the drive to the hall, slipping along over the satin-smooth roads with the snow crisping under the runners. There was a magnificent sunset, and the snowy hills and deep blue water of the St. Lawrence Gulf seemed to rim in the splendor like a huge bowl of pearl and sapphire brimmed with wine and fire. Tinkles of sleigh bells and distant laughter, that seemed like the mirth of wood elves, came from every quarter.

"Oh, Diana," breathed Anne, squeezing Diana's mittened hand under the fur robe, "isn't it all like a beautiful dream? Do I really look the same as usual? I feel so different that it seems to me it must show in my looks."

"You look awfully nice," said Diana, who having just received a compliment from one of her cousins, felt that she ought to pass it on. "You've got the loveliest color."

The program that night was a series of "thrills" for at least one listener in the audience, and, as Anne assured Diana, every succeeding thrill was thrillier than the last. When Prissy Andrews, attired in a new pink silk waist with a string of pearls about her smooth white throat and real carnations in her hair—rumor whispered that the master had sent all the way to town for them for her—"climbed the slimy ladder, dark without one ray of light," Anne shivered in luxurious sympathy; when the choir sang "Far Above the Gentle Daisies" Anne gazed at the ceiling as if it were frescoed with angels; when Sam Sloane proceeded to explain and illustrate "How Sockery Set a Hen" Anne laughed until people sitting near her laughed too, more out of sympathy with her than with amusement at a selection that was rather threadbare even in Avonlea; and when Mr. Phillips gave Mark Antony's oration over the dead body of Caesar in the most heart-stirring tones—looking at Prissy Andrews at the end of every sentence—Anne felt that she could rise and mutiny on the spot if but one Roman citizen led the way.

Only one number on the program failed to interest her. When Gilbert Blythe recited "Bingen on the Rhine" Anne picked up Rhoda

Murray's library book and read it until he had finished, when she sat
rigidly stiff and motionless while Diana clapped her hands until they
tingled.

It was eleven when they got home, sated with dissipation, but with
the exceeding sweet pleasure of talking it all over still to come.
Everybody seemed asleep and the house was dark and silent. Anne
and Diana tiptoed into the parlor, a long narrow room out of which the
spare room opened. It was pleasantly warm and dimly lighted by the
embers of a fire in the grate.

"Let's undress here," said Diana. "It's so nice and warm."

"Hasn't it been a delightful time?" sighed Anne rapturously. "It
must be splendid to get up and recite there. Do you suppose we will
ever be asked to do it, Diana?"

"Yes, of course, some day. They're always wanting the big scholars to recite. Gilbert Blythe does often and he's only two years older
than us. Oh, Anne, how could you pretend not to listen to him? When
he came to the line,

"'There's another, not a sister,
he looked right down at you."

"Diana," said Anne with dignity, "you are my bosom friend, but I
cannot allow even you to speak to me of that person. Are you ready for
bed? Let's run a race and see who'll get to the bed first."

The suggestion appealed to Diana. The two little white-clad figures flew down the long room, through the spare room door, and
bounded on the bed at the same moment. And then—something—
moved beneath them, there was a gasp and a cry—and somebody said
in muffled accents:

"Merciful goodness!"

Anne and Diana were never able to tell just how they got off
that bed and out of the room. They only knew that after one frantic
rush they found themselves tiptoeing shiveringly upstairs.

"Oh, who was it—what was it?" whispered Anne, her teeth chattering with cold and fright.

"It was Aunt Josephine," said Diana, gasping with laughter. "Oh,
Anne, it was Aunt Josephine, however she came to be there. Oh, and

I know she will be furious. It's dreadful—it's really dreadful—but did you ever know anything so funny, Anne?"

"Who is your aunt Josephine?"

"She's father's aunt and she lives in Charlottetown. She's awfully old—seventy anyhow—and I don't believe she was *ever* a little girl. We were expecting her out for a visit, but not so soon. She's awfully prim and proper and she'll scold dreadfully about this, I know. Well, we'll have to sleep with Minnie May—and you can't think how she kicks."

Miss Josephine Barry did not appear at the early breakfast the next morning. Mrs. Barry smiled kindly at the two little girls.

"Did you have a good time last night? I tried to stay awake until you came home, for I wanted to tell you Aunt Josephine had come and that you would have to go upstairs after all, but I was so tired I fell asleep. I hope you didn't disturb your aunt, Diana."

Diana preserved a discreet silence, but she and Anne exchanged furtive smiles of guilty amusement across the table. Anne hurried home after breakfast and so remained in blissful ignorance of the disturbance which presently resulted in the Barry household until the late afternoon, when she went down to Mrs. Lynde's on an errand for Marilla.

"So you and Diana nearly frightened poor old Miss Barry to death last night?" said Mrs. Lynde severely, but with a twinkle in her eye. "Mrs. Barry was here a few minutes ago on her way to Carmody. She's feeling real worried over it. Old Miss Barry was in a terrible temper when she got up this morning—and Josephine Barry's temper is no joke, I can tell you that. She wouldn't speak to Diana at all."

"It wasn't Diana's fault," said Anne contritely. "It was mine. I suggested racing to see who would get into bed first."

"I knew it!" said Mrs. Lynde with the exultation of a correct guesser. "I knew that idea came out of your head. Well, it's made a nice lot of trouble, that's what. Old Miss Barry came out to stay for a month, but she declares she won't stay another day and is going right back to town tomorrow, Sunday and all as it is. She'd have gone today if they could have taken her. She had promised to pay for a quarter's music lessons for Diana, but now she is determined to do nothing at all for such a tomboy. Oh, I guess they had a lively time of it there this morning.

The Barrys must feel cut up. Old Miss Barry is rich and they'd like to keep on the good side of her. Of course, Mrs. Barry didn't say just that to me, but I'm a pretty good judge of human nature, that's what."

"I'm such an unlucky girl," mourned Anne. "I'm always getting into scrapes myself and getting my best friends—people I'd shed my heart's blood for—into them, too. Can you tell me why it is so, Mrs. Lynde?"

"It's because you're too heedless and impulsive, child, that's what. You never stop to think—whatever comes into your head to say or do you say or do it without a moment's reflection."

"Oh, but that's the best of it," protested Anne. "Something just flashes into your mind, so exciting, and you must out with it. If you stop to think it over you spoil it all. Haven't you never felt that yourself, Mrs. Lynde?"

No, Mrs. Lynde had not. She shook her head sagely.

"You must learn to think a little, Anne, that's what. The proverb you need to go by is 'Look before you leap'—especially into spare room beds."

Mrs. Lynde laughed comfortably over her mild joke, but Anne remained pensive. She saw nothing to laugh at in the situation, which to her eyes appeared very serious. When she left Mrs. Lynde's she took her way across the crusted fields to Orchard Slope. Diana met her at the kitchen door.

"Your Aunt Josephine was very cross about it, wasn't she?" whispered Anne.

"Yes," answered Diana, stifling a giggle with an apprehensive glance over her shoulder at the closed sitting room door. "She was fairly dancing with rage, Anne. Oh, how she scolded. She said I was the worst-behaved girl she ever saw and that my parents ought to be ashamed of the way they had brought me up. She says she won't stay and I'm sure I don't care. But father and mother do."

"Why didn't you tell them it was my fault?" demanded Anne.

"It's likely I'd do such a thing, isn't it?" said Diana with just scorn. "I'm no telltale, Anne Shirley, and anyhow I was just as much to blame as you."

"Well, I'm going in to tell her myself," said Anne resolutely. Diana stared.

"Anne Shirley, you'd never! why—she'll eat you alive!"

"Don't frighten me any more than I am frightened," implored Anne. "I'd rather walk up to a cannon's mouth. But I've got to do it, Diana. It was my fault and I've got to confess. I've had practice in confessing fortunately."

"Well, she's in the room," said Diana. "You can go in if you want to. I wouldn't dare. And I don't believe you'll do a bit of good."

With this encouragement Anne bearded the lion in its den— that is to say, walked resolutely up to the sitting-room door and knocked faintly. A sharp "Come in" followed.

Miss Josephine Barry, thin, prim and rigid, was knitting fiercely by the fire, her wrath quite unappeased and her eyes snapping through her gold-rimmed glasses. She wheeled around in her chair, expecting to see Diana, and beheld a white-faced girl whose great eyes were brimmed up with a mixture of desperate courage and shrinking terror.

"Who are you?" demanded Miss Josephine Barry without ceremony.

"I'm Anne of Green Gables," said the small visitor tremulously, clasping her hands with her characteristic gesture, "and I've come to confess, if you please."

"Confess what?"

"That it was all my fault about jumping into bed on you last night. I suggested it. Diana would never have thought of such a thing, I am sure. Diana is a very ladylike girl, Miss Barry. So you must see how unjust it is to blame her."

"Oh, I must, hey? I rather think Diana did her share of the jumping at least. Such carryings-on in a respectable house!"

"But we were only in fun," persisted Anne. "I think you ought to forgive us, Miss Barry, now that we've apologized. And anyhow, please forgive Diana and let her have her music lessons. Diana's heart is set on her music lessons, Miss Barry, and I know too well what it is to set your heart on a thing and not get it. If you must be cross with any one, be cross with me. I've been so used in my early days to having people cross at me that I can endure it much better than Diana can."

Much of the snap had gone out of the old lady's eyes by this time and was replaced by a twinkle of amused interest. But she still said severely:

"I don't think it is any excuse for you that you were only in fun. Little girls never indulged in that kind of fun when I was young. You don't know what it is to be awakened out of a sound sleep, after a long and arduous journey, by two great girls coming bounce down on you."

"I don't *know,* but I can *imagine,*" said Anne eagerly. "I'm sure it must have been very disturbing. But then, there is our side of it too. Have you any imagination, Miss Barry? If you have, just put yourself in our place. We didn't know there was anybody in that bed and you nearly scared us to death. It was simply awful the way we felt. And then we couldn't sleep in the spare room after being promised. I suppose you are used to sleeping in spare rooms. But just imagine what you would feel like if you were a little orphan girl who had never had such an honor."

All the snap had gone by this time. Miss Barry actually laughed— a sound which caused Diana, waiting in speechless anxiety in the kitchen outside, to give a great gasp of relief.

"I'm afraid my imagination is a little rusty—it's so long since I used it," she said. "I dare say your claim to sympathy is just as strong as mine. It all depends on the way we look at it. Sit down here and tell me about yourself."

"I am very sorry I can't," said Anne firmly. "I would like to, because you seem like an interesting lady, and you might even be a kindred spirit although you don't look very much like it. But it is my duty to go home to Miss Marilla Cuthbert. Miss Marilla Cuthbert is a very kind lady who has taken me to bring up properly. She is doing her best, but it is very discouraging work. You must not blame her because I jumped on the bed. But before I go I do wish you would tell me if you will forgive Diana and stay just as long as you meant to in Avonlea."

"I think perhaps I will if you will come over and talk to me occasionally," said Miss Barry.

That evening Miss Barry gave Diana a silver bangle bracelet and told the senior members of the household that she had unpacked her valise.

"I've made up my mind to stay simply for the sake of getting better acquainted with that Anne-girl," she said frankly. "She amuses me, and at my time of life an amusing person is a rarity."

Marilla's only comment when she heard the story was, "I told you so." This was for Matthew's benefit.

Miss Barry stayed her month out and over. She was a more agreeable guest than usual, for Anne kept her in good humor. They became firm friends.

When Miss Barry went away she said:

"Remember, you Anne-girl, when you come to town you're to visit me and I'll put you in my very sparest spare-room bed to sleep."

"Miss Barry was a kindred spirit, after all," Anne confided to Marilla. "You wouldn't think so to look at her, but she is. You don't find it right out at first, as in Matthew's case, but after awhile you come to see it. Kindred spirits are not so scarce as I used to think. It's splendid to find out there are so many of them in the world."

20

A Good Imagination Gone Wrong

pring had come once more to Green Gables—the beautiful, capricious, reluctant Canadian spring, lingering along through April and May in a succession of sweet, fresh, chilly days, with pink sunsets and miracles of resurrection and growth. The maples in Lovers' Lane were red-budded and little curly ferns pushed up around the Dryad's Bubble. Away up in the barrens, behind Mr. Silas Sloane's place, the Mayflowers blossomed out, pink and white stars of sweetness under their brown leaves. All the school girls and boys had one golden afternoon gathering them, coming home in the clear, echoing twilight with arms and baskets full of flowery spoil.

"I'm so sorry for people who live in lands where there are no Mayflowers," said Anne. "Diana says perhaps they have something better, but there couldn't be anything better than Mayflowers, could there, Marilla? And Diana says if they don't know what they are like they don't miss them. But I think that is the saddest thing of all. I think it would be *tragic*, Marilla, not to know what Mayflowers are like and *not* to miss them. Do you know what I think Mayflowers are, Marilla? I think they must be the souls of the flowers that died last summer and this is their heaven. But we had a splendid time today, Marilla. We had our lunch down in a big mossy hollow by an old well—such a *romantic* spot. Charlie Sloane dared Arty Gillis to jump over it, and Arty did because he wouldn't take a dare. Nobody would in school. It is very *fashionable* to dare. Mr. Phillips gave all the Mayflowers he found to Prissy Andrews and I heard him say 'sweets to the sweet.' He got that out of a book, I know; but it shows he has some imagination. I was offered some Mayflowers too, but I rejected them with scorn. I can't tell you the person's name because I have vowed never to let it cross my lips. We made wreaths of the Mayflowers and put them on our hats; and when the time came to go home we marched in procession down the road, two by two, with our bouquets and wreaths, singing 'My Home on the Hill.' Oh, it was so thrilling, Marilla. All Mr. Silas Sloane's folks rushed out to see us and everybody we met on the road stopped and stared after us. We made a real sensation."

"Not much wonder! Such silly doings!" was Marilla's response.

After the Mayflowers came the violets, and Violet Vale was empurpled with them. Anne walked through it on her way to school with reverent steps and worshipping eyes, as if she trod on holy ground.

"Somehow," she told Diana, "when I'm going through here I don't really care whether Gil—whether anybody gets ahead of me in class or not. But when I'm up in school it's all different and I care as much as ever. There's such a lot of different Annes in me. I sometimes think that is why I'm such a troublesome person. If I was just the one Anne it would be ever so much more comfortable, but then it wouldn't be half so interesting."

One June evening, when the orchards were pink-blossomed again, when the frogs were singing silvery sweet in the marshes about the head of the Lake of Shining Waters, and the air was full of the savor of clover fields and balsamic fir woods, Anne was sitting by her gable window. She had been studying her lessons, but it had grown too dark to see the book, so she had fallen into wide-eyed reverie, looking out past the boughs of the Snow Queen, once more bestarred with its tufts of blossom.

In all essential respects the little gable chamber was unchanged. The walls were as white, the pincushion as hard, the chairs as stiffly and yellowly upright as ever. Yet the whole character of the room was altered. It was full of a new vital, pulsing personality that seemed to pervade it and to be quite independent of schoolgirl books and dresses and ribbons, and even of the cracked blue jug full of apple blossoms on the table. It was as if all the dreams, sleeping and waking, of its vivid occupant had taken a visible although immaterial form and had tapestried the bare room with splendid filmy tissues of rainbow and moonshine. Presently Marilla came briskly in with some of Anne's freshly ironed school aprons. She hung them over a chair and sat down with a short sigh. She had had one of her headaches that afternoon, and although the pain had gone she felt weak and "tuckered out," as she expressed it. Anne looked at her with eyes limpid with sympathy.

"I do truly wish I could have had the headache in your place, Marilla. I would have endured it joyfully for your sake."

"I guess you did your part in attending to the work and letting me rest," said Marilla. "You seem to have got on fairly well and made fewer mistakes than usual. Of course it wasn't exactly necessary to starch Matthew's handkerchiefs! And most people when they put a pie in the oven to warm up for dinner take it out and eat it when it gets hot instead of leaving it to be burned to a crisp. But that doesn't seem to be your way evidently."

Headaches always left Marilla somewhat sarcastic.

"Oh, I'm so sorry," said Anne penitently. "I never thought about that pie from the moment I put it in the oven till now, although I felt *instinctively* that there was something missing on the dinner table. I was firmly resolved, when you left me in charge this morning, not to imagine anything, but keep my thoughts on facts. I did pretty well until I put the pie in, and then an irresistible temptation came to me to imagine I was an enchanted princess shut up in a lonely tower with a handsome knight riding to my rescue on a coal-black steed. So that is how I came to forget the pie. I didn't know I starched the handkerchiefs. All the time I was ironing I was trying to think of a name for a new island Diana and I have discovered up the brook. It's the most ravishing spot, Marilla. There are two maple-trees on it and the brook flows right around it. At last it struck me that it would be splendid to call it Victoria Island because we found it on the Queen's birthday. Both Diana and I are very loyal. But I'm very sorry about the pie and the handkerchiefs. I wanted to be extra good today because it's an anniversary. Do you remember what happened this day last year, Marilla?"

"No, I can't think of anything special."

"Oh, Marilla, it was the day I came to Green Gables. I shall never forget it. It was the turning point in my life. Of course it wouldn't seem so important to you. I've been here for a year and I've been so happy. Of course, I've had my troubles, but one can live down troubles. Are you sorry you kept me, Marilla?"

"No, I can't say I'm sorry," said Marilla, who sometimes wondered how she could have lived before Anne came to Green Gables, "no, not exactly sorry. If you've finished your lessons, Anne, I want you to run over and ask Mrs. Barry if she'll lend me Diana's apron pattern."

"Oh—it's—it's too dark," cried Anne.

"Too dark? Why, it's only twilight. And goodness knows you've gone over often enough after dark."

"I'll go over early in the morning," said Anne eagerly. "I'll get up at sunrise and go over, Marilla."

"What has got into your head now, Anne Shirley? I want that pattern to cut out your new apron this evening. Go at once and be smart, too."

"I'll have to go around by the road, then," said Anne, taking up her hat reluctantly.

"Go by the road and waste half an hour! I'd like to catch you!"

"I can't go through the Haunted Wood, Marilla," cried Anne desperately.

Marilla stared.

"The Haunted Wood! Are you crazy? What under the canopy is the Haunted Wood?"

"The spruce wood over the brook," said Anne in a whisper.

"Fiddlesticks! There is no such thing as a haunted wood anywhere. Who has been telling you such stuff?"

"Nobody," confessed Anne. "Diana and I just imagined the wood was haunted. All the places around here are so—so—*commonplace*. We just got this up for our own amusement. We began it in April. A haunted wood is so very romantic, Marilla. We chose the spruce grove because it's so gloomy. Oh, we have imagined the most harrowing things. There's a white lady walks along the brook just about this time of the night and wrings her hands and utters wailing cries. She appears when there is to be a death in the family. And the ghost of a little murdered child haunts the corner up by Idlewild; it creeps up behind you and lays its cold fingers on your hand—so. Oh, Marilla, it gives me a shudder to think of it. And there's a headless man stalks up and down the path and skeletons glower at you between the boughs. Oh, Marilla, I wouldn't go through the Haunted Wood after dark now for anything. I'd be sure that white things would reach out from behind the trees and grab me."

"Did ever any one hear the like!" ejaculated Marilla, who had listened in dumb amazement. "Anne Shirley, do you mean to tell me you believe all that wicked nonsense of your own imagination?"

"Not believe *exactly*," faltered Anne. "At least, I don't believe it in the daylight. But after dark, Marilla, it's different. That is when ghosts walk."

"There are no such things as ghosts, Anne."

"Oh, but there are, Marilla," cried Anne eagerly. "I know people who have seen them. And they are respectable people. Charlie Sloane says that his grandmother saw his grandfather driving home the cows one night after he'd been buried for a year. You know Charlie Sloane's grandmother wouldn't tell a story for anything. She's a very religious woman. And Mrs. Thomas' father was pursued home one night by a lamb of fire with its head cut off hanging by a strip of skin. He said he knew it was the spirit of his brother and that it was a warning he would die within nine days. He didn't, but he died two years after, so you see it was really true. And Ruby Gillis says—"

"Anne Shirley," interrupted Marilla firmly, "I never want to hear you talking in this fashion again. I've had my doubts about that imagination of yours right along, and if this is going to be the outcome of it, I won't countenance any such doings. You'll go right over to Barry's, and you'll go through that spruce grove, just for a lesson and a warning to you. And never let me hear a word out of your head about haunted woods again."

Anne might plead and cry as she liked—and did, for her terror was very real. Her imagination had run away with her and she held the spruce grove in mortal dread after nightfall. But Marilla was inexorable. She marched the shrinking ghostseer down to the spring and ordered her to proceed straightway over the bridge and into the dusky retreats of wailing ladies and headless specters beyond.

"Oh, Marilla, how can you be so cruel?" sobbed Anne. "What would you feel like if a white thing did snatch me up and carry me off?"

"I'll risk it," said Marilla unfeelingly. "You know I always mean what I say. I'll cure you of imagining ghosts into places. March, now."

Anne marched. That is, she stumbled over the bridge and went shuddering up the horrible dim path beyond. Anne never forgot that walk. Bitterly did she repent the license she had given to her imagination. The goblins of her fancy lurked in every shadow about her, reaching out their cold, fleshless hands to grasp the terrified small girl who had called them into being. A white strip of birch bark blowing up from the hollow over the brown floor of the grove made her heart stand still. The long-drawn wail of two old boughs rubbing against each other brought out the perspiration in beads on her forehead. The swoop of bats in the darkness over her was as the wings of unearthly creatures. When she reached Mr. William Bell's field she fled across it as if pursued by an army of white things, and arrived at the Barry kitchen door so out of breath that she could hardly gasp out her request for the apron pattern. Diana was away so that she had no excuse to linger. The dreadful return journey had to be faced. Anne went back over it with shut eyes, preferring to take the risk of dashing her brains out among the boughs to that of seeing a white thing. When she finally stumbled over the log bridge she drew one long shivering breath of relief.

"Well, so nothing caught you?" said Marilla unsympathetically.

"Oh, Mar—Marilla," chattered Anne, "I'll b-b-be cont-t-tented with c-c-commonplace places after this."

21

A New Departure in Flavorings

"Dear me, there is nothing but meetings and partings in this world, as Mrs. Lynde says," remarked Anne plaintively, putting her slate and books down on the kitchen table on the last day of June and wiping her red eyes with a very damp handkerchief. "Wasn't it fortunate, Marilla, that I took an extra handkerchief to school today? I had a presentiment that it would be needed."

"I never thought you were so fond of Mr. Phillips that you'd require two handkerchiefs to dry your tears just because he was going away," said Marilla.

"I don't think I was crying because I was really so very fond of him," reflected Anne. "I just cried because all the others did. It was Ruby Gillis started it. Ruby Gillis has always declared she hated Mr. Phillips, but just as soon as he got up to make his farewell speech she burst into tears. Then all the girls began to cry, one after the other. I tried to hold out, Marilla. I tried to remember the time Mr. Phillips made me sit with Gil—with a boy; and the time he spelled my name without an *e* on the blackboard; and how he said I was the worst dunce he ever saw at geometry and laughed at my spelling; and all the times he had been so horrid and sarcastic; but somehow I couldn't, Marilla, and I just had to cry too. Jane Andrews has been talking for a month about how glad she'd be when Mr. Phillips went away and she declared she'd never shed a tear. Well, she was worse than any of us and had to borrow a handkerchief from her brother—of course the boys didn't cry—because she hadn't brought one of her own, not expecting to need it. Oh, Marilla, it was heartrending. Mr. Phillips made such a beautiful farewell speech beginning, 'The time has come for us to part.' It was very affecting. And he had tears in his eyes too, Marilla. Oh, I felt dreadfully sorry and remorseful for all the times I'd talked in school and drawn pictures of him on my slate and made fun of him and Prissy. I can tell you I wished I'd been a model pupil like Minnie Andrews. She hadn't anything on her conscience. The girls cried all the way home from school. Carrie Sloane kept saying every few minutes, 'The time has come for us to part,' and that would start us off again whenever we were in any danger of cheering up. I do feel dreadfully sad, Marilla. But one can't feel quite in the depths of despair with two months vacation before them, can they, Marilla? And besides, we met the new minister and his wife coming from the station. For all I was feeling so bad about Mr. Phillips going away I couldn't help taking a little interest in a new minister, could I? His wife is very pretty. Not exactly regally lovely, of course—it wouldn't do, I suppose, for a minister to have a regally lovely wife, because it might set a bad example. Mrs. Lynde says the minister's wife over at Newbridge sets a very bad example because she dresses so fashionably. Our new minister's wife was dressed in blue muslin with lovely puffed sleeves and a hat trimmed with roses. Jane Andrews said she thought puffed sleeves were too worldly for a minister's wife, but I didn't make any such uncharitable remark, Marilla, because I know what it is to long for puffed sleeves. Besides, she's only been a minister's wife for a little while, so one should make allowances, shouldn't they? They are going to board with Mrs. Lynde until the manse is ready."

If Marilla, in going down to Mrs. Lynde's that evening, was actuated by any motive save her avowed one of returning the quilting-frames she had borrowed the preceding winter, it was an amiable weakness shared by most of the Avonlea people. Many a thing Mrs. Lynde had lent, sometimes never expecting to see it again, came home that night in charge of the borrowers thereof. A new minister, and moreover a minister with a wife, was a lawful object of curiosity in a quiet little country settlement where sensations were few and far between.

Old Mr. Bentley, the minister whom Anne had found lacking in imagination, had been pastor of Avonlea for eighteen years. He was a widower when he came, and a widower he remained, despite the fact that gossip regularly married him to this, that or the other one, every year of his sojourn. In the preceding February he had resigned his charge and departed amid the regrets of his people, most of whom had the affection born of long intercourse for their good old minister in spite of his shortcomings as an orator. Since then the Avonlea church had enjoyed a variety of religious dissipation in listening to the many and various candidates and "supplies" who came Sunday after Sunday to preach on trial. These stood or fell by the judgment of the fathers and mothers in Israel; but a certain small, red-haired girl who sat meekly in the corner of the old Cuthbert pew also had her opinions about them and discussed the same in full with Matthew, Marilla always declining from principle to criticize ministers in any shape or form.

"I don't think Mr. Smith would have done, Matthew," was Anne's final summing up. "Mrs. Lynde says his delivery was so poor, but I think his worst fault was just like Mr. Bentley's—he had no imagination. And Mr. Terry had too much; he let it run away with him just as I did mine in the matter of the Haunted Wood. Besides, Mrs. Lynde says his theology wasn't sound. Mr. Gresham was a very good man and a very religious man, but he told too many funny stories and made the people laugh in church; he was undignified, and you must have some dignity about a minister, mustn't you, Matthew? I thought Mr. Marshall was decidedly attractive; but Mrs. Lynde says he isn't married, or even engaged, because she made special inquiries about him, and she says it would never do to have a young unmarried minister in Avonlea, because he might marry in the congregation and that would make trouble. Mrs. Lynde is a very farseeing woman, isn't she, Matthew? I'm very glad they've called Mr. Allan. I liked him because his sermon was interesting and he prayed as if he meant it and not just as if he did it because he was in the habit of it. Mrs. Lynde says he isn't perfect, but she says she supposes we couldn't expect a perfect minister for seven hundred and fifty dollars a year, and anyhow his theology is sound because she questioned him thoroughly on all the points of doctrine. And she knows his wife's people and they are most respectable and the women are all good housekeepers. Mrs. Lynde says that sound doctrine in the man and good housekeeping in the woman make an ideal combination for a minister's family."

The new minister and his wife were a young, pleasant-faced couple, still in their honeymoon, and full of all good and beautiful enthusiasms for their chosen lifework. Avonlea opened its heart to them from the start. Old and young liked the frank, cheerful young man with his high ideals, and the bright, gentle little lady who assumed the mistress-ship of the manse. With Mrs. Allan Anne fell promptly and wholeheartedly in love. She had discovered another kindred spirit.

"Mrs. Allan is perfectly lovely," she announced one Sunday afternoon. "She's taken our class and she's a splendid teacher. She said right away she didn't think it was fair for the teacher to ask all the questions, and you know, Marilla, that is exactly what I've always thought. She said we could ask her any question we liked, and I asked ever so many. I'm good at asking questions, Marilla."

"I believe you," was Marilla's emphatic comment.

"Nobody else asked any except Ruby Gillis, and she asked if there was to be a Sunday school picnic this summer. I didn't think that was a very proper question to ask because it hadn't any connection with the lesson—the lesson was about Daniel in the lions' den—but Mrs. Allan just smiled and said she thought there would be. Mrs. Allan has a lovely smile; she has such *exquisite* dimples in her cheeks. I wish I had dimples in my cheeks, Marilla. I'm not half so skinny as I was when I came here, but I have no dimples yet. If I had perhaps I could influence people for good. Mrs. Allan said we ought always to try to influence other people for good. She talked so nice about everything. I never knew before that religion was such a cheerful thing. I always thought it was kind of melancholy, but Mrs. Allan's isn't, and I'd like to be a Christian if I could be one like her. I wouldn't want to be one like Mr. Superintendent Bell."

"It's very naughty of you to speak so about Mr. Bell," said Marilla severely. "Mr. Bell is a real good man."

"Oh, of course he's good," agreed Anne. "But he doesn't seem to get any comfort out of it. If I could be good I'd dance and sing all day because I was glad of it. I suppose Mrs. Allan is too old to dance and sing and of course it wouldn't be dignified in a minister's wife. But I can just feel she's glad she's a Christian and that she'd be one even if she could get to heaven without it."

"I suppose we must have Mr. and Mrs. Allan up to tea some day soon," said Marilla reflectively. "They've been most everywhere but here. Let me see. Next Wednesday would be a good time to have them. But don't say a word to Matthew about it, for if he knew they were coming he'd find some excuse to be away that day. He'd got so used to Mr. Bentley he didn't mind him, but he's going to find it hard to get acquainted with a new minister, and a new minister's wife will frighten him to death."

"I'll be as secret as the dead," assured Anne. "But oh, Marilla, will you let me make a cake for the occasion? I'd love to do something for Mrs. Allan, and you know I can make a pretty good cake by this time."

"You can make a layer cake," promised Marilla.

Monday and Tuesday great preparations went on at Green Gables. Having the minister and his wife to tea was a serious and important undertaking, and Marilla was determined not to be eclipsed by any of the Avonlea housekeepers. Anne was wild with excitement and delight. She talked it all over with Diana Tuesday night in the twilight, as they sat on the big red stones by the Dryad's Bubble and made rainbows in the water with little twigs dipped in fir balsam.

"Everything is ready, Diana, except my cake which I'm to make in the morning, and the baking-powder biscuits which Marilla will make just before teatime. I assure you, Diana, that Marilla and I have had a busy two days of it. It's such a responsibility having a minister's family to tea. I never went through such an experience before. You should just see our pantry. It's a sight to behold. We're going to have jellied chicken and cold tongue. We're to have two kinds of jelly, red and yellow, and whipped cream and lemon pie, and cherry pie, and three kinds of cookies, and fruitcake, and Marilla's famous yellow plum preserves that she keeps especially for ministers, and pound cake and layer cake, and biscuits as aforesaid; and new bread and old both, in case the minister is dyspeptic and can't eat new. Mrs. Lynde says ministers mostly are dyspeptic, but I don't think Mr. Allan has been a minister long enough for it to have had a bad effect on him. I just grow cold when I think of my layer cake. Oh, Diana, what if it shouldn't be good! I dreamed last night that I was chased all around by a fearful goblin with a big layer cake for a head."

"It'll be good, all right," assured Diana, who was a very comfortable sort of friend. "I'm sure that piece of the one you made that we had for lunch in Idlewild two weeks ago was perfectly elegant."

"Yes; but cakes have such a terrible habit of turning out bad just when you especially want them to be good," sighed Anne, setting a particularly well-balsamed twig afloat. "However, I suppose I shall just have to trust to Providence and be careful to put in the flour. Oh, look, Diana, what a lovely rainbow! Do you suppose the dryad will come out after we go away and take it for a scarf?"

"You know there is no such thing as a dryad," said Diana. Diana's mother had found out about the Haunted Wood and had been decidedly angry over it. As a result Diana had abstained from any further imitative flights of imagination and did not think it prudent to cultivate a spirit of belief even in harmless dryads.

"But it's so easy to imagine there is," said Anne. "Every night, before I go to bed, I look out of my window and wonder if the dryad is really sitting here, combing her locks with the spring for a mirror. Sometimes I look for her footprints in the dew in the morning. Oh, Diana, don't give up your faith in the dryad!"

Wednesday morning came. Anne got up at sunrise because she was too excited to sleep. She had caught a severe cold in the head by reason of her dabbling in the spring on the preceding evening; but nothing short of absolute pneumonia could have quenched her interest in culinary matters that morning. After breakfast she proceeded to make her cake. When she finally shut the oven door upon it she drew a long breath.

"I'm sure I haven't forgotten anything this time, Marilla. But do you think it will rise? Just suppose perhaps the baking powder isn't good? I used it out of the new can. And Mrs. Lynde says you can never be sure of getting good baking powder nowadays when everything is so adulterated. Mrs. Lynde says the Government ought to take the matter up, but she says we'll never see the day when a Tory Government will do it. Marilla, what if that cake doesn't rise?"

"We'll have plenty without it," was Marilla's unimpassioned way of looking at the subject.

The cake did rise, however, and came out of the oven as light and feathery as golden foam. Anne, flushed with delight, clapped it together with layers of ruby jelly and, in imagination, saw Mrs. Allan eating it and possibly asking for another piece!

"You'll be using the best tea set, of course, Marilla," she said. "Can I fix up the table with ferns and wild roses?"

"I think that's all nonsense," sniffed Marilla. "In my opinion it's the eatables that matter and not flummery decorations."

"Mrs. Barry had *her* table decorated," said Anne, who was not entirely guiltless of the wisdom of the serpent, "and the minister paid her an elegant compliment. He said it was a feast for the eye as well as the palate."

"Well, do as you like," said Marilla, who was quite determined not to be surpassed by Mrs. Barry or anybody else. "Only mind you leave enough room for the dishes and the food."

Anne laid herself out to decorate in a manner and after a fashion that should leave Mrs. Barry's nowhere. Having abundance of roses and ferns and a very artistic taste of her own, she made that tea table such a thing of beauty that when the minister and his wife sat down to it they exclaimed in chorus over its loveliness.

"It's Anne's doings," said Marilla, grimly just; and Anne felt that Mrs. Allan's approving smile was almost too much happiness for this world.

Matthew was there, having been inveigled into the party only goodness and Anne knew how. He had been in such a state of shyness and nervousness that Marilla had given him up in despair, but Anne took him in hand so successfully that he now sat at the table in his best clothes and white collar and talked to the minister not uninterestingly. He never said a word to Mrs. Allan, but that perhaps was not to be expected.

All went merry as a marriage bell until Anne's layer cake was passed. Mrs. Allan, having already been helped to a bewildering variety, declined it. But Marilla, seeing the disappointment on Anne's face, said smilingly:

"Oh, you must take a piece of this, Mrs. Allan. Anne made it on purpose for you."

"In that case I must sample it," laughed Mrs. Allan, helping herself to a plump triangle, as did also the minister and Marilla.

Mrs. Allan took a mouthful of hers and a most peculiar expression crossed her face; not a word did she say, however, but steadily ate away at it. Marilla saw the expression and hastened to taste the cake.

"Anne Shirley!" she exclaimed, "what on earth did you put into that cake?"

"Nothing but what the recipe said, Marilla," cried Anne with a look of anguish. "Oh, isn't it all right?"

"All right! It's simply horrible. Mrs. Allan, don't try to eat it. Anne, taste it yourself. What flavoring did you use?"

"Vanilla," said Anne, her face scarlet with mortification after tasting the cake. "Only vanilla. Oh, Marilla, it must have been the baking powder. I had my suspicions of that bak—"

"Baking powder fiddlesticks! Go and bring me the bottle of vanilla you used."

Anne fled to the pantry and returned with a small bottle partially filled with a brown liquid and labelled yellowly, "Best Vanilla."

Marilla took it, uncorked it, smelled it.

"Mercy on us, Anne, you've flavored that cake with *anodyne liniment*. I broke the liniment bottle last week and poured what was left into an old empty vanilla bottle. I suppose it's partly my fault—I should have warned you—but for pity's sake why couldn't you have smelled it?"

Anne dissolved into tears under this double disgrace.

"I couldn't—I had such a cold" and with this she fairly fled to the gable chamber, where she cast herself on the bed and wept as one who refuses to be comforted.

Presently a light step sounded on the stairs and somebody entered the room.

"Oh, Marilla," sobbed Anne without looking up, "I'm disgraced for ever. I shall never be able to live this down. It will get out—things always do get out in Avonlea. Diana will ask me how my cake turned out and I shall have to tell her the truth. I shall always be pointed at as the girl who flavored a cake with anodyne liniment. Gil—the boys in school will never get over laughing at it. Oh, Marilla, if you have a spark of Christian pity don't tell me that I must go down and wash the dishes after this. I'll wash them when the minister and his wife are gone, but I cannot ever look Mrs. Allan in the face again. Perhaps she'll think I tried to poison her. Mrs. Lynde says she knows an orphan girl who tried to poison her benefactor. But the liniment isn't poisonous. It's meant to be taken internally—although not in cakes. Won't you tell Mrs. Allan so, Marilla?"

"Suppose you jump up and tell her so yourself," said a merry voice.

Anne flew up, to find Mrs. Allan standing by her bed, surveying her with laughing eyes.

"My dear little girl, you mustn't cry like this," she said, genuinely disturbed by Anne's tragic face. "Why, it's all just a funny mistake that anybody might make."

"Oh, no, it takes me to make such a mistake," said Anne forlornly. "And I wanted to have that cake so nice for you, Mrs. Allan."

"Yes, I know, dear. And I assure you I appreciate your kindness and thoughtfulness just as much as if it had turned out all right. Now, you mustn't cry any more, but come down with me and show me your flower garden. Miss Cuthbert tells me you have a little plot all your own. I want to see it, for I'm very much interested in flowers."

Anne permitted herself to be led down and comforted, reflecting that it was really providential that Mrs. Allan was a kindred spirit. Nothing more was said about the liniment cake, and when the guests went away Anne found that she had enjoyed the evening more than could have been expected, considering that terrible incident. Nevertheless she sighed deeply.

"Marilla, isn't it nice to think that tomorrow is a new day with no mistakes in it yet?"

"I'll warrant you'll make plenty in it," said Marilla. "I never saw your beat for making mistakes, Anne."

"Yes, and well I know it," admitted Anne mournfully. "But have you ever noticed one encouraging thing about me, Marilla? I never make the same mistake twice."

"I don't know as that's much benefit when you're always making new ones."

"Oh, don't you see, Marilla? There *must* be a limit to the mistakes one person can make, and when I get to the end of them, then I'll be through with them. That's a very comforting thought."

"Well, you'd better go and give that cake to the pigs," said Marilla. "It isn't fit for any human to eat, not even Jerry Buote."

22

Anne is Invited out to Tea

"nd what are your eyes popping out of your head about now?" asked Marilla, when Anne had just come in from a run to the post office. "Have you discovered another kindred spirit?"

Excitement hung around Anne like a garment, shone in her eyes, kindled in every feature. She had come dancing up the lane, like a wind-blown sprite, through the mellow sunshine and lazy shadows of the August evening.

"No, Marilla, but oh, what do you think? I am invited to tea at the manse tomorrow afternoon! Mrs. Allan left the letter for me at the post office. Just look at it, Marilla. 'Miss Anne Shirley, Green Gables.' That is the first time I was ever called 'Miss.' Such a thrill as it gave me! I shall cherish it for ever among my choicest treasures."

"Mrs. Allan told me she meant to have all the members of her Sunday school class to tea in turn," said Marilla, regarding the wonderful event very coolly. "You needn't get in such a fever over it. Do learn to take things calmly, child."

For Anne to take things calmly would have been to change her nature. All "spirit and fire and dew," as she was, the pleasures and pains of life came to her with trebled intensity. Marilla felt this and was vaguely troubled over it, realizing that the ups and downs of existence would probably bear hardly on this impulsive soul and not sufficiently understanding that the equally great capacity for delight might more than compensate. Therefore Marilla conceived it to be her duty to drill Anne into a tranquil uniformity of disposition as impossible and alien to her as to a dancing sunbeam in one of the brook shallows. She did not make much headway, as she sorrowfully admitted to herself.

The downfall of some dear hope or plan plunged Anne into "deeps of affliction." The fulfilment thereof exalted her to dizzy realms of delight. Marilla had almost begun to despair of ever fashioning this waif of the world into her model little girl of demure manners and prim deportment. Neither would she have believed that she really liked Anne much better as she was.

Anne went to bed that night speechless with misery because Matthew had said the wind was round northeast and he feared it would be a rainy day tomorrow. The rustle of the poplar leaves about the house worried her, it sounded so like pattering rain drops, and the dull, far-away roar of the gulf, to which she listened delightedly at other times, loving its strange, sonorous, haunting rhythm, now seemed like a prophecy of storm and disaster to a small maiden who particularly wanted a fine day. Anne thought that the morning would never come.

But all things have an end, even nights before the day on which you are invited to take tea at the manse. The morning, in spite of Matthew's predictions, was fine and Anne's spirits soared to their highest.

"Oh, Marilla, there is something in me today that makes me just love everybody I see," she exclaimed as she washed the breakfast dishes. "You don't know how good I feel! Wouldn't it be nice if it could last? I believe I could be a model child if I were just invited out to tea every day. But oh, Marilla, it's a solemn occasion, too. I feel so anxious. What if I shouldn't behave properly? You know I never had tea at a manse before, and I'm not sure that I know all the rules of etiquette, although I've been studying the rules given in the Etiquette Department of the *Family Herald* ever since I came here. I'm so afraid I'll do something silly or forget to do something I should do. Would it be good manners to take a second helping of anything if you wanted to *very* much?"

"The trouble with you, Anne, is that you're thinking too much about yourself. You should just think of Mrs. Allan and what would be nicest and most agreeable for her," said Marilla, hitting for once in her life on a very sound and pithy piece of advice. Anne instantly realized this.

"You are right, Marilla. I'll try not to think about myself at all."

Anne evidently got through her visit without any serious breach of "etiquette" for she came home through the twilight, under a great, high-sprung sky gloried over with trails of saffron and rosy cloud, in a beatified state of mind and told Marilla all about it happily, sitting on the big red sandstone slab at the kitchen door with her tired curly head in Marilla's gingham lap.

A cool wind was blowing down over the long harvest fields from the rims of firry western hills and whistling through the poplars. One clear star hung above the orchard and the fireflies were flitting over in Lovers' Lane, in and out among the ferns and rustling boughs. Anne watched them as she talked and somehow felt that wind and stars and fireflies were all tangled up together into something unutterably sweet and enchanting.

"Oh, Marilla, I've had a most *fascinating* time. I feel that I have not lived in vain and I shall always feel like that even if I should never be invited to tea at a manse again. When I got there Mrs. Allan met me at the door. She was dressed in the sweetest dress of pale pink organdy, with dozens of frills and elbow sleeves, and she looked just like a seraph. I really think I'd like to be a minister's wife when I grow up, Marilla. A minister mightn't mind my red hair because he wouldn't be thinking of such worldly things. But then of course one would have to be naturally good and I'll never be that, so I suppose there's no use in thinking about it. Some people are naturally good, you know, and others are not. I'm one of the others, Mrs. Lynde says I'm full of original sin. No matter how hard I try to be good I can never make such a success of it as those who are naturally good. It's a good deal like geometry, I expect. But don't you think the trying so hard ought to count for something? Mrs. Allan is one of the naturally good people. I love her passionately. You know there are some people, like Matthew and Mrs. Allan, that you can love right off without any trouble. And there are others, like Mrs. Lynde, that you have to try very hard to love. You know you *ought* to love them because they know so much and are such active workers in the church, but you have to keep reminding yourself of it all the time or else you forget. There was another little girl at the manse to tea, from the White Sands Sunday school. Her name was Lauretta Bradley, and she was a very nice little girl. Not exactly a kindred spirit, you know, but still very nice. We had an elegant tea, and I think I kept all the rules of etiquette pretty well. After tea Mrs. Allan played and sang and she got Lauretta and me to sing, too. Mrs. Allan says I have a good voice and she says I must sing in the Sunday school choir after this. You can't think how I was thrilled at the mere thought. I've longed so to sing in the Sunday school choir, as Diana does, but I feared it was an honor I could never aspire to. Lauretta had to go home early because there is a big concert in the White Sands hotel tonight and her sister is to recite at it. Lauretta says that the Americans at the hotel give a concert every fortnight in aid of the Charlottetown hospital, and they ask lots of the White Sands people to recite. Lauretta said she expected to be asked herself some day. I just gazed at her in awe. After she had gone Mrs. Allan and I had a heart to heart talk. I told her everything— about Mrs. Thomas and the twins and Katie Maurice and Violetta and coming to Green Gables and my troubles over geometry. And would you believe it, Marilla? Mrs. Allan told me she was a dunce at geometry, too. You don't know how that encouraged me. Mrs. Lynde came to the manse just before I left, and what do you think, Marilla? The trustees have hired a new teacher and it's a lady. Her name is Miss Muriel Stacy. Isn't that a romantic name? Mrs. Lynde says they've never had a female teacher in Avonlea before and she thinks it is a dangerous innovation. But I think it will be splendid to have a lady teacher, and I really don't see how I'm going to live through the two weeks before school begins, I'm so impatient to see her."

23

Anne Comes to Grief in an Affair of Honor

nne had to live through more than two weeks, as it happened. Almost a month having elapsed since the liniment cake episode, it was high time for her to get into fresh trouble of some sort, little mistakes, such as absentmindedly emptying a pan of skim milk into a basket of yarn balls in the pantry instead of into the pigs' bucket, and walking clean over the edge of the log bridge into the brook while wrapped in imaginative reverie, not really being worth counting.

A week after the tea at the manse Diana Barry gave a party.

"Small and select," Anne assured Marilla. "Just the girls in our class."

They had a very good time and nothing untoward happened until after tea, when they found themselves in the Barry garden, a little tired of all their games and ripe for an enticing form of mischief which might present itself. This presently took the form of "daring."

Daring was the fashionable amusement among the Avonlea small fry just then. It had begun among the boys, but soon spread to the girls, and all the silly things that were done in Avonlea that summer because the doers thereof were "dared" to do them would fill a book by themselves.

First of all Carrie Sloane dared Ruby Gillis to climb to a certain point in the huge old willow tree before the front door, which Ruby Gillis, albeit in mortal dread of the fat green caterpillars with which said tree was infested and with the fear of her mother before her eyes if she should tear her new muslin dress, nimbly did, to the discomfiture of the aforesaid Carrie Sloane.

Then Josie Pye dared Jane Andrews to hop on her left leg around the garden without stopping once or putting her right foot to the ground; which Jane Andrews gamely tried to do, but gave out at the third corner and had to confess herself defeated.

Josie's triumph being rather more pronounced than good taste permitted, Anne Shirley dared her to walk along the top of the board fence which bounded the garden to the east. Now, to "walk" board fences requires more skill and steadiness of head and heel than one might suppose who has never tried it. But Josie Pye, if deficient in some qualities that make for popularity, had at least a natural and inborn gift, duly cultivated, for walking board fences. Josie walked the Barry fence with an airy unconcern which seemed to imply that a little thing like that wasn't worth a "dare." Reluctant admiration greeted her exploit, for most of the other girls could appreciate it, having suffered many things themselves in their efforts to walk fences. Josie descended from her perch, flushed with victory, and darted a defiant glance at Anne.

Anne tossed her red braids.

"I don't think it's such a very wonderful thing to walk a little, low, board fence," she said. "I knew a girl in Marysville who could walk the ridgepole of a roof."

"I don't believe it," said Josie flatly. "I don't believe anybody could walk a ridgepole. *You* couldn't, anyhow."

"Couldn't I?" cried Anne rashly.

"Then I dare you to do it," said Josie defiantly. "I dare you to climb up there and walk the ridgepole of Mr. Barry's kitchen roof."

Anne turned pale, but there was clearly only one thing to be done. She walked towards the house, where a ladder was leaning against the kitchen roof. All the fifth-class girls said, "Oh!" partly in excitement, partly in dismay.

"Don't you do it, Anne," entreated Diana. "You'll fall off and be killed. Never mind Josie Pye. It isn't fair to dare anybody to do anything so dangerous."

"I must do it. My honor is at stake," said Anne solemnly. "I shall walk that ridgepole, Diana, or perish in the attempt. If I am killed you are to have my pearl bead ring."

Anne climbed the ladder amid breathless silence, gained the ridge-pole, balanced herself uprightly on that precarious footing, and started to walk along it, dizzily conscious that she was uncomfortably high up in the world and that walking ridgepoles was not a thing in which your imagination helped you out much. Nevertheless, she managed to take several steps before the catastrophe came. Then she swayed, lost her balance, stumbled, staggered and fell, sliding down over the sun-baked roof and crashing off it through the tangle of Virginia creeper beneath—all before the dismayed circle below could give a simultaneous, terrified shriek.

If Anne had tumbled off the roof on the side up which she ascended Diana would probably have fallen heir to the pearl bead ring then and there. Fortunately she fell on the other side, where the roof extended down over the porch so nearly to the ground that a fall therefrom was a much less serious thing. Nevertheless, when Diana and the other girls had rushed frantically around the house—except Ruby Gillis, who remained as if rooted to the ground and went into hysterics—they found Anne lying all white and limp among the wreck and ruin of the Virginia creeper.

"Anne, are you killed?" shrieked Diana, throwing herself on her knees beside her friend. "Oh, Anne, dear Anne, speak just one word to me and tell me if you're killed."

To the immense relief of all the girls, and especially of Josie Pye, who, in spite of lack of imagination, had been seized with horrible visions of a future branded as the girl who was the cause of Anne Shirley's early and tragic death, Anne sat dizzily up and answered uncertainly:

"No, Diana, I am not killed, but I think I am rendered unconscious."

"Where?" sobbed Carrie Sloane. "Oh, where, Anne?"

Before Anne could answer Mrs. Barry appeared on the scene. At sight of her Anne tried to scramble to her feet, but sank back again with a sharp little cry of pain.

"What's the matter? Where have you hurt yourself?" demanded Mrs. Barry.

"My ankle," gasped Anne. "Oh, Diana, please find your father and ask him to take me home. I know I can never walk there. And I'm sure I couldn't hop so far on one foot when Jane couldn't even hop around the garden."

Marilla was out in the orchard picking a panful of summer apples when she saw Mr. Barry coming over the log bridge and up the slope, with Mrs. Barry beside him and a whole procession of little girls trailing after him. In his arms he carried Anne whose head lay limply against his shoulder.

At that moment Marilla had a revelation. In the sudden stab of fear that pierced to her very heart she realized what Anne had come to mean to her. She would have admitted that she liked Anne—nay, that she was very fond of Anne. But now she knew as she hurried wildly down the slope that Anne was dearer to her than anything on earth.

"Mr. Barry, what has happened to her?" she gasped, more white and shaken than the self-contained, sensible Marilla had been for many years.

Anne herself answered, lifting her head.

"Don't be very frightened, Marilla. I was walking the ridgepole and I fell off. I expect I have sprained my ankle. But, Marilla, I might have broken my neck. Let us look on the bright side of things."

"I might have known you'd go and do something of the sort when I let you go to that party," said Marilla, sharp and shrewish in her very relief. "Bring her in here, Mr. Barry, and lay her on the sofa. Mercy me, the child has gone and fainted!"

It was quite true. Overcome by the pain of her injury, Anne had one more of her wishes granted to her. She had fainted dead away.

Matthew, hastily summoned from the harvest field, was straightway dispatched for the doctor, who in due time came, to discover that the injury was more serious than they had supposed. Anne's ankle was broken.

That night, when Marilla went up to the east gable, where a white-faced girl was lying, a plaintive voice greeted her from the bed.

"Aren't you very sorry for me, Marilla?"

"It was your own fault," said Marilla, twitching down the blind and lighting a lamp.

"And that is just why you should be sorry for me," said Anne, "because the thought that it is all my own fault is what makes it so hard. If I could blame it on anybody I would feel so much better. But what would you have done, Marilla, if you had been dared to walk a ridgepole?"

"I'd have stayed on good firm ground and let them dare away. Such absurdity!" said Marilla.

Anne sighed.

"But you have such strength of mind, Marilla. I haven't. I just felt that I couldn't bear Josie Pye's scorn. She would have crowed over me all my life. And I think I have been punished so much that you needn't be very cross with me, Marilla. It's not a bit nice to faint, after all. And the doctor hurt me dreadfully when he was setting my ankle. I won't be able to go around for six or seven weeks and I'll miss the new lady teacher. She won't be new any more by the time I'm able to go to school. And Gil—everybody will get ahead of me in class. Oh, I am an afflicted mortal. But I'll try to bear it all bravely if only you won't be cross with me, Marilla."

"There, there, I'm not cross," said Marilla. "You're an unlucky child, there's no doubt about that; but, as you say, you'll have the suffering of it. Here now, try and eat some supper."

"Isn't it fortunate I've got such an imagination?" said Anne. "It will help me through splendidly, I expect. What do people who haven't any imagination do when they break their bones, do you suppose, Marilla?"

Anne had good reason to bless her imagination many a time and oft during the tedious seven weeks that followed. But she was not solely dependent on it. She had many visitors and not a day passed without one or more of the schoolgirls dropping in to bring her flowers and books and tell her all the happenings in the juvenile world of Avonlea.

"Everybody has been so good and kind, Marilla," sighed Anne happily, on the day when she could first limp across the floor. "It isn't very pleasant to be laid up; but there *is* a bright side to it, Marilla. You find out how many friends you have. Why, even Superintendent Bell came to see me, and he's really a very fine man. Not a kindred spirit, of course; but still I like him and I'm awfully sorry I ever criticized his prayers. I believe now he really does mean them, only he has got into the habit of saying them as if he didn't. He could get over that if he'd take a little trouble. I gave him a good broad hint. I told him how hard

I tried to make my own little private prayers interesting. He told me all about the time he broke his ankle when he was a boy. It does seem so strange to think of Superintendent Bell ever being a boy. Even my imagination has its limits for I can't imagine *that*. When I try to imagine him as a boy I see him with gray whiskers and spectacles, just as he looks in Sunday school, only small. Now, it's so easy to imagine Mrs. Allan as a little girl. Mrs. Allan has been to see me fourteen times. Isn't that something to be proud of Marilla? When a minister's wife has so many claims on her time! She is such a cheerful person to have visit you, too. She never tells you it's your own fault and she hopes you'll be a better girl on account of it. Mrs. Lynde always told me that when she came to see me; and she said it in a kind of way that made me feel she might hope I'd be a better girl, but didn't really believe I would. Even Josie Pye came to see me. I received her as politely as I could, because I think she was sorry she dared me to walk a ridgepole. If I had been killed she would have to carry a dark burden of remorse all her life. Diana has been a faithful friend. She's been over every day to cheer my lonely pillow. But oh, I shall be so glad when I can go to school for I've heard such exciting things about the new teacher. The girls all think she is perfectly sweet. Diana says she has the loveliest fair curly hair and such fascinating eyes. She dresses beautifully, and her sleeve puffs are bigger than anybody else's in Avonlea. Every other Friday afternoon she has recitations and everybody has to say a piece or take part in a dialogue. Oh, it's just glorious to think of it. Josie Pye says she hates it, but that is just because Josie has so little imagination. Diana and Ruby Gillis and Jane Andrews are preparing a dialogue, called 'A Morning Visit,' for next Friday. And the Friday afternoons they don't have recitations Miss Stacy takes them all to the woods for a 'field' day and they study ferns and flowers and birds. And they have physical culture exercises every morning and evening. Mrs. Lynde says she never heard of such goings-on and it all comes of having a lady teacher. But I think it must be splendid and I believe I shall find that Miss Stacy is a kindred spirit."

"There's one thing plain to be seen, Anne," said Marilla, "and that is that your fall off the Barry roof hasn't injured your tongue at all."

24

Miss Stacy and Her Pupils Get Up a Concert

It was October again when Anne was ready to go back to school—a glorious October, all red and gold, with mellow mornings when the valleys were filled with delicate mists as if the spirit of autumn had poured them in for the sun to drain—amethyst, pearl, silver, rose, and smoke-blue. The dews were so heavy that the fields glistened like cloth of silver and there were such heaps of rustling leaves in the hollows of many-stemmed woods to run crisply through. The Birch Path was a canopy of yellow and the ferns were sear and brown all along it. There was a tang in the very air that inspired the hearts of small maidens tripping, unlike snails, swiftly and willingly to school; and it *was* jolly to be back again at the little brown desk beside Diana, with Ruby Gillis nodding across the aisle and Carrie Sloane sending up notes and Julia Bell passing a "chew" of gum down from the back seat. Anne drew a long breath of happiness as she sharpened her pencil and arranged her picture cards in her desk. Life was certainly very interesting.

In the new teacher she found another true and helpful friend. Miss Stacy was a bright, sympathetic young woman with the happy gift of winning and holding the affections of her pupils and bringing out the best that was in them mentally and morally. Anne expanded like a flower under this wholesome influence and carried home to the admiring Matthew and the critical Marilla glowing accounts of school work and aims.

"I love Miss Stacy with my whole heart, Marilla. She is so ladylike and she has such a sweet voice. When she pronounces my name I feel *instinctively* that she's spelling it with an *e*. We had recitations this afternoon. I just wish you could have been there to hear me recite 'Mary,

Queen of Scots.' I just put my whole soul into it. Ruby Gillis told me coming home that the way I said the line, 'Now for my father's arm, she said, my woman's heart farewell,' just made her blood run cold."

"Well now, you might recite it for me some of these days, out in the barn," suggested Matthew.

"Of course I will," said Anne meditatively, "but I won't be able to do it so well, I know. It won't be so exciting as it is when you have a whole schoolful before you hanging breathlessly on your words. I know I won't be able to make your blood run cold."

"Mrs. Lynde says it made *her* blood run cold to see the boys climbing to the very tops of those big trees on Bell's hill after crows' nests last Friday," said Marilla. "I wonder at Miss Stacy for encouraging it."

"But we wanted a crow's nest for nature study," explained Anne. "That was on our field afternoon. Field afternoons are splendid, Marilla. And Miss Stacy explains everything so beautifully. We have to write compositions on our field afternoons and I write the best ones."

"It's very vain of you to say so then. You'd better let your teacher say it."

"But she *did* say it, Marilla. And indeed I'm not vain about it. How can I be, when I'm such a dunce at geometry? Although I'm really beginning to see through it a little, too. Miss Stacy makes it so clear. Still, I'll never be good at it and I assure you it is a humbling reflection. But I love writing compositions. Mostly Miss Stacy lets us choose our own subjects; but next week we are to write a composition on some remarkable person. It's hard to choose among so many remarkable people who have lived. Mustn't it be splendid to be remarkable and have compositions written about you after you're dead? Oh, I would dearly love to be remarkable. I think when I grow up I'll be a trained nurse and go with the Red Crosses to the field of battle as a messenger of mercy. That is, if I don't go out as a foreign missionary. That would be very romantic, but one would have to be very good to be a missionary, and that would be a stumbling-block. We have physical culture exercises every day, too. They make you graceful and promote digestion."

"Promote fiddlesticks!" said Marilla, who honestly thought it was all nonsense.

But all the field afternoons and recitation Fridays and physical culture contortions paled before a project which Miss Stacy brought forward in November. This was that the scholars of Avonlea school should get up a concert and hold it in the hall on Christmas night, for the laudable purpose of helping to pay for a schoolhouse flag. The pupils one and all taking graciously to this plan, the preparations for a program were begun at once. And of all the excited performers-elect none was so excited as Anne Shirley, who threw herself into the undertaking heart and soul, hampered as she was by Marilla's disapproval. Marilla thought it all rank foolishness.

"It's just filling your heads up with nonsense and taking time that ought to be put on your lessons," she grumbled. "I don't approve of children's getting up concerts and racing about to practices. It makes them vain and forward and fond of gadding."

"But think of the worthy object," pleaded Anne. "A flag will cultivate a spirit of patriotism, Marilla."

"Fudge! There's precious little patriotism in the thoughts of any of you. All you want is a good time."

"Well, when you can combine patriotism and fun, isn't it all right? Of course it's real nice to be getting up a concert. We're going to have six choruses and Diana is to sing a solo. I'm in two dialogues—'The Society for the Suppression of Gossip' and 'The Fairy Queen.' The boys are going to have a dialogue, too. And I'm to have two recitations, Marilla. I just tremble when I think of it, but it's a nice thrilly kind of tremble. And we're to have a tableau at the last—'Faith, Hope and Charity.' Diana and Ruby and I are to be in it, all draped in white with flowing hair. I'm to be Hope, with my hands clasped—so—and my eyes uplifted. I'm going to practice my recitations in the garret. Don't be alarmed if you hear me groaning. I have to groan heartrendingly in one of them, and it's really hard to get up a good artistic groan, Marilla. Josie Pye is sulky because she didn't get the part she wanted in the dialogue. She wanted to be the fairy queen. That would have been ridiculous, for who ever heard of a fairy queen as fat as Josie? Fairy queens must be slender. Jane Andrews is to be the queen and I am to be one of her maids of honor. Josie says she thinks a redhaired fairy is just as ridiculous as a fat one, but I do not let myself mind what Josie says. I'm to have a wreath of white roses on my hair and Ruby Gillis is going to lend me her slippers because I haven't any of my own. It's necessary for fairies to have slippers, you know. You couldn't imagine a fairy wearing boots, could you? Especially with copper toes? We are going to decorate the hall with creeping spruce and fir mottoes with pink tissue paper roses in them. And we are all to march in two by two after the audience is seated, while Emma White plays a march on the organ. Oh, Marilla, I know you are not so enthusiastic about it as I am, but don't you hope your little Anne will distinguish herself?"

"All I hope is that you'll behave yourself. I'll be heartily glad when all this fuss is over and you'll be able to settle down. You are simply good for nothing just now with your head stuffed full of dialogues and groans and tableaus. As for your tongue, it's a marvel it's not clean worn out."

Anne sighed and betook herself to the back yard, over which a young new moon was shining through the leafless poplar boughs from an apple-green western sky, and where Matthew was splitting wood. Anne perched herself on a block and talked the concert over with him, sure of an appreciative and sympathetic listener in this instance at least.

"Well now, I reckon it's going to be a pretty good concert. And I expect you'll do your part fine," he said, smiling down into her eager, vivacious little face. Anne smiled back at him. Those two were the best of friends and Matthew thanked his stars many a time and oft that he had nothing to do with bringing her up. That was Marilla's exclusive duty; if it had been his he would have been worried over frequent conflicts between inclination and said duty. As it was, he was free to "spoil Anne"—Marilla's phrasing—as much as he liked. But it was not such a bad arrangement after all; a little "appreciation" sometimes does quite as much good as all the conscientious "bringing up" in the world.

25

Matthew Insists on Puffed Sleeves

Matthew was having a bad ten minutes of it. He had come into the kitchen, in the twilight of a cold, gray December evening, and had sat down in the woodbox corner to take off his heavy boots, unconscious of the fact that Anne and a bevy of her schoolmates were having a practice of "The Fairy Queen" in the sitting room. Presently they came trooping through the hall and out into the kitchen, laughing and chattering gaily. They did not see Matthew, who shrank bashfully back into the shadows beyond the woodbox with a boot in one hand and a bootjack in the other, and he watched them shyly for the aforesaid ten minutes as they put on caps and jackets and talked about the dialogue and the concert. Anne stood among them, bright-eyed and animated as they; but Matthew suddenly became conscious that there was something about her different from her mates. And what worried Matthew was that the difference impressed him as being something that should not exist. Anne had a brighter face, and bigger, starrier eyes, and more delicate features than the others; even shy, unobservant Matthew had learned to take note of these things; but the difference that disturbed him did not consist in any of these respects. Then in what did it consist?

Matthew was haunted by this question long after the girls had gone, arm in arm, down the long, hard-frozen lane and Anne had betaken herself to her books. He could not refer it to Marilla, who, he felt, would be quite sure to sniff scornfully and remark that the only difference she saw between Anne and the other girls was that they sometimes kept their tongues quiet while Anne never did. This, Matthew felt, would be no great help.

He had recourse to his pipe that evening to help him study it out, much to Marilla's disgust. After two hours of smoking and hard reflection Matthew arrived at a solution of his problem. Anne was not dressed like the other girls!

The more Matthew thought about the matter the more he was convinced that Anne never had been dressed like the other girls— never since she had come to Green Gables. Marilla kept her clothed in plain, dark dresses, all made after the same unvarying pattern. If Matthew knew there was such a thing as fashion in dress it is as much as he did; but he was quite sure that Anne's sleeves did not look at all like the sleeves the other girls wore. He recalled the cluster of little girls he had seen around her that evening—all gay in waists of red and blue and pink and white—and he wondered why Marilla always kept her so plainly and soberly gowned.

Of course, it must be all right. Marilla knew best and Marilla was bringing her up. Probably some wise, inscrutable motive was to be served thereby. But surely it would do no harm to let the child have one pretty dress—something like Diana Barry always wore. Matthew decided that he would give her one; that surely could not be objected to as an unwarranted putting in of his oar. Christmas was only a fortnight off. A nice new dress would be the very thing for a present. Matthew, with a sigh of satisfaction, put away his pipe and went to bed, while Marilla opened all the doors and aired the house.

The very next evening Matthew betook himself to Carmody to buy the dress, determined to get the worst over and have done with it. It would be, he felt assured, no trifling ordeal. There were some things Matthew could buy and prove himself no mean bargainer; but he knew he would be at the mercy of shopkeepers when it came to buying a girl's dress.

After much cogitation Matthew resolved to go to Samuel Lawson's store instead of William Blair's. To be sure, the Cuthberts always had gone to William Blair's; it was almost as much a matter of conscience with them as to attend the Presbyterian church and vote Conservative. But William Blair's two daughters frequently waited on customers there and Matthew held them in absolute dread. He could contrive to deal with them when he knew exactly what he wanted and could point it out; but in such a matter as this, requiring explanation and consultation, Matthew felt that he must be sure of a man behind the counter. So he would go to Lawson's, where Samuel or his son would wait on him.

Alas! Matthew did not know that Samuel, in the recent expansion of his business, had set up a lady clerk also; she was a niece of his wife's and a very dashing young person indeed, with a huge, drooping pompadour, big, rolling brown eyes, and a most extensive and bewildering smile. She was dressed with exceeding smartness and wore several bangle bracelets that glittered and rattled and tinkled with every movement of her hands. Matthew was covered with confusion at finding her there at all; and those bangles completely wrecked his wits at one fell swoop.

"What can I do for you this evening, Mr. Cuthbert?" Miss Lucilla Harris inquired, briskly and ingratiatingly, tapping the counter with both hands.

"Have you any—any—any—well now, say any garden rakes?" stammered Matthew.

Miss Harris looked somewhat surprised, as well she might, to hear a man inquiring for garden rakes in the middle of December.

"I believe we have one or two left over," she said, "but they're upstairs in the lumber room. I'll go and see."

During her absence Matthew collected his scattered senses for another effort.

When Miss Harris returned with the rake and cheerfully inquired: "Anything else tonight, Mr. Cuthbert?" Matthew took his courage in both hands and replied: "Well now, since you suggest it, I might as well—take—that is—look at—buy some—some hayseed."

Miss Harris had heard Matthew Cuthbert called odd. She now concluded that he was entirely crazy.

"We only keep hayseed in the spring," she explained loftily. "We've none on hand just now."

"Oh, certainly—certainly—just as you say," stammered unhappy Matthew, seizing the rake and making for the door. At the threshold he recollected that he had not paid for it and he turned miserably back. While Miss Harris was counting out his change he rallied his powers for a final desperate attempt.

"Well now—if it isn't too much trouble—I might as well—that is—I'd like to look at—at—some sugar."

"White or brown?" queried Miss Harris patiently.

"Oh—well now—brown," said Matthew feebly.

"There's a barrel of it over there," said Miss Harris, shaking her bangles at it. "It's the only kind we have."

"I'll—I'll take twenty pounds of it," said Matthew, with beads of perspiration standing on his forehead.

Matthew had driven halfway home before he was his own man again. It had been a gruesome experience, but it served him right, he thought, for committing the heresy of going to a strange store. When he reached home he hid the rake in the tool-house, but the sugar he carried in to Marilla.

"Brown sugar!" exclaimed Marilla. "Whatever possessed you to get so much? You know I never use it except for the hired man's porridge or black fruitcake. Jerry's gone and I've made my cake long ago. It's not good sugar, either—it's coarse and dark—William Blair doesn't usually keep sugar like that."

"I—I thought it might come in handy sometime," said Matthew, making good his escape.

When Matthew came to think the matter over he decided that a woman was required to cope with the situation. Marilla was out of the question. Matthew felt sure she would throw cold water on his project at once. Remained only Mrs. Lynde; for of no other woman in Avonlea would Matthew have dared to ask advice. To Mrs. Lynde he went accordingly, and that good lady promptly took the matter out of the harassed man's hands.

"Pick out a dress for you to give Anne? To be sure I will. I'm going to Carmody tomorrow and I'll attend to it. Have you something particular in mind? No? Well, I'll just go by my own judgment then. I believe a nice rich brown would just suit Anne, and William Blair has some new gloria in that's real pretty. Perhaps you'd like me to make it up for her, too, seeing that if Marilla was to make it Anne would probably get wind of it before the time and spoil the surprise? Well, I'll do it. No, it isn't a mite of trouble. I like sewing. I'll make it to fit my niece, Jenny Gillis, for she and Anne are as like as two peas as far as figure goes."

"Well now, I'm much obliged," said Matthew, "and—and—I dunno—but I'd like—I think they make the sleeves different nowadays to what they used to be. If it wouldn't be asking too much I—I'd like them made in the new way."

"Puffs? Of course. You needn't worry a speck more about it, Matthew. I'll make it up in the very latest fashion," said Mrs. Lynde. To herself she added when Matthew had gone:

"It'll be a real satisfaction to see that poor child wearing something decent for once. The way Marilla dresses her is positively ridiculous, that's what, and I've ached to tell her so plainly a dozen times. I've held my tongue though, for I can see Marilla doesn't want advice and she thinks she knows more about bringing children up than I do for all she's an old maid. But that's always the way. Folks that has brought up children know that there's no hard and fast method in the world that'll suit every child. But them as never have think it's all as plain and easy as Rule of Three—just set your three terms down so fashion, and the sum'll work out correct. But flesh and blood don't come under the head of arithmetic and that's where Marilla Cuthbert makes her mistake. I suppose she's trying to cultivate a spirit of humility in Anne by dressing her as she does; but it's more likely to cultivate envy and discontent. I'm sure the child must feel the difference between her clothes and the other girls'. But to think of Matthew taking notice of it! That man is waking up after being asleep for over sixty years."

Marilla knew all the following fortnight that Matthew had something on his mind, but what it was she could not guess, until Christmas Eve, when Mrs. Lynde brought up the new dress. Marilla behaved pretty well on the whole, although it is very likely she distrusted Mrs. Lynde's diplomatic explanation that she had made the dress because Matthew was afraid Anne would find out about it too soon if Marilla made it.

"So this is what Matthew has been looking so mysterious over and grinning about to himself for two weeks, is it?" she said a little stiffly but tolerantly. "I knew he was up to some foolishness. Well, I must say I don't think Anne needed any more dresses. I made her three good, warm, serviceable ones this fall, and anything more is sheer extravagance. There's enough material in those sleeves alone to make a waist, I· declare there is. You'll just pamper Anne's vanity, Matthew, and she's as vain as a peacock now. Well, I hope she'll be satisfied at last, for I know she's been hankering after these silly sleeves ever since they came in, although she never said a word after the first. The puffs have been getting bigger and more ridiculous right along; they're as big as balloons now. Next year anybody who wears them will have to go through a door sideways."

Christmas morning broke on a beautiful white world. It had been a very mild December and people had looked forward to a green Christmas; but just enough snow fell softly in the night to transfigure Avonlea. Anne peeped out from her frosted gable window with delighted eyes. The firs in the Haunted Wood were all feathery and wonderful; the birches and wild cherry trees were outlined in pearl; the ploughed fields were stretches of snowy dimples; and there was a crisp tang in the air that was glorious. Anne ran downstairs singing until her voice reechoed through Green Gables.

"Merry Christmas, Marilla! Merry Christmas, Matthew! Isn't it a lovely Christmas? I'm so glad it's white. Any other kind of Christmas doesn't seem real, does it? I don't like green Christmases. They're *not* green—they're just nasty faded browns and grays. What makes people call them green? Why—why—Matthew, is that for me? Oh, Matthew!"

Matthew had sheepishly unfolded the dress from its paper swathings and held it out with a deprecatory glance at Marilla, who feigned to be contemptuously filling the teapot, but nevertheless watched the scene out of the corner of her eye with a rather interested air.

Anne took the dress and looked at it in reverent silence. Oh, how pretty it was—a lovely soft brown gloria with all the gloss of silk; a skirt with dainty frills and shirrings; a waist elaborately pin-tucked in the most fashionable way, with a little ruffle of filmy lace at the neck. But the sleeves—they were the crowning glory! Long elbow cuffs, and above them two beautiful puffs divided by rows of shirring and bows of brown silk ribbon.

"That's a Christmas present for you, Anne," said Matthew shyly. "Why—why—Anne, don't you like it? Well now—well now."

For Anne's eyes had suddenly filled with tears.

"*Like* it! Oh, Matthew!" Anne laid the dress over a chair and clasped her hands. "Matthew, it's perfectly exquisite. Oh, I can never thank you enough. Look at those sleeves! Oh, it seems to me this must be a happy dream."

"Well, well, let us have breakfast," interrupted Marilla. "I must say, Anne, I don't think you needed the dress; but since Matthew has got it for you, see that you take good care of it. There's a hair ribbon Mrs. Lynde left for you. It's brown, to match the dress. Come now, sit in."

"I don't see how I'm going to eat breakfast," said Anne rapturously. "Breakfast seems so commonplace at such an exciting moment. I'd rather feast my eyes on that dress. I'm so glad that puffed sleeves are still fashionable. It did seem to me that I'd never get over it if they went out before I had a dress with them. I'd never have felt quite sat-. isfied, you see. It was lovely of Mrs. Lynde to give me the ribbon, too. I feel that I ought to be a very good girl indeed. It's at times like this I'm sorry I'm not a model little girl; and I always resolve that I will be in future. But somehow it's hard to carry out your resolutions when irresistible temptations come. Still, I really will make an extra effort after this."

When the commonplace breakfast was over Diana appeared, crossing the white log bridge in the hollow, a gay little figure in her crimson ulster. Anne flew down the slope to meet her.

"Merry Christmas, Diana! And oh, it's a wonderful Christmas. I've something splendid to show you. Matthew has given me the loveli-est dress, with *such* sleeves. I couldn't even imagine any nicer."

"I've got something more for you," said Diana breathlessly. "Here—this box. Aunt Josephine sent us out a big box with ever so many things in it—and this is for you. I'd have brought it over last night, but it didn't come until after dark, and I never feel very comfortable coming through the Haunted Wood in the dark now."

Anne opened the box and peeped in. First a card with "For the Anne-girl and Merry Christmas," written on it; and then, a pair of the daintiest little kid slippers, with beaded toes and satin bows and glistening buckles.

"Oh," said Anne, "Diana, this is too much. I must be dreaming."

"*I* call it providential," said Diana. "You won't have to borrow Ruby's slippers now, and that's a blessing, for they're two sizes too big for you, and it would be awful to hear a fairy shuffling. Josie Pye would be delighted. Mind you, Rob Wright went home with Gertie Pye from the practice night before last. Did you ever hear anything equal to that?"

All the Avonlea scholars were in a fever of excitement that day, for the hall had to be decorated and a last grand rehearsal held.

The concert came off in the evening and was a pronounced success. The little hall was crowded; all the performers did excellently well, but Anne was the bright particular star of the occasion, as even envy, in the shape of Josie Pye, dared not deny.

"Oh, hasn't it been a brilliant evening?" sighed Anne, when it was all over and she and Diana were walking home together under a dark, starry sky.

"Everything went off very well," said Diana practically. "I guess we must have made as much as ten dollars. Mind you, Mr. Allan is going to send an account of it to the Charlottetown papers."

"Oh, Diana, will we really see our names in print? It makes me thrill to think of it. Your solo was perfectly elegant, Diana. I felt prouder than you did when it was encored. I just said to myself, 'It is my dear bosom friend who is so honored.'"

"Well, your recitations just brought down the house, Anne. That sad one was simply splendid."

"Oh, I was so nervous, Diana. When Mr. Allan called out my name I really cannot tell how I ever got up on that platform. I felt as if a million eyes were looking at me and through me, and for one dreadful moment I was sure I couldn't begin at all. Then I thought of my lovely puffed sleeves and took courage. I knew that I must live up to those sleeves, Diana. So I started in, and my voice seemed to be coming from ever so far away. I just felt like a parrot. It's providential that I practised those recitations so often up in the garret, or I'd never have been able to get through. Did I groan all right?"

"Yes, indeed, you groaned lovely," assured Diana.

"I saw old Mrs. Sloane wiping away tears when I sat down. It was splendid, to think I had touched somebody's heart. It's so romantic to take part in a concert, isn't it? Oh, it's been a very memorable occasion indeed."

"Wasn't the boys' dialogue fine?" said Diana. "Gilbert Blythe was just splendid. Anne, I do think it's awful mean the way you treat Gil. Wait till I tell you. When you ran off the platform after the fairy dialogue one of your roses fell out of your hair. I saw Gil pick it up and put it in his breast-pocket. There now. You're so romantic that I'm sure you ought to be pleased at that."

"It's nothing to me what that person does," said Anne loftily. "I simply never waste a thought on him, Diana."

That night Marilla and Matthew, who had been out to a concert for the first time in twenty years, sat for awhile by the kitchen fire after Anne had gone to bed.

"Well, now, I guess our Anne did as well as any of them," said Matthew proudly.

"Yes, she did," admitted Marilla. "She's a bright child, Matthew. And she looked real nice, too. I've been kind of opposed to this concert scheme, but I suppose there's no real harm in it after all. Anyhow, I was proud of Anne tonight, although I'm not going to tell her so."

"Well now, I was proud of her and I did tell her so 'fore she went upstairs," said Matthew. "We must see what we can do for her some of these days, Marilla. I guess she'll need something more than Avonlea school by and by."

"There's time enough to think of that," said Marilla. "She's only thirteen in March. Though tonight it struck me she was growing quite a big girl. Mrs. Lynde made that dress a mite too long, and it makes Anne look so tall. She's quick to learn and I guess the best thing we can do for her will be to send her to Queen's after a spell. But nothing need be said about that for a year or two yet."

"Well now, it'll do no harm to be thinking it over off and on," said Matthew. "Things like that are all the better for lots of thinking over."

26

The Story Club is Formed

Junior Avonlea found it hard to settle down to humdrum existence again. To Anne in particular things seemed fearfully flat, stale, and unprofitable after the goblet of excitement she had been sipping for weeks. Could she go back to the former quiet pleasures of those faraway days before the concert? At first, as she told Diana, she did not really think she could.

"I'm positively certain, Diana, that life can never be quite the same again as it was in those olden days," she said mournfully, as if referring to a period of at least fifty years back. "Perhaps after awhile I'll get used to it, but I'm afraid concerts spoil people for everyday life. I suppose that is why Marilla disapproves of them. Marilla is such a sensible woman. It must be a great deal better to be sensible; but still, I don't believe I'd really want to be a sensible person, because they are so unromantic. Mrs. Lynde says there is no danger of my ever being one, but you can never tell. I feel just now that I may grow up to be sensible yet. But perhaps that is only because I'm tired. I simply couldn't sleep last night for ever so long. I just lay awake and imagined the concert over and over again. That's one splendid thing about such affairs— it's so lovely to look back to them."

Eventually, however, Avonlea school slipped back into its old groove and took up its old interests. To be sure, the concert left traces. Ruby Gillis and Emma White, who had quarreled over a point of precedence in their platform seats, no longer sat at the same desk, and a promising friendship of three years was broken up. Josie Pye and Julia Bell did not "speak" for three months, because Josie Pye had told Bessie Wright that Julia Bell's bow when she got up to recite made her think of a chicken jerking its head, and Bessie told Julia. None of the Sloanes would have any dealings with the Bells, because the Bells had declared that the Sloanes had too much to do in the programme, and the Sloanes had retorted that the Bells were not capable of doing the little they had to do properly. Finally, Charlie Sloane fought Moody Spurgeon MacPherson, because Moody Spurgeon had said that Anne Shirley put on airs about her recitations, and Moody Spurgeon was "licked;" consequently Moody Spurgeon's sister, Ella May, would not "speak" to Anne Shirley all the rest of the winter. With the exception of these trifling frictions, work in Miss Stacy's little kingdom went on with regularity and smoothness.

The winter weeks slipped by. It was an unusually mild winter, with so little snow that Anne and Diana could go to school nearly every day by way of the Birch Path. On Anne's birthday they were tripping lightly down it, keeping eyes and ears alert amid all their chatter, for Miss Stacy had told them that they must soon write a composition on "A Winter's Walk in the Woods," and it behooved them to be observant.

"Just think, Diana, I'm thirteen years old today," remarked Anne in an awed voice. "I can scarcely realize that I'm in my teens. When I woke this morning it seemed to me that everything must be different. You've been thirteen for a month, so I suppose it doesn't seem such a novelty to you as it does to me. It makes life seem so much more interesting. In two more years I'll be really grown up. It's a great comfort to think that I'll be able to use big words then without being laughed at."

"Ruby Gillis says she means to have a beau as soon as she's fifteen," said Diana.

"Ruby Gillis thinks of nothing but beaus," said Anne disdainfully. "She's actually delighted when any one writes her name up in a take-notice for all she pretends to be so mad. But I'm afraid that is an uncharitable speech. Mrs. Allan says we should never make uncharitable speeches; but they do slip out so often before you think, don't they? I simply can't talk about Josie Pye without making an uncharitable speech, so I never mention her at all. You may have noticed that. I'm trying to be as much like Mrs. Allan as I possibly can, for I think she's perfect. Mr. Allan thinks so too. Mrs. Lynde says he just worships the ground she treads on and she doesn't really think it right for a minister to set his affections so much on a mortal being. But then, Diana, even ministers are human and have their besetting sins just like everybody else. I had such an interesting talk with Mrs. Allan about besetting sins last Sunday afternoon. There are just a few things it's proper to talk about on Sundays and that is one of them. My besetting sin is imagining too much and forgetting my duties. I'm striving very hard to overcome it and now that I'm really thirteen perhaps I'll get on better."

"In four more years we'll be able to put our hair up," said Diana. "Alice Bell is only sixteen and she is wearing hers up, but I think that's ridiculous. I shall wait until I'm seventeen."

"If I had Alice Bell's crooked nose," said Anne decidedly, "I wouldn't—but there! I won't say what I was going to because it was extremely uncharitable. Besides, I was comparing it with my own nose and that's vanity. I'm afraid I think too much about my nose ever since I heard that compliment about it long ago. It really is a great comfort to me. Oh, Diana, look, there's a rabbit. That's something to remember for our woods composition. I really think the woods are just as lovely in winter as in summer. They're so white and still, as if they were asleep and dreaming pretty dreams."

"I won't mind writing that composition when its time comes," sighed Diana. "I can manage to write about the woods, but the one we're to hand in Monday is terrible. The idea of Miss Stacy telling us to write a story out of our own heads!"

"Why, it's as easy as wink," said Anne.

"It's easy for you because you have an imagination," retorted Diana, "but what would you do if you had been born without one? I suppose you have your composition all done?"

Anne nodded, trying hard not to look virtuously complacent and failing miserably.

"I wrote it last Monday evening. It's called 'The Jealous Rival; or, in Death Not Divided.' I read it to Marilla and she said it was stuff and nonsense. Then I read it to Matthew and he said it was fine. That is the kind of critic I like. It's a sad, sweet story. I just cried like a child while I was writing it. It's about two beautiful maidens called Cordelia

Montmorency and Geraldine Seymour who lived in the same village and were devotedly attached to each other. Cordelia was a regal brunette with a coronet of midnight hair and duskly flashing eyes. Geraldine was a queenly blonde with hair like spun gold and velvety purple eyes."

"I never saw anybody with purple eyes," said Diana dubiously.

"Neither did I. I just imagined them. I wanted something out of the common. Geraldine had an alabaster brow, too. I've found out what an alabaster brow is. That is one of the advantages of being thirteen. You know so much more than you did when you were only twelve."

"Well, what became of Cordelia and Geraldine?" asked Diana, who was beginning to feel rather interested in their fate.

"They grew in beauty side by side until they were sixteen. Then Bertram DeVere came to their native village and fell in love with the fair Geraldine. He saved her life when her horse ran away with her in a carriage, and she fainted in his arms and he carried her home three miles; because, you understand, the carriage was all smashed up. I found it rather hard to imagine the proposal because I had no experience to go by. I asked Ruby Gillis if she knew anything about how men proposed because I thought she'd likely be an authority on the subject, having so many sisters married. Ruby told me she was hid in the hall pantry when Malcolm Andrews proposed to her sister Susan. She said Malcolm told Susan that his dad had given him the farm in his own name and then said, 'What do you say, darling pet, if we get hitched this fall?' And Susan said, 'Yes—no—I don't know—let me see,'—and there they were, engaged as quick as that. But I didn't think that sort of a proposal was a very romantic one, so in the end I had to imagine it out as well as I could. I made it very flowery and poetical and Bertram went on his knees, although Ruby Gillis says it isn't done nowadays. Geraldine accepted him in a speech a page long. I can tell you I took a lot of trouble with that speech. I rewrote it five times and I look upon it as my masterpiece. Bertram gave her a diamond ring and a ruby necklace and told her they would go to Europe for a wedding tour, for he was immensely wealthy. But then, alas, shadows began to darken over their path. Cordelia was secretly in love with Bertram herself and when Geraldine told her about the engagement she was simply furious, especially when she saw the necklace and the diamond ring. All her affection for Geraldine turned to bitter hate and she vowed that she should never marry Bertram. But she pretended to be Geraldine's friend the same as ever. One evening they were standing on the bridge over a rushing turbulent stream and Cordelia, thinking they were alone, pushed Geraldine over the brink with a wild, mocking, 'Ha, ha, ha.' But Bertram saw it all and he at once plunged into the current, exclaiming, 'I will save thee, my peerless Geraldine.' But alas, he had forgotten he couldn't swim, and they were both drowned, clasped in each other's arms. Their bodies were washed ashore soon afterwards. They were buried in the one grave and their funeral was most impos-ing, Diana. It's so much more romantic to end a story up with a funeral than a wedding. As for Cordelia, she went insane with remorse and was shut up in a lunatic asylum. I thought that was a poetical retribution for her crime."

"How perfectly lovely!" sighed Diana, who belonged to Matthew's school of critics. "I don't see how you can make up such thrilling things out of your own head, Anne. I wish my imagination was as good as yours."

"It would be if you'd only cultivate it," said Anne cheeringly. "I've just thought of a plan, Diana. Let you and I have a story club all our own and write stories for practice. I'll help you along until you can do them by yourself. You ought to cultivate your imagination, you know. Miss Stacy says so. Only we must take the right way. I told her about the Haunted Wood, but she said we went the wrong way about it in that."

This was how the story club came into existence. It was limited to Diana and Anne at first, but soon it was extended to include Jane Andrews and Ruby Gillis and one or two others who felt that their imaginations needed cultivating. No boys were allowed in—although Ruby Gillis opined that their admission would make it more exciting—and each member had to produce one story a week.

"It's extremely interesting," Anne told Marilla. "Each girl has to read her story out loud and then we talk it over. We are going to keep them all sacredly and have them to read to our descendants. We each write under a nom de plume. Mine is Rosamond Montmorency. All the girls do pretty well. Ruby Gillis is rather sentimental. She puts too much lovemaking into her stories and you know too much is worse than too little. Jane never puts any because she says it makes her feel so silly when she has to read it out loud. Jane's stories are extremely sensible. Then Diana puts too many murders into hers. She says most of the time she doesn't know what to do with the people so she kills them off to get rid of them. I mostly always have to tell them what to write about, but that isn't hard for I've millions of ideas."

"I think this story writing business is the foolishest yet," scoffed Marilla. "You'll get a pack of nonsense into your heads and waste time that should be put on your lessons. Reading stories is bad enough but writing them is worse."

"But we're so careful to put a moral into them all, Marilla," explained Anne. "I insist upon that. All the good people are rewarded and all the bad ones are suitably punished. I'm sure that must have a wholesome effect. The moral is the great thing. Mr. Allan says so. I read one of my stories to him and Mrs. Allan and they both agreed that the moral was excellent. Only they laughed in the wrong places. I like it better when people cry. Jane and Ruby almost always cry when I come to the pathetic parts. Diana wrote her Aunt Josephine about our club and her Aunt Josephine wrote back that we were to send her some of our stories. So we copied out four of our very best and sent them. Miss Josephine Barry wrote back that she had never read anything so amusing in her life. That kind of puzzled us because the stories were all very pathetic and almost everybody died. But I'm glad Miss Barry liked them. It shows our club is doing some good in the world. Mrs. Allan says that ought to be our object in everything. I do really try to make it my object but I forget so often when I'm having fun. I hope I shall be a little like Mrs. Allan when I grow up. Do you think there is any prospect of it, Marilla?"

"I shouldn't say there was a great deal," was Marilla's encouraging answer. "I'm sure Mrs. Allan was never such a silly, forgetful little girl as you are."

"No; but she wasn't always so good as she is now either," said Anne seriously. "She told me so herself—that is, she said she was a dreadful mischief when she was a girl and was always getting into scrapes. I felt so encouraged when I heard that. Is it very wicked of me, Marilla, to feel encouraged when I hear that other people have been bad and mischievous? Mrs. Lynde says it is. Mrs. Lynde says she always feels shocked when she hears of any one ever having been naughty, no matter how small they were. Mrs. Lynde says she once heard a minister confess that when he was a boy he stole a strawberry tart out of his aunt's pantry and she never had any respect for that minister again. Now, I wouldn't have felt that way. I'd have thought that it was real noble of him to confess it, and I'd have thought what an encouraging thing it would be for small boys nowadays who do naughty things and are sorry for them to know that perhaps they may grow up to be ministers in spite of it. That's how I'd feel, Marilla."

"The way I feel at present, Anne," said Marilla, "is that it's high time you had those dishes washed. You've taken half an hour longer than you should with all your chattering. Learn to work first and talk afterwards."

27

Vanity and Vexation of Spirit

Marilla, walking home one late April evening from an Aid meeting, realized that the winter was over and gone with the thrill of delight that spring never fails to bring to the oldest and saddest as well as to the youngest and merriest. Marilla was not given to subjective analysis of her thoughts and feelings. She probably imagined that she was thinking about the Aids and their missionary box and the new carpet for the vestry room, but under these reflections was a harmonious consciousness of red fields smoking into pale purply mists in the declining sun, of long, sharp-pointed fir shadows falling over the meadow beyond the brook, of still, crimson-budded maples around a mirror-like wood-pool, of a wakening in the world and a stir of hidden pulses under the gray sod. The spring was abroad in the land and Marilla's sober, middle-aged step was lighter and swifter because of its deep, primal gladness.

Her eyes dwelt affectionately on Green Gables, peering through its network of trees and reflecting the sunlight back from its windows in several little coruscations of glory. Marilla, as she picked her steps along the damp lane, thought that it was really a satisfaction to know that she was going home to a briskly snapping wood fire and a table nicely spread for tea, instead of to the cold comfort of old Aid meeting evenings before Anne had come to Green Gables.

Consequently, when Marilla entered her kitchen and found the fire black out, with no sign of Anne anywhere, she felt justly disappointed and irritated. She had told Anne to be sure and have tea ready at five o'clock, but now she must hurry to take off her second-best dress and prepare the meal herself against Matthew's return from plowing.

"I'll settle Miss Anne when she comes home," said Marilla grimly, as she shaved up kindlings with a carving knife and more vim than was strictly necessary. Matthew had come in and was waiting patiently for his tea in his corner. "She's gadding off somewhere with Diana, writing stories or practicing dialogues or some such tomfoolery, and never thinking once about the time or her duties. She's just got to be pulled up short and sudden on this sort of thing. I don't care if Mrs. Allan does say she's the brightest and sweetest child she ever knew. She may be bright and sweet enough, but her head is full of nonsense and there's never any knowing what shape it'll break out in next. Just as soon as she grows out of one freak she takes up with another. But there! Here I am saying the very thing I was so riled with Rachel Lynde for saying at the Aid today. I was real glad when Mrs. Allan spoke up for Anne, for if she hadn't I know I'd have said something too sharp to Rachel before everybody. Anne's got plenty of faults, goodness knows, and far be it from me to deny it. But I'm bringing her up and not Rachel Lynde, who'd pick faults in the Angel Gabriel himself if he lived in Avonlea. Just the same, Anne has no business to leave the house like this when I told her she was to stay home this afternoon and look after things. I must say, with all her faults, I never found her disobedient or untrustworthy before and I'm real sorry to find her so now."

"Well now, I dunno," said Matthew, who, being patient and wise and, above all, hungry, had deemed it best to let Marilla talk her wrath out unhindered, having learned by experience that she got through with whatever work was on hand much quicker if not delayed by untimely argument. "Perhaps you're judging her too hasty, Marilla. Don't call her untrustworthy until you're sure she has disobeyed you. Mebbe it can all be explained—Anne's a great hand at explaining."

"She's not here when I told her to stay," retorted Marilla. "I reckon she'll find it hard to explain that to my satisfaction. Of course I knew you'd take her part, Matthew. But I'm bringing her up, not you."

It was dark when supper was ready, and still no sign of Anne, coming hurriedly over the log bridge or up Lovers' Lane, breathless and repentant with a sense of neglected duties. Marilla washed and put away the dishes grimly. Then, wanting a candle to light her down cellar, she went up to the east gable for the one that generally stood on Anne's table. Lighting it, she turned around to see Anne herself lying on the bed, face downward among the pillows.

"Mercy on us," said astonished Marilla, "have you been asleep, Anne?"

"No," was the muffled reply.

"Are you sick then?" demanded Marilla anxiously, going over to the bed.

Anne cowered deeper into her pillows as if desirous of hiding herself forever from mortal eyes.

"No. But please, Marilla, go away and don't look at me. I'm in the depths of despair and I don't care who gets head in class or writes the best composition or sings in the Sunday school choir any more. Little things like that are of no importance now because I don't suppose I'll ever be able to go anywhere again. My career is closed. Please, Marilla, go away and don't look at me."

"Did any one ever hear the like?" the mystified Marilla wanted to know. "Anne Shirley, whatever is the matter with you? What have you done? Get right up this minute and tell me. This minute, I say. There now, what is it?"

Anne had slid to the floor in despairing obedience.

"Look at my hair, Marilla," she whispered.

Accordingly, Marilla lifted her candle and looked scrutinizingly at Anne's hair, flowing in heavy masses down her back. It certainly had a very strange appearance.

"Anne Shirley, what have you done to your hair? Why it's *green!*"

Green it might be called, if it were any earthly color—a queer, dull, bronzy green, with streaks here and there of the original red to heighten the ghastly effect. Never in all her life had Marilla seen anything so grotesque as Anne's hair at that moment.

"Yes, it's green," moaned Anne. "I thought nothing could be as bad as red hair. But now I know it's ten times worse to have green hair. Oh, Marilla, you little know how utterly wretched I am."

"I little know how you got into this fix, but I mean to find out," said Marilla. "Come right down to the kitchen—it's too cold up here—

and tell me just what you've done. I've been expecting something queer for some time. You haven't got into any scrape for over two months, and I was sure another one was due. Now, then, what did you do to your hair?"

"I dyed it."

"Dyed it! Dyed your hair! Anne Shirley, didn't you know it was a wicked thing to do?"

"Yes, I knew it was a little wicked," admitted Anne. "But I thought it was worthwhile to be a little wicked to get rid of red hair. I counted the cost, Marilla. Besides, I meant to be extra good in other ways to make up for it."

"Well," said Marilla sarcastically, "if I'd decided it was worthwhile to dye my hair I'd have dyed it a decent color at least. I wouldn't have dyed it green."

"But I didn't mean to dye it green, Marilla," protested Anne dejectedly. "If I was wicked I meant to be wicked to some purpose. He said it would turn my hair a beautiful raven black—he positively assured me that it would. How could I doubt his word, Marilla? I know what it feels like to have your word doubted. And Mrs. Allan says we should never suspect any one of not telling us the truth unless we have proof that they're not. I have proof now—green hair is proof enough for anybody. But I hadn't then and I believed every word he said *implicitly*."

"Who said? Who are you talking about?"

"The peddler that was here this afternoon. I bought the dye from him."

"Anne Shirley, how often have I told you never to let one of those Italians in the house! I don't believe in encouraging them to come around at all."

"Oh, I didn't let him in the house. I remembered what you told me, and I went out, carefully shut the door, and looked at his things on the step. Besides, he wasn't an Italian—he was a German Jew. He had a big box full of very interesting things and he told me he was working hard to make enough money to bring his wife and children out from Germany. He spoke so feelingly about them that it touched my heart. I wanted to buy something from him to help him in such a worthy object. Then all at once I saw the bottle of hair dye. The peddler said it was warranted to dye any hair a beautiful raven black and wouldn't wash off. In a trice I saw myself with beautiful raven black hair and the temptation was irresistible. But the price of the bottle was seventy-five cents and I had only fifty cents left out of my chicken money. I think the peddler had a very kind heart, for he said that seeing it was me, he'd sell it for fifty cents and that was just giving it away. So I bought it, and as soon as he had gone I came up here and applied it with an old hairbrush as the directions said. I used up the whole bottle, and oh, Marilla, when I saw the dreadful color it turned my hair I repented of being wicked, I can tell you. And I've been repenting ever since."

"Well, I hope you'll repent to good purpose," said Marilla severely, "and that you've got your eyes opened to where your vanity has led you, Anne. Goodness knows what's to be done. I suppose the first thing is to give your hair a good washing and see if that will do any good."

Accordingly, Anne washed her hair, scrubbing it vigorously with soap and water, but for all the difference it made she might as well have been scouring its original red. The peddler had certainly spoken the truth when he declared that the dye wouldn't wash off, however his veracity might be impeached in other respects.

"Oh, Marilla, what shall I do?" questioned Anne in tears. "I can never live this down. People have pretty well forgotten my other mistakes—the liniment cake and setting Diana drunk and flying into a temper with Mrs. Lynde. But they'll never forget this. They will think I am not respectable. Oh, Marilla, 'what a tangled web we weave when first we practice to deceive.' That is poetry, but it is true. And oh, how Josie Pye will laugh! Marilla, I *cannot* face Josie Pye. I am the unhappiest girl in Prince Edward Island."

Anne's unhappiness continued for a week. During that time she went nowhere and shampooed her hair every day. Diana alone of outsiders knew the fatal secret, but she promised solemnly never to tell, and it may be stated here and now that she kept her word. At the end of the week Marilla said decidedly:

"It's no use, Anne. That is fast dye if ever there was any. Your hair must be cut off; there is no other way. You can't go out with it looking like that."

Anne's lips quivered, but she realized the bitter truth of Marilla's remarks. With a dismal sigh she went for the scissors.

"Please cut it off at once, Marilla, and have it over. Oh, I feel that my heart is broken. This is such an unromantic affliction. The girls in books lose their hair in fevers or sell it to get money for some good deed, and I'm sure I wouldn't mind losing my hair in some such fashion half so much. But there is nothing comforting in having your hair cut off because you've dyed it a dreadful color, is there? I'm going to weep all the time you're cutting it off, if it won't interfere. It seems such a tragic thing."

Anne wept then, but later on, when she went upstairs and looked in the glass, she was calm with despair. Marilla had done her work thoroughly and it had been necessary to shingle the hair as closely as possible. The result was not becoming, to state the case as mildly as may be. Anne promptly turned her glass to the wall.

"I'll never, never look at myself again until my hair grows," she exclaimed passionately.

Then she suddenly righted the glass.

"Yes, I will, too. I'll do penance for being wicked that way. I'll look at myself every time I come to my room and see how ugly I am. And I won't try to imagine it away, either. I never thought I was vain about my hair, of all things, but now I know I was, in spite of its being red, because it was so long and thick and curly. I expect something will happen to my nose next."

Anne's clipped head made a sensation in school on the following Monday, but to her relief nobody guessed the real reason for it, not even Josie Pye, who, however, did not fail to inform Anne that she looked like a perfect scarecrow.

"I didn't say anything when Josie said that to me," Anne confided that evening to Marilla, who was lying on the sofa after one of her headaches, "because I thought it was part of my punishment and I ought to bear it patiently. It's hard to be told you look like a scarecrow and I wanted to say something back. But I didn't. I just swept her one scornful look and then I forgave her. It makes you feel very virtuous when you forgive people, doesn't it? I mean to devote all my energies to being good after this and I shall never try to be beautiful again. Of course it's better to be good. I know it is, but it's sometimes so hard to believe a thing even when you know it. I do really want to be good, Marilla, like you and Mrs. Allan and Miss Stacy, and grow up to be a credit to you. Diana says when my hair begins to grow to tie a black velvet ribbon around my head with a bow at one side. She says she thinks it will be very becoming. I will call it a snood—that sounds so romantic. But am I talking too much, Marilla? Does it hurt your head?"

"My head is better now. It was terrible bad this afternoon, though. These headaches of mine are getting worse and worse. I'll have to see a doctor about them. As for your chatter, I don't know that I mind it— I've got so used to it."

Which was Marilla's way of saying that she liked to hear it.

28

An Unfortunate Lily Maid

"Of course you must be Elaine, Anne," said Diana. "I could never have the courage to float down there."

"Nor I," said Ruby Gillis with a shiver. "I don't mind floating down when there's two or three of us in the flat and we can sit up. It's fun then. But to lie down and pretend I was dead—I just couldn't. I'd die really of fright."

"Of course it would be romantic," conceded Jane Andrews. "But I know I couldn't keep still. I'd be popping up every minute or so to see where I was and if I wasn't drifting too far out. And you know, Anne, that would spoil the effect."

"But it's so ridiculous to have a red-headed Elaine," mourned Anne. "I'm not afraid to float down and I'd *love* to be Elaine. But it's ridiculous just the same. Ruby ought to be Elaine because she is so fair and has such lovely long golden hair—Elaine had 'all her bright hair streaming down,' you know. And Elaine was the lily maid. Now, a red-haired person cannot be a lily maid."

"Your complexion is just as fair as Ruby's," said Diana earnestly, "and your hair is ever so much darker than it used to be before you cut it."

"Oh, do you really think so?" exclaimed Anne, flushing sensitively with delight. "I've sometimes thought it was myself—but I never dared to ask any one for fear she would tell me it wasn't. Do you think it could be called auburn now, Diana?"

"Yes, and I think it is real pretty," said Diana, looking admiringly at the short, silky curls that clustered over Anne's head and were held in place by a very jaunty black velvet ribbon and bow.

They were standing on the bank of the pond, below Orchard Slope, where a little headland fringed with birches ran out from the bank; at its tip was a small wooden platform built out into the water for the convenience of fishermen and duck hunters. Ruby and Jane were spending the midsummer afternoon with Diana, and Anne had come over to play with them.

Anne and Diana had spent most of their playtime that summer on and about the pond. Idlewild was a thing of the past, Mr. Bell having ruthlessly cut down the little circle of trees in his back pasture in the spring. Anne had sat among the stumps and wept, not without an eye to the romance of it; but she was speedily consoled, for, after all, as she and Diana said, big girls of thirteen, going on fourteen, were too old for such childish amusements as playhouses, and there were more fascinating sports to be found about the pond. It was splendid to fish for trout over the bridge and the two girls learned to row themselves about in the little flat-bottomed dory Mr. Barry kept for duck shooting.

It was Anne's idea that they dramatize Elaine. They had studied Tennyson's poem in school the preceding winter, the Superintendent of Education having prescribed it in the English course for the Prince Edward Island schools. They had analyzed and parsed it and torn it to pieces in general until it was a wonder there was any meaning at all left in it for them, but at least the fair lily maid and Lancelot and Guinevere and King Arthur had become very real people to them, and Anne was devoured by secret regret that she had not been born in Camelot. Those days, she said, were so much more romantic than the present.

Anne's plan was hailed with enthusiasm. The girls had discovered that if the flat were pushed off from the landing place it would drift down with the current under the bridge and finally strand itself on another headland lower down which ran out at a curve in the pond. They had often gone down like this and nothing could be more convenient for playing Elaine.

"Well, I'll be Elaine," said Anne, yielding reluctantly, for, although she would have been delighted to play the principal character, yet her artistic sense demanded fitness for it and this, she felt, her limitations made impossible. "Ruby, you must be King Arthur and Jane will be Guinevere and Diana must be Lancelot. But first you must be the brothers and the father. We can't have the old dumb servitor because there isn't room for two in the flat when one is lying down. We must pall the barge all its length in blackest samite. That old black shawl of your mother's will be just the thing, Diana."

The black shawl having been procured, Anne spread it over the flat and then lay down on the bottom, with closed eyes and hands folded over her breast.

"Oh, she does look really dead," whispered Ruby Gillis nervously, watching the still, white little face under the flickering shadows of the birches. "It makes me feel frightened, girls. Do you suppose it's really right to act like this? Mrs. Lynde says that all playacting is abominably wicked."

"Ruby, you shouldn't talk about Mrs. Lynde," said Anne severely. "It spoils the effect because this is hundreds of years before Mrs. Lynde was born. Jane, you arrange this. It's silly for Elaine to be talking when she's dead."

Jane rose to the occasion. Cloth of gold for coverlet there was none, but an old piano scarf of yellow Japanese crêpe was an excellent substitute. A white lily was not obtainable just then, but the effect of a tall blue iris placed in one of Anne's folded hands was all that could be desired.

"Now, she's all ready," said Jane. "We must kiss her quiet brows and, Diana, you say, 'Sister, farewell for ever,' and Ruby, you say, 'Farewell, sweet sister,' both of you as sorrowfully as you possibly can. Anne, for goodness sake smile a little. You know Elaine 'lay as though she smiled.' That's better. Now push the flat off."

The flat was accordingly pushed off, scraping roughly over an old embedded stake in the process. Diana and Jane and Ruby only waited long enough to see it caught in the current and headed for the bridge before scampering up through the woods, across the road, and down to the lower headland where, as Lancelot and Guinevere and the King, they were to be in readiness to receive the lily maid.

For a few minutes Anne, drifting slowly down, enjoyed the romance of her situation to the full. Then something happened not at all romantic. The flat began to leak. In a very few moments it was necessary for Elaine to scramble to her feet, pick up her cloth of gold coverlet and pall of blackest samite and gaze blankly at a big crack in the bottom of her barge through which the water was literally pouring. That sharp stake at the landing had torn off the strip of batting nailed on the flat. Anne did not know this, but it did not take her long to realize that she was in a dangerous plight. At this rate the flat would fill and sink long before it could drift to the lower headland. Where were the oars? Left behind at the landing!

Anne gave one gasping little scream which nobody ever heard; she was white to the lips, but she did not lose her self-possession. There was one chance—just one.

"I was horribly frightened," she told Mrs. Allan the next day, "and it seemed like years while the flat was drifting down to the bridge and the water rising in it every moment. I prayed, Mrs. Allan, most earnestly, but I didn't shut my eyes to pray, for I knew the only way God could save me was to let the flat float close enough to one of the bridge piles for me to climb up on it. You know the piles are just old tree trunks and there are lots of knots and old branch stubs on them. It was proper to pray, but I had to do my part by watching out and right well I knew it. I just said, 'Dear God, please take the flat close to a pile and I'll do the rest,' over and over again. Under such circumstances you don't think much about making a flowery prayer. But mine was answered, for the flat bumped right into a pile for a minute and I flung the scarf and the shawl over my shoulder and scrambled up on a big providential stub. And there I was, Mrs. Allan, clinging to that slippery old pile with no way of getting up or down. It was a very unromantic position, but I didn't think about that at the time. You don't think much about romance when you have just escaped from a watery grave. I said a grateful prayer at once and then I gave all my attention to holding on tight, for I knew I should probably have to depend on human aid to get back to dry land."

The flat drifted under the bridge and then promptly sank in midstream. Ruby, Jane, and Diana, already awaiting it on the lower headland, saw it disappear before their very eyes and had not a doubt but that Anne had gone down with it. For a moment they stood still, white as sheets, frozen with horror at the tragedy; then, shrieking at the tops of their voices, they started on a frantic run up through the woods, never pausing as they crossed the main road to glance the way of the bridge. Anne, clinging desperately to her precarious foothold, saw their flying forms and heard their shrieks. Help would soon come, but meanwhile her position was a very uncomfortable one.

The minutes passed by, each seeming an hour to the unfortunate lily maid. Why didn't somebody come? Where had the girls gone? Suppose they had fainted, one and all! Suppose nobody ever came! Suppose she grew so tired and cramped that she could hold on no longer! Anne looked at the wicked green depths below her, wavering with long, oily shadows, and shivered. Her imagination began to suggest all manner of gruesome possibilities to her.

Then, just as she thought she really could not endure the ache in her arms and wrists another moment, Gilbert Blythe came rowing under the bridge in Harmon Andrews' dory!

Gilbert glanced up and, much to his amazement, beheld a little white scornful face looking down upon him with big, frightened but also scornful gray eyes.

"Anne Shirley! How on earth did you get there?" he exclaimed.

Without waiting for an answer he pulled close to the pile and extended his hand. There was no help for it; Anne, clinging to Gilbert Blythe's hand, scrambled down into the dory, where she sat, drabbled and furious, in the stern with her arms full of dripping shawl and wet crêpe. It was certainly extremely difficult to be dignified under the circumstances!

"What has happened, Anne?" asked Gilbert, taking up his oars.

"We were playing Elaine," explained Anne frigidly, without even looking at her rescuer, "and I had to drift down to Camelot in the barge— I mean the flat. The flat began to leak and I climbed out on the pile. The girls went for help. Will you be kind enough to row me to the landing?"

Gilbert obligingly rowed to the landing and Anne, disdaining assistance, sprang nimbly on shore.

"I'm very much obliged to you," she said haughtily as she turned away. But Gilbert had also sprung from the boat and now laid a detaining hand on her arm.

"Anne," he said hurriedly, "look here. Can't we be good friends? I'm awfully sorry I made fun of your hair that time. I didn't mean to vex you and I only meant it for a joke. Besides, it's so long ago. I think your hair is awfully pretty now—honest I do. Let's be friends."

For a moment Anne hesitated. She had an odd, newly awakened consciousness under all her outraged dignity that the half-shy, half-eager expression in Gilbert's hazel eyes was something that was very good to see. Her heart gave a quick, queer little beat. But the bitterness of her old grievance promptly stiffened up her wavering determination. That scene of two years before flashed back into her recollection as vividly as if it had taken place yesterday. Gilbert had called her "carrots" and had brought about her disgrace before the whole school. Her resentment, which to other and older people might be as laughable as its cause, was in no whit allayed and softened by time seemingly. She hated Gilbert Blythe! She would never forgive him!

"No," she said coldly, "I shall never be friends with you, Gilbert Blythe; and I don't want to be!"

"All right!" Gilbert sprang into his skiff with an angry color in his cheeks. "I'll never ask you to be friends again, Anne Shirley. And I don't care either!"

He pulled away with swift defiant strokes, and Anne went up the steep, ferny little path under the maples. She held her head very high, but she was conscious of an odd feeling of regret. She almost wished she had answered Gilbert differently. Of course, he had insulted her terribly, but still—! Altogether, Anne rather thought it would be a relief to sit down and have a good cry. She was really quite unstrung, for the reaction from her fright and cramped clinging was making itself felt.

Halfway up the path she met Jane and Diana rushing back to the pond in a state narrowly removed from positive frenzy. They had found nobody at Orchard Slope, both Mr. and Mrs. Barry being away. Here Ruby Gillis had succumbed to hysterics, and was left to recover from them as best she might, while Jane and Diana flew through the Haunted Wood and across the brook to Green Gables. There they had found nobody either, for Marilla had gone to Carmody and Matthew was making hay in the back field.

"Oh, Anne," gasped Diana, fairly falling on the former's neck and weeping with relief and delight, "Oh, Anne—we thought—you were—drowned—and we felt like murderers—because we had made—you be—Elaine. And Ruby is in hysterics—oh, Anne, how did you escape?"

"I climbed up on one of the piles," explained Anne wearily, "and Gilbert Blythe came along in Mr. Andrews' dory and brought me to land."

"Oh, Anne, how splendid of him! Why, it's so romantic!" said Jane, finding breath enough for utterance at last. "Of course you'll speak to him after this."

"Of course I won't," flashed Anne with a momentary return of her old spirit. "And I don't want ever to hear the word romantic again, Jane Andrews. I'm awfully sorry you were so frightened, girls. It is all my fault. I feel sure I was born under an unlucky star. Everything I do gets me or my dearest friends into a scrape. We've gone and lost your father's flat, Diana, and I have a presentiment that we'll not be allowed to row on the pond any more."

Anne's presentiment proved more trustworthy than presentiments are apt to do. Great was the consternation in the Barry and Cuthbert households when the events of the afternoon became known.

"Will you *ever* have any sense, Anne?" groaned Marilla.

"Oh, yes, I think I will, Marilla," returned Anne optimistically. A good cry, indulged in the grateful solitude of the east gable, had soothed her nerves and restored her to her wonted cheerfulness. "I think my prospects of becoming sensible are brighter now than ever."

"I don't see how," said Marilla.

"Well," explained Anne, "I've learned a new and valuable lesson today. Ever since I came to Green Gables I've been making mistakes, and each mistake has helped to cure me of some great shortcoming. The affair of the amethyst brooch cured me of meddling with things that didn't belong to me. The Haunted Wood mistake cured me of letting my imagination run away with me. The liniment cake mistake cured me of carelessness in cooking. Dyeing my hair cured me of vanity. I never think about my hair and nose now—at least, very seldom. And today's mistake is going to cure me of being too romantic. I have come to the conclusion that it is no use trying to be romantic in Avonlea. It was probably easy enough in towered Camelot hundreds of years ago, but romance is not appreciated now. I feel quite sure that you will soon see a great improvement in me in this respect, Marilla."

"I'm sure I hope so," said Marilla skeptically.

But Matthew, who had been sitting mutely in his corner, laid a hand on Anne's shoulder when Marilla had gone out.

"Don't give up all your romance, Anne," he whispered shyly, "a little of it is a good thing—not too much, of course—but keep a little of it, Anne, keep a little of it."

29

An Epoch in Anne's Life

nne was bringing the cows home from the back pasture by way of Lovers' Lane. It was a September evening and all the gaps and clearings in the woods were brimmed up with ruby sunset light. Here and there the lane was splashed with it, but for the most part it was already quite shadowy beneath the maples, and the spaces under the firs were filled with a clear violet dusk like airy wine. The winds were out in their tops, and there is no sweeter music on earth than that which the wind makes in the fir-trees at evening.

The cows swung placidly down the lane, and Anne followed them dreamily, repeating aloud the battle canto from "Marmion"—which had also been part of their English course the preceding winter and which Miss Stacy had made them learn off by heart—and exulting in its rushing lines and the clash of spears in its imagery. When she came to the lines:

> "The stubborn spearsmen still made good
> Their dark impenetrable wood,"

she stopped in ecstasy to shut her eyes that she might the better fancy herself one of that heroic ring. When she opened them again it was to behold Diana coming through the gate that led into the Barry field and looking so important that Anne instantly divined there was news to be told. But betray too eager curiosity she would not.

"Isn't this evening just like a purple dream, Diana? It makes me so glad to be alive. In the mornings I always think the mornings are best; but when evening comes I think it's lovelier still."

"It's a very fine evening," said Diana, "but oh, I have such news, Anne. Guess. You can have three guesses."

"Charlotte Gillis is going to be married in the church after all and Mrs. Allan wants us to decorate it," cried Anne.

"No. Charlotte's beau won't agree to that, because nobody ever has been married in the church yet, and he thinks it would seem too much like a funeral. It's too mean, because it would be such fun. Guess again."

"Jane's mother is going to let her have a birthday party?"

Diana shook her head, her black eyes dancing with merriment.

"I can't think what it can be," said Anne in despair, "unless it's that Moody Spurgeon MacPherson saw you home from prayer meeting last night. Did he?"

"I should think not," exclaimed Diana indignantly. "I wouldn't be likely to boast of it if he did, the horrid creature! I knew you couldn't guess it. Mother had a letter from Aunt Josephine today, and Aunt Josephine wants you and me to go to town next Tuesday and stop with her for the Exhibition. There!"

"Oh, Diana," whispered Anne, finding it necessary to lean up against a maple tree for support, "do you really mean it? But I'm afraid Marilla won't let me go. She will say that she can't encourage gadding about. That was what she said last week when Jane invited me to go with them in their double-seated buggy to the American concert at the White Sands Hotel. I wanted to go, but Marilla said I'd be better at home learning my lessons and so would Jane. I was bitterly disappointed, Diana. I felt so heart-broken that I wouldn't say my prayers when I went to bed. But I repented of that and got up in the middle of the night and said them."

"I'll tell you," said Diana, "we'll get mother to ask Marilla. She'll be more likely to let you go then; and if she does we'll have the time of our lives, Anne. I've never been to an Exhibition, and it's so aggravating to hear the other girls talking about their trips. Jane and Ruby have been twice, and they're going this year again."

"I'm not going to think about it at all until I know whether I can go or not," said Anne resolutely. "If I did and then was disappointed, it would be more than I could bear. But in case I do go I'm very glad my new coat will be ready by that time. Marilla didn't think I needed a new coat. She said my old one would do very well for another winter and that I ought to be satisfied with having a new dress. The dress is very pretty, Diana—navy blue and made so fashionably. Marilla always makes my dresses fashionably now, because she says she doesn't intend to have Matthew going to Mrs. Lynde to make them. I'm so glad. It is ever so much easier to be good if your clothes are fashionable. At least, it is easier for me. I suppose it doesn't make such a difference to naturally good people. But Matthew said I must have a new coat, so Marilla bought a lovely piece of blue broadcloth, and it's being made by a real dressmaker over at Carmody. It's to be done Saturday night, and I'm trying not to imagine myself walking up the church aisle on Sunday in my new suit and cap, because I'm afraid it isn't right to imagine such things. But it just slips into my mind in spite of me. My cap is so pretty. Matthew bought it for me the day we were over at Carmody. It is one of those little blue velvet ones that are all the rage, with gold cord and tassels. Your new hat is elegant, Diana, and so becoming. When I saw you come into church last Sunday my heart swelled with pride to think you were my dearest friend. Do you suppose it's wrong for us to think so much about our clothes? Marilla says it is very sinful. But it *is* such an interesting subject, isn't it?"

Marilla agreed to let Anne go to town, and it was arranged that Mr. Barry should take the girls in on the following Tuesday. As Charlottetown was thirty miles away and Mr. Barry wished to go and return the same day, it was necessary to make a very early start. But Anne counted it all joy, and was up before sunrise on Tuesday morning. A glance from her window assured her that the day would be fine, for the eastern sky behind the firs of the Haunted Wood was all silvery and cloudless. Through the gap in the trees a light was shining in the western gable of Orchard Slope, a token that Diana was also up.

Anne was dressed by the time Matthew had the fire on and had the breakfast ready when Marilla came down, but for her own part was much too excited to eat. After breakfast the jaunty new cap and jacket were donned, and Anne hastened over the brook and up through the firs to Orchard Slope. Mr. Barry and Diana were waiting for her, and they were soon on the road.

It was a long drive, but Anne and Diana enjoyed every minute of it. It was delightful to rattle along over the moist roads in the early red sunlight that was creeping across the shorn harvest fields. The air was fresh and crisp, and little smoke-blue mists curled through the valleys and floated off from the hills. Sometimes the road went through woods where maples were beginning to hang out scarlet banners; sometimes it crossed rivers on bridges that made Anne's flesh cringe with the old, half-delightful fear; sometimes it wound along a harbor shore and passed by a little cluster of weather-gray fishing huts; again it mounted to hills whence a far sweep of curving upland or misty blue sky could be seen; but wherever it went there was much of interest to discuss. It was almost noon when they reached town and found their way to "Beechwood." It was quite a fine old mansion, set back from the street in a seclusion of green elms and branching beeches. Miss Barry met them at the door with a twinkle in her sharp black eyes.

"So you've come to see me at last, you Anne-girl," she said. "Mercy, child, how you have grown! You're taller than I am, I declare. And you're ever so much better-looking than you used to be, too. But I dare say you know that without being told."

"Indeed I didn't," said Anne radiantly. "I know I'm not so freckled as I used to be, so I've much to be thankful for, but I really hadn't dared to hope there was any other improvement. I'm so glad you think there is, Miss Barry."

Miss Barry's house was furnished with "great magnificence," as Anne told Marilla afterwards. The two little country girls were rather abashed by the splendor of the parlor where Miss Barry left them when she went to see about dinner.

"Isn't it just like a palace?" whispered Diana. "I never was in Aunt Josephine's house before, and I'd no idea it was so grand. I just wish Julia Bell could see this—she puts on such airs about her mother's parlor."

"Velvet carpet," sighed Anne luxuriously, "*and* silk curtains! I've dreamed of such things, Diana. But do you know I don't believe I feel very comfortable with them after all. There are so many things in this room and all so splendid that there is no scope for imagination. That is one consolation when you are poor—there are so many more things you can imagine about."

Their sojourn in town was something that Anne and Diana dated from for years. From first to last it was crowded with delights.

On Wednesday Miss Barry took them to the Exhibition grounds and kept them there all day.

"It was splendid," Anne related to Marilla later on. "I never imagined anything so interesting. I don't really know which department was the most interesting. I think I liked the horses and the flowers and the fancy work best. Josie Pye took first prize for knitted lace. I was real glad she did. And I was glad that I felt glad, for it shows I'm improving, don't you think, Marilla, when I can rejoice in Josie's success? Mr. Harmon Andrews took second prize for Gravenstein apples and Mr. Bell took first prize for a pig. Diana said she thought it was ridiculous for a Sunday school superintendent to take a prize in pigs, but I don't see why. Do you? She said she would always think of it after this when he was praying so solemnly. Clara Louise MacPherson took a prize for painting, and Mrs. Lynde got first prize for homemade butter and cheese. So Avonlea was pretty well represented, wasn't it? Mrs. Lynde was there that day, and I never knew how much I really liked her until I saw her familiar face among all those strangers. There were thousands of people there, Marilla. It made me feel dreadfully insignificant. And Miss Barry took us up to the grand stand to see the horse races. Mrs. Lynde wouldn't go; she said horse racing was an abomination, and she being a church member, thought it her bounden duty to set a good example by staying away. But there were so many there I don't believe Mrs. Lynde's absence would ever be noticed. I don't think, though, that I ought to go very often to horse races, because they *are* awfully fascinating. Diana got so excited that she offered to bet me ten cents that the red horse would win. I didn't believe he would, but I refused to bet, because I wanted to tell Mrs. Allan all about everything, and I felt sure it wouldn't do to tell her that. It's always wrong to do anything you can't tell the minister's wife. It's as good as an extra conscience to have a minister's wife for your friend. And I was very glad I didn't bet, because the red horse *did* win, and I would have lost ten cents. So you see that virtue was its own reward. We saw a man go up in a balloon. I'd love to go up in a balloon, Marilla; it would be simply thrilling; and we saw a man selling fortunes. You paid him ten cents and a little bird picked out your fortune for you. Miss Barry gave Diana and me ten cents each to have our fortunes told. Mine was that I would marry a dark complected man who was very wealthy, and I would go across water to live. I looked carefully at all the dark men I saw after that, but I didn't care much for any of them, and anyhow I suppose it's too early to be looking out for him yet. Oh, it was a never-to-be-forgotten day, Marilla. I was so tired I couldn't sleep at night. Miss Barry put us in the spare room, according to promise. It was an elegant room, Marilla, but somehow sleeping in a spare room isn't what I used to think it was. That's the worst of growing up, and I'm beginning to realize it. The things you wanted so much when you were a child don't seem half so wonderful to you when you get them."

Thursday the girls had a drive in the park, and in the evening Miss Barry took them to a concert in the Academy of Music, where a noted prima donna was to sing. To Anne the evening was a glittering vision of delight.

"Oh, Marilla, it was beyond description. I was so excited I couldn't even talk, so you may know what it was like. I just sat in enraptured silence. Madame Selitsky was perfectly beautiful, and wore white satin and diamonds. But when she began to sing I never thought about anything else. Oh, I can't tell you how I felt. But it seemed to me that it could never be hard to be good any more. I felt like I do when I look up to the stars. Tears came into my eyes, but, oh, they were such happy tears I was so sorry when it was all over, and I told Miss Barry I didn't see how I was ever to return to common life again. She said she thought if we went over to the restaurant across the street and had an ice cream it might help me. That sounded so prosaic; but to my surprise I found it true. The ice cream was delicious, Marilla, and it was so lovely and dissipated to be sitting there eating it at eleven o'clock at night. Diana said she believed she was born for city life. Miss Barry asked me what my opinion was, but I said I would have to think it over very seriously before I could tell her what I really thought. So I thought it over after I went to bed. That is the best time to think things out. And I came to the conclusion, Marilla, that I wasn't born for city life and that I was glad of it. It's nice to be eating ice cream at brilliant restaurants at eleven o'clock at night once in awhile; but as a regular thing I'd rather be in the east gable at eleven, sound asleep, but kind of knowing even in my sleep that the stars were shining outside and that the wind was blowing in the firs across the brook. I told Miss Barry so at breakfast the next morning and she laughed. Miss Barry generally laughed at anything I said, even when I said the most solemn things. I don't think I liked it, Marilla, because I wasn't trying to be funny. But she is a most hospitable lady and treated us royally."

Friday brought going-home time, and Mr. Barry drove in for the girls.

"Well, I hope you've enjoyed yourselves," said Miss Barry, as she bade them good-bye.

"Indeed we have," said Diana.

"And you, Anne-girl?"

"I've enjoyed every minute of the time," said Anne, throwing her arms impulsively about the old woman's neck and kissing her wrinkled cheek. Diana would never have dared to do such a thing, and felt rather aghast at Anne's freedom. But Miss Barry was pleased, and she stood on her veranda and watched the buggy out of sight. Then she went back into her big house with a sigh. It seemed very lonely, lacking those fresh young lives. Miss Barry was a rather selfish old lady, if the truth must be told, and had never cared much for anybody but herself. She valued people only as they were of service to her or amused her. Anne had amused her, and consequently stood high in the old lady's good graces. But Miss Barry found herself thinking less about Anne's quaint speeches than of her fresh enthusiasms, her transparent emotions, her little winning ways, and the sweetness of her eyes and lips.

"I thought Marilla Cuthbert was an old fool when I heard she'd adopted a girl out of an orphan asylum," she said to herself, "but I guess she didn't make much of a mistake after all. If I'd a child like Anne in the house all the time I'd be a better and happier woman."

Anne and Diana found the drive home as pleasant as the drive in—pleasanter, indeed, since there was the delightful consciousness of home waiting at the end of it. It was sunset when they passed through White Sands and turned into the shore road. Beyond, the Avonlea hills came out darkly against the saffron sky. Behind them the moon was rising out of the sea that grew all radiant and transfigured in her light. Every little cove along the curving road was a marvel of dancing ripples. The waves broke with a soft swish on the rocks below them, and the tang of the sea was in the strong, fresh air.

"Oh, but it's good to be alive and to be going home," breathed Anne.

When she crossed the log bridge over the brook the kitchen light of Green Gables winked her a friendly welcome back, and through the open door shone the hearth fire, sending out its warm red glow athwart the chilly autumn night. Anne ran blithely up the hill and into the kitchen, where a hot supper was waiting on the table.

"So you've got back?" said Marilla, folding up her knitting.

"Yes, and, oh, it's so good to be back," said Anne joyously. "I could kiss everything, even to the clock. Marilla, a broiled chicken! You don't mean to say you cooked that for me!"

"Yes, I did," said Marilla. "I thought you'd be hungry after such a drive and need something real appetizing. Hurry and take off your things, and we'll have supper as soon as Matthew comes in. I'm glad you've got back, I must say. It's been fearful lonesome here without you, and I never put in four longer days."

After supper Anne sat before the fire between Matthew and Marilla, and gave them a full account of her visit.

"I've had a splendid time," she concluded happily, "and I feel that it marks an epoch in my life. But the best of it all was the coming home."

30

The Queen's Class is Organized

arilla laid her knitting on her lap and leaned back in her chair. Her eyes were tired, and she thought vaguely that she must see about having her glasses changed the next time she went to town, for her eyes had grown tired very often of late.

It was nearly dark, for the dull November twilight had fallen around Green Gables, and the only light in the kitchen came from the dancing red flames in the stove.

Anne was curled up Turk-fashion on the hearth-rug, gazing into that joyous glow where the sunshine of a hundred summers was being distilled from the maple cordwood. She had been reading, but her book had slipped to the floor, and now she was dreaming, with a smile on her parted lips. Glittering castles in Spain were shaping themselves out of the mists and rainbows of her lively fancy; adventures wonderful and enthralling were happening to her in cloudland—adventures that always turned out triumphantly and never involved her in scrapes like those of actual life.

Marilla looked at her with a tenderness that would never have been suffered to reveal itself in any clearer light than that soft mingling of fireshine and shadow. The lesson of a love that should display itself easily in spoken word and open look was one Marilla could never learn. But she had learned to love this slim, gray-eyed girl with an affection all the deeper and stronger from its very undemonstrativeness. Her love made her afraid of being unduly indulgent, indeed. She had an uneasy feeling that it was rather sinful to set one's heart so intensely on any human creature as she had set hers on Anne, and perhaps she performed a sort of unconscious penance for this by being stricter and more critical than if the girl had been less dear to her. Certainly Anne herself had no idea how Marilla loved her. She sometimes thought wistfully that Marilla was very hard to please and distinctly lacking in sympathy and understanding. But she always checked the thought reproachfully, remembering what she owed to Marilla.

"Anne," said Marilla abruptly, "Miss Stacy was here this afternoon when you were out with Diana."

Anne came back from her other world with a start and a sigh.

"Was she? Oh, I'm so sorry I wasn't in. Why didn't you call me, Marilla? Diana and I were only over in the Haunted Wood. It's lovely in the woods now. All the little wood things—the ferns and the satin leaves and the crackerberries—have gone to sleep, just as if somebody had tucked them away until spring under a blanket of leaves. I think it was a little gray fairy with a rainbow scarf that came tiptoeing along the last moonlight night and did it. Diana wouldn't say much about that, though. Diana has never forgotten the scolding her mother gave her about imagining ghosts into the Haunted Wood. It had a very bad effect on Diana's imagination. It blighted it. Mrs. Lynde says Myrtle Bell is a blighted being. I asked Ruby Gillis why Myrtle was blighted, and Ruby said she guessed it was because her young man had gone back on her. Ruby Gillis thinks of nothing but young men, and the older she gets the worse she is. Young men are all very well in their place, but it doesn't do to drag them into everything, does it? Diana and I are thinking seriously of promising each other that we will never marry but be nice old maids and live together for ever. Diana hasn't quite made up her mind though, because she thinks perhaps it would be nobler to marry some wild, dashing, wicked young man and reform him. Diana and I talk a great deal about serious subjects now, you know. We feel that we are so much older than we used to be that it isn't becoming to talk of childish matters. It's such a solemn thing to be almost fourteen, Marilla. Miss Stacy took all us girls who are in our teens down to the brook last Wednesday, and talked to us about it. She said we couldn't be too careful what habits we formed and what ideals we acquired in our teens, because by the time we were twenty our characters would be developed and the foundation laid for our whole future life. And she said if the foundation was shaky we could never build anything really worthwhile on it. Diana and I talked the matter over coming home from school. We felt extremely solemn, Marilla. And we decided that we would try to be very careful indeed and form respectable habits and learn all we could and be as sensible as possible, so that by the time we were twenty our characters would be properly developed. It's perfectly appalling to think of being twenty, Marilla. It sounds so fearfully old and grown up. But why was Miss Stacy here this afternoon?"

"That is what I want to tell you, Anne, if you'll ever give me a chance to get a word in edgewise. She was talking about you."

"About me?" Anne looked rather scared. Then she flushed and exclaimed:

"Oh, I know what she was saying. I meant to tell you, Marilla, honestly I did, but I forgot. Miss Stacy caught me reading 'Ben Hur' in school yesterday afternoon when I should have been studying my Canadian history. Jane Andrews lent it to me. I was reading it at dinner hour, and I had just got to the chariot-race when school went in. I was simply wild to know how it turned out—although I felt sure 'Ben Hur' must win, because it wouldn't be poetical justice if he didn't—so I spread the history open on my desk-lid and then tucked 'Ben Hur' between the desk and my knee. It just looked as if I were studying Canadian history, you know, while all the while I was reveling in 'Ben Hur.' I was so interested in it that I never noticed Miss Stacy coming down the aisle until all at once I just looked up and there she was looking down at me, so reproachful like. I can't tell you how ashamed I felt, Marilla, especially when I heard Josie Pye giggling. Miss Stacy took 'Ben Hur' away, but she never said a word then. She kept me in at recess and talked to me. She said I had done very wrong in two respects. First, I was wasting the time I ought to have put on my studies; and secondly I was deceiving my teacher in trying to make it appear I was reading a history when it was a storybook instead. I had never realized until that moment, Marilla, that what I was doing was deceitful. I was shocked. I cried bitterly, and asked Miss Stacy to forgive me and I'd never do such a thing again; and I offered to do penance by never so much as looking at 'Ben Hur' for a whole week, not even to see how the chariot-race turned out. But Miss Stacy said she wouldn't require that, and she forgave me freely. So I think it wasn't very kind of her to come up here to you about it after all."

"Miss Stacy never mentioned such a thing to me, Anne, and it's only your guilty conscience that's the matter with you. You have no business to be taking storybooks to school. You read too many novels anyhow. When I was a girl I wasn't so much as allowed to look at a novel."

"Oh, how can you call 'Ben Hur' a novel when it's really such a religious book?" protested Anne. "Of course it's a little too exciting to be proper reading for Sunday, and I only read it on weekdays. And I never read *any* book now unless either Miss Stacy or Mrs. Allan thinks it is a proper book for a girl thirteen and three-quarters to read. Miss Stacy made me promise that. She found me reading a book one day called, 'The Lurid Mystery of the Haunted Hall.' It was one Ruby Gillis had lent me, and, oh, Marilla, it was so fascinating and creepy. It just curdled the blood in my veins. But Miss Stacy said it was a very silly, unwholesome book, and she asked me not to read any more of it or any like it. I didn't mind promising not to read any more like it, but it was *agonizing* to give back that book without knowing how it turned out. But my love for Miss Stacy stood the test and I did. It's really wonderful, Marilla, what you can do when you're truly anxious to please a certain person."

"Well, I guess I'll light the lamp and get to work," said Marilla. "I see plainly that you don't want to hear what Miss Stacy had to say. You're more interested in the sound of your own tongue than in anything else."

"Oh, indeed, Marilla, I do want to hear it," cried Anne contritely. "I won't say another word—not one. I know I talk too much, but I am really trying to overcome it, and although I say far too much, yet if you only knew how many things I want to say and don't, you'd give me some credit for it. Please tell me, Marilla."

"Well, Miss Stacy wants to organize a class among her advanced students who mean to study for the entrance examination into Queen's. She intends to give them extra lessons for an hour after school. And she came to ask Matthew and me if we would like to have you join it. What do you think about it yourself, Anne? Would you like to go to Queen's and pass for a teacher?"

"Oh, Marilla!" Anne straightened to her knees and clasped her hands. "It's been the dream of my life—that is, for the last six months, ever since Ruby and Jane began to talk of studying for the entrance. But I didn't say anything about it, because I supposed it would be perfectly useless. I'd love to be a teacher. But won't it be dreadfully expensive? Mr. Andrews says it cost him one hundred and fifty dollars to put Prissy through, and Prissy wasn't a dunce in geometry."

"I guess you needn't worry about that part of it. When Matthew and I took you to bring up we resolved we would do the best we could for you and give you a good education. I believe in a girl being fitted to earn her own living whether she ever has to or not. You'll always have a home at Green Gables as long as Matthew and I are here, but nobody knows what is going to happen in this uncertain world, and it's just as well to be prepared. So you can join the Queen's class if you like, Anne."

"Oh, Marilla, thank you." Anne flung her arms about Marilla's waist and looked up earnestly into her face. "I'm extremely grateful to you and Matthew. And I'll study as hard as I can and do my very best to be a credit to you. I warn you not to expect much in geometry, but I think I can hold my own in anything else if I work hard."

"I dare say you'll get along well enough. Miss Stacy says you are bright and diligent." Not for worlds would Marilla have told Anne just what Miss Stacy had said about her; that would have been to pamper vanity. "You needn't rush to any extreme of killing yourself over your books. There is no hurry. You won't be ready to try the entrance for a year and a half yet. But it's well to begin in time and be thoroughly grounded, Miss Stacy says."

"I shall take more interest than ever in my studies now," said Anne blissfully, "because I have a purpose in life. Mr. Allan says everybody should have a purpose in life and pursue it faithfully. Only he says we must first make sure that it is a worthy purpose. I would call it a worthy purpose to want to be a teacher like Miss Stacy, wouldn't you, Marilla? I think it's a very noble profession."

The Queen's class was organized in due time. Gilbert Blythe, Anne Shirley, Ruby Gillis, Jane Andrews, Josie Pye, Charlie Sloane, and Moody Spurgeon MacPherson joined it. Diana Barry did not, as her parents did not intend to send her to Queen's. This seemed nothing short of a calamity to Anne. Never, since the night on which Minnie May had had the croup, had she and Diana been separated in anything. On the evening when the Queen's class first remained in school for the extra lessons and Anne saw Diana go slowly out with the others, to walk home alone through the Birch Path and Violet Vale, it was all the former could do to keep her seat and refrain from rushing impulsively after her chum. A lump came into her throat, and she hastily retired behind the pages of her uplifted Latin grammar to hide the tears in her eyes. Not for worlds would Anne have had Gilbert Blythe or Josie Pye see those tears.

"But, oh, Marilla, I really felt that I had tasted the bitterness of death, as Mr. Allan said in his sermon last Sunday, when I saw Diana go out alone," she said mournfully that night. "I thought how splendid it would have been if Diana had only been going to study for the Entrance, too. But we can't have things perfect in this imperfect world, as Mrs. Lynde says. Mrs. Lynde isn't exactly a comforting person sometimes, but there's no doubt she says a great many very true things. And I think the Queen's class is going to be extremely interesting. Jane and Ruby are just going to study to be teachers. That is the height of their ambition. Ruby says she will only teach for two years after she gets through, and then she intends to be married. Jane says she will devote her whole life to teaching, and never, never marry, because you are paid a salary for teaching, but a husband won't pay you anything, and growls if you ask for a share in the egg and butter money. I expect Jane speaks from mournful experience, for Mrs. Lynde says that her father is a perfect old crank, and meaner than second skimmings. Josie Pye says she is just going to college for education's sake, because she won't have to earn her own living; she says of course it is different with orphans who are living on charity—*they* have to hustle. Moody Spurgeon is going to be a minister. Mrs. Lynde says he couldn't be anything else with a name like that to live up to. I hope it isn't wicked of me, Marilla, but really the thought of Moody Spurgeon being a minister makes me laugh. He's such a funny looking boy with that big fat face, and his little blue eyes, and his ears sticking out like flaps. But perhaps he will be more intellectual looking when he grows up. Charlie Sloane says he's going to go into politics and be a member of Parliament, but Mrs. Lynde says he'll never succeed at that, because the Sloanes are all honest people, and it's only rascals that get on in politics nowadays."

"What is Gilbert Blythe going to be?" queried Marilla, seeing that Anne was opening her Caesar.

"I don't happen to know what Gilbert Blythe's ambition in life is—if he has any," said Anne scornfully.

There was open rivalry between Gilbert and Anne now. Previously the rivalry had been rather one-sided, but there was no longer any doubt that Gilbert was as determined to be first in class as Anne was. He was a foeman worthy of her steel. The other members of the class tacitly acknowledged their superiority, and never dreamed of trying to compete with them.

Since the day by the pond when she had refused to listen to his plea for forgiveness, Gilbert, save for the aforesaid determined rivalry, had evinced no recognition whatever of the existence of Anne Shirley. He talked and jested with the other girls, exchanged books and puzzles with them, discussed lessons and plans, sometimes walked home with one or the other of them from prayer meeting or Debating Club. But Anne Shirley he simply ignored, and Anne found out that it is not pleasant to be ignored. It was in vain that she told herself with a toss of her head that she did not care. Deep down in her wayward, feminine little heart she knew that she did care, and that if she had that chance of the Lake of Shining Waters again she would answer very differently. All at once, as it seemed, and to her secret dismay, she found that the old resentment she had cherished against him was gone—gone just when she most needed its sustaining power. It was in vain that she recalled every incident and emotion of that memorable occasion and tried to feel the old satisfying anger. That day by the pond had witnessed its last spasmodic flicker.

Anne realized that she had forgiven and forgotten without knowing it. But it was too late.

And at least neither Gilbert nor anybody else, not even Diana, should ever suspect how sorry she was and how much she wished she hadn't been so proud and horrid! She determined to "shroud her feelings in deepest oblivion," and it may be stated here and now that she did it, so successfully that Gilbert, who possibly was not quite so indifferent as he seemed, could not console himself with any belief that Anne felt his retaliatory scorn. The only poor comfort he had was that she snubbed Charlie Sloane, unmercifully, continually and undeservedly.

Otherwise the winter passed away in a round of pleasant duties and studies. For Anne the days slipped by like golden beads on the necklace of the year. She was happy, eager, interested; there were lessons to be learned and honors to be won; delightful books to read; new pieces to be practiced for the Sunday school choir; pleasant Saturday afternoons at the manse with Mrs. Allan; and then, almost before Anne realized it, spring had come again to Green Gables and all the world was abloom once more.

Studies palled just a wee bit then; the Queen's class, left behind in school while the others scattered to green lanes and leafy wood cuts and meadow byways, looked wistfully out of the windows and discovered that Latin verbs and French exercises had somehow lost the tang and zest they had possessed in the crisp winter months. Even Anne and Gilbert lagged and grew indifferent. Teacher and taught were alike glad when the term was ended and the glad vacation days stretched rosily before them.

"But you've done good work this past year," Miss Stacy told them on the last evening, "and you deserve a good, jolly vacation. Have the best time you can in the out-of-door world and lay in a good stock of health and vitality and ambition to carry you through next year. It will be the tug of war, you know—the last year before the Entrance."

"Are you going to be back next year, Miss Stacy?" asked Josie Pye.

Josie Pye never scrupled to ask questions; in this instance the rest of the class felt grateful to her; none of them would have dared to ask it of Miss Stacy, but all wanted to, for there had been alarming rumors running at large through the school for some time that Miss Stacy was not coming back the next year—that she had been offered a position in the graded school of her own home district and meant to accept. The Queen's class listened in breathless suspense for her answer.

"Yes, I think I will," said Miss Stacy. "I thought of taking another school, but I have decided to come back to Avonlea. To tell the truth, I've grown so interested in my pupils here that I found I couldn't leave them. So I'll stay and see you through."

"Hurrah!" said Moody Spurgeon. Moody Spurgeon had never been so carried away by his feelings before, and he blushed uncomfortably every time he thought about it for a week.

"Oh, I'm so glad," said Anne with shining eyes. "Dear Miss Stacy, it would be perfectly dreadful if you didn't come back. I don't believe I could have the heart to go on with my studies at all if another teacher came here."

When Anne got home that night she stacked all her textbooks away in an old trunk in the attic, locked it, and threw the key into the blanket box.

"I'm not even going to look at a school book in vacation," she told Marilla. "I've studied as hard all the term as I possibly could and I've pored over that geometry until I know every proposition in the first book off by heart, even when the letters *are* changed. I just feel tired of everything sensible and I'm going to let my imagination run riot for the summer. Oh, you needn't be alarmed, Marilla. I'll only let it run riot within reasonable limits. But I want to have a real good jolly time this summer, for maybe it's the last summer I'll be a little girl. Mrs. Lynde says that if I keep stretching out next year as I've done this I'll have to put on longer skirts. She says I'm all running to legs and eyes. And when I put on longer skirts I shall feel that I have to live up to them and be very dignified. It won't even do to believe in fairies then, I'm afraid; so I'm going to believe in them with all my whole heart this summer. I think we're going to have a very gay vacation. Ruby Gillis is going to have a birthday party soon and there's the Sunday-school picnic and the missionary concert next month. And Mr. Barry says that some evening he'll take Diana and me over to the White Sands Hotel and have dinner there. They have dinner there in the evening, you know. Jane Andrews was over once last summer and she says it was a dazzling sight to see the electric lights and the flowers and all the lady guests in such beautiful dresses. Jane says it was her first glimpse into high life and she'll never forget it to her dying day."

Mrs. Lynde came up the next afternoon to find out why Marilla had not been at the Aid meeting on Thursday. When Marilla was not at Aid meeting people knew there was something wrong at Green Gables.

"Matthew had a bad spell with his heart Thursday," Marilla explained, "and I didn't feel like leaving him. Oh, yes, he's all right again now, but he takes them spells oftener than he used to and I'm anxious about him. The doctor says he must be careful to avoid excitement. That's easy enough, for Matthew doesn't go about looking for excitement by any means and never did, but he's not to do any very heavy work either and you might as well tell Matthew not to breathe as not to work. Come and lay off your things, Rachel. You'll stay to tea?"

"Well, seeing you're so pressing, perhaps I might as well stay," said Mrs. Rachel, who had not the slightest intention of doing anything else.

Mrs. Rachel and Marilla sat comfortably in the parlor while Anne got the tea and made hot biscuits that were light and white enough to defy even Mrs. Rachel's criticism.

"I must say Anne has turned out a real smart girl," admitted Mrs. Rachel, as Marilla accompanied her to the end of the lane at sunset. "She must be a great help to you."

"She is," said Marilla, "and she's real steady and reliable now. I used to be afraid she'd never get over her featherbrained ways, but she has and I wouldn't be afraid to trust her in anything now."

"I never would have thought she'd have turned out so well that first day I was here three years ago," said Mrs. Rachel. "Lawful heart, shall I ever forget that tantrum of hers! When I went home that night I says to Thomas, says I, 'Mark my words, Thomas, Marilla Cuthbert'll live to rue the step she's took.' But I was mistaken and I'm real glad of it. I ain't one of those kind of people, Marilla, as can never be brought to own up that they've made a mistake. No, that never was my way, thank goodness. I did make a mistake in judging Anne, but it weren't no wonder, for an odder, unexpecteder witch of a child there never was in this world, that's what. There was no ciphering her out by the rules that worked with other children. It's nothing short of wonderful how she's improved these three years, but especially in looks. She's a real pretty girl got to be, though I can't say I'm overly partial to that pale, big-eyed style myself. I like more snap and color, like Diana Barry has or Ruby Gillis. Ruby Gillis' looks are real showy. But somehow—I don't know how it is but when Anne and them are together, though she ain't half as handsome, she makes them look kind of common and overdone—something like them white June lilies she calls narcissus alongside of the big, red peonies, that's what."

31

Where the Brook and River Meet

Anne had her "good" summer and enjoyed it whole-heartedly. She and Diana fairly lived outdoors, reveling in all the delights that Lovers' Lane and the Dryad's Bubble and Willowmere and Victoria Island afforded. Marilla offered no objections to Anne's gypsyings. The Spencervale doctor who had come the night Minnie May had the croup met Anne at the house of a patient one afternoon early in vacation, looked her over sharply, screwed up his mouth, shook his head, and sent a message to Marilla Cuthbert by another person. It was:

"Keep that redheaded girl of yours in the open air all summer and don't let her read books until she gets more spring into her step."

This message frightened Marilla wholesomely. She read Anne's death warrant by consumption in it unless it was scrupulously obeyed. As a result, Anne had the golden summer of her life as far as freedom and frolic went. She walked, rowed, berried and dreamed to her heart's content; and when September came she was bright-eyed and alert, with a step that would have satisfied the Spencervale doctor and a heart full of ambition and zest once more.

"I feel just like studying with might and main," she declared as she brought her books down from the attic. "Oh, you good old friends, I'm glad to see your honest faces once more—yes, even you, geometry. I've had a perfectly beautiful summer, Marilla, and now I'm rejoicing as a strong man to run a race, as Mr. Allan said last Sunday. Doesn't Mr. Allan preach magnificent sermons? Mrs. Lynde says he is improving every day and the first thing we know some city church will gobble him up and then we'll be left and have to turn to and break in another green preacher. But I don't see the use of meeting trouble halfway, do you, Marilla? I think it would be better just to enjoy Mr. Allan while we have him. If I were a man I think I'd be a minister. They can have such an influence for good, if their theology is sound; and it must be thrilling to preach splendid sermons and stir your hearers' hearts. Why can't women be ministers, Marilla? I asked Mrs. Lynde that and she was shocked and said it would be a scandalous thing. She said there might be female ministers in the States and she believed there was, but thank goodness we hadn't got to that stage in Canada yet and she hoped we never would. But I don't see why. I think women would make splendid ministers. When there is a social to be got up or a church tea or anything else to raise money the women have to turn to and do the work. I'm sure Mrs. Lynde can pray every bit as well as Superintendent Bell and I've no doubt she could preach too with a little practice."

"Yes, I believe she could," said Marilla drily. "She does plenty of unofficial preaching as it is. Nobody has much of a chance to go wrong in Avonlea with Rachel to oversee them."

"Marilla," said Anne in a burst of confidence, "I want to tell you something and ask you what you think about it. It has worried me terribly—on Sunday afternoons, that is, when I think specially about such matters. I do really want to be good; and when I'm with you or Mrs. Allan or Miss Stacy I want it more than ever and I want to do just what would please you and what you would approve of. But mostly when I'm with Mrs. Lynde I feel desperately wicked and as if I wanted to go and do the very thing she tells me I oughtn't to do. I feel irresistibly tempted to do it. Now, what do you think is the reason I feel like that? Do you think it's because I'm really bad and unregenerate?"

Marilla looked dubious for a moment. Then she laughed.

"If you are I guess I am too, Anne, for Rachel often has that very effect on me. I sometimes think she'd have more of an influence for good, as you say yourself, if she didn't keep nagging people to do right. There should have been a special commandment against nagging. But there, I shouldn't talk so. Rachel is a good Christian woman and she means well. There isn't a kinder soul in Avonlea and she never shirks her share of work."

"I'm very glad you feel the same," said Anne decidedly. "It's so encouraging. I sha'n't worry so much over that after this. But I dare say there'll be other things to worry me. They keep coming up new all the time—things to perplex you, you know. You settle one question and there's another right after. There are so many things to be thought over and decided when you're beginning to grow up. It keeps me busy all the time thinking them over and deciding what is right. It's a serious thing to grow up, isn't it, Marilla? But when I have such good friends as you and Matthew and Mrs. Allan and Miss Stacy I ought to grow up successfully, and I'm sure it will be my own fault if I don't. I feel it's a great responsibility because I have only the one chance. If I don't grow up right I can't go back and begin over again. I've grown two inches this summer, Marilla. Mr. Gillis measured me at Ruby's party. I'm so glad you made my new dresses longer. That dark green one is so pretty and it was sweet of you to put on the flounce. Of course I know it wasn't really necessary, but flounces are so stylish this fall and Josie Pye has flounces on all her dresses. I know I'll be able to study better because of mine. I shall have such a comfortable feeling deep down in my mind about that flounce."

"It's worth something to have that," admitted Marilla.

Miss Stacy came back to Avonlea school and found all her pupils eager for work once more. Especially did the Queen's class gird up their loins for the fray, for at the end of the coming year, dimly shadowing their pathway already, loomed up that fateful thing known as "the Entrance," at the thought of which one and all felt their hearts sink into their very shoes. Suppose they did not pass! That thought was doomed to haunt Anne through the waking hours of that winter, Sunday afternoons inclusive, to the almost entire exclusion of moral and theological problems. When Anne had bad dreams she found herself staring miserably at pass lists of the Entrance exams, where Gilbert Blythe's name was blazoned at the top and in which hers did not appear at all.

But it was a jolly, busy, happy swift-flying winter. School work was as interesting, class rivalry as absorbing, as of yore. New worlds of thought, feeling, and ambition, fresh, fascinating fields of unexplored knowledge seemed to be opening out before Anne's eager eyes.

"Hills peeped o'er hill and Alps on Alps arose."

Much of all this was due to Miss Stacy's tactful, careful, broad-minded guidance. She led her class to think and explore and discover for themselves and encouraged straying from the old beaten paths to a degree that quite shocked Mrs. Lynde and the school trustees, who viewed all innovations on established methods rather dubiously.

Apart from her studies Anne expanded socially, for Marilla, mindful of the Spencervale doctor's dictum, no longer vetoed occasional outings. The Debating Club flourished and gave several concerts; there were one or two parties almost verging on grown-up affairs; there were sleigh drives and skating frolics galore.

Between times Anne grew, shooting up so rapidly that Marilla was astonished one day, when they were standing side by side, to find the girl was taller than herself.

"Why, Anne, how you've grown!" she said, almost unbelievingly. A sigh followed on the words. Marilla felt a queer regret over Anne's inches. The child she had learned to love had vanished somehow and here was this tall, serious-eyed girl of fifteen, with the thoughtful brow and the proudly poised little head, in her place. Marilla loved the girl as much as she had loved the child, but she was conscious of a queer sorrowful sense of loss. And that night when Anne had gone to prayer meeting with Diana, Marilla sat alone in the wintry twilight and indulged in the weakness of a cry. Matthew, coming in with a lantern, caught her at it and gazed at her in such consternation that Marilla had to laugh through her tears.

"I was thinking about Anne," she explained. "She's got to be such a big girl—and she'll probably be away from us next winter. I'll miss her terrible."

"She'll be able to come home often," comforted Matthew, to whom Anne was as yet and always would be the little, eager girl he had brought home from Bright River on that June evening four years before. "The branch railroad will be built to Carmody by that time."

"It won't be the same thing as having her here all the time," sighed Marilla gloomily, determined to enjoy her luxury of grief uncomforted. "But there—men can't understand these things!"

There were other changes in Anne no less real than the physical change. For one thing, she became much quieter. Perhaps she thought all the more and dreamed as much as ever, but she certainly talked less. Marilla noticed and commented on this also.

"You don't chatter half as much as you used to, Anne, nor use half as many big words. What has come over you?"

Anne colored and laughed a little, as she dropped her book and looked dreamily out of the window, where big fat red buds were bursting out on the creeper in response to the lure of the spring sunshine.

"I don't know—I don't want to talk as much," she said, denting her chin thoughtfully with her forefinger. "It's nicer to think dear, pretty thoughts and keep them in one's heart, like treasures. I don't like to have them laughed at or wondered over. And somehow I don't want to use big words any more. It's almost a pity, isn't it, now that I'm really growing big enough to say them if I did want to. It's fun to be almost grown up in some ways, but it's not the kind of fun I expected, Marilla. There's so much to learn and do and think that there isn't time for big words. Besides, Miss Stacy says the short ones are much stronger and better. She makes us write all our essays as simply as possible. It was hard at first. I was so used to crowding in all the fine big words I could think of—and I thought of any number of them. But I've got used to it now and I see it's so much better."

"What has become of your story club? I haven't heard you speak of it for a long time."

"The story club isn't in existence any longer. We hadn't time for it—and anyhow I think we had got tired of it. It was silly to be writing about love and murder and elopements and mysteries. Miss Stacy sometimes has us write a story for training in composition, but she won't let us write anything but what might happen in Avonlea in our own lives, and she criticizes it very sharply and makes us criticize our own too. I never thought my compositions had so many faults until I began to look for them myself. I felt so ashamed I wanted to give up altogether, but Miss Stacy said I could learn to write well if I only trained myself to be my own severest critic. And so I am trying to."

"You've only two more months before the Entrance," said Marilla. "Do you think you'll be able to get through?"

Anne shivered.

"I don't know. Sometimes I think I'll be all right—and then I get horribly afraid. We've studied hard and Miss Stacy has drilled us thoroughly, but we mayn't get through for all that. We've each got a stumbling-block. Mine is geometry of course, and Jane's is Latin and Ruby's and Charlie's is algebra and Josie's is arithmetic. Moody Spurgeon says he feels it in his bones that he is going to fail in English history. Miss Stacy is going to give us examinations in June just as hard as we'll have at the Entrance and mark us just as strictly, so we'll have some idea. I wish it was all over, Marilla. It haunts me. Sometimes I wake up in the night and wonder what I'll do if I don't pass."

"Why, go to school next year and try again," said Marilla unconcernedly.

"Oh, I don't believe I'd have the heart for it. It would be such a disgrace to fail, especially if Gil—if the others passed. And I get so nervous in an examination that I'm likely to make a mess of it. I wish I had nerves like Jane Andrews. Nothing rattles her."

Anne sighed and, dragging her eyes from the witcheries of the spring world, the beckoning day of breeze and blue, and the green things upspringing in the garden, buried herself resolutely in her book. There would be other springs, but if she did not succeed in passing the Entrance Anne felt convinced that she would never recover sufficiently to enjoy them.

32

The Pass List is Out

ith the end of June came the close of the term and the close of Miss Stacy's rule in Avonlea school. Anne and Diana walked home that evening feeling very sober indeed. Red eyes and damp handkerchiefs bore convincing testimony to the fact that Miss Stacy's farewell words must have been quite as touching as Mr. Phillips' had been under similar circumstances three years before. Diana looked back at the schoolhouse from the foot of the spruce hill and sighed deeply.

"It does seem as if it was the end of everything, doesn't it?" she said dismally.

"You oughtn't to feel half as badly as I do," said Anne, hunting vainly for a dry spot on her handkerchief. "You'll be back again next winter, but I suppose I've left the dear old school forever—if I have good luck, that is."

"It won't be a bit the same. Miss Stacy won't be there, nor you nor Jane nor Ruby probably. I shall have to sit all alone, for I couldn't bear to have another deskmate after you. Oh, we have had jolly times, haven't we, Anne? It's dreadful to think they're all over."

Two big tears rolled down by Diana's nose.

"If you would stop crying I could," said Anne imploringly. "Just as soon as I put away my hanky I see you brimming up and that starts me off again. As Mrs. Lynde says, 'If you can't be cheerful, be as cheerful as you can.' After all, I dare say I'll be back next year. This is one of the times I *know* I'm not going to pass. They're getting alarmingly frequent."

"Why, you came out splendidly in the exams Miss Stacy gave."

"Yes, but those exams didn't make me nervous. When I think of the real thing you can't imagine what a horrid cold fluttery feeling comes round my heart. And then my number is thirteen and Josie Pye says it's so unlucky. I am *not* superstitious and I know it can make no difference. But still I wish it wasn't thirteen."

"I do wish I were going in with you," said Diana. "Wouldn't we have a perfectly elegant time? But I suppose you'll have to cram in the evenings."

"No; Miss Stacy has made us promise not to open a book at all. She says it would only tire and confuse us and we are to go out walking and not think about the exams at all and go to bed early. It's good advice, but I expect it will be hard to follow; good advice is apt to be, I think. Prissy Andrews told me that she sat up half the night every night of her Entrance week and crammed for dear life; and I had determined to sit up *at least* as long as she did. It was so kind of your Aunt Josephine to ask me to stay at Beechwood while I'm in town."

"You'll write to me while you're in, won't you?"

"I'll write Tuesday night and tell you how the first day goes," promised Anne.

"I'll be haunting the post office Wednesday," vowed Diana.

Anne went to town the following Monday and on Wednesday Diana haunted the post office, as agreed, and got her letter.

"Dearest Diana," wrote Anne, "here it is Tuesday night and I'm writing this in the library at Beechwood. Last night I was horribly lonesome all alone in my room and wished so much you were with me. I couldn't 'cram' because I'd promised Miss Stacy not to, but it was as hard to keep from opening my history as it used to be to keep me from reading a story before my lessons were learned.

"This morning Miss Stacy came for me and we went to the Academy, calling for Jane and Ruby and Josie on our way. Ruby asked me to feel her hands and they were cold as ice. Josie said I looked as if I hadn't slept a wink and she didn't believe I was strong enough to stand the grind of the teacher's course even if I did get through. There are times and seasons even yet when I don't feel that I've made any great headway in learning to like Josie Pye!

"When we reached the Academy there were scores of students

there from all over the island. The first person we saw was Moody Spurgeon sitting on the steps and muttering away to himself. Jane asked him what on earth he was doing and he said he was repeating the multiplication table over and over to steady his nerves and for pity's sake not to interrupt him, because if he stopped for a moment he got frightened and forgot everything he ever knew, but the multiplication table kept all his facts firmly in their proper place!

"When we were assigned to our rooms Miss Stacy had to leave us. Jane and I sat together and Jane was so composed that I envied her. No need of the multiplication table for good, steady, sensible Jane! I wondered if I looked as I felt and if they could hear my heart thumping clear across the room. Then a man came in and began distributing the English examination sheets. My hands grew cold then and my head fairly whirled round as I picked it up. Just one awful moment,— Diana, I felt exactly as I did four years ago when I asked Marilla if I might stay at Green Gables—and then everything cleared up in my mind and my heart began beating again—I forgot to say that it had stopped altogether!—for I knew I could do something with *that* paper anyhow.

"At noon we went home for dinner and then back again for history in the afternoon. The history was a pretty hard paper and I got dreadfully mixed up in the dates. Still, I think I did fairly well today. But oh, Diana, tomorrow the geometry exam comes off and when I think of it it takes every bit of determination I possess to keep from opening my Euclid. If I thought the multiplication table would help me any I would recite it from now till tomorrow morning.

"I went down to see the other girls this evening. On my way I met Moody Spurgeon wandering distractedly around. He said he knew he had failed in history and he was born to be a disappointment to his parents and he was going home on the morning train; and it would be easier to be a carpenter than a minister, anyhow. I cheered him up and persuaded him to stay to the end because it would be unfair to Miss Stacy if he didn't. Sometimes I wished I was born a boy, but when I see Moody Spurgeon I'm always glad I'm a girl and not his sister.

"Ruby was in hysterics when I reached their boarding-house; she had just discovered a fearful mistake she had made in her English paper. When she recovered we went up-town and had an ice-cream. How we wished you had been with us.

"Oh, Diana, if only the geometry examination were over! But there, as Mrs. Lynde would say, the sun will go on rising and setting whether I fail in geometry or not. That is true but not especially comforting. I think I'd rather it *didn't* go on if I failed!

"Yours devotedly.

"ANNE."

The geometry examination and all the others were over in due time and Anne arrived home on Friday evening, rather tired but with an air of chastened triumph about her. Diana was over at Green Gables when she arrived and they met as if they had been parted for years.

"You old darling, it's perfectly splendid to see you back again. It seems like an age since you went to town and oh, Anne, how did you get along?"

"Pretty well, I think, in everything but the geometry. I don't know whether I passed in it or not and I have a creepy, crawly presentiment that I didn't. Oh, how good it is to be back! Green Gables is the dearest, loveliest spot in the world."

"How did the others do?"

"The girls say they know they didn't pass, but I think they did pretty well. Josie says the geometry was so easy a child of ten could do it! Moody Spurgeon still thinks he failed in history and Charlie says he failed in algebra. But we don't really know anything about it and won't until the pass list is out. That won't be for a fortnight. Fancy living a fortnight in such suspense! I wish I could go to sleep and never wake up until it is over."

Diana knew it would be useless to ask how Gilbert Blythe had fared, so she merely said:

"Oh, you'll pass all right. Don't worry."

"I'd rather not pass at all than not come out pretty well up on the list," flashed Anne, by which she meant—and Diana knew she meant—

that success would be incomplete and bitter if she did not come out ahead of Gilbert Blythe.

With this end in view Anne had strained every nerve during the examinations. So had Gilbert. They had met and passed each other on the street a dozen times without any sign of recognition and every time Anne had held her head a little higher and wished a little more earnestly that she had made friends with Gilbert when he asked her, and vowed a little more determinedly to surpass him in the examination. She knew that all Avonlea junior was wondering which would come out first; she even knew that Jimmy Glover and Ned Wright had a bet on the question and that Josie Pye had said there was no doubt in the world that Gilbert would be first; and she felt that her humiliation would be unbearable if she failed.

But she had another and nobler motive for wishing to do well. She wanted to "pass high" for the sake of Matthew and Marilla—especially Matthew. Matthew had declared to her his conviction that she "would beat the whole Island." That, Anne felt, was something it would be foolish to hope for even in the wildest dreams. But she did hope fervently that she would be among the first ten at least, so that she might see Matthew's kindly brown eyes gleam with pride in her achievement. That, she felt, would be a sweet reward indeed for all her hard work and patient grubbing among unimaginative equations and conjugations.

At the end of the fortnight Anne took to "haunting" the post office also, in the distracted company of Jane, Ruby and Josie, opening the Charlottetown dailies with shaking hands and cold, sinkaway feelings as bad as any experienced during the Entrance week. Charlie and Gilbert were not above doing this too, but Moody Spurgeon stayed resolutely away.

"I haven't got the grit to go there and look at a paper in cold blood," he told Anne. "I'm just going to wait until somebody comes and tells me suddenly whether I've passed or not."

When three weeks had gone by without the pass list appearing Anne began to feel that she really couldn't stand the strain much longer. Her appetite failed and her interest in Avonlea doings languished. Mrs. Lynde wanted to know what else you could expect with a Tory superintendent of education at the head of affairs, and Matthew, noting Anne's paleness and indifference and the lagging steps that bore her home from the post office every afternoon, began seriously to wonder if he hadn't better vote Grit at the next election.

But one evening the news came. Anne was sitting at her open window, for the time forgetful of the woes of examinations and the cares of the world, as she drank in the beauty of the summer dusk, sweet-scented with flower-breaths from the garden below and sibilant and rustling from the stir of poplars. The eastern sky above the firs was flushed faintly pink from the reflection of the west, and Anne was wondering dreamily if the spirit of color looked like that, when she saw Diana come flying down through the firs, over the log bridge, and up the slope, with a fluttering newspaper in her hand.

Anne sprang to her feet, knowing at once what that paper contained. The pass list was out! Her head whirled and her heart beat until it hurt her. She could not move a step. It seemed an hour to her before Diana came rushing along the hall and burst into the room without even knocking, so great was her excitement.

"Anne, you've passed," she cried, "passed the *very first*—you and Gilbert both—you're ties—but your name is first. Oh, I'm so proud!"

Diana flung the paper on the table and herself on Anne's bed, utterly breathless and incapable of further speech. Anne lighted the lamp, oversetting the match-safe and using up half a dozen matches before her shaking hands could accomplish the task. Then she snatched up the paper. Yes, she had passed—there was her name at the very top of a list of two hundred! That moment was worth living for.

"You did just splendidly, Anne," puffed Diana, recovering sufficiently to sit up and speak, for Anne, starry-eyed and rapt, had not uttered a word. "Father brought the paper home from Bright River not ten minutes ago—it came out on the afternoon train, you know, and won't be here till tomorrow by mail—and when I saw the pass list I just rushed over like a wild thing. You've all passed, every one of you, Moody Spurgeon and all, although he's conditioned in history. Jane and Ruby did pretty well—they're half-way up—and so did Charlie. Josie just scraped through with three marks to spare, but you'll see she'll put on as many airs as if she'd led. Won't Miss Stacy be delighted? Oh, Anne, what does it feel like to see your name at the head of a pass list like that? If it were me I know I'd go crazy with joy. I am pretty near crazy as it is, but you're as calm and cool as a spring evening."

"I'm just dazzled inside," said Anne. "I want to say a hundred things, and I can't find words to say them in. I never dreamed of this— yes, I did, too, just once! I let myself think *once,* 'What if I should come out first?' quakingly, you know, for it seemed so vain and presumptuous to think I could lead the Island. Excuse me a minute, Diana. I must run right out to the field to tell Matthew. Then we'll go up the road and tell the good news to the others."

They hurried to the hayfield below the barn where Matthew was coiling hay, and, as luck would have it, Mrs. Lynde was talking to Marilla at the lane fence.

"Oh, Matthew," exclaimed Anne, "I've passed and I'm first—or one of the first! I'm not vain, but I'm thankful."

"Well now, I always said it," said Matthew, gazing at the pass list delightedly. "I knew you could beat them all easy."

"You've done pretty well, I must say, Anne," said Marilla, trying to hide her extreme pride in Anne from Mrs. Rachel's critical eye. But that good soul said heartily:

"I just guess she has done well, and far be it from me to be backward in saying it. You're a credit to your friends, Anne, that's what, and we're all proud of you."

That night Anne, who had wound up a delightful evening by a serious little talk with Mrs. Allan at the manse, knelt sweetly by her open window in a great sheen of moonshine and murmured a prayer of gratitude and aspiration that came straight from her heart. There was in it thankfulness for the past and reverent petition for the future; and when she slept on her white pillow her dreams were as fair and bright and beautiful as maidenhood might desire.

33

The Hotel Concert

"Put on your white organdy, by all means, Anne," advised Diana decidedly.

They were together in the east gable chamber; outside it was only twilight—a lovely yellowish-green twilight with a clear blue cloudless sky. A big round moon, slowly deepening from her pallid luster into burnished silver, hung over the Haunted Wood; the air was full of sweet summer sounds—sleepy birds twittering, freakish breezes, far-away voices and laughter. But in Anne's room the blind was drawn and the lamp lighted, for an important toilet was being made.

The east gable was a very different place from what it had been on that night four years before, when Anne had felt its bareness penetrate to the marrow of her spirit with its inhospitable chill. Changes had crept in, Marilla conniving at them resignedly, until it was as sweet and dainty a nest as a young girl could desire.

The velvet carpet with the pink roses and the pink silk curtains of Anne's early visions had certainly never materialized; but her dreams had kept pace with her growth, and it is not probable she lamented them. The floor was covered with a pretty matting, and the curtains that softened the high window and fluttered in the vagrant breezes were of pale green art muslin. The walls, hung not with gold and silver brocade tapestry, but with a dainty apple blossom paper, were adorned with a few good pictures given Anne by Mrs. Allan. Miss Stacy's photograph occupied the place of honor, and Anne made a sentimental point of keeping fresh flowers on the bracket under it. Tonight a spike of white lilies faintly perfumed the room like the dream of a fragrance. There was no "mahogany furniture," but there was a white-painted bookcase filled with books, a cushioned wicker rocker, a toilet table befrilled with white muslin, a quaint, gilt-framed mirror with chubby pink cupids and purple grapes painted over its arched top, that used to hang in the spare room, and a low white bed.

Anne was dressing for a concert at the White Sands Hotel. The guests had got it up in aid of the Charlottetown hospital, and had hunted out all the available amateur talent in the surrounding districts to help it along. Bertha Sampson and Pearl Clay of the White Sands Baptist choir had been asked to sing a duet; Milton Clark of Newbridge was to give a violin solo; Winnie Adella Blair of Carmody was to sing a Scotch ballad; and Laura Spencer of Spencervale and Anne Shirley of Avonlea were to recite.

As Anne would have said at one time, it was "an epoch in her life," and she was deliciously athrill with the excitement of it. Matthew was in the seventh heaven of gratified pride over the honor conferred on his Anne, and Marilla was not far behind, although she would have died rather than admit it, and said she didn't think it was very proper for a lot of young folks to be gadding over to the hotel without any responsible person with them.

Anne and Diana were to drive over with Jane Andrews and her brother Billy in their double-seated buggy; and several other Avonlea girls and boys were going, too. There was a party of visitors expected out from town, and after the concert a supper was to be given to the performers.

"Do you really think the organdy will be best?" queried Anne anxiously. "I don't think it's as pretty as my blue-flowered muslin—and it certainly isn't so fashionable."

"But it suits you ever so much better," said Diana. "It's so soft and frilly and clinging. The muslin is stiff, and makes you look too dressed up. But the organdy seems as if it grew on you."

Anne sighed and yielded. Diana was beginning to have a reputation for notable taste in dressing, and her advice on such subjects was much sought after. She was looking very pretty herself on this particular night in a dress of the lovely wild-rose pink, from which Anne was forever debarred; but she was not to take any part in the concert, so her appearance was of minor importance. All her pains were bestowed upon Anne, who, she vowed, must, for the credit of Avonlea, be dressed and combed and adorned to the queen's taste.

"Pull out that frill a little more—so, here, let me tie your sash; now for your slippers. I'm going to braid your hair in two thick braids, and tie them halfway up with big white bows—no, don't pull out a single curl over your forehead—just have the soft part. There is no way you do your hair suits you so well, Anne, and Mrs. Allan says you look like a Madonna when you part it so. I shall fasten this little white house rose just behind your ear. There was just one on my bush, and I saved it for you."

"Shall I put my pearl beads on?" asked Anne. "Matthew brought me a string from town last week, and I know he'd like to see them on me."

Diana pursed up her lips, put her black head on one side critically, and finally pronounced in favor of the beads, which were thereupon tied around Anne's slim milk white throat.

"There's something so stylish about you, Anne," said Diana, with unenvious admiration. "You hold your head with such an air. I suppose it's your figure. I am just a dumpling. I've always been afraid of it, and now I know it is so. Well, I suppose I shall just have to resign myself to it."

"But you have such dimples," said Anne, smiling affectionately into the pretty, vivacious face so near her own. "Lovely dimples, like little dents in cream. I have given up all hope of dimples. My dimple-dream will never come true; but so many of my dreams have that I mustn't complain. Am I all ready now?"

"All ready," assured Diana, as Marilla appeared in the doorway, a gaunt figure with grayer hair than of yore and no fewer angles, but with a much softer face. "Come right in and look at our elocutionist, Marilla. Doesn't she look lovely?"

Marilla emitted a sound between a sniff and a grunt.

"She looks neat and proper. I like that way of fixing her hair. But I expect she'll ruin that dress driving over there in the dust and dew with it, and it looks most too thin for these damp nights. Organdy's the most unserviceable stuff in the world anyhow, and I told Matthew so when he got it. But there is no use in saying anything to Matthew nowadays. Time was when he would take my advice, but now he just buys things for Anne regardless, and the clerks at Carmody know they can palm anything off on him. Just let them tell him a thing is pretty and fashionable, and Matthew plunks his money down for it. Mind you keep your skirt clear of the wheel, Anne, and put your warm jacket on."

Then Marilla stalked downstairs, thinking proudly how sweet Anne looked, with that

"One moonbeam from the forehead to the crown"

and regretting that she could not go to the concert herself to hear her girl recite.

"I wonder if it *is* too damp for my dress," said Anne anxiously.

"Not a bit of it," said Diana, pulling up the window blind. "It's a perfect night, and there won't be any dew. Look at the moonlight."

"I'm so glad my window looks east into the sunrising," said Anne, going over to Diana. "It's so splendid to see the morning coming up over those long hills and glowing through those sharp fir tops. It's new every morning, and I feel as if I washed my very soul in that bath of earliest sunshine. Oh, Diana, I love this little room so dearly. I don't know how I'll get along without it when I go to town next month."

"Don't speak of your going away tonight," begged Diana. "I don't want to think of it, it makes me so miserable, and I do want to have a good time this evening. What are you going to recite, Anne? And are you nervous?"

"Not a bit. I've recited so often in public I don't mind at all now. I've decided to give 'The Maiden's Vow.' It's so pathetic. Laura Spencer is going to give a comic recitation, but I'd rather make people cry than laugh."

"What will you recite if they encore you?"

"They won't dream of encoring me," scoffed Anne, who was not without her own secret hopes that they would, and already visioned herself telling Matthew all about it at the next morning's breakfast-table. "There are Billy and Jane now—I hear the wheels. Come on."

Billy Andrews insisted that Anne should ride on the front seat with him, so she unwillingly climbed up. She would have much preferred to sit back with the girls, where she could have laughed and chattered to her heart's content. There was not much of either laughter or chatter in Billy. He was a big, fat, stolid youth of twenty, with a round, expressionless face, and a painful lack of conversational gifts. But he admired Anne immensely, and was puffed up with pride over the prospect of driving to White Sands with that slim, upright figure beside him.

Anne, by dint of talking over her shoulder to the girls and occasionally passing a sop of civility to Billy—who grinned and chuckled and never could think of any reply until it was too late—contrived to enjoy the drive in spite of all. It was a night for enjoyment. The road was full of buggies, all bound for the hotel, and laughter, silver-clear, echoed and re-echoed along it. When they reached the hotel it was a blaze of light from top to bottom. They were met by the ladies of the concert committee, one of whom took Anne off to the performers' dressing room, which was filled with the members of a Charlottetown Symphony Club, among whom Anne felt suddenly shy and frightened and countrified. Her dress, which, in the east gable, had seemed so dainty and pretty, now seemed simple and plain—too simple and plain, she thought, among all the silks and laces that glistened and rustled around her. What were her pearl beads compared to the diamonds of the big, handsome lady near her? And how poor her one wee white rose must look beside all the hot house flowers the others wore! Anne laid her hat and jacket away, and shrank miserably into a corner. She wished herself back in the white room at Green Gables.

It was still worse on the platform of the big concert hall of the hotel, where she presently found herself. The electric lights dazzled her eyes, the perfume and hum bewildered her. She wished she were sitting down in the audience with Diana and Jane, who seemed to be having a splendid time away at the back. She was wedged in between a stout lady in pink silk and a tall, scornful looking girl in a white lace dress. The stout lady occasionally turned her head squarely around and surveyed Anne through her eyeglasses until Anne, acutely sensitive of being so scrutinized, felt that she must scream aloud; and the white lace girl kept talking audibly to her next neighbor about the "country bumpkins" and "rustic belles" in the audience, languidly anticipating "such fun" from the displays of local talent on the program. Anne believed that she would hate that white lace girl to the end of life.

Unfortunately for Anne, a professional elocutionist was staying at the hotel and had consented to recite. She was a lithe, dark-eyed woman in a wonderful gown of shimmering gray stuff like woven moonbeams, with gems on her neck and in her dark hair. She had a marvelously flexible voice and wonderful power of expression; the audience went wild over her selection. Anne, forgetting all about herself and her troubles for the time, listened with rapt and shining eyes; but when the recitation ended she suddenly put her hands over her face. She could never get up and recite after that—never. Had she ever thought she could recite? Oh, if she were only back at Green Gables!

At this unpropitious moment her name was called. Somehow, Anne—who did not notice the rather guilty little start of surprise the white lace girl gave, and would not have understood the subtle compliment implied therein if she had—got on her feet, and moved dizzily out to the front. She was so pale that Diana and Jane, down in the audience, clasped each other's hands in nervous sympathy.

Anne was the victim of an overwhelming attack of stage fright. Often as she had recited in public, she had never before faced such an audience as this, and the sight of it paralyzed her energies completely. Everything was so strange, so brilliant, so bewildering—the rows of ladies in evening dress, the critical faces, the whole atmosphere of wealth and culture about her. Very different this from the plain benches at the Debating Club, filled with the homely, sympathetic faces of friends and neighbors. These people, she thought, would be merciless critics. Perhaps, like the white lace girl, they anticipated amusement from her "rustic" efforts. She felt hopelessly, helplessly ashamed and miserable. Her knees trembled, her heart fluttered, a horrible faintness came over her; not a word could she utter, and the next moment she would have fled from the platform despite the humiliation which, she felt, must ever after be her portion if she did so.

But suddenly, as her dilated, frightened eyes gazed out over the audience, she saw Gilbert Blythe away at the back of the room, bending forward with a smile on his face—a smile which seemed to Anne at once triumphant and taunting. In reality it was nothing of the kind. Gilbert was merely smiling with appreciation of the whole affair in general and of the effect produced by Anne's slender white form and spiritual face against a background of palms in particular. Josie Pye, whom he had driven over, sat beside him, and her face certainly was both triumphant and taunting. But Anne did not see Josie, and would not have cared if she had. She drew a long breath and flung her head up proudly, courage and determination tingling over her like an electric shock. She *would not* fail before Gilbert Blythe—he should never be able to laugh at her, never, never! Her fright and nervousness vanished; and she began her recitation, her clear, sweet voice reaching to the farthest corner of the room without a tremor or a break. Self-possession was fully restored to her, and in the reaction from that horrible moment of powerlessness she recited as she had never done before. When she finished there were bursts of honest applause. Anne, stepping back to her seat, blushing with shyness and delight, found her hand vigorously clasped and shaken by the stout lady in pink silk.

"My dear, you did splendidly," she puffed. "I've been crying like a baby, actually I have. There, they're encoring you—they're bound to have you back!"

"Oh, I can't go," said Anne confusedly. "But yet—I must, or Matthew will be disappointed. He said they would encore me."

"Then don't disappoint Matthew," said the pink lady, laughing.

Smiling, blushing, limpid-eyed, Anne tripped back and gave a quaint, funny little selection that captivated her audience still further. The rest of the evening was quite a little triumph for her.

When the concert was over, the stout pink lady—who was the wife of an American millionaire—took her under her wing, and introduced her to everybody; and everybody was very nice to her. The professional elocutionist, Mrs. Evans, came and chatted with her, telling her that she had a charming voice and "interpreted" her selections beautifully. Even the white lace girl paid her a languid little compliment. They had supper in the big, beautifully decorated dining-room; Diana and Jane were invited to partake of this, also, since they had come with Anne, but Billy was nowhere to be found, having decamped in mortal fear of some such invitation. He was in waiting for them, with the team, however, when it was all over, and the three girls came merrily out into the calm, white moonshine radiance. Anne breathed deeply, and looked into the clear sky beyond the dark boughs of the firs.

Oh, it was good to be out again in the purity and silence of the night! How great and still and wonderful everything was, with the murmur of the sea sounding through it and the darkling cliffs beyond like grim giants guarding enchanted coasts.

"Hasn't it been a perfectly splendid time?" sighed Jane, as they drove away. "I just wish I was a rich American and could spend my summer at a hotel and wear jewels and low-necked dresses and have ice cream and chicken salad every blessed day. I'm sure it would be ever so much more fun than teaching school. Anne, your recitation was simply great, although I thought at first you were never going to begin. I think it was better than Mrs. Evans'."

"Oh, no, don't say things like that, Jane," said Anne quickly, "because it sounds silly. It couldn't be better than Mrs. Evans,' you know, for she is a professional, and I'm only a schoolgirl, with a little knack of reciting. I'm quite satisfied if the people just liked mine pretty well."

"I've a compliment for you, Anne," said Diana. "At least I think it must be a compliment because of the tone he said it in. Part of it was anyhow. There was an American sitting behind Jane and me—such a romantic looking man, with coal-black hair and eyes. Josie Pye says he is a distinguished artist, and that her mother's cousin in Boston is married to a man that used to go to school with him. Well, we heard him say—didn't we, Jane?—Who is that girl on the platform with the splendid Titian hair? She has a face I should like to paint.' There now, Anne. But what does Titian hair mean?"

"Being interpreted it means plain red, I guess," laughed Anne. "Titian was a very famous artist who liked to paint red-haired women."

"*Did* you see all the diamonds those ladies wore?" sighed Jane. "They were simply dazzling. Wouldn't you just love to be rich, girls?"

"We *are* rich," said Anne staunchly. "Why, we have sixteen years to our credit, and we're happy as queens, and we've all got imaginations, more or less. Look at that sea, girls—all silver and shadow and vision of things not seen. We couldn't enjoy its loveliness any more if we had millions of dollars and ropes of diamonds. You wouldn't change into any of those women if you could. Would you want to be that white lace girl and wear a sour look all your life, as if you'd been born turning up your nose at the world? Or the pink lady, kind and nice as she is, so stout and short that you'd really no figure at all? Or even Mrs. Evans, with that sad, sad look in her eyes? She must have been dreadfully unhappy sometime to have such a look. You *know* you wouldn't, Jane Andrews!"

"I *don't* know—exactly," said Jane unconvinced. "I think diamonds would comfort a person for a good deal."

"Well, I don't want to be any one but myself, even if I go uncomforted by diamonds all my life," declared Anne. "I'm quite content to be Anne of Green Gables, with my string of pearl beads. I know Matthew gave me as much love with them as ever went with Madame the Pink Lady's jewels."

34

A Queen's Girl

he next three weeks were busy ones at Green Gables, for Anne was getting ready to go to Queen's, and there was much sewing to be done, and many things to be talked over and arranged. Anne's outfit was ample and pretty, for Matthew saw to that, and Marilla for once made no objections whatever to anything he purchased or suggested. More—one evening she went up to the east gable with her arms full of a delicate pale green material.

"Anne, here's something for a nice light dress for you. I don't suppose you really need it; you've plenty of pretty waists; but I thought maybe you'd like something real dressy to wear if you were asked out anywhere of an evening in town, to a party or anything like that. I hear that Jane and Ruby and Josie have got 'evening dresses,' as they call them, and I don't mean you shall be behind them. I got Mrs. Allan to help me pick it in town last week, and we'll get Emily Gillis to make it for you. Emily has got taste, and her fits aren't to be equaled."

"Oh, Marilla, it's just lovely," said Anne. "Thank you so much. I don't believe you ought to be so kind to me—it's making it harder every day for me to go away."

The green dress was made up with as many tucks and frills and shirrings as Emily's taste permitted. Anne put it on one evening for Matthew's and Marilla's benefit, and recited "The Maiden's Vow" for them in the kitchen. As Marilla watched the bright, animated face and graceful motions her thoughts went back to the evening Anne had arrived at Green Gables, and memory recalled a vivid picture of the odd, frightened child in her preposterous yellowish-brown wincey dress, the heartbreak looking out of her tearful eyes. Something in the memory brought tears to Marilla's own eyes.

"I declare, my recitation has made you cry, Marilla," said Anne gaily, stooping over Marilla's chair to drop a butterfly kiss on that lady's cheek. "Now, I call that a positive triumph."

"No, I wasn't crying over your piece," said Marilla, who would have scorned to be betrayed into such weakness by any "poetry stuff." "I just couldn't help thinking of the little girl you used to be, Anne. And I was wishing you could have stayed a little girl, even with all your queer ways. You've grown up now and you're going away; and you look so tall and stylish and so—so—different altogether in that dress—as if you didn't belong in Avonlea at all—and I just got lonesome thinking it all over."

"Marilla!" Anne sat down on Marilla's gingham lap, took Marilla's lined face between her hands, and looked gravely and tenderly into Marilla's eyes. "I'm not a bit changed—not really. I'm only just pruned down and branched out. The real *me*—back here—is just the same. It won't make a bit of difference where I go or how much I change outwardly; at heart I shall always be your little Anne, who will love you and Matthew and dear Green Gables more and better every day of her life."

Anne laid her fresh young cheek against Marilla's faded one, and reached out a hand to pat Matthew's shoulder. Marilla would have given much just then to have possessed Anne's power of putting her feelings into words; but nature and habit had willed it otherwise, and she could only put her arms close about her girl and hold her tenderly to her heart, wishing that she need never let her go.

Matthew, with a suspicious moisture in his eyes, got up and went out-of-doors. Under the stars of the blue summer night he walked agitatedly across the yard to the gate under the poplars.

"Well now, I guess she ain't been much spoiled," he muttered, proudly. "I guess my putting in my oar occasional never did much harm after all. She's smart and pretty, and loving, too, which is better than all the rest. She's been a blessing to us, and there never was a luckier mistake than what Mrs. Spencer made—if it *was* luck. I don't believe it was any such thing. It was Providence, because the Almighty saw we needed her, I reckon."

The day finally came when Anne must go to town. She and

Matthew drove in one fine September morning, after a tearful parting with Diana and an untearful, practical one—on Marilla's side at least—with Marilla. But when Anne had gone Diana dried her tears and went to a beach picnic at White Sands with some of her Carmody cousins, where she contrived to enjoy herself tolerably well; while Marilla plunged fiercely into unnecessary work and kept at it all day long with the bitterest kind of a heartache—the ache that burns and gnaws and cannot wash itself away in ready tears. But that night, when Marilla went to bed, acutely and miserably conscious that the little gable room at the end of the hall was untenanted by any vivid young life and unstirred by any soft breathing, she buried her face in her pillow, and wept for her girl in a passion of sobs that appalled her when she grew calm enough to reflect how very wicked it must be to take on so about a sinful fellow creature.

Anne and the rest of the Avonlea scholars reached town just in time to hurry off to the Academy. That first day passed pleasantly enough in a whirl of excitement, meeting all the new students, learning to know the professors by sight and being assorted and organized into classes. Anne intended taking up the Second Year work, being advised to do so by Miss Stacy; Gilbert Blythe elected to do the same. This meant getting a First Class teacher's license in one year instead of two, if they were successful; but it also meant much more and harder work. Jane, Ruby, Josie, Charlie, and Moody Spurgeon, not being troubled with the stirrings of ambition, were content to take up the Second Class work. Anne was conscious of a pang of loneliness when she found herself in a room with fifty other students, not one of whom she knew, except the tall, brown-haired boy across the room; and knowing him in the fashion she did, did not help her much, as she reflected pessimistically. Yet she was undeniably glad that they were in the same class; the old rivalry could still be carried on, and Anne would hardly have known what to do if it had been lacking.

"I wouldn't feel comfortable without it," she thought. "Gilbert looks awfully determined. I suppose he's making up his mind, here and now, to win the medal. What a splendid chin he has! I never noticed it before. I do wish Jane and Ruby had gone in for First Class, too. I suppose I won't feel so much like a cat in a strange garret when I get acquainted, though. I wonder which of the girls here are going to be my friends. It's really an interesting speculation. Of course I promised Diana that no Queen's girl, no matter how much I liked her, should ever be as dear to me as she is; but I've lots of second-best affections to bestow. I like the look of that girl with the brown eyes and the crimson waist. She looks vivid and red-rosy; there's that pale, fair one gazing out of the window. She has lovely hair, and looks as if she knew a thing or two about dreams. I'd like to know them both—know them well—well enough to walk with my arm about their waists, and call them nicknames. But just now I don't know them and they don't know me, and probably don't want to know me particularly. Oh, it's lonesome!"

It was lonesomer still when Anne found herself alone in her hall bedroom that night at twilight. She was not to board with the other girls, who all had relatives in town to take pity on them. Miss Josephine Barry would have liked to board her, but Beechwood was so far from the Academy that it was out of the question; so Miss Barry hunted up a boarding-house, assuring Matthew and Marilla that it was the very place for Anne.

"The lady who keeps it is a reduced gentlewoman," explained Miss Barry. "Her husband was a British officer, and she is very careful what sort of boarders she takes. Anne will not meet with any objectionable persons under her roof. The table is good, and the house is near the Academy, in a quiet neighborhood."

All this might be quite true, and indeed, proved to be so, but it did not materially help Anne in the first agony of homesickness that seized upon her. She looked dismally about her narrow little room, with its dull-papered, pictureless walls, its small iron bedstead and empty bookcase; and a horrible choke came into her throat as she thought of her own white room at Green Gables, where she would have the pleasant consciousness of a great green still outdoors, of sweet peas growing in the garden, and moonlight falling on the orchard, of the brook below the slope and the spruce boughs tossing in the night wind beyond it, of a vast starry sky, and the light from Diana's window shining out through the gap in the trees. Here there was nothing of this; Anne knew that outside of her window was a hard street, with a network of telephone wires shutting out the sky, the tramp of alien feet, and a thousand lights gleaming on stranger faces. She knew that she was going to cry, and fought against it.

"I *won't* cry. It's silly—and weak—there's the third tear splashing down by my nose. There are more coming! I must think of something funny to stop them. But there's nothing funny except what is connected with Avonlea, and that only makes things worse—four—five— I'm going home next Friday, but that seems a hundred years away. Oh, Matthew is nearly home by now—and Marilla is at the gate, looking down the lane for him—six—seven—eight—oh, there's no use in counting them! They're coming in a flood presently. I can't cheer up— I don't *want* to cheer up. It's nicer to be miserable!"

The flood of tears would have come, no doubt, had not Josie Pye appeared at that moment. In the joy of seeing a familiar face Anne forgot that there had never been much love lost between her and Josie. As a part of Avonlea life even a Pye was welcome.

"I'm so glad you came up," Anne said sincerely.

"You've been crying," remarked Josie, with aggravating pity. "I suppose you're homesick—some people have so little self-control in that respect. I've no intention of being homesick, I can tell you. Town's too jolly after that poky old Avonlea. I wonder how I ever existed there so long. You shouldn't cry, Anne; it isn't becoming, for your nose and eyes get red, and then you seem *all* red. I'd a perfectly scrumptious time in the Academy today. Our French professor is simply a duck. His moustache would give you kerwollops of the heart. Have you anything eatable around, Anne? I'm literally starving. Ah, I guessed likely Marilla'd load you up with cake. That's why I called round. Otherwise I'd have gone to the park to hear the band play with Frank Stockley. He boards same place as I do, and he's a sport. He noticed you in class today, and asked me who the red-headed girl was. I told him you were an orphan that the Cuthberts had adopted, and nobody knew very much about what you'd been before that."

Anne was wondering if, after all, solitude and tears were not more satisfactory than Josie Pye's companionship when Jane and Ruby appeared, each with an inch of Queen's color ribbon—purple and scarlet—pinned proudly to her coat. As Josie was not "speaking" to Jane just then she had to subside into comparative harmlessness.

"Well," said Jane with a sigh, "I feel as if I'd lived many moons since the morning. I ought to be home studying my Virgil—that horrid old professor gave us twenty lines to start in on tomorrow. But I simply couldn't settle down to study tonight. Anne, methinks I see the traces of tears. If you've been crying *do* own up. It will restore my self-respect, for I was shedding tears freely before Ruby came along. I don't mind being a goose so much if somebody else is goosey, too. Cake? You'll give me a teeny piece, won't you? Thank you. It has the real Avonlea flavor."

Ruby, perceiving the Queen's calendar lying on the table, wanted to know if Anne meant to try for the gold medal.

Anne blushed and admitted she was thinking of it.

"Oh, that reminds me," said Josie, "Queen's is to get one of the Avery scholarships after all. The word came today. Frank Stockley told me—his uncle is one of the board of governors, you know. It will be announced in the Academy tomorrow."

An Avery scholarship! Anne felt her heart beat more quickly, and the horizons of her ambition shifted and broadened as if by magic. Before Josie had told the news Anne's highest pinnacle of aspiration had been a teacher's provincial license, Class First, at the end of the year, and perhaps the medal! But now in one moment Anne saw herself winning the Avery scholarship, taking an Arts course at Redmond College, and graduating in a gown and mortar-board, all before the echo of Josie's words had died away. For the Avery scholarship was in English, and Anne felt that here her foot was on her native heath.

A wealthy manufacturer of New Brunswick had died and left part of his fortune to endow a large number of scholarships to be distributed among the various high schools and academics of the Maritime Provinces, according to their respective standings. There had been much doubt whether one would be allotted to Queen's, but the matter was settled at last, and at the end of the year the graduate who made the highest mark in English and English literature would win the scholarship—two hundred and fifty dollars a year for four years at Redmond College. No wonder that Anne went to bed that night with tingling cheeks!

"I'll win that scholarship if hard work can do it," she resolved. "Wouldn't Matthew be proud if I got to be a B. A.? Oh, it's delightful to have ambitions. I'm so glad I have such a lot. And there never seems to be any end to them—that's the best of it. Just as soon as you attain to one ambition you see another one glittering higher up still. It does make life so interesting."

The Winter at Queen's

nne's homesickness wore off, greatly helped in the wearing by her weekend visits home. As long as the open weather lasted the Avonlea students went out to Carmody on the new branch railway every Friday night. Diana and several other Avonlea young folks were generally on hand to meet them and they all walked over to Avonlea in a merry party. Anne thought those Friday evening gypsyings over the autumnal hills in the crisp golden air, with the home-lights of Avonlea twinkling beyond, were the best and dearest hours in the whole week.

Gilbert Blythe nearly always walked with Ruby Gillis and carried her satchel for her. Ruby was a very handsome young lady, now thinking herself quite as grown up as she really was; she wore her skirts as long as her mother would let her and did her hair up in town, though she had to take it down when she went home. She had large, bright-blue eyes, a brilliant complexion, and a plump showy figure. She laughed a great deal, was cheerful and good-tempered, and enjoyed the pleasant things of life frankly.

"But I shouldn't think she was the sort of girl Gilbert would like," whispered Jane to Anne. Anne did not think so either, but she would not have said so for the Avery scholarship. She could not help thinking, too, that it would be very pleasant to have such a friend as Gilbert to jest and chatter with and exchange ideas about books and studies and ambitions. Gilbert had ambitions, she knew, and Ruby Gillis did not seem the sort of person with whom such could be profitably discussed.

There was no silly sentiment in Anne's ideas concerning Gilbert. Boys were to her, when she thought about them at all, merely possible good comrades. If she and Gilbert had been friends she would not have cared how many other friends he had nor with whom he walked. She had a genius for friendship; girl friends she had in plenty; but she had a vague consciousness that masculine friendship might also be a good thing to round out one's conceptions of companionship and furnish broader standpoints of judgment and comparison. Not that Anne could have put her feelings on the matter into just such clear definition. But she thought that if Gilbert had ever walked home with her from the train, over the crisp fields and along the ferny byways, they might have had many and merry and interesting conversations about the new world that was opening around them and their hopes and ambitions therein. Gilbert was a clever young fellow, with his own thoughts about things and a determination to get the best out of life and put the best into it. Ruby Gillis told Jane Andrews that she didn't understand half the things Gilbert Blythe said; he talked just like Anne Shirley did when she had a thoughtful fit on and for her part she didn't think it any fun to be bothering about books and that sort of thing when you didn't have to. Frank Stockley had lots more dash and go, but then he wasn't half as good-looking as Gilbert and she really couldn't decide which she liked best!

In the Academy Anne gradually drew a little circle of friends about her, thoughtful, imaginative, ambitious students like herself. With the "rose-red" girl, Stella Maynard, and the "dream girl," Priscilla Grant, she soon became intimate, finding the latter pale spiritual-looking maiden to be full to the brim of mischief and pranks and fun, while the vivid, black-eyed Stella had a heartful of wistful dreams and fancies, as aerial and rainbow-like as Anne's own.

After the Christmas holidays the Avonlea students gave up going home on Fridays and settled down to hard work. By this time all the Queen's scholars had gravitated into their own places in the ranks and the various classes had assumed distinct and settled shadings of individuality. Certain facts had become generally accepted. It was admitted that the medal contestants had practically narrowed down to three—Gilbert Blythe, Anne Shirley, and Lewis Wilson; the Avery scholarship was more doubtful, any one of a certain six being a possible winner. The bronze medal for mathematics was considered as good

as won by a fat, funny little up-country boy with a bumpy forehead and
a patched coat.

Ruby Gillis was the handsomest girl of the year at the Academy;
in the Second Year classes Stella Maynard carried off the palm for
beauty, with small but critical minority in favor of Anne Shirley. Ethel
Marr was admitted by all competent judges to have the most stylish
modes of hairdressing, and Jane Andrews—plain, plodding, conscientious Jane—carried off the honors in the domestic science course. Even
Josie Pye attained a certain preeminence as the sharpest-tongued
young lady in attendance at Queen's. So it may be fairly stated that Miss
Stacy's old pupils held their own in the wider arena of the academical
course.

Anne worked hard and steadily. Her rivalry with Gilbert was as
intense as it had ever been in Avonlea school, although it was not
known in the class at large, but somehow the bitterness had gone out
of it. Anne no longer wished to win for the sake of defeating Gilbert;
rather, for the proud consciousness of a well-won victory over a worthy foeman. It would be worthwhile to win, but she no longer thought
life would be insupportable if she did not.

In spite of lessons the students found opportunities for pleasant
times. Anne spent many of her spare hours at Beechwood and generally ate her Sunday dinners there and went to church with Miss Barry.
The latter was, as she admitted, growing old, but her black eyes were
not dim nor the vigor of her tongue in the least abated. But she never
sharpened the latter on Anne, who continued to be a prime favorite
with the critical old lady.

"That Anne-girl improves all the time," she said. "I get tired of
other girls—there is such a provoking and eternal sameness about
them. Anne has as many shades as a rainbow and every shade is the
prettiest while it lasts. I don't know that she is as amusing as she was
when she was a child, but she makes me love her and I like people
who make me love them. It saves me so much trouble in making
myself love them."

Then, almost before anybody realized it, spring had come; out in
Avonlea the Mayflowers were peeping pinkly out on the sere barrens

where snow-wreaths lingered; and the "mist of green" was on the woods and in the valleys. But in Charlottetown harassed Queen's students thought and talked only of examinations.

"It doesn't seem possible that the term is nearly over," said Anne. "Why, last fall it seemed so long to look forward to—a whole winter of studies and classes. And here we are, with the exams looming up next week. Girls, sometimes I feel as if those exams meant everything, but when I look at the big buds swelling on those chestnut trees and the misty blue air at the end of the streets they don't seem half so important."

Jane and Ruby and Josie, who had dropped in, did not take this view of it. To them the coming examinations were constantly very important indeed—far more important than chestnut buds or Maytime hazes. It was all very well for Anne, who was sure of passing at least, to have her moments of belittling them, but when your whole future depended on them—as the girls truly thought theirs did—you could not regard them philosophically.

"I've lost seven pounds in the last two weeks," sighed Jane. "It's no use to say don't worry. I *will* worry. Worrying helps you some—it seems as if you were doing something when you're worrying. It would be dreadful if I failed to get my license after going to Queen's all winter and spending so much money."

"*I* don't care," said Josie Pye. "If I don't pass this year I'm coming back next. My father can afford to send me. Anne, Frank Stockley says that Professor Tremaine said Gilbert Blythe was sure to get the medal and that Emily Clay would likely win the Avery scholarship."

"That may make me feel badly tomorrow, Josie," laughed Anne, "but just now I honestly feel that as long as I know the violets are coming out all purple down in the hollow below Green Gables and that little ferns are poking their heads up in Lovers' Lane, it's not a great deal of difference whether I win the Avery or not. I've done my best and I begin to understand what is meant by the 'joy of the strife.' Next to trying and winning, the best thing is trying and failing. Girls, don't talk about exams! Look at that arch of pale green sky over those houses and picture to yourselves what it must look like over the purply-dark beech-woods back of Avonlea."

"What are you going to wear for commencement, Jane?" asked Ruby practically.

Jane and Josie both answered at once and the chatter drifted into a side eddy of fashions. But Anne, with her elbows on the window sill, her soft cheek laid against her clasped hands, and her eyes filled with visions, looked out unheedingly across city roof and spire to that glorious dome of sunset sky and wove her dreams of a possible future from the golden tissue of youth's own optimism. All the Beyond was hers with its possibilities lurking rosily in the oncoming year—each year a rose of promise to be woven into an immortal chaplet.

36

The Glory and the Dream

n the morning when the final results of all the examinations were to be posted on the bulletin board at Queen's, Anne and Jane walked down the street together. Jane was smiling and happy; examinations were over and she was comfortably sure she had made a pass at least; further considerations troubled Jane not at all; she had no soaring ambitions and consequently was not affected with the unrest attendant thereon. For we pay a price for everything we get or take in this world; and although ambitions are well worth having, they are not to be cheaply won, but exact their dues of work and self-denial, anxiety and discouragement. Anne was pale and quiet; in ten more minutes she would know who had won the medal and who the Avery. Beyond those ten minutes there did not seem, just then, to be anything worth being called Time.

"Of course you'll win one of them anyhow," said Jane, who couldn't understand how the faculty could be so unfair as to order it otherwise.

"I have no hope of the Avery," said Anne. "Everybody says Emily Clay will win it. And I'm not going to march up to that bulletin board and look at it before everybody. I haven't the moral courage. I'm going straight to the girls' dressing room. You must read the announcements and then come and tell me, Jane. And I implore you in the name of our old friendship to do it as quickly as possible. If I have failed just say so, without trying to break it gently; and whatever you do *don't* sympathize with me. Promise me this, Jane."

Jane promised solemnly; but, as it happened, there was no necessity for such a promise. When they went up the entrance steps of Queen's they found the hall full of boys who were carrying Gilbert

Blythe around on their shoulders and yelling at the tops of their voices, "Hurrah for Blythe, Medalist!"

For a moment Anne felt one sickening pang of defeat and disappointment. So she had failed and Gilbert had won! Well, Matthew would be sorry—he had been so sure she would win.

And then!

Somebody called out:

"Three cheers for Miss Shirley, winner of the Avery!"

"Oh, Anne," gasped Jane, as they fled to the girls' dressing room amid hearty cheers. "Oh, Anne, I'm so proud! Isn't it splendid?"

And then the girls were around them and Anne was the center of a laughing, congratulating group. Her shoulders were thumped and her hands shaken vigorously. She was pushed and pulled and hugged and among it all she managed to whisper to Jane:

"Oh, won't Matthew and Marilla be pleased! I must write the news home right away."

Commencement was the next important happening. The exercises were held in the big assembly hall of the Academy. Addresses were given, essays read, songs sung, the public award of diplomas, prizes and medals made.

Matthew and Marilla were there, with eyes and ears for only one student on the platform—a tall girl in pale green, with faintly flushed cheeks and starry eyes, who read the best essay and was pointed out and whispered about as the Avery winner.

"Reckon you're glad we kept her, Marilla?" whispered Matthew, speaking for the first time since he had entered the hall, when Anne had finished her essay.

"It's not the first time I've been glad," retorted Marilla. "You do like to rub things in, Matthew Cuthbert."

Miss Barry, who was sitting behind them, leaned forward and poked Marilla in the back with her parasol.

"Aren't you proud of that Anne-girl? I am," she said.

Anne went home to Avonlea with Matthew and Marilla that evening. She had not been home since April and she felt that she could not wait another day. The apple blossoms were out and the world was fresh and young. Diana was at Green Gables to meet her. In her own white room, where Marilla had set a flowering house rose on the window sill, Anne looked about her and drew a long breath of happiness.

"Oh, Diana, it's so good to be back again. It's so good to see those pointed firs coming out against the pink sky—and that white orchard and the old Snow Queen. Isn't the breath of the mint delicious? And that tea rose—why, it's a song and a hope and a prayer all in one. And it's *good* to see you again, Diana!"

"I thought you liked that Stella Maynard better than me," said Diana reproachfully. "Josie Pye told me you did. Josie said you were *infatuated* with her."

Anne laughed and pelted Diana with the faded "June lilies" of her bouquet.

"Stella Maynard is the dearest girl in the world except one and you are that one, Diana," she said. "I love you more than ever—and I've so many things to tell you. But just now I feel as if it were joy enough to sit here and look at you. I'm tired, I think—tired of being studious and ambitious. I mean to spend at least two hours tomorrow lying out in the orchard grass, thinking of absolutely nothing."

"You've done splendidly, Anne. I suppose you won't be teaching now that you've won the Avery?"

"No. I'm going to Redmond in September. Doesn't it seem wonderful? I'll have a brand new stock of ambition laid in by that time after three glorious, golden months of vacation. Jane and Ruby are going to teach. Isn't it splendid to think we all got through even to Moody Spurgeon and Josie Pye?"

"The Newbridge trustees have offered Jane their school already," said Diana. "Gilbert Blythe is going to teach, too. He has to. His father can't afford to send him to college next year, after all, so he means to earn his own way through. I expect he'll get the school here if Miss Ames decides to leave."

Anne felt a queer little sensation of dismayed surprise. She had not known this; she had expected that Gilbert would be going to Redmond also. What would she do without their inspiring rivalry?

Would not work, even at a coeducational college with a real degree in prospect, be rather flat without her friend the enemy?

The next morning at breakfast it suddenly struck Anne that Matthew was not looking well. Surely he was much grayer than he had been a year before.

"Marilla," she said hesitatingly when he had gone out, "is Matthew quite well?"

"No, he isn't," said Marilla in a troubled tone. "He's had some real bad spells with his heart this spring and he won't spare himself a mite. I've been real worried about him, but he's some better this while back and we've got a good hired man, so I'm hoping he'll kind of rest and pick up. Maybe he will now you're home. You always cheer him up."

Anne leaned across the table and took Marilla's face in her hands.

"You are not looking as well yourself as I'd like to see you, Marilla. You look tired. I'm afraid you've been working too hard. You must take a rest, now that I'm home. I'm just going to take this one day off to visit all the dear old spots and hunt up my old dreams, and then it will be your turn to be lazy while I do the work."

Marilla smiled affectionately at her girl.

"It's not the work—it's my head. I've a pain so often now—behind my eyes. Doctor Spencer's been fussing with glasses, but they don't do me any good. There is a distinguished oculist coming to the Island the last of June and the doctor says I must see him. I guess I'll have to. I can't read or sew with any comfort now. Well, Anne, you've done real well at Queen's I must say. To take First Class License in one year and win the Avery scholarship—well, well, Mrs. Lynde says pride goes before a fall and she doesn't believe in the higher education of women at all; she says it unfits them for woman's true sphere. I don't believe a word of it. Speaking of Rachel reminds me—did you hear anything about the Abbey Bank lately, Anne?"

"I heard that it was shaky," answered Anne. "Why?"

"That is what Rachel said. She was up here one day last week and said there was some talk about it. Matthew felt real worried. All we have saved is in that bank—every penny. I wanted Matthew to put it in the Savings Bank in the first place, but old Mr. Abbey was a great friend of father's and he'd always banked with him. Matthew said any bank with him at the head of it was good enough for anybody."

"I think he has only been its nominal head for many years," said Anne. "He is a very old man; his nephews are really at the head of the institution."

"Well, when Rachel told us that, I wanted Matthew to draw our money right out and he said he'd think of it. But Mr. Russell told him yesterday that the bank was all right."

Anne had her good day in the companionship of the outdoor world. She never forgot that day; it was so bright and golden and fair, so free from shadow and so lavish of blossom. Anne spent some of its rich hours in the orchard; she went to the Dryad's Bubble and Willowmere and Violet Vale; she called at the manse and had a satisfying talk with Mrs. Allan; and finally in the evening she went with Matthew for the cows, through Lovers' Lane to the back pasture. The woods were all gloried through with sunset and the warm splendor of it streamed down through the hill gaps in the west. Matthew walked slowly with bent head; Anne, tall and erect, suited her springing step to his.

"You've been working too hard today, Matthew," she said reproachfully. "Why won't you take things easier?"

"Well now, I can't seem to," said Matthew, as he opened the yard gate to let the cows through. "It's only that I'm getting old, Anne, and keep forgetting it. Well, well, I've always worked pretty hard and I'd rather drop in harness."

"If I had been the boy you sent for," said Anne wistfully, "I'd be able to help you so much now and spare you in a hundred ways. I could find it in my heart to wish I had been, just for that."

"Well now, I'd rather have you than a dozen boys, Anne," said Matthew patting her hand. "Just mind you that—rather than a dozen boys. Well now, I guess it wasn't a boy that took the Avery scholarship, was it? It was a girl—my girl—my girl that I'm proud of."

He smiled his shy smile at her as he went into the yard. Anne took the memory of it with her when she went to her room that night and sat for a long while at her open window, thinking of the past and dreaming of the future. Outside the Snow Queen was mistily white in the moonshine; the frogs were singing in the marsh beyond Orchard Slope. Anne always remembered the silvery, peaceful beauty and fragrant calm of that night. It was the last night before sorrow touched her life; and no life is ever quite the same again when once that cold, sanctifying touch has been laid upon it.

37

The Reaper Whose Name is Death

"Matthew—Matthew—what is the matter? Matthew, are you sick?"

It was Marilla who spoke, alarm in every jerky word. Anne came through the hall, her hands full of white narcissus,—it was long before Anne could love the sight or odor of white narcissus again,—in time to hear her and to see Matthew standing in the porch doorway, a folded paper in his hand, and his face strangely drawn and gray. Anne dropped her flowers and sprang across the kitchen to him at the same moment as Marilla. They were both too late; before they could reach him Matthew had fallen across the threshold.

"He's fainted," gasped Marilla. "Anne, run for Martin—quick, quick! He's at the barn."

Martin, the hired man, who had just driven home from the post office, started at once for the doctor, calling at Orchard Slope on his way to send Mr. and Mrs. Barry over. Mrs. Lynde, who was there on an errand, came too. They found Anne and Marilla distractedly trying to restore Matthew to consciousness.

Mrs. Lynde pushed them gently aside, tried his pulse, and then laid her ear over his heart. She looked at their anxious faces sorrowfully and the tears came into her eyes.

"Oh, Marilla," she said gravely. "I don't think—we can do anything for him."

"Mrs. Lynde, you don't think—you can't think Matthew is—is" Anne could not say the dreadful word; she turned sick and pallid.

"Child, yes, I'm afraid of it. Look at his face. When you've seen that look as often as I have you'll know what it means."

Anne looked at the still face and there beheld the seal of the Great Presence.

When the doctor came he said that death had been instantaneous and probably painless, caused in all likelihood by some sudden shock. The secret of the shock was discovered to be in the paper Matthew had held and which Martin had brought from the office that morning. It contained an account of the failure of the Abbey Bank.

The news spread quickly through Avonlea, and all day friends and neighbors thronged Green Gables and came and went on errands of kindness for the dead and living. For the first time shy, quiet Matthew Cuthbert was a person of central importance; the white majesty of death had fallen on him and set him apart as one crowned.

When the calm night came softly down over Green Gables the old house was hushed and tranquil. In the parlor lay Matthew Cuthbert in his coffin, his long gray hair framing his placid face on which there was a little kindly smile as if he but slept, dreaming pleasant dreams. There were flowers about him—sweet old-fashioned flowers which his mother had planted in the homestead garden in her bridal days and for which Matthew had always had a secret, wordless love. Anne had gathered them and brought them to him, her anguished, tearless eyes burning in her white face. It was the last thing she could do for him.

The Barrys and Mrs. Lynde stayed with them that night. Diana, going to the east gable, where Anne was standing at her window, said gently:

"Anne dear, would you like to have me sleep with you tonight?"

"Thank you, Diana." Anne looked earnestly into her friend's face. "I think you won't misunderstand me when I say that I want to be alone. I'm not afraid. I haven't been alone one minute since it happened—and I want to be. I want to be quite silent and quiet and try to realize it. I *can't* realize it. Half the time it seems to me that Matthew can't be dead; and the other half it seems as if he must have been dead for a long time and I've had this horrible dull ache ever since."

Diana did not quite understand. Marilla's impassioned grief, breaking all the bounds of natural reserve and lifelong habit in its stormy rush, she could comprehend better than Anne's tearless agony.

But she went away kindly, leaving Anne alone to keep her first vigil with sorrow.

Anne hoped that tears would come in solitude. It seemed to her a terrible thing that she could not shed a tear for Matthew, whom she had loved so much and who had been so kind to her, Matthew, who had walked with her last evening at sunset and was now lying in the dim room below with that awful peace on his brow. But no tears came at first, even when she knelt by her window in the darkness and prayed, looking up to the stars beyond the hills—no tears, only the same horrible dull ache of misery that kept on aching until she fell asleep, worn out with the day's pain and excitement.

In the night she awakened, with the stillness and the darkness about her, and the recollection of the day came over her like a wave of sorrow. She could see Matthew's face smiling at her as he had smiled when they parted at the gate that last evening—she could hear his voice saying, "My girl—my girl that I'm proud of." Then the tears came and Anne wept her heart out. Marilla heard her and crept in to comfort her.

"There—there—don't cry so, dearie. It can't bring him back. It—it—isn't right to cry so. I knew that today, but I couldn't help it then. He'd always been such a good, kind brother to me—but God knows best."

"Oh, just let me cry, Marilla," sobbed Anne. "The tears don't hurt me like that ache did. Stay here for a little while with me and keep your arm round me—so. I couldn't have Diana stay, she's good and kind and sweet—but it's not her sorrow—she's outside of it and she couldn't come close enough to my heart to help me. It's our sorrow—yours and mine. Oh, Marilla, what will we do without him?"

"We've got each other, Anne. I don't know what I'd do if you weren't here—if you'd never come. Oh, Anne, I know I've been kind of strict and harsh with you maybe—but you mustn't think I didn't love you as well as Matthew did, for all that. I want to tell you now when I can. It's never been easy for me to say things out of my heart, but at times like this it's easier. I love you as dear as if you were my own flesh and blood and you've been my joy and comfort ever since you came to Green Gables."

Two days afterwards they carried Matthew Cuthbert over his homestead threshold and away from the fields he had tilled and the orchards he had loved and the trees he had planted; and then Avonlea settled back to its usual placidity and even at Green Gables affairs slipped into their old groove and work was done and duties fulfilled with regularity as before, although always with the aching sense of "loss in all familiar things." Anne, new to grief, thought it almost sad that it could be so—that they *could* go on in the old way without Matthew. She felt something like shame and remorse when she discovered that the sunrises behind the firs and the pale pink buds opening in the garden gave her the old inrush of gladness when she saw them— that Diana's visits were pleasant to her and that Diana's merry words and ways moved her to laughter and smiles—that, in brief, the beautiful world of blossom and love and friendship had lost none of its power to please her fancy and thrill her heart, that life still called to her with many insistent voices.

"It seems like disloyalty to Matthew, somehow, to find pleasure in these things now that he has gone," she said wistfully to Mrs. Allan one evening when they were together in the manse garden. "I miss him so much—all the time—and yet, Mrs. Allan, the world and life seem very beautiful and interesting to me for all. Today Diana said something funny and I found myself laughing. I thought when it happened I could never laugh again. And it somehow seems as if I oughtn't to."

"When Matthew was here he liked to hear you laugh and he liked to know that you found pleasure in the pleasant things around you," said Mrs. Allan gently. "He is just away now; and he likes to know it just the same. I am sure we should not shut our hearts against the healing influences that nature offers us. But I understand your feeling. I think we all experience the same thing. We resent the thought that anything can please us when someone we love is no longer here to share the pleasure with us, and we almost feel as if we were unfaithful to our sorrow when we find our interest in life returning to us."

"I was down to the graveyard to plant a rosebush on Matthew's grave this afternoon," said Anne dreamily. "I took a slip of the little white Scotch rosebush his mother brought out from Scotland long ago; Matthew always liked those roses the best—they were so small and sweet on their thorny stems. It made me feel glad that I could plant it by his grave—as if I were doing something that must please him in taking it there to be near him. I hope he has roses like them in heaven. Perhaps the souls of all those little white roses that he has loved so many summers were all there to meet him. I must go home now. Marilla is all alone and she gets lonely at twilight."

"She will be lonelier still, I fear, when you go away again to college," said Mrs. Allan.

Anne did not reply; she said good night and went slowly back to Green Gables. Marilla was sitting on the front door-steps and Anne sat down beside her. The door was open behind them, held back by a big pink conch shell with hints of sea sunsets in its smooth inner convolutions.

Anne gathered some sprays of pale yellow honeysuckle and put them in her hair. She liked the delicious hint of fragrance, as of some aerial benediction, above her every time she moved.

"Doctor Spencer was here while you were away," Marilla said. "He says that the specialist will be in town tomorrow and he insists that I must go in and have my eyes examined. I suppose I'd better go and have it over. I'll be more than thankful if the man can give me the right kind of glasses to suit my eyes. You won't mind staying here alone while I'm away, will you? Martin will have to drive me in and there's ironing and baking to do."

"I shall be all right. Diana will come over for company for me. I shall attend to the ironing and baking beautifully—you needn't fear that I'll starch the handkerchiefs or flavor the cake with liniment."

Marilla laughed.

"What a girl you were for making mistakes in them days, Anne. You were always getting into scrapes. I did use to think you were possessed. Do you mind the time you dyed your hair?"

"Yes, indeed. I shall never forget it," smiled Anne, touching the heavy braid of hair that was wound about her shapely head. "I laugh a little now sometimes when I think what a worry my hair used to be to me—but I don't laugh *much*, because it was a very real trouble then. I did suffer terribly over my hair and my freckles. My freckles are really gone; and people are nice enough to tell me my hair is auburn now— all but Josie Pye. She informed me yesterday that she really thought it was redder than ever, or at least my black dress made it took redder, and she asked me if people who had red hair ever got used to having it. Marilla, I've almost decided to give up trying to like Josie Pye. I've made what I would once have called a heroic effort to like her, but Josie Pye won't *be* liked."

"Josie is a Pye," said Marilla sharply, "so she can't help being dis-agreeable. I suppose people of that kind serve some useful purpose in society, but I must say I don't know what it is any more than I know the use of thistles. Is Josie going to teach?"

"No, she is going back to Queen's next year. So are Moody Spurgeon and Charlie Sloane. Jane and Ruby are going to teach and they have both got schools—Jane at Newbridge and Ruby at some place up west."

"Gilbert Blythe is going to teach too, isn't he?"

"Yes"—briefly.

"What a nice looking young fellow he is," said Marilla absently. "I saw him in church last Sunday and he seemed so tall and manly. He looks a lot like his father did at the same age. John Blythe was a nice boy. We used to be real good friends, he and I. People called him my beau."

Anne looked up with swift interest.

"Oh, Marilla—and what happened?—why didn't you—"

"We had a quarrel. I wouldn't forgive him when he asked me to. I meant to, after awhile—but I was sulky and angry and I wanted to punish him first. He never came back—the Blythes were all mighty independent. But I always felt—rather sorry. I've always kind of wished I'd forgiven him when I had the chance."

"So you've had a bit of romance in your life, too," said Anne softly.

"Yes, I suppose you might call it that. You wouldn't think so to look at me, would you? But you never can tell about people from their outsides. Everybody has forgot about me and John. I'd forgotten myself. But it all came back to me when I saw Gilbert last Sunday."

38

The Bend in the Road

arilla went to town the next day and returned in the evening. Anne had gone over to Orchard Slope with Diana and came back to find Marilla in the kitchen, sitting by the table with her head leaning on her hand. Something in her dejected attitude struck a chill to Anne's heart. She had never seen Marilla sit limply inert like that.

"Are you very tired, Marilla?"

"Yes—no—I don't know," said Marilla wearily, looking up. "I suppose I am tired but I haven't thought about it. It's not that."

"Did you see the oculist? What did he say?" asked Anne anxiously.

"Yes, I saw him. He examined my eyes. He says that if I give up all reading and sewing entirely and any kind of work that strains the eyes, and if I'm careful not to cry, and if I wear the glasses he's given me he thinks my eyes may not get any worse and my headaches will be cured. But if I don't he says I'll certainly be stone blind in six months. Blind! Anne, just think of it!"

For a minute Anne, after her first quick exclamation of dismay, was silent. It seemed to her that she could *not* speak. Then she said bravely, but with a catch in her voice:

"Marilla, *don't* think of it. You know he has given you hope. If you are careful you won't lose your sight altogether; and if his glasses cure your headaches it will be a great thing."

"I don't call it much hope," said Marilla bitterly. "What am I to live for if I can't read or sew or do anything like that? I might as well be blind—or dead. And as for crying, I can't help that when I get lonesome. But there, it's no good talking about it. If you'll get me a cup of tea I'll be thankful. I'm about done out. Don't say anything about this to any one for a spell yet, anyway. I can't bear that folks should come here to question and sympathize and talk about it."

When Marilla had eaten her lunch Anne persuaded her to go to bed. Then Anne went herself to the east gable and sat down by her window in the darkness alone with her tears and her heaviness of heart. How sadly things had changed since she had sat there the night after coming home! Then she had been full of hope and joy and the future had looked rosy with promise. Anne felt as if she had lived years since then, but before she went to bed there was a smile on her lips and peace in her heart. She had looked her duty courageously in the face and found it a friend—as duty ever is when we meet it frankly.

One afternoon a few days later Marilla came slowly in from the yard where she had been talking to a caller—a man whom Anne knew by sight as John Sadler from Carmody. Anne wondered what he could have been saying to bring that look to Marilla's face.

"What did Mr. Sadler want, Marilla?"

Marilla sat down by the window and looked at Anne. There were tears in her eyes in defiance of the oculist's prohibition and her voice broke as she said:

"He heard that I was going to sell Green Gables and he wants to buy it."

"Buy it! Buy Green Gables?" Anne wondered if she had heard right. "Oh, Marilla, you don't mean to sell Green Gables!"

"Anne, I don't know what else is to be done. I've thought it all over. If my eyes were strong I could stay here and make out to look after things and manage, with a good hired man. But as it is I can't. I may lose my sight altogether; and anyway I'll not be fit to run things. Oh, I never thought I'd live to see the day when I'd have to sell my home. But things would only go behind worse and worse all the time, till nobody would want to buy it. Every cent of our money went in that bank; and there's some notes Matthew gave last fall to pay. Mrs. Lynde advises me to sell the farm and board somewhere— with her I suppose. It won't bring much—it's small and the buildings are old. But it'll be enough for me to live on I reckon. I'm thankful you're provided for with that scholarship, Anne. I'm sorry you won't have a home to come to in your vacations, that's all, but I suppose you'll manage somehow."

Marilla broke down and wept bitterly.

"You mustn't sell Green Gables," said Anne resolutely.

"Oh, Anne, I wish I didn't have to. But you can see for yourself. I can't stay here alone. I'd go crazy with trouble and loneliness. And my sight would go—I know it would."

"You won't have to stay here alone, Marilla. I'll be with you. I'm not going to Redmond."

"Not going to Redmond!" Marilla lifted her worn face from her hands and looked at Anne. "Why, what do you mean?"

"Just what I say. I'm not going to take the scholarship. I decided so the night after you came home from town. You surely don't think I could leave you alone in your trouble, Marilla, after all you've done for me. I've been thinking and planning. Let me tell you my plans. Mr. Barry wants to rent the farm for next year. So you won't have any bother over that. And I'm going to teach. I've applied for the school here—but I don't expect to get it for I understand the trustees have promised it to Gilbert Blythe. But I can have the Carmody school—Mr. Blair told me so last night at the store. Of course that won't be quite as nice or convenient as if I had the Avonlea school. But I can board home and drive myself over to Carmody and back, in the warm weather at least. And even in winter I can come home Fridays. We'll keep a horse for that. Oh, I have it all planned out, Marilla. And I'll read to you and keep you cheered up. You sha'n't be dull or lonesome. And we'll be real cozy and happy here together, you and I."

Marilla had listened like a woman in a dream.

"Oh, Anne, I could get on real well if you were here, I know. But I can't let you sacrifice yourself so for me. It would be terrible."

"Nonsense!" Anne laughed merrily. "There is no sacrifice. Nothing could be worse than giving up Green Gables—nothing could hurt me more. We must keep the dear old place. My mind is quite made up, Marilla. I'm *not* going to Redmond; and I *am* going to stay here and teach. Don't you worry about me a bit."

"But your ambitions—and—"

"I'm just as ambitious as ever. Only, I've changed the object of my ambitions. I'm going to be a good teacher—and I'm going to save your eyesight. Besides, I mean to study at home here and take a little college course all by myself. Oh, I've dozens of plans, Marilla. I've been thinking them out for a week. I shall give life here my best, and I believe it will give its best to me in return. When I left Queen's my future seemed to stretch out before me like a straight road. I thought I could see along it for many a milestone. Now there is a bend in it. I don't know what lies around the bend, but I'm going to believe that the best does. It has a fascination of its own, that bend, Marilla. I wonder how the road beyond it goes—what there is of green glory and soft, checkered light and shadows—what new landscapes—what new beauties—what curves and hills and valleys further on."

"I don't feel as if I ought to let you give it up," said Marilla, referring to the scholarship.

"But you can't prevent me. I'm sixteen and a half, 'obstinate as a mule,' as Mrs. Lynde once told me," laughed Anne. "Oh, Marilla, don't you go pitying me. I don't like to be pitied, and there is no need for it. I'm heart glad over the very thought of staying at dear Green Gables. Nobody could love it as you and I do—so we must keep it."

"You blessed girl!" said Marilla, yielding. "I feel as if you'd given me new life. I guess I ought to stick out and make you go to college—but I know I can't, so I ain't going to try. I'll make it up to you though, Anne."

When it became noised abroad in Avonlea that Anne Shirley had given up the idea of going to college and intended to stay home and teach there was a good deal of discussion over it. Most of the good folks, not knowing about Marilla's eyes, thought she was foolish. Mrs. Allan did not. She told Anne so in approving words that brought tears of pleasure to the girl's eyes. Neither did good Mrs. Lynde. She came up one evening and found Anne and Marilla sitting at the front door in the warm, scented summer dusk. They liked to sit there when the twilight came down and the white moths flew about in the garden and the odor of mint filled the dewy air.

Mrs. Rachel deposited her substantial person upon the stone

bench by the door, behind which grew a row of tall pink and yellow hollyhocks, with a long breath of mingled weariness and relief.

"I declare I'm glad to sit down. I've been on my feet all day, and two hundred pounds is a good bit for two feet to carry round. It's a great blessing not to be fat, Marilla. I hope you appreciate it. Well, Anne, I hear you've given up your notion of going to college. I was real glad to hear it. You've got as much education now as a woman can be comfortable with. I don't believe in girls going to college with the men and cramming their heads full of Latin and Greek and all that nonsense."

"But I'm going to study Latin and Greek just the same, Mrs. Lynde," said Anne laughing. "I'm going to take my Arts course right here at Green Gables, and study everything that I would at college."

Mrs. Lynde lifted her hands in holy horror.

"Anne Shirley, you'll kill yourself."

"Not a bit of it. I shall thrive on it. Oh, I'm not going to overdo things. As 'Josiah Allen's wife' says, I shall be 'mejum.' But I'll have lots of spare time in the long winter evenings, and I've no vocation for fancy work. I'm going to teach over at Carmody, you know."

"I don't know it. I guess you're going to teach right here in Avonlea. The trustees have decided to give you the school."

"Mrs. Lynde!" cried Anne, springing to her feet in her surprise. "Why, I thought they had promised it to Gilbert Blythe!"

"So they did. But as soon as Gilbert heard that you had applied for it he went to them—they had a business meeting at the school last night, you know—and told them that he withdrew his application, and suggested that they accept yours. He said he was going to teach at White Sands. Of course he gave up the school just to oblige you, because he knew how much you wanted to stay with Marilla, and I must say I think it was real kind and thoughtful in him, that's what. Real self-sacrificing, too, for he'll have his board to pay at White Sands, and everybody knows he's got to earn his own way through college. So the trustees decided to take you. I was tickled to death when Thomas came home and told me."

"I don't feel that I ought to take it," murmured Anne. "I mean—I don't think I ought to let Gilbert make such a sacrifice for—for me."

"I guess you can't prevent him now. He's signed papers with the White Sands trustees. So it wouldn't do him any good now if you were to refuse. Of course you'll take the school. You'll get along all right, now that there are no Pyes going. Josie was the last of them, and a good thing she was, that's what. There's been some Pye or other going to Avonlea school for the last twenty years, and I guess their mission in life was to keep schoolteachers reminded that earth isn't their home. Bless my heart! What does all that winking and blinking at the Barry gable mean?"

"Diana is signaling for me to go over," laughed Anne. "You know we keep up the old custom. Excuse me while I run over and see what she wants."

Anne ran down the clover slope like a deer, and disappeared in the firry shadows of the Haunted Wood. Mrs. Lynde looked after her indulgently.

"There's a good deal of the child about her yet in some ways."

"There's a good deal more of the woman about her in others," retorted Marilla, with a momentary return of her old crispness.

But crispness was no longer Marilla's distinguishing characteristic. As Mrs. Lynde told her Thomas that night.

"Marilla Cuthbert has got *mellow*. That's what."

Anne went to the little Avonlea graveyard the next evening to put fresh flowers on Matthew's grave and water the Scotch rosebush. She lingered there until dusk, liking the peace and calm of the little place, with its poplars whose rustle was like low, friendly speech, and its whispering grasses growing at will among the graves. When she finally left it and walked down the long hill that sloped to the Lake of Shining Waters it was past sunset and all Avonlea lay before her in a dreamlike afterlight—"a haunt of ancient peace." There was a freshness in the air as of a wind that had blown over honey-sweet fields of clover. Home lights twinkled out here and there among the homestead trees. Beyond lay the sea, misty and purple, with its haunting, unceasing murmur. The west was a glory of soft mingled hues, and the pond reflected them all in still softer shadings. The beauty of it all thrilled Anne's heart, and she gratefully opened the gates of her soul to it.

"Dear old world," she murmured, "you are very lovely, and I am glad to be alive in you."

Halfway down the hill a tall lad came whistling out of a gate before the Blythe homestead. It was Gilbert and the whistle died on his lips as he recognized Anne. He lifted his cap courteously, but he would have passed on in silence, if Anne had not stopped and held out her hand.

"Gilbert," she said, with scarlet cheeks, "I want to thank you for giving up the school for me. It was very good of you—and I want you to know that I appreciate it."

Gilbert took the offered hand eagerly.

"It wasn't particularly good of me at all, Anne. I was pleased to be able to do you some small service. Are we going to be friends after this? Have you really forgiven me my old fault?"

Anne laughed and tried unsuccessfully to withdraw her hand.

"I forgave you that day by the pond landing, although I didn't know it. What a stubborn little goose I was. I've been—I may as well make a complete confession—I've been sorry ever since."

"We are going to be the best of friends," said Gilbert, jubilantly. "We were born to be good friends, Anne. You've thwarted destiny long enough. I know we can help each other in many ways. You are going to keep up your studies, aren't you? So am I. Come, I'm going to walk home with you."

Marilla looked curiously at Anne when the latter entered the kitchen.

"Who was that came up the lane with you, Anne?"

"Gilbert Blythe," answered Anne, vexed to find herself blushing. "I met him on Barry's hill."

"I didn't think you and Gilbert Blythe were such good friends that you'd stand for half an hour at the gate talking to him," said Marilla, with a dry smile.

"We haven't been—we've been good enemies. But we have decided that it will be much more sensible to be good friends in future. Were we really there half an hour? It seemed just a few minutes. But, you see, we have five years' lost conversations to catch up with, Marilla."

Anne sat long at her window that night companioned by a glad content. The wind purred softly in the cherry boughs, and the mint breaths came up to her. The stars twinkled over the pointed firs in the hollow and Diana's light gleamed through the old gap.

Anne's horizons had closed in since the night she had sat there after coming home from Queen's; but if the path set before her feet was to be narrow she knew that flowers of quiet happiness would bloom along it. The joys of sincere work and worthy aspiration and congenial friendship were to be hers; nothing could rob her of her birthright of fancy or her ideal world of dreams. And there was always the bend in the road!

"'God's in his heaven, all's right with the world,'" whispered Anne softly.

Anne
of
Avonlea

Flowers spring to blossom where she walks
The careful ways of duty,
Our hard, stiff lines of life with her
Are flowing lines of beauty.

WHITTIER

CONTENTS

1

An Irate Neighbor

tall, slim girl, "half-past sixteen," with serious gray eyes and hair which her friends called auburn, had sat down on the broad red sandstone doorstep of a Prince Edward Island farmhouse one ripe afternoon in August, firmly resolved to construe so many lines of Virgil.

But an August afternoon, with blue hazes scarfing the harvest slopes, little winds whispering elfishly in the poplars, and a dancing splendor of red poppies outflaming against the dark coppice of young firs in a corner of the cherry orchard, was fitter for dreams than dead languages. The Virgil soon slipped unheeded to the ground, and Anne, her chin propped on her clasped hands, and her eyes on the splendid mass of fluffy clouds that were heaping up just over Mr. J. A. Harrison's house like a great white mountain, was far away in a delicious world where a certain schoolteacher was doing a wonderful work, shaping the destinies of future statesmen, and inspiring youthful minds and hearts with high and lofty ambitions.

To be sure, if you came down to harsh facts . . . which, it must be confessed, Anne seldom did until she had to . . . it did not seem likely that there was much promising material for celebrities in Avonlea school; but you could never tell what might happen if a teacher used her influence for good. Anne had certain rosetinted ideals of what a teacher might accomplish if she only went the right way about it; and she was in the midst of a delightful scene, forty years hence, with a famous personage . . . just exactly what he was to be famous for was left in convenient haziness, but Anne thought it would be rather nice to have him a college president or a Canadian premier . . . bowing low over her wrinkled hand and assuring her that it was she who had first kindled his ambition, and that all his success in life was due to the lessons she had instilled so long ago in Avonlea school. This pleasant vision was shattered by a most unpleasant interruption.

A demure little Jersey cow came scuttling down the lane and five seconds later Mr. Harrison arrived . . . if "arrived" be not too mild a term to describe the manner of his irruption into the yard.

He bounced over the fence without waiting to open the gate, and angrily confronted astonished Anne, who had risen to her feet and stood looking at him in some bewilderment. Mr. Harrison was their new righthand neighbor and she had never met him before, although she had seen him once or twice.

In early April, before Anne had come home from Queen's, Mr. Robert Bell, whose farm adjoined the Cuthbert place on the west, had sold out and moved to Charlottetown. His farm had been bought by a certain Mr. J. A. Harrison, whose name, and the fact that he was a New Brunswick man, were all that was known about him. But before he had been a month in Avonlea he had won the reputation of being an odd person . . . "a crank," Mrs. Rachel Lynde said. Mrs. Rachel was an outspoken lady, as those of you who may have already made her acquaintance will remember. Mr. Harrison was certainly different from other people . . . and that is the essential characteristic of a crank, as everybody knows.

In the first place he kept house for himself and had publicly stated that he wanted no fools of women around his diggings. Feminine Avonlea took its revenge by the gruesome tales it related about his housekeeping and cooking. He had hired little John Henry Carter of White Sands and John Henry started the stories. For one thing, there was never any stated time for meals in the Harrison establishment. Mr. Harrison "got a bite" when he felt hungry, and if John Henry were around at the time, he came in for a share, but if he were not, he had to wait until Mr. Harrison's next hungry spell. John Henry mournfully averred that he would have starved to death if it wasn't that he got home on Sundays and got a good filling up, and that his mother always gave him a basket of "grub" to take back with him on Monday mornings.

As for washing dishes, Mr. Harrison never made any pretence of doing it unless a rainy Sunday came. Then he went to work and washed them all at once in the rainwater hogshead, and left them to drain dry.

Again, Mr. Harrison was "close." When he was asked to subscribe to the Rev. Mr. Allan's salary he said he'd wait and see how many dollars' worth of good he got out of his preaching first . . . *he* didn't believe in buying a pig in a poke. And when Mrs. Lynde went to ask for a contribution to missions . . . and incidentally to see the inside of the house . . . he told her there were more heathens among the old woman gossips in Avonlea than anywhere else he knew of, and he'd cheerfully contribute to a mission for Christianizing them if she'd undertake it. Mrs. Rachel got herself away and said it was a mercy poor Mrs. Robert Bell was safe in her grave, for it would have broken her heart to see the state of her house in which she used to take so much pride.

"Why, she scrubbed the kitchen floor every second day," Mrs. Lynde told Marilla Cuthbert indignantly, "and if you could see it now! I had to hold up my skirts as I walked across it."

Finally, Mr. Harrison kept a parrot called Ginger. Nobody in Avonlea had ever kept a parrot before; consequently that proceeding was considered barely respectable. And such a parrot! If you took John Henry Carter's word for it, never was such an unholy bird. It swore terribly. Mrs. Carter would have taken John Henry away at once if she had been sure she could get another place for him. Besides, Ginger had bitten a piece right out of the back of John Henry's neck one day when he had stooped down too near the cage. Mrs. Carter showed everybody the mark when the luckless John Henry went home on Sundays.

All these things flashed through Anne's mind as Mr. Harrison stood, quite speechless with wrath apparently, before her. In his most amiable mood Mr. Harrison could not have been considered a handsome man; he was short and fat and bald; and now, with his round face purple with rage and his prominent blue eyes almost sticking out of his head, Anne thought he was really the ugliest person she had ever seen.

All at once Mr. Harrison found his voice.

"I'm not going to put up with this," he spluttered, "not a day longer, do you hear, miss. Bless my soul, this is the third time, miss . . . the third time! Patience has ceased to be a virtue, miss. I warned your aunt the last time not to let it occur again . . . and she's let it . . . she's done it . . . what does she mean by it, that is what I want to know. That is what I'm here about, miss."

"Will you explain what the trouble is?" asked Anne, in her most dignified manner. She had been practicing it considerably of late to have it in good working order when school began; but it had no apparent effect on the irate J. A. Harrison.

"Trouble, is it? Bless my soul, trouble enough, I should think. The trouble is, miss, that I found that Jersey cow of your aunt's in my oats again, not half an hour ago. The third time, mark you. I found her in last Tuesday and I found her in yesterday. I came here and told your aunt not to let it occur again. She *has* let it occur again. Where's your aunt, miss? I just want to see her for a minute and give her a piece of my mind . . . a piece of J. A. Harrison's mind, miss."

"If you mean Miss Marilla Cuthbert, she is *not* my aunt, and she has gone down to East Grafton to see a distant relative of hers who is very ill," said Anne, with due increase of dignity at every word. "I am very sorry that my cow should have broken into your oats . . . she *is* my cow and not Miss Cuthbert's . . . Matthew gave her to me three years ago when she was a little calf and he bought her from Mr. Bell."

"Sorry, miss! Sorry isn't going to help matters any. You'd better go and look at the havoc that animal has made in my oats . . . trampled them from center to circumference, miss."

"I am very sorry," repeated Anne firmly, "but perhaps if you kept your fences in better repair Dolly might not have broken in. It is your part of the line fence that separates your oatfield from our pasture and I noticed the other day that it was not in very good condition."

"My fence is all right," snapped Mr. Harrison, angrier than ever at this carrying of the war into the enemy's country. "The jail fence couldn't keep a demon of a cow like that out. And I can tell you, you redheaded snippet, that if the cow is yours, as you say, you'd be better employed in watching her out of other people's grain than in sitting round reading yellow-covered novels," . . . with a scathing glance at the innocent tan-colored Virgil by Anne's feet.

Something at that moment was red besides Anne's hair . . . which had always been a tender point with her.

"I'd rather have red hair than none at all, except a little fringe round my ears," she flashed.

The shot told, for Mr. Harrison was really very sensitive about his bald head. His anger choked him up again and he could only glare speechlessly at Anne, who recovered her temper and followed up her advantage.

"I can make allowance for you, Mr. Harrison, because I have an imagination. I can easily imagine how very trying it must be to find a cow in your oats and I shall not cherish any hard feelings against you for the things you've said. I promise you that Dolly shall never break into your oats again. I give you my word of honor on *that* point."

"Well, mind you she doesn't," muttered Mr. Harrison in a somewhat subdued tone; but he stamped off angrily enough and Anne heard him growling to himself until he was out of earshot.

Grievously disturbed in mind, Anne marched across the yard and shut the naughty Jersey up in the milking pen.

"She can't possibly get out of that unless she tears the fence down," she reflected. "She looks pretty quiet now. I daresay she has sickened herself on those oats. I wish I'd sold her to Mr. Shearer when he wanted her last week, but I thought it was just as well to wait until we had the auction of the stock and let them all go together. I believe it is true about Mr. Harrison being a crank. Certainly there's nothing of the kindred spirit about *him*."

Anne had always a weather eye open for kindred spirits.

Marilla Cuthbert was driving into the yard as Anne returned from the house, and the latter flew to get tea ready. They discussed the matter at the tea table.

"I'll be glad when the auction is over," said Marilla. "It is too much responsibility having so much stock about the place and nobody but that unreliable Martin to look after them. He has never come back yet and he promised that he would certainly be back last night if I'd give him the day off to go to his aunt's funeral. I don't know how many aunts he has got, I am sure. That's the fourth that's died since he hired here a year ago. I'll be more than thankful when the crop is in and Mr. Barry takes over the farm. We'll have to keep Dolly shut up in the pen till Martin comes, for she must be put in the back pasture and the fences there have to be fixed. I declare, it is a world of trouble, as Rachel says. Here's poor Mary Keith dying and what is to become of those two children of hers is more than I know. She has a brother in British Columbia and she has written to him about them, but she hasn't heard from him yet."

"What are the children like? How old are they?"

"Six past . . . they're twins."

"Oh, I've always been especially interested in twins ever since Mrs. Hammond had so many," said Anne eagerly. "Are they pretty?"

"Goodness, you couldn't tell . . . they were too dirty. Davy had been out making mud pies and Dora went out to call him in. Davy pushed her headfirst into the biggest pie and then, because she cried, he got into it himself and wallowed in it to show her it was nothing to cry about. Mary said Dora was really a very good child but that Davy was full of mischief. He has never had any bringing up you might say. His father died when he was a baby and Mary has been sick almost ever since."

"I'm always sorry for children that have had no bringing up," said Anne soberly. "You know I hadn't any till you took me in hand. I hope their uncle will look after them. Just what relation is Mrs. Keith to you?"

"Mary? None in the world. It was her husband . . . he was our third cousin. There's Mrs. Lynde coming through the yard. I thought she'd be up to hear about Mary."

"Don't tell her about Mr. Harrison and the cow," implored Anne.

Marilla promised; but the promise was quite unnecessary, for Mrs. Lynde was no sooner fairly seated than she said,

"I saw Mr. Harrison chasing your Jersey out of his oats today when I was coming home from Carmody. I thought he looked pretty mad. Did he make much of a rumpus?"

Anne and Marilla furtively exchanged amused smiles. Few things in Avonlea ever escaped Mrs. Lynde. It was only that morning Anne had said,

"If you went to your own room at midnight, locked the door, pulled down the blind, and *sneezed,* Mrs. Lynde would ask you the next day how your cold was!"

"I believe he did," admitted Marilla. "I was away. He gave Anne a piece of his mind."

"I think he is a very disagreeable man," said Anne, with a resentful toss of her ruddy head.

"You never said a truer word," said Mrs. Rachel solemnly. "I knew there'd be trouble when Robert Bell sold his place to a New Brunswick man, that's what. I don't know what Avonlea is coming to, with so many strange people rushing into it. It'll soon not be safe to go to sleep in our beds."

"Why, what other strangers are coming in?" asked Marilla.

"Haven't you heard? Well, there's a family of Donnells, for one thing. They've rented Peter Sloane's old house. Peter has hired the man to run his mill. They belong down east and nobody knows anything about them. Then that shiftless Timothy Cotton family are going to move up from White Sands and they'll simply be a burden on the public. He is in consumption . . . when he isn't stealing . . . and his wife is a slack-twisted creature that can't turn her hand to a thing. She washes her dishes *sitting down*. Mrs. George Pye has taken her husband's orphan nephew, Anthony Pye. He'll be going to school to you, Anne, so you may expect trouble, that's what. And you'll have another strange pupil, too. Paul Irving is coming from the States to live with his grandmother. You remember his father, Marilla . . . Stephen Irving, him that jilted Lavendar Lewis over at Grafton?"

"I don't think he jilted her. There was a quarrel . . . I suppose there was blame on both sides."

"Well, anyway, he didn't marry her, and she's been as queer as possible ever since, they say . . . living all by herself in that little stone house she calls Echo Lodge. Stephen went off to the States and went into business with his uncle and married a Yankee. He's never been home since, though his mother has been up to see him once or twice. His wife died two years ago and he's sending the boy home to his mother for a spell. He's ten years old and I don't know if he'll be a very desirable pupil. You can never tell about those Yankees."

Mrs. Lynde looked upon all people who had the misfortune to be born or brought up elsewhere than in Prince Edward Island with a decided can-any-good-thing-come-out-of-Nazareth air. They *might* be good people, of course; but you were on the safe side in doubting it. She had a special prejudice against "Yankees." Her husband had been cheated out of ten dollars by an employer for whom he had once worked in Boston and neither angels nor principalities nor powers could have convinced Mrs. Rachel that the whole United States was not responsible for it.

"Avonlea school won't be the worse for a little new blood," said Marilla drily, "and if this boy is anything like his father he'll be all right. Steve Irving was the nicest boy that was ever raised in these parts, though some people did call him proud. I should think Mrs. Irving would be very glad to have the child. She has been very lonesome since her husband died."

"Oh, the boy may be well enough, but he'll be different from Avonlea children," said Mrs. Rachel, as if that clinched the matter. Mrs. Rachel's opinions concerning any person, place, or thing, were always warranted to wear. "What's this I hear about your going to start up a Village Improvement Society, Anne?"

"I was just talking it over with some of the girls and boys at the last Debating Club," said Anne, flushing. "They thought it would be rather nice . . . and so do Mr. and Mrs. Allan. Lots of villages have them now."

"Well, you'll get into no end of hot water if you do. Better leave it alone, Anne, that's what. People don't like being improved."

"Oh, we are not going to try to improve the *people*. It is Avonlea itself. There are lots of things which might be done to make it prettier. For instance, if we could coax Mr. Levi Boulter to pull down that dreadful old house on his upper farm wouldn't that be an improvement?"

"It certainly would," admitted Mrs. Rachel. "That old ruin has been an eyesore to the settlement for years. But if you Improvers can coax Levi Boulter to do anything for the public that he isn't to be paid for doing, may I be there to see and hear the process, that's what. I don't want to discourage you, Anne, for there may be something in your idea, though I suppose you did get it out of some rubbishy Yankee magazine; but you'll have your hands full with your school and I advise you as a friend not to bother with your improvements, that's what. But there, I know you'll go ahead with it if you've set your mind on it. You were always one to carry a thing through somehow."

Something about the firm outlines of Anne's lips told that Mrs. Rachel was not far astray in this estimate. Anne's heart was bent on forming the Improvement Society. Gilbert Blythe, who was to teach in White Sands but would always be home from Friday night to Monday morning, was enthusiastic about it; and most of the other young folks were willing to go in for anything that meant occasional meetings and consequently some "fun." As for what the "improvements" were to be, nobody had any very clear idea except Anne and Gilbert. They had talked them over and planned them out until an ideal Avonlea existed in their minds, if nowhere else.

Mrs. Rachel had still another item of news.

"They've given the Carmody school to a Priscilla Grant. Didn't you go to Queen's with a girl of that name, Anne?"

"Yes, indeed. Priscilla to teach at Carmody! How perfectly lovely!" exclaimed Anne, her gray eyes lighting up until they looked like evening stars, causing Mrs. Lynde to wonder anew if she would ever get it settled to her satisfaction whether Anne Shirley were really a pretty girl or not.

2

Selling in Haste and
Repenting at Leisure

nne drove over to Carmody on a shopping expedition the next afternoon and took Diana Barry with her. Diana was, of course, a pledged member of the Improvement Society, and the two girls talked about little else all the way to Carmody and back.

"The very first thing we ought to do when we get started is to have that hall painted," said Diana, as they drove past the Avonlea hall, a rather shabby building set down in a wooded hollow, with spruce trees hooding it about on all sides. "It's a disgraceful looking place and we must attend to it even before we try to get Mr. Levi Boulter to pull his house down. Father says we'll never succeed in doing *that* . . . Levi Boulter is too mean to spend the time it would take."

"Perhaps he'll let the boys take it down if they promise to haul the boards and split them up for him for kindling wood," said Anne hopefully. "We must do our best and be content to go slowly at first. We can't expect to improve everything all at once. We'll have to educate public sentiment first, of course."

Diana wasn't exactly sure what educating public sentiment meant; but it sounded fine and she felt rather proud that she was going to belong to a society with such an aim in view.

"I thought of something last night that we could do, Anne. You know that three-cornered piece of ground where the roads from Carmody and Newbridge and White Sands meet? It's all grown over with young spruce; but wouldn't it be nice to have them all cleared out, and just leave the two or three birch trees that are on it?"

"Splendid," agreed Anne gaily. "And have a rustic seat put under the birches. And when spring comes we'll have a flower-bed made in the middle of it and plant geraniums."

"Yes; only we'll have to devise some way of getting old Mrs. Hiram Sloane to keep her cow off the road, or she'll eat our geraniums up," laughed Diana. "I begin to see what you mean by educating public sentiment, Anne. There's the old Boulter house now. Did you ever see such a rookery? And perched right close to the road too. An old house with its windows gone always makes me think of something dead with its eyes picked out."

"I think an old, deserted house is such a sad sight," said Anne dreamily. "It always seems to me to be thinking about its past and mourning for its old-time joys. Marilla says that a large family was raised in that old house long ago, and that it was a real pretty place, with a lovely garden and roses climbing all over it. It was full of little children and laughter and songs; and now it is empty, and nothing ever wanders through it but the wind. How lonely and sorrowful it must feel! Perhaps they all come back on moonlit nights . . . the ghosts of the little children of long ago and the roses and the songs . . . and for a little while the old house can dream it is young and joyous again."

Diana shook her head.

"I never imagine things like that about places now, Anne. Don't you remember how cross mother and Marilla were when we imagined ghosts into the Haunted Wood? To this day I can't go through that bush comfortably after dark; and if I began imagining such things about the old Boulter house I'd be frightened to pass it too. Besides, those children aren't dead. They're all grown up and doing well . . . and one of them is a butcher. And flowers and songs couldn't have ghosts anyhow."

Anne smothered a little sigh. She loved Diana dearly and they had always been good comrades. But she had long ago learned that when she wandered into the realm of fancy she must go alone. The way to it was by an enchanted path where not even her dearest might follow her.

A thunder-shower came up while the girls were at Carmody; it did not last long, however, and the drive home, through lanes where the raindrops sparkled on the boughs and little leafy valleys where the drenched ferns gave out spicy odors, was delightful. But just as they turned into the Cuthbert lane Anne saw something that spoiled the beauty of the landscape for her.

Before them on the right extended Mr. Harrison's broad, gray-green field of late oats, wet and luxuriant; and there, standing squarely in the middle of it, up to her sleek sides in the lush growth, and blinking at them calmly over the intervening tassels, was a Jersey cow!

Anne dropped the reins and stood up with a tightening of the lips that boded no good to the predatory quadruped. Not a word said she, but she climbed nimbly down over the wheels, and whisked across the fence before Diana understood what had happened.

"Anne, come back," shrieked the latter, as soon as she found her voice. "You'll ruin your dress in that wet grain . . . ruin it. She doesn't hear me! Well, she'll never get that cow out by herself. I must go and help her, of course."

Anne was charging through the grain like a mad thing. Diana hopped briskly down, tied the horse securely to a post, turned the skirt of her pretty gingham dress over her shoulders, mounted the fence, and started in pursuit of her frantic friend. She could run faster than Anne, who was hampered by her clinging and drenched skirt, and soon overtook her. Behind them they left a trail that would break Mr. Harrison's heart when he should see it.

"Anne, for mercy's sake, stop," panted poor Diana. "I'm right out of breath and you are wet to the skin."

"I must . . . get . . . that cow . . . out . . . before . . . Mr. Harrison . . . sees her," gasped Anne. "I don't . . . care . . . if I'm . . . drowned . . . if we . . . can . . . only . . . do that."

But the Jersey cow appeared to see no good reason for being hustled out of her luscious browsing ground. No sooner had the two breathless girls got near her than she turned and bolted squarely for the opposite corner of the field.

"Head her off," screamed Anne. "Run, Diana, run."

Diana did run. Anne tried to, and the wicked Jersey went around the field as if she were possessed. Privately, Diana thought she was. It was fully ten minutes before they headed her off and drove her through the corner gap into the Cuthbert lane.

There is no denying that Anne was in anything but an angelic temper at that precise moment. Nor did it soothe her in the least to behold a buggy halted just outside the lane, wherein sat Mr. Shearer of Carmody and his son, both of whom wore a broad smile.

"I guess you'd better have sold me that cow when I wanted to buy her last week, Anne," chuckled Mr. Shearer.

"I'll sell her to you now, if you want her," said her flushed and disheveled owner. "You may have her this very minute."

"Done. I'll give you twenty for her as I offered before, and Jim here can drive her right over to Carmody. She'll go to town with the rest of the shipment this evening. Mr. Reed of Brighton wants a Jersey cow."

Five minutes later Jim Shearer and the Jersey cow were marching up the road, and impulsive Anne was driving along the Green Gables lane with her twenty dollars.

"What will Marilla say?" asked Diana.

"Oh, she won't care. Dolly was my own cow and it isn't likely she'd bring more than twenty dollars at the auction. But oh dear, if Mr. Harrison sees that grain he will know she has been in again, and after my giving him my word of honor that I'd never let it happen! Well, it has taught me a lesson not to give my word of honor about cows. A cow that could jump over or break through our milk-pen fence couldn't be trusted anywhere."

Marilla had gone down to Mrs. Lynde's, and when she returned knew all about Dolly's sale and transfer, for Mrs. Lynde had seen most of the transaction from her window and guessed the rest.

"I suppose it's just as well she's gone, though you *do* do things in a dreadful headlong fashion, Anne. I don't see how she got out of the pen, though. She must have broken some of the boards off."

"I didn't think of looking," said Anne, "but I'll go and see now. Martin has never come back yet. Perhaps some more of his aunts have died. I think it's something like Mr. Peter Sloane and the octogenarians. The other evening Mrs. Sloane was reading a newspaper and she said to Mr. Sloane, 'I see here that another octogenarian has just died. What *is* an octogenarian, Peter?' And Mr. Sloane said he didn't know, but they must be very sickly creatures, for you never heard tell of them but they were dying. That's the way with Martin's aunts."

"Martin's just like all the rest of those French," said Marilla in disgust. "You can't depend on them for a day."

Marilla was looking over Anne's Carmody purchases when she heard a shrill shriek in the barnyard. A minute later Anne dashed into the kitchen, wringing her hands.

"Anne Shirley, what's the matter now?"

"Oh, Marilla, whatever shall I do? This is terrible. And it's all my fault. Oh, will I *ever* learn to stop and reflect a little before doing reckless things? Mrs. Lynde always told me I would do something dreadful some day, and now I've done it!"

"Anne, you are the most exasperating girl! *What* is it you've done?"

"Sold Mr. Harrison's Jersey cow . . . the one he bought from Mr. Bell . . . to Mr. Shearer! Dolly is out in the milking pen this very minute."

"Anne Shirley, are you dreaming?"

"I only wish I were. There's no dream about it, though it's very like a nightmare. And Mr. Harrison's cow is in Charlottetown by this time. Oh, Marilla, I thought I'd finished getting into scrapes, and here I am in the very worst one I ever was in in my life. What can I do?"

"Do? There's nothing to do, child, except go and see Mr. Harrison about it. We can offer him our Jersey in exchange if he doesn't want to take the money. She is just as good as his."

"I'm sure he'll be awfully cross and disagreeable about it, though," moaned Anne.

"I daresay he will. He seems to be an irritable sort of a man. I'll go and explain to him if you like."

"No, indeed, I'm not as mean as that," exclaimed Anne. "This is all my fault and I'm certainly not going to let you take my punishment. I'll go myself and I'll go at once. The sooner it's over the better, for it will be terribly humiliating."

Poor Anne got her hat and her twenty dollars and was passing out when she happened to glance through the open pantry door. On the table reposed a nut cake which she had baked that morning . . . a particularly toothsome concoction iced with pink icing and adorned with walnuts. Anne had intended it for Friday evening, when the youth of Avonlea were to meet at Green Gables to organize the Improvement Society. But what were they compared to the justly offended Mr. Harrison? Anne thought that cake ought to soften the heart of any man, especially one who had to do his own cooking, and she promptly popped it into a box. She would take it to Mr. Harrison as a peace offering.

"That is, if he gives me a chance to say anything at all," she thought ruefully, as she climbed the lane fence and started on a short cut across the fields, golden in the light of the dreamy August evening. "I know now just how people feel who are being led to execution."

3

Mr. Harrison at Home

Mr. Harrison's house was an old-fashioned, low-eaved, whitewashed structure, set against a thick spruce grove.

Mr. Harrison himself was sitting on his vine-shaded veranda, in his shirt sleeves, enjoying his evening pipe. When he realized who was coming up the path he sprang suddenly to his feet, bolted into the house, and shut the door. This was merely the uncomfortable result of his surprise, mingled with a good deal of shame over his outburst of temper the day before. But it nearly swept the remnant of her courage from Anne's heart.

"If he's so cross now what will he be when he hears what I've done," she reflected miserably, as she rapped at the door.

But Mr. Harrison opened it, smiling sheepishly, and invited her to enter in a tone quite mild and friendly, if somewhat nervous. He had laid aside his pipe and donned his coat; he offered Anne a very dusty chair very politely, and her reception would have passed off pleasantly enough if it had not been for that telltale of a parrot who was peering through the bars of his cage with wicked golden eyes. No sooner had Anne seated herself than Ginger exclaimed,

"Bless my soul, what's that redheaded snippet coming here for?"

It would be hard to say whose face was the redder, Mr. Harrison's or Anne's.

"Don't you mind that parrot," said Mr. Harrison, casting a furious glance at Ginger. "He's . . . he's always talking nonsense. I got him from my brother who was a sailor. Sailors don't always use the choicest language, and parrots are very imitative birds."

"So I should think," said poor Anne, the remembrance of her errand quelling her resentment. She couldn't afford to snub Mr. Harrison under the circumstances, that was certain. When you had just sold a man's Jersey cow offhand, without his knowledge or consent, you must not mind if his parrot repeated uncomplimentary things. Nevertheless, the "redheaded snippet" was not quite so meek as she might otherwise have been.

"I've come to confess something to you, Mr. Harrison," she said resolutely. "It's . . . it's about . . . that Jersey cow."

"Bless my soul," exclaimed Mr. Harrison nervously, "has she gone and broken into my oats again? Well, never mind . . . never mind if she has. It's no difference . . . none at all. I . . . I was too hasty yesterday, that's a fact. Never mind if she has."

"Oh, if it were only that," sighed Anne. "But it's ten times worse. I don't . . ."

"Bless my soul, do you mean to say she's got into my wheat?"

"No . . . no . . . not the wheat. But . . ."

"Then it's the cabbages! She's broken into my cabbages that I was raising for Exhibition, hey?"

"It's *not* the cabbages, Mr. Harrison. I'll tell you everything . . . that is what I came for—but please don't interrupt me. It makes me so nervous. Just let me tell my story and don't say anything till I get through—and then no doubt you'll say plenty," Anne concluded, but in thought only.

"I won't say another word," said Mr. Harrison, and he didn't. But Ginger was not bound by any contract of silence and kept ejaculating, "Redheaded snippet" at intervals until Anne felt quite wild.

"I shut my Jersey cow up in our pen yesterday. This morning I went to Carmody and when I came back I saw a Jersey cow in your oats. Diana and I chased her out and you can't imagine what a hard time we had. I was so dreadfully wet and tired and vexed—and Mr. Shearer came by that very minute and offered to buy the cow. I sold her to him on the spot for twenty dollars. It was wrong of me. I should have waited and consulted Marilla, of course. But I'm dreadfully given to doing things without thinking—everybody who knows me will tell you that. Mr. Shearer took the cow right away to ship her on the afternoon train."

"Redheaded snippet," quoted Ginger in a tone of profound contempt.

At this point Mr. Harrison arose and, with an expression that would have struck terror into any bird but a parrot, carried Ginger's cage into an adjoining room and shut the door. Ginger shrieked, swore, and otherwise conducted himself in keeping with his reputation, but finding himself left alone, relapsed into sulky silence.

"Excuse me and go on," said Mr. Harrison, sitting down again. "My brother the sailor never taught that bird any manners."

"I went home and after tea I went out to the milking pen. Mr. Harrison," . . . Anne leaned forward, clasping her hands with her old childish gesture, while her big gray eyes gazed imploringly into Mr. Harrison's embarrassed face . . . "I found my cow still shut up in the pen. It was *your* cow I had sold to Mr. Shearer."

"Bless my soul," exclaimed Mr. Harrison, in blank amazement at this unlooked-for conclusion. "What a *very* extraordinary thing!"

"Oh, it isn't in the least extraordinary that I should be getting myself and other people into scrapes," said Anne mournfully. "I'm noted for that. You might suppose I'd have grown out of it by this time . . . I'll be seventeen next March . . . but it seems that I haven't. Mr. Harrison, is it too much to hope that you'll forgive me? I'm afraid it's too late to get your cow back, but here is the money for her . . . or you can have mine in exchange if you'd rather. She's a very good cow. And I can't express how sorry I am for it all."

"Tut, tut," said Mr. Harrison briskly, "don't say another word about it, miss. It's of no consequence . . . no consequence whatever. Accidents will happen. I'm too hasty myself sometimes, miss . . . far too hasty. But I can't help speaking out just what I think and folks must take me as they find me. If that cow had been in my cabbages now . . . but never mind, she wasn't, so it's all right. I think I'd rather have your cow in exchange, since you want to be rid of her."

"Oh, thank you, Mr. Harrison. I'm so glad you are not vexed. I was afraid you would be."

"And I suppose you were scared to death to come here and tell me, after the fuss I made yesterday, hey? But you mustn't mind me, I'm a terrible outspoken old fellow, that's all . . . awful apt to tell the truth, no matter if it is a bit plain."

"So is Mrs. Lynde," said Anne, before she could prevent herself.

"Who? Mrs. Lynde? Don't you tell me I'm like that old gossip," said Mr. Harrison irritably. "I'm not . . . not a bit. What have you got in that box?"

"A cake," said Anne archly. In her relief at Mr. Harrison's unexpected amiability her spirits soared upward feather-light. "I brought it over for you . . . I thought perhaps you didn't have cake very often."

"I don't, that's a fact, and I'm mighty fond of it, too. I'm much obliged to you. It looks good on top. I hope it's good all the way through."

"It is," said Anne, gaily confident. "I have made cakes in my time that were *not,* as Mrs. Allan could tell you, but this one is all right. I made it for the Improvement Society, but I can make another for them."

"Well, I'll tell you what, miss, you must help me eat it. I'll put the kettle on and we'll have a cup of tea. How will that do?"

"Will you let me make the tea?" said Anne dubiously.

Mr. Harrison chuckled.

"I see you haven't much confidence in my ability to make tea. You're wrong . . . I can brew up as good a jorum of tea as you ever drank. But go ahead yourself. Fortunately it rained last Sunday, so there's plenty clean dishes."

Anne hopped briskly up and went to work. She washed the teapot in several waters before she put the tea to steep. Then she swept the stove and set the table, bringing the dishes out of the pantry. The state of that pantry horrified Anne, but she wisely said nothing. Mr. Harrison told her where to find the bread and butter and a can of peaches. Anne adorned the table with a bouquet from the garden and shut her eyes to the stains on the tablecloth. Soon the tea was ready and Anne found herself sitting opposite Mr. Harrison at his own table, pouring his tea for him, and chatting freely to him about her school and friends and plans. She could hardly believe the evidence of her senses.

Mr. Harrison had brought Ginger back, averring that the poor bird would be lonesome; and Anne, feeling that she could forgive everybody and everything, offered him a walnut. But Ginger's feelings had been grievously hurt and he rejected all overtures of friendship. He sat moodily on his perch and ruffled his feathers up until he looked like a mere ball of green and gold.

"Why do you call him Ginger?" asked Anne, who liked appropriate names and thought Ginger accorded not at all with such gorgeous plumage.

"My brother the sailor named him. Maybe it had some reference to his temper. I think a lot of that bird though . . . you'd be surprised if you knew how much. He has his faults of course. That bird has cost me a good deal one way and another. Some people object to his swearing habits but he can't be broken of them. I've tried . . . other people have tried. Some folks have prejudices against parrots. Silly, ain't it? I like them myself. Ginger's a lot of company to me. Nothing would induce me to give that bird up . . . nothing in the world, miss."

Mr. Harrison flung the last sentence at Anne as explosively as if he suspected her of some latent design of persuading him to give Ginger up. Anne, however, was beginning to like the queer, fussy, fidgety little man, and before the meal was over they were quite good friends. Mr. Harrison found out about the Improvement Society and was disposed to approve of it.

"That's right. Go ahead. There's lots of room for improvement in this settlement . . . and in the people too."

"Oh, I don't know," flashed Anne. To herself, or to her particular cronies, she might admit that there were some small imperfections, easily removable, in Avonlea and its inhabitants. But to hear a practical outsider like Mr. Harrison saying it was an entirely different thing. "I think Avonlea is a lovely place; and the people in it are very nice, too."

"I guess you've got a spice of temper," commented Mr. Harrison, surveying the flushed cheeks and indignant eyes opposite him. "It goes with hair like yours, I reckon. Avonlea is a pretty decent place or I wouldn't have located here; but I suppose even you will admit that it has *some* faults?"

"I like it all the better for them," said loyal Anne. "I don't like places or people either that haven't any faults. I think a truly perfect person would be very uninteresting. Mrs. Milton White says she never met a perfect person, but she's heard enough about one . . . her husband's first wife. Don't you think it must be very uncomfortable to be married to a man whose first wife was perfect?"

"It would be more uncomfortable to be married to the perfect wife," declared Mr. Harrison, with a sudden and inexplicable warmth.

When tea was over Anne insisted on washing the dishes, although Mr. Harrison assured her that there were enough in the house to do for weeks yet. She would dearly have loved to sweep the floor also, but no broom was visible and she did not like to ask where it was for fear there wasn't one at all.

"You might run across and talk to me once in a while," suggested Mr. Harrison when she was leaving. "'Tisn't far and folks ought to be neighborly. I'm kind of interested in that society of yours. Seems to me there'll be some fun in it. Who are you going to tackle first?"

"We are not going to meddle with *people* . . . it is only *places* we mean to improve," said Anne, in a dignified tone. She rather suspected that Mr. Harrison was making fun of the project.

When she had gone Mr. Harrison watched her from the window . . . a lithe, girlish shape, tripping lightheartedly across the fields in the sunset afterglow.

"I'm a crusty, lonesome, crabbed old chap," he said aloud, "but there's something about that little girl makes me feel young again . . . and it's such a pleasant sensation I'd like to have it repeated once in a while."

"Redheaded snippet," croaked Ginger mockingly.

Mr. Harrison shook his fist at the parrot.

"You ornery bird," he muttered, "I almost wish I'd wrung your neck when my brother the sailor brought you home. Will you never be done getting me into trouble?"

Anne ran home blithely and recounted her adventures to Marilla, who had been not a little alarmed by her long absence and was on the point of starting out to look for her.

"It's a pretty good world, after all, isn't it, Marilla?" concluded Anne happily. "Mrs. Lynde was complaining the other day that it wasn't much of a world. She said whenever you looked forward to anything pleasant you were sure to be more or less disappointed . . . that nothing ever came up to your expectations. Well, perhaps that is true. But there is a good side to it too. The bad things don't always come up to your expectations either . . . they nearly always turn out ever so much better than you think. I looked forward to a dreadfully unpleasant experience when I went over to Mr. Harrison's tonight; and instead he was quite kind and I had almost a nice time. I think we're going to be real good friends if we make plenty of allowances for each other, and everything has turned out for the best. But all the same, Marilla, I shall certainly never again sell a cow before making sure to whom she belongs. And I do *not* like parrots!"

4

Different Opinions

ne evening at sunset, Jane Andrews, Gilbert Blythe, and
Anne Shirley were lingering by a fence in the shadow of
gently swaying spruce boughs, where a wood cut known
as the Birch Path joined the main road. Jane had been up
to spend the afternoon with Anne, who walked part of the way home
with her; at the fence they met Gilbert, and all three were now talking
about the fateful morrow; for that morrow was the first of September
and the schools would open. Jane would go to Newbridge and Gilbert
to White Sands.

"You both have the advantage of me," sighed Anne. "You're
going to teach children who don't know you, but I have to teach my
own old schoolmates, and Mrs. Lynde says she's afraid they won't
respect me as they would a stranger unless I'm very cross from the
first. But I don't believe a teacher should be cross. Oh, it seems to me
such a responsibility!"

"I guess we'll get on all right," said Jane comfortably. Jane was not
troubled by any aspirations to be an influence for good. She meant to
earn her salary fairly, please the trustees, and get her name on the School
Inspector's roll of honor. Further ambitions Jane had none. "The main
thing will be to keep order and a teacher has to be a little cross to do that.
If my pupils won't do as I tell them I shall punish them."

"How?"

"Give them a good whipping, of course."

"Oh, Jane, you wouldn't," cried Anne, shocked. "Jane, you *couldn't!*"

"Indeed, I could and would, if they deserved it," said Jane decidedly.

"I could *never* whip a child," said Anne with equal decision. "I
don't believe in it *at all.* Miss Stacy never whipped any of us and she had

perfect order; and Mr. Phillips was always whipping and he had no
order at all. No, if I can't get along without whipping I shall not try to
teach school. There are better ways of managing. I shall try to win my
pupils' affections and then they will *want* to do what I tell them."

"But suppose they don't?" said practical Jane.

"I wouldn't whip them anyhow. I'm sure it wouldn't do any good.
Oh, don't whip your pupils, Jane dear, no matter what they do."

"What do you think about it, Gilbert?" demanded Jane. "Don't
you think there are some children who really need a whipping now
and then?"

"Don't you think it's a cruel, barbarous thing to whip a child . . .
any child?" exclaimed Anne, her face flushing with earnestness.

"Well," said Gilbert slowly, torn between his real convictions
and his wish to measure up to Anne's ideal, "there's something to be
said on both sides. I don't believe in whipping children *much*. I think,
as you say, Anne, that there are better ways of managing as a rule, and
that corporal punishment should be a last resort. But on the other
hand, as Jane says, I believe there is an occasional child who can't be
influenced in any other way and who, in short, needs a whipping and
would be improved by it. Corporal punishment as a last resort is to be
my rule."

Gilbert, having tried to please both sides, succeeded, as is usual
and eminently right, in pleasing neither. Jane tossed her head.

"I'll whip my pupils when they're naughty. It's the shortest and
easiest way of convincing them."

Anne gave Gilbert a disappointed glance.

"I shall never whip a child," she repeated firmly. "I feel sure it isn't
either right or necessary."

"Suppose a boy sauced you back when you told him to do something?" said Jane.

"I'd keep him in after school and talk kindly and firmly to him,"
said Anne. "There is some good in every person if you can find it. It is
a teacher's duty to find and develop it. That is what our School
Management professor at Queen's told us, you know. Do you suppose
you could find any good in a child by whipping him? It's far more

important to influence the children aright than it is even to teach them the three R's, Professor Rennie says."

"But the Inspector examines them in the three R's, mind you, and he won't give you a good report if they don't come up to his standard," protested Jane.

"I'd rather have my pupils love me and look back to me in after years as a real helper than be on the roll of honor," asserted Anne decidedly.

"Wouldn't you punish children at all, when they misbehaved?" asked Gilbert.

"Oh, yes, I suppose I shall have to, although I know I'll hate to do it. But you can keep them in at recess or stand them on the floor or give them lines to write."

"I suppose you won't punish the girls by making them sit with the boys?" said Jane slyly.

Gilbert and Anne looked at each other and smiled rather foolishly. Once upon a time, Anne had been made to sit with Gilbert for punishment and sad and bitter had been the consequences thereof.

"Well, time will tell which is the best way," said Jane philosophically as they parted.

Anne went back to Green Gables by way of the Birch Path, shadowy, rustling, fern-scented, through Violet Vale and past Willowmere, where dark and light kissed each other under the firs, and down through Lover's Lane . . . spots she and Diana had so named long ago. She walked slowly, enjoying the sweetness of wood and field and the starry summer twilight, and thinking soberly about the new duties she was to take up on the morrow. When she reached the yard at Green Gables Mrs. Lynde's loud, decided tones floated out through the open kitchen window.

"Mrs. Lynde has come up to give me good advice about tomorrow," thought Anne with a grimace, "but I don't believe I'll go in. Her advice is much like pepper, I think . . . excellent in small quantities but rather scorching in her doses. I'll run over and have a chat with Mr. Harrison instead."

This was not the first time Anne had run over and chatted with Mr. Harrison since the notable affair of the Jersey cow. She had been there several evenings and Mr. Harrison and she were very good friends, although there were times and seasons when Anne found the outspokenness on which he prided himself rather trying. Ginger still continued to regard her with suspicion, and never failed to greet her sarcastically as "redheaded snippet." Mr. Harrison had tried vainly to break him of the habit by jumping excitedly up whenever he saw Anne coming and exclaiming,

"Bless my soul, here's that pretty little girl again," or something equally flattering. But Ginger saw through the scheme and scorned it. Anne was never to know how many compliments Mr. Harrison paid her behind her back. He certainly never paid her any to her face.

"Well, I suppose you've been back in the woods laying in a supply of switches for tomorrow?" was his greeting as Anne came up the veranda steps.

"No, indeed," said Anne indignantly. She was an excellent target for teasing because she always took things so seriously. "I shall never have a switch in my school, Mr. Harrison. Of course, I shall have to have a pointer, but I shall use it for pointing *only*."

"So you mean to strap them instead? Well, I don't know but you're right. A switch stings more at the time but the strap smarts longer, that's a fact."

"I shall not use anything of the sort. I'm not going to whip my pupils."

"Bless my soul," exclaimed Mr. Harrison in genuine astonishment, "how do you lay out to keep order then?"

"I shall govern by affection, Mr. Harrison."

"It won't do," said Mr. Harrison, "won't do at all, Anne. 'Spare the rod and spoil the child.' When I went to school the master whipped me regular every day because he said if I wasn't in mischief just then I was plotting it."

"Methods have changed since your schooldays, Mr. Harrison."

"But human nature hasn't. Mark my words, you'll never manage the young fry unless you keep a rod in pickle for them. The thing is impossible."

"Well, I'm going to try my way first," said Anne, who had a fairly strong will of her own and was apt to cling very tenaciously to her theories.

"You're pretty stubborn, I reckon," was Mr. Harrison's way of putting it. "Well, well, we'll see. Some day when you get riled up . . . and people with hair like yours are desperate apt to get riled . . . you'll forget all your pretty little notions and give some of them a whaling. You're too young to be teaching anyhow . . . far too young and childish."

Altogether, Anne went to bed that night in a rather pessimistic mood. She slept poorly and was so pale and tragic at breakfast next morning that Marilla was alarmed and insisted on making her take a cup of scorching ginger tea. Anne sipped it patiently, although she could not imagine what good ginger tea would do. Had it been some magic brew, potent to confer age and experience, Anne would have swallowed a quart of it without flinching.

"Marilla, what if I fail!"

"You'll hardly fail completely in one day and there's plenty more days coming," said Marilla. "The trouble with you, Anne, is that you'll expect to teach those children everything and reform all their faults right off, and if you can't you'll think you've failed."

5

A Full-fledged Schoolma'am

hen Anne reached the school that morning . . . for the first time in her life she had traversed the Birch Path deaf and blind to its beauties . . . all was quiet and still. The preceding teacher had trained the children to be in their places at her arrival, and when Anne entered the schoolroom she was confronted by prim rows of "shining morning faces" and bright, inquisitive eyes. She hung up her hat and faced her pupils, hoping that she did not look as frightened and foolish as she felt and that they would not perceive how she was trembling.

She had sat up until nearly twelve the preceding night composing a speech she meant to make to her pupils upon opening the school. She had revised and improved it painstakingly, and then she had learned it off by heart. It was a very good speech and had some very fine ideas in it, especially about mutual help and earnest striving after knowledge. The only trouble was that she could not now remember a word of it.

After what seemed to her a year . . . about ten seconds in reality . . . she said faintly,

"Take your Testaments, please," and sank breathlessly into her chair under cover of the rustle and clatter of desk lids that followed. While the children read their verses Anne marshalled her shaky wits into order and looked over the array of little pilgrims to the Grown-up Land.

Most of them were, of course, quite well known to her. Her own classmates had passed out in the preceding year but the rest had all gone to school with her, excepting the primer class and ten newcomers to Avonlea. Anne secretly felt more interest in these ten than in those whose possibilities were already fairly well mapped out to her. To be sure, they might be just as commonplace as the rest; but on the other hand there *might* be a genius among them. It was a thrilling idea.

Sitting by himself at a corner desk was Anthony Pye. He had a dark, sullen little face, and was staring at Anne with a hostile expression in his black eyes. Anne instantly made up her mind that she would win that boy's affection and discomfit the Pyes utterly.

In the other corner another strange boy was sitting with Arty Sloane . . . a jolly looking little chap, with a snub nose, freckled face, and big, light blue eyes, fringed with whitish lashes . . . probably the Donnell boy; and if resemblance went for anything, his sister was sitting across the aisle with Mary Bell. Anne wondered what sort of a mother the child had, to send her to school dressed as she was. She wore a faded pink silk dress, trimmed with a great deal of cotton lace, soiled white kid slippers, and silk stockings. Her sandy hair was tortured into innumerable kinky and unnatural curls, surmounted by a flamboyant bow of pink ribbon bigger than her head. Judging from her expression she was very well satisfied with herself.

A pale little thing, with smooth ripples of fine, silky, fawn-colored hair flowing over her shoulders, must, Anne thought, be Annetta Bell, whose parents had formerly lived in the Newbridge school district, but, by reason of hauling their house fifty yards north of its old site were now in Avonlea. Three pallid little girls crowded into one seat were certainly Cottons; and there was no doubt that the small beauty with the long brown curls and hazel eyes, who was casting coquettish looks at Jack Gillis over the edge of her Testament, was Prillie Rogerson, whose father had recently married a second wife and brought Prillie home from her grandmother's in Grafton. A tall, awkward girl in a back seat, who seemed to have too many feet and hands, Anne could not place at all, but later on discovered that her name was Barbara Shaw and that she had come to live with an Avonlea aunt. She was also to find that if Barbara ever managed to walk down the aisle without falling over her own or somebody else's feet the Avonlea scholars wrote the unusual fact up on the porch wall to commemorate it.

But when Anne's eyes met those of the boy at the front desk facing her own, a queer little thrill went over her, as if she had found her

genius. She knew this must be Paul Irving and that Mrs. Rachel Lynde
had been right for once when she prophesied that he would be unlike
the Avonlea children. More than that, Anne realized that he was
unlike other children anywhere, and that there was a soul subtly akin
to her own gazing at her out of the very dark blue eyes that were
watching her so intently.

She knew Paul was ten but he looked no more than eight. He had
the most beautiful little face she had ever seen in a child . . . features of
exquisite delicacy and refinement, framed in a halo of chestnut curls.
His mouth was delicious, being full without pouting, the crimson lips
just softly touching and curving into finely finished little corners that
narrowly escaped being dimpled. He had a sober, grave, meditative
expression, as if his spirit was much older than his body; but when
Anne smiled softly at him it vanished in a sudden answering smile,
which seemed an illumination of his whole being, as if some lamp had
suddenly kindled into flame inside of him, irradiating him from top to
toe. Best of all, it was involuntary, born of no external effort or motive,
but simply the outflashing of a hidden personality, rare and fine and
sweet. With that quick interchange of smiles Anne and Paul were fast
friends forever before a word had passed between them.

The day went by like a dream. Anne could never clearly recall it
afterwards. It almost seemed as if it were not she who was teaching but
somebody else. She heard classes and worked sums and set copies
mechanically. The children behaved quite well; only two cases of dis-
cipline occurred. Morley Andrews was caught driving a pair of trained
crickets in the aisle. Anne stood Morley on the platform for an hour
and . . . which Morley felt much more keenly . . . confiscated his crickets. She put them in a box and on the way from school set them free in
Violet Vale; but Morley believed, then and ever afterwards, that she
took them home and kept them for her own private amusement.

The other culprit was Anthony Pye, who poured the last drops of
water from his slate bottle down the back of Aurelia Clay's neck. Anne
kept Anthony in at recess and talked to him about what was expected
of gentlemen, admonishing him that they never poured water down
ladies' necks. She wanted all her boys to be gentlemen, she said. Her

little lecture was quite kind and touching; but unfortunately Anthony remained absolutely untouched. He listened to her in silence, with the same sullen expression, and whistled scornfully as he went out. Anne sighed; and then cheered herself up by remembering that winning a Pye's affections, like the building of Rome, wasn't the work of a day. In fact, it was doubtful whether some of the Pyes had any affections to win; but Anne hoped better things of Anthony, who looked as if he might be a rather nice boy if one ever got behind his sullenness.

When school was dismissed and the children had gone Anne dropped wearily into her chair. Her head ached and she felt woefully discouraged. There was no real reason for discouragement, since nothing very dreadful had occurred; but Anne was very tired and inclined to believe that she would never learn to like teaching. And how terrible it would be to be doing something you didn't like every day for ... well, say forty years. Anne was of two minds whether to have her cry out then and there, or wait till she was safely in her own white room at home. Before she could decide there was a click of heels and a silken swish on the porch floor, and Anne found herself confronted by a lady whose appearance made her recall a recent criticism of Mr. Harrison's on an overdressed female he had seen in a Charlottetown store. "She looked like a head-on collision between a fashion plate and a nightmare."

The newcomer was gorgeously arrayed in a pale blue summer silk, puffed, frilled, and shirred wherever puff, frill, or shirring could possibly be placed. Her head was surmounted by a huge white chiffon hat, bedecked with three long but rather stringy ostrich feathers. A veil of pink chiffon, lavishly sprinkled with huge black dots, hung like a flounce from the hat brim to her shoulders and floated off in two airy streamers behind her. She wore all the jewelry that could be crowded on one small woman, and a very strong odor of perfume attended her.

"I am Mrs. Donnell . . . Mrs. H. B. Donnell," announced this vision, "and I have come in to see you about something Clarice Almira told me when she came home to dinner today. It annoyed me *excessively.*"

"I'm sorry," faltered Anne, vainly trying to recollect any incident of the morning connected with the Donnell children.

"Clarice Almira told me that you pronounced our name *Don*nell. Now, Miss Shirley, the correct pronunciation of our name is Don*nell* . . . accent on the last syllable. I *hope* you'll remember this in future."

"I'll try to," gasped Anne, choking back a wild desire to laugh. "I know by experience that it's very unpleasant to have one's name *spelled* wrong and I suppose it must be even worse to have it pronounced wrong."

"Certainly it is. And Clarice Almira also informed me that you call my son Jacob."

"He told me his name was Jacob," protested Anne.

"I might have expected that," said Mrs. H. B. Don*nell,* in a tone which implied that gratitude in children was not to be looked for in this degenerate age. "That boy has such plebeian tastes, Miss Shirley. When he was born I wanted to call him St. Clair . . . it sounds *so* aristocratic, doesn't it? But his father insisted he should be called Jacob after his uncle. I yielded, because Uncle Jacob was a rich old bachelor. And what do you think, Miss Shirley? When our innocent boy was five years old Uncle Jacob actually went and got married and now he has three boys of his own. Did you ever hear of such ingratitude? The moment the invitation to the wedding . . . for he had the impertinence to send us an invitation, Miss Shirley . . . came to the house I said, 'No more Jacobs for me, thank you.' From that day I called my son St. Clair and St. Clair I am determined he shall be called. His father obstinately continues to call him Jacob, and the boy himself has a perfectly unaccountable preference for the vulgar name. But St. Clair he is and St. Clair he shall remain. You will kindly remember this, Miss Shirley, will you not? *Thank* you. I told Clarice Almira that I was sure it was only a misunderstanding and that a word would set it right. Don*nell* . . . accent on last syllable . . . and St. Clair . . . on *no* account Jacob. You'll remember? *Thank* you."

When Mrs. H. B. Don*nell* had skimmed away Anne locked the school door and went home. At the foot of the hill she found Paul Irving by the Birch Path. He held out to her a cluster of the dainty little wild orchids which Avonlea children called "rice lillies."

"Please, teacher, I found these in Mr. Wright's field," he said shyly, "and I came back to give them to you because I thought you were the kind of lady that would like them, and because . . ." he lifted his big, beautiful eyes . . . "I like you, teacher."

"You darling," said Anne, taking the fragrant spikes. As if Paul's words had been a spell of magic, discouragement and weariness passed from her spirit, and hope upwelled in her heart like a dancing fountain. She went through the Birch Path light-footedly, attended by the sweetness of her orchids as by a benediction.

"Well, how did you get along?" Marilla wanted to know.

"Ask me that a month later and I may be able to tell you. I can't now . . . I don't know myself . . . I'm too near it. My thoughts feel as if they had been all stirred up until they were thick and muddy. The only thing I feel really sure of having accomplished today is that I taught Cliffie Wright that A is A. He never knew it before. Isn't it something to have started a soul along a path that may end in Shakespeare and Paradise Lost?"

Mrs. Lynde came up later on with more encouragement. That good lady had waylaid the schoolchildren at her gate and demanded of them how they liked their new teacher.

"And every one of them said they liked you splendid, Anne, except Anthony Pye. I must admit he didn't. He said you 'weren't any good, just like all girl teachers.' There's the Pye leaven for you. But never mind."

"I'm not going to mind," said Anne quietly, "and I'm going to make Anthony Pye like me yet. Patience and kindness will surely win him."

"Well, you can never tell about a Pye," said Mrs. Rachel cautiously. "They go by contraries, like dreams, often as not. As for that *Donnell* woman, she'll get no *Don*nelling from me, I can assure you. The name is *Donn*ell and always has been. The woman is crazy, that's what. She has a pug dog she calls Queenie and it has its meals at the table along with the family, eating off a china plate. I'd be afraid of a judgment if I was her. Thomas says Donnell himself is a sensible, hardworking man, but he hadn't much gumption when he picked out a wife, that's what."

6

All Sorts and Conditions
of Men . . . and Women

September day on Prince Edward Island hills; a crisp wind blowing up over the sand dunes from the sea; a long red road, winding through fields and woods, now looping itself about a corner of thick set spruces, now threading a plantation of young maples with great feathery sheets of ferns beneath them, now dipping down into a hollow where a brook flashed out of the woods and into them again, now basking in open sunshine between ribbons of goldenrod and smoke-blue asters; air athrill with the pipings of myriads of crickets, those glad little pensioners of the summer hills; a plump brown pony ambling along the road; two girls behind him, full to the lips with the simple, priceless joy of youth and life.

"Oh, this is a day left over from Eden, isn't it, Diana?" . . . and Anne sighed for sheer happiness. "The air has magic in it. Look at the purple in the cup of that harvest valley, Diana. And oh, do smell the dying fir! It's coming up from that little sunny hollow where Mr. Eben Wright has been cutting fence poles. Bliss is it on such a day to be alive; but to smell dying fir is very heaven. That's two thirds Wordsworth and one third Anne Shirley. It doesn't seem possible that there should be dying fir in heaven, does it? And yet it doesn't seem to me that heaven would be quite perfect if you couldn't get a whiff of dead fir as you went through its woods. Perhaps we'll have the odor there without the death. Yes, I think that will be the way. That delicious aroma must be the souls of the firs . . . and of course it will be just souls in heaven."

"Trees haven't souls," said practical Diana, "but the smell of dead fir is certainly lovely. I'm going to make a cushion and fill it with fir needles. You'd better make one too, Anne."

"I think I shall . . . and use it for my naps. I'd be certain to dream I was a dryad or a wood-nymph then. But just this minute I'm well content to be Anne Shirley, Avonlea schoolma'am, driving over a road like this on such a sweet, friendly day."

"It's a lovely day but we have anything but a lovely task before us," sighed Diana. "Why on earth did you offer to canvass this road, Anne? Almost all the cranks in Avonlea live along it, and we'll probably be treated as if we were begging for ourselves. It's the very worst road of all."

"That is why I chose it. Of course Gilbert and Fred would have taken this road if we had asked them. But you see, Diana, I feel myself responsible for the A.V.I.S., since I was the first to suggest it, and it seems to me that I ought to do the most disagreeable things. I'm sorry on your account; but you needn't say a word at the cranky places. I'll do all the talking . . . Mrs. Lynde would say I was well able to. Mrs. Lynde doesn't know whether to approve of our enterprise or not. She inclines to, when she remembers that Mr. and Mrs. Allan are in favor of it; but the fact that village improvement societies first originated in the States is a count against it. So she is halting between two opinions and only success will justify us in Mrs. Lynde's eyes. Priscilla is going to write a paper for our next Improvement meeting, and I expect it will be good, for her aunt is such a clever writer and no doubt it runs in the family. I shall never forget the thrill it gave me when I found out that Mrs. Charlotte E. Morgan was Priscilla's aunt. It seemed so wonderful that I was a friend of the girl whose aunt wrote 'Edgewood Days' and 'The Rosebud Garden.'"

"Where does Mrs. Morgan live?"

"In Toronto. And Priscilla says she is coming to the Island for a visit next summer, and if it is possible Priscilla is going to arrange to have us meet her. That seems almost too good to be true—but it's something pleasant to imagine after you go to bed."

The Avonlea Village Improvement Society was an organized fact. Gilbert Blythe was president, Fred Wright vice-president, Anne Shirley secretary, and Diana Barry treasurer. The "Improvers," as they were promptly christened, were to meet once a fortnight at the homes of the members. It was admitted that they could not expect to affect many improvements so late in the season; but they meant to plan the next summer's campaign, collect and discuss ideas, write and read papers, and, as Anne said, educate public sentiment generally.

There was some disapproval, of course, and . . . which the Improvers felt much more keenly . . . a good deal of ridicule. Mr. Elisha Wright was reported to have said that a more appropriate name for the organization would be Courting Club. Mrs. Hiram Sloane declared she had heard the Improvers meant to plough up all the roadsides and set them out with geraniums. Mr. Levi Boulter warned his neighbors that the Improvers would insist that everybody pull down his house and rebuild it after plans approved by the society. Mr. James Spencer sent them word that he wished they would kindly shovel down the church hill. Eben Wright told Anne that he wished the Improvers could induce old Josiah Sloane to keep his whiskers trimmed. Mr. Lawrence Bell said he would whitewash his barns if nothing else would please them but he would *not* hang lace curtains in his cowstable windows. Mr. Major Spencer asked Clifton Sloane, an Improver who drove the milk to the Carmody cheese factory, if it was true that everybody would have to have his milk-stand hand-painted next summer and keep an embroidered centerpiece on it.

In spite of . . . or perhaps, human nature being what it is, because of . . . this, the Society went gamely to work at the only improvement they could hope to bring about that fall. At the second meeting, in the Barry parlor, Oliver Sloane moved that they start a subscription to re-shingle and paint the hall; Julia Bell seconded it, with an uneasy feeling that she was doing something not exactly ladylike. Gilbert put the motion, it was carried unanimously, and Anne gravely recorded it in her minutes. The next thing was to appoint a committee, and Gertie Pye, determined not to let Julia Bell carry off all the laurels, boldly moved that Miss Jane Andrews be chairman of said committee. This motion being also duly seconded and carried, Jane returned the compliment by appointing Gertie on the committee, along with Gilbert, Anne, Diana, and Fred Wright. The committee chose their routes in private conclave. Anne and Diana were told off for the Newbridge road, Gilbert and Fred for the White Sands road, and Jane and Gertie for the Carmody road.

"Because," explained Gilbert to Anne, as they walked home together through the Haunted Wood, "the Pyes all live along that road and they won't give a cent unless one of themselves canvasses them."

The next Saturday Anne and Diana started out. They drove to the end of the road and canvassed homeward, calling first on the "Andrews girls."

"If Catherine is alone we may get something," said Diana, "but if Eliza is there we won't."

Eliza was there . . . very much so . . . and looked even grimmer than usual. Miss Eliza was one of those people who give you the impression that life is indeed a vale of tears, and that a smile, never to speak of a laugh, is a waste of nervous energy truly reprehensible. The Andrews girls had been "girls" for fifty odd years and seemed likely to remain girls to the end of their earthly pilgrimage. Catherine, it was said, had not entirely given up hope, but Eliza, who was born a pessimist, had never had any. They lived in a little brown house built in a sunny corner scooped out of Mark Andrews' beech woods. Eliza complained that it was terrible hot in summer, but Catherine was wont to say it was lovely and warm in winter.

Eliza was sewing patchwork, not because it was needed but simply as a protest against the frivolous lace Catherine was crocheting. Eliza listened with a frown and Catherine with a smile, as the girls explained their errand. To be sure, whenever Catherine caught Eliza's eye she discarded the smile in guilty confusion; but it crept back the next moment.

"If I had money to waste," said Eliza grimly, "I'd burn it up and have the fun of seeing a blaze maybe; but I wouldn't give it to that hall, not a cent. It's no benefit to the settlement . . . just a place for young folks to meet and carry on when they's better be home in their beds."

"Oh, Eliza, young folks must have some amusement," protested Catherine.

"I don't see the necessity. We didn't gad about to halls and places when we were young, Catherine Andrews. This world is getting worse every day."

"I think it's getting better," said Catherine firmly.

"*You* think!" Miss Eliza's voice expressed the utmost contempt. "It doesn't signify what you *think,* Catherine Andrews. Facts is facts."

"Well, I always like to look on the bright side, Eliza."

"There isn't any bright side."

"Oh, indeed there is," cried Anne, who couldn't endure such heresy in silence. "Why, there are ever so many bright sides, Miss Andrews. It's really a beautiful world."

"You won't have such a high opinion of it when you've lived as long in it as I have," retorted Miss Eliza sourly, "and you won't be so enthusiastic about improving it either. How is your mother, Diana? Dear me, but she has failed of late. She looks terrible run down. And how long is it before Marilla expects to be stone blind, Anne?"

"The doctor thinks her eyes will not get any worse if she is very careful," faltered Anne.

Eliza shook her head.

"Doctors always talk like that just to keep people cheered up. I wouldn't have much hope if I was her. It's best to be prepared for the worst."

"But oughtn't we to be prepared for the best too?" pleaded Anne. "It's just as likely to happen as the worst."

"Not in my experience, and I've fifty-seven years to set against your sixteen," retorted Eliza. "Going, are you? Well, I hope this new society of yours will be able to keep Avonlea from running any further down hill but I haven't much hope of it."

Anne and Diana got themselves thankfully out, and drove away as fast as the fat pony could go. As they rounded the curve below the beech wood a plump figure came speeding over Mr. Andrews' pasture, waving to them excitedly. It was Catherine Andrews and she was so out of breath that she could hardly speak, but she thrust a couple of quarters into Anne's hand.

"That's my contribution to painting the hall," she gasped. "I'd like to give you a dollar but I don't dare take more from my egg money for Eliza would find it out if I did. I'm real interested in your society and I believe you're going to do a lot of good. I'm an optimist. I *have* to be, living with Eliza. I must hurry back before she misses me . . . she thinks I'm feeding the hens. I hope you'll have good luck canvassing, and don't be cast down over what Eliza said. The world *is* getting better . . . it certainly is."

The next house was Daniel Blair's.

"Now, it all depends on whether his wife is home or not," said Diana, as they jolted along a deep-rutted lane. "If she is we won't get a cent. Everybody says Dan Blair doesn't dare have his hair cut without asking her permission; and it's certain she's very close, to state it moderately. She says she has to be just before she's generous. But Mrs. Lynde says she's so much 'before' that generosity never catches up with her at all."

Anne related their experience at the Blair place to Marilla that evening.

"We tied the horse and then rapped at the kitchen door. Nobody came but the door was open and we could hear somebody in the pantry, going on dreadfully. We couldn't make out the words but Diana says she knows they were swearing by the sound of them. I can't believe that of Mr. Blair, for he is always so quiet and meek; but at least he had great provocation, for Marilla, when that poor man came to the door, red as a beet, with perspiration streaming down his face, he had on one of his wife's big gingham aprons. 'I can't get this durned thing off,' he said, 'for the strings are tied in a hard knot and I can't bust 'em, so you'll have to excuse me, ladies.' We begged him not to mention it and went in and sat down. Mr. Blair sat down too; he twisted the apron around to his back and rolled it up, but he did look so ashamed and worried that I felt sorry for him, and Diana said she feared we had called at an inconvenient time. 'Oh, not at all,' said Mr. Blair, trying to smile . . . you know he is always very polite . . . 'I'm a little busy . . . getting ready to bake a cake as it were. My wife got a telegram today that her sister from Montreal is coming tonight and she's gone to the train to meet her and left orders for me to make a cake for tea. She writ out the recipe and told me what to do but I've clean forgot half the directions already. And it says, "flavor according to taste." What does that mean? How can you tell? And what if my taste doesn't happen to be other people's taste? Would a tablespoon of vanilla be enough for a small layer cake?'

"I felt sorrier than ever for the poor man. He didn't seem to be in his proper sphere at all. I had heard of henpecked husbands and now I felt that I saw one. It was on my lips to say, 'Mr. Blair, if you'll give us a subscription for the hall I'll mix up your cake for you.' But I suddenly thought it wouldn't be neighborly to drive too sharp a bargain with a fellow creature in distress. So I offered to mix the cake for him without any conditions at all. He just jumped at my offer. He said he'd been used to making his own bread before he was married but he feared cake was beyond him, and yet he hated to disappoint his wife. He got me another apron, and Diana beat the eggs and I mixed the cake. Mr. Blair ran about and got us the materials. He had forgotten all about his apron and when he ran it streamed out behind him and Diana said she thought she would die to see it. He said he could bake the cake all right . . . he was used to that . . . and then he asked for our list and he put down four dollars. So you see we were rewarded. But even if he hadn't given a cent I'd always feel that we had done a truly Christian act in helping him."

Theodore White's was the next stopping place. Neither Anne nor Diana had ever been there before, and they had only a very slight acquaintance with Mrs. Theodore, who was not given to hospitality. Should they go to the back or front door? While they held a whispered consultation Mrs. Theodore appeared at the front door with an armful of newspapers. Deliberately she laid them down one by one on the porch floor and the porch steps, and then down the path to the very feet of her mystified callers.

"Will you please wipe your feet carefully on the grass and then walk on these papers?" she said anxiously. "I've just swept the house all over and I can't have any more dust tracked in. The path's been real muddy since the rain yesterday."

"Don't you dare laugh," warned Anne in a whisper, as they marched along the newspapers. "And I implore you, Diana, not to look at me, no matter what she says, or I shall not be able to keep a sober face."

The papers extended across the hall and into a prim, fleckless parlor. Anne and Diana sat down gingerly on the nearest chairs and explained their errand. Mrs. White heard them politely, interrupting only twice, once to chase out an adventurous fly, and once to pick up a tiny wisp of grass that had fallen on the carpet from Anne's dress. Anne felt wretchedly guilty; but Mrs. White subscribed two dollars and paid the money down . . . "to prevent us from having to go back for it," Diana said when they got away. Mrs. White had the newspapers gathered up before they had their horse untied and as they drove out of the yard they saw her busily wielding a broom in the hall.

"I've always heard that Mrs. Theodore White was the neatest woman alive and I'll believe it after this," said Diana, giving way to her suppressed laughter as soon as it was safe.

"I am glad she has no children," said Anne solemnly. "It would be dreadful beyond words for them if she had."

At the Spencers' Mrs. Isabella Spencer made them miserable by saying something ill-natured about everyone in Avonlea. Mr. Thomas Boulter refused to give anything because the hall, when it had been built, twenty years before, hadn't been built on the site he recommended. Mrs. Esther Bell, who was the picture of health, took half an hour to detail all her aches and pains, and sadly put down fifty cents because she wouldn't be there that time next year to do it . . . no, she would be in her grave.

Their worst reception, however, was at Simon Fletcher's. When they drove into the yard they saw two faces peering at them through the porch window. But although they rapped and waited patiently and persistently nobody came to the door. Two decidedly ruffled and indignant girls drove away from Simon Fletcher's. Even Anne admitted that she was beginning to feel discouraged. But the tide turned after that. Several Sloane homesteads came next, where they got liberal subscriptions, and from that to the end they fared well, with only an occasional snub. Their last place of call was at Robert Dickson's by the pond bridge. They stayed to tea here, although they were nearly home, rather than risk offending Mrs. Dickson, who had the reputation of being a very "touchy" woman.

While they were there old Mrs. James White called in.

"I've just been down to Lorenzo's," she announced. "He's the proudest man in Avonlea this minute. What do you think? There's a brand new boy there . . . and after seven girls that's quite an event, I can tell you."

Anne pricked up her ears, and when they drove away she said,

"I'm going straight to Lorenzo White's."

"But he lives on the White Sands road and it's quite a distance out of our way," protested Diana. "Gilbert and Fred will canvass him."

"They are not going around until next Saturday and it will be too late by then," said Anne firmly. "The novelty will be worn off. Lorenzo White is dreadfully mean but he will subscribe to *anything* just now. We mustn't let such a golden opportunity slip, Diana."

The result justified Anne's foresight. Mr. White met them in the yard, beaming like the sun upon an Easter day. When Anne asked for a subscription he agreed enthusiastically.

"Certain, certain. Just put me down for a dollar more than the highest subscription you've got."

"That will be five dollars . . . Mr. Daniel Blair put down four," said Anne, half afraid. But Lorenzo did not flinch.

"Five it is . . . and here's the money on the spot. Now, I want you to come into the house. There's something in there worth seeing . . . something very few people have seen as yet. Just come in and pass *your* opinion."

"What will we say if the baby isn't pretty?" whispered Diana in trepidation as they followed the excited Lorenzo into the house.

"Oh, there will certainly be something else nice to say about it," said Anne easily. "There always is about a baby."

The baby *was* pretty, however, and Mr. White felt that he got his five dollars' worth out of the girls' honest delight over the plump little newcomer. But that was the first, last, and only time that Lorenzo White ever subscribed to anything.

Anne, tired as she was, made one more effort for the public weal that night, slipping over the fields to interview Mr. Harrison, who was as usual smoking his pipe on the veranda with Ginger beside him. Strictly speaking he was on the Carmody road; but Jane and Gertie, who were not acquainted with him save by doubtful report, had nervously begged Anne to canvass him.

Mr. Harrison, however, flatly refused to subscribe a cent, and all Anne's wiles were in vain.

"But I thought you approved of our society, Mr. Harrison," she mourned.

"So I do . . . so I do . . . but my approval doesn't go as deep as my pocket, Anne."

"A few more experiences such as I have had today would make me as much of a pessimist as Miss Eliza Andrews," Anne told her reflection in the east gable mirror at bedtime.

7

The Pointing of Duty

nne leaned back in her chair one mild October evening and sighed. She was sitting at a table covered with text books and exercises, but the closely written sheets of paper before her had no apparent connection with studies or school work.

"What is the matter?" asked Gilbert, who had arrived at the open kitchen door just in time to hear the sigh.

Anne colored, and thrust her writing out of sight under some school compositions.

"Nothing very dreadful. I was just trying to write out some of my thoughts, as Professor Hamilton advised me, but I couldn't get them to please me. They seem so stiff and foolish directly they're written down on white paper with black ink. Fancies are like shadows . . . you can't cage them, they're such wayward, dancing things. But perhaps I'll learn the secret some day if I keep on trying. I haven't a great many spare moments, you know. By the time I finish correcting school exercises and compositions, I don't always feel like writing any of my own."

"You are getting on splendidly in school, Anne. All the children like you," said Gilbert, sitting down on the stone step.

"No, not all. Anthony Pye doesn't and *won't* like me. What is worse, he doesn't respect me . . . no, he doesn't. He simply holds me in contempt and I don't mind confessing to you that it worries me miserably. It isn't that he is so very bad . . . he is only rather mischievous, but no worse than some of the others. He seldom disobeys me; but he obeys with a scornful air of toleration as if it wasn't worthwhile disputing the point or he would . . . and it has a bad effect on the others. I've tried every way to win him but I'm beginning to fear I never shall. I want to, for he's rather a cute little lad, if he *is* a Pye, and I could like him if he'd let me."

"Probably it's merely the effect of what he hears at home."

"Not altogether. Anthony is an independent little chap and makes up his own mind about things. He has always gone to men before and he says girl teachers are no good. Well, we'll see what patience and kindness will do. I like overcoming difficulties and teaching is really very interesting work. Paul Irving makes up for all that is lacking in the others. That child is a perfect darling, Gilbert, and a genius into the bargain. I'm persuaded the world will hear of him some day," concluded Anne in a tone of conviction.

"I like teaching, too," said Gilbert. "It's good training, for one thing. Why, Anne, I've learned more in the weeks I've been teaching the young ideas of White Sands than I learned in all the years I went to school myself. We all seem to be getting on pretty well. The Newbridge people like Jane, I hear; and I think White Sands is tolerably satisfied with your humble servant . . . all except Mr. Andrew Spencer. I met Mrs. Peter Blewett on my way home last night and she told me she thought it her duty to inform me that Mr. Spencer didn't approve of my methods."

"Have you ever noticed," asked Anne reflectively, "that when people say it is their duty to tell you a certain thing you may prepare for something disagreeable? Why is it that they never seem to think it a duty to tell you the pleasant things they hear about you? Mrs. H. B. Don*nell* called at the school again yesterday and told me she thought it *her* duty to inform me that Mrs. Harmon Andrews didn't approve of my reading fairy tales to the children, and that Mr. Rogerson thought Prillie wasn't coming on fast enough in arithmetic. If Prillie would spend less time making eyes at the boys over her slate she might do better. I feel quite sure that Jack Gillis works her class sums for her, though I've never been able to catch him red-handed."

"Have you succeeded in reconciling Mrs. Don*nell's* hopeful son to his saintly name?"

"Yes," laughed Anne, "but it was really a difficult task. At first, when I called him 'St. Clair' he would not take the least notice until I'd spoken two or three times; and then, when the other boys nudged him, he would look up with such an aggrieved air, as if I'd called him John or Charlie and he couldn't be expected to know I meant him. So I kept him in after school one night and talked kindly to him. I told him his mother wished me to call him St. Clair and I couldn't go against her wishes. He saw it when it was all explained out . . . he's really a very reasonable little fellow . . . and he said *I* could call him St. Clair but that he'd 'lick the stuffing' out of any of the boys that tried it. Of course, I had to rebuke him again for using such shocking language. Since then *I* call him St. Clair and the boys call him Jake and all goes smoothly. He informs me that he means to be a carpenter, but Mrs. Don*nell* says I am to make a college professor out of him."

The mention of college gave a new direction to Gilbert's thoughts, and they talked for a time of their plans and wishes . . . gravely, earnestly, hopefully, as youth love to talk, while the future is yet an untrodden path full of wonderful possibilities.

Gilbert had finally made up his mind that he was going to be a doctor.

"It's a splendid profession," he said enthusiastically. "A fellow has to fight something all through life . . . didn't somebody once define man as a fighting animal? . . . and I want to fight disease and pain and ignorance . . . which are all members one of another. I want to do my share of honest, real work in the world, Anne . . . add a little to the sum of human knowledge that all the good men have been accumulating since it began. The folks who lived before me have done so much for me that I want to show my gratitude by doing something for the folks who will live after me. It seems to me that is the only way a fellow can get square with his obligations to the race."

"I'd like to add some beauty to life," said Anne dreamily. "I don't exactly want to make people *know* more . . . though I know that *is* the noblest ambition . . . but I'd love to make them have a pleasanter time because of me . . . to have some little joy or happy thought that would never have existed if I hadn't been born."

"I think you're fulfilling that ambition every day," said Gilbert admiringly.

And he was right. Anne was one of the children of light by birthright. After she had passed through a life with a smile or a word thrown across it like a gleam of sunshine the owner of that life saw it, for the time being at least, as hopeful and lovely and of good report.

Finally Gilbert rose regretfully.

"Well, I must run up to MacPhersons'. Moody Spurgeon came home from Queen's today for Sunday and he was to bring me out a book Professor Boyd is lending me."

"And I must get Marilla's tea. She went to see Mrs. Keith this evening and she will soon be back."

Anne had tea ready when Marilla came home; the fire was crackling cheerily, a vase of frost-bleached ferns and ruby-red maple leaves adorned the table, and delectable odors of ham and toast pervaded the air. But Marilla sank into her chair with a deep sigh.

"Are your eyes troubling you? Does your head ache?" queried Anne anxiously.

"No. I'm only tired . . . and worried. It's about Mary and those children . . . Mary is worse . . . she can't last much longer. And as for the twins, *I* don't know what is to become of them."

"Hasn't their uncle been heard from?"

"Yes, Mary had a letter from him. He's working in a lumber camp and 'shacking it,' whatever that means. Anyway, he says he can't possibly take the children till the spring. He expects to be married then and will have a home to take them to; but he says she must get some of the neighbors to keep them for the winter. She says she can't bear to ask any of them. Mary never got on any too well with the East Grafton people and that's a fact. And the long and short of it is, Anne, that I'm sure Mary wants me to take those children . . . she didn't say so but she *looked* it."

"Oh!" Anne clasped her hands, all athrill with excitement. "And of course you will, Marilla, won't you?"

"I haven't made up my mind," said Marilla rather tartly. "I don't rush into things in your headlong way, Anne. Third cousinship is a pretty slim claim. And it will be a fearful responsibility to have two children of six years to look after . . . twins, at that."

Marilla had an idea that twins were just twice as bad as single children.

"Twins are very interesting . . . at least one pair of them," said Anne. "It's only when there are two or three pairs that it gets monotonous. And I think it would be real nice for you to have something to amuse you when I'm away in school."

"I don't reckon there'd be much amusement in it . . . more worry and bother than anything else, I should say. It wouldn't be so risky if they were even as old as you were when I took you. I wouldn't mind Dora so much . . . she seems good and quiet. But that Davy is a limb."

Anne was fond of children and her heart yearned over the Keith twins. The remembrance of her own neglected childhood was very vivid with her still. She knew that Marilla's only vulnerable point was her stern devotion to what she believed to be her duty, and Anne skillfully marshalled her arguments along this line.

"If Davy is naughty it's all the more reason why he should have good training, isn't it, Marilla? If we don't take them we don't know who will, nor what kind of influences may surround them. Suppose Mrs. Keith's next door neighbors, the Sprotts, were to take them. Mrs. Lynde says Henry Sprott is the most profane man that ever lived and you can't believe a word his children say. Wouldn't it be dreadful to have the twins learn anything like that? Or suppose they went to the Wiggins'. Mrs. Lynde says that Mr. Wiggins sells everything off the place that can be sold and brings his family up on skim milk. You wouldn't like your relations to be starved, even if they were only third cousins, would you? It seems to me, Marilla, that it is our duty to take them."

"I suppose it is," assented Marilla gloomily. "I daresay I'll tell Mary I'll take them. You needn't look so delighted, Anne. It will mean a good deal of extra work for you. I can't sew a stitch on account of my eyes, so you'll have to see to the making and mending of their clothes. And you don't like sewing."

"I hate it," said Anne calmly, "but if you are willing to take those children from a sense of duty surely I can do their sewing from a sense of duty. It does people good to have to do things they don't like . . . in moderation."

8

Marilla Adopts Twins

Mrs. Rachel Lynde was sitting at her kitchen window, knitting a quilt, just as she had been sitting one evening several years previously when Matthew Cuthbert had driven down over the hill with what Mrs. Rachel called "his imported orphan." But that had been in springtime; and this was late autumn, and all the woods were leafless and the fields sere and brown. The sun was just setting with a great deal of purple and golden pomp behind the dark woods west of Avonlea when a buggy drawn by a comfortable brown nag came down the hill. Mrs. Rachel peered at it eagerly.

"There's Marilla getting home from the funeral," she said to her husband, who was lying on the kitchen lounge. Thomas Lynde lay more on the lounge nowadays than he had been used to do, but Mrs. Rachel, who was so sharp at noticing anything beyond her own household, had not as yet noticed this. "And she's got the twins with her . . . yes, there's Davy leaning over the dashboard grabbing at the pony's tail and Marilla jerking him back. Dora's sitting up on the seat as prim as you please. She always looks as if she'd just been starched and ironed. Well, poor Marilla is going to have her hands full this winter and no mistake. Still, I don't see that she could do anything less than take them, under the circumstances, and she'll have Anne to help her. Anne's tickled to death over the whole business, and she has a real knacky way with children, I must say. Dear me, it doesn't seem a day since poor Matthew brought Anne herself home and everybody laughed at the idea of Marilla bringing up a child. And now she has adopted twins. You're never safe from being surprised till you're dead."

The fat pony jogged over the bridge in Lynde's Hollow and along the Green Gables lane. Marilla's face was rather grim. It was ten miles from East Grafton and Davy Keith seemed to be possessed with a passion for perpetual motion. It was beyond Marilla's power to make him sit still and she had been in an agony the whole way lest he fall over the back of the wagon and break his neck, or tumble over the dashboard under the pony's heels. In despair she finally threatened to whip him soundly when she got him home. Whereupon Davy climbed into her lap, regardless of the reins, flung his chubby arms about her neck and gave her a bear-like hug.

"I don't believe you mean it," he said, smacking her wrinkled cheek affectionately. "You don't *look* like a lady who'd whip a little boy just 'cause he couldn't keep still. Didn't you find it awful hard to keep still when you was only 's old as me?"

"No, I always kept still when I was told," said Marilla, trying to speak sternly, albeit she felt her heart waxing soft within her under Davy's impulsive caresses.

"Well, I s'pose that was 'cause you was a girl," said Davy, squirming back to his place after another hug. "You *was* a girl once, I s'pose, though it's awful funny to think of it. Dora can sit still . . . but there ain't much fun in it *I* don't think. Seems to me it must be slow to be a girl. Here, Dora, let me liven you up a bit."

Davy's method of "livening up" was to grasp Dora's curls in his fingers and give them a tug. Dora shrieked and then cried.

"How can you be such a naughty boy and your poor mother just laid in her grave this very day?" demanded Marilla despairingly.

"But she was glad to die," said Davy confidentially. "I know, 'cause she told me so. She was awful tired of being sick. We'd a long talk the night before she died. She told me you was going to take me and Dora for the winter and I was to be a good boy. I'm going to be good, but can't you be good running round just as well as sitting still? And she said I was always to be kind to Dora and stand up for her, and I'm going to."

"Do you call pulling her hair being kind to her?"

"Well, I ain't going to let anybody else pull it," said Davy, doubling up his fists and frowning. "They'd just better try it. I didn't hurt her much . . . she just cried 'cause she's a girl. I'm glad I'm a boy but I'm sorry

I'm a twin. When Jimmy Sprott's sister conterdicks him he just says, 'I'm older'n you, so of course I know better,' and that settles *her*. But I can't tell Dora that, and she just goes on thinking diffrunt from me. You might let me drive the gee-gee for a spell, since I'm a man."

Altogether, Marilla was a thankful woman when she drove into her own yard, where the wind of the autumn night was dancing with the brown leaves. Anne was at the gate to meet them and lift the twins out. Dora submitted calmly to be kissed, but Davy responded to Anne's welcome with one of his hearty hugs and the cheerful announcement, "I'm Mr. Davy Keith."

At the supper table Dora behaved like a little lady, but Davy's manners left much to be desired.

"I'm so hungry I ain't got time to eat p'litely," he said when Marilla reproved him. "Dora ain't half as hungry as I am. Look at all the ex'cise I took on the road here. That cake's awful nice and plummy. We haven't had any cake at home for ever'n ever so long, 'cause mother was too sick to make it and Mrs. Sprott said it was as much as she could do to bake our bread for us. And Mrs. Wiggins never puts any plums in *her* cakes. Catch her! Can I have another piece?"

Marilla would have refused but Anne cut a generous second slice. However, she reminded Davy that he ought to say "Thank you" for it. Davy merely grinned at her and took a huge bite. When he had finished the slice he said,

"If you'll give me *another* piece I'll say thank you for *it*."

"No, you have had plenty of cake," said Marilla in a tone which Anne knew and Davy was to learn to be final.

Davy winked at Anne, and then, leaning over the table, snatched Dora's first piece of cake, from which she had just taken one dainty little bite, out of her very fingers and, opening his mouth to the fullest extent, crammed the whole slice in. Dora's lip trembled and Marilla was speechless with horror. Anne promptly exclaimed, with her best "schoolma'am" air,

"Oh, Davy, gentlemen don't do things like that."

"I know they don't," said Davy, as soon as he could speak, "but I ain't a gemplum."

"But don't you want to be?" said shocked Anne.

"Course I do. But you can't be a gemplum till you grow up."

"Oh, indeed you can," Anne hastened to say, thinking she saw a chance to sow good seed betimes. "You can begin to be a gentleman when you are a little boy. And gentlemen *never* snatch things from ladies. . . . or forget to say thank you . . . or pull anybody's hair."

"They don't have much fun, that's a fact," said Davy frankly. "I guess I'll wait till I'm grown up to be one."

Marilla, with a resigned air, had cut another piece of cake for Dora. She did not feel able to cope with Davy just then. It had been a hard day for her, what with the funeral and the long drive. At that moment she looked forward to the future with a pessimism that would have done credit to Eliza Andrews herself.

The twins were not noticeably alike, although both were fair. Dora had long sleek curls that never got out of order. Davy had a crop of fuzzy little yellow ringlets all over his round head. Dora's hazel eyes were gentle and mild; Davy's were as roguish and dancing as an elf's. Dora's nose was straight, Davy's was a positive snub; Dora had a "prunes and prisms" mouth, Davy's was all smiles; and besides, he had a dimple in one cheek and none in the other, which gave him a dear, comical, lopsided look when he laughed. Mirth and mischief lurked in every corner of his little face.

"They'd better go to bed," said Marilla, who thought it was the easiest way to dispose of them. "Dora will sleep with me and you can put Davy in the west gable. You're not afraid to sleep alone, are you, Davy?"

"No; but I ain't going to bed for ever so long yet," said Davy comfortably.

"Oh, yes, you are." That was all the much-tried Marilla said, but something in her tone squelched even Davy. He trotted obediently upstairs with Anne.

"When I'm grown up the very first thing I'm going to do is stay up *all* night just to see what it would be like," he told her confidentially.

In after years Marilla never thought of that first week of the twins' sojourn at Green Gables without a shiver. Not that it really was so much worse than the weeks that followed it; but it seemed so by reason of its novelty. There was seldom a waking minute of any day when Davy was not in mischief or devising it; but his first notable exploit occurred two days after his arrival, on Sunday morning . . . a fine, warm day, as hazy and mild as September. Anne dressed him for church while Marilla attended to Dora. Davy at first objected strongly to having his face washed.

"Marilla washed it yesterday . . . and Mrs. Wiggins scoured me with hard soap the day of the funeral. That's enough for one week. I don't see the good of being so awful clean. It's lots more comfable being dirty."

"Paul Irving washes his face every day of his own accord," said Anne astutely.

Davy had been an inmate of Green Gables for little over forty-eight hours; but he already worshipped Anne and hated Paul Irving, whom he had heard Anne praising enthusiastically the day after his arrival. If Paul Irving washed his face every day, that settled it. He, Davy Keith, would do it too, if it killed him. The same consideration induced him to submit meekly to the other details of his toilet, and he was really a handsome little lad when all was done. Anne felt an almost maternal pride in him as she led him into the old Cuthbert pew.

Davy behaved quite well at first, being occupied in casting covert glances at all the small boys within view and wondering which was Paul Irving. The first two hymns and the Scripture reading passed off uneventfully. Mr. Allan was praying when the sensation came.

Lauretta White was sitting in front of Davy, her head slightly bent and her fair hair hanging in two long braids, between which a tempting expanse of white neck showed, encased in a loose lace frill. Lauretta was a fat, placid-looking child of eight, who had conducted herself irreproachably in church from the very first day her mother carried her there, an infant of six months.

Davy thrust his hand into his pocket and produced . . . a caterpillar, a furry, squirming caterpillar. Marilla saw and clutched at him but she was too late. Davy dropped the caterpillar down Lauretta's neck.

Right into the middle of Mr. Allan's prayer burst a series of piercing shrieks. The minister stopped appalled and opened his eyes. Every head in the congregation flew up. Lauretta White was dancing up and down in her pew, clutching frantically at the back of her dress.

"Ow ... mommer ... mommer ... ow ... take it off ... ow ... get it out ... ow ... that bad boy put it down my neck ... ow ... mommer ... it's going further down. ... ow ... ow ... ow. ..."

Mrs. White rose and with a set face carried the hysterical, writhing Lauretta out of church. Her shrieks died away in the distance and Mr. Allan proceeded with the service. But everybody felt that it was a failure that day. For the first time in her life Marilla took no notice of the text and Anne sat with scarlet cheeks of mortification.

When they got home Marilla put Davy to bed and made him stay there for the rest of the day. She would not give him any dinner but allowed him a plain tea of bread and milk. Anne carried it to him and sat sorrowfully by him while he ate it with an unrepentant relish. But Anne's mournful eyes troubled him.

"I s'pose," he said reflectively, "that Paul Irving wouldn't have dropped a caterpillar down a girl's neck in church, would he?"

"Indeed he wouldn't," said Anne sadly.

"Well, I'm kind of sorry I did it, then," conceded Davy. "But it was such a jolly big caterpillar ... I picked him up on the church steps just as we went in. It seemed a pity to waste him. And say, wasn't it fun to hear that girl yell?"

Tuesday afternoon the Aid Society met at Green Gables. Anne hurried home from school, for she knew that Marilla would need all the assistance she could give. Dora, neat and proper, in her nicely starched white dress and black sash, was sitting with the members of the Aid in the parlor, speaking demurely when spoken to, keeping silence when not, and in every way comporting herself as a model child. Davy, blissfully dirty, was making mud pies in the barnyard.

"I told him he might," said Marilla wearily. "I thought it would keep him out of worse mischief. He can only get dirty at that. We'll have our teas over before we call him to his. Dora can have hers with us, but I would never dare to let Davy sit down at the table with all the Aids here."

When Anne went to call the Aids to tea she found that Dora was not in the parlor. Mrs. Jasper Bell said Davy had come to the front door and called her out. A hasty consultation with Marilla in the pantry resulted in a decision to let both children have their teas together later on.

Tea was half over when the dining room was invaded by a forlorn figure. Marilla and Anne stared in dismay, the Aids in amazement. Could that be Dora . . . that sobbing nondescript in a drenched, dripping dress and hair from which the water was streaming on Marilla's new coin-spot rug?

"Dora, what has happened to you?" cried Anne, with a guilty glance at Mrs. Jasper Bell, whose family was said to be the only one in the world in which accidents never occurred.

"Davy made me walk the pigpen fence," wailed Dora. "I didn't want to but he called me a fraid-cat. And I fell off into the pigpen and my dress got all dirty and the pig runned right over me. My dress was just awful but Davy said if I'd stand under the pump he'd wash it clean, and I did and he pumped water all over me but my dress ain't a bit cleaner and my pretty sash and shoes is all spoiled."

Anne did the honors of the table alone for the rest of the meal while Marilla went upstairs and redressed Dora in her old clothes. Davy was caught and sent to bed without any supper. Anne went to his room at twilight and talked to him seriously . . . a method in which she had great faith, not altogether unjustified by results. She told him she felt very badly over his conduct.

"I feel sorry now myself," admitted Davy, "but the trouble is I never feel sorry for doing things till after I've did them. Dora wouldn't help me make pies 'cause she was afraid of messing her clo'es and that made me hopping mad. I s'pose Paul Irving wouldn't have made *his* sister walk a pigpen fence if he knew she'd fall in?"

"No, he would never dream of such a thing. Paul is a perfect little gentleman."

Davy screwed his eyes tight shut and seemed to meditate on this for a time. Then he crawled up and put his arms about Anne's neck, snuggling his flushed little face down on her shoulder.

"Anne, don't you like me a little bit, even if I ain't a good boy like Paul?"

"Indeed I do," said Anne sincerely. Somehow, it was impossible to help liking Davy. "But I'd like you better still if you weren't so naughty."

"I . . . did something else today," went on Davy in a muffled voice. "I'm sorry now but I'm awful scared to tell you. You won't be very cross, will you? And you won't tell Marilla, will you?"

"I don't know, Davy. Perhaps I ought to tell her. But I think I can promise you I won't if you promise me that you will never do it again, whatever it is."

"No, I never will. Anyhow, it's not likely I'd find any more of them this year. I found this one on the cellar steps."

"Davy, what is it you've done?"

"I put a toad in Marilla's bed. You can go and take it out if you like. But say, Anne, wouldn't it be fun to leave it there?"

"Davy Keith!" Anne sprang from Davy's clinging arms and flew across the hall to Marilla's room. The bed was slightly rumpled. She threw back the blankets in nervous haste and there in very truth was the toad, blinking at her from under a pillow.

"How can I carry that awful thing out?" moaned Anne with a shudder. The fire shovel suggested itself to her and she crept down to get it while Marilla was busy in the pantry. Anne had her own troubles carrying that toad downstairs, for it hopped off the shovel three times and once she thought she had lost it in the hall. When she finally deposited it in the cherry orchard she drew a long breath of relief.

"If Marilla knew she'd never feel safe getting into bed again in her life. I'm so glad that little sinner repented in time. There's Diana signaling to me from her window. I'm glad . . . I really feel the need of some diversion, for what with Anthony Pye in school and Davy Keith at home my nerves have had about all they can endure for one day."

9

A Question of Color

"That old nuisance of a Rachel Lynde was here again today, pestering me for a subscription towards buying a carpet for the vestry room," said Mr. Harrison wrathfully. "I detest that woman more than anybody I know. She can put a whole sermon, text, comment, and application, into six words, and throw it at you like a brick."

Anne, who was perched on the edge of the veranda, enjoying the charm of a mild west wind blowing across a newly ploughed field on a gray November twilight and piping a quaint little melody among the twisted firs below the garden, turned her dreamy face over her shoulder.

"The trouble is, you and Mrs. Lynde don't understand one another," she explained. "That is always what is wrong when people don't like each other. I didn't like Mrs. Lynde at first either; but as soon as I came to understand her I learned to."

"Mrs. Lynde may be an acquired taste with some folks; but I didn't keep on eating bananas because I was told I'd learn to like them if I did," growled Mr. Harrison. "And as for understanding her, I understand that she is a confirmed busybody and I told her so."

"Oh, that must have hurt her feelings very much," said Anne reproachfully. "How could you say such a thing? I said some dreadful things to Mrs. Lynde long ago but it was when I had lost my temper. I couldn't say them *deliberately*."

"It was the truth and I believe in telling the truth to everybody."

"But you don't tell the whole truth," objected Anne. "You only tell the disagreeable part of the truth. Now, you've told me a dozen times that my hair was red, but you've never once told me that I had a nice nose."

"I daresay you know it without any telling," chuckled Mr. Harrison.

"I know I have red hair too . . . although it's *much* darker than it used to be . . . so there's no need of telling me that either."

"Well, well, I'll try and not mention it again since you're so sensitive. You must excuse me, Anne. I've got a habit of being outspoken and folks mustn't mind it."

"But they can't help minding it. And I don't think it's any help that it's your habit. What would you think of a person who went about sticking pins and needles into people and saying, 'Excuse me, you mustn't mind it . . . it's just a habit I've got.' You'd think he was crazy, wouldn't you? And as for Mrs. Lynde being a busybody, perhaps she is. But did you tell her she had a very kind heart and always helped the poor, and never said a word when Timothy Cotton stole a crock of butter out of her dairy and told his wife he'd bought it from her? Mrs. Cotton cast it up to her the next time they met that it tasted of turnips and Mrs. Lynde just said she was sorry it had turned out so poorly."

"I suppose she has some good qualities," conceded Mr. Harrison grudgingly. "Most folks have. I have some myself, though you might never suspect it. But anyhow I ain't going to give anything to that carpet. Folks are everlasting begging for money here, it seems to me. How's your project of painting the hall coming on?"

"Splendidly. We had a meeting of the A.V.I.S. last Friday night and found that we had plenty of money subscribed to paint the hall and shingle the roof too. *Most* people gave very liberally, Mr. Harrison."

Anne was a sweet-souled lass, but she could instill some venom into innocent italics when occasion required.

"What color are you going to have it?"

"We have decided on a very pretty green. The roof will be dark red, of course. Mr. Roger Pye is going to get the paint in town today."

"Who's got the job?"

"Mr. Joshua Pye of Carmody. He has nearly finished the shingling. We had to give him the contract, for every one of the Pyes . . . and there are four families, you know . . . said they wouldn't give a cent unless Joshua got it. They had subscribed twelve dollars between them and we thought that was too much to lose, although some people think we shouldn't have given in to the Pyes. Mrs. Lynde says they try to run everything."

"The main question is will this Joshua do his work well. If he does I don't see that it matters whether his name is Pye or Pudding."

"He has the reputation of being a good workman, though they say he's a very peculiar man. He hardly ever talks."

"He's peculiar enough all right then," said Mr. Harrison drily. "Or at least, folks here will call him so. I never was much of a talker till I came to Avonlea and then I had to begin in self-defense or Mrs. Lynde would have said I was dumb and started a subscription to have me taught sign language. You're not going yet, Anne?"

"I must. I have some sewing to do for Dora this evening. Besides, Davy is probably breaking Marilla's heart with some new mischief by this time. This morning the first thing he said was, 'Where does the dark go, Anne? I want to know.' I told him it went around to the other side of the world but after breakfast he declared it didn't . . . that it went down the well. Marilla says she caught him hanging over the well-box four times today, trying to reach down to the dark."

"He's a limb," declared Mr. Harrison. "He came over here yesterday and pulled six feathers out of Ginger's tail before I could get in from the barn. The poor bird has been moping ever since. Those children must be a sight of trouble to you folks."

"Everything that's worth having is some trouble," said Anne, secretly resolving to forgive Davy's next offence, whatever it might be, since he had avenged her on Ginger.

Mr. Roger Pye brought the hall paint home that night and Mr. Joshua Pye, a surly, taciturn man, began painting the next day. He was not disturbed in his task. The hall was situated on what was called "the lower road." In late autumn this road was always muddy and wet, and people going to Carmody traveled by the longer "upper" road. The hall was so closely surrounded by fir woods that it was invisible unless you were near it. Mr. Joshua Pye painted away in the solitude and independence that were so dear to his unsociable heart.

Friday afternoon he finished his job and went home to Carmody. Soon after his departure Mrs. Rachel Lynde drove by, having braved the mud of the lower road out of curiosity to see what the hall looked like in its new coat of paint. When she rounded the spruce curve she saw.

The sight affected Mrs. Lynde oddly. She dropped the reins, held up her hands, and said "Gracious Providence!" She stared as if she could not believe her eyes. Then she laughed almost hysterically.

"There must be some mistake . . . there *must*. I knew those Pyes would make a mess of things."

Mrs. Lynde drove home, meeting several people on the road and stopping to tell them about the hall. The news flew like wildfire. Gilbert Blythe, poring over a text book at home, heard it from his father's hired boy at sunset, and rushed breathlessly to Green Gables, joined on the way by Fred Wright. They found Diana Barry, Jane Andrews, and Anne Shirley, despair personified, at the yard gate of Green Gables, under the big leafless willows.

"It isn't true surely, Anne?" exclaimed Gilbert.

"It *is* true," answered Anne, looking like the muse of tragedy. "Mrs. Lynde called on her way from Carmody to tell me. Oh, it is simply dreadful! *What* is the use of trying to improve anything?"

"What is dreadful?" asked Oliver Sloane, arriving at this moment with a bandbox he had brought from town for Marilla.

"Haven't you heard?" said Jane wrathfully. "Well, it's simply this . . . Joshua Pye *has gone and painted the hall blue instead of green* . . . a deep, brilliant blue, the shade they use for painting carts and wheelbarrows. And Mrs. Lynde says it is the most hideous color for a building, especially when combined with a red roof, that she ever saw or imagined. You could simply have knocked me down with a feather when I heard it. It's heartbreaking, after all the trouble we've had."

"How on earth could such a mistake have happened?" wailed Diana.

The blame of this unmerciful disaster was eventually narrowed down to the Pyes. The Improvers had decided to use Morton-Harris paints and the Morton-Harris paint cans were numbered according to a color card. A purchaser chose his shade on the card and ordered by the accompanying number. Number 147 was the shade of green desired and when Mr. Roger Pye sent word to the Improvers by his son, John Andrew, that he was going to town and would get their paint for them, the Improvers told John Andrew to tell his father to get 147. John Andrew always averred that he did so, but Mr. Roger Pye as stanchly declared that John Andrew told him 157; and there the matter stands to this day.

That night there was blank dismay in every Avonlea house where an Improver lived. The gloom at Green Gables was so intense that it quenched even Davy. Anne wept and would not be comforted.

"I *must* cry, even if I am almost seventeen, Marilla," she sobbed. "It's so mortifying. And it sounds the death knell of our society. We'll simply be laughed out of existence."

In life, as in dreams, however, things often go by contraries. The Avonlea people did not laugh; they were too angry. *Their* money had gone to paint the hall and consequently *they* felt themselves bitterly aggrieved by the mistake. Public indignation centered on the Pyes. Roger Pye and John Andrew had bungled the matter between them; and as for Joshua Pye, he must be a born fool not to suspect there was something wrong when he opened the cans and saw the color of the paint. Joshua Pye, when thus animadverted upon, retorted that the Avonlea taste in colors was no business of his, whatever his private opinion of it might be; he had been hired to paint the hall, not to talk about it; and he meant to have his money for it.

The Improvers paid him his money in bitterness of spirit, after consulting Mr. Peter Sloane, who was a magistrate.

"You'll have to pay it," Peter told him. "You can't hold him responsible for the mistake, since he claims he was never told what the color was supposed to be but just given the cans and told to go ahead. But it's a burning shame and that hall certainly does look awful."

The luckless Improvers expected that Avonlea would be more prejudiced than ever against them; but instead, public sympathy veered around in their favor. People thought the eager, enthusiastic little band who had worked so hard for their object had been badly used. Mrs. Lynde told them to keep on and show the Pyes that there really were people in the world who could do things without making a muddle of them. Mr. Major Spencer sent them word that he would clean out all the stumps along the road front of his farm and seed it down with grass at his own expense; and Mrs. Hiram Sloane called at the school one day and beckoned Anne mysteriously out into the porch to tell her that if the "Sassiety" wanted to make a geranium bed at the crossroads in the spring they needn't be afraid of her cow, for she would see that the marauding animal was kept within safe bounds. Even Mr. Harrison chuckled, if he chuckled at all, in private, and was all sympathy outwardly.

"Never mind, Anne. Most paints fade uglier every year but that blue is as ugly as it can be to begin with, so it's bound to fade prettier. And the roof is shingled and painted all right. Folks will be able to sit in the hall after this without being leaked on. You've accomplished so much anyhow."

"But Avonlea's blue hall will be a byword in all the neighboring settlements from this time out," said Anne bitterly.

And it must be confessed that it was.

10

Davy in Search of a Sensation

nne, walking home from school through the Birch Path one November afternoon, felt convinced afresh that life was a very wonderful thing. The day had been a good day; all had gone well in her little kingdom. St. Clair Donnell had *not* fought any of the other boys over the question of his name; Prillie Rogerson's face had been so puffed up from the effects of toothache that she did not once try to coquette with the boys in her vicinity. Barbara Shaw had met with only *one* accident . . . spilling a dipper of water over the floor . . . and Anthony Pye had not been in school at all.

"What a nice month this November has been!" said Anne, who had never quite got over her childish habit of talking to herself. "November is usually such a disagreeable month . . . as if the year had suddenly found out that she was growing old and could do nothing but weep and fret over it. This year is growing old gracefully . . . just like a stately old lady who knows she can be charming even with gray hair and wrinkles. We've had lovely days and delicious twilights. This last fortnight has been so peaceful, and even Davy has been almost well-behaved. I really think he is improving a great deal. How quiet the woods are today . . . not a murmur except that soft wind purring in the treetops! It sounds like surf on a faraway shore. How dear the woods are! You beautiful trees! I love every one of you as a friend."

Anne paused to throw her arm about a slim young birch and kiss its cream-white trunk. Diana, rounding a curve in the path, saw her and laughed.

"Anne Shirley, you're only pretending to be grown up. I believe when you're alone you're as much a little girl as you ever were."

"Well, one can't get over the habit of being a little girl all at once," said Anne gaily. "You see, I was little for fourteen years and I've only been grown-uppish for scarcely three. I'm sure I shall always feel like a child in the woods. These walks home from school are almost the only time I have for dreaming . . . except the half hour or so before I go to sleep. I'm so busy with teaching and studying and helping Marilla with the twins that I haven't another moment for imagining things. You don't know what splendid adventures I have for a little while after I go to bed in the east gable every night. I always imagine I'm something very brilliant and triumphant and splendid . . . a great prima donna or a Red Cross nurse or a queen. Last night I was a queen. It's really splendid to imagine you are a queen. You have all the fun of it without any of the inconveniences and you can stop being a queen whenever you want to, which you couldn't in real life. But here in the woods I like best to imagine quite different things . . . I'm a dryad living in an old pine, or a little brown wood-elf hiding under a crinkled leaf. That white birch you caught me kissing is a sister of mine. The only difference is, she's a tree and I'm a girl, but that's no real difference. Where are you going, Diana?"

"Down to the Dicksons. I promised to help Alberta cut out her new dress. Can't you walk down in the evening, Anne, and come home with me?"

"I might . . . since Fred Wright is away in town," said Anne with a rather too innocent face.

Diana blushed, tossed her head, and walked on. She did not look offended, however.

Anne fully intended to go down to the Dicksons' that evening, but she did not. When she arrived at Green Gables she found a state of affairs which banished every other thought from her mind. Marilla met her in the yard . . . a wild-eyed Marilla.

"Anne, Dora is lost!"

"Dora! Lost!" Anne looked at Davy, who was swinging on the yard gate, and detected merriment in his eyes. "Davy, do you know where she is?"

"No, I don't," said Davy stoutly. "I haven't seen her since dinner time, cross my heart."

"I've been away ever since one o'clock," said Marilla. "Thomas Lynde took sick all of a sudden and Rachel sent up for me to go at once. When I left here Dora was playing with her doll in the kitchen and Davy was making mud pies behind the barn. I only got home half an hour ago . . . and no Dora to be seen. Davy declares he never saw her since I left."

"Neither I did," avowed Davy solemnly.

"She must be somewhere around," said Anne. "She would never wander far away alone . . . you know how timid she is. Perhaps she has fallen asleep in one of the rooms."

Marilla shook her head.

"I've hunted the whole house through. But she may be in some of the buildings."

A thorough search followed. Every corner of house, yard, and outbuildings was ransacked by those two distracted people. Anne roved the orchards and the Haunted Wood, calling Dora's name. Marilla took a candle and explored the cellar. Davy accompanied each of them in turn, and was fertile in thinking of places where Dora could possibly be. Finally they met again in the yard.

"It's a most mysterious thing," groaned Marilla.

"Where can she be?" said Anne miserably.

"Maybe she's tumbled into the well," suggested Davy cheerfully.

Anne and Marilla looked fearfully into each other's eyes. The thought had been with them both through their entire search but neither had dared to put it into words.

"She . . . she might have," whispered Marilla.

Anne, feeling faint and sick, went to the well-box and peered over. The bucket sat on the shelf inside. Far down below was a tiny glimmer of still water. The Cuthbert well was the deepest in Avonlea. If Dora . . . but Anne could not face the idea. She shuddered and turned away.

"Run across for Mr. Harrison," said Marilla, wringing her hands.

"Mr. Harrison and John Henry are both away . . . they went to town today. I'll go for Mr. Barry."

Mr. Barry came back with Anne, carrying a coil of rope to which was attached a claw-like instrument that had been the business end of a grubbing fork. Marilla and Anne stood by, cold and shaken with horror and dread, while Mr. Barry dragged the well, and Davy, astride the gate, watched the group with a face indicative of huge enjoyment.

Finally Mr. Barry shook his head, with a relieved air.

"She can't be down there. It's a mighty curious thing where she could have got to, though. Look here, young man, are you sure you've no idea where your sister is?"

"I've told you a dozen times that I haven't," said Davy, with an injured air. "Maybe a tramp come and stole her."

"Nonsense," said Marilla sharply, relieved from her horrible fear of the well. "Anne, do you suppose she could have strayed over to Mr. Harrison's? She has always been talking about his parrot ever since that time you took her over."

"I can't believe Dora would venture so far alone but I'll go over and see," said Anne.

Nobody was looking at Davy just then or it would have been seen that a very decided change came over his face. He quietly slipped off the gate and ran, as fast as his fat legs could carry him, to the barn.

Anne hastened across the fields to the Harrison establishment in no very hopeful frame of mind. The house was locked, the window shades were down, and there was no sign of anything living about the place. She stood on the veranda and called Dora loudly.

Ginger, in the kitchen behind her, shrieked and swore with sudden fierceness; but between his outbursts Anne heard a plaintive cry from the little building in the yard which served Mr. Harrison as a toolhouse. Anne flew to the door, unhasped it, and caught up a small mortal with a tearstained face who was sitting forlornly on an upturned nail keg.

"Oh, Dora, Dora, what a fright you have given us! How came you to be here?"

"Davy and I come over to see Ginger," sobbed Dora, "but we couldn't see him after all, only Davy made him swear by kicking the door. And then Davy brought me here and run out and shut the door; and I couldn't get out. I cried and cried, I was so frightened, and oh, I'm so hungry and cold; and I thought you'd never come, Anne."

"Davy?" But Anne could say no more. She carried Dora home with a heavy heart. Her joy at finding the child safe and sound was drowned out in the pain caused by Davy's behavior. The freak of shutting Dora up might easily have been pardoned. But Davy had told falsehoods . . . downright cold-blooded falsehoods about it. That was the ugly fact and Anne could not shut her eyes to it. She could have sat down and cried with sheer disappointment. She had grown to love Davy dearly . . . how dearly she had not known until this minute . . . and it hurt her unbearably to discover that he was guilty of deliberate falsehood.

Marilla listened to Anne's tale in a silence that boded no good Davy-ward; Mr. Barry laughed and advised that Davy be summarily dealt with. When he had gone home Anne soothed and warmed the sobbing, shivering Dora, got her her supper and put her to bed. Then she returned to the kitchen, just as Marilla came grimly in, leading, or rather pulling, the reluctant, cobwebby Davy, whom she had just found hidden away in the darkest corner of the stable.

She jerked him to the mat on the middle of the floor and then went and sat down by the east window. Anne was sitting limply by the west window. Between them stood the culprit. His back was toward Marilla and it was a meek, subdued, frightened back; but his face was toward Anne and although it was a little shamefaced there was a gleam of comradeship in Davy's eyes, as if he knew he had done wrong and was going to be punished for it, but could count on a laugh over it all with Anne later on.

But no half hidden smile answered him in Anne's gray eyes, as there might have done had it been only a question of mischief. There was something else . . . something ugly and repulsive.

"How could you behave so, Davy?" she asked sorrowfully.

Davy squirmed uncomfortably.

"I just did it for fun. Things have been so awful quiet here for so long that I thought it would be fun to give you folks a big scare. It was, too."

In spite of fear and a little remorse Davy grinned over the recollection.

"But you told a falsehood about it, Davy," said Anne, more sorrowfully than ever.

Davy looked puzzled.

"What's a falsehood? Do you mean a whopper?"

"I mean a story that was not true."

"Course I did," said Davy frankly. "If I hadn't you wouldn't have been scared. I *had* to tell it."

Anne was feeling the reaction from her fright and exertions. Davy's impenitent attitude gave the finishing touch. Two big tears brimmed up in her eyes.

"Oh, Davy, how could you?" she said, with a quiver in her voice. "Don't you know how wrong it was?"

Davy was aghast. Anne crying . . . he had made Anne cry! A flood of real remorse rolled like a wave over his warm little heart and engulfed it. He rushed to Anne, hurled himself into her lap, flung his arms around her neck, and burst into tears.

"I didn't know it was wrong to tell whoppers," he sobbed. "How did you expect me to know it was wrong? All Mr. Sprott's children told them *regular* every day, and cross their hearts too. I s'pose Paul Irving never tells whoppers and here I've been trying awful hard to be as good as him, but now I s'pose you'll never love me again. But I think you might have told me it was wrong. I'm awful sorry I've made you cry, Anne, and I'll never tell a whopper again."

Davy buried his face in Anne's shoulder and cried stormily. Anne, in a sudden glad flash of understanding, held him tight and looked over his curly thatch at Marilla.

"He didn't know it was wrong to tell falsehoods, Marilla. I think we must forgive him for that part of it this time if he will promise never to say what isn't true again."

"I never will, now that I know it's bad," asseverated Davy between sobs. "If you ever catch me telling a whopper again you can . . ." Davy groped mentally for a suitable penance . . . "you can skin me alive, Anne."

"Don't say 'whopper,' Davy . . . say 'falsehood,'" said the schoolma'am.

"Why?" queried Davy, settling comfortably down and looking up with a tearstained, investigating face. "Why ain't whopper as good as falsehood? I want to know. It's just as big a word."

"It's slang; and it's wrong for little boys to use slang."

"There's an awful lot of things it's wrong to do," said Davy with a sigh. "I never s'posed there was so many. I'm sorry it's wrong to tell whop . . . falsehoods, 'cause it's awful handy, but since it is I'm never going to tell any more. What are you going to do to me for telling them this time? I want to know." Anne looked beseechingly at Marilla.

"I don't want to be too hard on the child," said Marilla. "I daresay nobody ever did tell him it was wrong to tell lies, and those Sprott children were no fit companions for him. Poor Mary was too sick to train him properly and I presume you couldn't expect a six-year-old child to know things like that by instinct. I suppose we'll just have to assume he doesn't know *anything* right and begin at the beginning. But he'll have to be punished for shutting Dora up, and I can't think of any way except to send him to bed without his supper and we've done that so often. Can't you suggest something else, Anne? I should think you ought to be able to, with that imagination you're always talking of."

"But punishments are so horrid and I like to imagine only pleasant things," said Anne, cuddling Davy. "There are so many unpleasant things in the world already that there is no use in imagining any more."

In the end Davy was sent to bed, as usual, there to remain until noon next day. He evidently did some thinking, for when Anne went up to her room a little later she heard him calling her name softly. Going in, she found him sitting up in bed, with his elbows on his knees and his chin propped on his hands.

"Anne," he said solemnly, "is it wrong for everybody to tell whop . . . falsehoods? I want to know."

"Yes, indeed."

"Is it wrong for a grown-up person?"

"Yes."

"Then," said Davy decidedly, "Marilla is bad, for *she* tells them. And she's worse'n me, for I didn't know it was wrong but she does."

"Davy Keith, Marilla never told a story in her life," said Anne indignantly.

"She did so. She told me last Tuesday that something dreadful would happen to me if I didn't say my prayers every night. And I haven't said them for over a week, just to see what *would* happen . . . and nothing has," concluded Davy in an aggrieved tone.

Anne choked back a mad desire to laugh with the conviction that it would be fatal, and then earnestly set about saving Marilla's reputation.

"Why, Davy Keith," she said solemnly, "something dreadful *has* happened to you this very day."

Davy looked sceptical.

"I s'pose you mean being sent to bed without any supper," he said scornfully, "but *that* isn't dreadful. Course, I don't like it, but I've been sent to bed so much since I come here that I'm getting used to it. And you don't save anything by making me go without supper either, for I always eat twice as much for breakfast."

"I don't mean your being sent to bed. I mean the fact that you told a falsehood today. And, Davy," . . . Anne leaned over the footboard of the bed and shook her finger impressively at the culprit . . . "for a boy to tell what isn't true is almost the worst thing that *could* happen to him . . . almost the very worst. So you see Marilla told you the truth."

"But I thought the something bad would be exciting," protested Davy in an injured tone.

"Marilla isn't to blame for what you thought. Bad things aren't always exciting. They're very often just nasty and stupid."

"It was awful funny to see Marilla and you looking down the well, though," said Davy, hugging his knees.

Anne kept a sober face until she got downstairs and then she collapsed on the sitting room lounge and laughed until her sides ached.

"I wish you'd tell me the joke," said Marilla, a little grimly. "I haven't seen much to laugh at today."

"You'll laugh when you hear this," assured Anne. And Marilla did laugh, which showed how much her education had advanced since the adoption of Anne. But she sighed immediately afterwards.

"I suppose I shouldn't have told him that, although I heard a minister say it to a child once. But he did aggravate me so. It was that night you were at the Carmody concert and I was putting him to bed. He said he didn't see the good of praying until he got big enough to be of some importance to God. Anne, I do not know what we are going to do with that child. I never saw him beat. I'm feeling clean discouraged."

"Oh, don't say that, Marilla. Remember how bad I was when I came here."

"Anne, you never were bad . . . *never*. I see that now, when I've learned what real badness is. You were always getting into terrible scrapes, I'll admit, but your motive was always good. Davy is just bad from sheer love of it."

"Oh, no, I don't think it is real badness with him either," pleaded Anne. "It's just mischief. And it is rather quiet for him here, you know. He has no other boys to play with and his mind has to have something to occupy it. Dora is so prim and proper she is no good for a boy's playmate. I really think it would be better to let them go to school, Marilla."

"No," said Marilla resolutely, "my father always said that no child should be cooped up in the four walls of a school until it was seven years old, and Mr. Allan says the same thing. The twins can have a few lessons at home but go to school they shan't till they're seven."

"Well, we must try to reform Davy at home then," said Anne cheerfully. "With all his faults he's really a dear little chap. I can't help loving him. Marilla, it may be a dreadful thing to say, but honestly, I like Davy better than Dora, for all she's so good."

"I don't know but that I do, myself," confessed Marilla, "and it isn't fair, for Dora isn't a bit of trouble. There couldn't be a better child and you'd hardly know she was in the house."

"Dora is too good," said Anne. "She'd behave just as well if there wasn't a soul to tell her what to do. She was born already brought up, so she doesn't need us; and I think," concluded Anne, hitting on a very vital truth, "that we always love best the people who need us. Davy needs us badly."

"He certainly needs something," agreed Marilla. "Rachel Lynde would say it was a good spanking."

11

Facts and Fancies

"Teaching is really very interesting work," wrote Anne to a Queen's Academy chum. "Jane says she thinks it is monotonous but I don't find it so. Something funny is almost sure to happen every day, and the children say such amusing things. Jane says she punishes her pupils when they make funny speeches, which is probably why she finds teaching monotonous. This afternoon little Jimmy Andrews was trying to spell 'speckled' and couldn't manage it. 'Well,' he said finally, 'I can't spell it but I know what it means.'

"'What?' I asked.

"'St. Clair Donnell's face, miss.'

"St. Clair is certainly very much freckled, although I try to prevent the others from commenting on it . . . for *I* was freckled once and well do I remember it. But I don't think St. Clair minds. It was because Jimmy called him 'St. Clair' that St. Clair pounded him on the way home from school. I heard of the pounding, but not officially, so I don't think I'll take any notice of it.

"Yesterday I was trying to teach Lottie Wright to do addition. I said, 'If you had three candies in one hand and two in the other, how many would you have altogether?' 'A mouthful,' said Lottie. And in the nature study class, when I asked them to give me a good reason why toads shouldn't be killed, Benjie Sloane gravely answered, 'Because it would rain the next day.'

"It's so hard not to laugh, Stella. I have to save up all my amusement until I get home, and Marilla says it makes her nervous to hear wild shrieks of mirth proceeding from the east gable without any apparent cause. She says a man in Grafton went insane once and that was how it began.

"Did you know that Thomas à Becket was canonized as a *snake?* Rose Bell says he was . . . also that William Tyndale *wrote* the New Testament. Claude White says a 'glacier' is a man who puts in window frames!

"I think the most difficult thing in teaching, as well as the most interesting, is to get the children to tell you their real thoughts about things. One stormy day last week I gathered them around me at dinner hour and tried to get them to talk to me just as if I were one of themselves. I asked them to tell me the things they most wanted. Some of the answers were commonplace enough . . . dolls, ponies, and skates. Others were decidedly original. Hester Boulter wanted 'to wear her Sunday dress every day and eat in the sitting room.' Hannah Bell wanted 'to be good without having to take any trouble about it.' Marjory White, aged ten, wanted to be a *widow.* Questioned why, she gravely said that if you weren't married people called you an old maid, and if you were your husband bossed you; but if you were a widow there'd be no danger of either. The most remarkable wish was Sally Bell's. She wanted a 'honeymoon.' I asked her if she knew what it was and she said she thought it was an extra nice kind of bicycle because her cousin in Montreal went on a honeymoon when he was married and he had always had the very latest in bicycles!

"Another day I asked them all to tell me the naughtiest thing they had ever done. I couldn't get the older ones to do so, but the third class answered quite freely. Eliza Bell had 'set fire to her aunt's carded rolls.' Asked if she meant to do it she said, 'not altogether.' She just tried a little end to see how it would burn and the whole bundle blazed up in a jiffy. Emerson Gillis had spent ten cents for candy when he should have put it in his missionary box. Annetta Bell's worst crime was 'eating some blueberries that grew in the graveyard.' Willie White had 'slid down the sheephouse roof a lot of times with his Sunday trousers on.' 'But I was punished for it 'cause I had to wear patched pants to Sunday School all summer, and when you're punished for a thing you don't have to repent of it,' declared Willie.

"I wish you could see some of their compositions . . . so much do I wish it that I'll send you copies of some written recently. Last week

I told the fourth class I wanted them to write me letters about anything they pleased, adding by way of suggestion that they might tell me of some place they had visited or some interesting thing or person they had seen. They were to write the letters on real note paper, seal them in an envelope, and address them to me, all without any assistance from other people. Last Friday morning I found a pile of letters on my desk and that evening I realized afresh that teaching has its pleasures as well as its pains. Those compositions would atone for much. Here is Ned Clay's, address, spelling, and grammar as originally penned.

"'Miss teacher ShiRley
"'Green gabels.
"'p. e. Island can

"'birds

"'Dear teacher I think I will write you a composition about birds. birds is very useful animals. my cat catches birds. His name is William but pa calls him tom, he is oll striped and he got one of his ears froz of last winter. only for that he would be a good-looking cat. My unkle has adopted a cat. it come to his house one day and woudent go away and unkle says it has forgot more than most people ever knowed. he lets it sleep on his rocking chare and my aunt says he thinks more of it than he does of his children, that is not right. we ought to be kind to cats and give them new milk but we ought not to be better to them than to our children. this is oll I can think of so no more at present from

"'edward blake ClaY.'

"St. Clair Donnell's is, as usual, short and to the point. St. Clair never wastes words. I do not think he chose his subject or added the postscript out of malice aforethought. It is just that he has not a great deal of tact or imagination.

"'Dear Miss Shirley

"'You told us to describe something strange we have seen. I will describe the Avonlea Hall. It has two doors, an inside one and an outside one. It has six windows and a chimney. It has two ends and two sides. It is painted blue. That is what makes it strange. It is built on the lower Carmody road. It is the third most important building in Avonlea. The others are the church and the blacksmith shop. They hold debating clubs and lectures in it and concerts.

"'Your truly,
"'Jacob Donnell.

"'P.S. The hall is a very bright blue.'

"Annetta Bell's letter was quite long, which surprised me, for writing essays is not Annetta's forte, and hers are generally as brief as St. Clair's. Annetta is a quiet little puss and a model of good behavior, but there isn't a shadow of originality in her. Here is her letter;—

"'Dearest teacher,

"'I think I will write you a letter to tell you how much I love you. I love you with my whole heart and soul and mind . . . with all there is of me to love . . . and I want to serve you for ever. It would be my highest privilege. That is why I try so hard to be good in school and learn my lessuns.

"'You are so beautiful, my teacher. Your voice is like music and your eyes are like pansies when the dew is on them. You are like a tall stately queen. Your hair is like rippling gold. Anthony Pye says it is red, but you needn't pay any attention to Anthony.

"'I have only known you for a few months but I cannot realize that there was ever a time when I did not know you . . . when you had not come into my life to bless and hallow it. I will always look back to this year as the most wonderful in my life because it brought you to me. Besides, it's the year we moved to Avonlea from new-bridge. My love for you has made my life very rich and it has kept me from much of harm and evil. I owe this all to you, my sweetest teacher.

"'I shall never forget how sweet you looked the last time I saw you in that black dress with flowers in your hair. I shall see you like that for ever, even when we are both old and gray. You will always be young and fair to me, dearest teacher. I am thinking of you all the time . . . in the morning and at the noontide and at the twilight. I love you when you laugh and when you sigh . . . even when you look disdainful. I never saw you look cross though Anthony Pye says you always look so but I don't wonder you look cross at him for he deserves it. I love you in every dress . . . you seem more adorable in each new dress than the last.

"'Dearest teacher, good night. The sun has set and the stars are shining . . . stars that are as bright and beautiful as your eyes. I kiss your hands and face, my sweet. May God watch over you and protect you from all harm.

"'Your afecksionate pupil
"'Annetta Bell.'

"This extraordinary letter puzzled me not a little. I knew Annetta couldn't have composed it any more than she could fly. When I went to school the next day I took her for a walk down to the brook at recess and asked her to tell me the truth about the letter. Annetta cried and 'fessed up freely. She said she had never written a letter and she didn't know how to, or what to say, but there was a bundle of love letters in her mother's top bureau drawer which had been written to her by an old 'beau.'

"'It wasn't father,' sobbed Annetta, 'it was someone who was studying for a minister, and so he could write lovely letters, but ma didn't marry him after all. She said she couldn't make out what he was driving at half the time. But I thought the letters were sweet and that I'd just copy things out of them here and there to write you. I put "teacher" where he put "lady" and I put in something of my own when I could think of it and I changed some words. I put "dress" in place of "mood." I didn't know just what a "mood" was but I s'posed it was something to wear. I didn't s'pose you'd know the difference. I don't see how you found out it wasn't all mine. You must be awful clever, teacher.'

"I told Annetta it was very wrong to copy another person's letter and pass it off as her own. But I'm afraid that all Annetta repented of was being found out.

"'And I *do* love you, teacher,' she sobbed. 'It was all true, even if the minister wrote it first. I do love you with all my heart.'

"It's very difficult to scold anybody properly under such circumstances.

"Here is Barbara Shaw's letter. I can't reproduce the blots of the original.

"'Dear teacher,

"'You said we might write about a visit. I never visited but once. It was at my Aunt Mary's last winter. My Aunt Mary is a very particular woman and a great housekeeper. The first night I was there we were at tea. I knocked over a jug and broke it. Aunt Mary said she had had that jug ever since she was married and nobody had ever broken it before. When we got up I stepped on her dress and all the gathers tore out of the skirt. The next morning when I got up I hit the pitcher against the basin and cracked them both and I upset a cup of tea on the tablecloth at breakfast. When I was helping Aunt Mary with the dinner dishes I dropped a china plate and it smashed. That evening I fell downstairs and sprained my ankle and had to stay in bed for a week. I heard Aunt Mary tell Uncle Joseph it was a mercy or I'd have broken everything in the house. When I got better it was time to go home. I don't like visiting very much. I like going to school better, especially since I came to Avonlea.

"'Yours respectfully,
"'Barbara Shaw.'

"Willie White's began,

"'Respected Miss,

"'I want to tell you about my Very Brave Aunt. She lives in Ontario and one day she went out to the barn and saw a dog in the yard. The dog had no business there so she got a stick and whacked him hard and drove him into the barn and shut him up. Pretty soon a man came looking for an imaginary lion' (Query;—Did Willie mean a menagerie lion?) 'that had run away from a circus. And it turned out that the dog was a lion and my Very Brave Aunt had druv him into the barn with a stick. It is a wonder she was not et up but she was very brave. Emerson Gillis says if she thought it was a dog she wasn't any braver than if it really was a dog. But Emerson is jealous because he hasn't got a Brave Aunt himself, nothing but uncles.'

"I have kept the best for the last. You laugh at me because I think Paul is a genius but I am sure his letter will convince you that he is a very uncommon child. Paul lives away down near the shore with his grandmother and he has no playmates . . . no *real* playmates. You remember our School Management professor told us that we must not have 'favorites' among our pupils, but I can't help loving Paul Irving the best of all mine. I don't think it does any harm, though, for everybody loves Paul, even Mrs. Lynde, who says she could never have believed she'd get so fond of a Yankee. The other boys in school like him too. There is nothing weak or girlish about him in spite of his dreams and fancies. He is very manly and can hold his own in all games. He fought St. Clair Donnell recently because St. Clair said the Union Jack was away ahead of the Stars and Stripes as a flag. The result was a drawn battle and a mutual agreement to respect each other's patriotism henceforth. St. Clair says he can hit the *hardest* but Paul can hit the *oftenest*.

"Paul's Letter.

"'My dear teacher,
"'You told us we might write you about some interesting people

we knew. I think the most interesting people I know are my rock people and I mean to tell you about them. I have never told anybody about them except grandma and father but I would like to have you know about them because you understand things. There are a great many people who do *not* understand things so there is no use in telling them.

"'My rock people live at the shore. I used to visit them almost every evening before the winter came. Now I can't go till spring, but they will be there, for people like that never change . . . that is the splendid thing about them. Nora was the first one of them I got acquainted with and so I think I love her the best. She lives in Andrews' Cove and she has black hair and black eyes, and she knows all about the mermaids and the water kelpies. You ought to hear the stories she can tell. Then there are the Twin Sailors. They don't live anywhere, they sail all the time, but they often come ashore to talk to me. They are a pair of jolly tars and they have seen everything in the world . . . and more than what is in the world. Do you know what happened to the youngest Twin Sailor once? He was sailing and he sailed right into a moonglade. A moonglade is the track the full moon makes on the water when it is rising from the sea, you know, teacher. Well, the youngest Twin Sailor sailed along the moonglade till he came right up to the moon, and there was a little golden door in the moon and he opened it and sailed right through. He had some wonderful adventures in the moon but it would make this letter too long to tell them.

"'Then there is the Golden Lady of the cave. One day I found a big cave down on the shore and I went away in and after a while I found the Golden Lady. She has golden hair right down to her feet and her dress is all glittering and glistening like gold that is alive. And she has a golden harp and plays on it all day long . . . you can hear the music any time along shore if you listen carefully but most people would think it was only the wind among the rocks. I've never told Nora about the Golden Lady. I was afraid it might hurt her feelings. It even hurt her feelings if I talked too long with the Twin Sailors.

"'I always met the Twin Sailors at the Striped Rocks. The youngest Twin Sailor is very good-tempered but the oldest Twin

Sailor can look dreadfully fierce at times. I have my suspicions about that oldest Twin. I believe he'd be a pirate if he dared. There's really something very mysterious about him. He swore once and I told him if he ever did it again he needn't come ashore to talk to me because I'd promised grandmother I'd never associate with anybody that swore. He was pretty well scared, I can tell you, and he said if I would forgive him he would take me to the sunset. So the next evening when I was sitting on the Striped Rocks the oldest Twin came sailing over the sea in an enchanted boat and I got in her. The boat was all pearly and rainbowy, like the inside of the mussel shells, and her sail was like moonshine. Well, we sailed right across to the sunset. Think of that, teacher, I've been in the sunset. And what do you suppose it is? The sunset is a land all flowers, like a great garden, and the clouds are beds of flowers. We sailed into a great harbor, all the color of gold, and I stepped right out of the boat on a big meadow all covered with buttercups as big as roses. I stayed there for ever so long. It seemed nearly a year but the Oldest Twin says it was only a few minutes. You see, in the sunset land the time is ever so much longer than it is here.

    "'Your loving pupil,
    "'Paul Irving.

    "'P.S. Of course, this letter isn't really true, teacher.
    p.i.'"

12

A Jonah Day

It really began the night before with a restless, wakeful vigil of grumbling toothache. When Anne arose in the dull, bitter winter morning she felt that life was flat, stale, and unprofitable.

She went to school in no angelic mood. Her cheek was swollen and her face ached. The schoolroom was cold and smoky, for the fire refused to burn and the children were huddled about it in shivering groups. Anne sent them to their seats with a sharper tone than she had ever used before. Anthony Pye strutted to his with his usual impertinent swagger and she saw him whisper something to his seat-mate and then glance at her with a grin.

Never, so it seemed to Anne, had there been so many squeaky pencils as there were that morning; and when Barbara Shaw came up to the desk with a sum she tripped over the coal scuttle with disastrous results. The coal rolled to every part of the room, her slate was broken into fragments, and when she picked herself up, her face, stained with coat dust, sent the boys into roars of laughter.

Anne turned from the second reader class which she was hearing.

"Really, Barbara," she said icily, "if you cannot move without falling over something you'd better remain in your seat. It is positively disgraceful for a girl of your age to be so awkward."

Poor Barbara stumbled back to her desk, her tears combining with the coal dust to produce an effect truly grotesque. Never before had her beloved, sympathetic teacher spoken to her in such a tone or fashion, and Barbara was heartbroken. Anne herself felt a prick of conscience but it only served to increase her mental irritation, and the second reader class remember that lesson yet, as well as the unmerciful infliction of arithmetic that followed. Just as Anne was snapping the sums out St. Clair Donnell arrived breathlessly.

"You are half an hour late, St. Clair," Anne reminded him frigidly. "Why is this?"

"Please, miss, I had to help ma make a pudding for dinner 'cause we're expecting company and Clarice Almira's sick," was St. Clair's answer, given in a perfectly respectful voice but nevertheless provocative of great mirth among his mates.

"Take your seat and work out the six problems on page eighty-four of your arithmetic for punishment," said Anne. St. Clair looked rather amazed at her tone but he went meekly to his desk and took out his slate. Then he stealthily passed a small parcel to Joe Sloane across the aisle. Anne caught him in the act and jumped to a fatal conclusion about that parcel.

Old Mrs. Hiram Sloane had lately taken to making and selling "nut cakes" by way of adding to her scanty income. The cakes were specially tempting to small boys and for several weeks Anne had had not a little trouble in regard to them. On their way to school the boys would invest their spare cash at Mrs. Hiram's, bring the cakes along with them to school, and, if possible, eat them and treat their mates during school hours. Anne had warned them that if they brought any more cakes to school they would be confiscated; and yet here was St. Clair Donnell coolly passing a parcel of them, wrapped up in the blue and white striped paper Mrs. Hiram used, under her very eyes.

"Joseph," said Anne quietly, "bring that parcel here."

Joe, startled and abashed, obeyed. He was a fat urchin who always blushed and stuttered when he was frightened. Never did anybody look more guilty than poor Joe at that moment.

"Throw it into the fire," said Anne.

Joe looked very blank.

"P . . . p . . . p . . . lease, m . . . m . . . miss," he began.

"Do as I tell you, Joseph, without any words about it."

"B . . . b . . . but m . . . m . . . miss . . . th . . . th . . . they're . . ." gasped Joe in desperation.

"Joseph, are you going to obey me or are you *not*?" said Anne.

A bolder and more self-possessed lad than Joe Sloane would have been overawed by her tone and the dangerous flash of her eyes. This was a new Anne whom none of her pupils had ever seen before. Joe, with an agonized glance at St. Clair, went to the stove, opened the big, square front door, and threw the blue and white parcel in, before St. Clair, who had sprung to his feet, could utter a word. Then he dodged back just in time.

For a few moments the terrified occupants of Avonlea school did not know whether it was an earthquake or a volcanic explosion that had occurred. The innocent looking parcel which Anne had rashly supposed to contain Mrs. Hiram's nut cakes really held an assortment of firecrackers and pinwheels for which Warren Sloane had sent to town by St. Clair Donnell's father the day before, intending to have a birthday celebration that evening. The crackers went off in a thunderclap of noise and the pinwheels bursting out of the door spun madly around the room, hissing and spluttering. Anne dropped into her chair white with dismay and all the girls climbed shrieking upon their desks. Joe Sloane stood as one transfixed in the midst of the commotion and St. Clair, helpless with laughter, rocked to and fro in the aisle. Prillie Rogerson fainted and Annetta Bell went into hysterics.

It seemed a long time, although it was really only a few minutes, before the last pinwheel subsided. Anne, recovering herself, sprang to open doors and windows and let out the gas and smoke which filled the room. Then she helped the girls carry the unconscious Prillie into the porch, where Barbara Shaw, in an agony of desire to be useful, poured a pailful of half frozen water over Prillie's face and shoulders before anyone could stop her.

It was a full hour before quiet was restored . . . but it was a quiet that might be felt. Everybody realized that even the explosion had not cleared the teacher's mental atmosphere. Nobody, except Anthony Pye, dared whisper a word. Ned Clay accidentally squeaked his pencil while working a sum, caught Anne's eye and wished the floor would open and swallow him up. The geography class were whisked through a continent with a speed that made them dizzy. The grammar class were parsed and analyzed within an inch of their lives. Chester Sloane, spelling "odoriferous" with two f's, was made to feel that he could never live down the disgrace of it, either in this world or that which is to come.

Anne knew that she had made herself ridiculous and that the incident would be laughed over that night at a score of tea-tables, but the knowledge only angered her further. In a calmer mood she could have carried off the situation with a laugh but now that was impossible; so she ignored it in icy disdain.

When Anne returned to the school after dinner all the children were as usual in their seats and every face was bent studiously over a desk except Anthony Pye's. He peered across his book at Anne, his black eyes sparkling with curiosity and mockery. Anne twitched open the drawer of her desk in search of chalk and under her very hand a lively mouse sprang out of the drawer, scampered over the desk, and leaped to the floor.

Anne screamed and sprang back, as if it had been a snake, and Anthony Pye laughed aloud.

Then a silence fell . . . a very creepy, uncomfortable silence. Annetta Bell was of two minds whether to go into hysterics again or not, especially as she didn't know just where the mouse had gone. But she decided not to. Who could take any comfort out of hysterics with a teacher so white-faced and so blazing-eyed standing before one?

"Who put that mouse in my desk?" said Anne. Her voice was quite low but it made a shiver go up and down Paul Irving's spine. Joe Sloane caught her eye, felt responsible from the crown of his head to the sole of his feet, but stuttered out wildly,

"N . . . n . . . not m . . . m . . . me t . . . t . . . teacher, n . . . n . . . not m . . . m . . . me."

Anne paid no attention to the wretched Joseph. She looked at Anthony Pye, and Anthony Pye looked back, unabashed and unashamed.

"Anthony, was it you?"

"Yes, it was," said Anthony insolently.

Anne took her pointer from her desk. It was a long, heavy hardwood pointer.

"Come here, Anthony."

It was far from being the most severe punishment Anthony Pye had ever undergone. Anne, even the stormy-souled Anne she was at that moment, could not have punished any child cruelly. But the pointer nipped keenly and finally Anthony's bravado failed him; he winced and the tears came to his eyes.

Anne, conscience-stricken, dropped the pointer and told Anthony to go to his seat. She sat down at her desk feeling ashamed, repentant, and bitterly mortified. Her quick anger was gone and she would have given much to have been able to seek relief in tears. So all her boasts had come to this . . . she had actually whipped one of her pupils. How Jane would triumph! And how Mr. Harrison would chuckle! But worse than this, bitterest thought of all, she had lost her last chance of winning Anthony Pye. Never would he like her now.

Anne, by what somebody has called "a Herculaneum effort," kept back her tears until she got home that night. Then she shut herself in the east gable room and wept all her shame and remorse and disappointment into her pillows . . . wept so long that Marilla grew alarmed, invaded the room, and insisted on knowing what the trouble was.

"The trouble is, I've got things the matter with my conscience," sobbed Anne. "Oh, this has been such a Jonah day, Marilla. I'm so ashamed of myself. I lost my temper and whipped Anthony Pye."

"I'm glad to hear it," said Marilla with decision. "It's what you should have done long ago."

"Oh, no, no, Marilla. And I don't see how I can ever look those children in the face again. I feel that I have humiliated myself to the very dust. You don't know how cross and hateful and horrid I was. I can't forget the expression in Paul Irving's eyes . . . he looked so surprised and disappointed. Oh, Marilla, I *have* tried so hard to be patient and to win Anthony's liking . . . and now it has all gone for nothing."

Marilla passed her hard work-worn hand over the girl's glossy, tumbled hair with a wonderful tenderness. When Anne's sobs grew quieter she said, very gently for her,

"You take things too much to heart, Anne. We all make mistakes . . . but people forget them. And Jonah days come to everybody. As for Anthony Pye, why need you care if he does dislike you? He is the only one."

"I can't help it. I want everybody to love me and it hurts me so when anybody doesn't. And Anthony never will now. Oh, I just made an idiot of myself today, Marilla. I'll tell you the whole story."

Marilla listened to the whole story, and if she smiled at certain parts of it Anne never knew. When the tale was ended she said briskly,

"Well, never mind. This day's done and there's a new one coming tomorrow, with no mistakes in it yet, as you used to say yourself. Just come downstairs and have your supper. You'll see if a good cup of tea and those plum puffs I made today won't hearten you up."

"Plum puffs won't minister to a mind diseased," said Anne disconsolately; but Marilla thought it a good sign that she had recovered sufficiently to adapt a quotation.

The cheerful supper table, with the twins' bright faces, and Marilla's matchless plum puffs . . . of which Davy ate four . . . did "hearten her up" considerably after all. She had a good sleep that night and awakened in the morning to find herself and the world transformed. It had snowed softly and thickly all through the hours of darkness and the beautiful whiteness, glittering in the frosty sunshine, looked like a mantle of charity cast over all the mistakes and humiliations of the past.

"Every morn is a fresh beginning,
Every morn is the world made new,"

sang Anne, as she dressed.

Owing to the snow she had to go around by the road to school and she thought it was certainly an impish coincidence that Anthony Pye should come ploughing along just as she left the Green Gables lane. She felt as guilty as if their positions were reversed; but to her unspeakable astonishment Anthony not only lifted his cap . . . which he had never done before . . . but said easily,

"Kind of bad walking, ain't it? Can I take those books for you, teacher?"

Anne surrendered her books and wondered if she could possibly be awake. Anthony walked on in silence to the school, but when Anne took her books she smiled down at him . . . not the stereotyped "kind" smile she had so persistently assumed for his benefit but a sudden out-flashing of good comradeship. Anthony smiled . . . no, if the truth must be told, Anthony *grinned* back. A grin is not generally supposed to be a respectful thing; yet Anne suddenly felt that if she had not yet won Anthony's liking she had, somehow or other, won his respect.

Mrs. Rachel Lynde came up the next Saturday and confirmed this.

"Well, Anne, I guess you've won over Anthony Pye, that's what. He says he believes you are some good after all, even if you are a girl. Says that whipping you gave him was 'just as good as a man's.'"

"I never expected to win him by whipping him, though," said Anne, a little mournfully, feeling that her ideals had played her false somewhere. "It doesn't seem right. I'm *sure* my theory of kindness *can't* be wrong."

"No, but the Pyes are an exception to every known rule, that's what," declared Mrs. Rachel with conviction.

Mr. Harrison said "Thought you'd come to it," when he heard it, and Jane rubbed it in rather unmercifully.

13

A Golden Picnic

nne, on her way to Orchard Slope, met Diana, bound for Green Gables, just where the mossy old log bridge spanned the brook below the Haunted Wood, and they sat down by the margin of the Dryad's Bubble, where tiny ferns were unrolling like curly-headed green pixy folk wakening up from a nap.

"I was just on my way over to invite you to help me celebrate my birthday on Saturday," said Anne.

"Your birthday? But your birthday was in March!"

"That wasn't my fault," laughed Anne. "If my parents had consulted me it would never have happened then. I should have chosen to be born in spring, of course. It must be delightful to come into the world with the mayflowers and violets. You would always feel that you were their foster sister. But since I didn't, the next best thing is to celebrate my birthday in the spring. Priscilla is coming over Saturday and Jane will be home. We'll all four start off to the woods and spend a golden day making the acquaintance of the spring. We none of us really know her yet, but we'll meet her back there as we never can anywhere else. I want to explore all those fields and lonely places anyhow. I have a conviction that there are scores of beautiful nooks there that have never really been *seen* although they may have been *looked* at. We'll make friends with wind and sky and sun, and bring home the spring in our hearts."

"It *sounds* awfully nice," said Diana, with some inward distrust of Anne's magic of words. "But won't it be very damp in some places yet?"

"Oh, we'll wear rubbers," was Anne's concession to practicalities. "And I want you to come over early Saturday morning and help me prepare lunch. I'm going to have the daintiest things possible . . . things that will match the spring, you understand . . . little jelly tarts and lady fingers, and drop cookies frosted with pink and yellow icing, and buttercup cake. And we must have sandwiches too, though they're *not* very poetical."

Saturday proved an ideal day for a picnic . . . a day of breeze and blue, warm, sunny, with a little rollicking wind blowing across meadow and orchard. Over every sunlit upland and field was a delicate, flower-starred green.

Mr. Harrison, harrowing at the back of his farm and feeling some of the spring witch-work even in his sober, middle-aged blood, saw four girls, basket laden, tripping across the end of his field where it joined a fringing woodland of birch and fir. Their blithe voices and laughter echoed down to him.

"It's so easy to be happy on a day like this, isn't it?" Anne was saying, with true Anneish philosophy. "Let's try to make this a really golden day, girls, a day to which we can always look back with delight. We're to seek for beauty and refuse to see anything else. 'Begone, dull care!' Jane, you are thinking of something that went wrong in school yesterday."

"How do you know?" gasped Jane, amazed.

"Oh, I know the expression . . . I've felt it often enough on my own face. But put it out of your mind, there's a dear. It will keep till Monday . . . or if it doesn't so much the better. Oh, girls, girls, see that patch of violets! There's something for memory's picture gallery. When I'm eighty years old . . . if I ever am . . . I shall shut my eyes and see those violets just as I see them now. That's the first good gift our day has given us."

"If a kiss could be seen I think it would look like a violet," said Priscilla.

Anne glowed.

"I'm so glad you *spoke* that thought, Priscilla, instead of just thinking it and keeping it to yourself. This world would be a much more interesting place . . . although it *is* very interesting anyhow . . . if people spoke out their real thoughts."

"It would be too hot to hold some folks," quoted Jane sagely.

"I suppose it might be, but that would be their own faults for thinking nasty things. Anyhow, we can tell all our thoughts today because we are going to have nothing but beautiful thoughts. Everybody can say just what comes into her head. *That* is conversation. Here's a little path I never saw before. Let's explore it."

The path was a winding one, so narrow that the girls walked in single file and even then the fir boughs brushed their faces. Under the firs were velvety cushions of moss, and further on, where the trees were smaller and fewer, the ground was rich in a variety of green growing things.

"What a lot of elephant's ears," exclaimed Diana. "I'm going to pick a big bunch, they're so pretty."

"How did such graceful feathery things ever come to have such a dreadful name?" asked Priscilla.

"Because the person who first named them either had no imagination at all or else far too much," said Anne. "Oh, girls, look at that!"

"That" was a shallow woodland pool in the center of a little open glade where the path ended. Later on in the season it would be dried up and its place filled with a rank growth of ferns; but now it was a glimmering placid sheet, round as a saucer and clear as crystal. A ring of slender young birches encircled it and little ferns fringed its margin.

"*How* sweet!" said Jane.

"Let us dance around it like wood-nymphs," cried Anne, dropping her basket and extending her hands.

But the dance was not a success for the ground was boggy and Jane's rubbers came off.

"You can't be a wood-nymph if you have to wear rubbers," was her decision.

"Well, we must name this place before we leave it," said Anne, yielding to the indisputable logic of facts. "Everybody suggest a name and we'll draw lots, Diana?"

"Birch Pool," suggested Diana promptly.

"Crystal Lake," said Jane.

Anne, standing behind them, implored Priscilla with her eyes not to perpetrate another such name and Priscilla rose to the occasion with "Glimmer-glass." Anne's selection was "The Fairies' Mirror."

The names were written on strips of birch bark with a pencil Schoolma'am Jane produced from her pocket, and placed in Anne's hat. Then Priscilla shut her eyes and drew one. "Crystal Lake," read Jane triumphantly. Crystal Lake it was, and if Anne thought that chance had played the pool a shabby trick she did not say so.

Pushing through the undergrowth beyond, the girls came out to the young green seclusion of Mr. Silas Sloane's back pasture. Across it they found the entrance to a lane striking up through the woods and voted to explore it also. It rewarded their quest with a succession of pretty surprises. First, skirting Mr. Sloane's pasture, came an archway of wild cherry trees all in bloom. The girls swung their hats on their arms and wreathed their hair with the creamy, fluffy blossoms. Then the lane turned at right angles and plunged into a spruce wood so thick and dark that they walked in a gloom as of twilight, with not a glimpse of sky or sunlight to be seen.

"This is where the bad wood elves dwell," whispered Anne. "They are impish and malicious but they can't harm us, because they are not allowed to do evil in the spring. There was one peeping at us around that old twisted fir; and didn't you see a group of them on that big freckly toadstool we just passed? The good fairies always dwell in the sunshiny places."

"I wish there really were fairies," said Jane. "Wouldn't it be nice to have three wishes granted you . . . or even only one? What would you wish for, girls, if you could have a wish granted? I'd wish to be rich and beautiful and clever."

"I'd wish to be tall and slender," said Diana.

"I would wish to be famous," said Priscilla.

Anne thought of her hair and then dismissed the thought as unworthy.

"I'd wish it might be spring all the time and in everybody's heart and all our lives," she said.

"But that," said Priscilla, "would be just wishing this world were like heaven."

"Only like a part of heaven. In the other parts there would be summer and autumn . . . yes, and a bit of winter, too. I think I want glittering snowy fields and white frosts in heaven sometimes. Don't you, Jane?"

"I . . . I don't know," said Jane uncomfortably. Jane was a good girl, a member of the church, who tried conscientiously to live up to her profession and believed everything she had been taught. But she never thought about heaven any more than she could help, for all that.

"Minnie May asked me the other day if we would wear our best dresses every day in heaven," laughed Diana.

"And didn't you tell her we would?" asked Anne.

"Mercy, no! I told her we wouldn't be thinking of dresses at all there."

"Oh, I think we will . . . a *little*," said Anne earnestly. "There'll be plenty of time in all eternity for it without neglecting more important things. I believe we'll all wear beautiful dresses . . . or I suppose *raiment* would be a more suitable way of speaking. I shall want to wear pink for a few centuries at first . . . it would take me that long to get tired of it, I feel sure. I do love pink so and I can never wear it in *this* world."

Past the spruces the lane dipped down into a sunny little open where a log bridge spanned a brook; and then came the glory of a sun-lit beechwood where the air was like transparent golden wine, and the leaves fresh and green, and the wood floor a mosaic of tremulous sun-shine. Then more wild cherries, and a little valley of lissome firs, and then a hill so steep that the girls lost their breath climbing it; but when they reached the top and came out into the open the prettiest surprise of all awaited them.

Beyond were the "back fields" of the farms that ran out to the upper Carmody road. Just before them, hemmed in by beeches and firs but open to the south, was a little corner and in it a garden . . . or what had once been a garden. A tumbledown stone dyke, over-grown with mosses and grass, surrounded it. Along the eastern side ran a row of garden cherry trees, white as a snowdrift. There were traces of old paths still and a double line of rosebushes through the middle; but all the rest of the space was a sheet of yellow and white narcissi, in their airiest, most lavish, wind-swayed bloom above the lush green grasses.

"Oh, how perfectly lovely!" three of the girls cried. Anne only gazed in eloquent silence.

"How in the world does it happen that there ever was a garden back here?" said Priscilla in amazement.

"It must be Hester Gray's garden," said Diana. "I've heard mother speak of it but I never saw it before, and I wouldn't have supposed that it could be in existence still. You've heard the story, Anne?"

"No, but the name seems familiar to me."

"Oh, you've seen it in the graveyard. She is buried down there in the poplar corner. You know the little brown stone with the opening gates carved on it and 'Sacred to the memory of Hester Gray, aged twenty-two.' Jordan Gray is buried right beside her but there's no stone to him. It's a wonder Marilla never told you about it, Anne. To be sure, it happened thirty years ago and everybody has forgotten."

"Well, if there's a story we must have it," said Anne. "Let's sit right down here among the narcissi and Diana will tell it. Why, girls, there are hundreds of them . . . they've spread over everything. It looks as if the garden were carpeted with moonshine and sunshine combined. This is a discovery worth making. To think that I've lived within a mile of this place for six years and have never seen it before! Now, Diana."

"Long ago," began Diana, "this farm belonged to old Mr. David Gray. He didn't live on it . . . he lived where Silas Sloane lives now. He had one son, Jordan, and he went up to Boston one winter to work and while he was there he fell in love with a girl named Hester Murray. She was working in a store and she hated it. She'd been brought up in the country and she always wanted to get back. When Jordan asked her to marry him she said she would if he'd take her away to some quiet spot where she'd see nothing but fields and trees. So he brought her to Avonlea. Mrs. Lynde said he was taking a fearful risk in marrying a Yankee, and it's certain that Hester was very delicate and a very poor housekeeper; but mother says she was very pretty and sweet and Jordan just worshipped the ground she walked on. Well, Mr. Gray gave Jordan this farm and he built a little house back here and Jordan and Hester lived in it for four years. She never went out much and hardly anybody went to see her except mother and Mrs. Lynde. Jordan made her this garden and she was crazy about it and spent most of her time in it. She wasn't much of a housekeeper but she had a knack with flowers. And then she got sick. Mother says she thinks she was in consumption before she ever came here. She never really laid up but just grew weaker and weaker all the time. Jordan wouldn't have anybody to wait on her. He did it all himself and mother says he was as tender and gentle as a woman. Every day he'd wrap her in a shawl and carry her out to the garden and she'd lie there on a bench quite happy. They say she used to make Jordan kneel down by her every night and morning and pray with her that she might die out in the garden when the time came. And her prayer was answered. One day Jordan carried her out to the bench and then he picked all the roses that were out and heaped them over her; and she just smiled up at him . . . and closed her eyes . . . and that," concluded Diana softly, "was the end."

"Oh, what a dear story," sighed Anne, wiping away her tears.

"What became of Jordan?" asked Priscilla.

"He sold the farm after Hester died and went back to Boston. Mr. Jabez Sloane bought the farm and hauled the little house out to the road. Jordan died about ten years after and he was brought home and buried beside Hester."

"I can't understand how she could have wanted to live back here, away from everything," said Jane.

"Oh, I can easily understand *that*," said Anne thoughtfully. "I wouldn't want it myself for a steady thing, because, although I love the fields and woods, I love people too. But I can understand it in Hester. She was tired to death of the noise of the big city and the crowds of people always coming and going and caring nothing for her. She just wanted to escape from it all to some still, green, friendly place where she could rest. And she got just what she wanted, which is something very few people do, I believe. She had four beautiful years before she died . . . four years of perfect happiness, so I think she was to be envied more than pitied. And then to shut your eyes and fall asleep among roses, with the one you loved best on earth smiling down at you . . . oh, I think it was beautiful!"

"She set out those cherry trees over there," said Diana. "She told mother she'd never live to eat their fruit, but she wanted to think that something she had planted would go on living and helping to make the world beautiful after she was dead."

"I'm so glad we came this way," said Anne, the shining-eyed. "This is my adopted birthday, you know, and this garden and its story is the birthday gift it has given me. Did your mother ever tell you what Hester Gray looked like, Diana?"

"No . . . only just that she was pretty."

"I'm rather glad of that, because I can imagine what she looked like, without being hampered by facts. I think she was very slight and small, with softly curling dark hair and big, sweet, timid brown eyes, and a little wistful, pale face."

The girls left their baskets in Hester's garden and spent the rest of the afternoon rambling in the woods and fields surrounding it, discovering many pretty nooks and lanes. When they got hungry they had lunch in the prettiest spot of all . . . on the steep bank of a gurgling brook where white birches shot up out of long feathery grasses. The girls sat down by the roots and did full justice to Anne's dainties, even the unpoetical sandwiches being greatly appreciated by hearty, unspoiled appetites sharpened by all the fresh air and exercise they had enjoyed. Anne had brought glasses and lemonade for her guests, but for her own part drank cold brook water from a cup fashioned out of birch bark. The cup leaked, and the water tasted of earth, as brook water is apt to do in spring; but Anne thought it more appropriate to the occasion than lemonade.

"Look, do you see that poem?" she said suddenly, pointing.

"Where?" Jane and Diana stared, as if expecting to see Runic rhymes on the birch trees.

"There . . . down in the brook . . . that old green, mossy log with the water flowing over it in those smooth ripples that look as if they'd been combed, and that single shaft of sunshine falling right athwart it, far down into the pool. Oh, it's the most beautiful poem I ever saw."

"I should rather call it a picture," said Jane. "A poem is lines and verses."

"Oh dear me, no." Anne shook her head with its fluffy wild cherry coronal positively. "The lines and verses are only the outward garments of the poem and are no more really it than your ruffles and flounces are *you,* Jane. The real poem is the soul within them . . . and that beautiful bit is the soul of an unwritten poem. It is not every day one sees a soul . . . even of a poem."

"I wonder what a soul . . . a person's soul . . . would look like," said Priscilla dreamily.

"Like that, I should think," answered Anne, pointing to a radiance of sifted sunlight streaming through a birch tree. "Only with shape and features of course. I like to fancy souls as being made of light. And some are all shot through with rosy stains and quivers . . . and some have a soft glitter like moonlight on the sea . . . and some are pale and transparent like mist at dawn."

"I read somewhere once that souls were like flowers," said Priscilla.

"Then your soul is a golden narcissus," said Anne, "and Diana's is like a red, red rose. Jane's is an apple blossom, pink and wholesome and sweet."

"And your own is a white violet, with purple streaks in its heart," finished Priscilla.

Jane whispered to Diana that she really could not understand what they were talking about. Could she?

The girls went home by the light of a calm golden sunset, their baskets filled with narcissus blossoms from Hester's garden, some of which Anne carried to the cemetery next day and laid upon Hester's grave. Minstrel robins were whistling in the firs and the frogs were singing in the marshes. All the basins among the hills were brimmed with topaz and emerald light.

"Well, we have had a lovely time after all," said Diana, as if she had hardly expected to have it when she set out.

"It has been a truly golden day," said Priscilla.

"I'm really awfully fond of the woods myself," said Jane.

Anne said nothing. She was looking afar into the western sky and thinking of little Hester Gray.

14

A Danger Averted

A nne, walking home from the post office one Friday evening, was joined by Mrs. Lynde, who was as usual cumbered with all the cares of church and state.

"I've just been down to Timothy Cotton's to see if I could get Alice Louise to help me for a few days," she said. "I had her last week, for, though she's too slow to stop quick, she's better than nobody. But she's sick and can't come. Timothy's sitting there, too, coughing and complaining. He's been dying for ten years and he'll go on dying for ten years more. That kind can't even die and have done with it . . . they can't stick to anything, even to being sick, long enough to finish it. They're a terrible shiftless family and what is to become of them I don't know, but perhaps Providence does."

Mrs. Lynde sighed as if she rather doubted the extent of Providential knowledge on the subject.

"Marilla was in about her eyes again Tuesday, wasn't she? What did the specialist think of them?" she continued.

"He was much pleased," said Anne brightly. "He says there is a great improvement in them and he thinks the danger of her losing her sight completely is past. But he says she'll never be able to read much or do any fine hand-work again. How are your preparations for your bazaar coming on?"

The Ladies' Aid Society was preparing for a fair and supper, and Mrs. Lynde was the head and front of the enterprise.

"Pretty well . . . and that reminds me. Mrs. Allan thinks it would be nice to fix up a booth like an old-time kitchen and serve a supper of baked beans, doughnuts, pie, and so on. We're collecting old-fashioned fixings everywhere. Mrs. Simon Fletcher is going to lend us her mother's braided rugs and Mrs. Levi Boulter some old chairs and Aunt Mary Shaw will lend us her cupboard with the glass doors. I suppose Marilla will let us have her brass candlesticks? And we want all the old dishes we can get. Mrs. Allan is specially set on having a real blue willow ware platter if we can find one. But nobody seems to have one. Do you know where we could get one?"

"Miss Josephine Barry has one. I'll write and ask her if she'll lend it for the occasion," said Anne.

"Well, I wish you would. I guess we'll have the supper in about a fortnight's time. Uncle Abe Andrews is prophesying rain and storms for about that time; and that's a pretty sure sign we'll have fine weather."

The said "Uncle Abe," it may be mentioned, was at least like other prophets in that he had small honor in his own country. He was, in fact, considered in the light of a standing joke, for few of his weather predictions were ever fulfilled. Mr. Elisha Wright, who labored under the impression that he was a local wit, used to say that nobody in Avonlea ever thought of looking in the Charlottetown dailies for weather probabilities. No; they just asked Uncle Abe what it was going to be tomorrow and expected the opposite. Nothing daunted, Uncle Abe kept on prophesying.

"We want to have the fair over before the election comes off," continued Mrs. Lynde, "for the candidates will be sure to come and spend lots of money. The Tories are bribing right and left, so they might as well be given a chance to spend their money honestly for once."

Anne was a red-hot Conservative, out of loyalty to Matthew's memory, but she said nothing. She knew better than to get Mrs. Lynde started on politics.

She had a letter for Marilla, postmarked from a town in British Columbia.

"It's probably from the children's uncle," she said excitedly, when she got home. "Oh, Marilla, I wonder what he says about them."

"The best plan might be to open it and see," said Marilla curtly. A close observer might have thought that she was excited also, but she would rather have died than show it.

Anne tore open the letter and glanced over the somewhat untidy and poorly written contents.

"He says he can't take the children this spring . . . he's been sick most of the winter and his wedding is put off. He wants to know if we can keep them till the fall and he'll try and take them then. We will, of course, won't we, Marilla?"

"I don't see that there is anything else for us to do," said Marilla rather grimly, although she felt a secret relief. "Anyhow they're not so much trouble as they were . . . or else we've got used to them. Davy has improved a great deal."

"His *manners* are certainly much better," said Anne cautiously, as if she were not prepared to say as much for his morals.

Anne had come home from school the previous evening, to find Marilla away at an Aid meeting, Dora asleep on the kitchen sofa, and Davy in the sitting room closet, blissfully absorbing the contents of a jar of Marilla's famous yellow plum preserves . . . "company jam," Davy called it . . . which he had been forbidden to touch. He looked very guilty when Anne pounced on him and whisked him out of the closet.

"Davy Keith, don't you know that it is very wrong of you to be eating that jam, when you were told never to meddle with anything in *that* closet?"

"Yes, I knew it was wrong," admitted Davy uncomfortably, "but plum jam is awful nice, Anne. I just peeped in and it looked so good I thought I'd take just a weeny taste. I stuck my finger in . . ." Anne groaned . . . "and licked it clean. And it was so much gooder than I'd ever thought that I got a spoon and just *sailed in.*"

Anne gave him such a serious lecture on the sin of stealing plum jam that Davy became conscience stricken and promised with repentant kisses never to do it again.

"Anyhow, there'll be plenty of jam in heaven, that's one comfort," he said complacently.

Anne nipped a smile in the bud.

"Perhaps there will . . . if we want it," she said, "But what makes you think so?"

"Why, it's in the catechism," said Davy.

"Oh, no, there is nothing like *that* in the catechism, Davy."

"But I tell you there is," persisted Davy. "It was in that question Marilla taught me last Sunday. 'Why should we love God?' It says, 'Because He makes preserves, and redeems us.' Preserves is just a holy way of saying jam."

"I must get a drink of water," said Anne hastily. When she came back it cost her some time and trouble to explain to Davy that a certain comma in the said catechism question made a great deal of difference in the meaning.

"Well, I thought it was too good to be true," he said at last, with a sigh of disappointed conviction. "And besides, I didn't see when He'd find time to make jam if it's one endless Sabbath day, as the hymn says. I don't believe I want to go to heaven. Won't there ever be any Saturdays in heaven, Anne?"

"Yes, Saturdays, and every other kind of beautiful days. And every day in heaven will be more beautiful than the one before it, Davy," assured Anne, who was rather glad that Marilla was not by to be shocked. Marilla, it is needless to say, was bringing the twins up in the good old ways of theology and discouraged all fanciful speculations thereupon. Davy and Dora were taught a hymn, a catechism question, and two Bible verses every Sunday. Dora learned meekly and recited like a little machine, with perhaps as much understanding or interest as if she were one. Davy, on the contrary, had a lively curiosity, and frequently asked questions which made Marilla tremble for his fate.

"Chester Sloane says we'll do nothing all the time in heaven but walk around in white dresses and play on harps; and he says he hopes he won't have to go till he's an old man, 'cause maybe he'll like it better then. And he thinks it will be horrid to wear dresses and I think so too. Why can't men angels wear trousers, Anne? Chester Sloane is interested in those things, 'cause they're going to make a minister of him. He's *got* to be a minister 'cause his grandmother left the money to send him to college and he can't have it unless he is a minister. She thought a minister was such a 'spectable thing to have in a family. Chester says he doesn't mind much . . . though he'd rather be a blacksmith . . . but he's bound to have all the fun he can before he begins to be a minister, 'cause he doesn't expect to have much afterwards. *I* ain't going to be a minister. I'm going to be a storekeeper, like Mr. Blair, and keep heaps of candy and bananas. But I'd rather like going to your kind of a heaven if they'd let me play a mouth organ instead of a harp. Do you s'pose they would?"

"Yes, I think they would if you wanted it," was all Anne could trust herself to say.

The A. V. I. S. met at Mr. Harmon Andrews' that evening and a full attendance had been requested, since important business was to be discussed. The A. V. I. S. was in a flourishing condition, and had already accomplished wonders. Early in the spring Mr. Major Spencer had redeemed his promise and had stumped, graded, and seeded down all the road front of his farm. A dozen other men, some prompted by a determination not to let a Spencer get ahead of them, others goaded into action by Improvers in their own households, had followed his example. The result was that there were long strips of smooth velvet turf where once had been unsightly undergrowth or brush. The farm fronts that had not been done looked so badly by contrast that their owners were secretly shamed into resolving to see what they could do another spring. The triangle of ground at the cross roads had also been cleared and seeded down, and Anne's bed of geraniums, unharmed by any marauding cow, was already set out in the center.

Altogether, the Improvers thought that they were getting on beautifully, even if Mr. Levi Boulter, tactfully approached by a carefully selected committee in regard to the old house on his upper farm, did bluntly tell them that he wasn't going to have it meddled with.

At this especial meeting they intended to draw up a petition to the school trustees, humbly praying that a fence be put around the school grounds; and a plan was also to be discussed for planting a few orna-mental trees by the church, if the funds of the society would permit of it . . . for, as Anne said, there was no use in starting another subscrip-tion as long as the hall remained blue. The members were assembled in the Andrews' parlor and Jane was already on her feet to move the appointment of a committee which should find out and report on the price of said trees, when Gertie Pye swept in, pompadoured and frilled within an inch of her life. Gertie had a habit of being late . . . "to make her entrance more effective," spiteful people said. Gertie's entrance in this instance was certainly effective, for she paused dramatically on the middle of the floor, threw up her hands, rolled her eyes, and exclaimed,

"I've just heard something perfectly awful. What *do* you think? Mr. Judson Parker *is going to rent all the road fence of his farm to a patent medicine company to paint advertisements on.*"

For once in her life Gertie Pye made all the sensation she desired. If she had thrown a bomb among the complacent Improvers she could hardly have made more.

"It *can't* be true," said Anne blankly.

"That's just what *I* said when I heard it first, don't you know," said Gertie, who was enjoying herself hugely. "*I* said it couldn't be true . . . that Judson Parker wouldn't have the *heart* to do it, don't you know. But father met him this afternoon and asked him about it and he said it *was* true. Just fancy! His farm is side-on to the Newbridge road and how perfectly awful it will look to see advertisements of pills and plasters all along it, don't you know?"

The Improvers *did* know, all too well. Even the least imaginative among them could picture the grotesque effect of half a mile of board fence adorned with such advertisements. All thought of church and school grounds vanished before this new danger. Parliamentary rules and regulations were forgotten, and Anne, in despair, gave up trying to keep minutes at all. Everybody talked at once and fearful was the hubbub.

"Oh, let us keep calm," implored Anne, who was the most excited of them all, "and try to think of some way of preventing him."

"I don't know how you're going to prevent him," exclaimed Jane bitterly. "Everybody knows what Judson Parker is. He'd do *anything* for money. He hasn't a *spark* of public spirit or *any* sense of the beautiful."

The prospect looked rather unpromising. Judson Parker and his sister were the only Parkers in Avonlea, so that no leverage could be exerted by family connections. Martha Parker was a lady of all too certain age who disapproved of young people in general and the Improvers in particular. Judson was a jovial, smooth-spoken man, so uniformly

good-natured and bland that it was surprising how few friends he had.
Perhaps he had got the better in too many business transactions . . .
which seldom makes for popularity. He was reputed to be very "sharp"
and it was the general opinion that he "hadn't much principle."

"If Judson Parker has a chance to 'turn an honest penny,' as he says
himself, he'll never lose it," declared Fred Wright.

"Is there *nobody* who has any influence over him?" asked Anne
despairingly.

"He goes to see Louisa Spencer at White Sands," suggested Carrie
Sloane. "Perhaps she could coax him not to rent his fences."

"Not she," said Gilbert emphatically. "I know Louisa Spencer
well. She doesn't 'believe' in Village Improvement Societies, but she *does*
believe in dollars and cents. She'd be more likely to urge Judson on than
to dissuade him."

"The only thing to do is to appoint a committee to wait on him
and protest," said Julia Bell, "and you must send girls, for he'd hardly be
civil to boys . . . but *I* won't go, so nobody need nominate me."

"Better send Anne alone," said Oliver Sloane. "She can talk
Judson over if anybody can."

Anne protested. She was willing to go and do the talking; but she
must have others with her "for moral support." Diana and Jane were
therefore appointed to support her morally and the Improvers broke
up, buzzing like angry bees with indignation. Anne was so worried
that she didn't sleep until nearly morning, and then she dreamed that
the trustees had put a fence around the school and painted "Try Purple
Pills" all over it.

The committee waited on Judson Parker the next afternoon.
Anne pleaded eloquently against his nefarious design and Jane and
Diana supported her morally and valiantly. Judson was sleek, suave,
flattering; paid them several compliments of the delicacy of sunflow-
ers; felt real bad to refuse such charming young ladies . . . but business
was business; couldn't afford to let sentiment stand in the way these
hard times.

"But I'll tell what I *will* do," he said, with a twinkle in his light, full
eyes. "I'll tell the agent he must use only handsome, tasty colors . . . red

and yellow and so on. I'll tell him he mustn't paint the ads *blue* on any account."

The vanquished committee retired, thinking things not lawful to be uttered.

"We have done all we can do and must simply trust the rest to Providence," said Jane, with an unconscious imitation of Mrs. Lynde's tone and manner.

"I wonder if Mr. Allan could do anything," reflected Diana.

Anne shook her head.

"No, it's no use to worry Mr. Allan, especially now when the baby's so sick. Judson would slip away from him as smoothly as from us, although he *has* taken to going to church quite regularly just now. That is simply because Louisa Spencer's father is an elder and very particular about such things."

"Judson Parker is the only man in Avonlea who would dream of renting his fences," said Jane indignantly. "Even Levi Boulter or Lorenzo White would never stoop to that, tightfisted as they are. They would have too much respect for public opinion."

Public opinion was certainly down on Judson Parker when the facts became known, but that did not help matters much. Judson chuckled to himself and defied it, and the Improvers were trying to reconcile themselves to the prospect of seeing the prettiest part of the Newbridge road defaced by advertisements, when Anne rose quietly at the president's call for reports of committees on the occasion of the next meeting of the Society, and announced that Mr. Judson Parker had instructed her to inform the Society that he was *not* going to rent his fences to the Patent Medicine Company.

Jane and Diana stared as if they found it hard to believe their ears. Parliamentary etiquette, which was generally very strictly enforced in the A. V. I. S., forbade them giving instant vent to their curiosity, but after the Society adjourned Anne was besieged for explanations. Anne had no explanation to give. Judson Parker had overtaken her on the road the preceding evening and told her that he had decided to humor the A. V. I. S. in its peculiar prejudice against patent medicine advertisements. That was all Anne would say, then or ever afterwards, and it was the simple truth; but when Jane Andrews, on her way home, confided to Oliver Sloane her firm belief that there was more behind Judson Parker's mysterious change of heart than Anne Shirley had revealed, she spoke the truth also.

Anne had been down to old Mrs. Irving's on the shore road the preceding evening and had come home by a short cut which led her first over the low-lying shore fields, and then through the beech wood below Robert Dickson's, by a little footpath that ran out to the main road just above the Lake of Shining Waters . . . known to unimaginative people as Barry's pond.

Two men were sitting in their buggies, reined off to the side of the road, just at the entrance of the path. One was Judson Parker; the other was Jerry Corcoran, a Newbridge man against whom, as Mrs. Lynde would have told you in eloquent italics, nothing shady had ever been *proved.* He was an agent for agricultural implements and a prominent personage in matters political. He had a finger . . . some people said *all* his fingers . . . in every political pie that was cooked; and as Canada was on the eve of a general election Jerry Corcoran had been a busy man for many weeks, canvassing the county in the interests of his party's candidate. Just as Anne emerged from under the overhanging beech boughs she heard Corcoran say,

"If you'll vote for Amesbury, Parker . . . well, I've a note for that pair of harrows you've got in the spring. I suppose you wouldn't object to having it back, eh?"

"We . . .ll, since you put it in that way," drawled Judson with a grin, "I reckon I might as well do it. A man must look out for his own interests in these hard times."

Both saw Anne at this moment and conversation abruptly ceased. Anne bowed frostily and walked on, with her chin slightly more tilted than usual. Soon Judson Parker overtook her.

"Have a lift, Anne?" he inquired genially.

"Thank you, no," said Anne politely, but with a fine, needle-like disdain in her voice that pierced even Judson Parker's none too sensitive consciousness. His face reddened and he twitched his reins angrily; but the next second prudential considerations checked him. He looked uneasily at Anne, as she walked steadily on, glancing neither to the right nor to the left. Had she heard Corcoran's unmistakable offer and his own too plain acceptance of it? Confound Corcoran! If he couldn't put his meaning into less dangerous phrases he'd get into trouble some of these long-come-shorts. And confound redheaded school-ma'ams with a habit of popping out of beechwoods where they had no business to be. If Anne had heard, Judson Parker, measuring her corn in his own half bushel, as the country saying went, and cheating himself thereby, as such people generally do, believed that she would tell it far and wide. Now, Judson Parker, as has been seen, was not overly regardful of public opinion; but to be known as having accepted a bribe would be a nasty thing; and if it ever reached Isaac Spencer's ears farewell forever to all hope of winning Louisa Jane with her comfortable prospects as the heiress of a well-to-do farmer. Judson Parker knew that Mr. Spencer looked somewhat askance at him as it was; he could not afford to take any risks.

"Ahem . . . Anne, I've been wanting to see you about that little matter we were discussing the other day. I've decided not to let my fences to that company after all. A society with an aim like yours ought to be encouraged."

Anne thawed out the merest trifle.

"Thank you," she said.

"And . . . and . . . you needn't mention that little conversation of mine with Jerry."

"I have no intention of mentioning it in any case," said Anne icily, for she would have seen every fence in Avonlea painted with advertisements before she would have stooped to bargain with a man who would sell his vote.

"Just so . . . just so," agreed Judson, imagining that they understood each other beautifully. "I didn't suppose you would. Of course, I was only stringing Jerry . . . he thinks he's so all-fired cute and smart. I've no intention of voting for Amesbury. I'm going to vote for Grant as I've always done . . . you'll see that when the election comes off. I just led Jerry on to see if he would commit himself. And it's all right about the fence . . . you can tell the Improvers that."

"It takes all sorts of people to make a world, as I've often heard, but I think there are some who could be spared," Anne told her reflection in the east gable mirror that night. "I wouldn't have mentioned the disgraceful thing to a soul anyhow, so my conscience is clear on *that* score. I really don't know who or what is to be thanked for this. I did nothing to bring it about, and it's hard to believe that Providence ever works by means of the kind of politics men like Judson Parker and Jerry Corcoran have."

15

The Beginning of Vacation

nne locked the schoolhouse door on a still, yellow evening, when the winds were purring in the spruces around the playground, and the shadows were long and lazy by the edge of the woods. She dropped the key into her pocket with a sigh of satisfaction. The school year was ended, she had been reëngaged for the next, with many expressions of satisfaction . . . only Mr. Harmon Andrews told her she ought to use the strap oftener . . . and two delightful months of a well-earned vacation beckoned her invitingly. Anne felt at peace with the world and herself as she walked down the hill with her basket of flowers in her hand. Since the earliest mayflowers Anne had never missed her weekly pilgrimage to Matthew's grave. Everybody else in Avonlea, except Marilla, had already forgotten quiet, shy, unimportant Matthew Cuthbert; but his memory was still green in Anne's heart and always would be. She could never forget the kind old man who had been the first to give her the love and sympathy her starved childhood had craved.

At the foot of the hill a boy was sitting on the fence in the shadow of the spruces . . . a boy with big, dreamy eyes and a beautiful, sensitive face. He swung down and joined Anne, smiling; but there were traces of tears on his cheeks.

"I thought I'd wait for you, teacher, because I knew you were going to the graveyard," he said, slipping his hand into hers. "I'm going there, too . . . I'm taking this bouquet of geraniums to put on Grandpa Irving's grave for grandma. And look, teacher, I'm going to put this bunch of white roses beside Grandpa's grave in memory of my little mother . . . because I can't go to her grave to put it there. But don't you think she'll know all about it, just the same?"

"Yes, I am sure she will, Paul."

"You see, teacher, it's just three years today since my little mother died. It's such a long, long time but it hurts just as much as ever . . . and I miss her just as much as ever. Sometimes it seems to me that I just can't bear it, it hurts so."

Paul's voice quivered and his lip trembled. He looked down at his roses, hoping that his teacher would not notice the tears in his eyes.

"And yet," said Anne, very softly, "you wouldn't want it to stop hurting . . . you wouldn't want to forget your little mother even if you could."

"No, indeed, I wouldn't . . . that's just the way I feel. You're so good at understanding, teacher. Nobody else understands so well . . . not even grandma, although she's so good to me. Father understood pretty well, but still I couldn't talk much to him about mother, because it made him feel so bad. When he put his hand over his face I always knew it was time to stop. Poor father, he must be dreadfully lonesome without me; but you see he has nobody but a housekeeper now and he thinks housekeepers are no good to bring up little boys, especially when he has to be away from home so much on business. Grandmothers are better, next to mothers. Someday, when I'm brought up, I'll go back to father and we're never going to be parted again."

Paul had talked so much to Anne about his mother and father that she felt as if she had known them. She thought his mother must have been very like what he was himself, in temperament and disposition; and she had an idea that Stephen Irving was a rather reserved man with a deep and tender nature which he kept hidden scrupulously from the world.

"Father's not very easy to get acquainted with," Paul had said once. "I never got really acquainted with him until after my little mother died. But he's splendid when you do get to know him. I love him the best in all the world, and Grandma Irving next, and then you, teacher. I'd love you next to father if it wasn't my *duty* to love Grandma Irving best, because she's doing so much for me. *You* know, teacher. I wish she would leave the lamp in my room till I go to sleep, though. She takes it right out as soon as she tucks me up because she says I mustn't be a coward. I'm *not* scared, but I'd *rather* have the light. My little mother used always to sit beside me and hold my hand till I went to sleep. I expect she spoiled me. Mothers do sometimes, you know."

No, Anne did not know this, although she might imagine it. She thought sadly of *her* "little mother," the mother who had thought her so "perfectly beautiful" and who had died so long ago and was buried beside her boyish husband in that unvisited grave far away. Anne could not remember her mother and for this reason she almost envied Paul.

"My birthday is next week," said Paul, as they walked up the long red hill, basking in the June sunshine, "and father wrote me that he is sending me something that he thinks I'll like better than anything else he could send. I believe it has come already, for Grandma is keeping the bookcase drawer locked and that is something new. And when I asked her why, she just looked mysterious and said little boys mustn't be too curious. It's very exciting to have a birthday, isn't it? I'll be eleven. You'd never think it to look at me, would you? Grandma says I'm very small for my age and that it's all because I don't eat enough porridge. I do my very best, but Grandma gives such *generous* platefuls . . . there's nothing mean about Grandma, I can tell you. Ever since you and I had that talk about praying going home from Sunday School that day, teacher . . . when you said we ought to pray about all our difficulties . . . I've prayed every night that God would give me enough grace to enable me to eat every bit of my porridge in the mornings. But I've never been able to do it yet, and whether it's because I have too little grace or too much porridge I really can't decide. Grandma says father was brought up on porridge, and it certainly did work well in his case, for you ought to see the shoulders he has. But sometimes," concluded Paul with a sigh and a meditative air, "I really think porridge will be the death of me."

Anne permitted herself a smile, since Paul was not looking at her. All Avonlea knew that old Mrs. Irving was bringing her grandson up in accordance with the good, old-fashioned methods of diet and morals.

"Let us hope not, dear," she said cheerfully. "How are your rock people coming on? Does the oldest Twin still continue to behave himself?"

"He *has* to," said Paul emphatically. "He knows I won't associate with him if he doesn't. He is really full of wickedness, *I* think."

"And has Nora found out about the Golden Lady yet?"

"No; but I think she suspects. I'm almost sure she watched me the last time I went to the cave. I don't mind if she finds out . . . it is only for *her* sake I don't want her to . . . so that her feelings won't be hurt. But if she is *determined* to have her feelings hurt it can't be helped."

"If I were to go to the shore some night with you do you think I could see your rock people too?"

Paul shook his head gravely.

"No, I don't think you could see *my* rock people. I'm the only person who can see them. But you could see rock people of your own. You're one of the kind that can. We're both that kind. *You* know, teacher," he added, squeezing her hand chummily. "Isn't it spendid to be that kind, teacher?"

"Spendid," Anne agreed, gray shining eyes looking down into blue shining ones. Anne and Paul both knew

"How fair the realm
Imagination opens to the view,"

and both knew the way to that happy land. There the rose of joy bloomed immortal by dale and stream; clouds never darkened the sunny sky; sweet bells never jangled out of tune; and kindred spirits abounded. The knowledge of that land's geography . . . "east o' the sun, west o' the moon" . . . is priceless lore, not to be bought in any market place. It must be the gift of the good fairies at birth and the years can never deface it or take it away. It is better to possess it, living in a garret, than to be the inhabitant of palaces without it.

The Avonlea graveyard was as yet the grass-grown solitude it had always been. To be sure, the Improvers had an eye on it, and Priscilla Grant had read a paper on cemeteries before the last meeting of the Society. At some future time the Improvers meant to have the lichened, wayward old board fence replaced by a neat wire railing, the grass mown and the leaning monuments straightened up.

Anne put on Matthew's grave the flowers she had brought for it, and then went over to the little poplar shaded corner where Hester

Gray slept. Ever since the day of the spring picnic Anne had put flowers on Hester's grave when she visited Matthew's. The evening before
she had made a pilgrimage back to the little deserted garden in the
woods and brought therefrom some of Hester's own white roses.

"I thought you would like them better than any others, dear," she
said softly.

Anne was still sitting there when a shadow fell over the grass and
she looked up to see Mrs. Allan. They walked home together.

Mrs. Allan's face was not the face of the girl-bride whom the
minister had brought to Avonlea five years before. It had lost some of
its bloom and youthful curves, and there were fine, patient lines about
eyes and mouth. A tiny grave in that very cemetery accounted for some
of them; and some new ones had come during the recent illness, now
happily over, of her little son. But Mrs. Allan's dimples were as sweet
and sudden as ever, her eyes as clear and bright and true; and what her
face lacked of girlish beauty was now more than atoned for in added
tenderness and strength.

"I suppose you are looking forward to your vacation, Anne?" she
said, as they left the graveyard.

Anne nodded.

"Yes. . . . I could roll the word as a sweet morsel under my tongue.
I think the summer is going to be lovely. For one thing, Mrs. Morgan
is coming to the Island in July and Priscilla is going to bring her up. I
feel one of my old 'thrills' at the mere thought."

"I hope you'll have a good time, Anne. You've worked very hard
this past year and you have succeeded."

"Oh, I don't know. I've come so far short in so many things.
I haven't done what I meant to do when I began to teach last fall. . . . I
haven't lived up to my ideals."

"None of us ever do," said Mrs. Allan with a sigh. "But then,
Anne, you know what Lowell says, 'Not failure but low aim is crime.'
We must have ideals and try to live up to them, even if we never quite
succeed. Life would be a sorry business without them. With them it's
grand and great. Hold fast to your ideals, Anne."

"I shall try. But I have let go most of my theories," said Anne, laughing a little. "I had the most beautiful set of theories you ever knew when I started out as a schoolma'am, but every one of them has failed me at some pinch or another."

"Even the theory on corporal punishment," teased Mrs. Allan.

But Anne flushed.

"I shall never forgive myself for whipping Anthony."

"Nonsense, dear, he deserved it. And it agreed with him. You have had no trouble with him since and he has come to think there's nobody like you. Your kindness won his love after the idea that a 'girl was no good' was rooted out of his stubborn mind."

"He may have deserved it, but that is not the point. If I had calmly and deliberately decided to whip him because I thought it a just punishment for him I would not feel over it as I do. But the truth is, Mrs. Allan, that I just flew into a temper and whipped him because of that. I wasn't thinking whether it was just or unjust . . . even if he hadn't deserved it I'd have done it just the same. That is what humiliates me."

"Well, we all make mistakes, dear, so just put it behind you. We should regret our mistakes and learn from them, but never carry them forward into the future with us. There goes Gilbert Blythe on his wheel . . . home for his vacation too, I suppose. How are you and he getting on with your studies?"

"Pretty well. We plan to finish the Virgil tonight . . . there are only twenty lines to do. Then we are not going to study any more until September."

"Do you think you will ever get to college?"

"Oh, I don't know." Anne looked dreamily afar to the opal-tinted horizon. "Marilla's eyes will never be much better than they are now, although we are so thankful to think that they will not get worse. And then there are the twins . . . somehow I don't believe their uncle will ever really send for them. Perhaps college may be around the bend in the road, but I haven't got to the bend yet and I don't think much about it lest I might grow discontented."

"Well, I should like to see you go to college, Anne; but if you never do, don't be discontented about it. We make our own lives wherever we are, after all . . . college can only help us to do it more easily. They are broad or narrow according to what we put into them, not what we get out. Life is rich and full here . . . everywhere . . . if we can only learn how to open our whole hearts to its richness and fulness."

"I think I understand what you mean," said Anne thoughtfully, "and I know I have so much to feel thankful for . . . oh, so much . . . my work, and Paul Irving, and the dear twins, and all my friends. Do you know, Mrs. Allan, I'm so thankful for friendship. It beautifies life so much."

"True friendship is a very helpful thing indeed," said Mrs. Allan, "and we should have a very high ideal of it, and never sully it by any failure in truth and sincerity. I fear the name of friendship is often degraded to a kind of intimacy that has nothing of real friendship in it."

"Yes . . . like Gertie Pye's and Julia Bell's. They are very intimate and go everywhere together; but Gertie is always saying nasty things of Julia behind her back and everybody thinks she is jealous of her because she is always so pleased when anybody criticizes Julia. I think it is desecration to call *that* friendship. If we have friends we should look only for the best in them and give them the best that is in us, don't you think? Then friendship would be the most beautiful thing in the world."

"Friendship *is* very beautiful," smiled Mrs. Allan, "but some day . . ."

Then she paused abruptly. In the delicate, whitebrowed face beside her, with its candid eyes and mobile features, there was still far more of the child than of the woman. Anne's heart so far harbored only dreams of friendship and ambition, and Mrs. Allan did not wish to brush the bloom from her sweet unconsciousness. So she left her sentence for the future years to finish.

16

The Substance of Things Hoped For

"A nne," said Davy appealingly, scrambling up on the shiny, leather-covered sofa in the Green Gables kitchen, where Anne sat, reading a letter, "Anne, I'm *awful* hungry. You've no idea."

"I'll get you a piece of bread and butter in a minute," said Anne absently. Her letter evidently contained some exciting news, for her cheeks were as pink as the roses on the big bush outside, and her eyes were as starry as only Anne's eyes could be.

"But I ain't bread and butter hungry," said Davy in a disgusted tone. "I'm plum cake hungry."

"Oh," laughed Anne, laying down her letter and putting her arm about Davy to give him a squeeze, "that's a kind of hunger that can be endured very comfortably, Davy-boy. You know it's one of Marilla's rules that you can't have anything but bread and butter between meals."

"Well, gimme a piece then . . . please."

Davy had been at last taught to say "please," but he generally tacked it on as an afterthought. He looked with approval at the generous slice Anne presently brought to him. "You always put such a nice lot of butter on it, Anne. Marilla spreads it pretty thin. It slips down a lot easier when there's plenty of butter."

The slice "slipped down" with tolerable ease, judging from its rapid disappearance. Davy slid head first off the sofa, turned a double somersault on the rug, and then sat up and announced decidedly,

"Anne, I've made up my mind about heaven. I don't want to go there."

"Why not?" asked Anne gravely.

"'Cause heaven is in Simon Fletcher's garret, and I don't like Simon Fletcher."

"Heaven in . . . Simon Fletcher's garret!" gasped Anne, too amazed even to laugh. "Davy Keith, whatever put such an extraordinary idea into your head?"

"Milty Boulter says that's where it is. It was last Sunday in Sunday School. The lesson was about Elijah and Elisha, and I up and asked Miss Rogerson where heaven was. Miss Rogerson looked awful offended. She was cross anyhow, because when she'd asked us what Elijah left Elisha when he went to heaven Milty Boulter said, 'His old clo'es,' and us fellows all laughed before we thought. I wish you could think first and do things afterwards, 'cause then you wouldn't do them. But Milty didn't mean to be disrespeckful. He just couldn't think of the name of the thing. Miss Rogerson said heaven was where God was and I wasn't to ask questions like that. Milty nudged me and said in a whisper, 'Heaven's in Uncle Simon's garret and I'll esplain about it on the road home.' So when we was coming home he esplained. Milty's a great hand at esplaining things. Even if he don't know anything about a thing he'll make up a lot of stuff and so you get it esplained all the same. His mother is Mrs. Simon's sister and he went with her to the funeral when his cousin, Jane Ellen, died. The minister said she'd gone to heaven, though Milty says she was lying right before them in the coffin. But he s'posed they carried the coffin up to the garret afterwards. Well, when Milty and his mother went upstairs after it was all over to get her bonnet he asked her where heaven was that Jane Ellen had gone to, and she pointed right to the ceiling and said, 'Up there.' Milty knew there wasn't anything but the garret over the ceiling, so that's how *he* found out. And he's been awful scared to go to his Uncle Simon's ever since."

Anne took Davy on her knee and did her best to straighten out this theological tangle also. She was much better fitted for the task than Marilla, for she remembered her own childhood and had an instinctive understanding of the curious ideas that seven-year-olds sometimes get about matters that are, of course, very plain and simple to grown up people. She had just succeeded in convincing Davy that heaven was *not* in Simon Fletcher's garret when Marilla came in from the garden, where she and Dora had been picking peas. Dora was an industrious little soul and never happier than when "helping" in various small tasks suited to her chubby fingers. She fed chickens, picked up chips, wiped dishes, and ran errands galore. She was neat, faithful and observant; she never had to be told how to do a thing twice and never forgot any of her little duties. Davy, on the other hand, was rather heedless and forgetful; but he had the born knack of winning love, and even yet Anne and Marilla liked him the better.

While Dora proudly shelled the peas and Davy made boats of the pods, with masts of matches and sails of paper, Anne told Marilla about the wonderful contents of her letter.

"Oh, Marilla, what do you think? I've had a letter from Priscilla and she says that Mrs. Morgan is on the Island, and that if it is fine Thursday they are going to drive up to Avonlea and will reach here about twelve. They will spend the afternoon with us and go to the hotel at White Sands in the evening, because some of Mrs. Morgan's American friends are staying there. Oh, Marilla, isn't it wonderful? I can hardly believe I'm not dreaming."

"I daresay Mrs. Morgan is a lot like other people," said Marilla drily, although she did feel a trifle excited herself. Mrs. Morgan was a famous woman and a visit from her was no commonplace occurrence. "They'll be here to dinner, then?"

"Yes; and oh, Marilla, may I cook every bit of the dinner myself? I want to feel that I can do something for the author of 'The Rosebud Garden,' if it is only to cook a dinner for her. You won't mind, will you?"

"Goodness, I'm not so fond of stewing over a hot fire in July that it would vex me very much to have someone else do it. You're quite welcome to the job."

"Oh, thank you," said Anne, as if Marilla had just conferred a tremendous favor, "I'll make out the menu this very night."

"You'd better not try to put on too much style," warned Marilla, a little alarmed by the high-flown sound of "menu." "You'll likely come to grief if you do."

"Oh, I'm not going to put on any 'style,' if you mean trying to do or have things we don't usually have on festal occasions," assured Anne.

"That would be affectation, and, although I know I haven't as much sense and steadiness as a girl of seventeen and a schoolteacher ought to have, I'm not so silly as *that*. But I want to have everything as nice and dainty as possible. Davy-boy, don't leave those peapods on the back stairs . . . someone might slip on them. I'll have a light soup to begin with . . . you know I can make lovely cream-of-onion soup . . . and then a couple of roast fowls. I'll have the two white roosters. I have a real affection for those roosters and they've been pets ever since the gray hen hatched out just the two of them . . . little balls of yellow down. But I know they would have to be sacrificed sometime, and surely there couldn't be a worthier occasion than this. But oh, Marilla, *I* cannot kill them . . . not even for Mrs. Morgan's sake. I'll have to ask John Henry Carter to come over and do it for me."

"I'll do it," volunteered Davy, "if Marilla'll hold them by the legs, 'cause I guess it'd take both my hands to manage the axe. It's awful jolly fun to see them hopping about after their heads are cut off."

"Then I'll have peas and beans and creamed potatoes and a lettuce salad, for vegetables," resumed Anne, "and for dessert, lemon pie with whipped cream, and coffee and cheese and lady fingers. I'll make the pies and lady fingers tomorrow and do up my white muslin dress. And I must tell Diana tonight, for she'll want to do up hers. Mrs. Morgan's heroines are nearly always dressed in white muslin, and Diana and I have always resolved that that was what we would wear if we ever met her. It will be such a delicate compliment, don't you think? Davy, dear, you mustn't poke peapods into the cracks of the floor. I must ask Mr. and Mrs. Allan and Miss Stacy to dinner, too, for they're all very anxious to meet Mrs. Morgan. It's so fortunate she's coming while Miss Stacy is here. Davy dear, don't sail the peapods in the water bucket . . . go out to the trough. Oh, I do hope it will be fine Thursday, and I think it will, for Uncle Abe said last night when he called at Mr. Harrison's, that it was going to rain most of this week."

"That's a good sign," agreed Marilla.

Anne ran across to Orchard Slope that evening to tell the news to Diana, who was also very much excited over it, and they discussed the matter in the hammock swung under the big willow in the Barry garden.

"Oh, Anne, mayn't I help you cook the dinner?" implored Diana. "You know I can make splendid lettuce salad."

"Indeed you may," said Anne unselfishly. "And I shall want you to help me decorate too. I mean to have the parlor simply a *bower* of blossoms . . . and the dining table is to be adorned with wild roses. Oh, I do hope everything will go smoothly. Mrs. Morgan's heroines *never* get into scrapes or are taken at a disadvantage, and they are always so self-possessed and such good housekeepers. They seem to be *born* good housekeepers. You remember that *Gertrude* in 'Edgewood Days' kept house for her father when she was only eight years old. When I was eight years old I hardly knew how to do a thing except bring up children. Mrs. Morgan must be an authority on girls when she has written so much about them, and I do want her to have a good opinion of us. I've imagined it all out a dozen different ways . . . what she'll look like, and what she'll say, and what I'll say. And I'm so anxious about my nose. There are seven freckles on it, as you can see. They came at the A. V. I. S. picnic, when I went around in the sun without my hat. I suppose it's ungrateful of me to worry over them, when I should be thankful they're not spread all over my face as they once were; but I do wish they hadn't come . . . all Mrs. Morgan's heroines have such perfect complexions. I can't recall a freckled one among them."

"Yours are not very noticeable," comforted Diana. "Try a little lemon juice on them tonight."

The next day Anne made her pies and lady fingers, did up her muslin dress, and swept and dusted every room in the house . . . a quite unnecessary proceeding, for Green Gables was, as usual, in the apple pie order dear to Marilla's heart. But Anne felt that a fleck of dust would be a desecration in a house that was to be honored by a visit from Charlotte E. Morgan. She even cleaned out the "catch-all" closet under the stairs, although there was not the remotest possibility of Mrs. Morgan's seeing its interior.

"But I want to *feel* that it is in perfect order, even if she isn't to see it," Anne told Marilla. "You know, in her book 'Golden Keys,' she makes her two heroines *Alice* and *Louisa* take for their motto that verse of Longfellow's,

> "*In the elder days of art*
> *Builders wrought with greatest care*
> *Each minute and unseen part,*
> *For the gods see everywhere,*'

and so they always kept their cellar stairs scrubbed and never forgot to sweep under the beds. I should have a guilty conscience if I thought this closet was in disorder when Mrs. Morgan was in the house. Ever since we read 'Golden Keys,' last April, Diana and I have taken that verse for our motto too."

That night John Henry Carter and Davy between them contrived to execute the two white roosters, and Anne dressed them, the usually distasteful task quite glorified in her eyes by the destination of the plump birds.

"I don't like picking fowls," she told Marilla, "but isn't it fortunate we don't have to put our souls into what our hands may be doing? I've been picking chickens with my hands but in imagination I've been roaming the Milky Way."

"I thought you'd scattered more feathers over the floor than usual," remarked Marilla.

Then Anne put Davy to bed and made him promise that he would behave perfectly the next day.

"If I'm as good as good can be all day tomorrow will you let me be just as bad as I like all the next day?" asked Davy.

"I couldn't do that," said Anne discreetly, "but I'll take you and Dora for a row in the flat right to the bottom of the pond, and we'll go ashore on the sandhills and have a picnic."

"It's a bargain," said Davy. "I'll be good, you bet. I meant to go over to Mr. Harrison's and fire peas from my new popgun at Ginger but another day'll do as well. I espect it will be just like Sunday, but a picnic at the shore'll make up for *that*."

17

A Chapter of Accidents

nne woke three times in the night and made pilgrimages to her window to make sure that Uncle Abe's prediction was not coming true. Finally the morning dawned pearly and lustrous in a sky full of silver sheen and radiance, and the wonderful day had arrived.

Diana appeared soon after breakfast, with a basket of flowers over one arm and *her* muslin dress over the other . . . for it would not do to don it until all the dinner preparations were completed. Meanwhile she wore her afternoon pink print and a lawn apron fearfully and wonderfully ruffled and frilled; and very neat and pretty and rosy she was.

"You look simply sweet," said Anne admiringly.

Diana sighed.

"But I've had to let out every one of my dresses *again*. I weigh four pounds more than I did in July. Anne, *where* will this end? Mrs. Morgan's heroines are all tall and slender."

"Well, let's forget our troubles and think of our mercies," said Anne gaily. "Mrs. Allan says that whenever we think of anything that is a trial to us we should also think of something nice that we can set over against it. If you are slightly too plump you've got the dearest dimples; and if I have a freckled nose the *shape* of it is all right. Do you think the lemon juice did any good?"

"Yes, I really think it did," said Diana critically; and, much elated, Anne led the way to the garden, which was full of airy shadows and wavering golden lights.

"We'll decorate the parlor first. We have plenty of time, for Priscilla said they'd be here about twelve or half past at the latest, so we'll have dinner at one."

There may have been two happier and more excited girls somewhere in Canada or the United States at that moment, but I doubt it.
Every snip of the scissors, as rose and peony and bluebell fell, seemed
to chirp, "Mrs. Morgan is coming today." Anne wondered how Mr.
Harrison *could* go on placidly mowing hay in the field across the lane,
just as if nothing were going to happen.

The parlor at Green Gables was a rather severe and gloomy apartment, with rigid horsehair furniture, stiff lace curtains, and white anti-
macassars that were always laid at a perfectly correct angle, except at
such times as they clung to unfortunate people's buttons. Even Anne
had never been able to infuse much grace into it, for Marilla would not
permit any alterations. But it is wonderful what flowers can accomplish
if you give them a fair chance; when Anne and Diana finished with the
room you would not have recognized it.

A great blue bowlful of snowballs overflowed on the polished
table. The shining black mantelpiece was heaped with roses and ferns.
Every shelf of the whatnot held a sheaf of bluebells; the dark corners on
either side of the grate were lighted up with jars full of glowing crimson peonies, and the grate itself was aflame with yellow poppies. All this
splendor and color, mingled with the sunshine falling through the honeysuckle vines at the windows in a leafy riot of dancing shadows over
walls and floor, made of the usually dismal little room the veritable
"bower" of Anne's imagination, and even extorted a tribute of admiration from Marilla, who came in to criticize and remained to praise.

"Now, we must set the table," said Anne, in the tone of a priest-
ess about to perform some sacred rite in honor of a divinity. "We'll have
a big vaseful of wild roses in the center and one single rose in front of
everybody's plate—and a special bouquet of rosebuds only by Mrs.
Morgan's—an allusion to 'The Rosebud Garden' you know."

The table was set in the sitting room, with Marilla's finest linen
and the best china, glass, and silver. You may be perfectly certain that
every article placed on it was polished or scoured to the highest possible perfection of gloss and glitter.

Then the girls tripped out to the kitchen, which was filled with
appetizing odors emanating from the oven, where the chickens were

already sizzling splendidly. Anne prepared the potatoes and Diana got the peas and beans ready. Then, while Diana shut herself into the pantry to compound the lettuce salad, Anne, whose cheeks were already beginning to glow crimson, as much with excitement as from the heat of the fire, prepared the bread sauce for the chickens, minced her onions for the soup, and finally whipped the cream for her lemon pies.

And what about Davy all this time? Was he redeeming his promise to be good? He was, indeed. To be sure, he insisted on remaining in the kitchen, for his curiosity wanted to see all that went on. But as he sat quietly in a corner, busily engaged in untying the knots in a piece of herring net he had brought home from his last trip to the shore, nobody objected to this.

At half past eleven the lettuce salad was made, the golden circles of the pies were heaped with whipped cream, and everything was sizzling and bubbling that ought to sizzle and bubble.

"We'd better go and dress now," said Anne, "for they may be here by twelve. We must have dinner at sharp one, for the soup must be served as soon as it's done."

Serious indeed were the toilet rites presently performed in the east gable. Anne peered anxiously at her nose and rejoiced to see that its freckles were not at all prominent, thanks either to the lemon juice or to the unusual flush on her cheeks. When they were ready they looked quite as sweet and trim and girlish as ever did any of "Mrs. Morgan's heroines."

"I do hope I'll be able to say something once in a while, and not sit like a mute," said Diana anxiously. "All Mrs. Morgan's heroines converse so beautifully. But I'm afraid I'll be tongue-tied and stupid. And I'll be sure to say 'I seen.' I haven't often said it since Miss Stacy taught here; but in moments of excitement it's sure to pop out. Anne, if I were to say 'I seen' before Mrs. Morgan I'd die of mortification. And it would be almost as bad to have nothing to say."

"I'm nervous about a good many things," said Anne, "but I don't think there is much fear that I won't be able to *talk*."

And, to do her justice, there wasn't.

Anne shrouded her muslin glories in a big apron and went down to concoct her soup. Marilla had dressed herself and the twins, and looked more excited than she had ever been known to look before. At half past twelve the Allans and Miss Stacy came. Everything was going well but Anne was beginning to feel nervous. It was surely time for Priscilla and Mrs. Morgan to arrive. She made frequent trips to the gate and looked as anxiously down the lane as ever her namesake in the Bluebeard story peered from the tower casement.

"Suppose they don't come at all?" she said piteously.

"Don't suppose it. It would be too mean," said Diana, who, however, was beginning to have uncomfortable misgivings on the subject.

"Anne," said Marilla, coming out from the parlor, "Miss Stacy wants to see Miss Barry's willowware platter."

Anne hastened to the sitting room closet to get the platter. She had, in accordance with her promise to Mrs. Lynde, written to Miss Barry of Charlottetown, asking for the loan of it. Miss Barry was an old friend of Anne's, and she promptly sent the platter out, with a letter exhorting Anne to be very careful of it, for she had paid twenty dollars for it. The platter had served its purpose at the Aid bazaar and had then been returned to the Green Gables closet, for Anne would not trust anybody but herself to take it back to town.

She carried the platter carefully to the front door where her guests were enjoying the cool breeze that blew up from the brook. It was examined and admired; then, just as Anne had taken it back into her own hands, a terrific crash and clatter sounded from the kitchen pantry. Marilla, Diana, and Anne fled out, the latter pausing only long enough to set the precious platter hastily down on the second step of the stairs.

When they reached the pantry a truly harrowing spectacle met their eyes . . . a guilty-looking small boy scrambling down from the table, with his clean print blouse liberally plastered with yellow filling, and on the table the shattered remnants of what had been two brave, becreamed lemon pies.

Davy had finished ravelling out his herring net and had wound the twine into a ball. Then he had gone into the pantry to put it up on the shelf above the table, where he already kept a score or so of similar balls, which, so far as could be discovered, served no useful purpose save to yield the joy of possession. Davy had to climb on the table and reach over to the shelf at a dangerous angle . . . something he had been forbidden by Marilla to do, as he had come to grief once before in the experiment. The result in this instance was disastrous. Davy slipped and came sprawling squarely down on the lemon pies. His clean blouse was ruined for that time and the pies for all time. It is, however, an ill wind that blows nobody good, and the pig was eventually the gainer by Davy's mischance.

"Davy Keith," said Marilla, shaking him by the shoulder, "didn't I forbid you to climb up on that table again? Didn't I?"

"I forgot," whimpered Davy. "You've told me not to do such an awful lot of things that I can't remember them all."

"Well, you march upstairs and stay there till after dinner. Perhaps you'll get them sorted out in your memory by that time. No, Anne, never you mind interceding for him. I'm not punishing him because he spoiled your pies . . . that was an accident. I'm punishing him for his disobedience. Go, Davy, I say."

"Ain't I to have any dinner?" wailed Davy.

"You can come down after dinner is over and have yours in the kitchen."

"Oh, all right," said Davy, somewhat comforted. "I know Anne'll save some nice bones for me, won't you, Anne? 'Cause you know I didn't mean to fall on the pies. Say, Anne, since they *are* spoiled can't I take some of the pieces upstairs with me?"

"No, no lemon pie for you, Master Davy," said Marilla, pushing him toward the hall.

"What shall we do for dessert?" asked Anne, looking regretfully at the wreck and ruin.

"Get out a crock of strawberry preserves," said Marilla consolingly. "There's plenty of whipped cream left in the bowl for it."

One o'clock came . . . but no Priscilla or Mrs. Morgan. Anne was in an agony. Everything was done to a turn and the soup was just what soup should be, but couldn't be depended on to remain so for any length of time.

"I don't believe they're coming after all," said Marilla crossly.

Anne and Diana sought comfort in each other's eyes.

At half past one Marilla again emerged from the parlor.

"Girls, we *must* have dinner. Everybody is hungry and it's no use waiting any longer. Priscilla and Mrs. Morgan are not coming, that's plain, and nothing is being improved by waiting."

Anne and Diana set about lifting the dinner, with all the zest gone out of the performance.

"I don't believe I'll be able to eat a mouthful," said Diana dolefully.

"Nor I. But I hope everything will be nice for Miss Stacy's and Mr. and Mrs. Allan's sakes," said Anne listlessly.

When Diana dished the peas she tasted them and a very peculiar expression crossed her face.

"Anne, did *you* put sugar in these peas?"

"Yes," said Anne, mashing the potatoes with the air of one expected to do her duty. "I put a spoonful of sugar in. We always do. Don't you like it?"

"But *I* put a spoonful in too, when I set them on the stove," said Diana.

Anne dropped her masher and tasted the peas also. Then she made a grimace.

"How awful! I never dreamed you had put sugar in, because I knew your mother never does. I happened to think of it, for a won-der . . . I'm always forgetting it . . . so I popped a spoonful in."

"It's a case of too many cooks, I guess," said Marilla, who had lis-tened to this dialogue with a rather guilty expression. "I didn't think you'd remember about the sugar, Anne, for I'm perfectly certain you never did before . . . so I put in a spoonful."

The guests in the parlor heard peal after peal of laughter from the kitchen, but they never knew what the fun was about. There were no green peas on the dinner table that day, however.

"Well," said Anne, sobering down again with a sigh of recollection, "we have the salad anyhow and I don't think anything has happened to the beans. Let's carry the things in and get it over."

It cannot be said that that dinner was a notable success socially.

The Allans and Miss Stacy exerted themselves to save the situation and Marilla's customary placidity was not noticeably ruffled. But Anne and Diana, between their disappointment and the reaction from their excitement of the forenoon, could neither talk nor eat. Anne tried heroically to bear her part in the conversation for the sake of her guests; but all the sparkle had been quenched in her for the time being, and, in spite of her love for the Allans and Miss Stacy, she couldn't help thinking how nice it would be when everybody had gone home and she could bury her weariness and disappointment in the pillows of the east gable.

There is an old proverb that really seems at times to be inspired . . . "it never rains but it pours." The measure of that day's tribulations was not yet full. Just as Mr. Allan had finished returning thanks there arose a strange, ominous sound on the stairs, as of some hard, heavy object bounding from step to step, finishing up with a grand smash at the bottom. Everybody ran out into the hall. Anne gave a shriek of dismay.

At the bottom of the stairs lay a big pink conch shell amid the fragments of what had been Miss Barry's platter; and at the top of the stairs knelt a terrified Davy, gazing down with wide-open eyes at the havoc.

"Davy," said Marilla ominously, "did you throw that conch down *on purpose?*"

"No, I never did," whimpered Davy. "I was just kneeling here, quiet as quiet, to watch you folks through the bannisters, and my foot struck that old thing and pushed it off . . . and I'm awful hungry . . . and I do wish you'd lick a fellow and have done with it, instead of always sending him upstairs to miss all the fun."

"Don't blame Davy," said Anne, gathering up the fragments with trembling fingers. "It was my fault. I set that platter there and forgot all about it. I am properly punished for my carelessness; but oh, what will Miss Barry say?"

"Well, you know she only bought it, so it isn't the same as if it was an heirloom," said Diana, trying to console.

The guests went away soon after, feeling that it was the most tactful thing to do, and Anne and Diana washed the dishes, talking less than they had ever been known to do before. Then Diana went home with a headache and Anne went with another to the east gable, where she stayed until Marilla came home from the post office at sunset, with a letter from Priscilla, written the day before. Mrs. Morgan had sprained her ankle so severely that she could not leave her room.

"And oh, Anne dear," wrote Priscilla, "I'm so sorry, but I'm afraid we won't get up to Green Gables at all now, for by the time Aunty's ankle is well she will have to go back to Toronto. She has to be there by a certain date."

"Well," sighed Anne, laying the letter down on the red sandstone step of the back porch, where she was sitting, while the twilight rained down out of a dappled sky, "I always thought it was too good to be true that Mrs. Morgan should really come. But there . . . that speech sounds as pessimistic as Miss Eliza Andrews and I'm ashamed of making it. After all, it was *not* too good to be true . . . things just as good and far better are coming true for me all the time. And I suppose the events of today have a funny side too. Perhaps when Diana and I are old and gray we shall be able to laugh over them. But I feel that I can't expect to do it before then, for it has truly been a bitter disappointment."

"You'll probably have a good many more and worse disappointments than that before you get through life," said Marilla, who honestly thought she was making a comforting speech. "It seems to me, Anne, that you are never going to outgrow your fashion of setting your heart so on things and then crashing down into despair because you don't get them."

"I know I'm too much inclined that way," agreed Anne ruefully. "When I think something nice is going to happen I seem to fly right up on the wings of anticipation; and then the first thing I realize I drop down to earth with a thud. But really, Marilla, the flying part *is* glorious as long as it lasts . . . it's like soaring through a sunset. I think it almost pays for the thud."

"Well, maybe it does," admitted Marilla. "I'd rather walk calmly along and do without both flying and thud. But everybody has her own way of living . . . I used to think there was only one right way . . . but since I've had you and the twins to bring up I don't feel so sure of it. What are you going to do about Miss Barry's platter?"

"Pay her back the twenty dollars she paid for it, I suppose. I'm so thankful it wasn't a cherished heirloom because then no money could replace it."

"Maybe you could find one like it somewhere and buy it for her."

"I'm afraid not. Platters as old as that are very scarce. Mrs. Lynde couldn't find one anywhere for the supper. I only wish I could, for of course Miss Barry would just as soon have one platter as another, if both were equally old and genuine. Marilla, look at that big star over Mr. Harrison's maple grove, with all that holy hush of silvery sky about it. It gives me a feeling that is like a prayer. After all, when one can see stars and skies like that, little disappointments and accidents can't matter so much, can they?"

"Where's Davy?" said Marilla, with an indifferent glance at the star.

"In bed. I've promised to take him and Dora to the shore for a picnic tomorrow. Of course, the original agreement was that he must be good. But he *tried* to be good . . . and I hadn't the heart to disappoint him."

"You'll drown yourself or the twins, rowing about the pond in that flat," grumbled Marilla. "I've lived here for sixty years and I've never been on the pond yet."

"Well, it's never too late to mend," said Anne roguishly. "Suppose you come with us tomorrow. We'll shut Green Gables up and spend the whole day at the shore, daffing the world aside."

"No, thank you," said Marilla, with indignant emphasis. "I'd be a nice sight, wouldn't I, rowing down the pond in a flat? I think I hear Rachel pronouncing on it. There's Mr. Harrison driving away somewhere. Do you suppose there is any truth in the gossip that Mr. Harrison is going to see Isabella Andrews?"

"No, I'm sure there isn't. He just called there one evening on business with Mr. Harmon Andrews and Mrs. Lynde saw him and said she knew he was courting because he had a white collar on. I don't believe Mr. Harrison will ever marry. He seems to have a prejudice against marriage."

"Well, you can never tell about those old bachelors. And if he had a white collar on I'd agree with Rachel that it looks suspicious, for I'm sure he never was seen with one before."

"I think he only put it on because he wanted to conclude a business deal with Harmon Andrews," said Anne. "I've heard him say that's the only time a man needs to be particular about his appearance, because if he looks prosperous the party of the second part won't be so likely to try to cheat him. I really feel sorry for Mr. Harrison; I don't believe he feels satisfied with his life. It must be very lonely to have no one to care about except a parrot, don't you think? But I notice Mr. Harrison doesn't like to be pitied. Nobody does, I imagine."

"There's Gilbert coming up the lane," said Marilla. "If he wants you to go for a row on the pond mind you put on your coat and rubbers. There's a heavy dew tonight."

18

An Adventure on the Tory Road

"nne," said Davy, sitting up in bed and propping his chin on his hands, "Anne, where is sleep? People go to sleep every night, and of course I know it's the place where I do the things I dream, but I want to know *where* it is and how I get there and back without knowing anything about it . . . and in my nighty too. Where is it?"

Anne was kneeling at the west gable window watching the sunset sky that was like a great flower with petals of crocus and a heart of fiery yellow. She turned her head at Davy's question and answered dreamily,

> *"'Over the mountains of the moon,*
> *Down the valley of the shadow.'"*

Paul Irving would have known the meaning of this, or made a meaning out of it for himself, if he didn't; but practical Davy, who, as Anne often despairingly remarked, hadn't a particle of imagination, was only puzzled and disgusted.

"Anne, I believe you're just talking nonsense."

"Of course I was, dear boy. Don't you know that it is only very foolish folk who talk sense all the time?"

"Well, I think you might give a sensible answer when I ask a sensible question," said Davy in an injured tone.

"Oh, you are too little to understand," said Anne. But she felt rather ashamed of saying it; for had she not, in keen remembrance of many similar snubs administered in her own early years, solemnly vowed that she would never tell any child it was too little to understand? Yet here she was doing it . . . so wide sometimes is the gulf between theory and practice.

"Well, I'm doing my best to grow," said Davy, "but it's a thing you can't hurry much. If Marilla wasn't so stingy with her jam I believe I'd grow a lot faster."

"Marilla is not stingy, Davy," said Anne severely. "It is very ungrateful of you to say such a thing."

"There's another word that means the same thing and sounds a lot better, but I don't just remember it," said Davy, frowning intently. "I heard Marilla say she was it, herself, the other day."

"If you mean *economical,* it's a *very* different thing from being stingy. It is an excellent trait in a person if she is economical. If Marilla had been stingy she wouldn't have taken you and Dora when your mother died. Would you have liked to live with Mrs. Wiggins?"

"You just bet I wouldn't!" Davy was emphatic on that point. "Nor I don't want to go out to Uncle Richard neither. I'd far rather live here, even if Marilla is that long-tailed word when it comes to jam, 'cause *you're* here, Anne. Say, Anne, won't you tell me a story 'fore I go to sleep? I don't want a fairy story. They're all right for girls, I s'pose, but I want something exciting . . . lots of killing and shooting in it, and a house on fire, and in'trusting things like that."

Fortunately for Anne, Marilla called out at this moment from her room.

"Anne, Diana's signaling at a great rate. You'd better see what she wants."

Anne ran to the east gable and saw flashes of light coming through the twilight from Diana's window in groups of five, which meant, according to their old childish code, "Come over at once for I have something important to reveal." Anne threw her white shawl over her head and hastened through the Haunted Wood and across Mr. Bell's pasture corner to Orchard Slope.

"I've good news for you, Anne," said Diana. "Mother and I have just got home from Carmody, and I saw Mary Sentner from Spencervale in Mr. Blair's store. She says the old Copp girls on the Tory Road have a willow-ware platter and she thinks it's exactly like the one we had at the supper. She says they'll likely sell it, for Martha Copp has never been known to keep anything she *could* sell; but if they won't there's a platter at Wesley Keyson's at Spencervale and she knows they'd sell it, but she isn't sure it's just the same kind as Aunt Josephine's."

"I'll go right over to Spencervale after it tomorrow," said Anne resolutely, "and you must come with me. It will be such a weight off my mind, for I have to go to town day after tomorrow and how can I face your Aunt Josephine without a willow-ware platter? It would be even worse than the time I had to confess about jumping on the spare room bed."

Both girls laughed over the old memory . . . concerning which, if any of my readers are ignorant and curious, I must refer them to Anne's earlier history.

The next afternoon the girls fared forth on their platter hunting expedition. It was ten miles to Spencervale and the day was not especially pleasant for traveling. It was very warm and windless, and the dust on the road was such as might have been expected after six weeks of dry weather.

"Oh, I do wish it would rain soon," sighed Anne. "Everything is so parched up. The poor fields just seem pitiful to me and the trees seem to be stretching out their hands pleading for rain. As for my garden, it hurts me every time I go into it. I suppose I shouldn't complain about a garden when the farmers' crops are suffering so. Mr. Harrison says his pastures are so scorched up that his poor cows can hardly get a bite to eat and he feels guilty of cruelty to animals every time he meets their eyes."

After a wearisome drive the girls reached Spencervale and turned down the "Tory" Road . . . a green, solitary highway where the strips of grass between the wheel tracks bore evidence to lack of travel. Along most of its extent it was lined with thick-set young spruces crowding down to the roadway, with here and there a break where the back field of a Spencervale farm came out to the fence or an expanse of stumps was aflame with fireweed and goldenrod.

"Why is it called the Tory Road?" asked Anne.

"Mr. Allan says it is on the principle of calling a place a grove because there are no trees in it," said Diana, "for nobody lives along the road except the Copp girls and old Martin Bovyer at the further end, who is a Liberal. The Tory government ran the road through when they were in power just to show they were doing something."

Diana's father was a Liberal, for which reason she and Anne never discussed politics. Green Gables folk had always been Conservatives.

Finally the girls came to the old Copp homestead . . . a place of such exceeding external neatness that even Green Gables would have suffered by contrast. The house was a very old-fashioned one, situated on a slope, which fact had necessitated the building of a stone basement under one end. The house and outbuildings were all whitewashed to a condition of blinding perfection and not a weed was visible in the prim kitchen garden surrounded by its white paling.

"The shades are all down," said Diana ruefully. "I believe that nobody is home."

This proved to be the case. The girls looked at each other in perplexity.

"I don't know what to do," said Anne. "If I were sure the platter was the right kind I would not mind waiting until they came home. But if it isn't it may be too late to go to Wesley Keyson's afterward."

Diana looked at a certain little square window over the basement.

"That is the pantry window, I feel sure," she said, "because this house is just like Uncle Charles' at Newbridge, and that is their pantry window. The shade isn't down, so if we climbed up on the roof of that little house we could look into the pantry and might be able to see the platter. Do you think it would be any harm?"

"No, I don't think so," decided Anne, after due reflection, "since our motive is not idle curiosity."

This important point of ethics being settled, Anne prepared to mount the aforesaid "little house," a construction of lathes, with a peaked roof, which had in times past served as a habitation for ducks. The Copp girls had given up keeping ducks . . . "because they were such untidy birds" . . . and the house had not been in use for some years, save as an abode of correction for setting hens. Although scrupulously white-washed it had become somewhat shaky, and Anne felt rather dubious as she scrambled up from the vantage point of a keg placed on a box.

"I'm afraid it won't bear my weight," she said as she gingerly stepped on the roof.

"Lean on the window sill," advised Diana, and Anne accordingly leaned. Much to her delight, she saw, as she peered through the pane, a willow-ware platter, exactly such as she was in quest of, on the shelf in front of the window. So much she saw before the catastrophe came. In her joy Anne forgot the precarious nature of her footing, incautiously ceased to lean on the window sill, gave an impulsive little hop of pleasure . . . and the next moment she had crashed through the roof up to her armpits, and there she hung, quite unable to extricate herself. Diana dashed into the duck house and, seizing her unfortunate friend by the waist, tried to draw her down.

"Ow . . . don't," shrieked poor Anne. "There are some long splinters sticking into me. See if you can put something under my feet . . . then perhaps I can draw myself up."

Diana hastily dragged in the previously mentioned keg and Anne found that it was just sufficiently high to furnish a secure resting place for her feet. But she could not release herself.

"Could I pull you out if I crawled up?" suggested Diana.

Anne shook her head hopelessly.

"No . . . the splinters hurt too badly. If you can find an axe you might chop me out, though. Oh dear, I do really begin to believe that I *was* born under an ill-omened star."

Diana searched faithfully but no axe was to be found.

"I'll have to go for help," she said, returning to the prisoner.

"No, indeed, you won't," said Anne vehemently. "If you do the story of this will get out everywhere and I shall be ashamed to show my face. No, we must just wait until the Copp girls come home and bind them to secrecy. They'll know where the axe is and get me out. I'm not uncomfortable as long as I keep perfectly still . . . not uncomfortable in *body* I mean. I wonder what the Copp girls value this house at. I shall have to pay for the damage I've done, but I wouldn't mind that if I were only sure they would understand my motive in peeping in at their pantry window. My sole comfort is that the platter is just the kind I want and if Miss Copp will only sell it to me I shall be resigned to what has happened."

"What if the Copp girls don't come home until after night . . . or till tomorrow?" suggested Diana.

"If they're not back by sunset you'll have to go for other assistance, I suppose," said Anne reluctantly, "but you mustn't go until you really have to. Oh dear, this is a dreadful predicament. I wouldn't mind my misfortunes so much if they were romantic, as Mrs. Morgan's heroines' always are, but they are always just simply ridiculous. Fancy what the Copp girls will think when they drive into their yard and see a girl's head and shoulders sticking out of the roof of one of their outhouses. Listen . . . is that a wagon? No, Diana, I believe it is thunder."

Thunder it was undoubtedly, and Diana, having made a hasty pilgrimage around the house, returned to announce that a very black cloud was rising rapidly in the northwest.

"I believe we're going to have a heavy thundershower," she exclaimed in dismay. "Oh, Anne, what will we do?"

"We must prepare for it," said Anne tranquilly. A thunderstorm seemed a trifle in comparison with what had already happened. "You'd better drive the horse and buggy into that open shed. Fortunately my parasol is in the buggy. Here . . . take my hat with you. Marilla told me I was a goose to put on my best hat to come to the Tory Road and she was right, as she always is."

Diana untied the pony and drove into the shed, just as the first heavy drops of rain fell. There she sat and watched the resulting downpour, which was so thick and heavy that she could hardly see Anne through it, holding the parasol bravely over her bare head. There was not a great deal of thunder, but for the best part of an hour the rain came merrily down. Occasionally Anne slanted back her parasol and waved an encouraging hand to her friend; but conversation at that distance and under the circumstances was quite out of the question. Finally the rain ceased, the sun came out, and Diana ventured across the puddles of the yard.

"Did you get very wet?" she asked anxiously.

"Oh, no," returned Anne cheerfully. "My head and shoulders are quite dry and my skirt is only a little damp where the rain beat through the lathes. Don't pity me, Diana, for I haven't minded it at all. I kept thinking how much good the rain will do and how glad my garden must be for it, and imagining what the flowers and buds would think when the drops began to fall. I imagined out a most interesting dialogue between the asters and the sweet peas and the wild canaries in the lilac bush and the guardian spirit of the garden. When I go home I mean to write it down. I wish I had a pencil and paper to do it now, because I daresay I'll forget the best parts before I reach home."

Diana the faithful had a pencil and discovered a sheet of wrapping paper in the box of the buggy. Anne folded up her dripping parasol, put on her hat, spread the wrapping paper on a shingle Diana handed up, and wrote out her garden idyl under conditions that could hardly be considered as favorable to literature. Nevertheless, the result was quite pretty, and Diana was "enraptured" when Anne read it to her.

"Oh, Anne, it's sweet . . . just sweet. *Do* send it to the *Canadian Woman.*"

Anne shook her head.

"Oh, no, it wouldn't be suitable at all. There is no *plot* in it, you see. It's just a string of fancies. I like writing such things, but of course nothing of the sort would ever do for publication, for editors insist on plots, so Priscilla says. Oh, there's Miss Sarah Copp now. *Please,* Diana, go and explain."

Miss Sarah Copp was a small person, garbed in shabby black, with a hat chosen less for vain adornment than for qualities that would wear well. She looked as amazed as might be expected on seeing the curious tableau in her yard, but when she heard Diana's explanation she was all sympathy. She hurriedly unlocked the back door, produced the axe, and with a few skillful blows set Anne free. The latter, somewhat tired and stiff, ducked down into the interior of her prison and thankfully emerged into liberty once more.

"Miss Copp," she said earnestly, "I assure you I looked into your pantry window *only* to discover if you had a willow-ware platter. I didn't see anything else—I didn't *look* for anything else."

"Bless you, that's all right," said Miss Sarah amiably. "You needn't worry—there's no harm done. Thank goodness, we Copps keep our pantries presentable at all times and don't care who sees into them. As for that old duckhouse, I'm glad it's smashed, for maybe now Martha will agree to having it taken down. She never would before for fear it might come in handy sometime and I've had to whitewash it every spring. But you might as well argue with a post as with Martha. She went to town today—I drove her to the station. And you want to buy my platter. Well, what will you give for it?"

"Twenty dollars," said Anne, who was never meant to match business wits with a Copp, or she would not have offered her price at the start.

"Well, I'll see," said Miss Sarah cautiously. "That platter is mine fortunately, or I'd never dare to sell it when Martha wasn't here. As it is, I daresay she'll raise a fuss. Martha's the boss of this establishment I can tell you. I'm getting awful tired of living under another woman's thumb. But come in, come in. You must be real tired and hungry. I'll do the best I can for you in the way of tea but I warn you not to expect anything but bread and butter and some cowcumbers. Martha locked up all the cake and cheese and preserves afore she went. She always does, because she says I'm too extravagant with them if company comes."

The girls were hungry enough to do justice to any fare, and they enjoyed Miss Sarah's excellent bread and butter and "cowcumbers" thoroughly. When the meal was over Miss Sarah said,

"I don't know as I mind selling the platter. But it's worth twenty-five dollars. It's a very old platter."

Diana gave Anne's foot a gentle kick under the table, meaning, "Don't agree—she'll let it go for twenty if you hold out." But Anne was not minded to take any chances in regard to that precious platter. She promptly agreed to give twenty-five and Miss Sarah looked as if she felt sorry she hadn't asked for thirty.

"Well, I guess you may have it. I want all the money I can scare up just now. The fact is—" Miss Sarah threw up her head importantly, with a proud flush on her thin cheeks—"I'm going to be married—to Luther Wallace. He wanted me twenty years ago. I liked him real well but he was poor then and father packed him off. I s'pose I shouldn't have let him go so meek but I was timid and frightened of father. Besides, I didn't know men were so skurse."

When the girls were safely away, Diana driving and Anne holding the coveted platter carefully on her lap, the green, rain-freshened solitudes of the Tory Road were enlivened by ripples of girlish laughter.

"I'll amuse your Aunt Josephine with the 'strange eventful history' of this afternoon when I go to town tomorrow. We've had a rather trying time but it's over now. I've got the platter, and that rain has laid the dust beautifully. So 'all's well that ends well.'"

"We're not home yet," said Diana rather pessimistically, "and there's no telling what may happen before we are. You're such a girl to have adventures, Anne."

"Having adventures comes natural to some people," said Anne serenely. "You just have a gift for them or you haven't."

19

Just a Happy Day

"fter all," Anne had said to Marilla once, "I believe the nicest and sweetest days are not those on which anything very splendid or wonderful or exciting happens but just those that bring simple little pleasures, following one another softly, like pearls slipping off a string."

Life at Green Gables was full of just such days, for Anne's adventures and misadventures, like those of other people, did not all happen at once, but were sprinkled over the year, with long stretches of harmless, happy days between, filled with work and dreams and laughter and lessons. Such a day came late in August. In the forenoon Anne and Diana rowed the delighted twins down the pond to the sandshore to pick "sweet grass" and paddle in the surf, over which the wind was harping an old lyric learned when the world was young.

In the afternoon Anne walked down to the old Irving place to see Paul. She found him stretched out on the grassy bank beside the thick fir grove that sheltered the house on the north, absorbed in a book of fairy tales. He sprang up radiantly at sight of her.

"Oh, I'm so glad you've come, teacher," he said eagerly, "because Grandma's away. You'll stay and have tea with me, won't you? It's so lonesome to have tea all by oneself. *You* know, teacher. I've had serious thoughts of asking Young Mary Joe to sit down and eat her tea with me, but I expect Grandma wouldn't approve. She says the French have to be kept in their place. And anyhow, it's difficult to talk with Young Mary Joe. She just laughs and says, 'Well, yous do beat all de kids I ever knowed.' That isn't my idea of conversation."

"Of course I'll stay to tea," said Anne gaily. "I was dying to be asked. My mouth has been watering for some more of your grandma's delicious shortbread ever since I had tea here before."

Paul looked very sober.

"If it depended on me, teacher," he said, standing before Anne with his hands in his pockets and his beautiful little face shadowed with sudden care, "you should have shortbread with a right good will. But it depends on Mary Joe. I heard Grandma tell her before she left that she wasn't to give me any shortcake because it was too rich for little boys' stomachs. But maybe Mary Joe will cut some for you if I promise I won't eat any. Let us hope for the best."

"Yes, let us," agreed Anne, whom this cheerful philosophy suited exactly, "and if Mary Joe proves hard-hearted and won't give me any shortbread it doesn't matter in the least, so you are not to worry over that."

"You're sure you won't mind if she doesn't?" said Paul anxiously.

"Perfectly sure, dear heart."

"Then I won't worry," said Paul, with a long breath of relief, "especially as I really think Mary Joe will listen to reason. She's not a naturally unreasonable person, but she has learned by experience that it doesn't do to disobey Grandma's orders. Grandma is an excellent woman but people must do as she tells them. She was very much pleased with me this morning because I managed at last to eat all my plateful of porridge. It was a great effort but I succeeded. Grandma says she thinks she'll make a man of me yet. But, teacher, I want to ask you a very important question. You will answer it truthfully, won't you?"

"I'll try," promised Anne.

"Do you think I'm wrong in my upper story?" asked Paul, as if his very existence depended on her reply.

"Goodness, no, Paul," exclaimed Anne in amazement. "Certainly you're not. What put such an idea into your head?"

"Mary Joe . . . but she didn't know I heard her. Mrs. Peter Sloane's hired girl, Veronica, came to see Mary Joe last evening and I heard them talking in the kitchen as I was going through the hall. I heard Mary Joe say, 'Dat Paul, he is de queeres' leetle boy. He talks dat queer. I tink dere's someting wrong in his upper story.' I couldn't sleep last night for ever so long, thinking of it, and wondering if Mary Joe was right. I couldn't bear to ask Grandma about it somehow, but I made up my mind I'd ask you. I'm so glad you think I'm all right in my upper story."

"Of course you are. Mary Joe is a silly, ignorant girl, and you are never to worry about anything she says," said Anne indignantly, secretly resolving to give Mrs. Irving a discreet hint as to the advisability of restraining Mary Joe's tongue.

"Well, that's a weight off my mind," said Paul. "I'm perfectly happy now, teacher, thanks to you. It wouldn't be nice to have something wrong in your upper story, would it, teacher? I suppose the reason Mary Joe imagines I have is because I tell her what I think about things sometimes."

"It *is* a rather dangerous practice," admitted Anne, out of the depths of her own experience.

"Well, by and by I'll tell you the thoughts I told Mary Joe and you can see for yourself if there's anything queer in them," said Paul, "but I'll wait till it begins to get dark. That is the time I ache to tell people things, and when nobody else is handy I just *have* to tell Mary Joe. But after this I won't, if it makes her imagine I'm wrong in my upper story. I'll just ache and bear it."

"And if the ache gets too bad you can come up to Green Gables and tell me your thoughts," suggested Anne, with all the gravity that endeared her to children, who so dearly love to be taken seriously.

"Yes, I will. But I hope Davy won't be there when I go because he makes faces at me. I don't mind *very* much because he is such a little boy and I am quite a big one, but still it is not pleasant to have faces made at you. And Davy makes such terrible ones. Sometimes I am frightened he will never get his face straightened out again. He makes them at me in church when I ought to be thinking of sacred things. Dora likes me though, and I like her, but not so well as I did before she told Minnie May Barry that she meant to marry me when I grew up. I may marry somebody when I grow up but I'm far too young to be thinking of it yet, don't you think, teacher?"

"Rather young," agreed teacher.

"Speaking of marrying, reminds me of another thing that has been troubling me of late," continued Paul. "Mrs. Lynde was down here one day last week having tea with Grandma, and Grandma made me show her my little mother's picture . . . the one father sent me for my birthday present. I didn't exactly want to show it to Mrs. Lynde. Mrs. Lynde is a good, kind woman, but she isn't the sort of person you want to show your mother's picture to. *You* know, teacher. But of course I obeyed Grandma. Mrs. Lynde said she was very pretty but kind of actressy looking, and must have been an awful lot younger than father. Then she said, 'Some of these days your pa will be marrying again likely. How will you like to have a new ma, Master Paul?' Well, the idea almost took my breath away, teacher, but I wasn't going to let Mrs. Lynde see *that*. I just looked her straight in the face . . . like this . . . and I said, 'Mrs. Lynde, father made a pretty good job of picking out my first mother and I could trust him to pick out just as good a one the second time.' And I *can* trust him, teacher. But still, I hope, if he ever does give me a new mother, he'll ask my opinion about her before it's too late. There's Mary Joe coming to call us to tea. I'll go and consult with her about the shortbread."

As a result of the "consultation," Mary Joe cut the shortbread and added a dish of preserves to the bill of fare. Anne poured the tea and she and Paul had a very merry meal in the dim old sitting room whose windows were open to the gulf breezes, and they talked so much "nonsense" that Mary Joe was quite scandalized and told Veronica the next evening that "de school mees" was as queer as Paul. After tea Paul took Anne up to his room to show her his mother's picture, which had been the mysterious birthday present kept by Mrs. Irving in the bookcase. Paul's little low-ceilinged room was a soft whirl of ruddy light from the sun that was setting over the sea and swinging shadows from the fir trees that grew close to the square, deep-set window. From out this soft glow and glamor shone a sweet, girlish face, with tender mother eyes, that was hanging on the wall at the foot of the bed.

"That's my little mother," said Paul with loving pride. "I got Grandma to hang it there where I'd see it as soon as I opened my eyes in the morning. I never mind not having the light when I go to bed now, because it just seems as if my little mother was right here with me. Father knew just what I would like for a birthday present, although he never asked me. Isn't it wonderful how much fathers *do* know?"

"Your mother was very lovely, Paul, and you look a little like her. But her eyes and hair are darker than yours."

"My eyes are the same color as father's," said Paul, flying about the room to heap all available cushions on the window seat, "but father's hair is gray. He has lots of it, but it is gray. You see, father is nearly fifty. That's ripe old age, isn't it? But it's only *outside* he's old. *Inside* he's just as young as anybody. Now, teacher, please sit here; and I'll sit at your feet. May I lay my head against your knee? That's the way my little mother and I used to sit. Oh, this is real splendid, I think."

"Now, I want to hear those thoughts which Mary Joe pronounces so queer," said Anne, patting the mop of curls at her side. Paul never needed any coaxing to tell his thoughts . . . at least, to congenial souls.

"I thought them out in the fir grove one night," he said dreamily. "Of course I didn't *believe* them but I *thought* them. *You* know, teacher. And then I wanted to tell them to somebody and there was nobody but Mary Joe. Mary Joe was in the pantry setting bread and I sat down on the bench beside her and I said, 'Mary Joe, do you know what I think? I think the evening star is a lighthouse on the land where the fairies dwell.' And Mary Joe said, 'Well, yous are de queer one. Dare ain't no such ting as fairies.' I was very much provoked. Of course, I knew there are no fairies; but that needn't prevent my thinking there is. *You* know, teacher. But I tried again quite patiently. I said, 'Well then, Mary Joe, do you know what I think? I think an angel walks over the world after the sun sets . . . a great, tall, white angel, with silvery folded wings . . . and sings the flowers and birds to sleep. Children can hear him if they know how to listen.' Then Mary Joe held up her hands all over flour and said, 'Well, yous are de queer leetle boy. Yous make me feel scare.' And she really did looked scared. I went out then and whispered the rest of my thoughts to the garden. There was a little birch tree in the garden and it died. Grandma says the salt spray killed it; but I think the dryad belonging to it was a foolish dryad who wandered away to see the world and got lost. And the little tree was so lonely it died of a broken heart."

"And when the poor, foolish little dryad gets tired of the world and comes back to her tree *her* heart will break," said Anne.

"Yes; but if dryads are foolish they must take the consequences, just as if they were real people," said Paul gravely. "Do you know what I think about the new moon, teacher? I think it is a little golden boat full of dreams."

"And when it tips on a cloud some of them spill out and fall into your sleep."

"Exactly, teacher. Oh, you *do* know. And I think the violets are little snips of the sky that fell down when the angels cut out holes for the stars to shine through. And the buttercups are made out of old sunshine; and I think the sweet peas will be butterflies when they go to heaven. Now, teacher, do you see anything so very queer about those thoughts?"

"No, laddie dear, they are not queer at all; they are strange and beautiful thoughts for a little boy to think, and so people who couldn't think anything of the sort themselves, if they tried for a hundred years, think them queer. But keep on thinking them, Paul . . . some day you are going to be a poet, I believe."

When Anne reached home she found a very different type of boyhood waiting to be put to bed. Davy was sulky; and when Anne had undressed him he bounced into bed and buried his face in the pillow.

"Davy, you have forgotten to say your prayers," said Anne rebukingly.

"No, I didn't forget," said Davy defiantly, "but I ain't going to say my prayers any more. I'm going to give up trying to be good, 'cause no matter how good I am you'd like Paul Irving better. So I might as well be bad and have the fun of it."

"I don't like Paul Irving *better*," said Anne seriously. "I like you just as well, only in a different way."

"But I want you to like me the same way," pouted Davy.

"You can't like different people the same way. You don't like Dora and me the same way, do you?"

Davy sat up and reflected.

"No . . . o . . . o," he admitted at last, "I like Dora because she's my sister but I like you because you're *you*."

"And I like Paul because he is Paul and Davy because he is Davy," said Anne gaily.

"Well, I kind of wish I'd said my prayers then," said Davy, convinced by this logic. "But it's too much bother getting out now to say them. I'll say them twice over in the morning, Anne. Won't that do as well?"

No, Anne was positive it would not do as well. So Davy scrambled out and knelt down at her knee. When he had finished his devotions he leaned back on his little, bare, brown heels and looked up at her.

"Anne, I'm gooder than I used to be."

"Yes, indeed you are, Davy," said Anne, who never hesitated to give credit where credit was due.

"I *know* I'm gooder," said Davy confidently, "and I'll tell you how I know it. Today Marilla give me two pieces of bread and jam, one for me and one for Dora. One was a good deal bigger than the other and Marilla didn't say which was mine. But I give the biggest piece to Dora. That was good of me, wasn't it?"

"Very good, and very manly, Davy."

"Of course," admitted Davy, "Dora wasn't very hungry and she only et half her slice and then she give the rest to me. But I didn't know she was going to do that when I give it to her, so I *was* good, Anne."

In the twilight Anne sauntered down to the Dryad's Bubble and saw Gilbert Blythe coming down through the dusky Haunted Wood. She had a sudden realization that Gilbert was a schoolboy no longer. And how manly he looked—the tall, frank-faced fellow, with the clear, straightforward eyes and the broad shoulders. Anne thought Gilbert was a very handsome lad, even though he didn't look at all like her ideal man. She and Diana had long ago decided what kind of a man they admired and their tastes seemed exactly similar. He must be very tall and distinguished looking, with melancholy, inscrutable eyes, and a melting, sympathetic voice. There was nothing either melancholy or inscrutable in Gilbert's physiognomy, but of course that didn't matter in friendship!

Gilbert stretched himself out on the ferns beside the Bubble and looked approvingly at Anne. If Gilbert had been asked to describe his

ideal woman the description would have answered point for point to
Anne, even to those seven tiny freckles whose obnoxious presence still
continued to vex her soul. Gilbert was as yet little more than a boy; but
a boy has his dreams as have others, and in Gilbert's future there was
always a girl with big, limpid gray eyes, and a face as fine and delicate
as a flower. He had made up his mind, also, that his future must be worthy of its goddess. Even in quiet Avonlea there were temptations to be
met and faced. White Sands youth were a rather "fast" set, and Gilbert
was popular wherever he went. But he meant to keep himself worthy of
Anne's friendship and perhaps some distant day her love; and he
watched over word and thought and deed as jealously as if her clear
eyes were to pass in judgment on it. She held over him the unconscious
influence that every girl, whose ideals are high and pure, wields over her
friends; an influence which would endure as long as she was faithful to
those ideals and which she would as certainly lose if she were ever false
to them. In Gilbert's eyes Anne's greatest charm was the fact that she
never stooped to the petty practices of so many of the Avonlea girls—
the small jealousies, the little deceits and rivalries, the palpable bids for
favor. Anne held herself apart from all this, not consciously or of design,
but simply because anything of the sort was utterly foreign to her transparent, impulsive nature, crystal clear in its motives and aspirations.

But Gilbert did not attempt to put his thoughts into words, for
he had already too good reason to know that Anne would mercilessly
and frostily nip all attempts at sentiment in the bud—or laugh at him,
which was ten times worse.

"You look like a real dryad under that birch tree," he said teasingly.

"I love birch trees," said Anne, laying her cheek against the creamy
satin of the slim bole, with one of the pretty, caressing gestures that
came so natural to her.

"Then you'll be glad to hear that Mr. Major Spencer has decided
to set out a row of white birches all along the road front of his farm, by
way of encouraging the A. V. I. S.," said Gilbert. "He was talking to me
about it today. Major Spencer is the most progressive and public-
spirited man in Avonlea. And Mr. William Bell is going to set out a
spruce hedge along his road front and up his lane. Our Society is getting

on splendidly, Anne. It is past the experimental stage and is an accepted fact. The older folks are beginning to take an interest in it and the White Sands people are talking of starting one too. Even Elisha Wright has come around since that day the Americans from the hotel had the picnic at the shore. They praised our roadsides so highly and said they were so much prettier than in any other part of the Island. And when, in due time, the other farmers follow Mr. Spencer's good example and plant ornamental trees and hedges along their road fronts Avonlea will be the prettiest settlement in the province."

"The Aids are talking of taking up the graveyard," said Anne, "and I hope they will, because there will have to be a subscription for that, and it would be no use for the Society to try it after the hall affair. But the Aids would never have stirred in the matter if the Society hadn't put it into their thoughts unofficially. Those trees we planted on the church grounds are flourishing, and the trustees have promised me that they will fence in the school grounds next year. If they do I'll have an arbor day and every scholar shall plant a tree; and we'll have a garden in the corner by the road."

"We've succeeded in almost all our plans so far, except in getting the old Boulter house removed," said Gilbert, "and I've given *that* up in despair. Levi won't have it taken down just to vex us. There's a contrary streak in all the Boulters and it's strongly developed in him."

"Julia Bell wants to send another committee to him, but I think the better way will just be to leave him severely alone," said Anne sagely.

"And trust to Providence, as Mrs. Lynde says," smiled Gilbert. "Certainly, no more committees. They only aggravate him. Julia Bell thinks you can do anything, if you only have a committee to attempt it. Next spring, Anne, we must start an agitation for nice lawns and grounds. We'll sow good seed betimes this winter. I've a treatise here on lawns and lawn-making and I'm going to prepare a paper on the subject soon. Well, I suppose our vacation is almost over. School opens Monday. Has Ruby Gillis got the Carmody school?"

"Yes; Priscilla wrote that she had taken her own home school, so the Carmody trustees gave it to Ruby. I'm sorry Priscilla is not coming back, but since she can't I'm glad Ruby has got the school. She will be home for Saturdays and it will seem like old times, to have her and Jane and Diana and myself all together again."

Marilla, just home from Mrs. Lynde's, was sitting on the back porch step when Anne returned to the house.

"Rachel and I have decided to have our cruise to town tomorrow," she said. "Mr. Lynde is feeling better this week and Rachel wants to go before he has another sick spell."

"I intend to get up extra early tomorrow morning, for I've ever so much to do," said Anne virtuously. "For one thing, I'm going to shift the feathers from my old bedtick to the new one. I ought to have done it long ago but I've just kept putting it off . . . it's such a detestable task. It's a very bad habit to put off disagreeable things, and I never mean to again, or else I can't comfortably tell my pupils not to do it. That would be inconsistent. Then I want to make a cake for Mr. Harrison and finish my paper on gardens for the A. V. I. S., and write Stella, and wash and starch my muslin dress, and make Dora's new apron."

"You won't get half done," said Marilla pessimistically. "I never yet planned to do a lot of things but something happened to prevent me."

20

The Way It Often Happens

Anne rose betimes the next morning and blithely greeted the fresh day, when the banners of the sunrise were shaken triumphantly across the pearly skies. Green Gables lay in a pool of sunshine, flecked with the dancing shadows of poplar and willow. Beyond the lane was Mr. Harrison's wheatfield, a great, wind-rippled expanse of pale gold. The world was so beautiful that Anne spent ten blissful minutes hanging idly over the garden gate drinking the loveliness in.

After breakfast Marilla made ready for her journey. Dora was to go with her, having been long promised this treat.

"Now, Davy, you try to be a good boy and don't bother Anne," she straitly charged him. "If you are good I'll bring you a striped candy cane from town."

For alas, Marilla had stooped to the evil habit of bribing people to be good!

"I won't be bad on purpose, but s'posen I'm bad zacksidentally?" Davy wanted to know.

"You'll have to guard against accidents," admonished Marilla. "Anne, if Mr. Shearer comes today get a nice roast and some steak. If he doesn't you'll have to kill a fowl for dinner tomorrow."

Anne nodded.

"I'm not going to bother cooking any dinner for just Davy and myself today," she said. "That cold ham bone will do for noon lunch and I'll have some steak fried for you when you come home at night."

"I'm going to help Mr. Harrison haul dulse this morning," announced Davy. "He asked me to, and I guess he'll ask me to dinner too. Mr. Harrison is an awful kind man. He's a real sociable man. I hope

I'll be like him when I grow up. I mean *behave* like him . . . I don't want to *look* like him. But I guess there's no danger, for Mrs. Lynde says I'm a very handsome child. Do you s'pose it'll last, Anne? I want to know."

"I daresay it will," said Anne gravely. "You *are* a handsome boy, Davy," . . . Marilla looked volumes of disapproval . . . "but you must live up to it and be just as nice and gentlemanly as you look to be."

"And you told Minnie May Barry the other day, when you found her crying 'cause some one said she was ugly, that if she was nice and kind and loving people wouldn't mind her looks," said Davy discontentedly. "Seems to me you can't get out of being good in this world for some reason or 'nother. You just *have* to behave."

"Don't you want to be good?" asked Marilla, who had learned a great deal but had not yet learned the futility of asking such questions.

"Yes, I want to be good but not *too* good," said Davy cautiously. "You don't have to be very good to be a Sunday School superintendent. Mr. Bell's that, and he's a real bad man."

"Indeed he's not," said Marilla indignantly.

"He is . . . he says he is himself," asseverated Davy. "He said it when he prayed in Sunday School last Sunday. He said he was a vile worm and a miserable sinner and guilty of the blackest 'niquity. What did he do that was so bad, Marilla? Did he kill anybody? Or steal the collection cents? I want to know."

Fortunately Mrs. Lynde came driving up the lane at this moment and Marilla made off, feeling that she had escaped from the snare of the fowler, and wishing devoutly that Mr. Bell were not quite so highly figurative in his public petitions, especially in the hearing of small boys who were always "wanting to know."

Anne, left alone in her glory, worked with a will. The floor was swept, the beds made, the hens fed, the muslin dress washed and hung out on the line. Then Anne prepared for the transfer of feathers. She mounted to the garret and donned the first old dress that came to hand . . . a navy blue cashmere she had worn at fourteen. It was decidedly on the short side and as "skimpy" as the notable wincey Anne had worn upon the occasion of her debut at Green Gables; but at least it would not be materially injured by down and feathers. Anne completed her toilet by tying a big red and white spotted handkerchief that had belonged to Matthew over her head, and, thus accoutred, betook herself to the kitchen chamber, whither Marilla, before her departure, had helped her carry the feather bed.

A cracked mirror hung by the chamber window and in an unlucky moment Anne looked into it. There were those seven freckles on her nose, more rampant than ever, or so it seemed in the glare of light from the unshaded window.

"Oh, I forgot to rub that lotion on last night," she thought. "I'd better run down to the pantry and do it now."

Anne had already suffered many things trying to remove those freckles. On one occasion the entire skin had peeled off her nose but the freckles remained. A few days previously she had found a recipe for a freckle lotion in a magazine and, as the ingredients were within her reach, she straightway compounded it, much to the disgust of Marilla, who thought that if Providence had placed freckles on your nose it was your bounden duty to leave them there.

Anne scurried down to the pantry, which, always dim from the big willow growing close to the window, was now almost dark by reason of the shade drawn to exclude flies. Anne caught the bottle containing the lotion from the shelf and copiously annointed her nose therewith by means of a little sponge sacred to the purpose. This important duty done, she returned to her work. Any one who has ever shifted feathers from one tick to another will not need to be told that when Anne finished she was a sight to behold. Her dress was white with down and fluff, and her front hair, escaping from under the handkerchief, was adorned with a veritable halo of feathers. At this auspicious moment a knock sounded at the kitchen door.

"That must be Mr. Shearer," thought Anne. "I'm in a dreadful mess but I'll have to run down as I am, for he's always in a hurry."

Down flew Anne to the kitchen door. If ever a charitable floor did open to swallow up a miserable, befeathered damsel the Green Gables porch floor should promptly have engulfed Anne at that moment. On the doorstep were standing Priscilla Grant, golden and fair in silk attire, a short, stout, gray-haired lady in a tweed suit, and another lady, tall, stately, wonderfully gowned, with a beautiful, highbred face and large, black-lashed violet eyes, whom Anne "instinctively felt," as she would have said in her earlier days, to be Mrs. Charlotte E. Morgan.

In the dismay of the moment one thought stood out from the confusion of Anne's mind and she grasped at it as at the proverbial straw. All Mrs. Morgan's heroines were noted for "rising to the occasion." No matter what their troubles were, they invariably rose to the occasion and showed their superiority over all ills of time, space, and quantity. Anne therefore felt it was *her* duty to rise to the occasion and she did it, so perfectly that Priscilla afterward declared she never admired Anne Shirley more than at that moment. No matter what her outraged feelings were she did not show them. She greeted Priscilla and was introduced to her companions as calmly and composedly as if she had been arrayed in purple and fine linen. To be sure, it was somewhat of a shock to find that the lady she had instinctively felt to be Mrs. Morgan was not Mrs. Morgan at all, but an unknown Mrs. Pendexter, while the stout little gray-haired woman was Mrs. Morgan; but in the greater shock the lesser lost its power. Anne ushered her guests to the spare room and thence into the parlor, where she left them while she hastened out to help Priscilla unharness her horse.

"It's dreadful to come upon you so unexpectedly as this," apologized Priscilla, "but I did not know till last night that we were coming. Aunt Charlotte is going away Monday and she had promised to spend today with a friend in town. But last night her friend telephoned to her not to come because they were quarantined for scarlet fever. So I suggested we come here instead, for I knew you were longing to see her. We called at the White Sands Hotel and brought Mrs. Pendexter with us. She is a friend of aunt's and lives in New York and her husband is a millionaire. We can't stay very long, for Mrs. Pendexter has to be back at the hotel by five o'clock."

Several times while they were putting away the horse Ann caught Priscilla looking at her in a furtive, puzzled way.

"She needn't stare at me so," Ann thought a little resentfully. "If she doesn't *know* what it is to change a feather bed she might *imagine* it."

When Priscilla had gone to the parlor, and before Anne could escape upstairs, Diana walked into the kitchen. Anne caught her astonished friend by the arm.

"Diana Barry, who do you suppose is in that parlor at this very moment? Mrs. Charlotte E. Morgan . . . and a New York millionaire's wife . . . and here I am like *this* . . . and *not a thing in the house for dinner but a cold ham bone,* Diana!"

By this time Anne had become aware that Diana was staring at her in precisely the same bewildered fashion as Priscilla had done. It was really too much.

"Oh, Diana, don't look at me so," she implored. "*You,* at least, must know that the neatest person in the world couldn't empty feathers from one tick into another and remain neat in the process."

"It . . . it . . . isn't the feathers," hesitated Diana. "It's . . . it's . . . your nose, Anne."

"My nose? Oh, Diana, surely nothing has gone wrong with it!"

Anne rushed to the little looking glass over the sink. One glance revealed the fatal truth. Her nose was a brilliant scarlet!

Anne sat down on the sofa, her dauntless spirit subdued at last.

"What is the matter with it?" asked Diana, curiosity overcoming delicacy.

"I thought I was rubbing my freckle lotion on it, but I must have used that red dye Marilla has for marking the pattern on her rugs," was the despairing response. "What shall I do?"

"Wash it off," said Diana practically.

"Perhaps it won't wash off. First I dye my hair; then I dye my nose. Marilla cut my hair off when I dyed it but that remedy would hardly be practicable in this case. Well, this is another punishment for vanity and I suppose I deserve it . . . though there's not much comfort in *that.* It is really almost enough to make one believe in ill-luck, though Mrs. Lynde says there is no such thing, because everything is foreordained."

Fortunately the dye washed off easily and Anne, somewhat consoled, betook herself to the east gable while Diana ran home. Presently Anne came down again, clothed and in her right mind. The muslin dress she had fondly hoped to wear was bobbing merrily about on the line outside, so she was forced to content herself with her black lawn. She had the fire on and the tea steeping when Diana returned; the latter wore *her* muslin, at least, and carried a covered platter in her hand.

"Mother sent you this," she said, lifting the cover and displaying a nicely carved and jointed chicken to Anne's grateful eyes.

The chicken was supplemented by light new bread, excellent butter and cheese, Marilla's fruit cake and a dish of preserved plums, floating in their golden syrup as in congealed summer sunshine. There was a big bowlful of pink-and-white asters also, by way of decoration; yet the spread seemed very meager beside the elaborate one formerly prepared for Mrs. Morgan.

Anne's hungry guests, however, did not seem to think anything was lacking and they ate the simple viands with apparent enjoyment. But after the first few moments Anne thought no more of what was or was not on her bill of fare. Mrs. Morgan's appearance might be somewhat disappointing, as even her loyal worshippers had been forced to admit to each other; but she proved to be a delightful conversationalist. She had traveled extensively and was an excellent storyteller. She had seen much of men and women, and crystalized her experiences into witty little sentences and epigrams which made her hearers feel as if they were listening to one of the people in clever books. But under all her sparkle there was a strongly felt undercurrent of true, womanly sympathy and kindheartedness which won affection as easily as her brilliancy won admiration. Nor did she monopolize the conversation. She could draw others out as skillfully and fully as she could talk herself, and Anne and Diana found themselves chattering freely to her. Mrs. Pendexter said little; she merely smiled with her lovely eyes and lips, and ate chicken and fruit cake and preserves with such exquisite grace that she conveyed the impression of dining on ambrosia and honeydew. But then, as Anne said to Diana later on, anybody so divinely beautiful as Mrs. Pendexter didn't need to talk; it was enough for her just to *look*.

After dinner they all had a walk through Lover's Lane and Violet Vale and the Birch Path, then back through the Haunted Wood to the Dryad's Bubble, where they sat down and talked for a delightful last half hour. Mrs. Morgan wanted to know how the Haunted Wood came by its name, and laughed until she cried when she heard the story and Anne's dramatic account of a certain memorable walk through it at the witching hour of twilight.

"It has indeed been a feast of reason and flow of soul, hasn't it?" said Anne, when her guests had gone and she and Diana were alone again. "I don't know which I enjoyed more ... listening to Mrs. Morgan or gazing at Mrs. Pendexter. I believe we had a nicer time than if we'd known they were coming and been cumbered with much serving. You must stay to tea with me, Diana, and we'll talk it all over."

"Priscilla says Mrs. Pendexter's husband's sister is married to an English earl; and yet she took a second helping of the plum preserves," said Diana, as if the two facts were somehow incompatible.

"I daresay even the English earl himself wouldn't have turned up his aristocratic nose at Marilla's plum preserves," said Anne proudly.

Anne did not mention the misfortune which had befallen *her* nose when she related the day's history to Marilla that evening. But she took the bottle of freckle lotion and emptied it out of the window.

"I shall never try any beautifying messes again," she said, darkly resolute. "They may do for careful, deliberate people; but for anyone so hopelessly given over to making mistakes as I seem to be it's tempting fate to meddle with them."

21

Sweet Miss Lavendar

chool opened and Anne returned to her work, with fewer theories but considerably more experience. She had several new pupils, six- and seven-year-olds just venturing, round-eyed, into a world of wonder. Among them were Davy and Dora. Davy sat with Milty Boulter, who had been going to school for a year and was therefore quite a man of the world. Dora had made a compact at Sunday School the previous Sunday to sit with Lily Sloane; but Lily Sloane not coming the first day, she was temporarily assigned to Mirabel Cotton, who was ten years old and therefore, in Dora's eyes, one of the "big girls."

"I think school is great fun," Davy told Marilla when he got home that night. "You said I'd find it hard to sit still and I did . . . you mostly do tell the truth, I notice . . . but you can wriggle your legs about under the desk and that helps a lot. It's splendid to have so many boys to play with. I sit with Milty Boulter and he's fine. He's longer than me but I'm wider. It's nicer to sit in the back seats but you can't sit there till your legs grow long enough to touch the floor. Milty drawed a picture of Anne on his slate and it was awful ugly and I told him if he made pictures of Anne like that I'd lick him at recess. I thought first I'd draw one of him and put horns and a tail on it, but I was afraid it would hurt his feelings, and Anne says you should never hurt anyone's feelings. It seems it's dreadful to have your feelings hurt. It's better to knock a boy down than hurt his feelings if you *must* do something. Milty said he wasn't scared of me but he'd just as soon call it somebody else to 'blige me, so he rubbed out Anne's name and printed Barbara Shaw's under it. Milty doesn't like Barbara 'cause she calls him a sweet little boy and once she patted him on his head."

Dora said primly that she liked school; but she was very quiet, even for her; and when at twilight Marilla bade her go upstairs to bed she hesitated and began to cry.

"I'm . . . I'm frightened," she sobbed. "I . . . I don't want to go upstairs alone in the dark."

"What notion have you got into your head now?" demanded Marilla. "I'm sure you've gone to bed alone all summer and never been frightened before."

Dora still continued to cry, so Anne picked her up, cuddled her sympathetically, and whispered,

"Tell Anne all about it, sweetheart. What are you frightened of?"

"Of . . . of Mirabel Cotton's uncle," sobbed Dora. "Mirabel Cotton told me all about her family today in school. Nearly everybody in her family has died . . . all her grandfathers and grandmothers and ever so many uncles and aunts. They have a habit of dying, Mirabel says. Mirabel's awful proud of having so many dead relations, and she told me what they all died of, and what they said, and how they looked in their coffins. And Mirabel says one of her uncles was seen walking around the house after he was buried. Her mother saw him. I don't mind the rest so much but I can't help thinking about that uncle."

Anne went upstairs with Dora and sat by her until she fell asleep. The next day Mirabel Cotton was kept in at recess and "gently but firmly" given to understand that when you were so unfortunate as to possess an uncle who persisted in walking about houses after he had been decently interred it was not in good taste to talk about that eccentric gentleman to your deskmate of tender years. Mirabel thought this very harsh. The Cottons had not much to boast of. How was she to keep up her prestige among her schoolmates if she were forbidden to make capital out of the family ghost?

September slipped by into a gold and crimson graciousness of October. One Friday evening Diana came over.

"I'd a letter from Ella Kimball today, Anne, and she wants us to go over to tea tomorrow afternoon to meet her cousin, Irene Trent, from town. But we can't get one of our horses to go, for they'll all be in use tomorrow, and your pony is lame . . . so I suppose we can't go."

"Why can't we walk?" suggested Anne. "If we go straight back through the woods we'll strike the West Grafton road not far from the Kimball place. I was through that way last winter and I know the road. It's no more than four miles and we won't have to walk home, for Oliver Kimball will be sure to drive us. He'll be only too glad of the excuse, for he goes to see Carrie Sloane and they say his father will hardly ever let him have a horse."

It was accordingly arranged that they should walk, and the following afternoon they set out, going by way of Lover's Lane to the back of the Cuthbert farm, where they found a road leading into the heart of acres of glimmering beech and maple woods, which were all in a wondrous glow of flame and gold, lying in a great purple stillness and peace.

"It's as if the year were kneeling to pray in a vast cathedral full of mellow stained light, isn't it?" said Anne dreamily. "It doesn't seem right to hurry through it, does it? It seems irreverent, like running in a church."

"We *must* hurry though," said Diana, glancing at her watch. "We've left ourselves little enough time as it is."

"Well, I'll walk fast but don't ask me to talk," said Anne, quickening her pace. "I just want to drink the day's loveliness in . . . I feel as if she were holding it out to my lips like a cup of airy wine and I'll take a sip at every step."

Perhaps it was because she was so absorbed in "drinking it in" that Anne took the left turning when they came to a fork in the road. She should have taken the right, but ever afterward she counted it the most fortunate mistake of her life. They came out finally to a lonely, grassy road, with nothing in sight along it but ranks of spruce saplings.

"Why, where are we?" exclaimed Diana in bewilderment. "This isn't the West Grafton road."

"No, it's the base line road in Middle Grafton," said Anne, rather shamefacedly. "I must have taken the wrong turning at the fork. I don't know where we are exactly, but we must be all of three miles from Kimballs' still."

"Then we can't get there by five, for it's half past four now," said Diana, with a despairing look at her watch. "We'll arrive after they have had their tea, and they'll have all the bother of getting ours over again."

"We'd better turn back and go home," suggested Anne humbly. But Diana, after consideration, vetoed this.

"No, we may as well go and spend the evening, since we have come this far."

A few yards further on the girls came to a place where the road forked again.

"Which of these do we take?" asked Diana dubiously.

Anne shook her head.

"I don't know and we can't afford to make any more mistakes. Here is a gate and a lane leading right into the wood. There must be a house at the other side. Let us go down and inquire."

"What a romantic old lane this is," said Diana, as they walked along its twists and turns. It ran under patriarchal old firs whose branches met above, creating a perpetual gloom in which nothing except moss could grow. On either hand were brown wood floors, crossed here and there by fallen lances of sunlight. All was very still and remote, as if the world and the cares of the world were far away.

"I feel as if we were walking through an enchanted forest," said Anne in a hushed tone. "Do you suppose we'll ever find our way back to the real world again, Diana? We shall presently come to a palace with a spellbound princess in it, I think."

Around the next turn they came in sight, not indeed of a palace, but of a little house almost as surprising as a palace would have been in this province of conventional wooden farmhouses, all as much alike in general characteristics as if they had grown from the same seed. Anne stopped short in rapture and Diana exclaimed,

"Oh, I know where we are now. That is the little stone house where Miss Lavendar Lewis lives . . . Echo Lodge, she calls it, I think. I've often heard of it but I've never seen it before. Isn't it a romantic spot?"

"It's the sweetest, prettiest place I ever saw or imagined," said Anne delightedly. "It looks like a bit out of a story book or a dream."

The house was a low-eaved structure built of undressed blocks of red Island sandstone, with a little peaked roof out of which peered two dormer windows, with quaint wooden hoods over them, and two great chimneys. The whole house was covered with a luxuriant growth of ivy, finding easy foothold on the rough stonework and turned by autumn frosts to most beautiful bronze and wine-red tints.

Before the house was an oblong garden into which the lane gate where the girls were standing opened. The house bounded it on one side; on the three others it was enclosed by an old stone dyke, so overgrown with moss and grass and ferns that it looked like a high, green bank. On the right and left the tall, dark spruces spread their palm-like branches over it; but below it was a little meadow, green with clover aftermath, sloping down to the blue loop of the Grafton River. No other house or clearing was in sight . . . nothing but hills and valleys covered with feathery young firs.

"I wonder what sort of a person Miss Lewis is," speculated Diana as they opened the gate into the garden. "They say she is very peculiar."

"She'll be interesting then," said Anne decidedly. "Peculiar people are always that at least, whatever else they are or are not. Didn't I tell you we would come to an enchanted palace? I knew the elves hadn't woven magic over that lane for nothing."

"But Miss Lavendar Lewis is hardly a spellbound princess," laughed Diana. "She's an old maid . . . she's forty-five and quite gray, I've heard."

"Oh, that's only part of the spell," asserted Anne confidently. "At heart she's young and beautiful still . . . and if we only knew how to unloose the spell she would step forth radiant and fair again. But we don't know how . . . it's always and only the prince who knows that . . . and Miss Lavendar's prince hasn't come yet. Perhaps some fatal mischance has befallen him . . . though *that's* against the law of all fairy tales."

"I'm afraid he came long ago and went away again," said Diana. "They say she used to be engaged to Stephen Irving . . . Paul's father . . . when they were young. But they quarreled and parted."

"Hush," warned Anne. "The door is open."

The girls paused in the porch under the tendrils of ivy and knocked at the open door. There was a patter of steps inside and a rather odd little personage presented herself . . . a girl of about fourteen, with a freckled face, a snub nose, a mouth so wide that it did really seem as if it stretched "from ear to ear," and two long braids of fair hair tied with two enormous bows of blue ribbon.

"Is Miss Lewis at home?" asked Diana.

"Yes, ma'am. Come in, ma'am . . . this way, ma'am . . . and sit down, ma'am. I'll tell Miss Lavendar you're here, ma'am. She's upstairs, ma'am."

With this the small handmaiden whisked out of sight and the girls, left alone, looked about them with delighted eyes. The interior of this wonderful little house was quite as interesting as its exterior.

The room had a low ceiling and two square, small-paned windows, curtained with muslin frills. All the furnishings were old-fashioned, but so well and daintily kept that the effect was delicious. But it must be candidly admitted that the most attractive feature, to two healthy girls who had just tramped four miles through autumn air, was a table, set out with pale blue china and laden with delicacies, while little golden-hued ferns scattered over the cloth gave it what Anne would have termed "a festal air."

"Miss Lavendar must be expecting company to tea," she whispered. "There are six places set. But what a funny little girl she has. She looked like a messenger from pixy land. I suppose she could have told us the road, but I was curious to see Miss Lavendar. S . . . s . . . sh, she's coming."

And with that Miss Lavendar Lewis was standing in the doorway. The girls were so surprised that they forgot good manners and simply stared. They had unconsciously been expecting to see the usual type of elderly spinster as known to their experience . . . a rather angular personage, with prim gray hair and spectacles. Nothing more unlike Miss Lavendar could possibly be imagined.

She was a little lady with snow-white hair beautifully wavy and thick, and carefully arranged in becoming puffs and coils. Beneath it was an almost girlish face, pink cheeked and sweet lipped, with big soft brown eyes and dimples . . . actually dimples. She wore a very dainty gown of cream muslin with pale-hued roses on it . . . a gown which would have seemed ridiculously juvenile on most women of her age, but which suited Miss Lavendar so perfectly that you never thought about it at all.

"Charlotta the Fourth says that you wished to see me," she said, in a voice that matched her appearance.

"We wanted to ask the right road to West Grafton," said Diana. "We are invited to tea at Mr. Kimball's, but we took the wrong path coming through the woods and came out to the base line instead of the West Grafton road. Do we take the right or left turning at your gate?"

"The left," said Miss Lavendar, with a hesitating glance at her tea table. Then she exclaimed, as if in a sudden little burst of resolution,

"But oh, won't you stay and have tea with me? Please, do. Mr. Kimball's will have tea over before you get there. And Charlotta the Fourth and I will be so glad to have you."

Diana looked mute inquiry at Anne.

"We'd like to stay," said Anne promptly, for she had made up her mind that she wanted to know more of this surprising Miss Lavendar, "if it won't inconvenience you. But you are expecting other guests, aren't you?"

Miss Lavendar looked at her tea table again, and blushed.

"I know you'll think me dreadfully foolish," she said. "I *am* foolish . . . and I'm ashamed of it when I'm found out, but never unless I *am* found out. I'm not expecting anybody . . . I was just pretending I was. You see, I was so lonely. I love company . . . that is, the right kind of company . . . but so few people ever come here because it is so far out of the way. Charlotta the Fourth was lonely too. So I just pretended I was going to have a tea party. I cooked for it . . . and decorated the table for it . . . and set it with my mother's wedding china . . . and I dressed up for it."

Diana secretly thought Miss Lavendar quite as peculiar as report had pictured her. The idea of a woman of forty-five playing at having a tea party, just as if she were a little girl! But Anne of the shining eyes exclaimed joyfully,

"Oh, do *you* imagine things too?"

That "too" revealed a kindred spirit to Miss Lavendar.

"Yes, I do," she confessed, boldly. "Of course it's silly in anybody as old as I am. But what is the use of being an independent old maid if you can't be silly when you want to, and when it doesn't hurt anybody? A person must have some compensations. I don't believe I could live at times if I didn't pretend things. I'm not often caught at it though, and Charlotta the Fourth never tells. But I'm glad to be caught today, for you have really come and I have tea all ready for you. Will you go up to the spare room and take off your hats? It's the white door at the head of the stairs. I must run out to the kitchen and see that Charlotta the Fourth isn't letting the tea boil. Charlotta the Fourth is a very good girl but she *will* let the tea boil."

Miss Lavendar tripped off to the kitchen on hospitable thoughts intent and the girls found their way up to the spare room, an apartment as white as its door, lighted by the ivy-hung dormer window and looking, as Anne said, like the place where happy dreams grew.

"This is quite an adventure, isn't it?" said Diana. "And isn't Miss Lavendar sweet, if she *is* a little odd? She doesn't look a bit like an old maid."

"She looks just as music sounds, I think," answered Anne.

When they went down Miss Lavendar was carrying in the teapot, and behind her, looking vastly pleased, was Charlotta the Fourth, with a plate of hot biscuits.

"Now, you must tell me your names," said Miss Lavendar. "I'm so glad you are young girls. I love young girls. It's so easy to pretend I'm a girl myself when I'm with them. I do hate" . . . with a little grimace . . . "to believe I'm old. Now, who are you . . . just for convenience' sake? Diana Barry? And Anne Shirley? May I pretend that I've known you for a hundred years and call you Anne and Diana right away?"

"You may," the girls said both together.

"Then just let's sit comfily down and eat everything," said Miss Lavendar happily. "Charlotta, you sit at the foot and help the chicken. It is so fortunate that I made the sponge cake and doughnuts. Of course, it was foolish to do it for imaginary guests. . . . I know Charlotta the Fourth thought so, didn't you, Charlotta? But you see how well it has turned out. Of course they wouldn't have been wasted, for Charlotta the Fourth and I could have eaten them through time. But sponge cake is not a thing that improves with time."

That was a merry and memorable meal; and when it was over they all went out to the garden, lying in the glamor of sunset.

"I do think you have the loveliest place here," said Diana, looking round her admiringly.

"Why do you call it Echo Lodge?" asked Anne.

"Charlotta," said Miss Lavendar, "go into the house and bring out the little tin horn that is hanging over the clock shelf."

Charlotta the Fourth skipped off and returned with the horn.

"Blow it, Charlotta," commanded Miss Lavendar.

Charlotta accordingly blew, a rather raucous, strident blast. There was a moment's stillness . . . and then from the woods over the river came a multitude of fairy echoes, sweet, elusive, silvery, as if all the "horns of elfland" were blowing against the sunset. Anne and Diana exclaimed in delight.

"Now laugh, Charlotta . . . laugh loudly."

Charlotta, who would probably have obeyed if Miss Lavendar had told her to stand on her head, climbed upon the stone bench and laughed loud and heartily. Back came the echoes, as if a host of pixy people were mimicking her laughter in the purple woodlands and along the fir-fringed points.

"People always admire my echoes very much," said Miss Lavendar, as if the echoes were her personal property. "I love them myself. They are very good company . . . with a little pretending. On calm evenings Charlotta the Fourth and I often sit out here and amuse ourselves with them. Charlotta, take back the horn and hang it carefully in its place."

"Why do you call her Charlotta the Fourth?" asked Diana, who was bursting with curiosity on this point.

"Just to keep her from getting mixed up with the other Charlottas in my thoughts," said Miss Lavendar seriously. "They all look so much alike there's no telling them apart. Her name isn't really Charlotta at all. It is . . . let me see . . . what is it? I *think* it's Leonora . . . yes, it *is* Leonora. You see, it is this way. When mother died ten years ago I couldn't stay here alone . . . and I couldn't afford to pay the wages of a grown-up girl. So I got little Charlotta Bowman to come and stay with me for board and clothes. Her name really was Charlotta . . . she was Charlotta the First. She was just thirteen. She stayed with me till she was sixteen and then she went away to Boston, because she could do better there. Her sister came to stay with me then. Her name was Julietta . . . Mrs. Bowman had a weakness for fancy names I think . . . but she looked so like Charlotta that I kept calling her that all the time . . . and she didn't mind. So I just gave up trying to remember her right name. She was Charlotta the Second, and when she went away Evelina came and she was Charlotta the Third. Now I have Charlotta the Fourth; but when she is sixteen . . . she's fourteen now . . . she will want to go to Boston too, and what I shall do then I really do not know. Charlotta the Fourth is the last of the Bowman girls, and the best. The other Charlottas always let me see that they thought it silly of me to pretend things but Charlotta the Fourth never does, no matter what she may really think. I don't care what people think about me if they don't let me see it."

"Well," said Diana looking regretfully at the setting sun. "I suppose we must go if we want to get to Mr. Kimball's before dark. We've had a lovely time, Miss Lewis."

"Won't you come again to see me?" pleaded Miss Lavendar.

Tall Anne put her arm about the little lady.

"Indeed we shall," she promised. "Now that we have discovered you we'll wear out our welcome coming to see you. Yes, we must go . . . 'we must tear ourselves away,' as Paul Irving says every time he comes to Green Gables."

"Paul Irving?" There was a subtle change in Miss Lavendar's voice. "Who is he? I didn't think there was anybody of that name in Avonlea."

Anne felt vexed at her own heedlessness. She had forgotten about Miss Lavendar's old romance when Paul's name slipped out.

"He is a little pupil of mine," she explained slowly. "He came from Boston last year to live with his grandmother, Mrs. Irving of the shore road."

"Is he Stephen Irving's son?" Miss Lavendar asked, bending over her namesake border so that her face was hidden.

"Yes."

"I'm going to give you girls a bunch of lavendar apiece," said Miss Lavendar brightly, as if she had not heard the answer to her question.

"It's very sweet, don't you think? Mother always loved it. She planted these borders long ago. Father named me Lavendar because he was so fond of it. The very first time he saw mother was when he visited her home in East Grafton with her brother. He fell in love with her at first sight; and they put him in the spare room bed to sleep and the sheets were scented with lavendar and he lay awake all night and thought of her. He always loved the scent of lavendar after that . . . and that was why he gave me the name. Don't forget to come back soon, girls dear. We'll be looking for you, Charlotta the Fourth and I."

She opened the gate under the firs for them to pass through. She looked suddenly old and tired; the glow and radiance had faded from her face; her parting smile was as sweet with ineradicable youth as ever, but when the girls looked back from the first curve in the lane they saw her sitting on the old stone bench under the silver poplar in the middle of the garden with her head leaning wearily on her hand.

"She does look lonely," said Diana softly. "We must come often to see her."

"I think her parents gave her the only right and fitting name that could possibly be given her," said Anne. "If they had been so blind as to name her Elizabeth or Nellie or Muriel she must have been called Lavendar just the same, I think. It's so suggestive of sweetness and old-fashioned graces and 'silk attire.' Now, my name just smacks of bread and butter, patchwork and chores."

"Oh, I don't think so," said Diana. "Anne seems to me real stately and like a queen. But I'd like Kerrenhappuch if it happened to be your name. I think people make their names nice or ugly just by what they are themselves. I can't bear Josie or Gertie for names now but before I knew the Pye girls I thought them real pretty."

"That's a lovely idea, Diana," said Anne enthusiastically. "Living so that you beautify your name, even if it wasn't beautiful to begin with . . . making it stand in people's thoughts for something so lovely and pleasant that they never think of it by itself. Thank you, Diana."

22

Odds and Ends

"So you had tea at the stone house with Lavendar Lewis?" said Marilla at the breakfast table next morning. "What is she like now? It's over fifteen years since I saw her last . . . it was one Sunday in Grafton church. I suppose she has changed a great deal. Davy Keith, when you want something you can't reach, ask to have it passed and don't spread yourself over the table in that fashion. Did you ever see Paul Irving doing that when he was here to meals?"

"But Paul's arms are longer'n mine," grumbled Davy. "They've had eleven years to grow and mine've only had seven. 'Sides, I *did* ask, but you and Anne was so busy talking you didn't pay any 'tention. 'Sides, Paul's never been here to any meal escept tea, and it's easier to be p'lite at tea than at breakfast. You ain't half as hungry. It's an awful long while between supper and breakfast. Now, Anne, that spoonful ain't any bigger than it was last year and *I'm* ever so much bigger."

"Of course, I don't know what Miss Lavendar used to look like but I don't fancy somehow that she has changed a great deal," said Anne, after she had helped Davy to maple syrup, giving him two spoonfuls to pacify him. "Her hair is snow-white but her face is fresh and almost girlish, and she has the sweetest brown eyes . . . such a pretty shade of wood-brown with little golden glints in them . . . and her voice makes you think of white satin and tinkling water and fairy bells all mixed up together."

"She was reckoned a great beauty when she was a girl," said Marilla. "I never knew her very well but I liked her as far as I did know her. Some folks thought her peculiar even then. *Davy,* if ever I catch you at such a trick again you'll be made to wait for your meals til everyone else is done, like the French."

Most conversations between Anne and Marilla in the presence of the twins, were punctuated by these rebukes Davy-ward. In this instance, Davy, sad to relate, not being able to scoop up the last drops of his syrup with his spoon, had solved the difficulty by lifting his plate in both hands and applying his small pink tongue to it. Anne looked at him with such horrified eyes that the little sinner turned red and said, half shamefacedly, half defiantly,

"There ain't any wasted that way."

"People who are different from other people are always called peculiar," said Anne. "And Miss Lavendar is certainly different, though it's hard to say just where the difference comes in. Perhaps it is because she is one of those people who never grow old."

"One might as well grow old when all your generation do," said Marilla, rather reckless of her pronouns. "If you don't, you don't fit in anywhere. Far as I can learn Lavendar Lewis has just dropped out of everything. She's lived in that out of the way place until everybody has forgotten her. That stone house is one of the oldest on the Island. Old Mr. Lewis built it eighty years ago when he came out from England. Davy, stop joggling Dora's elbow. Oh, I saw you! You needn't try to look innocent. What does make you behave so this morning?"

"Maybe I got out of the wrong side of the bed," suggested Davy. "Milty Boulter says if you do that things are bound to go wrong with you all day. His grandmother told him. But which *is* the right side? And what are you to do when your bed's against the wall? I want to know."

"I've always wondered what went wrong between Stephen Irving and Lavendar Lewis," continued Marilla, ignoring Davy. "They were certainly engaged twenty-five years ago and then all at once it was broken off. I don't know what the trouble was but it must have been something terrible, for he went away to the States and never come home since."

"Perhaps it was nothing very dreadful after all. I think the little things in life often make more trouble than the big things," said Anne, with one of those flashes of insight which experience could not have bettered. "Marilla, please don't say anything about my being at Miss Lavendar's to Mrs. Lynde. She'd be sure to ask a hundred questions and somehow I wouldn't like it . . . nor Miss Lavendar either if she knew, I feel sure."

"I daresay Rachel would be curious," admitted Marilla, "though she hasn't as much time as she used to have for looking after other people's affairs. She's tied home now on account of Thomas; and she's feeling pretty downhearted, for I think she's beginning to lose hope of his ever getting better. Rachel will be left pretty lonely if anything happens to him, with all her children settled out west, except Eliza in town; and she doesn't like her husband."

Marilla's pronouns slandered Eliza, who was very fond of her husband.

"Rachel says if he'd only brace up and exert his will power he'd get better. But what is the use of asking a jellyfish to sit up straight?" continued Marilla. "Thomas Lynde never had any will power to exert. His mother ruled him till he married and then Rachel carried it on. It's a wonder he dared to get sick without asking her permission. But there, I shouldn't talk so. Rachel has been a good wife to him. He'd never have amounted to anything without her, that's certain. He was born to be ruled; and it's well he fell into the hands of a clever, capable manager like Rachel. He didn't mind her way. It saved him the bother of ever making up his own mind about anything. Davy, do stop squirming like an eel."

"I've nothing else to do," protested Davy. "I can't eat any more, and it's no fun watching you and Anne eat."

"Well, you and Dora go out and give the hens their wheat," said Marilla. "And don't you try to pull any more feathers out of the white rooster's tail either."

"I wanted some feathers for an Injun headdress," said Davy sulkily. "Milty Boulter has a dandy one, made out of the feathers his mother give him when she killed their old white gobbler. You might let me have some. That rooster's got ever so many more'n he wants."

"You may have the old feather duster in the garret," said Anne, "and I'll dye them green and red and yellow for you."

"You do spoil that boy dreadfully," said Marilla, when Davy, with a radiant face, had followed prim Dora out. Marilla's education had made great strides in the past six years; but she had not yet been able to rid herself of the idea that it was very bad for a child to have too many of its wishes indulged.

"All the boys of his class have Indian headdresses, and Davy wants one too," said Anne. "*I* know how it feels . . . I'll never forget how I used to long for puffed sleeves when all the other girls had them. And Davy isn't being spoiled. He is improving every day. Think what a difference there is in him since he came here a year ago."

"He certainly doesn't get into as much mischief since he began to go to school," acknowledged Marilla. "I suppose he works off the tendency with the other boys. But it's a wonder to me we haven't heard from Richard Keith before this. Never a word since last May."

"I'll be afraid to hear from him," sighed Anne, beginning to clear away the dishes. "If a letter should come I'd dread opening it, for fear it would tell us to send the twins to him."

A month later a letter did come. But it was not from Richard Keith. A friend of his wrote to say that Richard Keith had died of consumption a fortnight previously. The writer of the letter was the executor of his will and by that will the sum of two thousand dollars was left to Miss Marilla Cuthbert in trust for David and Dora Keith until they came of age or married. In the meantime the interest was to be used for their maintenance.

"It seems dreadful to be glad of anything in connection with a death," said Anne soberly. "I'm sorry for poor Mr. Keith; but I *am* glad that we can keep the twins."

"It's a very good thing about the money," said Marilla practically. "I wanted to keep them but I really didn't see how I could afford to do it, especially when they grew older. The rent of the farm doesn't do any more than keep the house and I was bound that not a cent of your money should be spent on them. You do far too much for them as it is. Dora didn't need that new hat you bought her any more than a cat needs two tails. But now the way is made clear and they are provided for."

Davy and Dora were delighted when they heard that they were to live at Green Gables "for good." The death of an uncle whom they had never seen could not weigh a moment in the balance against that. But Dora had one misgiving.

"Was Uncle Richard buried?" she whispered to Anne.

"Yes, dear, of course."

"He . . . he . . . isn't like Mirabel Cotton's uncle, is he?" in a still more agitated whisper. "He won't walk about houses after being buried, will he, Anne?"

23

Miss Lavendar's Romance

"I think I'll take a walk through to Echo Lodge this evening," said Anne, one Friday afternoon in December.

"It looks like snow," said Marilla dubiously.

"I'll be there before the snow comes and I mean to stay all night. Diana can't go because she has company, and I'm sure Miss Lavendar will be looking for me tonight. It's a whole fortnight since I was there."

Anne had paid many a visit to Echo Lodge since that October day. Sometimes she and Diana drove around by the road; sometimes they walked through the woods. When Diana could not go Anne went alone. Between her and Miss Lavendar had sprung up one of those fervent, helpful friendships possible only between a woman who has kept the freshness of youth in her heart and soul, and a girl whose imagination and intuition supplied the place of experience. Anne had at last discovered a real "kindred spirit," while into the little lady's lonely, sequestered life of dreams Anne and Diana came with the wholesome joy and exhilaration of the outer existence, which Miss Lavendar, "the world forgetting, by the world forgot," had long ceased to share; they brought an atmosphere of youth and reality to the little stone house. Charlotta the Fourth always greeted them with her very widest smile . . . and Charlotta's smiles *were* fearfully wide . . . loving them for the sake of her adored mistress as well as for their own. Never had there been such "high jinks" held in the little stone house as were held there that beautiful, late-lingering autumn, when November seemed October over again, and even December aped the sunshine and hazes of summer.

But on this particular day it seemed as if December had remembered that it was time for winter and had turned suddenly dull and brooding, with a windless hush predictive of coming snow. Never-theless, Anne keenly enjoyed her walk through the great gray maze of the beechlands; though alone she never found it lonely; her imagina-tion peopled her path with merry companions, and with these she car-ried on a gay, pretended conversation that was wittier and more fascinating than conversations are apt to be in real life, where people sometimes fail most lamentably to talk up to the requirements. In a "make believe" assembly of choice spirits everybody says just the thing you want her to say and so gives you the chance to say just what *you* want to say. Attended by this invisible company, Anne traversed the woods and arrived at the fir lane just as broad, feathery flakes began to flutter down softly.

At the first bend she came upon Miss Lavendar, standing under a big, broad-branching fir. She wore a gown of warm, rich red, and her head and shoulders were wrapped in a silvery gray silk shawl.

"You look like the queen of the fir wood fairies," called Anne merrily.

"I thought you would come tonight, Anne," said Miss Lavendar, running forward. "And I'm doubly glad, for Charlotta the Fourth is away. Her mother is sick and she had to go home for the night. I should have been very lonely if you hadn't come . . . even the dreams and the echoes wouldn't have been enough company. Oh, Anne, how pretty you are," she added suddenly, looking up at the tall, slim girl with the soft rose-flush of walking on her face. "How pretty and how young! It's so delightful to be seventeen, isn't it? I do envy you," concluded Miss Lavendar candidly.

"But you are only seventeen at heart," smiled Anne.

"No, I'm old . . . or rather middle-aged, which is far worse," sighed Miss Lavendar. "Sometimes I can pretend I'm not, but at other times I realize it. And I can't reconcile myself to it as most women seem to. I'm just as rebellious as I was when I discovered my first gray hair. Now, Anne, don't look as if you were trying to understand. Seventeen *can't* understand. I'm going to pretend right away that I am seventeen too, and I can do it, now that you're here. You always bring youth in your hand like a gift. We're going to have a jolly evening. Tea first . . . what do you want for tea? We'll have whatever you like. Do think of something nice and indigestible."

There were sounds of riot and mirth in the little stone house that night. What with cooking and feasting and making candy and laughing and "pretending," it is quite true that Miss Lavendar and Anne comported themselves in a fashion entirely unsuited to the dignity of a spinster of forty-five and a sedate schoolma'am. Then, when they were tired, they sat down on the rug before the grate in the parlor, lighted only by the soft fireshine and perfumed deliciously by Miss Lavendar's open rose-jar on the mantel. The wind had risen and was sighing and wailing around the eaves and the snow was thudding softly against the windows, as if a hundred storm sprites were tapping for entrance.

"I'm so glad you're here, Anne," said Miss Lavendar, nibbling at her candy. "If you weren't I should be blue . . . very blue . . . almost navy blue. Dreams and make-believes are all very well in the daytime and the sunshine, but when dark and storm come they fail to satisfy. One wants real things then. But you don't know this . . . seventeen never knows it. At seventeen dreams *do* satisfy because you think the realities are waiting for you further on. When I was seventeen, Anne, I didn't think forty-five would find me a white-haired little old maid with nothing but dreams to fill my life."

"But you aren't an old maid," said Anne, smiling into Miss Lavendar's wistful wood-brown eyes. "Old maids are *born* . . . they don't *become.*"

"Some are born old maids, some achieve old maidenhood, and some have old maidenhood thrust upon them," parodied Miss Lavendar whimsically.

"You are one of those who have achieved it then," laughed Anne, "and you've done it so beautifully that if every old maid were like you they would come into the fashion, I think."

"I always like to do things as well as possible," said Miss Lavendar meditatively, "and since an old maid I had to be I was determined to be a very nice one. People say I'm odd; but it's just because I follow my own way of being an old maid and refuse to copy the traditional pattern. Anne, did anyone ever tell you anything about Stephen Irving and me?"

"Yes," said Anne candidly, "I've heard that you and he were engaged once."

"So we were . . . twenty-five years ago . . . a lifetime ago. And we were to have been married the next spring. I had my wedding dress made, although nobody but mother and Stephen ever knew *that*. We'd been engaged in a way almost all our lives, you might say. When Stephen was a little boy his mother would bring him here when she came to see my mother; and the second time he ever came . . . he was nine and I was six . . . he told me out in the garden that he had pretty well made up his mind to marry me when he grew up. I remember that I said 'Thank you'; and when he was gone I told mother very gravely that there was a great weight off my mind, because I wasn't frightened any more about having to be an old maid. How poor mother laughed!"

"And what went wrong?" asked Anne breathlessly.

"We had just a stupid, silly, commonplace quarrel. So commonplace that, if you'll believe me, I don't even remember just how it began. I hardly know who was the more to blame for it. Stephen did really begin it, but I suppose I provoked him by some foolishness of mine. He had a rival or two, you see. I was vain and coquettish and liked to tease him a little. He was a very high-strung, sensitive fellow. Well, we parted in a temper on both sides. But I thought it would all come right; and it would have if Stephen hadn't come back too soon. Anne, my dear, I'm sorry to say" . . . Miss Lavendar dropped her voice as if she were about to confess a predilection for murdering people, "that I am a dreadfully sulky person. Oh, you needn't smile, . . . it's only too true. I *do* sulk; and Stephen came back before I had finished sulking. I wouldn't listen to him and I wouldn't forgive him; and so he went away for good. He was too proud to come again. And then I sulked because he didn't come. I might have sent for him perhaps, but I couldn't humble myself to do that. I was just as proud as he was . . . pride and sulkiness make a very bad combination, Anne. But I could never care for anybody else and I didn't want to. I knew I would rather be an old maid for a thousand years than marry anybody who wasn't Stephen Irving. Well, it all seems like a dream now, of course. How sympathetic you look, Anne . . . as sympathetic as only seventeen can look. But don't overdo it. I'm really a very happy, contented little person in spite of my broken heart. My heart did break, if ever a heart did, when I realized that Stephen Irving was not coming back. But, Anne, a broken heart in real life isn't half as dreadful as it is in books. It's a good deal like a bad tooth . . . though you won't think *that* a very romantic simile. It takes spells of aching and gives you a sleepless night now and then, but between times it lets you enjoy life and dreams and echoes and peanut candy as if there were nothing the matter with it. And now you're looking disappointed. You don't think I'm half as interesting a person as you did five minutes ago when you believed I was always the prey of a tragic memory bravely hidden beneath external smiles. That's the worst . . . or the best . . . of real life, Anne. It *won't* let you be miserable. It keeps on trying to make you comfortable . . . and succeeding . . . even when you're determined to be unhappy and romantic. Isn't this candy scrumptious? I've eaten far more than is good for me already but I'm going to keep recklessly on."

After a little silence Miss Lavendar said abruptly,

"It gave me a shock to hear about Stephen's son that first day you were here, Anne. I've never been able to mention him to you since, but I've wanted to know all about him. What sort of a boy is he?"

"He is the dearest, sweetest child I ever knew, Miss Lavendar . . . and he pretends things too, just as you and I do."

"I'd like to see him," said Miss Lavendar softly, as if talking to herself. "I wonder if he looks anything like the little dream-boy who lives here with me . . . *my* little dream-boy."

"If you would like to see Paul I'll bring him through with me sometime," said Anne.

"I *would* like it . . . but not too soon. I want to get used to the thought. There might be more pain than pleasure in it . . . if he looked too much like Stephen . . . or if he didn't look enough like him. In a month's time you may bring him."

Accordingly, a month later Anne and Paul walked through the woods to the stone house, and met Miss Lavendar in the lane. She had not been expecting them just then and she turned very pale.

"So this is Stephen's boy," she said in a low tone, taking Paul's hand and looking at him as he stood, beautiful and boyish, in his smart little fur coat and cap. "He . . . he is very like his father."

"Everybody says I'm a chip off the old block," remarked Paul, quite at his ease.

Anne, who had been watching the little scene, drew a relieved breath. She saw that Miss Lavendar and Paul had "taken" to each other, and that there would be no constraint or stiffness. Miss Lavendar was a very sensible person, in spite of her dreams and romance, and after that first little betrayal she tucked her feelings out of sight and entertained Paul as brightly and naturally as if he were anybody's son who had come to see her. They all had a jolly afternoon together and such a feast of fat things by way of supper as would have made old Mrs. Irving hold up her hands in horror, believing that Paul's digestion would be ruined for ever.

"Come again, laddie," said Miss Lavendar, shaking hands with him at parting.

"You may kiss me if you like," said Paul gravely.

Miss Lavendar stooped and kissed him.

"How did you know I wanted to?" she whispered.

"Because you looked at me just as my little mother used to do when she wanted to kiss me. As a rule, I don't like to be kissed. Boys don't. *You* know, Miss Lewis. But I think I rather like to have you kiss me. And of course I'll come to see you again. I think I'd like to have you for a particular friend of mine, if you don't object."

"I . . . I don't think I shall object," said Miss Lavendar. She turned and went in very quickly; but a moment later she was waving a gay and smiling goodbye to them from the window.

"I like Miss Lavendar," announced Paul, as they walked through the beech woods. "I like the way she looked at me, and I like her stone house, and I like Charlotta the Fourth. I wish Grandma Irving had a Charlotta the Fourth instead of Mary Joe. I feel sure Charlotta the Fourth wouldn't think I was wrong in my upper story when I told her what I think about things. Wasn't that a splendid tea we had, teacher? Grandma says a boy shouldn't be thinking about what he gets to eat, but he can't help it sometimes when he is real hungry. *You* know, teacher. I don't think Miss Lavendar would make a boy eat porridge for breakfast if he didn't like it. She'd get things for him he did like. But of course" . . . Paul was nothing if not fair-minded . . . "that mightn't be very good for him. It's very nice for a change though, teacher. *You* know."

24

A Prophet in His Own Country

ne May day Avonlea folks were mildly excited over some "Avonlea Notes," signed "Observer," which appeared in the Charlottetown *Daily Enterprise.* Gossip ascribed the authorship thereof to Charlie Sloane, partly because the said Charlie had indulged in similar literary flights in times past, and partly because one of the notes seemed to embody a sneer at Gilbert Blythe. Avonlea juvenile society persisted in regarding Gilbert Blythe and Charlie Sloane as rivals in the good graces of a certain damsel with gray eyes and an imagination.

Gossip, as usual, was wrong. Gilbert Blythe, aided and abetted by Anne, had written the notes, putting in the one about himself as a blind. Only two of the notes have any bearing on this history.

"Rumor has it that there will be a wedding in our village ere the daisies are in bloom. A new and highly respected citizen will lead to the hymeneal altar one of our most popular ladies."

"Uncle Abe, our well-known weather prophet, predicts a violent storm of thunder and lightning for the evening of the twenty-third of May, beginning at seven o'clock sharp. The area of the storm will extend over the greater part of the Province. People traveling that evening will do well to take umbrellas and mackintoshes with them."

"Uncle Abe really has predicted a storm for sometime this spring," said Gilbert, "but do you suppose Mr. Harrison really does go to see Isabella Andrews?"

"No," said Anne, laughing, "I'm sure he only goes to play checkers with Mr. Harmon Andrews, but Mrs. Lynde says she knows Isabella Andrews must be going to get married, she's in such good spirits this spring."

Poor old Uncle Abe felt rather indignant over the notes. He suspected that "Observer" was making fun of him. He angrily denied having assigned any particular date for his storm but nobody believed him.

Life in Avonlea continued on the smooth and even tenor of its
way. The "planting" was put in; the Improvers celebrated an Arbor Day.
Each Improver set out, or caused to be set out, five ornamental trees.
As the society now numbered forty members, this meant a total of two
hundred young trees. Early oats greened over the red fields; apple
orchards flung great blossoming arms about the farmhouses and the
Snow Queen adorned itself as a bride for her husband. Anne liked
to sleep with her window open and let the cherry fragrance blow over
her face all night. She thought it very poetical. Marilla thought she was
risking her life.

"Thanksgiving should be celebrated in the spring," said Anne one
evening to Marilla, as they sat on the front door steps and listened to
the silver-sweet chorus of the frogs. "I think it would be ever so much
better than having it in November when everything is dead or asleep.
Then you have to remember to be thankful; but in May one simply
can't help being thankful . . . that they are alive, if for nothing else. I feel
exactly as Eve must have felt in the garden of Eden before the trouble
began. Is that grass in the hollow green or golden? It seems to me,
Marilla, that a pearl of a day like this, when the blossoms are out and
the winds don't know where to blow from next for sheer crazy delight
must be pretty near as good as heaven."

Marilla looked scandalized and glanced apprehensively around to
make sure the twins were not within earshot. They came around the
corner of the house just then.

"Ain't it an awful nice-smelling evening?" asked Davy, sniffing
delightedly as he swung a hoe in his grimy hands. He had been working in his garden. That spring Marilla, by way of turning Davy's passion
for reveling in mud and clay into useful channels, had given him and
Dora a small plot of ground for a garden. Both had eagerly gone to
work in a characteristic fashion. Dora planted, weeded, and watered
carefully, systematically, and dispassionately. As a result, her plot was
already green with prim, orderly little rows of vegetables and annuals.

Davy, however, worked with more zeal than discretion; he dug and hoed and raked and watered and transplanted so energetically that his seeds had no chance for their lives.

"How is your garden coming on, Davy-boy?" asked Anne.

"Kind of slow," said Davy with a sigh. "I don't know why the things don't grow better. Milty Boulter says I must have planted them in the dark of the moon and that's the whole trouble. He says you must never sow seeds or kill pork or cut your hair or do any 'portant thing in the wrong time of the moon. Is that true, Anne? I want to know."

"Maybe if you didn't pull your plants up by the roots every other day to see how they're getting on 'at the other end,' they'd do better," said Marilla sarcastically.

"I only pulled six of them up," protested Davy. "I wanted to see if there was grubs at the roots. Milty Boulter said if it wasn't the moon's fault it must be grubs. But I only found one grub. He was a great big juicy curly grub. I put him on a stone and got another stone and smashed him flat. He made a jolly sqush I tell you. I was sorry there wasn't more of them. Dora's garden was planted same time's mine and her things are growing all right. It *can't* be the moon," Davy concluded in a reflective tone.

"Marilla, look at that apple tree," said Anne. "Why, the thing is human. It is reaching out long arms to pick its own pink skirts daintily up and provoke us to admiration."

"Those Yellow Duchess trees always bear well," said Marilla complacently. "That tree'll be loaded this year. I'm real glad . . . they're great for pies."

But neither Marilla nor Anne nor anybody else was fated to make pies out of Yellow Duchess apples that year.

The twenty-third of May came . . . an unseasonably warm day, as none realized more keenly than Anne and her little beehive of pupils, sweltering over fractions and syntax in the Avonlea schoolroom. A hot breeze blew all the forenoon; but after noon hour it died away into a heavy stillness. At half past three Anne heard a low rumble of thunder. She promptly dismissed school at once, so that the children might get home before the storm came.

As they went out to the playground Anne perceived a certain shadow and gloom over the world in spite of the fact that the sun was still shining brightly. Annetta Bell caught her hand nervously.

"Oh, teacher, look at that awful cloud!"

Anne looked and gave an exclamation of dismay. In the northwest a mass of cloud, such as she had never in all her life beheld before, was rapidly rolling up. It was dead black, save where its curled and fringed edges showed a ghastly, livid white. There was something about it indescribably menacing as it gloomed up in the clear blue sky; now and again a bolt of lightning shot across it, followed by a savage growl. It hung so low that it almost seemed to be touching the tops of the wooded hills.

Mr. Harmon Andrews came clattering up the hill in his truck wagon, urging his team of grays to their utmost speed. He pulled them to a halt opposite the school.

"Guess Uncle Abe's hit it for once in his life, Anne," he shouted. "His storm's coming a leetle ahead of time. Did ye ever see the like of that cloud? Here, all you young ones, that are going my way, pile in, and those that ain't scoot for the post office if ye've more'n a quarter of a mile to go, and stay there till the shower's over."

Anne caught Davy and Dora by the hands and flew down the hill, along the Birch Path, and past Violet Vale and Willowmere, as fast as the twins' fat legs could go. They reached Green Gables not a moment too soon and were joined at the door by Marilla, who had been hustling her ducks and chickens under shelter. As they dashed into the kitchen the light seemed to vanish, as if blown out by some mighty breath; the awful cloud rolled over the sun and a darkness as of late twilight fell across the world. At the same moment, with a crash of thunder and a blinding glare of lightning, the hail swooped down and blotted the landscape out in one white fury.

Through all the clamor of the storm came the thud of torn branches striking the house and the sharp crack of breaking glass. In three minutes every pane in the west and north windows was broken and the hail poured in through the apertures, covering the floor with stones, the smallest of which was as big as a hen's egg. For three quarters of an hour the storm raged unabated and no one who underwent it ever forgot it. Marilla, for once in her life shaken out of her composure by sheer terror, knelt by her rocking chair in a corner of the kitchen, gasping and sobbing between the deafening thunder peals. Anne, white as paper, had dragged the sofa away from the window and sat on it with a twin on either side. Davy at the first crash had howled, "Anne, Anne, is it the Judgment Day? Anne, Anne, I never *meant* to be naughty," and then had buried his face in Anne's lap and kept it there, his little body quivering. Dora, somewhat pale but quite composed, sat with her hand clasped in Anne's, quiet and motionless. It is doubtful if an earthquake would have disturbed Dora.

Then, almost as suddenly as it began, the storm ceased. The hail stopped, the thunder rolled and muttered away to the eastward, and the sun burst out merry and radiant over a world so changed that it seemed an absurd thing to think that a scant three quarters of an hour could have effected such a transformation.

Marilla rose from her knees, weak and trembling, and dropped on her rocker. Her face was haggard and she looked ten years older.

"Have we all come out of that alive?" she asked solemnly.

"You bet we have," piped Davy cheerfully, quite his own man again. "I wasn't a bit scared either . . . only just at the first. It come on a fellow so sudden. I made up my mind quick as a wink that I wouldn't fight Teddy Sloane Monday as I'd promised; but now maybe I will. Say, Dora, was you scared?"

"Yes, I was a little scared," said Dora primly, "but I held tight to Anne's hand and said my prayers over and over again."

"Well, I'd have said my prayers too if I'd have thought of it," said Davy; "but," he added triumphantly, "you see I came through just as safe as you for all I didn't say them."

Anne got Marilla a glassful of her potent currant wine . . . *how* potent it was Anne, in her earlier days, had had all too good reason to know . . . and then they went to the door to look out on the strange scene.

Far and wide was a white carpet, knee deep, of hailstones; drifts of them were heaped up under the eaves and on the steps. When, three or four days later, those hailstones melted, the havoc they had wrought was plainly seen, for every green growing thing in field or garden was cut off. Not only was every blossom stripped from the apple trees but great boughs and branches were wrenched away. And out of the two hundred trees set out by the Improvers by far the greater number were snapped off or torn to shreds.

"Can it possibly be the same world it was an hour ago?" asked Anne, dazedly. "It *must* have taken longer than that to play such havoc."

"The like of this has never been known in Prince Edward Island," said Marilla, "never. I remember when I was a girl there was a bad storm, but it was nothing to this. We'll hear of terrible destruction, you may be sure."

"I do hope none of the children were caught out in it," murmured Anne anxiously. As it was discovered later, none of the children had been, since all those who had any distance to go had taken Mr. Andrews' excellent advice and sought refuge at the post office.

"There comes John Henry Carter," said Marilla.

John Henry came wading through the hailstones with a rather scared grin.

"Oh, ain't this awful, Miss Cuthbert? Mr. Harrison sent me over to see if yous had come out all right."

"We're none of us killed," said Marilla grimly, "and none of the buildings was struck. I hope you got off equally well."

"Yas'm. Not quite so well, ma'am. We was struck. The lightning knocked over the kitchen chimbly and come down the flue and knocked over Ginger's cage and tore a hole in the floor and went into the sullar. Yas'm."

"Was Ginger hurt?" queried Anne.

"Yas'm. He was hurt pretty bad. He was killed." Later on Anne went over to comfort Mr. Harrison. She found him sitting by the table, stroking Ginger's gay dead body with a trembling hand.

"Poor Ginger won't call you any more names, Anne," he said mournfully.

Anne could never have imagined herself crying on Ginger's account, but the tears came into her eyes.

"He was all the company I had, Anne . . . and now he's dead. Well, well, I'm an old fool to care so much. I'll let on I don't care. I know you're going to say something sympathetic as soon as I stop talking . . . but don't. If you did I'd cry like a baby. Hasn't this been a terrible storm? I guess folks won't laugh at Uncle Abe's predictions again. Seems as if all the storms that he's been prophesying all his life that never happened came all at once. Beats all how he struck the very day though, don't it? Look at the mess we have here. I must hustle round and get some boards to patch up that hole in the floor."

Avonlea folks did nothing the next day but visit each other and compare damages. The roads were impassable for wheels by reason of the hailstones, so they walked or rode on horseback. The mail came late with ill tidings from all over the province. Houses had been struck, people killed and injured; the whole telephone and telegraph system had been disorganized, and any number of young stock exposed in the fields had perished.

Uncle Abe waded out to the blacksmith's forge early in the morning and spent the whole day there. It was Uncle Abe's hour of triumph and he enjoyed it to the full. It would be doing Uncle Abe an injustice to say that he was glad the storm had happened; but since it had to be he was very glad he had predicted it . . . to the very day, too. Uncle Abe forgot that he had ever denied setting the day. As for the trifling discrepancy in the hour, that was nothing.

Gilbert arrived at Green Gables in the evening and found Marilla and Anne busily engaged in nailing strips of oilcloth over the broken windows.

"Goodness only knows when we'll get glass for them," said Marilla. "Mr. Barry went over to Carmody this afternoon but not a pane could he get for love or money. Lawson and Blair were cleaned out by the Carmody people by ten o'clock. Was the storm bad at White Sands, Gilbert?"

"I should say so. I was caught in the school with all the children and I thought some of them would go mad with fright. Three of them fainted, and two girls took hysterics, and Tommy Blewett did nothing but shriek at the top of his voice the whole time."

"I only squealed once," said Davy proudly. "My garden was all smashed flat," he continued mournfully, "but so was Dora's," he added in a tone which indicated that there was yet balm in Gilead.

Anne came running down from the west gable.

"Oh, Gilbert, have you heard the news? Mr. Levi Boulter's old house was struck and burned to the ground. It seems to me that I'm dreadfully wicked to feel glad over *that,* when so much damage has been done. Mr. Boulter says he believes the A. V. I. S. magicked up that storm on purpose."

"Well, one thing is certain," said Gilbert, laughing, "'Observer' has made Uncle Abe's reputation as a weather prophet. 'Uncle Abe's storm' will go down in local history. It is a most extraordinary coincidence that it should have come on the very day we selected. I actually have a half guilty feeling, as if I really had 'magicked' it up. We may as well rejoice over the old house being removed, for there's not much to rejoice over where our young trees are concerned. Not ten of them have escaped."

"Ah well, we'll just have to plant them over again next spring," said Anne philosophically. "That is one good thing about this world . . . there are always sure to be more springs."

25

An Avonlea Scandal

ne blithe June morning, a fortnight after Uncle Abe's storm, Anne came slowly through the Green Gables yard from the garden, carrying in her hands two blighted stalks of white narcissus.

"Look, Marilla," she said sorrowfully, holding up the flowers before the eyes of a grim lady, with her hair coifed in a green gingham apron, who was going into the house with a plucked chicken, "these are the only buds the storm spared . . . and even they are imperfect. I'm so sorry . . . I wanted some for Matthew's grave. He was always so fond of June lilies."

"I kind of miss them myself," admitted Marilla, "though it doesn't seem right to lament over them when so many worse things have happened . . . all the crops destroyed as well as the fruit."

"But people have sown their oats over again," said Anne comfortingly, "and Mr. Harrison says he thinks if we have a good summer they will come out all right though late. And my annuals are all coming up again . . . but oh, nothing can replace the June lilies. Poor little Hester Gray will have none either. I went all the way back to her garden last night but there wasn't one. I'm sure she'll miss them."

"I don't think it's right for you to say such things, Anne, I really don't," said Marilla severely. "Hester Gray has been dead for thirty years and her spirit is in heaven . . . I hope."

"Yes, but I believe she loves and remembers her garden here still," said Anne. "I'm sure no matter how long I'd lived in heaven I'd like to look down and see somebody putting flowers on my grave. If I had had a garden here like Hester Gray's it would take me more than thirty years, even in heaven, to forget being homesick for it by spells."

"Well, don't let the twins hear you talking like that," was Marilla's feeble protest, as she carried her chicken into the house.

Anne pinned her narcissi on her hair and went to the lane gate, where she stood for awhile sunning herself in the June brightness before going in to attend to her Saturday morning duties. The world was growing lovely again; old Mother Nature was doing her best to remove the traces of the storm, and, though she was not to succeed fully for many a moon, she was really accomplishing wonders.

"I wish I could just be idle all day today," Anne told a bluebird, who was singing and swinging on a willow bough, "but a schoolma'am, who is also helping to bring up twins, can't indulge in laziness, birdie. How sweet you are singing, little bird. You are just putting the feelings of my heart into song ever so much better than I could myself. Why, who is coming?"

An express wagon was jolting up the lane, with two people on the front seat and a big trunk behind. When it drew near Anne recognized the driver as the son of the station agent at Bright River; but his companion was a stranger ... a scrap of a woman who sprang nimbly down at the gate almost before the horse came to a standstill. She was a very pretty little person, evidently nearer fifty than forty, but with rosy cheeks, sparkling black eyes, and shining black hair, surmounted by a wonderful beflowered and beplumed bonnet. In spite of having driven eight miles over a dusty road she was as neat as if she had just stepped out of the proverbial bandbox.

"Is this where Mr. James A. Harrison lives?" she inquired briskly.

"No, Mr. Harrison lives over there," said Anne, quite lost in astonishment.

"Well, I *did* think this place seemed too tidy ... *much* too tidy for James A. to be living here, unless he has greatly changed since I knew him," chirped the little lady. "Is it true that James A. is going to be married to some woman living in this settlement?"

"No, oh no," cried Anne, flushing so guiltily that the stranger looked curiously at her, as if she half suspected her of matrimonial designs on Mr. Harrison.

"But I saw it in an Island paper," persisted the Fair Unknown. "A friend sent a marked copy to me . . . friends are always so ready to do such things. James A.'s name was written in over 'new citizen.'"

"Oh, that note was only meant as a joke," gasped Anne. "Mr. Harrison has no intention of marrying *anybody*. I assure you he hasn't."

"I'm very glad to hear it," said the rosy lady, climbing nimbly back to her seat in the wagon, "because he happens to be married already. *I* am his wife. Oh, you may well look surprised. I suppose he has been masquerading as a bachelor and breaking hearts right and left. Well, well, James A.," nodding vigorously over the fields at the long white house, "your fun is over. I am here . . . though I wouldn't haven't bothered coming if I hadn't thought you were up to some mischief. I suppose," turning to Anne, "that parrot of his is as profane as ever?"

"His parrot . . . is dead . . . I *think*," gasped poor Anne, who couldn't have felt sure of her own name at that precise moment.

"Dead! Everything will be all right then," cried the rosy lady jubilantly. "I can manage James A. if that bird is out of the way."

With which cryptic utterance she went joyfully on her way and Anne flew to the kitchen door to meet Marilla.

"Anne, who was that woman?"

"Marilla," said Anne solemnly, but with dancing eyes, "do I look as if I were crazy?"

"Not more so than usual," said Marilla, with no thought of being sarcastic.

"Well then, do you think I am awake?"

"Anne, what nonsense has got into you? Who was that woman, I say?"

"Marilla, if I'm not crazy and not asleep she can't be such stuff as dreams are made of . . . she must be real. Anyway, I'm sure I couldn't have imagined such a bonnet. She says she is Mr. Harrison's wife, Marilla."

Marilla stared in her turn.

"His wife! Anne Shirley! Then what has he been passing himself off as an unmarried man for?"

"I don't suppose he did, really," said Anne, trying to be just. "He never said he wasn't married. People simply took it for granted. Oh Marilla, what will Mrs. Lynde say to this?"

They found out what Mrs. Lynde had to say when she came up that evening. Mrs. Lynde wasn't surprised! Mrs. Lynde had always expected something of the sort! Mrs. Lynde had always known there was *something* about Mr. Harrison!

"To think of his deserting his wife!" she said indignantly. "It's like something you'd read of in the States, but who would expect such a thing to happen right here in Avonlea?"

"But we don't know that he deserted her," protested Anne, determined to believe her friend innocent till he was proved guilty. "We don't know the rights of it at all."

"Well, we soon will. I'm going straight over there," said Mrs. Lynde, who had never learned that there was such a word as delicacy in the dictionary. "I'm not supposed to know anything about her arrival, and Mr. Harrison was to bring some medicine for Thomas from Carmody today, so that will be a good excuse. I'll find out the whole story and come in and tell you on my way back."

Mrs. Lynde rushed in where Anne had feared to tread. Nothing would have induced the latter to go over to the Harrison place; but she had her natural and proper share of curiosity and she felt secretly glad that Mrs. Lynde was going to solve the mystery. She and Marilla waited expectantly for that good lady's return, but waited in vain. Mrs. Lynde did not revisit Green Gables that night. Davy, arriving home at nine o'clock from the Boulter place, explained why.

"I met Mrs. Lynde and some strange woman in the Hollow," he said, "and gracious, how they were talking both at once! Mrs. Lynde said to tell you she was sorry it was too late to call tonight. Anne, I'm awful hungry. We had tea at Milty's at four and I think Mrs. Boulter is real mean. She didn't give us any preserves or cake . . . and even the bread was skurce."

"Davy, when you go visiting you must never criticize anything you are given to eat," said Anne solemnly. "It is very bad manners."

"All right . . . I'll only think it," said Davy cheerfully. "Do give a fellow some supper, Anne."

Anne looked at Marilla, who followed her into the pantry and shut the door cautiously.

"You can give him some jam on his bread, Anne. I know what tea at Levi Boulter's is apt to be."

Davy took his slice of bread and jam with a sigh.

"It's a kind of disappointing world after all," he remarked. "Milty has a cat that takes fits . . . she's took a fit regular every day for three weeks. Milty says it's awful fun to watch her. I went down today on purpose to see her have one but the mean old thing wouldn't take a fit and just kept healthy as healthy, though Milty and me hung round all the afternoon and waited. But never mind" . . . Davy brightened up as the insidious comfort of the plum jam stole into his soul . . . "maybe I'll see her in one sometime yet. It doesn't seem likely she'd stop having them all at once when she's been so in the habit of it, does it? This jam is awful nice."

Davy had no sorrows that plum jam could not cure.

Sunday proved so rainy that there was no stirring abroad; but by Monday everybody had heard some version of the Harrison story. The school buzzed with it and Davy came home, full of information.

"Marilla, Mr. Harrison has a new wife . . . well, not ezackly new, but they've stopped being married for quite a spell, Milty says. I always s'posed people had to keep on being married once they'd begun, but Milty says no, there's ways of stopping if you can't agree. Milty says one way is just to start off and leave your wife, and that's what Mr. Harrison did. Milty says Mr. Harrison left his wife because she throwed things at him . . . *hard* things . . . and Arty Sloane says it was because she wouldn't let him smoke, and Ned Clay says it was 'cause she never let up scolding him. I wouldn't leavy *my* wife for anything like that. I'd just put my foot down and say, 'Mrs. Davy, you've just got to do what'll please *me* 'cause I'm a *man*.' *That'd* settle her pretty quick I guess. But Annetta Clay says *she* left *him* because he wouldn't scrape his boots at the door and she doesn't blame her. I'm going right over to Mr. Harrison's this minute to see what she's like."

Davy soon returned, somewhat cast down.

"Mrs. Harrison was away . . . she's gone to Carmody with Mrs. Rachel Lynde to get new paper for the parlor. And Mr. Harrison said to tell Anne to go over and see him 'cause he wants to have a talk with her. And say, the floor is scrubbed, and Mr. Harrison is shaved, though there wasn't any preaching yesterday."

The Harrison kitchen wore a very unfamiliar look to Anne. The floor was indeed scrubbed to a wonderful pitch of purity and so was every article of furniture in the room; the stove was polished until she could see her face in it; the walls were whitewashed and the window panes sparkled in the sunlight. By the table sat Mr. Harrison in his working clothes, which on Friday had been noted for sundry rents and tatters but which were now neatly patched and brushed. He was sprucely shaved and what little hair he had was carefully trimmed.

"Sit down, Anne, sit down," said Mr. Harrison, in a tone but two degrees removed from that which Avonlea people used at funerals. "Emily's gone over to Carmody with Rachel Lynde . . . she's struck up a lifelong friendship already with Rachel Lynde. Beats all how contrary women are. Well, Anne, my easy times are over . . . all over. It's neatness and tidiness for me for the rest of my natural life, I suppose."

Mr. Harrison did his best to speak dolefully, but an irrepressible twinkle in his eye betrayed him.

"Mr. Harrison, you are glad your wife is come back," cried Anne, shaking her finger at him. "You needn't pretend you're not, because I can see it plainly."

Mr. Harrison relaxed into a sheepish smile.

"Well . . . well . . . I'm getting used to it," he conceded. "I can't say I was sorry to see Emily. A man really needs some protection in a community like this, where he can't play a game of checkers with a neighbor without being accused of wanting to marry that neighbor's sister and having it put in the paper."

"Nobody would have supposed you went to see Isabella Andrews if you hadn't pretended to be unmarried," said Anne severely.

"I didn't pretend I was. If anybody'd have asked me if I was married I'd have said I was. But they just took it for granted. I wasn't anxious to talk about the matter . . . I was feeling too sore over it. It would have been nuts for Mrs. Rachel Lynde if she had known my wife had left me, wouldn't it now?"

"But some people say that you left her."

"She started it, Anne, she started it. I'm going to tell you the whole story, for I don't want you to think worse of me than I deserve . . . nor of Emily neither. But let's go out on the veranda. Everything is so fearful neat in here that it kind of makes me homesick. I suppose I'll get used to it after awhile but it eases me up to look at the yard. Emily hasn't had time to tidy *it* up yet."

As soon as they were comfortably seated on the veranda Mr. Harrison began his tale of woe.

"I lived in Scottsford, New Brunswick, before I came here, Anne. My sister kept house for me and she suited me fine; she was just reasonably tidy and she let me alone and spoiled me . . . so Emily says. But three years ago she died. Before she died she worried a lot about what was to become of me and finally she got me to promise I'd get married. She advised me to take Emily Scott because Emily had money of her own and was a pattern housekeeper. I said, says I, 'Emily Scott wouldn't look at me.' 'You ask her and see,' says my sister; and just to ease her mind I promised her I would . . . and I did. And Emily said she'd have me. Never was so surprised in my life, Anne . . . a smart pretty little woman like her and an old fellow like me. I tell you I thought at first I was in luck. Well, we were married and took a little wedding trip up to St. John for a fortnight and then we went home. We got home at ten o'clock at night, and I give you my word, Anne, that in half an hour that woman was at work housecleaning. Oh, I know you're thinking my house needed it . . . you've got a very expressive face, Anne; your thoughts just come out on it like print . . . but it didn't, not that bad. It had got pretty mixed up while I was keeping bachelor's hall, I admit, but I'd got a woman to come in and clean it up before I was married and there'd been considerable painting and fixing done. I tell you if you took Emily into a brand new white marble palace she'd be into the scrubbing as soon as she could get an old dress on. Well, she cleaned house till one o'clock that night and at four she was up and at it again. And she kept on that way . . . far's I could see she never stopped. It was scour and sweep and dust everlasting, except on Sundays, and then she was just longing for Monday to begin again. But it was her way of amusing herself and I could have reconciled myself to it if she'd left me alone. But that she wouldn't do. She'd set out to make me over but she hadn't caught me young enough. I wasn't allowed to come into the house unless I changed my boots for slippers at the door. I darsn't smoke a pipe for my life unless I went to the barn. And I didn't use good enough grammar. Emily'd been a schoolteacher in her early life and she'd never got over it. Then she hated to see me eating with my knife. Well, there it was, pick and nag everlasting. But I s'pose, Anne, to be fair, I was cantankerous too. I didn't try to improve as I might have done . . . I just got cranky and disagreeable when she found fault. I told her one day she hadn't complained of my grammar when I proposed to her. It wasn't an overly tactful thing to say. A woman would forgive a man for beating her sooner than for hinting she was too much pleased to get him. Well, we bickered along like that and it wasn't exactly pleasant, but we might have got used to each other after a spell if it hadn't been for Ginger. Ginger was the rock we split on at last. Emily didn't like parrots and she couldn't stand Ginger's profane habits of speech. I was attached to the bird for my brother the sailor's sake. My brother the sailor was a pet of mine when we were little tads and he'd sent Ginger to me when he was dying. I didn't see any sense in getting worked up over his swearing. There's nothing I hate worse'n profanity in a human being, but in a parrot, that's just repeating what it's heard with no more understanding of it than I'd have of Chinese, allowances might be made. But Emily couldn't see it that way. Women ain't logical. She tried to break Ginger of swearing but she hadn't any better success than she had in trying to make me stop saying 'I seen' and 'them things.' Seemed as if the more she tried the worse Ginger got, same as me.

"Well, things went on like this, both of us getting raspier, till the *climax* came. Emily invited our minister and his wife to tea, and another minister and *his* wife that was visiting them. I'd promised to put Ginger away in some safe place where nobody would hear him . . . Emily wouldn't touch his cage with a ten-foot pole . . . and I meant to do it, for I didn't want the ministers to hear anything unpleasant in my house. But it slipped my mind . . . Emily was worrying me so much about clean collars and grammar that it wasn't any wonder . . . and I never thought of that poor parrot till we sat down to tea. Just as minister number one was in the very middle of saying grace, Ginger, who was on the veranda outside the dining room window, lifted up *his* voice. The gobbler had come into view in the yard and the sight of a gobbler always had an unwholesome effect on Ginger. He surpassed himself that time. You can smile, Anne, and I don't deny I've chuckled some over it since myself, but at the time I felt almost as much mortified as Emily. I went out and carried Ginger to the barn. I can't say I enjoyed that meal. I knew by the look of Emily that there was trouble brewing for Ginger and James A. When the folks went away I started for the cow pasture and on the way I did some thinking. I felt sorry for Emily and kind of fancied I hadn't been so thoughtful of her as I might; and besides, I wondered if the ministers would think that Ginger had learned his vocabulary from *me*. The long and short of it was, I decided that Ginger would have to be mercifully disposed of and when I'd druv the cows home I went in to tell Emily so. But there was no Emily and there *was* a letter on the table . . . just according to the rule in story books. Emily writ that I'd have to choose between her and Ginger; she'd gone back to her own house and there she would stay till I went and told her I'd got rid of that parrot.

"I was all riled up, Anne, and I said she might stay till doomsday if she waited for that; and I stuck to it. I packed up her belongings and sent them after her. It made an awful lot of talk . . . Scottsford was pretty near as bad as Avonlea for gossip . . . and everybody sympathized with Emily. It kept me all cross and cantankerous and I saw I'd have to get out or I'd never have any peace. I concluded I'd come to the Island. I'd been here when I was a boy and I liked it; but Emily had always said she wouldn't live in a place where folks were scared to walk out after dark for fear they'd fall off the edge. So, just to be contrary, I moved over here. And that's all there is to it. I hadn't ever heard a word from or about Emily till I come home from the back field Saturday and found her scrubbing the floor but with the first decent dinner I'd had since she left me all ready on the table. She told me to eat it first and then we'd talk . . . by which I concluded that Emily had learned some lessons about getting along with a man. So she's here and she's going to stay . . . seeing that Ginger's dead and the Island's some bigger than she thought. There's Mrs. Lynde and her now. No, don't go, Anne. Stay and get acquainted with Emily. She took quite a notion to you Saturday . . . wanted to know who that handsome redhaired girl was at the next house."

Mrs. Harrison welcomed Anne radiantly and insisted on her staying to tea.

"James A. has been telling me all about you and how kind you've been, making cakes and things for him," she said. "I want to get acquainted with all my new neighbors just as soon as possible. Mrs. Lynde is a lovely woman, isn't she? So friendly."

When Anne went home in the sweet June dusk, Mrs. Harrison went with her across the fields where the fireflies were lighting their starry lamps.

"I suppose," said Mrs. Harrison confidentially, "that James A. has told you our story?"

"Yes."

"Then I needn't tell it, for James A. is a just man and he would tell the truth. The blame was far from being all on his side. I can see that now. I wasn't back in my own house an hour before I wished I hadn't been so hasty but I wouldn't give in. I see now that I expected too much of a man. And I was real foolish to mind his bad grammar. It doesn't matter if a man does use bad grammar so long as he is a good provider and doesn't go poking round the pantry to see how much sugar you've used in a week. I feel that James A. and I are going to be real happy now. I wish I knew who 'Observer' is, so that I could thank him. I owe him a real debt of gratitude."

Anne kept her own counsel and Mrs. Harrison never knew that her gratitude found its way to its object. Anne felt rather bewildered over the far-reaching consequences of those foolish "notes." They had reconciled a man to his wife and made the reputation of a prophet.

Mrs. Lynde was in the Green Gables kitchen. She had been telling the whole story to Marilla.

"Well, and how do you like Mrs. Harrison?" she asked Anne.

"Very much. I think she's a real nice little woman."

"That's exactly what she is," said Mrs. Rachel with emphasis, "and as I've just been sayin' to Marilla, I think we ought all to overlook Mr. Harrison's peculiarities for her sake and try to make her feel at home here, that's what. Well, I must get back. Thomas'll be wearying for me. I get out a little since Eliza came and he's seemed a lot better these past few days, but I never like to be long away from him. I hear Gilbert Blythe has resigned from White Sands. He'll be off to college in the fall, I suppose."

Mrs. Rachel looked sharply at Anne, but Anne was bending over a sleepy Davy nodding on the sofa and nothing was to be read in her face. She carried Davy away, her oval girlish cheek pressed against his curly yellow head. As they went up the stairs Davy flung a tired arm about Anne's neck and gave her a warm hug and a sticky kiss.

"You're awful nice, Anne. Milty Boulter wrote on his slate today and showed it to Jennie Sloane,

"'Roses red and vi'lets blue,
Sugar's sweet, and so are you,'

and that 'spresses my feelings for you ezackly, Anne."

26

Around the Bend

homas Lynde faded out of life as quietly and unobtrusively as he had lived it. His wife was a tender, patient, unwearied nurse. Sometimes Rachel had been a little hard on her Thomas in health, when his slowness or meekness had provoked her; but when he became ill no voice could be lower, no hand more gently skillful, no vigil more uncomplaining.

"You've been a good wife to me, Rachel," he once said simply, when she was sitting by him in the dusk, holding his thin, blanched old hand in her work-hardened one. "A good wife. I'm sorry I ain't leaving you better off; but the children will look after you. They're all smart, capable children, just like their mother. A good mother . . . a good woman. . . ."

He had fallen asleep then; and the next morning, just as the white dawn was creeping up over the pointed firs in the hollow, Marilla went softly into the east gable and wakened Anne.

"Anne, Thomas Lynde is gone . . . their hired boy just brought the word. I'm going right down to Rachel."

On the day after Thomas Lynde's funeral Marilla went about Green Gables with a strangely preoccupied air. Occasionally she looked at Anne, seemed on the point of saying something, then shook her head and buttoned up her mouth. After tea she went down to see Mrs. Rachel; and when she returned she went to the east gable, where Anne was correcting school exercises.

"How is Mrs. Lynde tonight?" asked the latter.

"She's feeling calmer and more composed," answered Marilla, sitting down on Anne's bed . . . a proceeding which betokened some unusual mental excitement, for in Marilla's code of household ethics to sit on a bed after it was made up was an unpardonable offense. "But she's very lonely. Eliza had to go home today . . . her son isn't well and she felt she couldn't stay any longer."

"When I've finished these exercises I'll run down and chat awhile with Mrs. Lynde," said Anne. "I had intended to study some Latin composition tonight but it can wait."

"I suppose Gilbert Blythe is going to college in the fall," said Marilla jerkily. "How would you like to go too, Anne?"

Anne looked up in astonishment.

"I would like it, of course, Marilla. But it isn't possible."

"I guess it can be made possible. I've always felt that you should go. I've never felt easy to think you were giving it all up on my account."

"But, Marilla, I've never been sorry for a moment that I stayed home. I've been so happy . . . Oh, these past two years have just been delightful."

"Oh yes, I know you've been contented enough. But that isn't the question exactly. You ought to go on with your education. You've saved enough to put you through one year at Redmond and the money the stock brought in will do for another year . . . and there's scholarships and things you might win."

"Yes, but I can't go, Marilla. Your eyes are better, of course; but I can't leave you alone with the twins. They need so much looking after."

"I won't be alone with them. That's what I want to discuss with you. I had a long talk with Rachel tonight. Anne, she's feeling dreadful bad over a good many things. She's not left very well off. It seems they mortgaged the farm eight years ago to give the youngest boy a start when he went west; and they've never been able to pay much more than the interest since. And then of course Thomas' illness has cost a good deal, one way and another. The farm will have to be sold and Rachel thinks there'll be hardly anything left after the bills are settled. She says she'll have to go and live with Eliza and it's breaking her heart to think of leaving Avonlea. A woman of her age doesn't make new friends and interests easy. And, Anne, as she talked about it the thought came to me that I would ask her to come and live with me, but I thought I ought to talk it over with you first before I said anything to her. If I had Rachel living with me you could go to college. How do you feel about it?"

"I feel . . . as if . . . somebody . . . had handed me . . . the moon . . . and I didn't know . . . exactly . . . what to do . . . with it," said Anne dazedly. "But as for asking Mrs. Lynde to come here, that is for you to decide, Marilla. Do you think . . . are you sure . . . you would like it? Mrs. Lynde is a good woman and a kind neighbor, but . . . but . . ."

"But she's got her faults, you mean to say? Well, she has, of course; but I think I'd rather put up with far worse faults than see Rachel go away from Avonlea. I'd miss her terrible. She's the only close friend I've got here and I'd be lost without her. We've been neighbors for forty-five years and we've never had a quarrel . . . though we came rather near it that time you flew at Mrs. Rachel for calling you homely and red-haired. Do you remember, Anne?"

"I should think I do," said Anne ruefully. "People don't forget things like that. How I hated poor Mrs. Rachel at that moment!"

"And then that 'apology' you made her. Well, you were a handful, in all conscience, Anne. I did feel so puzzled and bewildered how to manage you. Matthew understood you better."

"Matthew understood everything," said Anne softly, as she always spoke of him.

"Well, I think it could be managed so that Rachel and I wouldn't clash at all. It's always seemed to me that the reason two women can't get along in one house is that they try to share the same kitchen and get in each other's way. Now, if Rachel came here, she could have the north gable for her bedroom and the spare room for a kitchen as well as not, for we don't really need a spare room at all. She could put her stove there and what furniture she wanted to keep, and be real comfortable and independent. She'll have enough to live on of course . . . her children'll see to that . . . so all I'd be giving her would be house room. Yes, Anne, far as I'm concerned I'd like it."

"Then ask her," said Anne promptly. "I'd be very sorry myself to see Mrs. Rachel go away."

"And if she comes," continued Marilla, "you can go to college as well as not. She'll be company for me and she'll do for the twins what I can't do, so there's no reason in the world why you shouldn't go."

Anne had a long meditation at her window that night. Joy and regret struggled together in her heart. She had come at last . . . suddenly and unexpectedly . . . to the bend in the road; and college *was* around it, with a hundred rainbow hopes and visions; but Anne realized as well that when she rounded that curve she must leave many sweet things behind . . . all the little simple duties and interests which had grown so dear to her in the last two years and which she had glorified into beauty and delight by the enthusiasm she had put into them. She must give up her school . . . and she loved every one of her pupils, even the stupid and naughty ones. The mere thought of Paul Irving made her wonder if Redmond were such a name to conjure with after all.

"I've put out a lot of little roots these two years," Anne told the moon, "and when I'm pulled up they're going to hurt a great deal. But it's best to go, I think, and, as Marilla says, there's no good reason why I shouldn't. I must get out all my ambitions and dust them."

Anne sent in her resignation the next day; and Mrs. Rachel, after a heart to heart talk with Marilla, gratefully accepted the offer of a home at Green Gables. She elected to remain in her own house for the summer, however; the farm was not to be sold until the fall and there were many arrangements to be made.

"I certainly never thought of living as far off the road as Green Gables," sighed Mrs. Rachel to herself. "But really, Green Gables doesn't seem as out of the world as it used to do . . . Anne has lots of company and the twins make it real lively. And anyhow, I'd rather live at the bottom of a well than leave Avonlea."

These two decisions being noised abroad speedily ousted the arrival of Mrs. Harrison in popular gossip. Sage heads were shaken over Marilla Cuthbert's rash step in asking Mrs. Rachel to live with her. People opined that they wouldn't get on together. They were both "too fond of their own way," and many doleful predictions were made, none of which disturbed the parties in question at all. They had come to a clear and distinct understanding of the respective duties and rights of their new arrangements and meant to abide by them.

"I won't meddle with you nor you with me," Mrs. Rachel had said decidedly, "and as for the twins, I'll be glad to do all I can for them; but I won't undertake to answer Davy's questions, that's what. I'm not an encyclopedia, neither am I a Philadelphia lawyer. You'll miss Anne for that."

"Sometimes Anne's answers were about as queer as Davy's questions," said Marilla drily. "The twins will miss her and no mistake; but her future can't be sacrificed to Davy's thirst for information. When he asks questions I can't answer I'll just tell him children should be seen and not heard. That was how *I* was brought up, and I don't know but what it was just as good a way as all these new-fangled notions for training children."

"Well, Anne's methods seem to have worked fairly well with Davy," said Mrs. Lynde smilingly. "He is a reformed character, that's what."

"He isn't a bad little soul," conceded Marilla. "I never expected to get as fond of those children as I have. Davy gets round you somehow . . . and Dora is a lovely child, although she is . . . kind of . . . well, kind of . . ."

"Monotonous? Exactly," supplied Mrs. Rachel. "Like a book where every page is the same, that's what. Dora will make a good, reliable woman but she'll never set the pond on fire. Well, that sort of folks are comfortable to have round, even if they're not as interesting as the other kind."

Gilbert Blythe was probably the only person to whom the news of Anne's resignation brought unmixed pleasure. Her pupils looked upon it as a sheer catastrophe. Annetta Bell had hysterics when she went home. Anthony Pye fought two pitched and unprovoked battles with other boys by way of relieving his feelings. Barbara Shaw cried all night. Paul Irving defiantly told his grandmother that she needn't expect him to eat any porridge for a week.

"I can't do it, Grandma," he said. "I don't really know if I can eat *anything*. I feel as if there was a dreadful lump in my throat. I'd have cried coming home from school if Jake Donnell hadn't been watching me. I believe I will cry after I go to bed. It wouldn't show on my eyes tomorrow, would it? And it would be such a relief. But anyway, I can't eat porridge. I'm going to need all my strength of mind to bear up against this, Grandma, and I won't have any left to grapple with porridge. Oh Grandma, I don't know what I'll do when my beautiful teacher goes away. Milty Boulter says he bets Jane Andrews will get the school. I suppose Miss Andrews is very nice. But I know she won't understand things like Miss Shirley."

Diana also took a very pessimistic view of affairs.

"It will be horribly lonesome here next winter," she mourned, one twilight when the moonlight was raining "airy silver" through the cherry boughs and filling the east gable with a soft, dream-like radiance in which the two girls sat and talked, Anne on her low rocker by the window, Diana sitting Turk-fashion on the bed. "You and Gilbert will be gone . . . and the Allans too. They are going to call Mr. Allan to Charlottetown and of course he'll accept. It's too mean. We'll be vacant all winter, I suppose, and have to listen to a long string of candidates . . . and half of them won't be any good."

"I hope they won't call Mr. Baxter from East Grafton here, anyhow," said Anne decidedly. "He wants the call but he does preach such gloomy sermons. Mr. Bell says he's a minister of the old school, but Mrs. Lynde says there's nothing whatever the matter with him but indigestion. His wife isn't a very good cook, it seems, and Mrs. Lynde says that when a man has to eat sour bread two weeks out of three his theology is bound to get a kink in it somewhere. Mrs. Allan feels very badly about going away. She says everybody has been so kind to her since she came here as a bride that she feels as if she were leaving lifelong friends. And then, there's the baby's grave, you know. She says she doesn't see how she can go away and leave that . . . it was such a little mite of a thing and only three months old, and she says she is afraid it will miss its mother, although she knows better and wouldn't say so to Mr. Allan for anything. She says she has slipped through the birch grove back of the manse nearly every night to the graveyard and sung a little lullaby to it. She told me all about it last evening when I was up putting some of those early wild roses on Matthew's grave. I promised her that as long as I was in Avonlea I would put flowers on the baby's grave and when I was away I felt sure that . . ."

"That I would do it," supplied Diana heartily. "Of course I will. And I'll put them on Matthew's grave too, for your sake, Anne."

"Oh, thank you. I meant to ask you to if you would. And on little Hester Gray's too? Please don't forget hers. Do you know, I've thought and dreamed so much about little Hester Gray that she has become strangely real to me. I think of her, back there in her little garden in that cool, still, green corner; and I have a fancy that if I could steal back there some spring evening, just at the magic time 'twixt light and dark, and tiptoe so softly up the beech hill that my footsteps could not frighten her, I would find the garden just as it used to be, all sweet with June lilies and early roses, with the tiny house beyond it all hung with vines; and little Hester Gray would be there, with her soft eyes, and the wind ruffling her dark hair, wandering about, putting her fingertips under the chins of the lilies and whispering secrets with the roses; and I would go forward, oh, so softly, and hold out my hands and say to her, 'Little Hester Gray, won't you let me be your playmate, for I love the roses too?' And we would sit down on the old bench and talk a little and dream a little, or just be beautifully silent together. And then the moon would rise and I would look around me . . . and there would be no Hester Gray and no little vine-hung house, and no roses . . . only an old waste garden starred with June lilies amid the grasses, and the wind sighing, oh, so sorrowfully in the cherry trees. And I would not know whether it had been real or if I had just imagined it all."

Diana crawled up and got her back against the headboard of the bed. When your companion of twilight hour said such spooky things it was just as well not to be able to fancy there was anything behind you.

"I'm afraid the Improvement Society will go down when you and Gilbert are both gone," she remarked dolefully.

"Not a bit of fear of it," said Anne briskly, coming back from dreamland to the affairs of practical life. "It is too firmly established for that, especially since the older people are becoming so enthusiastic about it. Look what they are doing this summer for their lawns and lanes. Besides, I'll be watching for hints at Redmond and I'll write a paper for it next winter and send it over. Don't take such a gloomy view of things, Diana. And don't grudge me my little hour of gladness and jubilation now. Later on, when I have to go away, I'll feel anything but glad."

"It's all right for you to be glad . . . you're going to college and you'll have a jolly time and make heaps of lovely new friends."

"I hope I shall make new friends," said Anne thoughtfully. "The possibilities of making new friends help to make life very fascinating. But no matter how many new friends I make they'll never be as dear to me as the old ones . . . especially a certain girl with black eyes and dimples. Can you guess who she is, Diana?"

"But there'll be so many clever girls at Redmond," sighed Diana, "and I'm only a stupid little country girl who says 'I seen' sometimes . . . though I really know better when I stop to think. Well, of course these past two years have really been too pleasant to last. I know *somebody* who is glad you are going to Redmond anyhow. Anne, I'm going to ask you a question . . . a serious question. Don't be vexed and do answer seriously. Do you care anything for Gilbert?"

"Ever so much as a friend and not a bit in the way you mean," said Anne calmly and decidedly; she also thought she was speaking sincerely.

Diana sighed. She wished, somehow, that Anne had answered differently.

"Don't you mean *ever* to be married, Anne?"

"Perhaps . . . some day . . . when I meet the right one," said Anne, smiling dreamily up at the moonlight.

"But how can you be sure when you do meet the right one?" persisted Diana.

"Oh, I should know him . . . *something* would tell me. You know what my ideal is, Diana."

"But people's ideals change sometimes."

"Mine won't. And I *couldn't* care for any man who didn't fulfill it."

"What if you never meet him?"

"Then I shall die an old maid," was the cheerful response. "I daresay it isn't the hardest death by any means."

"Oh, I suppose the dying would be easy enough; it's the living an old maid I shouldn't like," said Diana, with no intention of being humorous. "Although I wouldn't mind being an old maid *very* much if

I could be one like Miss Lavendar. But I never could be. When I'm forty-five I'll be horribly fat. And while there might be some romance about a thin old maid there couldn't possibly be any about a fat one. Oh, mind you, Nelson Atkins proposed to Ruby Gillis three weeks ago. Ruby told me all about it. She says she never had any intention of taking him, because any one who married him will have to go in with the old folks; but Ruby says that he made such a perfectly beautiful and romantic proposal that it simply swept her off her feet. But she didn't want to do anything rash so she asked for a week to consider; and two days later she was at a meeting of the Sewing Circle at his mother's and there was a book called 'The Complete Guide To Etiquette,' lying on the parlor table. Ruby said she simply couldn't describe her feelings when in a section of it headed, 'The Deportment of Courtship And Marriage,' she found the very proposal Nelson had made, word for word. She went home and wrote him a perfectly scathing refusal; and she says his father and mother have taken turns watching him ever since for fear he'll drown himself in the river; but Ruby says they needn't be afraid; for in the Deportment of Courtship and Marriage it told how a rejected lover should behave and there's nothing about drowning in *that*. And she says Wilbur Blair is literally pining away for her but she's perfectly helpless in the matter."

Anne made an impatient movement.

"I hate to say it . . . it seems so disloyal . . . but, well, I don't like Ruby Gillis now. I liked her when we went to school and Queen's together . . . though not so well as you and Jane of course. But this last year at Carmody she seems so different . . . so . . . so."

"I know," nodded Diana. "It's the Gillis coming out in her . . . she can't help it. Mrs. Lynde says that if ever a Gillis girl thought about anything but the boys she never showed it in her walk and conversation. She talks about nothing but boys and what compliments they pay her, and how crazy they all are about her at Carmody. And the strange thing is, they *are*, too . . ." Diana admitted this somewhat resentfully. "Last night when I saw her in Mr. Blair's store she whispered to me that she'd just made a new 'mash.' I wouldn't ask her who it was, because I knew she was dying to *be* asked. Well, it's what Ruby always wanted,

I suppose. You remember even when she was little she always said she meant to have dozens of beaus when she grew up and have the very gayest time she could before she settled down. She's so different from Jane, isn't she? Jane is such a nice, sensible, lady-like girl."

"Dear old Jane is a jewel," agreed Anne, "but," she added, leaning forward to bestow a tender pat on the plump, dimpled little hand hanging over her pillow, "there's nobody like my own Diana after all. Do you remember that evening we first met, Diana, and 'swore' eternal friendship in your garden? We've kept that 'oath,' I think . . . we've never had a quarrel nor even a coolness. I shall never forget the thrill that went over me the day you told me you loved me. I had had such a lonely, starved heart all through my childhood. I'm just beginning to realize how starved and lonely it really was. Nobody cared anything for me or wanted to be bothered with me. I should have been miserable if it hadn't been for that strange little dream-life of mine, wherein I imagined all the friends and love I craved. But when I came to Green Gables everything was changed. And then I met you. You don't know what your friendship meant to me. I want to thank you here and now, dear, for the warm and true affection you've always given me."

"And always, always will," sobbed Diana. "I shall *never* love anybody . . . any *girl* . . . half as well as I love you. And if I ever do marry and have a little girl of my own I'm going to name her *Anne*."

27

An Afternoon at the Stone House

here are you going, all dressed up, Anne?" Davy wanted to know. "You look bully in that dress."

Anne had come down to dinner in a new dress of pale green muslin . . . the first color she had worn since Matthew's death. It became her perfectly, bringing out all the delicate, flower-like tints of her face and the gloss and burnish of her hair.

"Davy, how many times have I told you that you mustn't use that word," she rebuked. "I'm going to Echo Lodge."

"Take me with you," entreated Davy.

"I would if I were driving. But I'm going to walk and it's too far for your eight-year-old legs. Besides, Paul is going with me and I fear you don't enjoy yourself in his company."

"Oh, I like Paul lots better'n I did," said Davy, beginning to make fearful inroads into his pudding. "Since I've got pretty good myself I don't mind his being gooder so much. If I can keep on I'll catch up with him some day, both in legs and goodness. 'Sides, Paul's real nice to us second primer boys in school. He won't let the other big boys meddle with us and he shows us lots of games."

"How came Paul to fall into the brook at noon hour yesterday?" asked Anne. "I met him on the playground, such a dripping figure that I sent him promptly home for dry clothes without waiting to find out what had happened."

"Well, it was partly a zacksident," explained Davy. "He stuck his head in on purpose but the rest of him fell in zacksidentally. We was all down at the brook and Prillie Rogerson got mad at Paul about something . . . she's awful mean and horrid anyway, if she *is* pretty . . . and said that his grandmother put his hair up in curl rags every night. Paul wouldn't have minded what she said, I guess, but Gracie Andrews laughed, and Paul got awful red, 'cause Gracie's his girl, you know. He's *clean gone* on her . . . brings her flowers and carries her books as far as the shore road. He got as red as a beet and said his grandmother didn't do any such thing and his hair was born curly. And then he laid down on the bank and stuck his head right into the spring to show them. Oh, it wasn't the spring we drink out of . . ." seeing a horrified look on Marilla's face . . . "it was the little one lower down. But the bank's awful slippy and Paul went right in. I tell you he made a bully splash. Oh, Anne, Anne, I didn't mean to say that . . . it just slipped out before I thought. He made a *splendid* splash. But he looked so funny when he crawled out, all wet and muddy. The girls laughed more'n ever, but Gracie didn't laugh. She looked sorry. Gracie's a nice girl but she's got a snub nose. When I get big enough to have a girl I won't have one with a snub nose . . . I'll pick one with a pretty nose like yours, Anne."

"A boy who makes such a mess of syrup all over his face when he is eating his pudding will never get a girl to look at him," said Marilla severely.

"But I'll wash my face before I go courting," protested Davy, trying to improve matters by rubbing the back of his hand over the smears. "And I'll wash behind my ears too, without being told. I remembered to this morning, Marilla. I don't forget half as often as I did. But . . ." and Davy sighed . . . "there's so many corners about a fellow that it's awful hard to remember them all. Well, if I can't go to Miss Lavendar's I'll go over and see Mrs. Harrison. Mrs. Harrison's an awful nice woman, I tell you. She keeps a jar of cookies in her pantry a-purpose for little boys, and she always gives me the scrapings out of a pan she's mixed up a plum cake in. A good many plums stick to the sides, you see. Mr. Harrison was always a nice man, but he's twice as nice since he got married over again. I guess getting married makes folks nicer. Why don't *you* get married, Marilla? I want to know."

Marilla's state of single blessedness had never been a sore point with her, so she answered amiably, with an exchange of significant looks with Anne, that she supposed it was because nobody would have her.

"But maybe you never asked anybody to have you," protested Davy.

"Oh, Davy," said Dora primly, shocked into speaking without being spoken to, "it's the *men* that have to do the asking."

"I don't know why they have to do it *always*," grumbled Davy. "Seems to me everything's put on the men in this world. Can I have some more pudding, Marilla?"

"You've had as much as was good for you," said Marilla; but she gave him a moderate second helping.

"I wish people could live on pudding. Why can't they, Marilla? I want to know."

"Because they'd soon get tired of it."

"I'd like to try that for myself," said skeptical Davy. "But I guess it's better to have pudding only on fish and company days than none at all. They never have any at Milty Boulter's. Milty says when company comes his mother gives them cheese and cuts it herself . . . one little bit apiece and one over for manners."

"If Milty Boulter talks like that about his mother at least you needn't repeat it," said Marilla severely.

"Bless my soul," . . . Davy had picked this expression up from Mr. Harrison and used it with great gusto . . . "Milty meant it as a compelment. He's awful proud of his mother 'cause folks say she could scratch a living on a rock."

"I . . . I suppose them pesky hens are in my pansy bed again," said Marilla, rising and going out hurriedly.

The slandered hens were nowhere near the pansy bed and Marilla did not even glance at it. Instead, she sat down on the cellar hatch and laughed until she was ashamed of herself.

When Anne and Paul reached the stone house that afternoon they found Miss Lavendar and Charlotta the Fourth in the garden, weeding, raking, clipping, and trimming as if for dear life. Miss Lavendar herself, all gay and sweet in the frills and laces she loved, dropped her shears and ran joyously to meet her guests, while Charlotta the Fourth grinned cheerfully.

"Welcome, Anne. I thought you'd come today. You belong to the afternoon so it brought you. Things that belong together are sure to come together. What a lot of trouble that would save some people if they only knew it. But they don't . . . and so they waste beautiful energy moving heaven and earth to bring things together that *don't* belong. And you, Paul . . . why, you've grown! You're half a head taller than when you were here before."

"Yes, I've begun to grow like pigweed in the night, as Mrs. Lynde says," said Paul, in frank delight over the fact. "Grandma says it's the porridge taking effect at last. Perhaps it is. Goodness knows . . ." Paul sighed deeply . . . "I've eaten enough to make anyone grow. I do hope, now that I've begun, I'll keep on till I'm as tall as father. He is six feet, you know, Miss Lavendar."

Yes, Miss Lavendar did know; the flush on her pretty cheeks deepened a little; she took Paul's hand on one side and Anne's on the other and walked to the house in silence.

"Is it a good day for the echoes, Miss Lavendar?" queried Paul anxiously. The day of his first visit had been too windy for echoes and Paul had been much disappointed.

"Yes, just the best kind of a day," answered Miss Lavendar, rousing herself from her reverie. "But first we are all going in to have something to eat. I know you two folks didn't walk all the way back here through those beechwoods without getting hungry, and Charlotta the Fourth and I can eat any hour of the day . . . we have such obliging appetites. So we'll just make a raid on the pantry. Fortunately it's lovely and full. I had a presentiment that I was going to have company today and Charlotta the Fourth and I prepared."

"I think you are one of the people who always have nice things in their pantry," declared Paul. "Grandma's like that too. But she doesn't approve of snacks between meals. I wonder," he added meditatively, "if I *ought* to eat them away from home when I know she doesn't approve."

"Oh, I don't think she would disapprove after you have had a long walk. That makes a difference," said Miss Lavendar, exchanging amused glances with Anne over Paul's brown curls. "I suppose that snacks *are* extremely unwholesome. That is why we have them so often at Echo Lodge. We . . . Charlotta the Fourth and I . . . live in defiance of every known law of diet. We eat all sorts of indigestible things whenever we happen to think of it, by day or night; and we flourish like green bay trees. We are always intending to reform. When we read any article in a paper warning us against something we like we cut it out and pin it up on the kitchen wall so that we'll remember it. But we never can somehow . . . until after we've gone and eaten that very thing. Nothing has ever killed us yet; but Charlotta the Fourth has been known to have bad dreams after we had eaten doughnuts and mince pie and fruit cake before we went to bed."

"Grandma lets me have a glass of milk and a slice of bread and butter before I go to bed; and on Sunday nights she puts jam on the bread," said Paul. "So I'm always glad when it's Sunday night . . . for more reasons than one. Sunday is a very long day on the shore road. Grandma says it's all too short for her and that father never found Sundays tiresome when he was a little boy. It wouldn't seem so long if I could talk to my rock people but I never do that because Grandma doesn't approve of it on Sundays. I think a good deal; but I'm afraid my thoughts are worldly. Grandma says we should never think anything but religious thoughts on Sundays. But teacher here said once that every really beautiful thought was religious, no matter what it was about, or what day we thought it on. But I feel sure Grandma thinks that sermons and Sunday School lessons are the only things you can think truly religious thoughts about. And when it comes to a difference of opinion between Grandma and teacher I don't know what to do. In my heart" . . . Paul laid his hand on his breast and raised very serious blue eyes to Miss Lavendar's immediately sympathetic face . . . "I agree with teacher. But then, you see, Grandma has brought father up *her* way and made a brilliant success of him; and teacher has never brought anybody up yet, though she's helping with Davy and Dora. But you can't tell how they'll turn out till they *are* grown up. So sometimes I feel as if it might be safer to go by Grandma's opinions."

"I think it would," agreed Anne solemnly. "Anyway, I daresay that if your Grandma and I both got down to what we really do mean, under our different ways of expressing it, we'd find out we both meant the same thing. You'd better go by her way of expressing it, since it's been the result of experience. We'll have to wait until we see how the twins do turn out before we can be sure that my way is equally good."

After lunch they went back to the garden, where Paul made the acquaintance of the echoes, to his wonder and delight, while Anne and Miss Lavendar sat on the stone bench under the poplar and talked.

"So you are going away in the fall?" said Miss Lavendar wistfully. "I ought to be glad for your sake, Anne . . . but I'm horribly, selfishly sorry. I shall miss you so much. Oh, sometimes I think it is of no use to make friends. They only go out of your life after awhile and leave a hurt that is worse than the emptiness before they came."

"That sounds like something Miss Eliza Andrews might say but never Miss Lavendar," said Anne. "*Nothing* is worse than emptiness . . . and I'm not going out of your life. There are such things as letters and vacations. Dearest, I'm afraid you're looking a little pale and tired."

"Oh . . . hoo . . . hoo . . . hoo," went Paul on the dyke, where he had been making noises diligently . . . not all of them melodious in the making, but all coming back transmuted into the very gold and silver of sound by the fairy alchemists over the river. Miss Lavendar made an impatient movement with her pretty hands.

"I'm just tired of everything . . . even of the echoes. There is nothing in my life but echoes . . . echoes of lost hopes and dreams and joys. They're beautiful and mocking. Oh Anne, it's horrid of me to talk like this when I have company. It's just that I'm getting old and it doesn't agree with me. I know I'll be fearfully cranky by the time I'm sixty. But perhaps all I need is a course of blue pills."

At this moment Charlotta the Fourth, who had disappeared after lunch, returned, and announced that the northeast corner of Mr. John Kimball's pasture was red with early strawberries, and wouldn't Miss Shirley like to go and pick some.

"Early strawberries for tea!" exclaimed Miss Lavendar. "Oh, I'm not so old as I thought . . . and I don't need a single blue pill! Girls, when you come back with your strawberries we'll have tea out here under the silver poplar. I'll have it all ready for you with home-grown cream."

Anne and Charlotta the Fourth accordingly betook themselves back to Mr. Kimball's pasture, a green remote place where the air was as soft as velvet and fragrant as a bed of violets and golden as amber.

"Oh, isn't it sweet and fresh back here?" breathed Anne. "I just feel as if I were drinking in the sunshine."

"Yes, ma'am, so do I. That's just exactly how I feel too, ma'am," agreed Charlotta the Fourth, who would have said precisely the same thing if Anne had remarked that she felt like a pelican of the wilderness. Always after Anne had visited Echo Lodge Charlotta the Fourth mounted to her little room over the kitchen and tried before her looking glass to speak and look and move like Anne. Charlotta could never flatter herself that she quite succeeded; but practice makes perfect, as Charlotta had learned at school, and she fondly hoped that in time she might catch the trick of that dainty uplift of chin, that quick, starry outflashing of eyes, that fashion of walking as if you were a bough swaying in the wind. It seemed so easy when you watched Anne. Charlotta the Fourth admired Anne wholeheartedly. It was not that she thought her so very handsome. Diana Barry's beauty of crimson cheek and black curls was much more to Charlotta the Fourth's taste than Anne's moonshine charm of luminous gray eyes and the pale, everchanging roses of her cheeks.

"But I'd rather look like you than be pretty," she told Anne sincerely.

Anne laughed, sipped the honey from the tribute, and cast away the sting. She was used to taking her compliments mixed. Public opinion never agreed on Anne's looks. People who had heard her called handsome met her and were disappointed. People who had heard her called plain saw her and wondered where other people's eyes were. Anne herself would never believe that she had any claim to beauty. When she looked in the glass all she saw was a little pale face with seven freckles on the nose thereof. Her mirror never revealed to her the elusive, ever-varying play of feeling that came and went over her features like a rosy illuminating flame, or the charm of dream and laughter alternating in her big eyes.

While Anne was not beautiful in any strictly defined sense of the word she possessed a certain evasive charm and distinction of appearance that left beholders with a pleasurable sense of satisfaction in that softly rounded girlhood of hers, with all its strongly felt potentialities. Those who knew Anne best felt, without realizing that they felt it, that

her greatest attraction was the aura of possibility surrounding her . . .
the power of future development that was in her. She seemed to walk
in an atmosphere of things about to happen.

As they picked, Charlotta the Fourth confided to Anne her fears
regarding Miss Lavendar. The warm-hearted little handmaiden was
honestly worried over her adored mistress' condition.

"Miss Lavendar isn't well, Miss Shirley, ma'am. I'm sure she isn't,
though she never complains. She hasn't seemed like herself this long
while, ma'am . . . not since that day you and Paul were here together
before. I feel sure she caught cold that night, ma'am. After you and him
had gone she went out and walked in the garden for long after dark with
nothing but a little shawl on her. There was a lot of snow on the walks
and I feel sure she got a chill, ma'am. Ever since then I've noticed her
acting tired and lonesome like. She don't seem to take an interest in anything, ma'am. She never pretends company's coming, nor fixes up for it,
nor nothing, ma'am. It's only when you come she seems to chirk up a bit.
And the worst sign of all, Miss Shirley, ma'am . . ." Charlotta the Fourth
lowered her voice as if she were about to tell some exceedingly weird and
awful symptom indeed . . . "is that she never gets cross now when I
breaks things. Why, Miss Shirley, ma'am, yesterday I bruk her green and
yaller bowl that's always stood on the bookcase. Her grandmother
brought it out from England and Miss Lavendar was awful choice of it.
I was dusting it just as careful, Miss Shirley, ma'am, and it slipped out,
so fashion, afore I could grab holt of it, and bruk into about forty mil-
lyun pieces. I tell you I was sorry and scared. I thought Miss Lavendar
would scold me awful, ma'am; and I'd ruther she had than take it the way
she did. She just come in and hardly looked at it and said, 'It's no matter, Charlotta. Take up the pieces and throw them away.' Just like that,
Miss Shirley, ma'am . . . 'take up the pieces and throw them away,' as if
it wasn't her grandmother's bowl from England. Oh, she isn't well and
I feel awful bad about it. She's got nobody to look after her but me."

Charlotta the Fourth's eyes brimmed up with tears. Anne patted
the little brown paw holding the cracked pink cup sympathetically.

"I think Miss Lavendar needs a change, Charlotta. She stays here
alone too much. Can't we induce her to go away for a little trip?"

Charlotta shook her head, with its rampant bows, disconsolately.

"I don't think so, Miss Shirley, ma'am. Miss Lavendar hates visiting. She's only got three relations she ever visits and she says she just goes to see them as a family duty. Last time when she come home she said she wasn't going to visit for family duty no more. 'I've come home in love with loneliness, Charlotta,' she says to me, 'and I never want to stray from my own vine and fig tree again. My relations try so hard to make an old lady of me and it has a bad effect on me.' Just like that, Miss Shirley, ma'am. 'It has a very bad effect on me.' So I don't think it would do any good to coax her to go visiting."

"We must see what can be done," said Anne decidedly, as she put the last possible berry in her pink cup. "Just as soon as I have my vacation I'll come through and spend a whole week with you. We'll have a picnic every day and pretend all sorts of interesting things, and see if we can't cheer Miss Lavendar up."

"That will be the very thing, Miss Shirley, ma'am," exclaimed Charlotta the Fourth in rapture. She was glad for Miss Lavendar's sake and for her own too. With a whole week in which to study Anne constantly she would surely be able to learn how to move and behave like her.

When the girls got back to Echo Lodge they found that Miss Lavendar and Paul had carried the little square table out of the kitchen to the garden and had everything ready for tea. Nothing ever tasted so delicious as those strawberries and cream, eaten under a great blue sky all curdled over with fluffy little white clouds, and in the long shadows of the wood with its lispings and its murmurings. After tea Anne helped Charlotta wash the dishes in the kitchen, while Miss Lavendar sat on the stone bench with Paul and heard all about his rock people. She was a good listener, this sweet Miss Lavendar, but just at the last it struck Paul that she had suddenly lost interest in the Twin Sailors.

"Miss Lavendar, why do you look at me like that?" he asked gravely.

"How do I look, Paul?"

"Just as if you were looking through me at somebody I put you in mind of," said Paul, who had such occasional flashes of uncanny insight that it wasn't quite safe to have secrets when he was about.

"You do put me in mind of somebody I knew long ago," said Miss Lavendar dreamily.

"When you were young?"

"Yes, when I was young. Do I seem very old to you, Paul?"

"Do you know, I can't make up my mind about that," said Paul confidentially. "Your hair looks old . . . I never knew a young person with white hair. But your eyes are as young as my beautiful teacher's when you laugh. I tell you what, Miss Lavendar" . . . Paul's voice and face were as solemn as a judge's . . . "I think you would make a splendid mother. You have just the right look in your eyes . . . the look my little mother always had. I think it's a pity you haven't any boys of your own."

"I have a little dream boy, Paul."

"Oh, have you really? How old is he?"

"About your age I think. He ought to be older because I dreamed him long before you were born. But I'll never let him get any older than eleven or twelve; because if I did some day he might grow up altogether and then I'd lose him."

"I know," nodded Paul. "That's the beauty of dream people . . . they stay any age you want them. You and my beautiful teacher and me myself are the only folks in the world that I know of that have dream people. Isn't it funny and nice we should all know each other? But I guess that kind of people always find each other out. Grandma never has dream people and Mary Joe thinks I'm wrong in the upper story because I have them. But I think it's splendid to have them. *You* know, Miss Lavendar. Tell me all about your little dream boy."

"He has blue eyes and curly hair. He steals in and wakens me with a kiss every morning. Then all day he plays here in the garden . . . and I play with him. Such games as we have. We run races and talk with the echoes; and I tell him stories. And when twilight comes . . ."

"*I* know," interrupted Paul eagerly. "He comes and sits beside you . . . *so* . . . because of course at twelve he'd be too big to climb into your lap . . . and lays his head on your shoulder . . . *so* . . . and you put your arms about him and hold him tight, tight, and rest your cheek on his head . . . yes, that's the very way. Oh, you *do* know, Miss Lavendar."

Anne found the two of them there when she came out of the stone house, and something in Miss Lavendar's face made her hate to disturb them.

"I'm afraid we must go, Paul, if we want to get home before dark. Miss Lavendar, I'm going to invite myself to Echo Lodge for a whole week pretty soon."

"If you come for a week I'll keep you for two," threatened Miss Lavendar.

28

The Prince Comes Back to the Enchanted Palace

he last day of school came and went. A triumphant "semi-annual examination" was held and Anne's pupils acquitted themselves splendidly. At the close they gave her an address and a writing desk. All the girls and ladies present cried, and some of the boys had it cast up to them later on that they cried too, although they always denied it.

Mrs. Harmon Andrews, Mrs. Peter Sloane, and Mrs. William Bell walked home together and talked things over.

"I do think it is such a pity Anne is leaving when the children seem so much attached to her," sighed Mrs. Peter Sloane, who had a habit of sighing over everything and even finished off her jokes that way. "To be sure," she added hastily, "we all know we'll have a good teacher next year too."

"Jane will do her duty, I've no doubt," said Mrs. Andrews rather stiffly. "I don't suppose she'll tell the children quite so many fairy tales or spend so much time roaming about the woods with them. But she has her name on the Inspector's Roll of Honor and the Newbridge people are in a terrible state over her leaving."

"I'm real glad Anne is going to college," said Mrs. Bell. "She has always wanted it and it will be a splendid thing for her."

"Well, I don't know." Mrs. Andrews was determined not to agree fully with anybody that day. "I don't see that Anne needs any more education. She'll probably be marrying Gilbert Blythe, if his infatuation for her lasts till he gets through college, and what good will Latin and Greek do her then? If they taught you at college how to manage a man there might be some sense in her going."

Mrs. Harmon Andrews, so Avonlea gossip whispered, had never

learned how to manage her "man," and as a result the Andrews household was not exactly a model of domestic happiness.

"I see that the Charlottetown call to Mr. Allan is up before the Presbytery," said Mrs. Bell. "That means we'll be losing him soon, I suppose."

"They're not going before September," said Mrs. Sloane. "It will be a great loss to the community . . . though I always did think that Mrs. Allan dressed rather too gay for a minister's wife. But we are none of us perfect. Did you notice how neat and snug Mr. Harrison looked today? I never saw such a changed man. He goes to church every Sunday and has subscribed to the salary."

"Hasn't that Paul Irving grown to be a big boy?" said Mrs. Andrews. "He was such a mite for his age when he came here. I declare I hardly knew him today. He's getting to look a lot like his father."

"He's a very smart boy," said Mrs. Bell.

"He's smart enough, but" . . . Mrs. Andrews lowered her voice . . . "I believe he tells queer stories. Gracie came home from school one day last week with the greatest rigmarole he had told her about people who lived down at the shore . . . stories there couldn't be a word of truth in, you know. I told Gracie not to believe them, and she said Paul didn't intend her to. But if he didn't what did he tell them to her for?"

"Anne says Paul is a genius," said Mrs. Sloane.

"He may be. You never know what to expect of them Americans," said Mrs. Andrews. Mrs. Andrews' only acquaintance with the word "genius" was derived from the colloquial fashion of calling any eccentric individual "a queer genius." She probably thought, with Mary Joe, that it meant a person with something wrong in his upper story.

Back in the schoolroom Anne was sitting alone at her desk, as she had sat on the first day of school two years before, her face leaning on her hand, her dewy eyes looking wistfully out of the window to the Lake of Shining Waters. Her heart was so wrung over the parting with her pupils that for the moment college had lost all its charm. She still felt the clasp of Annetta Bell's arms about her neck and heard the childish wail, "I'll *never* love any teacher as much as you, Miss Shirley, never, never."

For two years she had worked earnestly and faithfully, making many mistakes and learning from them. She had had her reward. She had taught her scholars something, but she felt that they had taught her much more . . . lessons of tenderness, self-control, innocent wisdom, lore of childish hearts. Perhaps she had not succeeded in "inspiring" any wonderful ambitions in her pupils, but she had taught them, more by her own sweet personality than by all her careful precepts, that it was good and necessary in the years that were before them to live their lives finely and graciously, holding fast to truth and courtesy and kindness, keeping aloof from all that savored of falsehood and meanness and vulgarity. They were, perhaps, all unconscious of having learned such lessons; but they would remember and practice them long after they had forgotten the capital of Afghanistan and the dates of the Wars of the Roses.

"Another chapter in my life is closed," said Anne aloud, as she locked her desk. She really felt very sad over it; but the romance in the idea of that "closed chapter" did comfort her a little.

Anne spent a fortnight at Echo Lodge early in her vacation and everybody concerned had a good time.

She took Miss Lavendar on a shopping expedition to town and persuaded her to buy a new organdy dress; then came the excitement of cutting and making it together, while the happy Charlotta the Fourth basted and swept up clippings. Miss Lavendar had complained that she could not feel much interest in anything; but the sparkle came back to her eyes over her pretty dress.

"What a foolish, frivolous person I must be," she sighed. "I'm wholesomely ashamed to think that a new dress . . . even if it is a forget-me-not organdy . . . should exhilarate me so, when a good conscience and an extra contribution to Foreign Missions couldn't do it."

Midway in her visit Anne went home to Green Gables for a day to mend the twins' stockings and settle up Davy's accumulated store of questions. In the evening she went down to the shore road to see Paul Irving. As she passed by the low, square window of the Irving sitting room she caught a glimpse of Paul on somebody's lap; but the next moment he came flying through the hall.

"Oh, Miss Shirley," he cried excitedly, "you can't think what has happened! Something so splendid. Father is here . . . just think of that! Father is here! Come right in. Father, this is my beautiful teacher. You know, father."

Stephen Irving came forward to meet Anne with a smile. He was a tall, handsome man of middle age, with iron-gray hair, deep-set, dark blue eyes, and a strong, sad face, splendidly modeled about chin and brow. Just the face for a hero of romance, Anne thought with a thrill of intense satisfaction. It was so disappointing to meet someone who ought to be a hero and find him bald or stooped, or otherwise lacking in manly beauty. Anne would have thought it dreadful if the object of Miss Lavendar's romance had not looked the part.

"So this is my little son's 'beautiful teacher,' of whom I have heard so much," said Mr. Irving with a hearty handshake. "Paul's letters have been so full of you, Miss Shirley, that I feel as if I were pretty well acquainted with you already. I want to thank you for what you have done for Paul. I think that your influence has been just what he needed. Mother is one of the best and dearest of women; but her robust, matter-of-fact Scotch common sense could not always understand a temperament like my laddie's. What was lacking in her you have supplied. Between you, I think Paul's training in these two past years has been as nearly ideal as a motherless boy's could be."

Everybody likes to be appreciated. Under Mr. Irving's praise Anne's face "burst flower-like into rosy bloom," and the busy, weary man of the world, looking at her, thought he had never seen a fairer, sweeter slip of girlhood than this little "down east" schoolteacher with her red hair and wonderful eyes.

Paul sat between them blissfully happy.

"I never dreamed father was coming," he said radiantly. "Even Grandma didn't know it. It was a great surprise. As a general thing . . ." Paul shook his brown curls gravely . . . "I don't like to be surprised. You lose all the fun of expecting things when you're surprised. But in a case like this it is all right. Father came last night after I had gone to bed. And after Grandma and Mary Joe had stopped being surprised he and Grandma came upstairs to look at me, not meaning to wake me up till morning. But I woke right up and saw father. I tell you I just sprang at him."

"With a hug like a bear's," said Mr. Irving, putting his arm around Paul's shoulder smilingly. "I hardly knew my boy, he had grown so big and brown and sturdy."

"I don't know which was the most pleased to see father, Grandma or I," continued Paul. "Grandma's been in kitchen all day making the things father likes to eat. She wouldn't trust them to Mary Joe, she says. That's *her* way of showing gladness. *I* like best just to sit and talk to father. But I'm going to leave you for a little while now if you'll excuse me. I must get the cows for Mary Joe. That is one of my daily duties."

When Paul had scampered away to do his "daily duty" Mr. Irving talked to Anne of various matters. But Anne felt that he was thinking of something else underneath all the time. Presently it came to the surface.

"In Paul's last letter he spoke of going with you to visit an old . . . friend of mine . . . Miss Lewis at the stone house in Grafton. Do you know her well?"

"Yes, indeed, she is a *very* dear friend of mine," was Anne's demure reply, which gave no hint of the sudden thrill that tingled over her from head to foot at Mr. Irving's question. Anne "felt instinctively" that romance was peeping at her around a corner.

Mr. Irving rose and went to the window, looking out on a great, golden, billowing sea where a wild wind was harping. For a few moments there was silence in the little, dark-walled room. Then he turned and looked down into Anne's sympathetic face with a smile, half-whimsical, half-tender.

"I wonder how much you know," he said.

"I know all about it," replied Anne promptly. "You see," she explained hastily, "Miss Lavendar and I are very intimate. She wouldn't tell things of such a sacred nature to everybody. We are kindred spirits."

"Yes, I believe you are. Well, I am going to ask a favor of you. I would like to go and see Miss Lavendar if she will let me. Will you ask her if I may come?"

Would she not? Oh, indeed she would! Yes, this was romance, the very, the real thing, with all the charm of rhyme and story and dream.

It was a little belated, perhaps, like a rose blooming in October which should have bloomed in June; but none the less a rose, all sweetness and fragrance, with the gleam of gold in its heart. Never did Anne's feet bear her on a more willing errand than on that walk through the beech-woods to Grafton the next morning. She found Miss Lavendar in the garden. Anne was fearfully excited. Her hands grew cold and her voice trembled.

"Miss Lavendar, I have something to tell you . . . something very important. Can you guess what it is?"

Anne never supposed that Miss Lavendar *could* guess; but Miss Lavendar's face grew very pale and Miss Lavendar said in a quiet, still voice, from which all the color and sparkle that Miss Lavendar's voice usually suggested had faded,

"Stephen Irving is home?"

"How did you know? Who told you?" cried Anne disappointedly, vexed that her great revelation had been anticipated.

"Nobody. I knew that must be it, just from the way you spoke."

"He wants to come and see you," said Anne. "May I send him word that he may?"

"Yes, of course," fluttered Miss Lavendar. "There is no reason why he shouldn't. He is only coming as any old friend might."

Anne had her own opinion about that as she hastened into the house to write a note at Miss Lavendar's desk.

"Oh, it's delightful to be living in a storybook," she thought gaily. "It will come out all right of course . . . it must . . . and Paul will have a mother after his own heart and everybody will be happy. But Mr. Irving will take Miss Lavendar away . . . and dear knows what will happen to the little stone house . . . and so there are two sides to it, as there seems to be to everything in this world."

The important note was written and Anne herself carried it to the Grafton post office, where she waylaid the mail carrier and asked him to leave it at the Avonlea office.

"It's so very important," Anne assured him anxiously. The mail carrier was a rather grumpy old personage who did not at all look the part of a messenger of Cupid; and Anne was none too certain that his memory was to be trusted. But he said he would do his best to remember and she had to be contented with that.

Charlotta the Fourth felt that some mystery pervaded the stone house that afternoon . . . a mystery from which she was excluded. Miss Lavendar roamed about the garden in a distracted fashion. Anne, too, seemed possessed by a demon of unrest, and walked to and fro and went up and down. Charlotta the Fourth endured it till patience ceased to be a virtue; then she confronted Anne on the occasion of that romantic young person's third aimless peregrination through the kitchen.

"Please, Miss Shirley, ma'am," said Charlotta the Fourth, with an indignant toss of her very blue bows, "it's plain to be seen you and Miss Lavendar have got a secret and I think, begging your pardon if I'm too forward, Miss Shirley, ma'am, that it's real mean not to tell me when we've all been such chums."

"Oh, Charlotta dear, I'd have told you all about it if it were my secret . . . but it's Miss Lavendar's, you see. However, I'll tell you this much . . . and if nothing comes of it you must never breathe a word about it to a living soul. You see, Prince Charming is coming tonight. He came long ago, but in a foolish moment went away and wandered afar and forgot the secret of the magic pathway to the enchanted castle, where the princess was weeping her faithful heart out for him. But at last he remembered it again and the princess is waiting still . . . because nobody but her own dear prince could carry her off."

"Oh, Miss Shirley, ma'am, what is that in prose?" gasped the mystified Charlotta.

Anne laughed.

"In prose, an old friend of Miss Lavendar's is coming to see her tonight."

"Do you mean an old beau of hers?" demanded the literal Charlotta.

"That is probably what I do mean . . . in prose," answered Anne gravely. "It is Paul's father . . . Stephen Irving. And goodness knows what will come of it, but let us hope for the best, Charlotta."

"I hope that he'll marry Miss Lavendar," was Charlotta's unequivocal response. "Some women's intended from the start to be old maids, and I'm afraid I'm one of them, Miss Shirley, ma'am, because I've awful little patience with the men. But Miss Lavendar never was. And I've been awful worried, thinking what on earth she'd do when I got so big I'd *have* to go to Boston. There ain't any more girls in our family and dear knows what she'd do if she got some stranger that might laugh at her pretendings and leave things lying round out of their place and not be willing to be called Charlotta the Fifth. She might get someone who wouldn't be as unlucky as me in breaking dishes but she'd never get anyone who'd love her better."

And the faithful little handmaiden dashed to the oven door with a sniff.

They went through the form of having tea as usual that night at Echo Lodge; but nobody really ate anything. After tea Miss Lavendar went to her room and put on her new forget-me-not organdy, while Anne did her hair for her. Both were dreadfully excited; but Miss Lavendar pretended to be very calm and indifferent.

"I must really mend that rent in the curtain tomorrow," she said anxiously, inspecting it as if it were the only thing of any importance just then. "Those curtains have not worn as well as they should, considering the price I paid. Dear me, Charlotta has forgotten to dust the stair railing *again*. I really *must* speak to her about it."

Anne was sitting on the porch steps when Stephen Irving came down the lane and across the garden.

"This is the one place where time stands still," he said, looking around him with delighted eyes. "There is nothing changed about this house or garden since I was here twenty-five years ago. It makes me feel young again."

"You know time always does stand still in an enchanted palace," said Anne seriously. "It is only when the prince comes that things begin to happen."

Mr. Irving smiled a little sadly into her uplifted face, all astar with its youth and promise.

"Sometimes the prince comes too late," he said. He did not ask Anne to translate her remark into prose. Like all kindred spirits he "understood."

"Oh, no, not if he is the real prince coming to the true princess," said Anne, shaking her red head decidedly, as she opened the parlor door. When he had gone in she shut it tightly behind him and turned to confront Charlotta the Fourth, who was in the hall, all "nods and becks and wreathed smiles."

"Oh, Miss Shirley, ma'am," she breathed, "I peeked from the kitchen window . . . and he's awful handsome . . . and just the right age for Miss Lavendar. And oh, Miss Shirley, ma'am, do you think it would be much harm to listen at the door?"

"It would be dreadful, Charlotta," said Anne firmly, "so just you come away with me out of the reach of temptation."

"I can't do anything, and it's awful to hang round just waiting," sighed Charlotta. "What if he don't propose after all, Miss Shirley, ma'am? You can never be sure of them men. My oldest sister, Charlotta the First, thought she was engaged to one once. But it turned out *he* had a different opinion and she says she'll never trust one of them again. And I heard of another case where a man thought he wanted one girl awful bad when it was really her sister he wanted all the time. When a man don't know his own mind, Miss Shirley, ma'am, how's a poor woman going to be sure of it?"

"We'll go to the kitchen and clean the silver spoons," said Anne. "That's a task which won't require much thinking fortunately . . . for I *couldn't* think tonight. And it will pass the time."

It passed an hour. Then, just as Anne laid down the last shining spoon, they heard the front door shut. Both sought comfort fearfully in each other's eyes.

"Oh, Miss Shirley, ma'am," gasped Charlotta, "if he's going away this early there's nothing into it and never will be."

They flew to the window. Mr. Irving had no intention of going away. He and Miss Lavendar were strolling slowly down the middle path to the stone bench.

"Oh, Miss Shirley, ma'am, he's got his arm around her waist," whispered Charlotta the Fourth delightedly. "He *must* have proposed to her or she'd never allow it."

Anne caught Charlotta the Fourth by her own plump waist and danced her around the kitchen until they were both out of breath.

"Oh, Charlotta," she cried gaily, "I'm neither a prophetess nor the daughter of a prophetess but I'm going to make a prediction. There'll be a wedding in this old stone house before the maple leaves are red. Do you want that translated into prose, Charlotta?"

"No, I can understand that," said Charlotta. "A wedding ain't poetry. Why, Miss Shirley, ma'am, you're crying! What for?"

"Oh, because it's all so beautiful . . . and story bookish . . . and romantic . . . and sad," said Anne, winking the tears out of her eyes. "It's all perfectly lovely . . . but there's a little sadness mixed up in it too, somehow."

"Oh, of course there's a resk in marrying anybody," conceded Charlotta the Fourth, "but, when all's said and done, Miss Shirley, ma'am, there's many a worse thing than a husband."

29

Poetry and Prose

or the next month Anne lived in what, for Avonlea, might be called a whirl of excitement. The preparation of her own modest outfit for Redmond was of secondary importance. Miss Lavendar was getting ready to be married and the stone house was the scene of endless consultations and plannings and discussions, with Charlotta the Fourth hovering on the outskirts of things in agitated delight and wonder. Then the dressmaker came, and there was the rapture and wretchedness of choosing fashions and being fitted. Anne and Diana spent half their time at Echo Lodge and there were nights when Anne could not sleep for wondering whether she had done right in advising Miss Lavendar to select brown rather than navy blue for her traveling dress, and to have her gray silk made princess.

Everybody concerned in Miss Lavendar's story was very happy. Paul Irving rushed to Green Gables to talk the news over with Anne as soon as his father had told him.

"I knew I could trust father to pick me out a nice little second mother," he said proudly. "It's a fine thing to have a father you can depend on, teacher. I just love Miss Lavendar. Grandma is pleased, too. She says she's real glad father didn't pick out an American for his second wife, because, although it turned out all right the first time, such a thing wouldn't be likely to happen twice. Mrs. Lynde says she thoroughly approves of the match and thinks it's likely Miss Lavendar will give up her queer notions and be like other people, now that she's going to be married. But I hope she won't give her queer notions up, teacher, because I like them. And I don't want her to be like other people. There are too many other people around as it is. *You* know, teacher."

Charlotta the Fourth was another radiant person.

"Oh, Miss Shirley, ma'am, it has all turned out so beautiful. When Mr. Irving and Miss Lavendar come back from their tower I'm to go up to Boston and live with them . . . and me only fifteen, and the other girls never went till they were sixteen. Ain't Mr. Irving splendid? He just worships the ground she treads on and it makes me feel so queer sometimes to see the look in his eyes when he's watching her. It beggars description, Miss Shirley, ma'am. I'm awful thankful they're so fond of each other. It's the best way, when all's said and done, though some folks can get along without it. I've got an aunt who has been married three times and she says she married the first time for love and the last two times for strictly business, and was happy with all three except at the times of the funerals. But I think she took a resk, Miss Shirley, ma'am."

"Oh, it's all so romantic," breathed Anne to Marilla that night. "If I hadn't taken the wrong path that day we went to Mr. Kimball's I'd never have known Miss Lavendar; and if I hadn't met her I'd never have taken Paul there . . . and he'd never have written to his father about visiting Miss Lavendar just as Mr. Irving was starting for San Francisco. Mr. Irving says whenever he got that letter he made up his mind to send his partner to San Francisco and come here instead. He hadn't heard anything of Miss Lavendar for fifteen years. Somebody had told him then that she was to be married and he thought she was and never asked anybody anything about her. And now everything has come right. And I had a hand in bringing it about. Perhaps, as Mrs. Lynde says, everything is foreordained and it was bound to happen anyway. But even so, it's nice to think one was an instrument used by predestination. Yes indeed, it's very romantic."

"I can't see that it's so terribly romantic at all," said Marilla rather crisply. Marilla thought Anne was too worked up about it and had plenty to do with getting ready for college without "traipsing" to Echo Lodge two days out of three helping Miss Lavendar. "In the first place two young fools quarrel and turn sulky; then Steve Irving goes to the States and after a spell gets married up there and is perfectly happy from all accounts. Then his wife dies and after a decent interval he thinks he'll come home and see if his first fancy'll have him. Meanwhile, she's been living single, probably because nobody nice enough came along to want her, and they meet and agree to be married after all. Now, where is the romance in all that?"

"Oh, there isn't any, when you put it that way," gasped Anne, rather as if somebody had thrown cold water over her. "I suppose that's how it looks in prose. But it's very different if you look at it through poetry . . . and *I* think it's nicer . . ." Anne recovered herself and her eyes shone and her cheeks flushed . . . "to look at it through poetry."

Marilla glanced at the radiant young face and refrained from further sarcastic comments. Perhaps some realization came to her that after all it was better to have, like Anne, "the vision and the faculty divine" . . . that gift which the world cannot bestow or take away, of looking at life through some transfiguring . . . or revealing? . . . medium, whereby everything seemed apparelled in celestial light, wearing a glory and a freshness not visible to those who, like herself and Charlotta the Fourth, looked at things only through prose.

"When's the wedding to be?" she asked after a pause.

"The last Wednesday in August. They are to be married in the garden under the honeysuckle trellis . . . the very spot where Mr. Irving proposed to her twenty-five years ago. Marilla, that *is* romantic, even in prose. There's to be nobody there except Mrs. Irving and Paul and Gilbert and Diana and I, and Miss Lavendar's cousins. And they will leave on the six o'clock train for a trip to the Pacific coast. When they come back in the fall Paul and Charlotta the Fourth are to go up to Boston to live with them. But Echo Lodge is to be left just as it is . . . only of course they'll sell the hens and cow, and board up the windows . . . and every summer they're coming down to live in it. I'm so glad. It would have hurt me dreadfully next winter at Redmond to think of that dear stone house all stripped and deserted, with empty rooms . . . or far worse still, with other people living in it. But I can think of it now, just as I've always seen it, waiting happily for the summer to bring life and laughter back to it again."

There was more romance in the world than that which had fallen to the share of the middle-aged lovers of the stone house. Anne stumbled suddenly on it one evening when she went over to Orchard Slope by the wood cut and came out into the Barry garden. Diana Barry and Fred Wright were standing together under the big willow. Diana was leaning against the gray trunk, her lashes cast down on very crimson cheeks. One hand was held by Fred, who stood with his face bent toward her, stammering something in low earnest tones. There were no other people in the world except their two selves at that magic moment; so neither of them saw Anne, who, after one dazed glance of comprehension, turned and sped noiselessly back through the spruce wood, never stopping till she gained her own gable room, where she sat breathlessly down by her window and tried to collect her scattered wits.

"Diana and Fred are in love with each other," she gasped. "Oh, it does seem so . . . so . . . so *hopelessly* grown up."

Anne, of late, had not been without her suspicions that Diana was proving false to the melancholy Byronic hero of her early dreams. But as "things seen are mightier than things heard," or suspected, the realization that it was actually so came to her with almost the shock of perfect surprise. This was succeeded by a queer, little lonely feeling . . . as if, somehow, Diana had gone forward into a new world, shutting a gate behind her, leaving Anne on the outside.

"Things are changing so fast it almost frightens me," Anne thought, a little sadly. "And I'm afraid that this can't help making some difference between Diana and me. I'm sure I can't tell her all my secrets after this . . . she might tell Fred. And what *can* she see in Fred? He's very nice and jolly . . . but he's just Fred Wright."

It is always a very puzzling question . . . what can somebody see in somebody else? But how fortunate after all that it is so, for if everybody saw alike . . . well, in that case, as the old Indian said, "Everybody would want my squaw." It was plain that Diana *did* see something in Fred Wright, however Anne's eyes might be holden. Diana came to Green Gables the next evening, a pensive, shy young lady, and told Anne the whole story in the dusky seclusion of the east gable. Both girls cried and kissed and laughed.

"I'm so happy," said Diana, "but it does seem ridiculous to think of me being engaged."

"What is it really like to be engaged?" asked Anne curiously.

"Well, that all depends on who you're engaged to," answered Diana, with that maddening air of superior wisdom always assumed by those who are engaged over those who are not. "It's perfectly lovely to be engaged to Fred . . . but I think it would be simply horrid to be engaged to anyone else."

"There's not much comfort for the rest of us in that, seeing that there is only one Fred," laughed Anne.

"Oh, Anne, you don't understand," said Diana in vexation. "I didn't mean *that* . . . it's so hard to explain. Never mind, you'll understand sometime, when your own turn comes."

"Bless you, dearest of Dianas, I understand now. What is an imagination for if not to enable you to peep at life through other people's eyes?"

"You must be my bridesmaid, you know, Anne. Promise me that . . . wherever you may be when I'm married."

"I'll come from the ends of the earth if necessary," promised Anne solemnly.

"Of course, it won't be for ever so long yet," said Diana, blushing. "Three years at the very least . . . for I'm only eighteen and mother says no daughter of hers shall be married before she's twenty-one. Besides, Fred's father is going to buy the Abraham Fletcher farm for him and he says he's got to have it two thirds paid for before he'll give it to him in his own name. But three years isn't any too much time to get ready for housekeeping, for I haven't a speck of fancy work made yet. But I'm going to begin crocheting doilies tomorrow. Myra Gillis had thirty-seven doilies when she was married and I'm determined I shall have as many as she had."

"I suppose it would be perfectly impossible to keep house with only thirty-six doilies," conceded Anne, with a solemn face but dancing eyes.

Diana looked hurt.

"I didn't think you'd make fun of me, Anne," she said reproachfully.

"Dearest, I wasn't making fun of you," cried Anne repentantly. "I was only teasing you a bit. I think you'll make the sweetest little housekeeper in the world. And I think it's perfectly lovely of you to be planning already for your home o' dreams."

Anne had no sooner uttered the phrase, "home o' dreams," than it captivated her fancy and she immediately began the erection of one of her own. It was, of course, tenanted by an ideal master, dark, proud, and melancholy; but oddly enough, Gilbert Blythe persisted in hanging about too, helping her arrange pictures, lay out gardens, and accomplish sundry other tasks which a proud and melancholy hero evidently considered beneath his dignity. Anne tried to banish Gilbert's image from her castle in Spain but, somehow, he went on being there, so Anne, being in a hurry, gave up the attempt and pursued her aerial architecture with such success that her "home o' dreams" was built and furnished before Diana spoke again.

"I suppose, Anne, you must think it's funny I should like Fred so well when he's so different from the kind of man I've always said I would marry . . . the tall, slender kind? But somehow I wouldn't want Fred to be tall and slender . . . because, don't you see, he wouldn't be Fred then. Of course," added Diana rather dolefully, "we will be a dreadfully pudgy couple. But after all that's better than one of us being short and fat and the other tall and lean, like Morgan Sloane and his wife. Mrs. Lynde says it always makes her think of the long and short of it when she sees them together."

"Well," said Anne to herself that night, as she brushed her hair before her gilt framed mirror, "I am glad Diana is so happy and satisfied. But when my turn comes . . . if it ever does . . . I do hope there'll be something a little more thrilling about it. But then Diana thought so too, once. I've heard her say time and again she'd never get engaged any poky commonplace way . . . he'd *have* to do something splendid to win her. But she has changed. Perhaps I'll change too. But I won't . . . I'm determined I won't. Oh, I think these engagements are dreadfully unsettling things when they happen to your intimate friends."

30

A Wedding at the Stone House

The last week in August came. Miss Lavendar was to be married in it. Two weeks later Anne and Gilbert would leave for Redmond College. In a week's time Mrs. Rachel Lynde would move to Green Gables and set up her lares and penates in the erstwhile spare room, which was already prepared for her coming. She had sold all her superfluous household plenishings by auction and was at present reveling in the congenial occupation of helping the Allans pack up. Mr. Allan was to preach his farewell sermon the next Sunday. The old order was changing rapidly to give place to the new, as Anne felt with a little sadness threading all her excitement and happiness.

"Changes ain't totally pleasant but they're excellent things," said Mr. Harrison philosophically. "Two years is about long enough for things to stay exactly the same. If they stayed put any longer they might grow mossy."

Mr. Harrison was smoking on his veranda. His wife had self-sacrificingly told him that he might smoke in the house if he took care to sit by an open window. Mr. Harrison rewarded this concession by going outdoors altogether to smoke in fine weather, and so mutual goodwill reigned.

Anne had come over to ask Mrs. Harrison for some of her yellow dahlias. She and Diana were going through to Echo Lodge that evening to help Miss Lavendar and Charlotta the Fourth with their final preparations for the morrow's bridal. Miss Lavendar herself never had dahlias; she did not like them and they would not have suited the fine retirement of her old-fashioned garden. But flowers of any kind were rather scarce in Avonlea and the neighboring districts that summer, thanks to Uncle

Abe's storm; and Anne and Diana thought that a certain old cream-colored stone jug, usually kept sacred to doughnuts, brimmed over with yellow dahlias, would be just the thing to set in a dim angle of the stone house stairs, against the dark background of red hall paper.

"I s'pose you'll be starting off for college in a fortnight's time?" continued Mr. Harrison. "Well, we're going to miss you an awful lot, Emily and me. To be sure, Mrs. Lynde'll be over there in your place. There ain't nobody but a substitute can be found for them."

The irony of Mr. Harrison's tone is quite untransferable to paper. In spite of his wife's intimacy with Mrs. Lynde, the best that could be said of the relationship between her and Mr. Harrison, even under the new regime, was that they preserved an armed neutrality.

"Yes, I'm going," said Anne. "I'm very glad with my head . . . and very sorry with my heart."

"I s'pose you'll be scooping up all the honors that are lying round loose at Redmond."

"I may try for one or two of them," confessed Anne, "but I don't care so much for things like that as I did two years ago. What I want to get out of my college course is some knowledge of the best way of living life and doing the most and best with it. I want to learn to understand and help other people and myself."

Mr. Harrison nodded.

"That's the idea exactly. That's what college ought to be for, instead of for turning out a lot of B.A.'s, so chock full of book-learning and vanity that there ain't room for anything else. You're all right. College won't be able to do you much harm, I reckon."

Diana and Anne drove over to Echo Lodge after tea, taking with them all the flowery spoil that several predatory expeditions in their own and their neighbors' gardens had yielded. They found the stone house agog with excitement. Charlotta the Fourth was flying around with such vim and briskness that her blue bows seemed really to possess the power of being everywhere at once. Like the helmet of Navarre, Charlotta's blue bows waved ever in the thickest of the fray.

"Praise be to goodness you've come," she said devoutly, "for there's heaps of things to do . . . and the frosting on that cake *won't* harden . . .

and there's all the silver to be rubbed up yet . . . and the horsehair trunk to be packed . . . and the roosters for the chicken salad are running out there beyant the henhouse yet, *crowing,* Miss Shirley, ma'am. And Miss Lavendar ain't to be trusted to do a thing. I was thankful when Mr. Irving came a few minutes ago and took her off for a walk in the woods. Courting's all right in its place, Miss Shirley, ma'am, but if you try to mix it up with cooking and scouring everything's spoiled. That's *my* opinion, Miss Shirley, ma'am."

Anne and Diana worked so heartily that by ten o'clock even Charlotta the Fourth was satisfied. She braided her hair in innumerable plaits and took her weary little bones off to bed.

"But I'm sure I shan't sleep a blessed wink, Miss Shirley, ma'am, for fear that something'll go wrong at the last minute . . . the cream won't whip . . . or Mr. Irving'll have a stroke and not be able to come."

"He isn't in the habit of having strokes, is he?" asked Diana, the dimpled corners of her mouth twitching. To Diana, Charlotta the Fourth was, if not exactly a thing of beauty, certainly a joy forever.

"They're not things that go by habit," said Charlotta the Fourth with dignity. "They just *happen* . . . and there you are. *Anybody* can have a stroke. You don't have to learn how. Mr. Irving looks a lot like an uncle of mine that had one once just as he was sitting down to dinner one day. But maybe everything'll go all right. In this world you've just got to hope for the best and prepare for the worst and take whatever God sends."

"The only thing I'm worried about is that it won't be fine tomorrow," said Diana. "Uncle Abe predicted rain for the middle of the week, and ever since the big storm I can't help believing there's a good deal in what Uncle Abe says."

Anne, who knew better than Diana just how much Uncle Abe had to do with the storm, was not much disturbed by this. She slept the sleep of the just and weary, and was roused at an unearthly hour by Charlotta the Fourth.

"Oh, Miss Shirley, ma'am, it's awful to call you so early," came wailing through the keyhole, "but there's so much to do yet . . . and oh, Miss Shirley, ma'am, I'm skeered it's going to rain and I wish you'd get up and tell me you think it ain't."

Anne flew to the window, hoping against hope that Charlotta the Fourth was saying this merely by way of rousing her effectually. But alas, the morning did look unpropitious. Below the window Miss Lavendar's garden, which should have been a glory of pale virgin sunshine, lay dim and windless; and the sky over the firs was dark with moody clouds.

"Isn't it too mean!" said Diana.

"We must hope for the best," said Anne determinedly. "If it only doesn't actually rain, a cool, pearly gray day like this would really be nicer than hot sunshine."

"But it will rain," mourned Charlotta, creeping into the room, a figure of fun, with her many braids wound about her head, the ends, tied up with white thread, sticking out in all directions. "It'll hold off till the last minute and then pour cats and dogs. And all the folks will get sopping . . . and track mud all over the house . . . and they won't be able to be married under the honeysuckle . . . and it's awful unlucky for no sun to shine on a bride, say what you will, Miss Shirley, ma'am. I *knew* things were going too well to last."

Charlotta the Fourth seemed certainly to have borrowed a leaf out of Miss Eliza Andrews' book.

It did not rain, though it kept on looking as if it meant to. By noon the rooms were decorated, the table beautifully laid; and upstairs was waiting a bride, "adorned for her husband."

"You do look sweet," said Anne rapturously.

"Lovely," echoed Diana.

"Everything's ready, Miss Shirley, ma'am, and nothing dreadful has happened *yet*," was Charlotta's cheerful statement as she betook herself to her little back room to dress. Out came all the braids; the resultant rampant crinkliness was plaited into two tails and tied, not with two bows alone, but with four, of brand-new ribbon, brightly blue. The two upper bows rather gave the impression of overgrown wings sprouting from Charlotta's neck, somewhat after the fashion of Raphael's cherubs. But Charlotta the Fourth thought them very beautiful, and after she had rustled into a white dress, so stiffly starched that it could stand alone, she surveyed herself in her glass with great satisfaction . . . a satisfaction which lasted until she went out in the hall and caught a glimpse through the spare room door of a tall girl in some softly clinging gown, pinning white, star-like flowers on the smooth ripples of her ruddy hair.

"Oh, I'll *never* be able to look like Miss Shirley," thought poor Charlotta despairingly. "You just have to be born so, I guess . . . don't seem's if any amount of practice could give you that *air*."

By one o'clock the guests had come, including Mr. and Mrs. Allan, for Mr. Allan was to perform the ceremony in the absence of the Grafton minister on his vacation. There was no formality about the marriage. Miss Lavendar came down the stairs to meet her bridegroom at the foot, and as he took her hand she lifted her big brown eyes to his with a look that made Charlotta the Fourth, who intercepted it, feel queerer than ever. They went out to the honeysuckle arbor, where Mr. Allan was awaiting them. The guests grouped themselves as they pleased. Anne and Diana stood by the old stone bench, with Charlotta the Fourth between them, desperately clutching their hands in her cold, tremulous little paws.

Mr. Allan opened his blue book and the ceremony proceeded. Just as Miss Lavendar and Stephen Irving were pronounced man and wife a very beautiful and symbolic thing happened. The sun suddenly burst through the gray and poured a flood of radiance on the happy bride. Instantly the garden was alive with dancing shadows and flickering lights.

"What a lovely omen," thought Anne, as she ran to kiss the bride. Then the three girls left the rest of the guests laughing around the bridal pair while they flew into the house to see that all was in readiness for the feast.

"Thanks be to goodness, it's over, Miss Shirley, ma'am," breathed Charlotta the Fourth, "and they're married safe and sound, no matter what happens now. The bags of rice are in the pantry, ma'am, and the old shoes are behind the door, and the cream for whipping is on the sullar steps."

At half past two Mr. and Mrs. Irving left, and everybody went to Bright River to see them off on the afternoon train. As Miss Lavendar . . . I beg her pardon, Mrs. Irving . . . stepped from the door of her old home Gilbert and the girls threw the rice and Charlotta the Fourth hurled an old shoe with such excellent aim that she struck Mr. Allan squarely on the head. But it was reserved for Paul to give the prettiest send-off. He popped out of the porch ringing furiously a huge old brass dinner bell which had adorned the dining room mantel. Paul's only motive was to make a joyful noise; but as the clangor died away, from point and curve and hill across the river came the chime of "fairy wedding bells," ringing clearly, sweetly, faintly and more faint, as if Miss Lavendar's beloved echoes were bidding her greeting and farewell. And so, amid this benediction of sweet sounds, Miss Lavendar drove away from the old life of dreams and make-believes to a fuller life of realities in the busy world beyond.

Two hours later Anne and Charlotta the Fourth came down the lane again. Gilbert had gone to West Grafton on an errand and Diana had to keep an engagement at home. Anne and Charlotta had come back to put things in order and lock up the little stone house. The garden was a pool of late golden sunshine, with butterflies hovering and bees booming; but the little house had already that indefinable air of desolation which always follows a festivity.

"Oh dear me, don't it look lonesome?" sniffed Charlotta the Fourth, who had been crying all the way home from the station. "A wedding ain't much cheerfuller than a funeral after all, when it's all over, Miss Shirley, ma'am."

A busy evening followed. The decorations had to be removed, the dishes washed, the uneaten delicacies packed into a basket for the delectation of Charlotta the Fourth's young brothers at home. Anne would not rest until everything was in apple-pie order; after Charlotta had gone home with her plunder Anne went over the still rooms, feeling like one who trod alone some banquet hall deserted, and closed the blinds. Then she locked the door and sat down under the silver poplar to wait for Gilbert, feeling very tired but still unweariedly thinking "long, long thoughts."

"What are you thinking of, Anne?" asked Gilbert, coming down the walk. He had left his horse and buggy out at the road.

"Of Miss Lavendar and Mr. Irving," answered Anne dreamily. "Isn't it beautiful to think how everything has turned out . . . how they have come together again after all the years of separation and misunderstanding?"

"Yes, it's beautiful," said Gilbert, looking steadily down into Anne's uplifted face, "but wouldn't it have been more beautiful still, Anne, if there had been *no* separation or misunderstanding . . . if they had come hand in hand all the way through life, with no memories behind them but those which belonged to each other?"

For a moment Anne's heart fluttered queerly and for the first time her eyes faltered under Gilbert's gaze and a rosy flush stained the paleness of her face. It was as if a veil that had hung before her inner consciousness had been lifted, giving to her view a revelation of unsuspected feelings and realities. Perhaps, after all, romance did not come into one's life with pomp and blare, like a gay knight riding down; perhaps it crept to one's side like an old friend through quiet ways; perhaps it revealed itself in seeming prose, until some sudden shaft of illumination flung athwart its pages betrayed the rhythm and the music; perhaps . . . perhaps . . . love unfolded naturally out of a beautiful friendship, as a golden-hearted rose slipping from its green sheath.

Then the veil dropped again; but the Anne who walked up the dark lane was not quite the same Anne who had driven gaily down it the evening before. The page of girlhood had been turned, as by an unseen finger, and the page of womanhood was before her with all its charm and mystery, its pain and gladness.

Gilbert wisely said nothing more; but in his silence he read the history of the next four years in the light of Anne's remembered blush. Four years of earnest, happy work . . . and then the guerdon of a useful knowledge gained and a sweet heart won.

Behind them in the garden the little stone house brooded among the shadows. It was lonely but not forsaken. It had not yet done with dreams and laughter and the joy of life; there were to be future summers for the little stone house; meanwhile, it could wait. And over the river in purple durance the echoes bided their time.

Anne
of the
Island

All precious things discovered late
To those that seek them issue forth,
For Love in sequel works with Fate,
And draws the veil from hidden worth.

TENNYSON

CONTENTS

1

The Shadow of Change

"Harvest is ended and summer is gone," quoted Anne Shirley, gazing across the shorn fields dreamily. She and Diana Barry had been picking apples in the Green Gables orchard, but were now resting from their labors in a sunny corner, where airy fleets of thistledown drifted by on the wings of a wind that was still summer-sweet with the incense of ferns in the Haunted Wood.

But everything in the landscape around them spoke of autumn. The sea was roaring hollowly in the distance, the fields were bare and sere, scarfed with golden rod, the brook valley below Green Gables overflowed with asters of ethereal purple, and the Lake of Shining Waters was blue—blue—blue; not the changeful blue of spring, nor the pale azure of summer, but a clear, steadfast, serene blue, as if the water were past all moods and tenses of emotion and had settled down to a tranquility unbroken by fickle dreams.

"It has been a nice summer," said Diana, twisting the new ring on her left hand with a smile. "And Miss Lavendar's wedding seemed to come as a sort of crown to it. I suppose Mr. and Mrs. Irving are on the Pacific coast now."

"It seems to me they have been gone long enough to go around the world," sighed Anne. "I can't believe it is only a week since they were married. Everything has changed. Miss Lavendar and Mr. and Mrs. Allan gone—how lonely the manse looks with the shutters all closed! I went past it last night, and it made me feel as if everybody in it had died."

"We'll never get another minister as nice as Mr. Allan," said Diana, with gloomy conviction. "I suppose we'll have all kinds of supplies this winter, and half the Sundays no preaching at all. And you and Gilbert gone—it will be awfully dull."

"Fred will be here," insinuated Anne slyly.

"When is Mrs. Lynde going to move up?" asked Diana, as if she had not heard Anne's remark.

"Tomorrow. I'm glad she's coming—but it will be another change. Marilla and I cleared everything out of the spare room yesterday. Do you know, I hated to do it? Of course, it was silly—but it did seem as if we were committing sacrilege. That old spare room has always seemed like a shrine to me. When I was a child I thought it the most wonderful apartment in the world. You remember what a consuming desire I had to sleep in a spare room bed—but not the Green Gables spare room. Oh, no, never there! It would have been too terrible—I couldn't have slept a wink from awe. I never *walked* through that room when Marilla sent me in on an errand—no, indeed, I tiptoed through it and held my breath, as if I were in church, and felt relieved when I got out of it. The pictures of George Whitefield and the Duke of Wellington hung there, one on each side of the mirror, and frowned so sternly at me all the time I was in, especially if I dared peep in the mirror, which was the only one in the house that didn't twist my face a little. I always wondered how Marilla dared houseclean that room. And now it's not only cleaned but stripped bare. George Whitefield and the Duke have been relegated to the upstairs hall. 'So passes the glory of this world,'" concluded Anne, with a laugh in which there was a little note of regret. It is never pleasant to have our old shrines desecrated, even when we have outgrown them.

"I'll be so lonesome when you go," moaned Diana for the hundredth time. "And to think you go next week!"

"But we're together still," said Anne cheerily. "We mustn't let next week rob us of this week's joy. I hate the thought of going myself—home and I are such good friends. Talk of being lonesome! It's I who should groan. *You'll* be here with any number of your old friends—*and* Fred! While I shall be alone among strangers, not knowing a soul!"

"*Except* Gilbert—*and* Charlie Sloane," said Diana, imitating Anne's italics and slyness.

"Charlie Sloane will be a great comfort, of course," agreed Anne sarcastically; whereupon both those irresponsible damsels laughed. Diana knew exactly what Anne thought of Charlie Sloane; but, despite sundry confidential talks, she did *not* know just what Anne thought of Gilbert Blythe. To be sure, Anne herself did not know that.

"The boys may be boarding at the other end of Kingsport, for all I know," Anne went on. "I am glad I'm going to Redmond, and I am sure I shall like it after a while. But for the first few weeks I know I won't. I shan't even have the comfort of looking forward to the weekend visit home, as I had when I went to Queen's. Christmas will seem like a thousand years away."

"Everything is changing—or going to change," said Diana sadly. "I have a feeling that things will never be the same again, Anne."

"We have come to a parting of the ways, I suppose," said Anne thoughtfully. "We had to come to it. Do you think, Diana, that being grown-up is really as nice as we used to imagine it would be when we were children?"

"I don't know—there are *some* nice things about it," answered Diana, again caressing her ring with that little smile which always had the effect of making Anne feel suddenly left out and inexperienced. "But there are so many puzzling things, too. Sometimes I feel as if being grown-up just frightened me—and then I would give anything to be a little girl again."

"I suppose we'll get used to being grown-up in time," said Anne cheerfully. "There won't be so many unexpected things about it by and by—though, after all, I fancy it's the unexpected things that give spice to life. We're eighteen, Diana. In two more years we'll be twenty. When I was ten I thought twenty was a green old age. In no time you'll be a staid, middle-aged matron, and I shall be nice, old maid Aunt Anne, coming to visit you in vacations. You'll always keep a corner for me, won't you, Di darling? Not the spare room, of course—old maids can't aspire to spare rooms, and I shall be as 'umble as *Uriah Heep*, and quite content with a little over-the-porch or off-the-parlor cubby hole."

"What nonsense you do talk, Anne," laughed Diana. "You'll marry somebody splendid and handsome and rich—and no spare room in

Avonlea will be half gorgeous enough for you—and you'll turn up your nose at all the friends of your youth."

"That would be a pity; my nose is quite nice, but I fear turning it up would spoil it," said Anne, patting that shapely organ. "I haven't so many good features that I could afford to spoil those I have; so, even if I should marry the King of the Cannibal Islands, I promise you I won't turn up my nose at *you*, Diana."

With another gay laugh the girls separated, Diana to return to Orchard Slope, Anne to walk to the Post Office. She found a letter awaiting her there, and when Gilbert Blythe overtook her on the bridge over the Lake of Shining Waters she was sparkling with the excitement of it.

"Priscilla Grant is going to Redmond, too," she exclaimed. "Isn't that splendid? I hoped she would, but she didn't think her father would consent. He has, however, and we're to board together. I feel that I can face an army with banners—or all the professors of Redmond in one fell phalanx—with a chum like Priscilla by my side."

"I think we'll like Kingsport," said Gilbert. "It's a nice old burg, they tell me, and has the finest natural park in the world. I've heard that the scenery in it is magnificent."

"I wonder if it will be—can be—any more beautiful than this," murmured Anne, looking around her with the loving, enraptured eyes of those to whom "home" must always be the loveliest spot in the world, no matter what fairer lands may lie under alien stars.

They were leaning on the bridge of the old pond, drinking deep of the enchantment of the dusk, just at the spot where Anne had climbed from her sinking Dory on the day Elaine floated down to Camelot. The fine, empurpling dye of sunset still stained the western skies, but the moon was rising and the water lay like a great, silver dream in her light. Remembrance wove a sweet and subtle spell over the two young creatures.

"You are very quiet, Anne," said Gilbert at last.

"I'm afraid to speak or move for fear all this wonderful beauty will vanish just like a broken silence," breathed Anne.

Gilbert suddenly laid his hand over the slender white one lying on the rail of the bridge. His hazel eyes deepened into darkness, his still boyish lips opened to say something of the dream and hope that thrilled his soul. But Anne snatched her hand away and turned quickly. The spell of the dusk was broken for her.

"I must go home," she exclaimed, with a rather overdone carelessness. "Marilla had a headache this afternoon, and I'm sure the twins will be in some dreadful mischief by this time. I really shouldn't have stayed away so long."

She chattered ceaselessly and inconsequently until they reached the Green Gabled lane. Poor Gilbert hardly had a chance to get a word in edgewise. Anne felt rather relieved when they parted. There had been a new, secret self-consciousness in her heart with regard to Gilbert, ever since that fleeting moment of revelation in the garden of Echo Lodge. Something alien had intruded into the old, perfect, school-day comradeship—something that threatened to mar it.

"I never felt glad to see Gilbert go before," she thought, half-resentfully, half-sorrowfully, as she walked alone up the lane. "Our friendship will be spoiled if he goes on with this nonsense. It mustn't be spoiled—I won't let it. Oh, *why* can't boys be just sensible!"

Anne had an uneasy doubt that it was not strictly "sensible" that she should still feel on her hand the warm pressure of Gilbert's, as distinctly as she had felt it for the swift second his had rested there; and still less sensible that the sensation was far from being an unpleasant one—very different from that which had attended a similar demonstration on Charlie Sloane's part, when she had been sitting out a dance with him at a White Sands party three nights before. Anne shivered over the disagreeable recollection. But all problems connected with infatuated swains vanished from her mind when she entered the homely, unsentimental atmosphere of the Green Gables kitchen where an eight-year-old boy was crying grievously on the sofa.

"What is the matter, Davy?" asked Anne, taking him up in her arms. "Where are Marilla and Dora?"

"Marilla's putting Dora to bed," sobbed Davy, "and I'm crying 'cause Dora fell down the outside cellar steps, heels over head, and scraped all the skin off her nose, and—"

"Oh, well, don't cry about it, dear. Of course, you are sorry for her, but crying won't help her any. She'll be all right tomorrow. Crying never helps any one, Davy-boy, and—"

"I ain't crying 'cause Dora fell down the cellar," said Davy, cutting short Anne's well-meant preachment with increasing bitterness. "I'm crying 'cause I wasn't there to see her fall. I'm always missing some fun or other, seems to me."

"Oh, Davy!" Anne choked back an unholy shriek of laughter. "Would you call it fun to see poor little Dora fall down the steps and get hurt?"

"She wasn't *much* hurt," said Davy defiantly. "'Course, if she'd been killed I'd have been real sorry, Anne. But the Keiths ain't so easy killed. They're like the Blewetts, I guess. Herb Blewett fell off the hayloft last Wednesday, and rolled right down through the turnip chute into the box stall, where they had a fearful wild, cross horse, and rolled right under his heels. And still he got out alive, with only three bones broke. Mrs. Lynde says there are some folks you can't kill with a meat-axe. Is Mrs. Lynde coming here tomorrow, Anne?"

"Yes, Davy, and I hope you'll be always very nice and good to her."

"I'll be nice and good. But will she ever put me to bed at nights, Anne?"

"Perhaps. Why?"

"'Cause," said Davy very decidedly, "if she does I won't say my prayers before her like I do before you, Anne."

"Why not?"

"'Cause I don't think it would be nice to talk to God before strangers. Anne. Dora can say hers to Mrs. Lynde if she likes, but *I* won't. I'll wait till she's gone and then say 'em. Won't that be all right, Anne?"

"Yes, if you are sure you won't forget to say them, Davy-boy."

"Oh, I won't forget, you bet I think saying my prayers is great fun. But it won't be as good fun saying them alone as saying them to you. I wish you'd stay home, Anne. I don't see what you want to go away and leave us for."

"I don't exactly *want* to; Davy, but I feel I ought to go."

"If you don't want to go you needn't. You're grown up. When *I'm* grown up I'm not going to do one single thing I don't want to do, Anne."

"All your life, Davy, you'll find yourself doing things you don't want to do."

"I won't," said Davy flatly. "Catch me! I have to do things I don't want to now, 'cause you and Marilla'll send me to bed if I don't. But when I grow up you can't do that, and there'll be nobody to tell me not to do things. Won't I have the time! Say, Anne, Milty Boulter says his mother says you're going to college to see if you can catch a man. Are you, Anne? I want to know."

For a second Anne burned with resentment. Then she laughed, reminding herself that Mrs. Boulter's crude vulgarity of thought and speech could not harm her.

"No, Davy, I'm not. I'm going to study and grow and learn about many things."

"What things?"

*"'Shoes and ships and sealing wax
And cabbages and kings,'"*

quoted Anne.

"But if you *did* want to catch a man how would you go about it? I want to know," persisted Davy, for whom the subject evidently possessed a certain fascination.

"You'd better ask Mrs. Boulter," said Anne thoughtlessly. "I think it's likely she knows more about the process than I do."

"I will, the next time I see her," said Davy gravely.

"Davy! If you do!" cried Anne, realizing her mistake.

"But you just told me to," protested Davy aggrieved.

"It's time you went to bed," decreed Anne, by way of getting out of the scrape.

After Davy had gone to bed Anne wandered down to Victoria Island and sat there alone, curtained with fine-spun, moonlit gloom, while the water laughed around her in a duet of brook and wind. Anne had always loved that brook. Many a dream had she spun over its sparkling water in days gone by. She forgot lovelorn youths, and the cayenne speeches of malicious neighbors, and all the problems of her girlish existence. In imagination she sailed over storied seas that wash the distant shining shores of "faëry lands forlorn," where lost Atlantis and Elysium lie, with the evening star for pilot, to the land of Heart's Desire. And she was richer in those dreams than in realities; for things seen pass away, but the things that are unseen are eternal.

2

Garlands of Autumn

The following week sped swiftly, crowded with Innumerable "last things," as Anne called them. Good-bye calls had to be made and received, being pleasant or otherwise, according to whether callers and called-upon were heartily in sympathy with Anne's hopes, or thought she was too much puffed-up over going to college and that it was their duty to "take her down a peg or two."

The A.V.I.S. gave a farewell party in honor of Anne and Gilbert one evening at the home of Josie Pye, choosing that place, partly because Mr. Pye's house was large and convenient, partly because it was strongly suspected that the Pye girls would have nothing to do with the affair if their offer of the house for the party was not accepted. It was a very pleasant little time, for the Pye girls were gracious, and said and did nothing to mar the harmony of the occasion—which was not according to their wont. Josie was unusually amiable—so much so that she even remarked condescendingly to Anne,

"Your new dress is rather becoming to you, Anne. Really, you look *almost pretty* in it."

"How kind of you to say so," responded Anne, with dancing eyes. Her sense of humor was developing, and the speeches that would have hurt her at fourteen were becoming merely food for amusement now. Josie suspected that Anne was laughing at her behind those wicked eyes; but she contented herself with whispering to Gertie, as they went downstairs, that Anne Shirley would put on more airs than ever now that she was going to college—you'd see!

All the "old crowd" was there, full of mirth and zest and youth-ful light-heartedness. Diana Barry, rosy and dimpled, shadowed by the faithful Fred; Jane Andrews, neat and sensible and plain; Ruby Gillis, looking her handsomest and brightest in a cream silk blouse, with red geraniums in her golden hair; Gilbert Blythe and Charlie Sloane, both trying to keep as near the elusive Anne as possible; Carrie Sloane, looking pale and melancholy because, so it was reported, her father would not allow Oliver Kimball to come near the place; Moody Spurgeon MacPherson, whose round face and objectionable ears were as round and objectionable as ever; and Billy Andrews, who sat in a corner all the evening, chuckled when any one spoke to him, and watched Anne Shirley with a grin of pleasure on his broad, freckled countenance.

Anne had known beforehand of the party, but she had not known that she and Gilbert were, as the founders of the Society, to be presented with a very complimentary "address" and "tokens of respect"—in her case a volume of Shakespeare's plays, in Gilbert's a fountain pen. She was so taken by surprise and pleased by the nice things said in the address, read in Moody Spurgeon's most solemn and ministerial tones, that the tears quite drowned the sparkle of her big gray eyes. She had worked hard and faithfully for the A.V.I.S., and it warmed the cockles of her heart that the members appreciated her efforts so sincerely. And they were all so nice and friendly and jolly—even the Pye girls had their merits; at that moment Anne loved all the world.

She enjoyed the evening tremendously, but the end of it rather spoiled all. Gilbert again made the mistake of saying something sentimental to her as they ate their supper on the moonlit verandah; and Anne, to punish him, was gracious to Charlie Sloane and allowed the latter to walk home with her. She found, however, that revenge hurts nobody quite so much as the one who tries to inflict it. Gilbert walked airily off with Ruby Gillis, and Anne could hear them laughing and talking gaily as they loitered along in the still, crisp autumn air. They were evidently having the best of good times, while she was horribly bored by Charlie Sloane, who talked unbrokenly on, and never, even by accident, said one thing that was worth listening to. Anne gave an occasional absent "yes" or "no," and thought how beautiful Ruby had looked that night, how very goggly Charlie's eyes were in the

moonlight—worse even than by daylight—and that the world, somehow, wasn't quite such a nice place as she had believed it to be earlier
in the evening.

"I'm just tired out—that is what is the matter with me," she said,
when she thankfully found herself alone in her own room. And she
honestly believed it was. But a certain little gush of joy, as from some
secret, unknown spring, bubbled up in her heart the next evening,
when she saw Gilbert striding down through the Haunted Wood and
crossing the old log bridge with that firm, quick step of his. So Gilbert
was not going to spend this last evening with Ruby Gillis after all!

"You look tired, Anne," he said.

"I am tired, and, worse than that, I'm disgruntled. I'm tired
because I've been packing my trunk and sewing all day. But I'm disgruntled because six women have been here to say good-bye to me, and
every one of the six managed to say something that seemed to take the
color right out of life and leave it as gray and dismal and cheerless as a
November morning."

"Spiteful old cats!" was Gilbert's elegant comment.

"Oh, no, they weren't," said Anne seriously. "That is just the trouble. If they had been spiteful cats I wouldn't have minded them. But
they are all nice, kind, motherly souls, who like me and whom I like, and
that is why what they said, or hinted, had such undue weight with me.
They let me see they thought I was crazy going to Redmond and trying to take a B.A., and ever since I've been wondering if I am. Mrs.
Peter Sloane sighed and said she hoped my strength would hold out till
I got through; and at once I saw myself a hopeless victim of nervous
prostration at the end of my third year; Mrs. Eben Wright said it must
cost an awful lot to put in four years at Redmond; and I felt all over me
that it was unpardonable in me to squander Marilla's money and my
own on such a folly; Mrs. Jasper Bell said she hoped I wouldn't let college spoil me, as it did some people; and I felt in my bones that the end
of my four Redmond years would see me a most insufferable creature,
thinking I knew it all, and looking down on everything and everybody
in Avonlea, Mrs. Elisha Wright said she understood that Redmond
girls, especially those who belonged to Kingsport, were 'dreadful dressy

and stuck-up,' and she guessed I wouldn't feel much at home among them; and I saw myself, a snubbed, dowdy, humiliated country girl, shuffling through Redmond's classic halls in copper-toned boots."

Anne ended with a laugh and a sigh commingled. With her sensitive nature all disapproval had weight, even the disapproval of those for whose opinions she had scant respect. For the time being life was savorless, and ambition had gone out like a snuffed candle.

"You surely don't care for what they said," protested Gilbert. "You know exactly how narrow their outlook on life is, excellent creatures though they are. To do anything *they* have never done is anathema maranatha. You are the first Avonlea girl who has ever gone to college; and you know that all pioneers are considered to be afflicted with moonstruck madness."

"Oh, I know. But *feeling* is so different from *knowing*. My common sense tells me all you can say, but there are times when common sense has no power over me. Common nonsense takes possession of my soul. Really, after Mrs. Elisha went away I hardly had the heart to finish packing."

"You're just tired, Anne. Come, forget it all and take a walk with me—a ramble back through the woods beyond the marsh. There should be something there I want to show you."

"Should be! Don't you know if it is there?"

"No. I only know it should be, from something I saw there in spring. Come on. We'll pretend we are two children again and we'll go the way of the wind."

They started gaily off. Anne, remembering the unpleasantness of the preceding evening, was very nice to Gilbert; and Gilbert, who was learning wisdom, took care to be nothing save the schoolboy comrade again. Mrs. Lynde and Marilla watched them from the kitchen window.

"That'll be a match some day," Mrs. Lynde said approvingly.

Marilla winced slightly. In her heart she hoped it would, but it went against her grain to hear the matter spoken of in Mrs. Lynde's gossipy matter-of-fact way.

"They're only children yet," she said shortly.

Mrs. Lynde laughed good-naturedly.

"Anne is eighteen; I was married when I was that age. We old folks, Marilla, are too much given to thinking children never grow up, that's what. Anne is a young woman and Gilbert's a man, and he worships the ground she walks on, as any one can see. He's a fine fellow, and Anne can't do better. I hope she won't get any romantic nonsense into her head at Redmond. I don't approve of them coeducational places and never did, that's what. I don't believe," concluded Mrs. Lynde solemnly, "that the students at such colleges ever do much else than flirt."

"They must study a little," said Marilla, with a smile.

"Precious little," sniffed Mrs. Rachel. "However, I think Anne will. She never was flirtatious. But she doesn't appreciate Gilbert at his full value, that's what. Oh, I know girls! Charlie Sloane is wild about her, too, but I'd never advise her to marry a Sloane. The Sloanes are good, honest, respectable people, of course. But when all's said and done, they're *Sloanes*."

Marilla nodded. To an outsider, the statement that Sloanes were Sloanes might not be very illuminating, but she understood. Every village has such a family; good, honest, respectable people they may be, but *Sloanes* they are and must ever remain, though they speak with the tongues of men and angels.

Gilbert and Anne, happily unconscious that their future was thus being settled by Mrs. Rachel, were sauntering through the shadows of the Haunted Wood. Beyond, the harvest hills were basking in an amber sunset radiance, under a pale, aerial sky of rose and blue. The distant spruce groves were burnished bronze, and their long shadows barred the upland meadows. But around them a little wind sang among the fir tassels, and in it there was the note of autumn.

"This wood really is haunted now—by old memories," said Anne, stooping to gather a spray of ferns, bleached to waxen whiteness by frost. "It seems to me that the little girls Diana and I used to be play here still, and sit by the Dryad's Bubble in the twilights, trysting with the ghosts. Do you know, I can never go up this path in the dusk without feeling a bit of the old fright and shiver? There was one especially horrifying phantom which we created—the ghost of the murdered child that crept up behind you and laid cold fingers on yours. I confess that, to this day, I cannot help fancying its little, furtive footsteps behind me when I come here after nightfall. I'm not afraid of the White Lady or the headless man or the skeletons, but I wish I had never imagined that baby's ghost into existence. How angry Marilla and Mrs. Barry were over that affair," concluded Anne, with reminiscent laughter.

The woods around the head of the marsh were full of purple vistas, threaded with gossamers. Past a dour plantation of gnarled spruces and a maple-fringed, sun-warm valley they found the "something" Gilbert was looking for.

"Ah, here it is," he said with satisfaction.

"An apple tree—and away back here!" exclaimed Anne delightedly.

"Yes, a veritable apple-bearing apple tree, too, here in the very midst of pines and beeches, a mile away from any orchard. I was here one day last spring and found it, all white with blossom. So I resolved I'd come again in the fall and see if it had been apples. See, it's loaded. They look good, too—tawny as russets but with a dusky red cheek. Most wild seedlings are green and uninviting."

"I suppose it sprang years ago from some chance-sown seed," said Anne dreamily. "And how it has grown and flourished and held its own here all alone among aliens, the brave determined thing!"

"Here's a fallen tree with a cushion of moss. Sit down, Anne—it will serve for a woodland throne. I'll climb for some apples. They all grow high—the tree had to reach up to the sunlight."

The apples proved to be delicious. Under the tawny skin was a white, white flesh, faintly veined with red; and, besides their own proper apple taste, they had a certain wild, delightful tang no orchard-grown apple ever possessed.

"The fatal apple of Eden couldn't have had a rarer flavor," commented Anne. "But it's time we were going home. See, it was twilight three minutes ago and now it's moonlight. What a pity we couldn't have caught the moment of transformation. But such moments never are caught, I suppose."

"Let's go back around the marsh and home by way of Lover's Lane. Do you feel as disgruntled now as when you started out, Anne?"

"Not I. Those apples have been as manna to a hungry soul. I feel that I shall love Redmond and have a splendid four years there."

"And after those four years—what?"

"Oh, there's another bend in the road at their end," answered Anne lightly. "I've no idea what may be around it—I don't want to have. It's nicer not to know."

Lover's Lane was a dear place that night, still and mysteriously dim in the pale radiance of the moonlight. They loitered through it in a pleasant chummy silence, neither caring to talk.

"If Gilbert were always as he has been this evening how nice and simple everything would be," reflected Anne.

Gilbert was looking at Anne, as she walked along. In her light dress, with her slender delicacy, she made him think of a white iris.

"I wonder if I can ever make her care for me," he thought, with a pang of self-distrust.

3

Greeting and Farewell

harlie Sloane, Gilbert Blythe and Anne Shirley left Avonlea the following Monday morning. Anne had hoped for a fine day. Diana was to drive her to the station and they wanted this, their last drive together for some time, to be a pleasant one. But when Anne went to bed Sunday night the east wind was moaning around Green Gables with an ominous prophecy which was fulfilled in the morning. Anne awoke to find raindrops pattering against her window and shadowing the pond's gray surface with widening rings; hills and sea were hidden in mist, and the whole world seemed dim and dreary. Anne dressed in the cheerless gray dawn, for an early start was necessary to catch the boat train; she struggled against the tears that *would* well up in her eyes in spite of herself. She was leaving the home that was so dear to her, and something told her that she was leaving it forever, save as a holiday refuge. Things would never be the same again; coming back for vacations would not be living there. And oh, how dear and beloved everything was—that little white porch room, sacred to the dreams of girlhood, the old Snow Queen at the window, the brook in the hollow, the Dryad's Bubble, the Haunted Wood, and Lover's Lane—all the thousand and one dear spots where memories of the old years bided. Could she ever be really happy anywhere else?

Breakfast at Green Gables that morning was a rather doleful meal. Davy, for the first time in his life probably, could not eat, but blubbered shamelessly over his porridge. Nobody else seemed to have much appetite, save Dora, who tucked away her rations comfortably. Dora, like the immortal and most prudent Charlotte, who "went on cutting bread and butter" when her frenzied lover's body had been carried past on a shutter, was one of those fortunate creatures who are seldom disturbed by anything. Even at eight it took a great deal to ruffle Dora's placidity. She was sorry Anne was going away, of course, but was that any reason why she should fail to appreciate a poached egg on toast? Not at all. And, seeing that Davy could not eat his, Dora ate it for him.

Promptly on time Diana appeared with horse and buggy, her rosy face glowing above her raincoat. The good-byes had to be said then somehow. Mrs. Lynde came in from her quarters to give Anne a hearty embrace and warn her to be careful of her health, whatever she did. Marilla, brusque and tearless, pecked Anne's cheek and said she supposed they'd hear from her when she got settled. A casual observer might have concluded that Anne's going mattered very little to her— unless said observer had happened to get a good look in her eyes. Dora kissed Anne primly and squeezed out two decorous little tears; but Davy, who had been crying on the back porch step ever since they rose from the table, refused to say good-bye at all. When he saw Anne coming towards him he sprang to his feet, bolted up the back stairs and hid in a clothes closet, out of which he would not come. His muffled howls were the last sounds Anne heard as she left Green Gables.

It rained heavily all the way to Bright River, to which station they had to go, since the branch line train from Carmody did not connect with the boat train. Charlie and Gilbert were on the station platform when they reached it, and the train was whistling. Anne had just time to get her ticket and trunk check, say a hurried farewell to Diana, and hasten on board. She wished she were going back with Diana to Avonlea, she knew she was going to die of homesickness. And oh, if only that dismal rain would stop pouring down as if the whole world were weeping over summer vanished and joys departed! Even Gilbert's presence brought her no comfort, for Charlie Sloane was there, too, and Sloanishness could be tolerated only in fine weather. It was absolutely insufferable in rain.

But when the boat steamed out of Charlottetown harbor things took a turn for the better. The rain ceased and the sun began to burst out goldenly now and again between the rents in the clouds, burnishing the gray seas with copper-hued radiance, and lighting up the mists that curtained the Island's red shores with gleams of gold foretokening a fine day after all Besides, Charlie Sloane promptly became so seasick that he had to go below, and Anne and Gilbert were left alone on deck.

"I am very glad that all the Sloanes get seasick as soon as they go on water," thought Anne mercilessly. "I am sure I couldn't take my farewell look at the 'ould sod' with Charlie standing there pretending to look sentimentally at it, too."

"Well, we're off," remarked Gilbert unsentimentally.

"Yes, I feel like Byron's 'Childe Harold'—only it isn't really my 'native shore' that I'm watching," said Anne, winking her gray eyes vigorously. "Nova Scotia is that, I suppose. But one's native shore is the land one loves the best, and that's good old P.E.I. for me. I can't believe I didn't always live here. Those eleven years before I came seem like a bad dream. It's seven years since I crossed on this boat—the evening Mrs. Spencer brought me over from Hopetown. I can see myself, in that dreadful old wincey dress and faded sailor hat, exploring decks and cabins with enraptured curiosity. It was a fine evening; and how those red Island shores did gleam in the sunshine. Now I'm crossing the strait again. Oh, Gilbert, I do hope I'll like Redmond and Kingsport, but I'm sure I won't!"

"Where's all your philosophy gone, Anne?"

"It's all submerged under a great, swamping wave of loneliness and homesickness. I've longed for three years to go to Redmond—and now I'm going—and I wish I weren't! Never mind! I shall be cheerful and philosophical again after I have just one good cry. I *must* have that, 'as a went'—and I'll have to wait until I get into my boardinghouse bed tonight, wherever it may be, before I can have it. Then Anne will be herself again. I wonder if Davy has come out of the closet yet."

It was nine that night when their train reached Kingsport, and they found themselves in the blue-white glare of the crowded station. Anne felt horribly bewildered, but a moment later she was seized by Priscilla Grant, who had come to Kingsport on Saturday.

"Here you are, beloved! And I suppose you're as tired as I was when I got here Saturday night."

"Tired! Priscilla, don't talk of it. I'm tired, and green, and provincial, and only about ten years old. For pity's sake take your poor, broken-down chum to some place where she can hear herself think."

"I'll take you right up to our boardinghouse. I've a cab ready outside."

"It's such a blessing you're here, Prissy. If you weren't I think I should just sit down on my suitcase, here and now, and weep bitter tears. What a comfort one familiar face is in a howling wilderness of strangers!"

"Is that Gilbert Blythe over there, Anne? How he has grown up this past year! He was only a schoolboy when I taught in Carmody. And of course that's Charlie Sloane. *He* hasn't changed—couldn't! He looked just like that when he was born, and he'll look like that when he's eighty. This way, dear. We'll be home in twenty minutes."

"Home!" groaned Anne. "You mean we'll be in some horrible boardinghouse, in a still more horrible hall bedroom, looking out on a dingy back yard."

"It isn't a horrible boardinghouse, Anne-girl. Here's our cab. Hop in—the driver will get your trunk. Oh, yes, the boardinghouse— it's really a very nice place of its kind, as you'll admit tomorrow morning when a rood night's sleep has turned your blues rosy pink. It's a big, old-fashioned, gray stone house on St. John Street, just a nice little constitutional from Redmond. It used to be the 'residence' of great folk, but fashion has deserted St. John Street and its houses only dream now of better days. They're so big that the people living in them have to take boarders just to fill up. At least, that is the reason our landladies are very anxious to impress on us. They're delicious, Anne—our landladies, I mean."

"How many are there?"

"Two. Miss Hannah Harvey and Miss Ada Harvey. They were born twins about fifty years ago."

"I can't get away from twins, it seems," smiled Anne. "Wherever I go they confront me."

"Oh, they're not twins now, dear. After they reached the age of thirty they never were twins again. Miss Hannah has grown old, not too gracefully, and Miss Ada has stayed thirty, less gracefully still. I don't know whether Miss Hannah can smile or not; I've never caught her at it so far, but Miss Ada smiles all the time and that's worse. However, they're nice, kind souls, and they take two boarders every year because Miss Hannah's economical soul cannot bear to 'waste room space'—not because they need to or have to, as Miss Ada has told me seven times since Saturday night. As for our rooms, I admit they are hall bedrooms, and mine does look out on the back yard. Your room is a front one and looks out on Old St. John's graveyard, which is just across the street."

"That sounds gruesome," shivered Anne. "I think I'd rather have the back yard view."

"Oh, no, you wouldn't. Wait and see. Old St. John's is a darling place. It's been a graveyard so long that it's ceased to be one and has become one of the sights of Kingsport. I was all through it yesterday for a pleasure exertion. There's a big stone wall and a row of enormous trees all around it, and rows of trees all through it, and the queerest old tombstones, with the queerest and quaintest inscriptions. You'll go there to study, Anne, see if you don't. Of course, nobody is ever buried there now. But a few years ago they put up a beautiful monument to the memory of Nova Scotian soldiers who fell in the Crimean War. It is just opposite the entrance gates and there's 'scope for imagination' in it, as you used to say. Here's your trunk at last—and the boys coming to say good night. Must I really shake hands with Charlie Sloane, Anne? His hands are always so cold and fishy-feeling. We must ask them to call occasionally. Miss Hannah gravely told me we could have 'young gentlemen callers' two evenings in the week, if they went away at a reasonable hour; and Miss Ada asked me, smiling, please to be sure they didn't sit on her beautiful cushions. I promised to see to it; but goodness knows where else they *can* sit, unless they sit on the floor, for there are cushions on *everything*. Miss Ada even has an elaborate Battenburg one on top of the piano."

Anne was laughing by this time. Priscilla's gay chatter had the intended effect of cheering her up; homesickness vanished for the time being, and did not even return in full force when she finally found herself alone in her little bedroom. She went to her window and looked out. The street below was dim and quiet. Across it the moon was shining above the trees in Old St. John's, just behind the great dark head of the lion on the monument. Anne wondered if it could have been only that morning that she had left Green Gables. She had the sense of a long passage of time which one day of change and travel gives.

"I suppose that very moon is looking down on Green Gables now," she mused. "But I won't think about it—that way homesickness lies. I'm not even going to have my good cry. I'll put that off to a more convenient season, and just now I'll go calmly and sensibly to bed and to sleep."

4

April's Lady

ingsport is a quaint old town, hearking back to early Colonial days, and wrapped in its ancient atmosphere, as some fine old dame in garments fashioned like those of her youth. Here and there it sprouts out into modernity, but at heart it is still unspoiled; it is full of curious relics, and haloed by the romance of many legends of the past. Once it was a mere frontier station on the fringe of the wilderness, and those were the days when Indians kept life from being monotonous to the settlers. Then it grew to be a bone of contention between the British and the French, being occupied now by the one and now by the other, emerging from each occupation with some fresh scar of battling nations branded on it.

It has in its park a martello tower, autographed all over by tourists, a dismantled old French fort on the hills beyond the town, and several antiquated cannon in its public squares. It has other historic spots also, which may be hunted out by the curious, and none is more quaint and delightful than Old St. John's Cemetery at the very core of the town, with streets of quiet, old-time houses on two sides, and busy, bustling, modern thoroughfares on the others. Every citizen of Kingsport feels a thrill of possessive pride in Old St. John's, for, if he be of any pretensions at all, he has an ancestor buried there, with a queer, crooked slab at his head, or else sprawling protectively over the grave, on which all the main facts of his history are recorded. For the most part no great art or skill was lavished on those old tombstones. The larger number are of roughly chiselled brown or gray native stone, and only in a few cases is there any attempt at ornamentation. Some are adorned with skull and crossbones, and this grizzly decoration is frequently coupled with a cherub's head. Many are prostrate and in ruins. Into almost all

Time's tooth has been gnawing, until some inscriptions have been completely effaced, and others can only be deciphered with difficulty. The graveyard is very full and very bowery, for it is surrounded and intersected by rows of elms and willows, beneath whose shade the sleepers must lie very dreamlessly, forever crooned to by the winds and leaves over them, and quite undisturbed by the clamor of traffic just beyond.

Anne took the first of many rambles in Old St. John's the next afternoon. She and Priscilla had gone to Redmond in the forenoon and registered as students, after which there was nothing more to do that day. The girls gladly made their escape, for it was not exhilarating to be surrounded by crowds of strangers, most of whom had a rather alien appearance, as if not quite sure where they belonged.

The "freshettes" stood about in detached groups of two or three, looking askance at each other; the "freshies," wiser in their day and generation, had banded themselves to ether on the big staircase of the entrance hall, where they were shouting out glees with all the vigor of youthful lungs, as a species of defiance to their traditional enemies, the Sophomores, a few of whom were prowling loftily about, looking properly disdainful of the "unlicked cubs" on the stairs. Gilbert and Charlie were nowhere to be seen.

"Little did I think the day would ever come when I'd be glad of the sight of a Sloane," said Priscilla, as they crossed the campus, "but I'd welcome Charlie's goggle eyes almost ecstatically. At least, they'd be familiar eyes."

"Oh," sighed Anne. "I can't describe how I felt when I was standing there, waiting my turn to be registered—as insignificant as the teeniest drop in a most enormous bucket. It's bad enough to feel insignificant, but it's unbearable to have it grained into your soul that you will never, *can* never, be anything but insignificant, and that is how I did feel—as if I were invisible to the naked eye and some of those Sophs might step on me. I knew I would go down to my grave unwept, unhonored and unsung."

"Wait till next year," comforted Priscilla. "Then we'll be able to look as bored and sophisticated as any Sophomore of them all. No doubt it is rather dreadful to feel insignificant; but I think it's better then to feel as big and awkward as I did—as if I were sprawled all over Redmond. That's how I felt—I suppose because I was a good two inches taller than any one else in the crowd. *I* wasn't afraid a Soph might walk over me; I was afraid they'd take me for an elephant, or an overgrown sample of a potato-fed Islander."

"I suppose the trouble is we can't forgive big Redmond for not being little Queen's," said Anne, gathering about her the shreds of her old cheerful philosophy to cover her nakedness of spirit. "When we left Queen's we knew everybody and had a place of our own. I suppose we have been unconsciously expecting to take life up at Redmond just where we left off at Queen's, and now we feel as if the ground had slipped from under our feet. I'm thankful that neither Mrs. Lynde nor Mrs. Elisha Wright know, or ever will know, my state of mind at present. They would exult in saying 'I told you so,' and be convinced it was the beginning of the end. Whereas it is just the end of the beginning."

"Exactly. That sounds more Anneish. In a little while we'll be acclimated and acquainted, and all will be well. Anne, did you notice the girl who stood alone just outside the door of the coeds' dressing room all the morning—the pretty one with the brown eyes and crooked mouth?"

"Yes, I did. I noticed her particularly because she seemed the only creature there who *looked* as lonely and friendless as I *felt*. I had *you*, but she had no one."

"I think she felt pretty all-by-herselfish, too. Several times I saw her make a motion as if to cross over to us, but she never did it—too shy, I suppose. I wished she would come. If I hadn't felt so much like the aforesaid elephant I'd have gone to her. But I couldn't lumber across that big hall with all those boys howling on the stairs. She was the prettiest freshette I saw today, but probably favor is deceitful and even beauty is vain on your first day at Redmond," concluded Priscilla with a laugh.

"I'm going across to Old St. John's after lunch," said Anne. "I don't know that a graveyard is a very good place to go to get cheered up, but it seems the only get-at-able place where there are trees, and trees

I must have. I'll sit on one of those old slabs and shut my eyes and imagine I'm in the Avonlea woods."

Anne did not do that, however, for she found enough of interest in Old St. John's to keep her eyes wide open. They went in by the entrance gates, past the simple, massive, stone arch surmounted by the great lion of England.

"'And on Inkerman yet the wild bramble is gory,
And those bleak heights henceforth shall be
famous in story,'"

quoted Anne, looking at it with a thrill. They found themselves in a dim, cool, green place where winds were fond of purring. Up and down the long grassy aisles they wandered, reading the quaint, voluminous epitaphs, carved in an age that had more leisure than our own.

"'Here lieth the body of Albert Crawford, Esq.,'" read Anne from a worn, gray slab, "'for many years Keeper of His Majesty's Ordnance at Kingsport. He served in the army till the peace of 1763, when he retired from bad health. He was a brave officer, the best of husbands, the best of fathers, the best of friends. He died October 29th, 1792, aged 84 years.' There's an epitaph for you, Prissy. There is certainly some 'scope for imagination' in it. How full such a life must have been of adventure! And as for his personal qualities, I'm sure human eulogy couldn't go further. I wonder if they told him he was all those best things while he was alive."

"Here's another," said Priscilla. "Listen—'To the memory of Alexander Ross, who died on the 22nd of September, 1840, aged 43 years. This is raised as a tribute of affection by one whom he served so faithfully for 27 years that he was regarded as a friend, deserving the fullest confidence and attachment.'"

"A very good epitaph," commented Anne thoughtfully. "I wouldn't wish a better. We are all servants of some sort, and if the fact that we are faithful can be truthfully inscribed on our tombstones nothing more need be added. Here's a sorrowful little gray stone, Prissy—'to the memory of a favorite child.' And here is another 'erected to the memory of one who is buried elsewhere.' I wonder where that unknown grave is. Really, Pris, the graveyards of today will never be as interesting as this. You were right—I shall come here often. I love it already. I see we're not alone here—there's a girl down at the end of this avenue."

"Yes, and I believe it's the very girl we saw at Redmond this morning. I've been watching her for five minutes. She has started to come up the avenue exactly half a dozen times, and half a dozen times has she turned and gone back. Either she's dreadfully shy or she has got something on her conscience. Let's go and meet her. It's easier to get acquainted in a graveyard than at Redmond, I believe."

They walked down the long grassy arcade towards the stranger, who was sitting on a gray slab under an enormous willow. She was certainly very pretty, with a vivid, irregular, bewitching type of prettiness. There was a gloss as of brown nuts on her satin-smooth hair and a soft, ripe glow on her round cheeks. Her eyes were big and brown and velvety, under oddly-pointed black brows, and her crooked mouth was rose-red. She wore a smart brown suit, with two very modish little shoes peeping from beneath it; and her hat of dull pink straw, wreathed with golden-brown poppies, had the indefinable, unmistakable air which pertains to the "creation" of an artist in millinery. Priscilla had a sudden stinging consciousness that her own hat had been trimmed by her village store milliner, and Anne wondered uncomfortably if the blouse she had made herself, and which Mrs. Lynde had fitted, looked *very* countrified and home-made besides the stranger's smart attire. For a moment both girls felt like turning back.

But they had already stopped and turned towards the gray slab. It was too late to retreat, for the brown-eyed girl had evidently concluded that they were coming to speak to her. Instantly she sprang up and came forward with outstretched hand and a gay, friendly smile in which there seemed not a shadow of either shyness or burdened conscience.

"Oh, I want to know who you two girls are," she exclaimed eagerly. "I've been *dying* to know. I saw you at Redmond this morning. Say, wasn't it *awful* there? For the time I wished I had stayed home and got married."

Anne and Priscilla both broke into unconstrained laughter at this unexpected conclusion. The brown-eyed girl laughed, too.

"I really did. I *could* have, you know. Come, let's all sit down on this gravestone and get acquainted. It won't be hard. I know we're going to adore each other—I knew it as soon as I saw you at Redmond this morning. I wanted so much to go right over and hug you both."

"Why didn't you?" asked Priscilla.

"Because I simply couldn't make up my mind to do it. I never can make up my mind about anything myself—I'm always afflicted with indecision. Just as soon as I decide to do something I feel in my bones that another course would be the correct one. It's a dreadful misfortune, but I was born that way, and there is no use in blaming me for it, as some people do. So I couldn't make up my mind to go and speak to you, much as I wanted to."

"We thought you were too shy," said Anne.

"No, no, dear. Shyness isn't among the many failings—or virtues— of Philippa Gordon—Phil for short. Do call me Phil right off. Now, what are your handles?"

"She's Priscilla Grant," said Anne, pointing.

"And *she's* Anne Shirley," said Priscilla, pointing in turn.

"And we're from the Island," said both together.

"I hail from Bolingbroke, Nova Scotia," said Philippa.

"Bolingbroke!" exclaimed Anne. "Why, that is where I was born."

"Do you really mean it? Why, that makes you a Bluenose after all."

"No, it doesn't," retorted Anne. "Wasn't It Dan O'Connell who said that if a man was born in a stable it didn't make him a horse? I'm Island to the core."

"Well, I'm glad you were born in Bolingbroke anyway. It makes us kind of neighbors, doesn't it? And I like that, because when I tell you secrets it won't be as if I were telling them to a stranger. I *have* to tell them. I can't keep secrets—it's no use to try. That's my worst failing—that, and indecision, as aforesaid. Would you believe it?—it took me half an hour to decide what hat to wear when I was coming here—*here*, to a graveyard! At first I inclined to my brown one with the feather; but as soon as I put it on I thought this pink one with the floppy brim would be more becoming. When I got *it* pinned in place I liked the brown one better. At last I put them close together on the bed, shut my eyes, and jabbed with a hat pin. The pin speared the pink one, so I put it on. It is becoming, isn't it? Tell me, what do you think of my looks?"

At this naïve demand, made in a perfectly serious tone, Priscilla laughed again. But Anne said, impulsively squeezing Philippa's hand,

"We thought this morning that you were the prettiest girl we saw at Redmond."

Philippa's crooked mouth flashed into a bewitching, crooked smile over very white little teeth.

"I thought that myself," was her next astounding statement, "but I wanted some one else's opinion to bolster mine up. I can't decide even on my own appearance. Just as soon as I've decided that I'm pretty I begin to feel miserably that I'm not. Besides, I have a horrible old great-aunt who is always saying to me, with a mournful sigh, 'You were such a pretty baby. It's strange how children change when they grow up.' I adore aunts, but I detest great-aunts. Please tell me quite often that I am pretty, if you don't mind. I feel so much more comfortable when I can believe I'm pretty. And I'll be just as obliging to you if you want me to—I *can* be, with a clear conscience."

"Thanks," laughed Anne, "but Priscilla and I are so firmly convinced of our own good looks that we don't need any assurance about them, so you needn't trouble."

"Oh, you're laughing at me. I know you think I'm abominably vain, but I'm not. There really isn't one spark of vanity in me. And I'm never a bit grudging about paying compliments to other girls when they deserve them. I'm so glad I know you folks. I came up on Saturday and I've nearly died of homesickness ever since. It's a horrible feeling, isn't it? In Bolingbroke I'm an important personage, and in Kingsport I'm just nobody! There were times when I could feel my soul turning a delicate blue. Where do you hang out?"

"Thirty-eight St. John's Street."

"Better and better. Why, I'm just around the corner on Wallace Street. I don't like my boardinghouse, though. It's bleak and lonesome, and my room looks out on such an unholy back yard. It's the ugliest place in the world. As for cats—well, surely *all* the Kingsport cats can't congregate there at night, but half of them must. I adore cats on hearth rugs, snoozing before nice, friendly fires, but cats in back yards at midnight are totally different animals. The first night I was here I cried all night, and so did the cats. You should have seen my nose in the morning. How I wished I had never left home!"

"I don't know how you managed to make up your mind to come to Redmond at all, if you are really such an undecided person," said amused Priscilla.

"Bless your heart, honey, I didn't. It was father who wanted me to come here. His heart was set on it—why, I don't know. It seems perfectly ridiculous to think of *me* studying for a B.A. degree, doesn't it? Not but what I can do it, all right. I have heaps of brains."

"Oh!" said Priscilla vaguely.

"Yes. But it's such hard work to use them. And B.A.'s are such learned, dignified, wise, solemn creatures—they must be. No, *I* didn't want to come to Redmond. I did it just to oblige father. He *is* such a duck. Besides, I knew if I stayed home I'd have to get married. Mother wanted that—wanted it decidedly. Mother has plenty of decision. But I really hated the thought of being married for a few years yet. I want to have heaps of fun before I settle down. And, ridiculous as the idea of my being a B.A. is, the idea of my being an old married woman is still more absurd, isn't it? I'm only eighteen. No, I concluded I would rather come to Redmond than be married. Besides, how could I ever have made up my mind which man to marry?"

"Were there so many?" laughed Anne.

"Heaps. The boys like me awfully—they really do. But there were only two that mattered. The rest were all too young and too poor. I must marry a rich man, you know."

"Why must you?"

"Honey, you couldn't imagine *me* being a poor man's wife, could you? I can't do a single useful thing, and I am *very* extravagant. Oh, no, my husband must have heaps of money. So that narrowed them down to two. But I couldn't decide between two any easier than between two hundred. I knew perfectly well that whichever one I chose I'd regret all my life that I hadn't married the other."

"Didn't you—love—either of them?" asked Anne, a little hesitatingly. It was not easy for her to speak to a stranger of the great mystery and transformation of life.

"Goodness, no. I couldn't love anybody. It isn't in me. Besides I wouldn't want to. Being in love makes you a perfect slave, I think. And it would give a man such power to hurt you. I'd be afraid. No, no, Alec and Alonzo are two dear boys, and I like them both so much that I really don't know which I like the better. That is the trouble. Alec is the best looking, of course, and I simply couldn't marry a man who wasn't handsome. He is good-tempered, too, and has lovely, curly, black hair. He's rather too perfect—I don't believe I'd like a perfect husband—somebody I could never find fault with."

"Then why not marry Alonzo?" asked Priscilla gravely.

"Think of marrying a name like Alonzo!" said Phil dolefully. "I don't believe I could endure it. But he has a classic nose, and it would be a comfort to have a nose in the family that could be depended on. I can't depend on mine. So far, it takes after the Gordon pattern, but I'm so afraid it will develop Byrne tendencies as I grow older. I examine it every day anxiously to make sure it's still Gordon. Mother was a Byrne and has the Byrne nose in the Byrnest degree. Wait till you see it. I adore nice noses. Your nose is awfully nice, Anne Shirley. Alonzo's nose nearly turned the balance in his favor. But Alonzo! No, I couldn't decide. If I could have done as I did with the hats—stood them both up together, shut my eyes, and jabbed with a hatpin—it would have been quite easy."

"What did Alec and Alonzo feel like when you came away?" queried Priscilla.

"Oh, they still have hope. I told them they'd have to wait till I could make up my mind. They're quite willing to wait. They both worship me, you know. Meanwhile, I intend to have a good time. I expect I shall have heaps of beaux at Redmond. I can't be happy unless I have, you know. But don't you think the freshmen are fearfully homely? I saw only one really handsome fellow among them. He went away before you came. I heard his chum call him Gilbert. His chum had eyes that stuck out *that far*. But you're not going yet, girls? Don't go yet."

"I think we must," said Anne, rather coldly. "It's getting late, and I've some work to do."

"But you'll both come to see me, won't you?" asked Philippa, getting up and putting an arm around each. "And let me come to see you. I want to be chummy with you. I've taken such a fancy to you both. And I haven't quite disgusted you with my frivolity, have I?"

"Not quite," laughed Anne, responding to Phil's squeeze, with a return of cordiality.

"Because I'm not half so silly as I seem on the surface, you know. You just accept Philippa Gordon, as the Lord made her, with all her faults, and I believe you'll come to like her. Isn't this graveyard a sweet place? I'd love to be buried here, Here's a grave I didn't see before—this one in the iron railing—oh, girls, look, see—the stone says it's the grave of a middy who was killed in the fight between the *Shannon* and the *Chesapeake*. Just fancy!"

Anne paused by the railing and looked at the worn stone, her pulses thrilling with sudden excitement. The old graveyard, with its over-arching trees and long aisles of shadows, faded from her sight. Instead, she saw the Kingsport Harbor of nearly a century agone. Out of the mist came slowly a great frigate, brilliant with "the meteor flag of England." Behind her was another, with a still, heroic form, wrapped in his own starry flag, lying on the quarter deck—the gallant *Lawrence*. Time's finger had turned back his pages, and that was the *Shannon* sailing triumphant up the bay with the *Chesapeake* as her prize.

"Come back, Anne Shirley—come back," laughed Philippa, pulling her arm. "You're a hundred years away from us. Come back."

Anne came back with a sigh; her eyes were shining softly.

"I've always loved that old story," she said, "and although the English won that victory, I think it was because of the brave, defeated commander I love it. This grave seems to bring it so near and make it so real. This poor little middy was only eighteen. He 'died of desperate wounds received in gallant action'—so reads his epitaph. It is such as a soldier might wish for."

Before she turned away, Anne unpinned the little cluster of purple pansies she wore and dropped it softly on the grave of the boy who had perished in the great sea-duel.

"Well, what do you think of our new friend?" asked Priscilla, when Phil had left them.

"I like her. There is something very lovable about her, in spite of all her nonsense. I believe, as she says herself, that she isn't half as silly as she sounds. She's a dear, kissable baby—and I don't know that she'll ever really grow up."

"I like her, too," said Priscilla decidedly. "She talks as much about boys as Ruby Gillis does. But it always enrages or sickens me to hear Ruby, whereas I just wanted to laugh good-naturedly at Phil. Now, what is the why of that?"

"There is a difference," said Anne meditatively. "I think it's because Ruby is really so *conscious* of boys. She plays at love and love-making. Besides, you feel, when she is boasting of her beaux that she is doing it to rub it well into you that you haven't half so many. Now, when Phil talks of her beaux it sounds as if she was just speaking of chums. She really looks upon boys as good comrades, and she is pleased when she has dozens of them tagging round, simply because she likes to be popular and to be thought popular. Even Alec and Alonzo—I'll never be able to think of those two names separately after this—are to her just two playfellows who want her to play with them all their lives. I'm glad we met her, and I'm glad we went to Old St. John's. I believe I've put forth a tiny soul-root into Kingsport soil this afternoon. I hope so. I hate to feel transplanted."

5

Letters from Home

or the next three weeks Anne and Priscilla continued to feel as strangers in a strange land. Then, suddenly, everything seemed to fall into focus—Redmond, professors, classes, students, studies, social doings. Life became homogeneous again, instead of being made up of detached fragments. The Freshmen, instead of being a collection of unrelated individuals, found themselves a class, with a class spirit, a class yell, class interests, class antipathies, and class ambitions. They won the day in the annual "Arts Rush" against the Sophomores, and thereby gained the respect of all the classes, and an enormous, confidence-giving opinion of themselves. For three years the Sophomores had won in the "rush"; that the victory of this year perched upon the Freshmen's banner was attributed to the strategic generalship of Gilbert Blythe, who marshalled the campaign and orig-inated certain new tactics, which demoralized the Sophs and swept the Freshmen to triumph. As a reward of merit he was elected president of the Freshman Class, a position of honor and responsibility—from a Fresh point of view, at least—coveted by many. He was also invited to join the "Lambs"—Redmondese for Lamba Theta—a compliment rarely paid to a Freshman. As a preparatory initiation ordeal he had to parade the principal business streets of Kingsport for a whole day wearing a sunbonnet and a voluminous kitchen apron of gaudily flowered calico. This he did cheerfully, doffing his sunbonnet with courtly grace when he met ladies of his acquaintance. Charlie Sloane, who had not been asked to join the Lambs, told Anne he did not see how Blythe could do it, and *he*, for his part, could never humiliate himself so.

"Fancy Charlie Sloane in a 'caliker' apron and a 'sunbunnit,'" gig-gled Priscilla. "He'd look exactly like his old Grandmother Sloane.

Gilbert, now, looked as much like a man in them as in his own proper habiliments."

Anne and Priscilla found themselves in the thick of the social life of Redmond. That this came about so speedily was due in great measure to Philippa Gordon. Philippa was the daughter of a rich and well-known man, and belonged to an old and exclusive "Bluenose" family. This, combined with her beauty and charm—a charm acknowledged by all who met her—promptly opened the gates of all cliques, clubs, and classes in Redmond to her; and where she went Anne and Priscilla went, too. Phil "adored" Anne and Priscilla, especially Anne. She was a loyal little soul, crystal-free from any form of snobbishness. "Love me, love my friends" seemed to be her unconscious motto. Without effort, she took them with her into her ever widening circle of acquaintance-ship, and the two Avonlea girls found their social pathway at Redmond made very easy and pleasant for them, to the envy and wonderment of the other freshettes, who, lacking Philippa's sponsorship, were doomed to remain rather on the fringe of things during their first college year.

To Anne and Priscilla, with their more serious views of life, Phil remained the amusing, lovable baby she had seemed on their first meeting. Yet, as she said herself, she had "heaps" of brains. When or where she found time to study was a mystery, for she seemed always in demand for some kind of "fun," and her home evenings were crowded with callers. She had all the "beaux" that heart could desire, for nine-tenths of the Freshmen and a big fraction of all the other classes were rivals for her smiles. She was naïvely delighted over this, and gleefully recounted each new conquest to Anne and Priscilla, with comments that might have made the unlucky lover's ears burn fiercely.

"Alec and Alonzo don't seem to have any serious rival yet," remarked Anne, teasingly.

"Not one," agreed Philippa. "I write them both every week and tell them all about my young men here. I'm sure it must amuse them. But, of course, the one I like best I can't get. Gilbert Blythe won't take any notice of me, except to look at me as if I were a nice little kitten he'd like to pat. Too well I know the reason. I owe you a grudge, Queen Anne. I really ought to hate you and instead I love you madly, and I'm miserable if I don't see you every day. You're different from any girl I ever knew before. When you look at me in a certain way I feel what an insignificant, frivolous little beast I am, and I long to be better and wiser and stronger. And then I make good resolutions; but the first nice-looking mannie who comes my way knocks them all out of my head. Isn't college life magnificent? It's so funny to think I hated it that first day. But if I hadn't I might never got really acquainted with you. Anne, please tell me over again that you like me a little bit. I yearn to hear it."

"I like you a big bit—and I think you're a dear, sweet, adorable, velvety, clawless, little—kitten," laughed Anne, "but I don't see when you ever get time to learn your lessons."

Phil must have found time for she held her own in every class of her year. Even the grumpy old professor of Mathematics, who detested coeds, and had bitterly opposed their admission to Redmond, couldn't floor her. She led the freshettes everywhere, except in English, where Anne Shirley left her far behind. Anne herself found the studies of her Freshman year very easy, thanks in great part to the steady work she and Gilbert had put in during those two past years in Avonlea. This left her more time for a social life which she thoroughly enjoyed. But never for a moment did she forget Avonlea and the friends there. To her, the happiest moments in each week were those in which letters came from home. It was not until she had got her first letters that she began to think she could ever like Kingsport or feel at home there. Before they came, Avonlea had seemed thousands of miles away; those letters brought it near and linked the old life to the new so closely that they began to seem one and the same, instead of two hopelessly segregated existences. The first batch contained six letters, from Jane Andrews, Ruby Gillis, Diana Barry, Marilla, Mrs. Lynde, and Davy. Jane's was a copper-plate production, with every "t" nicely crossed and every "i" precisely dotted, and not an interesting sentence in it. She never mentioned the school, concerning which Anne was avid to hear; she never answered one of the questions Anne had asked in her letter. But she told Anne how many yards of lace she had recently crocheted, and the kind of weather they were having in Avonlea, and how she intended to have her new dress made, and the way she felt when her head ached. Ruby Gillis wrote a gushing epistle deploring Anne's absence, assuring her she was horribly missed in everything, asking what the Redmond "fellows" were like, and filling the rest with accounts of her own harrowing experiences with her numerous admirers. It was a silly, harmless letter, and Anne would have laughed over it had it not been for the postscript. "Gilbert seems to be enjoying Redmond, judging from his letters," wrote Ruby. "I don't think Charlie is so stuck on it."

So Gilbert was writing to Ruby! Very well. He had a perfect right to, of course. Only—!! Anne did not know that Ruby had written the first letter and that Gilbert had answered it from mere courtesy. She tossed Ruby's letter aside contemptuously. But it took all Diana's breezy, newsy, delightful epistle to banish the sting of Ruby's postscript. Diana's letter contained a little too much Fred, but was otherwise crowded and crossed with items of interest, and Anne almost felt herself back in Avonlea while reading it. Marilla's was a rather prim and colorless epistle, severely innocent of gossip or emotion. Yet somehow it conveyed to Anne a whiff of the wholesome, simple life at Green Gables, with its savor of ancient peace, and the steadfast abiding love that was there for her. Mrs. Lynde's letter was full of church news. Having broken up housekeeping, Mrs. Lynde had more time than ever to devote to church affairs and had flung herself into them heart and soul. She was at present much worked up over the poor "supplies" they were having in the vacant Avonlea pulpit.

"I don't believe any but fools enter the ministry nowadays," she wrote bitterly. "Such candidates as they have sent us, and such stuff as they preach! Half of it ain't true, and, what's worse, it ain't sound doctrine. The one we have now is the worst of the lot. He mostly takes a text and preaches about something else. And he says he doesn't believe all the heathen will be eternally lost. The idea! If they won't all the money we've been giving to Foreign Missions will be clean wasted, that's, what! Last Sunday night he announced that next Sunday he'd preach on the axe-head that swam. I think he'd better confine himself to the Bible and leave sensational subjects alone. Things have come to a pretty pass if a minister can't find enough in Holy Writ to preach about, that's what. What church do you attend, Anne? I hope you go regularly. People are apt to get so careless about church-going away from home, and I understand college students are great sinners in this respect. I'm told many of them actually study their lessons on Sunday. I hope you'll never sink that low, Anne. Remember how you were brought up. And be very careful what friends you make. You never know what sort of creatures are in them colleges. Outwardly they may be as whited sepulchers and inwardly as ravening wolves, that's what. You'd better not have anything to say to any young man who isn't from the Island.

"I forgot to tell you what happened the day the minister called here. It was the funniest thing I ever saw. I said to Marilla, 'If Anne had been here wouldn't she have had a laugh?' Even Marilla laughed. You know he's a very short, fat little man with bow legs. Well, that old pig of Mr. Harrison's—the big, tall one—had wandered over here that day again and broke into the yard, and it got into the back porch, unbeknowns to us, and it was there when the minister appeared in the doorway. It made one wild bolt to get out, but there was nowhere to bolt to except between them bow legs. So there it went, and, being as it was so big and the minister so little, it took him clean off his feet and carried him away. His hat went one way and his cane another, just as Marilla and I got to the door. I'll never forget the look of him. And that poor pig was near scared to death. I'll never be able to read that account in the Bible of the swine that rushed madly down the steep place into the sea without seeing Mr. Harrison's pig careering down the hill with that minister. I guess the pig thought he had the Old Boy on his back instead of inside of him. I was thankful the twins weren't about. It wouldn't have been the right thing for them to have seen a minister in such an undignified predicament. Just before they got to the brook the minister jumped off or fell off. The pig rushed through the brook like mad and up through the woods. Marilla and I run down and helped the minister get up and brush his coat. He wasn't hurt, but he was mad. He seemed to hold Marilla and me responsible for it all, though we told him the pig didn't belong to us, and had been pestering us all summer. Besides, what did he come to the back door for? You'd never have caught Mr. Allan doing that. It'll be a long time before we get a man like Mr. Allan. But it's an ill wind that blows no good. We've never seen hoof or hair of that pig since, and it's my belief we never will.

"Things is pretty quiet in Avonlea. I don't find Green Gables as lonesome as I expected. I think I'll start another cotton warp quilt this winter. Mrs. Silas Sloane has a handsome new apple-leaf pattern.

"When I feel that I must have some excitement I read the murder trials in that Boston paper my niece sends me. I never used to do it, but they're real interesting. The States must be an awful place. I hope you'll never go there, Anne. But the way girls roam over the earth now is something terrible. It always makes me think of Satan in the Book of Job, going to and fro and walking up and down. I don't believe the Lord ever intended it, that's what.

"Davy has been pretty good since you went away. One day he was bad and Marilla punished him by making him wear Dora's apron all day, and then he went and cut all Dora's aprons up. I spanked him for that and then he went and chased my rooster to death.

"The MacPhersons have moved down to my place. She's a great housekeeper and very particular. She's rooted all my June lilies up because she says they make a garden look so untidy. Thomas set them lilies out when we were married. Her husband seems a nice sort of a man, but she can't get over being an old maid, that's what.

"Don't study too hard, and be sure and put your winter underclothes on as soon as the weather gets cool. Marilla worries a lot about you, but I tell her you've got a lot more sense than I ever thought you would have at one time, and that you'll be all right."

Davy's letter plunged into a grievance at the start.

"Dear anne, please write and tell marilla not to tie me to the rale of the bridge when I go fishing the boys make fun of me when she does. Its awful lonesome here without you but grate fun in school. Jane andrews is crosser than you. I scared mrs. lynde with a jacky lantern last nite. She was offel mad and she was mad cause I chased her old rooster round the yard till he fell down ded. I didn't mean to make him fall down ded. What made him die, anne, I want to know. Mrs. lynde threw him into the pig pen she mite of sold him to mr. blair. mr. blair is giving 50 sense apeace for good ded roosters now. I herd mrs. lynde asking the minister to pray for her. What did she do that was so bad, anne, I want to know. I've got a kite with a magnificent tail, anne. Milty bolter told me a grate story in school yesterday. it is troo. old Joe Mosey and Leon were playing cards one nite last week in the woods. The cards were on a stump and a big black man bigger than the trees come along and grabbed the cards and the stump and disapered with a noys like thunder. Ill bet they were skared. Milty says the black man was the old harry. was he, anne, I want to know. Mr. kimball over at spenservale is very sick and will have to go to the hospitable. please excuse me while I ask marilla if thats spelled rite. Marilla says its the silem he has to go to not the other place. He thinks he has a snake inside of him. whats it like to have a snake inside of you, anne. I want to know. mrs. lawrence bell is sick to. mrs. lynde says that all that is the matter with her is that she thinks too much about her insides."

"I wonder," said Anne, as she folded up her letters, "what Mrs. Lynde would think of Philippa."

6

In the Park

"What are you going to do with yourselves today, girls?" asked Philippa, popping into Anne's room one Saturday afternoon.

"We are going for a walk in the park," answered Anne. "I ought to stay in and finish my blouse. But I couldn't sew on a day like this. There's something in the air that gets into my blood and makes a sort of glory in my soul. My fingers would twitch and I'd sew a crooked seam. So it's ho for the park and the pines."

"Does 'we' include any one but yourself and Priscilla?"

"Yes, it includes Gilbert and Charlie, and we'll be very glad if it will include you, also."

"But," said Philippa dolefully, "if I go I'll have to be gooseberry, and that will be a new experience for Philippa Gordon."

"Well, new experiences are broadening. Come along, and you'll be able to sympathize with all poor souls who have to play gooseberry often. But where are all the victims?"

"Oh, I was tired of them all and simply couldn't be bothered with any of them today. Besides, I've been feeling a little blue—just a pale, elusive azure. It isn't serious enough for anything darker. I wrote Alec and Alonzo last week. I put the letters into envelopes and addressed them, but I didn't seal them up. That evening something funny happened. That is, Alec would think it funny, but Alonzo wouldn't be likely to. I was in a hurry, so I snatched Alec's letter—as I thought—out of the envelope and scribbled down a postscript. Then I mailed both letters. I got Alonzo's reply this morning. Girls, I had put that postscript to *his* letter and he was furious. Of course he'll get over it—and I don't care if he doesn't—but it spoiled my day. So I thought

I'd come to you darlings to get cheered up. After the football season opens I won't have any spare Saturday afternoons. I adore football. I've got the most gorgeous cap and sweater striped in Redmond colors to wear to the games. To be sure, a little way off I'll look like a walking barber's pole. Do you know that that Gilbert of yours has been elected Captain of the Freshman football team?"

"Yes, he told us so last evening," said Priscilla, seeing that outraged Anne would not answer. "He and Charlie were down. We knew they were coming, so we painstakingly put out of sight or out of reach all Miss Ada's cushions. That very elaborate one with the raised embroidery I dropped on the floor in the corner behind the chair it was on. I thought it would be safe there. But would you believe it? Charlie Sloane made for that chair, noticed the cushion behind it, solemnly fished it up, and sat on it the whole evening. Such a wreck of a cushion as it was! Poor Miss Ada asked me today, still smiling, but oh, so reproachfully, why I had allowed it to be sat upon. I told her I hadn't—that it was a matter of predestination coupled with inveterate Sloanishness and I wasn't a match for both combined."

"Miss Ada's cushions are really getting on my nerves," said Anne. "She finished two new ones last week, stuffed and embroidered within an inch of their lives. There being absolutely no other cushionless place to put them she stood them up against the wall on the stair landing. They topple over half the time and if we come up or down the stairs in the dark we fall over them. Last Sunday, when Dr. Davis prayed for all those exposed to the perils of the sea, I added in thought 'and for all those who live in houses where cushions are loved not wisely but too well!' There! we're ready, and I see the boys coming through Old St. John's. Do you cast in your lot with us, Phil?"

"I'll go, if I can walk with Priscilla and Charlie. That will be a bearable degree of gooseberry. That Gilbert of yours is a darling, Anne, but why *does* he go around so much with Goggle-eyes?"

Anne stiffened. She had no great liking for Charlie Sloane; but he was of Avonlea, so no outsider had any business to laugh at him.

"Charlie and Gilbert have always been friends," she said coldly. "Charlie is a nice boy. He's not to blame for his eyes."

"Don't tell me that! He is! He must have done something dreadful in a previous existence to be punished with such eyes. Pris and I are going to have such sport with him this afternoon. We'll make fun of him to his face and he'll never know it."

Doubtless, "the abandoned P's," as Anne called them, did carry out their amiable intentions. But Sloane was blissfully ignorant; he thought he was quite a fine fellow to be walking with two such coeds, especially Philippa Gordon, the class beauty and belle. It must surely impress Anne. She would see that some people appreciated him at his real value.

Gilbert and Anne loitered a little behind the others, enjoying the calm, still beauty of the autumn afternoon under the pines of the park, on the road that climbed and twisted around the harbor shore.

"The silence here is like a prayer, isn't it?" said Anne, her face upturned to the shining sky. "How I love the pines! They seem to strike their roots deep into the romance of all the ages. It is so comforting to creep away now and then for a good talk with them. I always feel so happy out here."

> "'And so in mountain solitudes o'ertaken
> As by some spell divine,
> Their cares drop from them like the needles shaken
> From out the gusty pine,'"

quoted Gilbert.

"They make our little ambitions seem rather petty, don't they, Anne?"

"I think, if ever any great sorrow came to me, I would come to the pines for comfort," said Anne dreamily.

"I hope no great sorrow ever will come to you, Anne," said Gilbert, who could not connect the idea of sorrow with the vivid, joyous creature beside him, unwitting that those who can soar to the highest heights can also plunge to the deepest depths, and that the natures which enjoy most keenly are those which also suffer most sharply.

"But there must—sometime," mused Anne. "Life seems like a cup of glory held to my lips just now. But there must be some bitterness in it—there is in every cup. I shall taste mine some day. Well, I hope I shall be strong and brave to meet it. And I hope it won't be through my own fault that it will come. Do you remember what Dr. Davis said last Sunday evening—that the sorrows God sent us brought comfort and strength with them, while the sorrows we brought on ourselves, through folly or wickedness, were by far the hardest to bear? But we mustn't talk of sorrow on an afternoon like this. It's meant for the sheer joy of living, isn't it?"

"If I had my way I'd shut everything out of your life but happiness and pleasure, Anne," said Gilbert in the tone that meant "danger ahead."

"Then you would be very unwise," rejoined Anne hastily. "I'm sure no life can be properly developed and rounded out without some trial and sorrow—though I suppose it is only when we are pretty comfortable that we admit it. Come—the others have got to the pavilion and are beckoning to us."

They all sat down in the little pavilion to watch an autumn sunset of deep red fire and pallid gold. To their left lay Kingsport, its roofs and spires dim in their shroud of violet smoke. To their right lay the harbor, taking on tints of rose and copper as it stretched out into the sunset. Before them the water shimmered, satin smooth and silver gray, and beyond, clean shaven William's Island loomed out of the mist, guarding the town like a sturdy bulldog. Its lighthouse beacon flared through the mist like a baleful star, and was answered by another in the far horizon.

"Did you ever see such a strong-looking place?" asked Philippa. "I don't want William's Island especially, but I'm sure I couldn't get it if I did. Look at that sentry on the summit of the fort, right beside the flag. Doesn't he look as if he had stepped out of a romance?"

"Speaking of romance," said Priscilla, "we've been looking for heather—but, of course, we couldn't find any. It's too late in the season, I suppose."

"Heather!" exclaimed Anne. "Heather doesn't grow in America, does it?"

"There are just two patches of it in the whole continent," said Phil, "one right here in the park, and one somewhere else in Nova Scotia, I forget where. The famous Highland Regiment, the Black Watch, camped here one year, and, when the men shook out the straw of their beds in the spring, some seeds of heather took root."

"Oh, how delightful!" said enchanted Anne.

"Let's go home around by Spofford Avenue," suggested Gilbert. "We can see all 'the handsome houses where the wealthy nobles dwell.' Spofford Avenue is the finest residential street in Kingsport. Nobody can build on it unless he's a millionaire."

"Oh, do," said Phil. "There's a perfectly killing little place I want to show you, Anne. *It* wasn't built by a millionaire. It's the first place after you leave the park, and must have grown while Spofford Avenue was still a country road. It *did* grow—it wasn't built! I don't care for the houses on the Avenue. They're too brand new and plate-glassy. But this little spot is a dream—and its name—but wait till you see it."

They saw it as they walked up the pine-fringed hill from the park. Just on the crest, where Spofford Avenue petered out into a plain road, was a little white frame house with groups of pines on either side of it, stretching their arms protectingly over its low roof. It was covered with red and gold vines, through which its green-shuttered windows peeped. Before it was a tiny garden, surrounded by a low stone wall. October though it was, the garden was still very sweet with dear, old-fashioned, unworldly flowers and shrubs—sweet may, southern-wood, lemon verbena, alyssum, petunias, marigolds, and chrysanthemums. A tiny brick wall, in herring-bone pattern, led from the gate to the front porch. The whole place might have been transplanted from some remote country village; yet there was something about it that made its nearest neighbor, the big lawn-encircled palace of a tobacco king, look exceedingly crude and showy and ill-bred by contrast. As Phil said, it was the difference between being born and being made.

"It's the dearest place I ever saw," said Anne delightedly. "It gives me one of my old, delightful, funny aches. It's dearer and quainter than even Miss Lavendar's stone house."

"It's the name I want you to notice especially," said Phil. "Look— in white letters, around the archway over the gate. 'Patty's Place.' Isn't that killing? Especially on this Avenue of Pinehursts and Elmwolds and Cedarcrofts? 'Patty's Place,' if you please! I adore it."

"Have you any idea who Patty is?" asked Priscilla.

"Patty Spofford is the name of the old lady who owns it, I've dis- covered. She lives there with her niece, and they've lived there for hundreds of years, more or less—maybe a little less, Anne. Exaggeration is merely a flight of poetic fancy. I understand that wealthy folk have tried to buy the lot time and again—it's really worth a small fortune now, you know—but 'Patty' won't sell upon any consideration. And there's an apple orchard behind the house in place of a back yard— you'll see it when we get a little past—a real apple orchard on Spofford Avenue!"

"I'm going to dream about 'Patty's Place' tonight," said Anne. "Why, I feel as if I belonged to it. I wonder if, by any chance, we'll ever see the inside of it."

"It isn't likely," said Priscilla.

Anne smiled mysteriously.

"No, it isn't likely. But I believe it will happen. I have a queer, creepy, crawly feeling—you can call it a presentiment, if you like—that 'Patty's Place' and I are going to be better acquainted yet."

7

Home Again

hose first three weeks at Redmond had seemed long; but the rest of the term flew by on wings of wind. Before they realized it the Redmond students found themselves in the grind of Christmas examinations, emerging therefrom more or less triumphantly. The honor of leading in the Freshman classes fluctuated between Anne, Gilbert, and Philippa, Priscilla did very well; Charlie Sloane scraped through respectably, and comported himself as complacently as if he had led in everything.

"I can't really believe that this time tomorrow I'll be in Green Gables," said Anne on the night before departure. "But I shall be. And you, Phil, will be in Bolingbroke with Alec and Alonzo."

"I'm longing to see them," admitted Phil, between the chocolate she was nibbling. "They really are such dear boys, you know. Oh, I'm going to have a splendid time in the holidays. There's to be no end of dances and drives and general jamborees. I shall never forgive you, Queen Anne, for not coming home with me for the holidays."

"'Never' means three days with you, Phil. It was dear of you to ask me—and I'd love to go to Bolingbroke some day. But I can't go this year—I *must* go home. You don't know how my heart longs for it."

"You won't have much of a time," said Phil scornfully. "There'll be one or two quilting parties, I suppose; and all the old gossips will talk you over to your face and behind your back. You'll die of lonesomeness, child."

"In Avonlea?" said Anne, highly amused.

"Now, if you'd come with me you'd have a perfectly gorgeous time. Bolingbroke would go wild over you, Queen Anne—your hair and your style and, oh, everything! You're so *different*. You'd be such a success—and I would bask in reflected glory—'not the rose but near the rose.' *Do* come, after all, Anne."

"Your picture of social triumphs is quite fascinating, Phil, but I'll paint one to offset it. I'm going home to an old country farmhouse, once green, rather faded now, set among leafless apple orchards. There is a brook below and a December fir wood beyond, where I've heard harps swept by the fingers of rain and wind. There is a pond nearby that will be gray and brooding now. There will be two oldish ladies in the house, one tall and thin, one short and fat; and there will be two twins, one a perfect model, the other what Mrs. Lynde calls a 'holy terror.' There will be a little room upstairs over the porch, where old dreams hang thick, and a big, fat, glorious feather bed which will almost seem the height of luxury after a boardinghouse mattress. How do you like my picture, Phil?"

"It seems a very dull one," said Phil, with a grimace.

"Oh, but I've left out the transforming thing," said Anne softly. "There'll be love there, Phil—faithful, tender love, such as I'll never find anywhere else in the world—love that's waiting for *me*. That makes my picture a masterpiece, doesn't it, even if the colors are not very brilliant?"

Phil silently got up, tossed her box of chocolates away, went up to Anne, and put her arms about her.

"Anne, I wish I was like you," she said soberly.

Diana met Anne at the Carmody station the next night, and they drove home together under silent, star-sown depths of sky. Green Gables had a very festal appearance as they drove up the lane. There was a light in every window, the glow breaking out through the darkness like flame-red blossoms swung against the dark background of the Haunted Wood. And in the yard was a brave bonfire with two gay little figures dancing around it, one of which gave an unearthly yell as the buggy turned in under the poplars.

"Davy means that for an Indian war-whoop," said Diana. "Mr. Harrison's hired boy taught it to him, and he's been practicing it up to welcome you with. Mrs. Lynde says it has worn her nerves to a frazzle. He creeps up behind her, you know, and then lets go. He was determined to have a bonfire for you, too. He's been piling up dry branches for a fortnight and pestering Marilla to be let pour some kerosene oil over it before setting it on fire. I guess she did, by the smell, though Mrs. Lynde said up to the last that Davy would blow himself and everybody else up if he was let."

Anne was out of the buggy by this time, and Davy was rapturously hugging her knees, while even Dora was clinging to her hand.

"Isn't that a bully bonfire, Anne? Just let me show you how to poke it—see the sparks? I did it for you, Anne, 'cause I was so glad you were coming home."

The kitchen door opened and Marilla's spare form darkened against the inner light. She preferred to meet Anne in the shadows, for she was horribly afraid that she was going to cry with joy—she, stern, repressed Marilla, who thought all display of deep emotion unseemly. Mrs. Lynde was behind her, sonsy, kindly, matronly, as of yore. The love that Anne had told Phil was waiting for her surrounded her and enfolded her with its blessing and its sweetness. Nothing, after all, could compare with old ties, old friends, and old Green Gables! How starry Anne's eyes were as they sat down to the loaded supper table, how pink her cheeks, how silver-clear her laughter! And Diana was going to stay all night, too. How like the dear old times it was! And the rose-bud tea-set graced the table! With Marilla the force of nature could no further go.

"I suppose you and Diana will now proceed to talk all night," said Marilla sarcastically, as the girls went upstairs. Marilla was always sarcastic after any self-betrayal.

"Yes," agreed Anne gaily, "but I'm going to put Davy to bed first. He insists on that."

"You bet," said Davy, as they went along the hall. "I want somebody to say my prayers to again. It's no fun saying them alone."

"You don't say them alone, Davy. God is always with you to hear you."

"Well, I can't see Him," objected Davy. "I want to pray to somebody I can see, but I *won't* say them to Mrs. Lynde or Marilla, there now!"

Nevertheless, when Davy was garbed in his gray flannel nighty, he did not seem in a hurry to begin. He stood before Anne, shuffling one bare foot over the other, and looked undecided.

"Come, dear, kneel down," said Anne.

Davy came and burled his head in Anne's lap, but he did not kneel down.

"Anne," he said in a muffled voice, "I don't feel like praying after all. I haven't felt like it for a week now. I—I *didn't* pray last night nor the night before."

"Why not, Davy?" asked Anne gently.

"You—you won't be mad if I tell you?" implored Davy.

Anne lifted the little gray-flannelled body on her knee and cuddled his head on her arm.

"Do I ever get 'mad' when you tell me things, Davy?"

"No-o-o, you never do. But you get sorry, and that's worse. You'll be awful sorry when I tell you this, Anne—and you'll be 'shamed of me, I s'pose."

"Have you done something naughty, Davy, and is that why you can't say your prayers?"

"No, I haven't done anything naughty—yet. But I want to do it."

"What is it, Davy?"

"I—I want to say a bad word, Anne," blurted out Davy, with a desperate effort. "I heard Mr. Harrison's hired boy say it one day last week, and ever since I've been wanting to say it *all* the time—even when I'm saying my prayers."

"Say it then, Davy."

Davy lifted his flushed face in amazement.

"But, Anne, it's an *awful* bad word."

"*Say it!*"

Davy gave her another incredulous look, then in a low voice he said the dreadful word. The next minute his face was burrowing against her.

"Oh, Anne, I'll never say it again—never. I'll never *want* to say it again. I knew it was bad, but I didn't s'pose it was so—so—I didn't s'pose it was like *that*."

"No, I don't think you'll ever want to say it again, Davy—or think it, either. And I wouldn't go about much with Mr. Harrison's hired boy if I were you."

"He can make bully war-whoops," said Davy a little regretfully.

"But you don't want your mind filled with bad words, do you, Davy—words that will poison it and drive out all that is good and manly?"

"No," said Davy, owl-eyed with introspection.

"Then don't go with those people who use them. And now do you feel as if you could say your prayers, Davy?"

"Oh, yes," said Davy, eagerly wriggling down on his knees, "I can say them now all right. I ain't scared now to say 'if I should die before I wake,' like I was when I was wanting to say that word."

Probably Anne and Diana did empty out their souls to each other that night, but no record of their confidences has been preserved. They both looked as fresh and bright-eyed at breakfast as only youth can look after unlawful hours of revelry and confession. There had been no snow up to this time, but as Diana crossed the old log bridge on her homeward way the white flakes were beginning to flutter down over the fields and woods, russet and gray in their dreamless sleep. Soon the far-away slopes and hills were dim and wraith-like through their gauzy scarfing, as if pale autumn had flung a misty bridal veil over her hair and was waiting for her wintry bridegroom. So they had a white Christmas after all, and a very pleasant day it was. In the forenoon letters and gifts came from Miss Lavendar and Paul; Anne opened them in the cheerful Green Gables kitchen, which was filled with what Davy, sniffing in ecstasy, called "pretty smells."

"Miss Lavendar and Mr. Irving are settled in their new home now," reported Anne. "I am sure Miss Lavendar is perfectly happy—I know it by the general tone of her letter—but there's a note from Charlotta the Fourth. She doesn't like Boston at all, and she is fearfully homesick. Miss Lavendar wants me to go through to Echo Lodge some day while I'm home and light a fire to air it, and see that the cushions aren't getting moldy. I think I'll get Diana to go over with me next week, and we can spend the evening with Theodora Dix. I want to see Theodora. By the way, is Ludovic Speed still going to see her?"

"They say so," said Marilla, "and he's likely to continue it. Folks have given up expecting that that courtship will ever arrive anywhere."

"I'd hurry him up a bit, if I was Theodora, that's what," said Mrs. Lynde. And there is not the slightest doubt but that she would.

There was also a characteristic scrawl from Philippa, full of Alec and Alonzo, what they said and what they did, and how they looked when they saw her.

"But I can't make up my mind yet which to marry," wrote Phil. "I do wish you had come with me to decide for me. Some one will have to. When I saw Alec my heart gave a great thump and I thought, 'He must be the right one.' And then, when Alonzo came, thump went my heart again. So that's no guide, though it should be, according to all the novels I've ever read. Now, Anne, *your* heart wouldn't thump for anybody but the genuine Prince Charming, would it? There must be something radically wrong with mine. But I'm having a perfectly gorgeous time. How I wish you were here! It's snowing today, and I'm rapturous. I was so afraid we'd have a green Christmas and I loathe them. You know, when Christmas is a dirty grayey-browney affair, looking as if it had been left over a hundred years ago and had been in soak ever since, it is called a *green* Christmas! Don't ask me why. As Lord Dundreary says 'there are thome thingth no fellow can underthtand.'

"Anne, did you ever get on a street car and then discover that you hadn't any money with you to pay your fare? I did, the other day. It's quite awful. I had a nickel with me when I got on the car. I thought it was in the left pocket of my coat. When I got settled down comfortably I felt for it. It wasn't there. I had a cold chill. I felt in the other pocket. Not there. I had another chill. Then I felt in a little inside pocket. All in vain. I had two chills at once.

"I took off my gloves, laid them on the seat, and went over all my pockets again. It was not there. I stood up and shook myself, and then looked on the floor. The car was full of people, who were going home from the opera, and they all stared at me, but I was past caring for a little thing like that.

"But I could not find my fare. I concluded I must have put it in my mouth and swallowed it inadvertently.

"I didn't know what to do. Would the conductor, I wondered, stop the car and put me off in ignominy and shame? Was it possible that I could convince him that I was merely the victim of my own absent-mindedness, and not an unprincipled creature trying to obtain a ride upon false pretenses? How I wished that Alec or Alonzo were there. But they weren't because I wanted them. If I *hadn't* wanted them they would have been there by the dozen. And I couldn't decide what to say to the conductor when he came around. As soon as I got one sentence of explanation mapped out in my mind I felt nobody could believe it and I must compose another. It seemed there was nothing to do but trust in Providence, and for all the comfort that gave me I might as well have been the old lady who, when told by the captain during a storm that she must put her trust in the Almighty exclaimed, 'Oh, Captain, is it as bad as that?'

"Just at the conventional moment, when all hope had fled, and the conductor was holding out his box to the passenger next to me, I suddenly remembered where I had put that wretched coin of the realm. I hadn't swallowed it after all. I meekly fished it out of the index finger of my glove and poked it in the box. I smiled at everybody and felt that it was a beautiful world."

The visit to Echo Lodge was not the least pleasant of many pleasant holiday outings. Anne and Diana went back to it by the old way of the beech woods, carrying a lunch basket with them. Echo Lodge, which had been closed ever since Miss Lavendar's wedding, was briefly thrown open to wind and sunshine once more, and firelight glimmered again in the little rooms. The perfume of Miss Lavendar's rose bowl still filled the air. It was hardly possible to believe that Miss Lavendar would not come tripping in presently, with her brown eyes a-star with welcome, and that Charlotta the Fourth, blue of bow and wide of smile, would not pop through the door. Paul, too, seemed hovering around, with his fairy fancies.

"It really makes me feel a little bit like a ghost revisiting the old time glimpses of the moon," laughed Anne. "Let's go out and see if the echoes are at home. Bring the old horn. It is still behind the kitchen door."

The echoes were at home, over the white river, as silver-clear and multitudinous as ever; and when they had ceased to answer the girls locked up Echo Lodge again and went away in the perfect half hour that follows the rose and saffron of a winter sunset.

8

Anne's First Proposal

The old year did not slip away in a green twilight, with a pinky-yellow sunset. Instead, it went out with a wild, white bluster and blow. It was one of the nights when the storm-wind hurtles over the frozen meadows and black hollows, and moans around the eaves like a lost creature, and drives the snow sharply against the shaking panes.

"Just the sort of night people like to cuddle down between their blankets and count their mercies," said Anne to Jane Andrews, who had come up to spend the afternoon and stay all night. But when they were cuddled between their blankets, in Anne's little porch room, it was not her mercies of which Jane was thinking.

"Anne," she said very solemnly, "I want to tell you something. May I?"

Anne was feeling rather sleepy after the party Ruby Gillis had given the night before. She would much rather have gone to sleep than listen to Jane's confidences, which she was sure would bore her. She had no prophetic inkling of what was coming. Probably Jane was engaged, too; rumor averred that Ruby Gillis was engaged to the Spencervale schoolteacher, about whom all the girls were said to be quite wild.

"I'll soon be the only fancy-free maiden of our old quartet," thought Anne, drowsily. Aloud she said, "Of course."

"Anne," said Jane, still more solemnly, "what do you think of my brother Billy?"

Anne gasped over this unexpected question, and floundered helplessly in her thoughts. Goodness, what *did* she think of Billy Andrews? She had never thought *anything* about him—round-faced, stupid, perpetually smiling, good-natured Billy Andrews. Did *anybody* ever think about Billy Andrews?

ANNE OF THE ISLAND 589

"I—I don't understand, Jane," she stammered. "What do you mean—exactly?"

"Do you like Billy?" asked Jane bluntly.

"Why—why—yes, I like him, of course," gasped Anne, wondering if she were telling the literal truth. Certainly she did not *dis*like Billy. But could the indifferent tolerance with which she regarded him, when he happened to be in her range of vision, be considered positive enough for liking? *What* was Jane trying to elucidate?

"Would you like him for a husband?" asked Jane calmly.

"A husband!" Anne had been sitting up in bed, the better to wrestle with the problem of her exact opinion of Billy Andrews. Now she fell flatly back on her pillows, the very breath gone out of her. "*Whose* husband?"

"Yours, of course," answered Jane. "Billy wants to marry you. He's always been crazy about you—and now father has given him the upper farm in his own name and there's nothing to prevent him from getting married. But he's so shy he couldn't ask you himself if you'd have him, so he got me to do it. I'd rather not have, but he gave me no peace till I said I would, if I got a good chance. What do you think about it, Anne?"

Was it a dream? Was it one of those nightmare things in which you find yourself engaged or married to some one you hate or don't know, without the slightest idea how it ever came about? No, she, Anne Shirley, was lying there, wide awake, in her own bed, and Jane Andrews was beside her, calmly proposing for her brother Billy. Anne did not know whether she wanted to writhe or laugh; but she could do neither, for Jane's feelings must not be hurt.

"I—I couldn't marry Billy, you know, Jane," she managed to gasp. "Why, such an idea never occurred to me—never!"

"I don't suppose it did," agreed Jane. "Billy has always been far too shy to think of courting. But you might think it over, Anne. Billy is a good fellow. I must say that, if he *is* my brother. He has no bad habits and he's a great worker, and you can depend on him. 'A bird in the hand is worth two in the bush.' He told me to tell you he'd be quite willing to wait till you got through college, if you insisted, though he'd *rather* get married this spring before the planting begins. He'd always be very good to you, I'm sure, and you know, Anne, I'd love to have you for a sister."

"I can't marry Billy," said Anne decidedly. She had recovered her wits, and was even feeling a little angry. It was all so ridiculous. "There is no use thinking of it, Jane. I don't care anything for him in that way, and you must tell him so."

"Well, I didn't suppose you would," said Jane with a resigned sigh, feeling that she had done her best. "I told Billy I didn't believe it was a bit of use to ask you, but he insisted. Well, you've made your decision, Anne, and I hope you won't regret it."

Jane spoke rather coldly. She had been perfectly sure that the enamored Billy had no chance at all of inducing Anne to marry him. Nevertheless, she felt a little resentment that Anne Shirley, who was, after all, merely an adopted orphan, without kith or kin, should refuse *her* brother—one of the Avonlea Andrews. Well, pride sometimes goes before a fall, Jane reflected ominously.

Anne permitted herself to smile in the darkness over the idea that she might ever regret not marrying Billy Andrews.

"I hope Billy won't feel very badly over it," she said nicely.

Jane made a movement as if she were tossing her head on her pillow.

"Oh, he won't break his heart. Billy has too much good sense for that. He likes Nettie Blewett pretty well, too, and mother would rather he married her than any one. She's such a good manager and saver. I think, when Billy is once sure you won't have him, he'll take Nettie. Please don't mention this to any one, will you, Anne?"

"Certainly not," said Anne, who had no desire whatever to publish abroad the fact that Billy Andrews wanted to marry her, preferring her, when all was said and done, to Nettie Blewett. Nettie Blewett!

"And now I suppose we'd better go to sleep," suggested Jane.

To sleep went Jane easily and speedily; but, though very unlike Macbeth in most respects, she had certainly contrived to murder sleep for Anne. That proposed-to damsel lay on a wakeful pillow until the wee sma's, but her meditations were far from being romantic. It was not, however, until the next morning that she had an opportunity to indulge in a good laugh over the whole affair. When Jane had gone home—still with a hint of frost in voice and manner because Anne had declined so ungratefully and decidedly the honor of an alliance with the House of Andrews—Anne retreated to the porch room, shut the door, and had her laugh out at last.

"If I could only share the joke with some one!" she thought. "But I can't. Diana is the only one I'd want to tell, and, even if I hadn't sworn secrecy to Jane, I can't tell Diana things now. She tells everything to Fred—I know she does. Well, I've had my first proposal. I supposed it would come some day—but I certainly never thought it would be by proxy. It's awfully funny—and yet there's a sting in it, too, somehow."

Anne knew quite well wherein the sting consisted, though she did not put it into words. She had had her secret dreams of the first time some one should ask her the great question. And it had, in those dreams, always been very romantic and beautiful: and the some one was to be very handsome and dark-eyed and distinguished-looking and eloquent, whether he were Prince Charming to be enraptured with "yes," or one to whom a regretful, beautifully worded, but hopeless refusal must be given. If the latter, the refusal was to be expressed so delicately that it would be next best thing to acceptance, and he would go away, after kissing her hand, assuring her of his unalterable, lifelong devotion. And it would always be a beautiful memory, to be proud of and a little sad about, also.

And now, this thrilling experience had turned out to be merely grotesque. Billy Andrews had got his sister to propose for him because his father had given him the upper farm; and if Anne wouldn't "have him" Nettie Blewett would. There was romance for you, with a vengeance! Anne laughed—and then sighed. The bloom had been brushed from one little maiden dream. Would the painful process go on until everything became prosaic and hum-drum?

9

An Unwelcome Lover and
a Welcome Friend

The second term at Redmond sped as quickly as had the first—"actually whizzed away," Philippa said. Anne enjoyed it thoroughly in all its phases—the stimulating class rivalry, the making and deepening of new and helpful friendships, the gay little social stunts, the doings of the various societies of which she was a member, the widening of horizons and interests. She studied hard, for she had made up her mind to win the Thorburn Scholarship in English. This being won, meant that she could come back to Redmond the next year without trenching on Marilla's small savings—something Anne was determined she would not do.

Gilbert, too, was in full chase after a scholarship, but found plenty of time for frequent calls at Thirty-eight, St. John's. He was Anne's escort at nearly all the college affairs, and she knew that their names were coupled in Redmond gossip. Anne raged over this but was helpless; she could not cast an old friend like Gilbert aside, especially when he had grown suddenly wise and wary, as behooved him in the dangerous proximity of more than one Redmond youth who would gladly have taken his place by the side of the slender, red-haired coed, whose gray eyes were as alluring as stars of evening. Anne was never attended by the crowd of willing victims who hovered around Philippa's conquering march through her Freshman year; but there was a lanky, brainy Freshie, a jolly, little, round Sophomore, and a tall, learned Junior who all liked to call at Thirty-eight, St. John's, and talk over 'ologies and 'isms, as well as lighter subjects, with Anne, in the be-cushioned parlor of that domicile. Gilbert did not love any of them, and he was exceedingly careful to give none of them the advantage over him by any untimely display of his real feelings Anne-ward. To her he had become again the boy-comrade of Avonlea days, and as such could hold his own against any smitten swain who had so far entered the lists against him. As a companion, Anne honestly acknowledged nobody could be so satisfactory as Gilbert; she was very glad, so she told herself, that he had evidently dropped all nonsensical ideas—though she spent considerable time secretly wondering why.

Only one disagreeable incident marred that winter. Charlie Sloane, sitting bolt upright on Miss Ada's most dearly beloved cushion, asked Anne one night if she would promise "to become Mrs. Charlie Sloane some day." Coming after Billy Andrews' proxy effort, this was not quite the shock to Anne's romantic sensibilities that it would otherwise have been; but it was certainly another heart-rending disillusion. She was angry, too, for she felt that she had never given Charlie the slightest encouragement to suppose such a thing possible. But what could you expect of a Sloane, as Mrs. Rachel Lynde would ask scornfully? Charlie's whole attitude, tone, air, words, fairly reeked with Sloanishness. He was conferring a great honor—no doubt whatever about that. And when Anne, utterly insensible to the honor, refused him, as delicately and considerately as she could—for even a Sloane had feelings which ought not to be unduly lacerated—Sloanishness still further betrayed itself. Charlie certainly did not take his dismissal as Anne's imaginary rejected suitors did. Instead, he became angry, and showed it; he said two or three quite nasty things; Anne's temper flashed up mutinously and she retorted with a cutting little speech whose keenness pierced even Charlie's protective Sloanishness and reached the quick; he caught up his hat and flung himself out of the house with a very red face; Anne rushed upstairs, falling twice over Miss Ada's cushions on the way, and threw herself on her bed, in tears of humiliation and rage. Had she actually stooped to quarrel with a Sloane? Was it possible anything Charlie Sloane could say had power to make her angry? Oh, this was degradation, indeed—worse even than being the rival of Nettie Blewett!

"I wish I need never see the horrible creature again," she sobbed vindictively into her pillows.

She could not avoid seeing him again, but the outraged Charlie took care that it should not be at very close quarters. Miss Ada's cushions were henceforth safe from his depredations, and when he met Anne on the street, or in Redmond's halls, his bow was icy in the extreme. Relations between these two old schoolmates continued to be thus strained for nearly a year! Then Charlie transferred his blighted affections to a round, rosy, snub-nosed, blue-eyed, little Sophomore who appreciated them as they deserved, whereupon he forgave Anne and condescended to be civil to her again; in a patronizing manner intended to show her just what she had lost.

One day Anne scurried excitedly into Priscilla's room.

"Read that," she cried, tossing Priscilla a letter. "It's from Stella—and she's coming to Redmond next year—and what do you think of her idea? I think it's a perfectly splendid one, if we can only carry it out. Do you suppose we can, Pris?"

"I'll be better able to tell you when I find out what it is," said Priscilla, casting aside a Greek lexicon and taking up Stella's letter. Stella Maynard had been one of their chums at Queen's Academy and had been teaching school ever since.

"But I'm going to give it up, Anne dear," she wrote, "and go to college next year. As I took the third year at Queen's I can enter the Sophomore year. I'm tired of teaching in a back country school. Some day I'm going to write a treatise' on 'The Trials of a Country Schoolmarm.' It will be a harrowing bit of realism. It seems to be the prevailing impression that we live in clover, and have nothing to do but draw our quarter's salary. My treatise shall tell the truth about us. Why, if a week should pass without some one telling me that I am doing easy work for big pay I would conclude that I might as well order my ascension robe 'immediately and to onct.' 'Well, you get your money easy,' some rate-payer will tell me, condescendingly. 'All you have to do is to sit there and hear lessons.' I used to argue the matter at first, but I'm wiser now. Facts are stubborn things, but, as some one has wisely said, not half so stubborn as fallacies. So I only smile loftily now in eloquent silence. Why, I have nine grades in my school and I have to teach a little of everything, from investigating the interiors of earthworms to the study of the solar system. My youngest pupil is four—his mother sends him to school to 'get him out of the way'—and my oldest twenty—it 'suddenly struck him' that it would be easier to go to school and get an education than follow the plough any longer. In the wild effort to cram all sorts of research into six hours a day I don't wonder if the children feel like the little boy who was taken to see the biograph. 'I have to look for what's coming next before I know what went last,' he complained. I feel like that myself.

"And the letters I get, Anne! Tommy's mother writes me that Tommy is not coming on in arithmetic as fast as she would like. He is only in simple reduction yet, and Johnny Johnson is in fractions, and Johnny isn't half as smart as her Tommy, and she can't understand it. And Susy's father wants to know why Susy can't write a letter without misspelling half the words, and Dick's aunt wants me to change his seat, because that bad Brown boy he is sitting with is teaching him to say naughty words.

"As to the financial part—but I'll not begin on *that*. Those whom the gods wish to destroy they first make country schoolmarms!

"There, I feel better, after that growl. After all, I've enjoyed these past two years. But I'm coming to Redmond.

"And now, Anne, I've a little plan. You know how I loathe boarding. I've boarded for four years and I'm so tired of it. I don't feel like enduring three years more of it. Now, why can't you and Priscilla and I club together, rent a little house somewhere in Kingsport, and board ourselves? It would be cheaper than any other way. Of course, we would have to have a housekeeper and I have one ready on the spot. You've heard me speak of Aunt Jamesina? She's the sweetest aunt that ever lived, in spite of her name. She can't help that! She was called Jamesina because her father, whose name was James, was drowned at sea a month before she was born. I always call her Aunt Jimsie. Well, her only daughter has recently married and gone to the foreign mission field. Aunt Jamesina is left alone in a great big house, and she is horribly lonesome. She will come to Kingsport and keep house for us if we want her, and I know you'll both love her. The more I think of the plan the more I like it. We could have such good, independent times.

"Now, if you and Priscilla agree to it, wouldn't it be a good idea for you, who are on the spot, to look around and see if you can find a suitable house this spring? That would be better than leaving it till the fall. If you could get a furnished one so much the better, but if not, we can scare up a few sticks of furniture between us and old family friends with attics. Anyhow, decide as soon as you can and write me, so that Aunt Jamesina will know what plans to make for next year."

"I think it's a good idea," said Priscilla.

"So do I," agreed Anne delightedly. "Of course, we have a nice boardinghouse here, but, when all's said and done, a boardinghouse isn't home. So let's go house-hunting at once, before exams come on."

"I'm afraid it will be hard enough to get a really suitable house," warned Priscilla. "Don't expect too much, Anne. Nice houses in nice localities will probably be away beyond our means. We'll likely have to content ourselves with a shabby little place on some street whereon live people whom to know is to be unknown, and make life inside compensate for the outside."

Accordingly they went house-hunting, but to find just what they wanted proved even harder than Priscilla had feared. Houses there were galore, furnished and unfurnished; but one was too big, another too small; this one too expensive, that one too far from Redmond. Exams were on and over; the last week of the term came and still their "house o' dreams," as Anne called it, remained a castle in the air.

"We shall have to give up and wait till the fall, I suppose," said Priscilla wearily, as they rambled through the park on one of April's darling days of breeze and blue, when the harbor was creaming and shimmering beneath the pearl-hued mists floating over it. "We may find some shack to shelter us then; and if not, boardinghouses we shall have always with us."

"I'm not going to worry about it just now, anyway, and spoil this lovely afternoon," said Anne, gazing around her with delight. The fresh chill air was faintly charged with the aroma of pine balsam, and the sky above was crystal clear and blue—a great inverted cup of blessing. "Spring is singing in my blood today, and the lure of April is abroad on the air. I'm seeing visions and dreaming dreams, Pris. That's because the wind is from the west. I do love the west wind. It sings of hope and gladness, doesn't it? When the east wind blows I always think of sorrowful rain on the eaves and sad waves on a gray shore. When I get old I shall have rheumatism when the wind is east."

"And isn't it jolly when you discard furs and winter garments for the first time and sally forth, like this, in spring attire?" laughed Priscilla. "Don't you feel as if you had been made over new?"

"Everything is new in the spring," said Anne. "Springs themselves are always so new, too. No spring is ever just like any other spring. It always has something of its own to be its own peculiar sweetness. See how green the grass is around that little pond, and how the willow buds are bursting."

"And exams are over and gone—the time of Convocation will soon come—next Wednesday. This day week we'll be home."

"I'm glad," said Anne dreamily. "There are so many things I want to do. I want to sit on the back porch steps and feel the breeze blowing down over Mr. Harrison's fields. I want to hunt ferns in the Haunted Wood and gather violets in Violet Vale. Do you remember the day of our golden picnic, Priscilla? I want to hear the frogs singing and the poplars whispering. But I've learned to love Kingsport, too, and I'm glad I'm coming back next fall. If I hadn't won the Thorburn I don't believe I could have. I *couldn't* take any of Marilla's little hoard."

"If we could only find a house!" sighed Priscilla. "Look over there at Kingsport, Anne—houses, houses everywhere, and not one for us."

"Stop it, Pris. 'The best is yet to be.' Like the old Roman, we'll find a house or build one. On a day like this there's no such word as fail in my bright lexicon."

They lingered in the park until sunset, living in the amazing miracle and glory and wonder of the springtide; and they went home as usual, by way of Spofford Avenue, that they might have the delight of looking at Patty's Place.

"I feel as if something mysterious were going to happen right away—'by the pricking of my thumbs,'" said Anne, as they went up the slope. "It's a nice story-bookish feeling. Why—why—why! Priscilla Grant, look over there and tell me if it's true, or am I seein' things?"

Priscilla looked. Anne's thumbs and eyes had not deceived her. Over the arched gateway of Patty's Place dangled a little, modest sign. It said "To Let, Furnished. Inquire Within."

"Priscilla," said Anne, in a whisper, "do you suppose it's possible that we could rent Patty's Place?"

"No, I don't," averred Priscilla. "It would be too good to be true. Fairy tales don't happen nowadays. I *won't* hope, Anne. The disappointment would be too awful to bear. They're sure to want more for it than we can afford. Remember, it's on Spofford Avenue."

"We must find out anyhow," said Anne resolutely. "It's too late to call this evening, but we'll come tomorrow. Oh, Pris, if we can get this darling spot! I've always felt that my fortunes were linked with Patty's Place, ever since I saw it first."

10

Patty's Place

he next evening found them treading resolutely the herring-bone walk through the tiny garden. The April wind was filling the pine trees with its roundelay, and the grove was alive with robins—great, plump, saucy fellows, strutting along the paths. The girls rang rather timidly, and were admitted by a grim and ancient handmaiden. The door opened directly into a large living-room, where by a cheery little fire sat two other ladies, both of whom were also grim and ancient. Except that one looked to be about seventy and the other fifty, there seemed little difference between them. Each had amazingly big, light-blue eyes behind steel-rimmed spectacles; each wore a cap and a gray shawl; each was knitting without haste and without rest; each rocked placidly and looked at the girls without speaking; and just behind each sat a large white china dog, with round green spots all over it, a green nose and green ears. Those dogs captured Anne's fancy on the spot; they seemed like the twin guardian deities of Patty's Place.

For a few minutes nobody spoke. The girls were too nervous to find words, and neither the ancient ladies nor the china dogs seemed conversationally inclined. Anne glanced about the room. What a dear place it was! Another door opened out of it directly into the pine grove and the robins came boldly up on the very step. The floor was spotted with round, braided mats, such as Marilla made at Green Gables, but which were considered out of date everywhere else, even in Avonlea. And yet here they were on Spofford Avenue! A big, polished grandfather's clock ticked loudly and solemnly in a corner. There were delightful little cupboards over the mantelpiece, behind whose glass doors gleamed quaint bits of china. The walls were hung with old prints and silhouettes. In one corner the stairs went up, and at the first low turn was a long window with an inviting seat. It was all just as Anne had known it must be.

By this time the silence had grown too dreadful, and Priscilla nudged Anne to intimate that she *must* speak.

"We—we—saw by your sign that this house is to let," said Anne faintly, addressing the older lady, who was evidently Miss Patty Spofford.

"Oh, yes," said Miss Patty. "I intended to take that sign down today."

"Then—then we are too late," said Anne sorrowfully. "You've let it to some one else?"

"No, but we have decided not to let it at all."

"Oh, I'm so sorry," exclaimed Anne impulsively. "I love this place so. I did hope we could have got it."

Then did Miss Patty lay down her knitting, take off her specs, rub them, put them on again, and for the first time look at Anne as at a human being. The other lady followed her example so perfectly that she might as well have been a reflection in a mirror.

"You *love* it," said Miss Patty with emphasis. "Does that mean that you really *love* it? Or that you merely like the looks of it? The girls nowadays indulge in such exaggerated statements that one never can tell what they *do* mean. It wasn't so in my young days. *Then* a girl did not say she *loved* turnips, in just the same tone as she might have said she loved her mother or her Savior."

Anne's conscience bore her up.

"I really do love it," she said gently. "I've loved it ever since I saw it last fall. My two college chums and I want to keep house next year instead of boarding, so we are looking for a little place to rent; and when I saw that this house was to let I was so happy."

"If you love it, you can have it," said Miss Patty. "Maria and I decided today that we would not let it after all, because we did not like any of the people who have wanted it. We don't *have* to let it. We can afford to go to Europe even if we don't let it. It would help us out, but not for gold will I let my home pass into the possession of such people as have come here and looked at it. *You* are different. I believe you do love it and will be good to it. You can have it."

"If—if we can afford to pay what you ask for it," hesitated Anne.

Miss Patty named the amount required. Anne and Priscilla looked at each other. Priscilla shook her head.

"I'm afraid we can't afford quite so much," said Anne, choking back her disappointment. "You see, we are only college girls and we are poor."

"What were you thinking you could afford?" demanded Miss Patty, ceasing not to knit.

Anne named her amount. Miss Patty nodded gravely.

"That will do. As I told you, it is not strictly necessary that we should let it at all. We are not rich, but we have enough to go to Europe on. I have never been in Europe in my life, and never expected or wanted to go. But my niece there, Maria Spofford, has taken a fancy to go. Now, you know a young person like Maria can't go globe-trotting alone."

"No—I—I suppose not," murmured Anne, seeing that Miss Patty was quite solemnly in earnest.

"Of course not. So I have to go along to look after her. I expect to enjoy it, too; I'm seventy years old, but I'm not tired of living yet. I daresay I'd have gone to Europe before if the idea had occurred to me. We shall be away for two years, perhaps three. We sail in June and we shall send you the key, and leave all in order for you to take possession when you choose. We shall pack away a few things we prize especially, but all the rest will be left."

"Will you leave the china dogs?" asked Anne timidly.

"Would you like me to?"

"Oh, indeed, yes. They are delightful."

A pleased expression came into Miss Patty's face.

"I think a great deal of those dogs," she said proudly. "They are over a hundred years old, and they have sat on either side of this fireplace ever since my brother Aaron brought them from London fifty years ago. Spofford Avenue was called after my brother Aaron."

"A fine man he was," said Miss Maria, speaking for the first time. "Ah, you don't see the like of him nowadays."

"He was a good uncle to you, Maria," said Miss Patty, with evident emotion. "You do well to remember him."

"I shall always remember him," said Miss Maria solemnly. "I can see him, this minute, standing there before that fire, with his hands under his coat-tails, beaming on us."

Miss Maria took out her handkerchief and wiped her eyes; but Miss Patty came resolutely back from the regions of sentiment to those of business.

"I shall leave the dogs where they are, if you will promise to be very careful of them," she said. "Their names are Gog and Magog. Gog looks to the right and Magog to the left. And there's just one thing more. You don't object, I hope, to this house being called Patty's Place?"

"No, indeed. We think that is one of the nicest things about it."

"You have sense, I see," said Miss Patty in a tone of great satisfaction. "Would you believe it? All the people who came here to rent the house wanted to know if they couldn't take the name off the gate during their occupation of it. I told them roundly that the name went with the house. This has been Patty's Place ever since my brother Aaron left it to me in his will, and Patty's Place it shall remain until I die and Maria dies. After that happens the next possessor can call it any fool name he likes," concluded Miss Patty, much as she might have said, "After that— the deluge." "And now, wouldn't you like to go over the house and see it all before we consider the bargain made?"

Further exploration still further delighted the girls. Besides the big living-room, there was a kitchen and a small bedroom downstairs. Upstairs were three rooms, one large and two small. Anne took an especial fancy to one of the small ones, looking out into the big pines, and hoped it would be hers. It was papered in pale blue and had a little, old-timey toilet table with sconces for candles. There was a diamond-paned window with a seat under the blue muslin frills that would be a satisfying spot for studying or dreaming.

"It's all so delicious that I know we are going to wake up and find it a fleeting vision of the night," said Priscilla as they went away.

"Miss Patty and Miss Maria are hardly such stuff as dreams are made of," laughed Anne. "Can you fancy them 'globe-trotting'— especially in those shawls and caps?"

"I suppose they'll take them off when they really begin to trot," said Priscilla, "but I know they'll take their knitting with them everywhere. They simply couldn't be parted from it. They will walk about Westminster Abbey and knit, I feel sure. Meanwhile, Anne, we shall be living in Patty's Place—*and* on Spofford Avenue. I feel like a millionairess even now."

"I feel like one of the morning stars that sang for joy," said Anne.

Phil Gordon crept into Thirty-eight, St. John's, that night and flung herself on Anne's bed.

"Girls, dear, I'm tired to death. I feel like the man without a country—or was it without a shadow? I forget which. Anyway. I've been packing up."

"And I suppose you are worn out because you couldn't decide which things to pack first, or where to put them," laughed Priscilla.

"E-zackly. And when I had got everything jammed in somehow, and my landlady and her maid had both sat on it while I locked it, I discovered I had packed a whole lot of things I wanted for Convocation at the very bottom. I had to unlock the old thing and poke and dive into it for an hour before I fished out what I wanted. I would get hold of something that felt like what I was looking for, and I'd yank it up, and it would be something else. No, Anne, I did not swear."

"I didn't say you did."

"Well, you looked it. But I admit my thoughts verged on the profane. And I have such a cold in the head—I can do nothing but sniffle, sigh, and sneeze. Isn't that alliterative agony for you? Queen Anne, do say something to cheer me up."

"Remember that next Thursday night you'll be back in the land of Alec and Alonzo," suggested Anne.

Phil shook her head dolefully.

"More alliteration. No, I don't want Alec and Alonzo when I have a cold in the head. But what has happened you two? Now that I look at you closely you seem all lighted up with an internal iridescence. Why, you're actually *shining!* What's up?"

"We are going to live in Patty's Place next winter," said Anne triumphantly. "*Live*, mark you, not board! We've rented it, and Stella Maynard is coming, and her aunt is going to keep house for us."

Phil bounced up, wiped her nose, and fell on her knees before Anne.

"Girls—girls—let me come, too. Oh, I'll be so good. If there's no room for me I'll sleep in the little doghouse in the orchard—I've seen it. Only let me come."

"Get up, you goose."

"I won't stir off my marrow bones till you tell me. I can live with you next winter."

Anne and Priscilla looked at each other. Then Anne said slowly, "Phil dear, we'd love to have you. But we may as well speak plainly. I'm poor—Pris is poor—Stella Maynard is poor—our housekeeping will have to be very simple and our table plain. You'd have to live as we would. Now, you are rich and your boardinghouse fare attests the fact."

"Oh, what do I care for that?" demanded Phil tragically. "Better a dinner of herbs where your chums are than a stalled ox in a lonely boardinghouse. Don't think I'm *all* stomach, girls. I'll be willing to live on bread and water—with just a *leetle* jam—if you'll let me come."

"And then," continued Anne, "there will be a good deal of work to be done. Stella's aunt can't do it all. We all expect to have our chores to do. Now, you—"

"Toil not, neither do I spin," finished Philippa. "But I'll learn to do things. You'll only have to show me once. I *can* make my own bed to begin with. And remember that, though I can't cook, I *can* keep my temper. That's something. And I *never* growl about the weather. That's more. Oh, please, please! I never wanted anything so much in my life—and this floor is awfully hard."

"There's just one more thing," said Priscilla resolutely. "You, Phil, as all Redmond knows, entertain callers almost every evening. Now, at Patty's Place we can't do that. We have decided that we shall be at home to our friends on Friday evenings only. If you come with us you'll have to abide by that rule,"

"Well, you don't think I'll mind that, do you? Why, I'm glad of it. I knew I should have had some such rule myself, but I hadn't enough decision to make it or stick to it. When I can shuffle off the responsibility on you it will be a real relief. If you won't let me cast in my lot with you I'll die of the disappointment and then I'll come back and haunt you. I'll camp on the very doorstep of Patty's Place and you won't be able to go out or come in without falling over my spook."

Again Anne and Priscilla exchanged eloquent looks.

"Well," said Anne, "of course we can't promise to take you until we've consulted with Stella; but I don't think she'll object, and, as far as we are concerned, you may come and glad welcome."

"If you get tired of our simple life you can leave us, and no questions asked," added Priscilla.

Phil sprang up, hugged them both jubilantly, and went on her way rejoicing.

"I hope things will go right," said Priscilla soberly.

"We must *make* them go right," avowed Anne. "I think Phil will fit into our 'appy little 'ome very well."

"Oh. Phil's a dear to rattle round with and be chums. And, of course, the more there are of us the easier it will be on our slim purses. But how will she be to live with? You have to summer and winter with any one before you know if she's *livable* or not."

"Oh, well, we'll all be put to the test, as far as that goes. And we must quit us like sensible folk, living and let live. Phil isn't selfish, though she's a little thoughtless, and I believe we will all get on beautifully in Patty's Place."

11

The Round of Life

Anne was back in Avonlea with the luster of the Thorburn Scholarship on her brow. People told her she hadn't changed much, in a tone which hinted they were surprised and a little disappointed she hadn't. Avonlea had not changed, either. At least, so it seemed at first. But as Anne sat in the Green Gables pew, on the first Sunday after her return, and looked over the congregation, she saw several little changes which, all coming home to her at once, made her realize that time did not quite stand still, even in Avonlea. A new minister was in the pulpit. In the pews more than one familiar face was missing forever. Old "Uncle Abe," his prophesying over and done with, Mrs. Peter Sloane, who had sighed, it was to be hoped, for the last time, Timothy Cotton, who, as Mrs. Rachel Lynde said "had actually managed to die at last after practicing at it for twenty years," and old Josiah Sloane, whom nobody knew in his coffin because he had his whiskers neatly trimmed, were all sleeping in the little graveyard behind the church. And Billy Andrews was married to Nettie Blewett! They "appeared out" that Sunday. When Billy, beaming with pride and happiness, showed his be-plumed and be-silked bride into the Harmon Andrews' pew, Anne dropped her lids to hide her dancing eyes. She recalled the stormy winter night of the Christmas holidays when Jane had proposed for Billy. He certainly had not broken his heart over his rejection. Anne wondered if Jane had also proposed to Nettie for him, or if he had mustered enough spunk to ask the fateful question himself. All the Andrews family seemed to share in his pride and pleasure, from Mrs. Harmon in the pew to Jane in the choir. Jane had resigned from the Avonlea school and intended to go West in the fall.

"Can't get a beau in Avonlea, that's what," said Mrs. Rachel Lynde scornfully. "*Says* she thinks she'll have better health out West. I never heard her health was poor before."

"Jane is a nice girl," Anne had said loyally. "She never tried to attract attention, as some did."

"Oh, she never chased the boys, if that's what you mean," said Mrs. Rachel. "But she'd like to be married, just as much as anybody, that's what. What else would take her out West to some forsaken place whose only recommendation is that men are plenty and women scarce? Don't you tell me!"

But it was not at Jane Anne gazed that day in dismay and surprise. It was at Ruby Gillis, who sat beside her in the choir. What had happened to Ruby? She was even handsomer than ever; but her blue eyes were too bright and lustrous, and the color of her cheeks was hectically brilliant; besides, she was very thin; the hands that held her hymn-book were almost transparent in their delicacy.

"Is Ruby Gillis ill?" Anne asked of Mrs. Lynde, as they went home from church.

"Ruby Gillis is dying of galloping consumption," said Mrs. Lynde bluntly. "Everybody knows it except herself and her family. *They* won't give in. If you ask *them*, she's perfectly well. She hasn't been able to teach since she had that attack of congestion in the winter, but she says she's going to teach again in the fall, and she's after the White Sands school. She'll be in her grave, poor girl, when White Sands school opens, that's what."

Anne listened in shocked silence. Ruby Gillis, her old school-chum, dying? Could it be possible? Of late years they had grown apart; but the old tie of schoolgirl intimacy was there, and made itself felt sharply in the tug the news gave at Anne's heartstrings. Ruby, the brilliant, the merry, the coquettish! It was impossible to associate the thought of her with anything like death. She had greeted Anne with gay cordiality after church, and urged her to come up the next evening.

"I'll be away Tuesday and Wednesday evenings," she had whispered triumphantly. "There's a concert at Carmody and a party at White Sands. Herb Spencer's going to take me. He's my *latest*. Be sure to come up tomorrow. I'm dying for a good talk with you. I want to hear all about your doings at Redmond."

Anne knew that Ruby meant that she wanted to tell Anne all about her own recent flirtations, but she promised to go, and Diana offered to go with her.

"I've been wanting to go to see Ruby for a long while," she told Anne, when they left Green Gables the next evening, "but I really couldn't go alone. It's so awful to hear Ruby rattling on as she does, and pretending there is nothing the matter with her, even when she can hardly speak for coughing. She's fighting so hard for her life, and yet she hasn't any chance at all, they say."

The girls walked silently down the red, twilit road. The robins were singing vespers in the high treetops, filling the golden air with their jubilant voices. The silver fluting of the frogs came from marshes and ponds, over fields where seeds were beginning to stir with life and thrill to the sunshine and rain that had drifted over them. The air was fragrant with the wild, sweet, wholesome smell of young raspberry copses. White mists were hovering in the silent hollows and violet stars were shining bluely on the brooklands.

"What a beautiful sunset," said Diana. "Look, Anne, it's just like a land in itself, isn't it? That long, low bank of purple cloud is the shore, and the clear sky further on is like a golden sea."

"If we could sail to it in the moonshine boat Paul wrote of in his old composition—you remember?—how nice it would be," said Anne, rousing from her reverie. "Do you think we could find all our yesterdays there, Diana—all our old springs and blossoms? The beds of flowers that Paul saw there are the roses that have bloomed for us in the past?"

"Don't!" said Diana. "You make me feel as if we were old women with everything in life behind us."

"I think I've almost felt as if we were since I heard about poor Ruby," said Anne. "If it is true that she is dying any other sad thing might be true, too."

"You don't mind calling in at Elisha Wright's for a moment, do you?" asked Diana. "Mother asked me to leave this little dish of jelly for Aunt Atossa."

"Who is Aunt Atossa?"

"Oh, haven't you heard? She's Mrs. Samson Coates of Spencervale—Mrs. Elisha Wright's aunt. She's father's aunt, too. Her husband died last winter and she was left very poor and lonely, so the Wrights took her to live with them. Mother thought we ought to take her, but father put his foot down. Live with Aunt Atossa he would not."

"Is she so terrible?" asked Anne absently.

"You'll probably see what she's like before we can get away," said Diana significantly. "Father says she has a face like a hatchet—it cuts the air. But her tongue is sharper still."

Late as it was Aunt Atossa was cutting potato sets in the Wright kitchen. She wore a faded old wrapper, and her gray hair was decidedly untidy. Aunt Atossa did not like being "caught in a kilter," so she went out of her way to be disagreeable.

"Oh, so you're Anne Shirley?" she said, when Diana introduced Anne. "I've heard of you." Her tone implied that she had heard nothing good. "Mrs. Andrews was telling me you were home. She said you had improved a good deal."

There was no doubt Aunt Atossa thought there was plenty of room for further improvement. She ceased not from cutting sets with much energy.

"Is it any use to ask you to sit down?" she inquired sarcastically. "Of course, there's nothing very entertaining here for you. The rest are all away."

"Mother sent you this little pot of rhubarb jelly," said Diana pleasantly. "She made it today and thought you might like some."

"Oh, thanks," said Aunt Atossa sourly. "I never fancy your mother's jelly—she always makes it too sweet. However, I'll try to worry some down. My appetite's been dreadful poor this spring. I'm far from well," continued Aunt Atossa solemnly, "but still I keep a-doing. People who can't work aren't wanted *here*. If it isn't too much trouble will you be condescending enough to set the jelly in the pantry? I'm in a hurry to get these spuds done tonight. I suppose you two *ladies* never do anything like this. You'd be afraid of spoiling your hands."

"I used to cut potato sets before we rented the farm," smiled Anne.

"I do it yet," laughed Diana. "I cut sets three days last week. Of course," she added teasingly, "I did my hands up in lemon juice and kid gloves every night after it."

Aunt Atossa sniffed.

"I suppose you got that notion out of some of those silly magazines you read so many of. I wonder your mother allows you. But she always spoiled you. We all thought when George married her she wouldn't be a suitable wife for him."

Aunt Atossa sighed heavily, as if all forebodings upon the occasion of George Barry's marriage had been amply and darkly fulfilled.

"Going, are you?" she inquired, as the girls rose. "Well, I suppose you can't find much amusement talking to an old woman like me. It's such a pity the boys ain't home."

"We want to run in and see Ruby Gillis a little while," explained Diana.

"Oh, anything does for an excuse, of course," said Aunt Atossa, amiably. "Just whip in and whip out before you have time to say how-do decently. It's college airs, I s'pose. You'd be wiser to keep away from Ruby Gillis. The doctors say consumption's catching. I always knew Ruby'd get something, gadding off to Boston last fall for a visit. People who ain't content to stay home always catch something."

"People who don't go visiting catch things, too. Sometimes they even die," said Diana solemnly.

"Then they don't have themselves to blame for it," retorted Aunt Atossa triumphantly. "I hear you are to be married in June, Diana."

"There is no truth in that report," said Diana, blushing.

"Well, don't put it off too long," said Aunt Atossa significantly. "You'll fade soon—you're all complexion and hair. And the Wrights are terrible fickle. You ought to wear a hat, *Miss Shirley*. Your nose is freckling scandalous. My, but you *are* redheaded! Well, I s'pose we're all as the Lord made us! Give Marilla Cuthbert my respects. She's never been to see me since I come to Avonlea, but I s'pose I oughtn't to complain. The Cuthberts always did think themselves a cut higher than any one else round here."

"Oh, isn't she dreadful?" gasped Diana, as they escaped down the lane.

"She's worse than Miss Eliza Andrews," said Anne. "But then think of living all your life with a name like Atossa! Wouldn't it sour almost any one? She should have tried to imagine her name was Cordelia. It might have helped her a great deal. It certainly helped me in the days when I didn't like *Anne*."

"Josie Pye will be just like her when she grows up," said Diana. "Josie's mother and Aunt Atossa are cousins, you know. Oh, dear, I'm glad that's over. She's so malicious—she seems to put a bad flavor in everything. Father tells such a funny story about her. One time they had a minister in Spencervale who was a very good, spiritual man but very deaf. He couldn't hear any ordinary conversation at all. Well, they used to have a prayer meeting on Sunday evenings, and all the church members present would get up and pray in turn, or say a few words on some Bible verse. But one evening Aunt Atossa bounced up. She didn't either pray or preach. Instead, she lit into everybody else in the church and gave them a fearful raking down, calling them right out by name and telling them how they all had behaved, and casting up all the quarrels and scandals of the past ten years. Finally she wound up by saying that she was disgusted with Spencervale church and she never meant to darken its door again, and she hoped a fearful judgment would come upon it. Then she sat down out of breath, and the minister, who hadn't heard a word she said, immediately remarked, in a very devout voice, 'Amen! The Lord grant our dear sister's prayer!' You ought to hear father tell the story."

"Speaking of stories, Diana," remarked Anne, in a significant, confidential tone, "do you know that lately I have been wondering if I could write a short story—a story that would be good enough to be published?"

"Why, of course you could," said Diana, after she has grasped the amazing suggestion. "You used to write perfectly thrilling stories years ago in our old Story Club."

"Well, I hardly meant one of that kind of stories," smiled Anne. "I've been thinking about it a little of late, but I'm almost afraid to try, for, if I should fail, it would be too humiliating."

"I heard Priscilla say once that all Mrs. Morgan's first stories were rejected. But I'm sure yours wouldn't be, Anne, for it's likely editors have more sense nowadays."

"Margaret Burton, one of the Junior girls at Redmond, wrote a story last winter and it was published in the *Canadian Woman*. I really do think I could write one at least as good."

"And will you have it published in the *Canadian Woman*?"

"I might try one of the bigger magazines first. It all depends on what kind of a story I write."

"What is it to be about?"

"I don't know yet. I want to get hold of a good plot. I believe that is very necessary from an editor's point of view. The only thing I've settled on is the heroine's name. It is to be *Averil Lester*. Rather pretty, don't you think? Don't mention this to any one, Diana. I haven't told anybody but you and Mr. Harrison. *He* wasn't very encouraging—he said there was far too much trash written nowadays as it was, and he'd expected something better of me, after a year at college."

"What does Mr. Harrison know about it?" demanded Diana scornfully.

They found the Gillis home gay with lights and callers. Leonard Kimball, of Spencervale, and Morgan Bell, of Carmody, were glaring at each other across the parlor. Several merry girls had dropped in: Ruby was dressed in white and her eyes and cheeks were very brilliant. She laughed and chattered incessantly, and after the other girls had gone she took Anne upstairs to display her new summer dresses.

"I've a blue silk to make up yet, but it's a little heavy for summer wear. I think I'll leave it until the fall. I'm going to teach in White Sands, you know. How do you like my hat? That one you had on in church yesterday was real dinky. But I like something brighter for myself. Did you notice those two ridiculous boys downstairs? They've both come determined to sit each other out. I don't care a single bit about either of them, you know. Herb Spencer is the one I like. Sometimes I really do think's he's *Mr. Right*. At Christmas I thought the Spencervale schoolmaster was that. But I found out something about him that turned me against him. He nearly went insane when I turned him down. I wish those two boys hadn't come tonight. I wanted to have a nice good talk with you, Anne, and tell you such heaps of things. You and I were always good chums, weren't we?"

Ruby slipped her arm about Anne's waist with a shallow little laugh. But just for a moment their eyes met, and, behind all the luster of Ruby's, Anne saw something that made her heart ache.

"Come up often, won't you, Anne?" whispered Ruby. "Come alone—I want you."

"Are you feeling quite well, Ruby?"

"Me! Why, I'm perfectly well. I never felt better in my life. Of course, that congestion last winter pulled me down a little. But just see my color. I don't look much like an invalid, I'm sure."

Ruby's voice was almost sharp. She pulled her arm away from Anne, as if in resentment, and ran downstairs, where she was gayer than ever, apparently so much absorbed in bantering her two swains that Diana and Anne felt rather out of it and soon went away.

12

"Averil's Atonement"

"What are you dreaming of, Anne?"

The two girls were loitering one evening in a fairy hollow of the brook. Ferns nodded in it, and little grasses were green, and wild pears hung finely-scented, white curtains around it.

Anne roused herself from her reverie with a happy sigh.

"I was thinking out my story, Diana."

"Oh, have you really begun it?" cried Diana, all alight with eager interest in a moment.

"Yes, I have only a few pages written, but I have it all pretty well thought out. I've had such a time to get a suitable plot. None of the plots that suggested themselves suited a girl named *Averil*."

"Couldn't you have changed her name?"

"No, the thing was impossible. I tried to, but I couldn't do it, any more than I could change yours. *Averil* was so real to me that no matter what other name I tried to give her I just thought of her as *Averil* behind it all. But finally I got a plot that matched her. Then came the excitement of choosing names for all my characters. You have no idea how fascinating that is. I've lain awake for hours thinking over those names. The hero's name is *Perceval Dalrymple*."

"Have you named *all* the characters?" asked Diana wistfully. "If you hadn't I was going to ask you to let me name *one*—just some unimportant person. I'd feel as if I had a share in the story then."

"You may name the little hired boy who lived with the *Lesters*," conceded Anne. "He is not very important, but he is the only one left unnamed."

"Call him *Raymond Fitzosborne*," suggested Diana, who had a store of such names laid away in her memory, relics of the old "Story Club," which she and Anne and Jane Andrews and Ruby Gillis had had in their schooldays.

Anne shook her head doubtfully.

"I'm afraid that is too aristocratic a name for a chore boy, Diana. I couldn't imagine a Fitzosborne feeding pigs and picking up chips, could you?"

Diana didn't see why, if you had an imagination at all, you couldn't stretch it to that extent; but probably Anne knew best, and the chore boy was finally christened *Robert Ray*, to be called *Bobby* should occasion require.

"How much do you suppose you'll get for it?" asked Diana.

But Anne had not thought about this at all. She was in pursuit of fame, not filthy lucre, and her literary dreams were as yet untainted by mercenary considerations.

"You'll let me read it, won't you?" pleaded Diana.

"When it is finished I'll read it to you and Mr. Harrison, and I shall want you to criticize it *severely*. No one else shall see it until it is published."

"How are you going to end it—happily or unhappily?"

"I'm not sure. I'd like it to end unhappily, because that would be so much more romantic. But I understand editors have a prejudice against sad endings. I heard Professor Hamilton say once that nobody but a genius should try to write an unhappy ending. And," concluded Anne modestly, "I'm anything but a genius."

"Oh, I like happy endings best. You'd better let him marry her," said Diana, who, especially since her engagement to Fred, thought this was how every story should end.

"But you like to cry over stories?"

"Oh, yes, in the middle of them. But I like everything to come right at last."

"I must have *one* pathetic scene in it," said Anne thoughtfully. "I might let *Robert Ray* be injured in an accident and have a death scene."

"No, you mustn't kill *Bobby* off," declared Diana, laughing. "He belongs to me and I want him to live and flourish. Kill somebody else if you have to."

For the next fortnight Anne writhed or reveled, according to mood, in her literary pursuits. Now she would be jubilant over a brilliant idea, now despairing because some contrary character would *not* behave properly. Diana could not understand this.

"*Make* them do as you want them to," she said.

"I can't," mourned Anne. "Averil is such an unmanageable heroine. She *will* do and say things I never meant her to. Then that spoils everything that went before and I have to write it all over again."

Finally, however, the story was finished, and Anne read it to Diana in the seclusion of the porch gable. She had achieved her "pathetic scene" without sacrificing *Robert Ray*, and she kept a watchful eye on Diana as she read it. Diana rose to the occasion and cried properly; but, when the end came, she looked a little disappointed.

"Why did you kill *Maurice Lennox*?" she asked reproachfully.

"He was the villain," protested Anne. "He had to be punished."

"I like him best of them all," said unreasonable Diana.

"Well, he's dead, and he'll have to stay dead," said Anne, rather resentfully. "If I had let him live he'd have gone on persecuting *Averil* and *Perceval*."

"Yes—unless you had reformed him."

"That wouldn't have been romantic, and, besides, it would have made the story too long."

"Well, anyway, it's a perfectly elegant story, Anne, and will make you famous, of that I'm sure. Have you got a title for it?"

"Oh, I decided on the title long ago. I call it *Averil's Atonement*. Doesn't that sound nice and alliterative? Now, Diana, tell me candidly, do you see any faults in my story?"

"Well," hesitated Diana, "that part where *Averil* makes the cake doesn't seem to me quite romantic enough to match the rest. It's just what anybody might do. Heroines shouldn't do cooking, *I* think."

"Why, that is where the humor comes in, and it's one of the best parts of the whole story," said Anne. And it may be stated that in this she was quite right.

Diana prudently refrained from any further criticism, but Mr. Harrison was much harder to please. First he told her there was entirely too much description in the story.

"Cut out all those flowery passages," he said unfeelingly.

Anne had an uncomfortable conviction that Mr. Harrison was right, and she forced herself to expunge most of her beloved descriptions, though it took three re-writings before the story could be pruned down to please the fastidious Mr. Harrison.

"I've left out *all* the descriptions but the sunset," she said at last. "I simply *couldn't* let it go. It was the best of them all."

"It hasn't anything to do with the story," said Mr. Harrison, "and you shouldn't have laid the scene among rich city people. What do you know of them? Why didn't you lay it right here in Avonlea—changing the name, of course, or else Mrs. Rachel Lynde would probably think she was the heroine."

"Oh, that would never have done," protested Anne. "Avonlea is the dearest place in the world, but it isn't quite romantic enough for the scene of a story."

"I daresay there's been many a romance in Avonlea—and many a tragedy, too," said Mr. Harrison drily. "But your folks ain't like real folks anywhere. They talk too much and use too high-flown language. There's one place where that *Dalrymple* chap talks even on for two pages, and never lets the girl get a word in edgewise. If he'd done that in real life she'd have pitched him."

"I don't believe it," said Anne flatly. In her secret soul she thought that the beautiful, poetical things said to *Averil* would win any girl's heart completely. Besides, it was gruesome to hear of *Averil*, the stately, queen-like *Averil*, "pitching" any one. *Averil* "declined her suitors."

"Anyhow," resumed the merciless Mr. Harrison, "I don't seer why *Maurice Lennox* didn't get her. He was twice the man the other is. He did bad things, but he *did* them. *Perceval* hadn't time for anything but mooning."

"Mooning." That was even worse than "pitching!"

"*Maurice Lennox* was the villain," said Anne indignantly. "I don't see why every one likes him better than *Perceval*."

"Perceval is too good. He's aggravating. Next time you write about a hero put a little spice of human nature in him."

"*Averil* couldn't have married *Maurice*. He was bad."

"She'd have reformed him. You *can* reform a man; you can't reform a jelly-fish, of course. Your story isn't bad—it's kind of interesting, I'll admit. But you're too young to write a story that would be worthwhile. Wait ten years."

Anne made up her mind that the next time she wrote a story she wouldn't ask anybody to criticize it. It was too discouraging. She would not read the story to Gilbert, although she told him about it.

"If it is a success you'll see it when it is published, Gilbert, but if it is a failure nobody shall ever see it."

Marilla knew nothing about the venture. In imagination Anne saw herself reading a story out of a magazine to Marilla, entrapping her into praise of it—for in imagination all things are possible—and then triumphantly announcing herself the author.

One day Anne took to the Post Office a long, bulky envelope, addressed, with the delightful confidence of youth and inexperience, to the very biggest of the "big" magazines. Diana was as excited over it as Anne herself.

"How long do you suppose it will be before you hear from it?" she asked.

"It shouldn't be longer than a fortnight. Oh, how happy and proud I shall be if it is accepted!"

"Of course it will be accepted, and they will likely ask you to send them more. You may be as famous as Mrs. Morgan some day, Anne, and then how proud I'll be of knowing you," said Diana, who possessed, at least, the striking merit of an unselfish admiration of the gifts and graces of her friends.

A week of delightful dreaming followed, and then came a bitter awakening. One evening Diana found Anne in the porch gable, with suspicious-looking eyes. On the table lay a long envelope and a crumpled manuscript.

"Anne, your story hasn't come back?" cried Diana incredulously.

"Yes, it has," said Anne shortly.

"Well, that editor must be crazy. What reason did he give?"

"No reason at all. There is just a printed slip saying that it wasn't found acceptable."

"I never thought much of that magazine, anyway," said Diana hotly. "The stories in it are not half as interesting as those in the *Canadian Woman*, although it costs so much more. I suppose the editor is prejudiced against any one who isn't a Yankee. Don't be discouraged, Anne. Remember how Mrs. Morgan's stories came back. Send yours to the *Canadian Woman*."

"I believe I will," said Anne, plucking up heart. "And if it is published I'll send that American editor a marked copy. But I'll cut the sunset out. I believe Mr. Harrison was right."

Out came the sunset; but in spite of this heroic mutilation the editor of the *Canadian Woman* sent *Averil's Atonement* back so promptly that the indignant Diana declared that it couldn't have been read at all, and vowed she was going to stop her subscription immediately. Anne took this second rejection with the calmness of despair. She locked the story away in the garret trunk where the old Story Club tales reposed; but first she yielded to Diana's entreaties and gave her a copy.

"This is the end of my literary ambitions," she said bitterly.

She never mentioned the matter to Mr. Harrison, but one evening he asked her bluntly if her story had been accepted.

"No, the editor wouldn't take it," she answered briefly.

Mr. Harrison looked sidewise at the flushed, delicate profile.

"Well, I suppose you'll keep on writing them," he said encouragingly.

"No, I shall never try to write a story again," declared Anne, with the hopeless finality of nineteen when a door is shut in its face.

"I wouldn't give up altogether," said Mr. Harrison reflectively. "I'd write a story once in a while, but I wouldn't pester editors with it. I'd write of people and places like I knew, and I'd make my characters talk everyday English; and I'd let the sun rise and set in the usual quiet way without much fuss over the fact. If I had to have villains at all, I'd give them a chance, Anne—I'd give them a chance. There *are* some terrible bad men in the world, I suppose, but you'd have to go a long piece to find them—though Mrs. Lynde believes we're all bad. But most of us have got a little decency somewhere in us. Keep on writing, Anne."

"No. It was very foolish of me to attempt it. When I'm through Redmond I'll stick to teaching. I *can* teach. I can't write stories."

"It'll be time for you to be getting a husband when you're through Redmond," said Mr. Harrison. "I don't believe in putting marrying off too long—like I did."

Anne got up and marched home. There were times when Mr. Harrison was really intolerable. "Pitching," "mooning," and "getting a husband." Ow!!

13

The Way of Transgressors

avy and Dora were ready for Sunday School. They were going alone, which did not often happen, for Mrs. Lynde always attended Sunday School. But Mrs. Lynde had twisted her ankle and was lame, so she was staying home this morning. The twins were also to represent the family at church, for Anne had gone away the evening before to spend Sunday with friends in Carmody, and Marilla had one of her headaches.

Davy came downstairs slowly. Dora was waiting in the hall for him, having been made ready by Mrs. Lynde. Davy had attended to his own preparations. He had a cent in his pocket for the Sunday School collection, and a five-cent piece for the church collection; he carried his Bible in one hand and his Sunday School quarterly in the other; he knew his lesson and his Golden Text and his catechism question perfectly. Had he not studied them—perforce—in Mrs. Lynde's kitchen, all last Sunday afternoon? Davy, therefore, should have been in a placid frame of mind. As a matter of fact, despite text and catechism, he was inwardly as a ravening wolf.

Mrs. Lynde limped out of her kitchen as he joined Dora.

"Are you clean?" she demanded severely.

"Yes—all of me that shows," Davy answered with a defiant scowl.

Mrs. Rachel sighed. She had her suspicions about Davy's neck and ears. But she knew that if she attempted to make a personal examination Davy would likely take to his heels and she could not pursue him today.

"Well, be sure you behave yourselves," she warned them. "Don't walk in the dust. Don't stop in the porch to talk to the other children.

Don't squirm or wriggle in your places. Don't forget the Golden Text. Don't lose your collection or forget to put it in. Don't whisper at prayer time, and don't forget to pay attention to the sermon."

Davy deigned no response. He marched away down the lane, followed by the meek Dora. But his soul seethed within him. Davy had suffered, or thought he had suffered, many things at the hands and tongue of Mrs. Rachel Lynde since she had come to Green Gables, for Mrs. Lynde could not live with anybody, whether they were nine or ninety, without trying to bring them up properly. And it was only the preceding afternoon that she had interfered to influence Marilla against allowing Davy to go fishing with the Timothy Cottons. Davy was still boiling over this.

As soon as he was out of the lane Davy stopped and twisted his countenance into such an unearthly and terrific contortion that Dora, although she knew his gifts in that respect, was honestly alarmed lest he should never in the world be able to get it straightened out again.

"Darn her," exploded Davy.

"Oh, Davy, don't swear," gasped Dora in dismay.

"'Darn' isn't swearing—not real swearing. And I don't care if it is," retorted Davy recklessly.

"Well, if you *must* say dreadful words don't say them on Sunday," pleaded Dora.

Davy was as yet far from repentance, but in his secret soul he felt that, perhaps, he had gone a little too far.

"I'm going to invent a swear word of my own," he declared.

"God will punish you if you do," said Dora solemnly.

"Then I think God is a mean old scamp," retorted Davy. "Doesn't He know a fellow must have some way of 'spressing his feelings?"

"Davy!!!" said Dora. She expected that Davy would be struck down dead on the spot. But nothing happened.

"Anyway, I ain't going to stand any more of Mrs. Lynde's bossing," spluttered Davy. "Anne and Marilla may have the right to boss me, but *she* hasn't. I'm going to do every single thing she told me not to do. You watch me."

In grim, deliberate silence, while Dora watched him with the fascination of horror, Davy stepped off the green grass of the roadside, ankle deep into the fine dust which four weeks of rainless weather had made on the road, and marched along in it, shuffling his feet viciously until he was enveloped in a hazy cloud.

"That's the beginning," he announced triumphantly. "And I'm going to stop in the porch and talk as long as there's anybody there to talk to. I'm going to squirm and wriggle and whisper, and I'm going to say I don't know the Golden Text. And I'm going to throw away both of my collections *right now*."

And Davy hurled cent and nickel over Mr. Barry's fence with fierce delight.

"Satan made you do that," said Dora reproachfully.

"He didn't," cried Davy indignantly. "I just thought it out for myself. And I've thought of something else. I'm not going to Sunday School or church at all. I'm going up to play with the Cottons. They told me yesterday they weren't going to Sunday School today, 'cause their mother was away and there was nobody to make them. Come along, Dora, we'll have a great time."

"I don't want to go," protested Dora.

"You've got to," said Davy. "If you don't come I'll tell Marilla that Frank Bell kissed you in school last Monday."

"I couldn't help it. I didn't know he was going to," cried Dora, blushing scarlet.

"Well, you didn't slap him or seem a bit cross," retorted Davy. "I'll tell her *that*, too, if you don't come. We'll take the short cut up this field."

"I'm afraid of those cows," protested poor Dora, seeing a prospect of escape.

"The very idea of your being scared of those cows," scoffed Davy. "Why, they're both younger than you."

"They're bigger," said Dora.

"They won't hurt you. Come along, now. This is great. When I grow up I ain't going to bother going to church at all. I believe I can get to heaven by myself."

"You'll go to the other place if you break the Sabbath day," said unhappy Dora, following him sorely against her will.

But Davy was not scared—yet. Hell was very far off, and the delights of a fishing expedition with the Cottons were very near. He wished Dora had more spunk. She kept looking back as if she were going to cry every minute, and that spoiled a fellow's fun. Hang girls, anyway. Davy did not say "darn" this time, even in thought. He was not sorry—yet—that he had said it once, but it might be as well not to tempt the Unknown Powers too far on one day.

The small Cottons were playing in their back yard, and hailed Davy's appearance with whoops of delight. Pete, Tommy, Adolphus, and Mirabel Cotton were all alone. Their mother and older sisters were away. Dora was thankful Mirabel was there, at least. She had been afraid she would be alone in a crowd of boys. Mirabel was almost as bad as a boy—she was so noisy and sunburned and reckless. But at least she wore dresses.

"We've come to go fishing," announced Davy.

"Whoop," yelled the Cottons. They rushed away to dig worms at once, Mirabel leading the van with a tin can. Dora could have sat down and cried. Oh, if only that hateful Frank Bell had never kissed her! Then she could have defied Davy, and gone to her beloved Sunday School.

They dared not, of course, go fishing on the pond, where they would be seen by people going to church. They had to resort to the brook in the woods behind the Cotton house. But it was full of trout, and they had a glorious time that morning—at least the Cottons certainly had, and Davy seemed to have it. Not being entirely bereft of prudence, he had discarded boots and stockings and borrowed Tommy Cotton's overalls. Thus accoutered, bog and marsh and undergrowth had no terrors for him. Dora was frankly and manifestly miserable. She followed the others in their peregrinations from pool to pool, clasping her Bible and quarterly tightly and thinking with bitterness of soul of her beloved class where she should be sitting that very moment, before a teacher she adored. Instead, here she was roaming the woods with those half-wild Cottons, trying to keep her boots clean and her pretty white dress free from rents and stains. Mirabel had offered the loan of an apron but Dora had scornfully refused.

The trout bit as they always do on Sundays. In an hour the transgressors had all the fish they wanted, so they returned to the house, much to Dora's relief. She sat primly on a hencoop in the yard while the others played an uproarious game of tag; and then they all climbed to the top of the pig-house roof and cut their initials on the saddleboard. The flat-roofed henhouse and a pile of straw beneath gave Davy another inspiration. They spent a splendid half hour climbing on the roof and diving off into the straw with whoops and yells.

But even unlawful pleasures must come to an end. When the rumble of wheels over the pond bridge told that people were going home from church Davy knew they must go. He discarded Tommy's overalls, resumed his own rightful attire, and turned away from his string of trout with a sigh. No use to think of taking them home.

"Well, hadn't we a splendid time?" he demanded defiantly, as they went down the hill field.

"I hadn't," said Dora flatly. "And I don't believe you had—really— either," she added, with a flash of insight that was not to be expected of her.

"I had so," cried Davy, but in the voice of one who doth protest too much. "No wonder *you* hadn't—just sitting there like a—like a mule."

"I ain't going to 'sociate with the Cottons," said Dora loftily.

"The Cottons are all right," retorted Davy. "And they have far better times than we have. They do just as they please and say just what they like before everybody. *I'm* going to do that, too, after this."

"There are lots of things you wouldn't dare say before everybody," averred Dora.

"No, there isn't."

"There is, too. Would you," demanded Dora gravely, "would you say 'tomcat' before the minister?"

This was a staggerer. Davy was not prepared for such a concrete example of the freedom of speech. But one did not have to be consistent with Dora.

"Of course not," he admitted sulkily. "'Tomcat' isn't a holy word. I wouldn't mention such an animal before a minister at all."

"But if you had to?" persisted Dora.

"I'd call it a Thomas pussy," said Davy.

"*I* think 'gentleman cat' would be more polite," reflected Dora.

"*You* thinking!" retorted Davy with withering scorn.

Davy was not feeling comfortable, though he would have died before he admitted it to Dora. Now that the exhilaration of truant delights had died away, his conscience was beginning to give him salutary twinges. After all, perhaps it would have been better to have gone to Sunday School and church. Mrs. Lynde might be bossy; but there was always a box of cookies in her kitchen cupboard and she was not stingy. At this inconvenient moment Davy remembered that when he had torn his new school pants the week before, Mrs. Lynde had mended them beautifully and never said a word to Marilla about them.

But Davy's cup of iniquity was not yet full. He was to discover that one sin demands another to cover it. They had dinner with Mrs. Lynde that day, and the first thing she asked Davy was,

"Were all your class in Sunday School today?"

"Yes'm," said Davy with a gulp. "All were there—'cept one."

"Did you say your Golden Text and catechism?"

"Yes'm."

"Did you put your collection in?"

"Yes'm."

"Was Mrs. Malcolm MacPherson in church?"

"I don't know." This, at least, was the truth, thought wretched Davy.

"Was the Ladies' Aid announced for next week?"

"Yes'm"—quakingly.

"Was prayer-meeting?"

"I—I don't know."

"You *should* know. You should listen more attentively to the announcements. What was Mr. Harvey's text?"

Davy took a frantic gulp of water and swallowed it and the last protest of conscience together. He glibly recited an old Golden Text learned several weeks ago. Fortunately Mrs. Lynde now stopped questioning him; but Davy did not enjoy his dinner. He could only eat one helping of pudding.

"What's the matter with you?" demanded justly astonished Mrs. Lynde. "Are you sick?"

"No," muttered Davy.

"You look pale. You'd better keep out of the sun this afternoon," admonished Mrs. Lynde.

"Do you know how many lies you told Mrs. Lynde?" asked Dora reproachfully, as soon as they were alone after dinner.

Davy, goaded to desperation, turned fiercely.

"I don't know and I don't care," he said. "You just shut up, Dora Keith."

Then poor Davy betook himself to a secluded retreat behind the woodpile to think over the way of transgressors.

Green Gables was wrapped in darkness and silence when Anne reached home. She lost no time going to bed, for she was very tired and sleepy. There had been several Avonlea jollifications the preceding week, involving rather late hours. Anne's head was hardly on her pillow before she was half asleep; but just then her door was softly opened and a pleading voice said, "Anne."

Anne sat up drowsily.

"Davy, is that you? What is the matter?"

A white-clad figure flung itself across the floor and on to the bed.

"Anne," sobbed Davy, getting his arms about her neck. "I'm awful glad you're home. I couldn't go to sleep till I'd told somebody."

"Told somebody what?"

"How mis'rubul I am."

"Why are you miserable, dear?"

"'Cause I was so bad today, Anne. Oh, I was awful bad—badder'n I've ever been yet."

"What did you do?"

"Oh, I'm afraid to tell you. You'll never like me again, Anne. I couldn't say my prayers tonight. I couldn't tell God what I'd done. I was 'shamed to have Him know."

"But He knew anyway, Davy."

"That's what Dora said. But I thought p'raps He mightn't have noticed just at the time. Anyway, I'd rather tell you first."

"*What* is it you did?"

Out it all came in a rush.

"I run away from Sunday School—and went fishing with the Cottons—and I told ever so many whoppers to Mrs. Lynde—oh! 'most half a dozen—and—and—I—I said a swear word, Anne—a pretty near swear word, anyhow—and I called God names."

There was a silence. Davy didn't know what to make of it. Was Anne so shocked that she never would speak to him again?

"Anne, what are you going to do to me?" he whispered.

"Nothing, dear. You've been punished already, I think."

"No, I haven't. Nothing's been done to me."

"You've been very unhappy ever since you did wrong, haven't you?"

"You bet!" said Davy emphatically.

"That was your conscience punishing you, Davy."

"What's my conscience? I want to know."

"It's something in you, Davy, that always tells you when you are doing wrong and makes you unhappy if you persist in doing it. Haven't you noticed that?"

"Yes, but I didn't know what it was. I wish I didn't have it. I'd have lots more fun. Where is my conscience, Anne? I want to know. Is it in my stomach?"

"No, it's in your soul," answered Anne, thankful for the darkness, since gravity must be preserved in serious matters.

"I s'pose I can't get clear of it then," said Davy with a sigh. "Are you going to tell Marilla and Mrs. Lynde on me, Anne?"

"No, dear, I'm not going to tell any one. You are sorry you were naughty, aren't you?"

"You bet!"

"And you'll never be bad like that again."

"No, but—" added Davy cautiously, "I might be bad some other way."

"You won't say naughty words, or run away on Sundays, or tell falsehoods to cover up your sins?"

"No. It doesn't pay," said Davy.

"Well, Davy, just tell God you are sorry and ask Him to forgive you."

"Have *you* forgive me, Anne?"

"Yes, dear."

"Then," said Davy joyously, "I don't care much whether God does or not."

"Davy!"

"Oh—I'll ask Him—I'll ask Him," said Davy quickly, scrambling off the bed, convinced by Anne's tone that he must have said something dreadful. "I don't mind asking him, Anne.—Please, God, I'm awful sorry I behaved bad today and I'll try to be good on Sundays always and please forgive me.—There now, Anne."

"Well, now, run off to bed like a good boy."

"All right. Say, I don't feel mis'rubul any more. I feel fine. Good night."

"Good night."

Anne slipped down on her pillows with a sigh of relief. Oh—how sleepy—she was! In another second—

"Anne!"

Davy was back again by her bed. Anne dragged her eyes open.

"What is it now, dear?" she asked, trying to keep a note of impatience out of her voice.

"Anne, have you ever noticed how Mr. Harrison spits? Do you s'pose, if I practice hard, I can learn to spit just like him?"

Anne sat up.

"Davy Keith," she said, "go straight to your bed and don't let me catch you out of it again tonight! Go, now!"

Davy went, and stood not upon the order of his going.

14

The Summons

Anne was sitting with Ruby Gillis in the Gillis' garden after the day had crept lingeringly through it and was gone. It had been a warm, smoky summer afternoon. The world was in a splendor of out-flowering. The idle valleys were full of hazes. The woodways were pranked with shadows and the fields with the purple of the asters.

Anne had given up a moonlight drive to the White Sands beach that she might spend the evening with Ruby. She had so spent many evenings that summer, although she often wondered what good it did any one, and sometimes went home deciding that she could not go again.

Ruby grew paler as the summer waned; the White Sands school was given up—"her father thought it better that she shouldn't teach till New Year's"—and the fancy work she loved oftener and oftener fell from hands grown too weary for it. But she was always gay, always hopeful, always chattering and whispering of her beaux, and their rivalries and despairs. It was this that made Anne's visits hard for her. What had once been silly or amusing was gruesome now; it was death peering through a wilful mask of life. Yet Ruby seemed to cling to her, and never let her go until she had promised to come again soon. Mrs. Lynde grumbled about Anne's frequent visits, and declared she would catch consumption; even Marilla was dubious.

"Every time you go to see Ruby you come home looking tired out," she said.

"It's so very sad and dreadful," said Anne in a low tone. "Ruby doesn't seem to realize her condition in the least. And yet I somehow feel she needs help—craves it—and I want to give it to her and can't.

All the time I'm with her I feel as if I were watching her struggle with an invisible foe—trying to push it back with such feeble resistance as she has. That is why I come home tired."

But tonight Anne did not feel this so keenly. Ruby was strangely quiet. She said not a word about parties and drives and dresses and "fellows." She lay in the hammock, with her untouched work beside her, and a white shawl wrapped about her thin shoulders. Her long yellow braids of hair—how Anne had envied those beautiful braids in old schooldays!—lay on either side of her. She had taken the pins out—they made her head ache, she said. The hectic flush was gone for the time, leaving her pale and childlike.

The moon rose in the silvery sky, empearling the clouds around her. Below, the pond shimmered in its hazy radiance. Just beyond the Gillis homestead was the church, with the old graveyard beside it. The moonlight shone on the white stones, bringing them out in clear-cut relief against the dark trees behind.

"How strange the graveyard looks by moonlight!" said Ruby suddenly. "How ghostly!" she shuddered. "Anne, it won't be long now before I'll be lying over there. You and Diana and all the rest will be going about, full of life—and I'll be there—in the old graveyard—dead!"

The surprise of it bewildered Anne. For a few moments she could not speak.

"You know it's so, don't you?" said Ruby insistently.

"Yes, I know," answered Anne in a low tone. "Dear Ruby, I know."

"Everybody knows it," said Ruby bitterly. "I know it—I've known it all summer, though I wouldn't give in. And, oh, Anne"—she reached out and caught Anne's hand pleadingly, impulsively—"I don't want to die. I'm *afraid* to die."

"Why should you be afraid, Ruby?" asked Anne quietly.

"Because—because—oh, I'm not afraid but that I'll go to heaven, Anne. I'm a church member. But—it'll be all so different. I think—and think—and I get so frightened—and—and—homesick. Heaven must be very beautiful, of course, the Bible says so—but, Anne, *it won't be what I've been used to.*"

Through Anne's mind drifted an intrusive recollection of a funny story she had heard Philippa Gordon tell—the story of some old man who had said very much the same thing about the world to come. It *had* sounded funny then—she remembered how she and Priscilla had laughed over it. But it did not seem in the least humorous now, coming from Ruby's pale, trembling lips. It was sad, tragic—and *true!* Heaven could not be what Ruby had been used to. There had been nothing in her gay, frivolous life, her shallow ideals and aspirations, to fit her for that great change, or make the life to come seem to her anything but alien and unreal and undesirable. Anne wondered helplessly what she could say that would help her. Could she say anything? "I think, Ruby," she began hesitatingly—for it was difficult for Anne to speak to any one of the deepest thoughts of her heart, or the new ideas that had vaguely begun to shape themselves in her mind, concerning the great mysteries of life here and hereafter, superseding her old childish conceptions, and it was hardest of all to speak of them to such as Ruby Gillis—"I think, perhaps, we have very mistaken ideas about heaven—what it is and what it holds for us. I don't think it can be so very different from life here as most people seem to think. I believe we'll just go on living, a good deal as we live here—and be *ourselves* just the same—only it will be easier to be good and to—follow the highest. All the hindrances and perplexities will be taken away, and we shall see clearly. Don't be afraid, Ruby."

"I can't help it," said Ruby pitifully. "Even if what you say about heaven is true—and you can't be sure—it may be only that imagination of yours—it won't be *just* the same. It *can't* be. I want to go on living *here*. I'm so young, Anne. I haven't had my life. I've fought so hard to live—and it isn't any use—I have to die—and leave *everything* I care for."

Anne sat in a pain that was almost intolerable. She could not tell comforting falsehoods; and all that Ruby said was so horribly true. She *was* leaving everything she cared for. She had laid up her treasures on earth only; she had lived solely for the little things of life—the things that pass—forgetting the great things that go onward into eternity, bridging the gulf between the two lives and making of death a mere passing from one dwelling to the other—from twilight to unclouded day. God would take care of her there—Anne believed—she would learn—but now it was no wonder her soul clung, in blind helplessness, to the only things she knew and loved.

Ruby raised herself on her arm and lifted up her bright, beautiful blue eyes to the moonlit skies.

"I want to live," she said, in a trembling voice. "I want to live like other girls. I—I want to be married, Anne—and—and—have little children. You know I always loved babies, Anne. I couldn't say this to any one but you. I know you understand. And then poor Herb—he—he loves me and I love him, Anne. The others meant nothing to me, but *he* does—and if I could live I would be his wife and be so happy. Oh, Anne, it's hard."

Ruby sank back on her pillows and sobbed convulsively. Anne pressed her hand in an agony of sympathy—silent sympathy, which perhaps helped Ruby more than broken, imperfect words could have done; for presently she grew calmer and her sobs ceased.

"I'm glad I've told you this, Anne," she whispered. "It has helped me just to say it all out. I've wanted to all summer—every time you came I wanted to talk it over with you—but I *couldn't*. It seemed as if it would make death so *sure* if I *said* I was going to die, or if any one else said it or hinted it. I wouldn't say it, or even think it. In the daytime, when people were around me and everything was cheerful, it wasn't so hard to keep from thinking of it. But in the night, when I couldn't sleep—it was so dreadful, Anne. I couldn't get away from it then. Death just came and stared me in the face, until I got so frightened I could have screamed."

"But you won't be frightened any more, Ruby, will you? You'll be brave, and believe that all is going to be well with you."

"I'll try. I'll think over what you have said, and try to believe it. And you'll come up as often as you can, won't you, Anne?"

"Yes, dear."

"It—it won't be very long now, Anne. I feel sure of that. And I'd rather have you than any one else. I always liked you best of all the girls I went to school with. You were never jealous, or mean, like some of them were. Poor Em White was up to see me yesterday. You remember

Em and I were such chums for three years when we went to school? And then we quarrelled the time of the school concert. We've never spoken to each other since. Wasn't it silly? Anything like that seems silly *now*. But Em and I made up the old quarrel yesterday. She said she'd have spoken years ago, only she thought I wouldn't. And I never spoke to her because I was sure she wouldn't speak to me. Isn't it strange how people misunderstand each other, Anne?"

"Most of the trouble in life comes from misunderstanding, I think," said Anne. "I must go now, Ruby. It's getting late—and you shouldn't be out in the damp."

"You'll come up soon again."

"Yes, very soon. And if there's anything I can do to help you I'll be so glad."

"I know. You *have* helped me already. Nothing seems quite so dreadful now. Good night, Anne."

"Good night, dear."

Anne walked home very slowly in the moonlight. The evening had changed something for her. Life held a different meaning, a deeper purpose. On the surface it would go on just the same; but the deeps had been stirred. It must not be with her as with poor butterfly Ruby. When she came to the end of one life it must not be to face the next with the shrinking terror of something wholly different—something for which accustomed thought and ideal and aspiration had unfitted her. The little things of life, sweet and excellent in their place, must not be the things lived for; the highest must be sought and followed; the life of heaven must be begun here on earth.

That good night in the garden was for all time. Anne never saw Ruby in life again. The next night the A.V.I.S. gave a farewell party to Jane Andrews before her departure for the West. And, while light feet danced and bright eyes laughed and merry tongues chattered, there came a summons to a soul in Avonlea that might not be disregarded or evaded. The next morning the word went from house to house that Ruby Gillis was dead. She had died in her sleep, painlessly and calmly, and on her face was a smile—as if, after all, death had come as a kindly friend to lead her over the threshold, instead of the grisly phantom she had dreaded.

Mrs. Rachel Lynde said emphatically after the funeral that Ruby Gillis was the handsomest corpse she ever laid eyes on. Her loveliness, as she lay, white-clad, among the delicate flowers that Anne had placed about her, was remembered and talked of for years in Avonlea. Ruby had always been beautiful; but her beauty had been of the earth, earthy; it had had a certain insolent quality in it, as if it flaunted itself in the beholder's eye; spirit had never shone through it, intellect had never refined it. But death had touched it and consecrated it, bringing out delicate modelings and purity of outline never seen before—doing what life and love and great sorrow and deep womanhood joys might have done for Ruby. Anne, looking down through a mist of tears, at her old playfellow, thought she saw the face God had meant Ruby to have, and remembered it so always.

Mrs. Gillis called Anne aside into a vacant room before the funeral procession left the house, and gave her a small packet.

"I want you to have this," she sobbed. "Ruby would have liked you to have it. It's the embroidered centerpiece she was working at. It isn't quite finished—the needle is sticking in it just where her poor little fingers put it the last time she laid it down, the afternoon before she died."

"There's always a piece of unfinished work left," said Mrs. Lynde, with tears in her eyes. "But I suppose there's always some one to finish it."

"How difficult it is to realize that one we have always known can really be dead," said Anne, as she and Diana walked home. "Ruby is the first of our schoolmates to go. One by one, sooner or later, all the rest of us must follow."

"Yes, I suppose so," said Diana uncomfortably. She did not want to talk of that. She would have preferred to have discussed the details of the funeral—the splendid white velvet casket Mr. Gillis had insisted on having for Ruby—"the Gillises must always make a splurge, even at funerals," quoth Mrs. Rachel Lynde—Herb Spencer's sad face, the uncontrolled, hysteric grief of one of Ruby's sisters—but Anne would not talk of these things. She seemed wrapped in a reverie in which Diana felt lonesomely that she had neither lot nor part.

"Ruby Gillis was a great girl to laugh," said Davy suddenly. "Will she laugh as much in heaven as she did in Avonlea. Anne? I want to know."

"Yes, I think she will," said Anne.

"Oh, Anne," protested Diana, with a rather shocked smile.

"Well, why not, Diana?" asked Anne seriously. "Do you think we'll never laugh in heaven?"

"Oh—I—I don't know," floundered Diana. "It doesn't seem just right, somehow. You know it's rather dreadful to laugh in church."

"But heaven won't be like church—all the time," said Anne.

"I hope it ain't," said Davy emphatically. "If it is *I* don't want to go. Church is awful dull. Anyway, I don't mean to go for ever so long. I mean to live to be a hundred years old, like Mr. Thomas Blewett of White Sands. He says he's lived so long 'cause he always smoked tobacco and it killed all the germs. Can I smoke tobacco pretty soon, Anne?"

"No, Davy. I hope you'll never use tobacco," said Anne absently.

"What'll you feel like if the germs kill me then?" demanded Davy.

15

A Dream Turned Upside Down

"Just one more week and we go back to Redmond," said Anne. She was happy at the thought of returning to work, classes, and Redmond friends. Pleasing visions were also being woven around Patty's Place. There was a warm pleasant sense of home in the thought of it, even though she had never lived there.

But the summer had been a very happy one, too—a time of glad living with summer suns and skies, a time of keen delight in wholesome things; a time of renewing and deepening of old friendships; a time in which she had learned to live more nobly, to work more patiently, to play more heartily.

"All life lessons are not learned at college," she thought. "Life teaches them everywhere."

But alas, the final week of that pleasant vacation was spoiled for Anne, by one of those impish happenings which are like a dream turned upside down.

"Been writing any more stories lately?" inquired Mr. Harrison genially one evening when Anne was taking tea with him and Mrs. Harrison.

"No," answered Anne, rather crisply.

"Well, no offense meant. Mrs. Hiram Sloane told me the other day that a big envelope addressed to the Rollings Reliable Baking Powder Company of Montreal had been dropped into the post office box a month ago, and she suspicioned that somebody was trying for the prize they'd offered for the best story that introduced the name of their baking powder. She said it wasn't addressed in your writing, but I thought maybe it was you."

"Indeed, no! I saw the prize offer, but I'd never dream of competing for it. I think it would be perfectly disgraceful to write a story to advertise a baking powder. It would be almost as bad as Judson Parker's patent medicine fence."

So spake Anne loftily, little dreaming of the valley of humiliation awaiting her. That very evening Diana popped into the porch gable, bright-eyed and rosy cheeked, carrying a letter.

"Oh, Anne, here's a letter for you. I was at the office, so I thought I'd bring it along. Do open it quick. If it is what I believe it is I shall just be wild with delight."

Anne, puzzled, opened the letter and glanced over the typewritten contents.

"Miss Anne Shirley.
"Green Gables,
"Avonlea, P.E. Island.

"Dear Madam: We have much pleasure in informing you that your charming story 'Averil's Atonement' has won the prize of twenty-five dollars offered in our recent competition. We enclose the check herewith. We are arranging for the publication of the story in several prominent Canadian newspapers, and we also intend to have it printed in pamphlet form for distribution among our patrons. Thanking you for the interest you have shown in our enterprise, we remain,

Yours very truly,
The Rollings Reliable Baking Powder Co."

"I don't understand," said Anne, blankly.

Diana clapped her hands.

"Oh, I *knew* it would win the prize—I was sure of it. *I* sent your story into the competition, Anne."

"Diana—Barry!"

"Yes, I did," said Diana gleefully, perching herself on the bed. "When I saw the offer I thought of your story in a minute, and at first

I thought I'd ask you to send it in. But then I was afraid you wouldn't—you had so little faith left in it. So I just decided I'd send the copy you gave me, and say nothing about it. Then, if it didn't win the prize, you'd never know and you wouldn't feel badly over it, because the stories that failed were not to be returned, and if it did you'd have such a delightful surprise."

Diana was not the most discerning of mortals, but just at this moment it struck her that Anne was not looking exactly overjoyed. The surprise was there, beyond doubt—but where was the delight?

"Why, Anne, you don't seem a bit pleased!" she exclaimed.

Anne instantly manufactured a smile and put it on.

"Of course I couldn't be anything but pleased over your unselfish wish to give me pleasure," she said slowly. "But you know—I'm so amazed—I can't realize it—and I don't understand. There wasn't a word in my story about—about—" Anne choked a little over the word—"baking powder."

"Oh, I put that in," said Diana, reassured. "It was as easy as wink—and of course my experience in our old Story Club helped me. You know the scene where Averil makes the cake? Well, I just stated that she used the Rollings Reliable in it, and that was why it turned out so well; and then, in the last paragraph, where *Perceval* clasps *Averil* in his arms and says, 'Sweetheart, the beautiful coming years will bring us the fulfilment of our home of dreams,' I added, 'in which we will never use any baking powder except Rollings Reliable.'"

"Oh," gasped poor Anne, as if some one had dashed cold water on her.

"And you've won the twenty-five dollars," continued Diana jubilantly. "Why, I heard Priscilla say once that the *Canadian Woman* only pays five dollars for a story!"

Anne held out the hateful pink slip in shaking fingers.

"I can't take it—it's yours by right, Diana. You sent the story in and made the alterations. I—I would certainly never have sent it. So you must take the check."

"I'd like to see myself," said Diana scornfully. "Why, what I did wasn't any trouble. The honor of being a friend of the prize-winner is enough for me. Well, I must go. I should have gone straight home from the post office for we have company. But I simply had to come and hear the news. I'm *so* glad for your sake, Anne."

Anne suddenly bent forward, put her arms about Diana. and kissed her cheek.

"I think you are the sweetest and truest friend in the world, Diana," she said, with a little tremble in her voice, "and I assure you I appreciate the motive of what you've done."

Diana, pleased and embarrassed, got herself away, and poor Anne, after flinging the innocent check into her bureau drawer as if it were blood-money, cast herself on her bed and wept tears of shame and outraged sensibility. Oh, she could never live this down—never!

Gilbert arrived at dusk, brimming over with congratulations, for he had called at Orchard Slope and heard the news. But his congratulations died on his lips at sight of Anne's face.

"Why, Anne, what is the matter? I expected to find you radiant over winning Rollings Reliable prize. Good for you!"

"Oh, Gilbert, not you," implored Anne, in an *et-tu Brute* tone. "I thought *you* would understand. Can't you see how awful it is?"

"I must confess I can't. *What* is wrong?"

"Everything," moaned Anne. "I feel as if I were disgraced forever. What do you think a mother would feel like if she found her child tattooed over with a baking powder advertisement? I feel just the same. I loved my poor little story, and I wrote it out of the best that was in me. And it is *sacrilege* to have it degraded to the level of a baking powder advertisement. Don't you remember what Professor Hamilton used to tell us in the literature class at Queen's? He said we were never to write a word for a low or unworthy motive, but always to cling to the very highest ideals. What will he think when he hears I've written a story to advertise Rollings Reliable? And, oh, when it gets out at Redmond! Think how I'll be teased and laughed at!"

"That you won't," said Gilbert, wondering uneasily if it were that confounded Junior's opinion in particular over which Anne was worried. "The Reds will think just as I thought—that you, being like nine out of ten of us, not overburdened with worldly wealth, had taken this way of earning an honest penny to help yourself through the year. I don't see that there's anything low or unworthy about that, or anything ridiculous either. One would rather write masterpieces of literature no doubt—but meanwhile board and tuition fees have to be paid."

This commonsense, matter-of-fact view of the case cheered Anne a little. At least it removed her dread of being laughed at, though the deeper hurt of an outraged ideal remained.

16

Adjusted Relationships

"It's the homiest spot I ever saw—it's homier than home," avowed Philippa Gordon, looking about her with delighted eyes. They were all assembled at twilight in the big living-room at Patty's Place—Anne and Priscilla, Phil and Stella, Aunt Jamesina, Rusty, Joseph, the Sarah-Cat, and Gog and Magog. The firelight shadows were dancing over the walls; the cats were purring; and a huge bowl of hothouse chrysanthemums, sent to Phil by one of the victims, shone through the golden gloom like creamy moons.

It was three weeks since they had considered themselves settled, and already all believed the experiment would be a success. The first fortnight after their return had been a pleasantly exciting one; they had been busy setting up their household goods, organizing their little establishment, and adjusting different opinions.

Anne was not over-sorry to leave Avonlea when the time came to return to college. The last few days of her vacation had not been pleasant. Her prize story had been published in the Island papers; and Mr. William Blair had, upon the counter of his store, a huge pile of pink, green, and yellow pamphlets, containing it, one of which he gave to every customer. He sent a complimentary bundle to Anne, who promptly dropped them all in the kitchen stove. Her humiliation was the consequence of her own ideals only, for Avonlea folks thought it quite splendid that she should have won the prize. Her many friends regarded her with honest admiration; her few foes with scornful envy. Josie Pye said she believed Anne Shirley had just copied the story; she was sure she remembered reading it in a paper years before. The Sloanes, who had found out or guessed that Charlie had been "turned down," said they didn't think it was much to be proud of; almost any one could have done it, if she tried. Aunt Atossa told Anne she was very sorry to hear she had taken to writing novels; nobody born and bred in Avonlea would do it; that was what came of adopting orphans from goodness knew where, with goodness knew what kind of parents. Even Mrs. Rachel Lynde was darkly dubious about the propriety of writing fiction, though she was almost reconciled to it by that twenty-five dollar check.

"It is perfectly amazing, the price they pay for such lies, that's what," she said, half-proudly, half-severely.

All things considered, it was a relief when going-away time came. And it was very jolly to be back at Redmond, a wise, experienced Soph with hosts of friends to greet on the merry opening day. Pris and Stella and Gilbert were there, Charlie Sloane, looking more important than ever Sophomore looked before, Phil, with the Alec-and-Alonzo question still unsettled, and Moody Spurgeon MacPherson. Moody Spurgeon had been teaching school ever since leaving Queen's, but his mother had concluded it was high time he gave it up and turned his attention to learning how to be a minister. Poor Moody Spurgeon fell on hard luck at the very beginning of his college career. Half a dozen ruthless Sophs, who were among his fellow-boarders, swooped down upon him one night and shaved half of his head. In this guise the luckless Moody Spurgeon had to go about until his hair grew again. He told Anne bitterly that there were times when he had his doubts as to whether he was really called to be a minister.

Aunt Jamesina did not come until the girls had Patty's Place ready for her. Miss Patty had sent the key to Anne, with a letter in which she said Gog and Magog were packed in a box under the spare-room bed, but might be taken out when wanted; in a postscript she added that she hoped the girls would be careful about putting up pictures. The living room had been newly papered five years before and she and Miss Maria did not want any more holes made in that new paper than was absolutely necessary. For the rest she trusted everything to Anne.

How those girls enjoyed putting their nest in order! As Phil said, it was almost as good as getting married. You had the fun of homemaking without the bother of a husband. All brought something with them to adorn or make comfortable the little house. Pris and Phil and Stella had knick-knacks and pictures galore, which latter they proceeded to hang according to taste, in reckless disregard of Miss Patty's new paper.

"We'll putty the holes up when we leave, dear—she'll never know," they said to protesting Anne.

Diana had given Anne a pine needle cushion and Miss Ada had given both her and Priscilla a fearfully and wonderfully embroidered one. Marilla had sent a big box of preserves, and darkly hinted at a hamper for Thanksgiving, and Mrs. Lynde gave Anne a patchwork quilt and loaned her five more.

"You take them," she said authoritatively. "They might as well be in use as packed away in that trunk in the garret for moths to gnaw."

No moths would ever have ventured near those quilts, for they reeked of mothballs to such an extent that they had to be hung in the orchard of Patty's Place a full fortnight before they could be endured indoors. Verily, aristocratic Spofford Avenue had rarely beheld such a display. The gruff old millionaire who lived "next door" came over and wanted to buy the gorgeous red and yellow "tulip-pattern" one which Mrs. Rachel had given Anne. He said his mother used to make quilts like that, and by Jove, he wanted one to remind him of her. Anne would not sell it, much to his disappointment, but she wrote all about it to Mrs. Lynde. That highly-gratified lady sent word back that she had one just like it to spare, so the tobacco king got his quilt after all, and insisted on having it spread on his bed, to the disgust of his fashionable wife.

Mrs. Lynde's quilts served a very useful purpose that winter. Patty's Place, for all its many virtues, had its faults also. It was really a rather cold house; and when the frosty nights came the girls were very glad to snuggle down under Mrs. Lynde's quilts, and hoped that the loan of them might be accounted unto her for righteousness. Anne had the blue room she had coveted at sight. Priscilla and Stella had the large one. Phil was blissfully content with the little one over the kitchen; and Aunt Jamesina was to have the downstairs one off the living-room. Rusty at first slept on the doorstep.

Anne, walking home from Redmond a few days after her return, became aware that the people that she met surveyed her with a covert, indulgent smile. Anne wondered uneasily what was the matter with her. Was her hat crooked? Was her belt loose? Craning her head to investigate, Anne, for the first time, saw Rusty.

Trotting along behind her, close to her heels, was quite the most forlorn specimen of the cat tribe she had ever beheld. The animal was well past kittenhood, lank, thin, disreputable-looking. Pieces of both ears were lacking, one eye was temporarily out of repair, and one jowl ludicrously swollen. As for color, if a once black cat had been well and thoroughly singed the result would have resembled the hue of this waif's thin, draggled, unsightly fur.

Anne "shooed," but the cat would not "shoo." As long as she stood he sat back on his haunches and gazed at her reproachfully out of his one good eye; when she resumed her walk he followed. Anne resigned herself to his company until she reached the gate of Patty's Place, which she coldly shut in his face, fondly supposing she had seen the last of him. But when, fifteen minutes later, Phil opened the door, there sat the rusty-brown cat on the step. More, he promptly darted in and sprang upon Anne's lap with a half-pleading, half-triumphant "miaow."

"Anne," said Stella severely, "do you own that animal?"

"No, I do *not*," protested disgusted Anne. "The creature followed me home from somewhere. I couldn't get rid of him. Ugh, get down. I like decent cats reasonably well; but I don't like beasties of your complexion."

Pussy, however, refused to get down. He coolly curled up in Anne's lap and began to purr.

"He has evidently adopted you," laughed Priscilla.

"I won't *be* adopted," said Anne stubbornly.

"The poor creature is starving," said Phil pityingly. "Why, his bones are almost coming through his skin."

"Well, I'll give him a square meal and then he must return to whence he came," said Anne resolutely.

The cat was fed and put out. In the morning he was still on the doorstep. On the doorstep he continued to sit, bolting in whenever the door was opened. No coolness of welcome had the least effect on him; of nobody save Anne did he take the least notice. Out of compassion the girls fed him; but when a week had passed they decided that something must be done. The cat's appearance had improved. His eye and cheek had resumed their normal appearance; he was not quite so thin; and he had been seen washing his face.

"But for all that we can't keep him," said Stella. "Aunt Jimsie is coming next week and she will bring the Sarah-cat with her. We can't keep two cats; and if we did this Rusty Coat would fight all the time with the Sarah-cat. He's a fighter by nature. He had a pitched battle last evening with the tobacco-king's cat and routed him, horse, foot and artillery."

"We must get rid of him," agreed Anne, looking darkly at the subject of their discussion, who was purring on the hearth rug with an air of lamb-like meekness. "But the question is—how? How can four unprotected females get rid of a cat who *won't* be got rid of?"

"We must chloroform him," said Phil briskly. "That is the most humane way."

"Who of us knows anything about chloroforming a cat?" demanded Anne gloomily.

"I do, honey. It's one of my few—sadly few—useful accomplishments. I've disposed of several at home. You take the cat in the morning and give him a good breakfast. Then you take an old burlap bag—there's one in the back porch—put the cat on it and turn over him a wooden box. Then take a two-ounce bottle of chloroform, uncork it, and slip it under the edge of the box. Put a heavy weight on top of the box and leave it till evening. The cat will be dead, curled up peacefully as if he were asleep. No pain—no struggle."

"It sounds easy," said Anne dubiously.

"It *is* easy. Just leave it to me. I'll see to it," said Phil reassuringly.

Accordingly the chloroform was procured, and the next morning Rusty was lured to his doom. He ate his breakfast, licked his chops, and climbed into Anne's lap. Anne's heart misgave her. This poor creature loved her—trusted her. How could she be a party to his destruction?

"Here, take him," she said hastily to Phil. "I feel like a murderess."

"He won't suffer, you know," comforted Phil, but Anne had fled.

The fatal deed was done in the back porch. Nobody went near it that day. But at dusk Phil declared that Rusty must be buried.

"Pris and Stella must dig his grave in the orchard," decreed Phil, "and Anne must come with me to lift the box off. That's the part I always hate."

The two conspirators tip-toed reluctantly to the back porch. Phil gingerly lifted the stone she had put on the box. Suddenly, faint but distinct, sounded an unmistakable mew under the box.

"He—he isn't dead," gasped Anne, sitting blankly down on the kitchen doorstep.

"He must be," said Phil incredulously.

Another tiny mew proved that he wasn't. The two girls stared at each other.

"What will we do?" questioned Anne.

"Why in the world don't you come?" demanded Stella, appearing in the doorway. "We've got the grave ready. 'What, silent still and silent all?'" she quoted teasingly.

"'Oh, no, the voices of the dead
Sound like the distant torrent's fall,'"

promptly counter-quoted Anne, pointing solemnly to the box.

A burst of laughter broke the tension.

"We must leave him here till morning," said Phil, replacing the stone. "He hasn't mewed for five minutes. Perhaps the mews we heard were his dying groan. Or perhaps we merely imagined them, under the strain of our guilty consciences."

But, when the box was lifted in the morning, Rusty bounded at one gay leap to Anne's shoulder where he began to lick her face affectionately. Never was there a cat more decidedly alive.

"Here's a knot hole in the box," groaned Phil. "I never saw it. That's why he didn't die. Now, we've got to do it all over again."

"No, we haven't," declared Anne suddenly. "Rusty isn't going to be killed again. He's my cat—and you've just got to make the best of it."

"Oh, well, if you'll settle with Aunt Jimsie and the Sarah-cat," said Stella, with the air of one washing her hands of the whole affair.

From that time Rusty was one of the family. He slept o' nights on the scrubbing cushion in the back porch and lived on the fat of the land.

By the time Aunt Jamesina came he was plump and glossy and tolerably respectable. But, like Kipling's cat, he "walked by himself." His paw was against every cat, and every cat's paw against him. One by one he vanquished the aristocratic felines of Spofford Avenue. As for human beings, he loved Anne and Anne alone. Nobody else even dared stroke him. An angry spit and something that sounded much like very improper language greeted any one who did.

"The airs that cat puts on are perfectly intolerable," declared Stella.

"Him was a nice old pussens, him was," vowed Anne, cuddling her pet defiantly.

"Well, I don't know how he and the Sarah-cat will ever make out to live together," said Stella pessimistically. "Cat-fights in the orchard o' nights are bad enough. But cat-fights here in the living-room are unthinkable."

In due time Aunt Jamesina arrived. Anne and Priscilla and Phil had awaited her advent rather dubiously; but when Aunt Jamesina was enthroned in the rocking chair before the open fire they figuratively bowed down and worshipped her.

Aunt Jamesina was a tiny old woman with a little, softly-triangular face, and large, soft blue eyes that were alight with unquenchable youth, and as full of hopes as a girl's. She had pink cheeks and snow-white hair which she wore in quaint little puffs over her ears.

"It's a very old-fashioned way," she said, knitting industriously at something as dainty and pink as a sunset cloud. "But *I* am old-fashioned. My clothes are, and it stands to reason my opinions are, too. I don't say they're any the better of that, mind you. In fact, I daresay they're a good deal the worse. But they've worn nice and easy. New shoes are smarter than old ones, but the old ones are more comfortable. I'm old enough to indulge myself in the matter of shoes and opinions. I mean to take it real easy here. I know you expect me to look after you and keep you proper, but I'm not going to do it. You're old enough to know how to behave if you're ever going to be. So, as far as I am concerned," concluded Aunt Jamesina, with a twinkle in her young eyes, "you can all go to destruction in your own way."

"Oh, will somebody separate those cats?" pleaded Stella, shudderingly.

Aunt Jamesina had brought with her not only the Sarah-cat but Joseph. Joseph, she explained, had belonged to a dear friend of hers who had gone to live in Vancouver.

"She couldn't take Joseph with her so she begged me to take him. I really couldn't refuse. He's a beautiful cat—that is, his disposition is beautiful. She called him Joseph because his coat is of many colors."

It certainly was. Joseph, as the disgusted Stella said, looked like a walking rag-bag. It was impossible to say what his ground color was. His legs were white with black spots on them. His back was gray with a huge patch of yellow on one side and a black patch on the other. His tail was yellow with a gray tip. One ear was black and one yellow. A black patch over one eye gave him a fearfully rakish look. In reality he was meek and inoffensive, of a sociable disposition. In one respect, if in no other, Joseph was like a lily of the field. He toiled not neither did he spin or catch mice. Yet Solomon in all his glory slept not on softer cushions; or feasted more fully on fat things.

Joseph and the Sarah-cat arrived by express in separate boxes. After they had been released and fed, Joseph selected the cushion and corner which appealed to him, and the Sarah-cat gravely sat her down before the fire and proceeded to wash her face. She was a large, sleek, gray-and-white cat, with an enormous dignity which was not at all impaired by any consciousness of her plebeian origin. She had been given to Aunt Jamesina by her washerwoman.

"Her name was Sarah, so my husband always called puss the Sarah-cat," explained Aunt Jamesina. "She is eight years old, and a remarkable mouser. Don't worry, Stella. The Sarah-cat *never* fights and Joseph rarely."

"They'll have to fight here in self-defense," said Stella.

At this juncture Rusty arrived on the scene. He bounded joyously half way across the room before he saw the intruders. Then he stopped short; his tail expanded until it was as big as three tails. The fur on his back rose up in a defiant arch; Rusty lowered his head, uttered a fearful shriek of hatred and defiance, and launched himself at the Sarah-cat.

That stately animal had stopped washing her face and was looking at him curiously. She met his onslaught with one contemptuous
sweep of her capable paw. Rusty went rolling helplessly over on the rug;
he picked himself up dazedly. What sort of a cat was this who had
boxed his ears? He looked dubiously at the Sarah-cat. Would he or
would he not? The Sarah-cat deliberately turned her back on him and
resumed her toilet operations. Rusty decided that he would not. He
never did. From that time on the Sarah-cat ruled the roost. Rusty
never again interfered with her.

But Joseph rashly sat up and yawned. Rusty, burning to avenge
his disgrace, swooped down upon him. Joseph, pacific by nature, could
fight upon occasion and fight well. The result was a series of drawn
battles. Every day Rusty and Joseph fought at sight. Anne took Rusty's
part and detested Joseph. Stella was in despair. But Aunt Jamesina
only laughed.

"Let them fight it out," she said tolerantly. "They'll make friends
after a bit. Joseph needs some exercise—he was getting too fat. And
Rusty has to learn he isn't the only cat in the world."

Eventually Joseph and Rusty accepted the situation and from
sworn enemies became sworn friends. They slept on the same cushion
with their paws about each other, and gravely washed each other's faces.

"We've all got used to each other," said Phil. "And I've learned
how to wash dishes and sweep a floor."

"But you needn't try to make us believe you can chloroform a cat,"
laughed Anne.

"It was all the fault of the knothole," protested Phil.

"It was a good thing the knothole was there," said Aunt Jamesina
rather severely. "Kittens *have* to be drowned, I admit, or the world
would be overrun. But no decent, grown-up cat should be done to
death—unless he sucks eggs."

"You wouldn't have thought Rusty very decent if you'd seen him
when he came here," said Stella. "He positively looked like the Old Nick."

"I don't believe Old Nick can be so very ugly," said Aunt Jamesina
reflectively. "He wouldn't do so much harm if he was. *I* always think of
him as a rather handsome gentleman."

17

A Letter from Davy

"It's beginning to snow, girls," said Phil, coming in one November evening, "and there are the loveliest little stars and crosses all over the garden walk. I never noticed before what exquisite things snowflakes really are. One has time to notice things like that in the simple life. Bless you all for permitting me to live it. It's really delightful to feel worried because butter has gone up five cents a pound."

"Has it?" demanded Stella, who kept the household accounts.

"It has—and here's your butter. I'm getting quite expert at marketing. It's better fun than flirting," concluded Phil gravely.

"Everything is going up scandalously," sighed Stella.

"Never mind. Thank goodness air and salvation are still free," said Aunt Jamesina.

"And so is laughter," added Anne. "There's no tax on it yet and that is well, because you're all going to laugh presently. I'm going to read you Davy's letter. His spelling has improved immensely this past year, though he is not strong on apostrophes, and he certainly possesses the gift of writing an interesting letter. Listen and laugh, before we settle down to the evening's study-grind."

"Dear Anne," ran Davy's letter, "I take my pen to tell you that we are all pretty well and hope this will find you the same. It's snowing some today and Marilla says the old woman in the sky is shaking her feather beds. Is the old woman in the sky God's wife, Anne? I want to know.

"Mrs. Lynde has been real sick but she is better now. She fell down the cellar stairs last week. When she fell she grabbed hold of the shelf with all the milk pails and stewpans on it, and it gave way and went down with her and made a splendid crash. Marilla thought it was an earthquake at first. One of the stewpans was all dinged up and Mrs. Lynde straned her ribs. The doctor come and gave her medicine to rub on her ribs but she didn't understand him and took it all inside instead. The doctor said it was a wonder it dident kill her but it dident and it cured her ribs and Mrs. Lynde says doctors dont know much anyhow. But we couldent fix up the stewpan. Marilla had to throw it out. Thanksgiving was last week. There was no school and we had a great dinner. I et mince pie and rost turkey and frut cake and donuts and cheese and jam and choklut cake. Marilla said I'd die but I dident. Dora had earake after it, only it wasent in her ears it was in her stummick. I dident have earake anywhere.

"Our new teacher is a man. He does things for jokes. Last week he made all us third-class boys write a composishun on what kind of a wife we'd like to have and the girls on what kind of a husband. He laughed fit to kill when he read them. This was mine. I thought youd like to see it.

"'The kind of a wife I'd like to Have.

"'She must have good manners and get my meals on time and do what I tell her and always be very polite to me. She must be fifteen yers old. She must be good to the poor and keep her house tidy and be good tempered and go to church regularly. She must be very handsome and have curly hair. If I get a wife that is just what I like Ill be an awful good husband to her. I think a woman ought to be awful good to her husband. Some poor women havent any husbands.

the end.'

"I was at Mrs. Isaac Wrights funeral at White Sands last week. The husband of the corpse felt real sorry. Mrs. Lynde says Mrs. Wrights grandfather stole a sheep but Marilla says we mustent speak ill of the dead. Why mustent we, Anne? I want to know. It's pretty safe, ain't it?

"Mrs. Lynde was awful mad the other day because I asked her if she was alive in Noah's time. I dident mean to hurt her feelings. I just wanted to know. Was she, Anne?

"Mr. Harrison wanted to get rid of his dog. So he hunged him once but he come to life and scooted for the barn while Mr. Harrison was digging the grave, so he hunged him again and he stayed dead that time. Mr. Harrison has a new man working for him. He's awful okward. Mr. Harrison says he is left handed in both his feet. Mr. Barry's hired man is lazy. Mrs. Barry says that but Mr. Barry says he aint lazy exactly only he thinks it easier to pray for things than to work for them.

"Mrs. Harmon Andrews prize pig that she talked so much of died in a fit. Mrs. Lynde says it was a judgment on her for pride. But I think it was hard on the pig. Milty Boulter has been sick. The doctor gave him medicine and it tasted horrid. I offered to take it for him for a quarter but the Boulters are so mean. Milty says he'd rather take it himself and save his money. I asked Mrs. Boulter how a person would go about catching a man and she got awful mad and said she dident know, shed never chased men.

"The A.V.I.S. is going to paint the hall again. They're tired of having it blue.

"The new minister was here to tea last night. He took three pieces of pie. If I did that Mrs. Lynde would call me piggy. And he et fast and took big bites and Marilla is always telling me not to do that. Why can ministers do what boys can't? I want to know.

"I haven't any more news. Here are six kisses. xxxxxx. Dora sends one. Heres hers. x.

"Your loving friend
"David Keith"

"P.S. Anne, who was the devils father? I want to know."

18

Miss Josephine Remembers
the Anne-Girl

When Christmas holidays came the girls of Patty's Place scattered to their respective homes, but Aunt Jamesina elected to stay where she was.

"I couldn't go to any of the places I've been invited and take those three cats," she said. "And I'm not going to leave the poor creatures here alone for nearly three weeks. If we had any decent neighbors who would feed them I might, but there's nothing except millionaires on this street. So I'll stay here and keep Patty's Place warm for you."

Anne went home with the usual joyous anticipations—which were not wholly fulfilled. She found Avonlea in the grip of such an early, cold, and stormy winter as even the "oldest inhabitant" could not recall. Green Gables was literally hemmed in by huge drifts. Almost every day of that ill-starred vacation it stormed fiercely; and even on fine days it drifted unceasingly. No sooner were the roads broken than they filled in again. It was almost impossible to stir out. The A.V.I.S. tried, on three evenings, to have a party in honor of the college students, and on each evening the storm was so wild that nobody could go, so they gave up the attempt in despair. Anne, despite her love of and loyalty to Green Gables, could not help thinking longingly of Patty's Place, its cosy open fire, Aunt Jamesina's mirthful eyes, the three cats, the merry chatter of the girls, the pleasantness of Friday evenings when college friends dropped in to talk of grave and gay.

Anne was lonely; Diana, during the whole of the holidays, was imprisoned at home with a bad attack of bronchitis. She could not come to Green Gables and it was rarely Anne could get to Orchard Slope, for the old way through the Haunted Wood was impassable with drifts, and the long way over the frozen Lake of Shining Waters was almost as bad. Ruby Gillis was sleeping in the white-heaped graveyard; Jane Andrews was teaching a school on western prairies. Gilbert, to be sure, was still faithful, and waded up to Green Gables every possible evening. But Gilbert's visits were not what they once were. Anne almost dreaded them. It was very disconcerting to look up in the midst of a sudden silence and find Gilbert's hazel eyes fixed upon her with a quite unmistakable expression in their grave depths; and it was still more disconcerting to find herself blushing hotly and uncomfortably under his gaze, just as if—just as if—well, it was very embarrassing. Anne wished herself back at Patty's Place, where there was always somebody else about to take the edge off a delicate situation. At Green Gables Marilla went promptly to Mrs. Lynde's domain when Gilbert came and insisted on taking the twins with her. The significance of this was unmistakable and Anne was in a helpless fury over it.

Davy, however, was perfectly happy. He reveled in getting out in the morning and shoveling out the paths to the well and henhouse. He gloried in the Christmas-tide delicacies which Marilla and Mrs. Lynde vied with each other in preparing for Anne, and he was reading an enthralling tale, in a school library book, of a wonderful hero who seemed blessed with a miraculous faculty for getting into scrapes from which he was usually delivered by an earthquake or a volcanic explosion, which blew him high and dry out of his troubles, handed him in a fortune, and closed the story with proper *éclat*.

"I tell you it's a bully story, Anne," he said ecstatically. "I'd ever so much rather read it than the Bible."

"Would you?" smiled Anne.

Davy peered curiously at her.

"You don't seem a bit shocked, Anne. Mrs. Lynde was awful shocked when I said it to her."

"No, I'm not shocked, Davy. I think it's quite natural that a nine-year-old boy would sooner read an adventure story than the Bible. But when you are older I hope and think that you will realize what a wonderful book the Bible is."

"Oh, I think some parts of it are fine," conceded Davy. "That story about Joseph now—it's bully. But if I'd been Joseph *I* wouldn't have forgive the brothers. No, siree, Anne. I'd have cut all their heads off. Mrs. Lynde was awful mad when I said that and shut the Bible up and said she'd never read me any more of it if I talked like that. So I don't talk now when she reads it Sunday afternoons; I just think things and say them to Milty Boulter next day in school. I told Milty the story about Elisha and the bears and it scared him so he's never made fun of Mr. Harrison's bald head since. Are there any bears on P.E. Island, Anne? I want to know."

"Not nowadays," said Anne, absently, as the wind blew a scud of snow against the window. "Oh, dear, will it ever stop storming."

"God knows," said Davy airily, preparing to resume his reading.

Anne *was* shocked this time.

"Davy!" she exclaimed reproachfully.

"Mrs. Lynde says that," protested Davy. "One night last week Marilla said 'Will Ludovic Speed and Theodora Dix *ever* get married,' and Mrs. Lynde said, 'God knows'—just like that."

"Well, it wasn't right for her to say it," said Anne, promptly deciding upon which horn of this dilemma to empale herself. "It isn't right for anybody to take that name in vain or speak it lightly, Davy. Don't ever do it again."

"Not if I say it slow and solemn, like the minister?" queried Davy gravely.

"No, not even then."

"Well, I won't. Ludovic Speed and Theodora Dix live in Middle Grafton and Mrs. Rachel says he has been courting her for a hundred years. Won't they soon be too old to get married, Anne? I hope Gilbert won't court *you* that long. When are you going to be married, Anne? Mrs. Lynde says it's a sure thing."

"Mrs. Lynde is a—" began Anne hotly; then stopped.

"Awful old gossip," completed Davy calmly. "That's what every one calls her. But *is* it a sure thing, Anne? I want to know."

"You're a very silly little boy, Davy," said Anne, stalking haughtily out of the room. The kitchen was deserted and she sat down by the window in the fast falling wintry twilight. The sun had set and the wind had died down. A pale chilly moon looked out behind a bank of purple clouds in the west. The sky faded out, but the strip of yellow along the western horizon grew brighter and fiercer, as if all the stray gleams of light were concentrating in one spot; the distant hills, rimmed with priest-like firs, stood out in dark distinctness against it. Anne looked across the still, white fields, cold and lifeless in the harsh light of that grim sunset, and sighed. She was very lonely; and she was sad at heart; for she was wondering if she would be able to return to Redmond next year. It did not seem likely. The only scholarship possible in the Sophomore year was a very small affair. She would not take Marilla's money; and there seemed little prospect of being able to earn enough in the summer vacation.

"I suppose I'll just have to drop out next year," she thought drearily, "and teach a district school again until I earn enough to finish my course. And by that time all my old class will have graduated and Patty's Place will be out of the question. But there! I'm not going to be a coward. I'm thankful I can earn my way through if necessary."

"Here's Mr. Harrison wading up the lane," announced Davy, running out. "I hope he's brought the mail. It's three days since we got it. I want to see what them pesky Grits are doing. I'm a Conservative, Anne. And I tell you, you have to keep your eye on them Grits."

Mr. Harrison had brought the mail, and merry letters from Stella and Priscilla and Phil soon dissipated Anne's blues. Aunt Jamesina, too, had written, saying that she was keeping the hearth-fire alight, and that the cats were all well, and the house plants doing fine.

"The weather has been real cold," she wrote, "so I let the cats sleep in the house—Rusty and Joseph on the sofa in the living-room, and the Sarah-cat on the foot of my bed. It's real company to hear her purring when I wake up in the night and think of my poor daughter in the foreign field. If it was anywhere but in India I wouldn't worry, but they say the snakes out there are terrible. It takes all the Sarah-cats's purring to drive away the thought of those snakes. I have enough faith for everything but the snakes. I can't think why Providence ever made them. Sometimes I don't think He did. I'm inclined to believe the Old Harry had a hand in making *them*."

Anne had left a thin, typewritten communication till the last, thinking it unimportant. When she had read it she sat very still, with tears in her eyes.

"What is the matter, Anne?" asked Marilla.

"Miss Josephine Barry is dead," said Anne, in a low tone.

"So she has gone at last," said Marilla. "Well, she has been sick for over a year, and the Barrys have been expecting to hear of her death any time. It is well she is at rest for she has suffered dreadfully, Anne. She was always kind to you."

"She has been kind to the last, Marilla. This letter is from her lawyer. She has left me a thousand dollars in her will."

"Gracious, ain't that an awful lot of money," exclaimed Davy. "She's the woman you and Diana lit on when you jumped into the spare room bed, ain't she? Diana told me that story. Is that why she left you so much?"

"Hush, Davy," said Anne gently. She slipped away to the porch gable with a full heart, leaving Marilla and Mrs. Lynde to talk over the news to their hearts' content.

"Do you s'pose Anne will ever get married now?" speculated Davy anxiously. "When Dorcas Sloane got married last summer she said if she'd had enough money to live on she'd never have been bothered with a man, but even a widower with eight children was better'n living with a sister-in-law."

"Davy Keith, do hold your tongue," said Mrs. Rachel severely. "The way you talk is scandalous for a small boy, that's what."

19

An Interlude

"To think that this is my twentieth birthday, and that I've left my teens behind me forever," said Anne, who was curled up on the hearth-rug with Rusty in her lap, to Aunt Jamesina who was reading in her pet chair. They were alone in the living room. Stella and Priscilla had gone to a committee meeting and Phil was upstairs adorning herself for a party.

"I suppose you feel kind of sorry," said Aunt Jamesina. "The teens are such a nice part of life. I'm glad I've never gone out of them myself."

Anne laughed.

"You never will, Aunty. You'll be eighteen when you should be a hundred. Yes, I'm sorry, and a little dissatisfied as well. Miss Stacy told me long ago that by the time I was twenty my character would be formed, for good or evil. I don't feel that it's what it should be. It's full of flaws."

"So's everybody's," said Aunt Jamesina cheerfully. "Mine's cracked in a hundred places. Your Miss Stacy likely meant that when you are twenty your character would have got its permanent bent in one direction or 'tother, and would go on developing in that line. Don't worry over it, Anne. Do your duty by God and your neighbor and yourself, and have a good time. That's my philosophy and it's always worked pretty well. Where's Phil off to tonight?"

"She's going to a dance, and she's got the sweetest dress for it— creamy yellow silk and cobwebby lace. It just suits those brown tints of hers."

"There's magic in the words 'silk' and 'lace,' isn't there?" said Aunt Jamesina. "The very sound of them makes me feel like skipping off to a dance. And *yellow* silk. It makes one think of a dress of sunshine.

I always wanted a yellow silk dress, but first my mother and then my husband wouldn't hear of it. The very first thing I'm going to do when I get to heaven is to get a yellow silk dress."

Amid Anne's peal of laughter Phil came downstairs, trailing clouds of glory, and surveyed herself in the long oval mirror on the wall.

"A flattering looking glass is a promoter of amiability," she said. "The one in my room does certainly make me green. Do I look pretty nice, Anne?"

"Do you really know how pretty you are, Phil?" asked Anne, in honest admiration.

"Of course I do. What are looking glasses and men for? That wasn't what I meant. Are all my ends tucked in? Is my skirt straight? And would this rose look better lower down? I'm afraid it's too high— it will make me look lop-sided. But I hate things tickling my ears."

"Everything is just right, and that southwest dimple of yours is lovely."

"Anne, there's one thing in particular I like about you—you're so ungrudging. There isn't a particle of envy in you."

"Why should she be envious?" demanded Aunt Jamesina. "She's not quite as good-looking as you, maybe, but she's got a far hand- somer nose."

"I know it," conceded Phil.

"My nose always has been a great comfort to me," confessed Anne.

"And I love the way your hair grows on your forehead, Anne. And that one wee curl, always looking as if it were going to drop, but never dropping, is delicious. But as for noses, mine is a dreadful worry to me. I know by the time I'm forty it will be Byrney. What do you think I'll look like when I'm forty, Anne?"

"Like an old, matronly, married woman," teased Anne.

"I won't," said Phil, sitting down comfortably to wait for her escort. "Joseph, you calico beastie, don't you dare jump on my lap. I won't go to a dance all over cat hairs. No, Anne, I *won't* look matronly. But no doubt I'll be married."

"To Alec or Alonzo?" asked Anne.

"To one of them, I suppose," sighed Phil, "if I can ever decide which."

"It shouldn't be hard to decide," scolded Aunt Jamesina.

"I was born a see-saw, Aunty, and nothing can ever prevent me from teetering."

"You ought to be more levelheaded, Philippa."

"It's best to be levelheaded, of course," agreed Philippa, "but you miss lots of fun. As for Alec and Alonzo, if you knew them you'd understand why it's difficult to choose between them. They're equally nice."

"Then take somebody who is nicer," suggested Aunt Jamesina. "There's that Senior who is so devoted to you—Will Leslie. He has such nice, large, mild eyes."

"They're a little bit too large and too mild—like a cow's," said Phil cruelly.

"What do you say about George Parker?"

"There's nothing to say about him except that he always looks as if he had just been starched and ironed."

"Marr Holworthy then. You can't find a fault with him."

"No, he would do if he wasn't poor. I must marry a rich man, Aunt Jamesina. That—and good looks—is an indispensable qualification. I'd marry Gilbert Blythe if he were rich."

"Oh, would you?" said Anne, rather viciously.

"We don't like that idea a little bit, although we don't want Gilbert ourselves, oh, no," mocked Phil. "But don't let's talk of disagreeable subjects. I'll have to marry sometime, I suppose, but I shall put off the evil day as long as I can."

"You mustn't marry anybody you don't love, Phil, when all's said and done," said Aunt Jamesina.

"'Oh, hearts that loved in the good old way,
Have been out o' the fashion this many a day,'"

trilled Phil mockingly. "There's the carriage. I fly—Bi-bi, you two old-fashioned darlings."

When Phil had gone Aunt Jamesina looked solemnly at Anne.

"That girl is pretty and sweet and good-hearted, but do you think she is quite right in her mind, by spells, Anne?"

"Oh, I don't think there's anything the matter with Phil's mind," said Anne, hiding a smile. "It's just her way of talking."

Aunt Jamesina shook her head.

"Well, I hope so, Anne. I do hope so, because I love her. But *I* can't understand her—she beats me. She isn't like any of the girls I ever knew, or any of the girls I was myself."

"How many girls were you, Aunt Jimsie?"

"About half a dozen, my dear."

20

Gilbert Speaks

"This has been a dull, prosy day," yawned Phil, stretching herself idly on the sofa, having previously dispossessed two exceedingly indignant cats.

Anne looked up from *Pickwick Papers*. Now that spring examinations were over she was treating herself to Dickens.

"It has been a prosy day for us," she said thoughtfully, "but to some people it has been a wonderful day. Some one has been rapturously happy in it. Perhaps a great deed has been done somewhere today—or a great poem written—or a great man born. And some heart has been broken, Phil."

"Why did you spoil your pretty thought by tagging that last sentence on, honey?" grumbled Phil. "I don't like to think of broken hearts—or anything unpleasant."

"Do you think you'll be able to unpleasant things all your life, Phil?"

"Dear me, no. Am I not up against them now? You don't call Alec and Alonzo pleasant things, do you, when they simply plague my life out?"

"You never take anything seriously, Phil."

"Why should I? There are enough folks who do. The world needs people like me, Anne, just to amuse it. It would be a terrible place if *everybody* were intellectual and serious and in deep, deadly earnest. *My* mission is, as *Josiah Allen* says, 'to charm and allure.' Confess now. Hasn't life at Patty's Place been really much brighter and pleasanter this past winter because I've been here to leaven you?"

"Yes, it has," owned Anne.

"And you all love me—even Aunt Jamesina, who thinks I'm stark mad. So why should I try to be different? Oh, dear, I'm so sleepy. I was awake until one last night, reading a harrowing ghost story. I read it in bed, and after I had finished it do you suppose I could get out of bed to put the light out? No! And if Stella had not fortunately come in late that lamp would have burned good and bright till morning. When I heard Stella I called her in, explained my predicament, and got her to put out the light. If I had got out myself to do it I knew something would grab me by the feet when I was getting in again. By the way, Anne, has Aunt Jamesina decided what to do this summer?"

"Yes, she's going to stay here. I know she's doing it for the sake of those blessed cats, although she says it's too much trouble to open her own house, and she hates visiting."

"What are you reading?"

"*Pickwick.*"

"That's a book that always makes me hungry," said Phil. "There's so much good eating in it. The characters seem always to be reveling on ham and eggs and milk punch. I generally go on a cupboard rummage after reading *Pickwick*. The mere thought reminds me that I'm starving. Is there any tidbit in the pantry, Queen Anne?"

"I made a lemon pie this morning. You may have a piece of it."

Phil dashed out to the pantry and Anne betook herself to the orchard in company with Rusty. It was a moist, pleasantly-odorous night in early spring. The snow was not quite all gone from the park; a little dingy bank of it yet lay under the pines of the harbor road, screened from the influence of April suns. It kept the harbor road muddy, and chilled the evening air. But grass was growing green in sheltered spots and Gilbert had found some pale, sweet arbutus in a hidden corner. He came up from the park, his hands full of it.

Anne was sitting on the big gray boulder in the orchard looking at the poem of a bare, birchen bough hanging against the pale red sunset with the very perfection of grace. She was building a castle in air— a wondrous mansion whose sunlit courts and stately halls were steeped in Araby's perfume, and where she reigned queen and chatelaine. She frowned as she saw Gilbert coming through the orchard. Of late she had managed not to be left alone with Gilbert. But he had caught her fairly now; and even Rusty had deserted her.

Gilbert sat down beside her on the boulder and held out his Mayflowers.

"Don't these remind you of home and our old schoolday picnics, Anne?"

Anne took them and buried her face in them.

"I'm in Mr. Silas Sloane's barrens this very minute," she said rapturously.

"I suppose you will be there in reality in a few days?"

"No, not for a fortnight. I'm going to visit with Phil in Bolingbroke before I go home. You'll be in Avonlea before I will."

"No, I shall not be in Avonlea at all this summer, Anne. I've been offered a job in the *Daily News* office and I'm going to take it."

"Oh," said Anne vaguely. She wondered what a whole Avonlea summer would be like without Gilbert. Somehow she did not like the prospect. "Well," she concluded flatly, "it is a good thing for you, of course."

"Yes, I've been hoping I would get it. It will help me out next year."

"You mustn't work *too* hard," said Anne, without any very clear idea of what she was saying. She wished desperately that Phil would come out. "You've studied very constantly this winter. Isn't this a delightful evening? Do you know, I found a cluster of white violets under that old twisted tree over there today? I felt as if I had discovered a gold mine."

"You are always discovering gold mines," said Gilbert—also absently.

"Let us go and see if we can find some more," suggested Anne eagerly. "I'll call Phil and—"

"Never mind Phil and the violets just now, Anne," said Gilbert quietly, taking her hand in a clasp from which she could not free it. "There is something I want to say to you."

"Oh, don't say it," cried Anne, pleadingly. "Don't—*please*. Gilbert."

"I must. Things can't go on like this any longer. Anne, I love you. You know I do. I—I can't tell you how much. Will you promise me that some day you'll be my wife?"

"I—I can't," said Anne miserably. "Oh, Gilbert—you—you've spoiled everything."

"Don't you care for me at all?" Gilbert asked after a very dreadful pause, during which Anne had not dared to look up.

"Not—not in that way. I do care a great deal for you as a friend. But I don't love you, Gilbert."

"But can't you give me some hope that you will—yet?"

"No, I can't," exclaimed Anne desperately. "I never, never can love you—in that way—Gilbert. You must never speak of this to me again,"

There was another pause—so long and so dreadful that Anne was driven at last to look up. Gilbert's face was white to the lips. And his eyes—but Anne shuddered and looked away. There was nothing romantic about this. Must proposals be either grotesque or—horrible? Could she ever forget Gilbert's face?

"Is there anybody else?" he asked at last in a low voice.

"No—no," said Anne eagerly. "I don't care for any one like *that*— and I *like* you better than anybody else in the world, Gilbert. And we must—we *must* go on being friends, Gilbert."

Gilbert gave a bitter little laugh.

"Friends! Your friendship can't satisfy me, Anne. I want your love—and you tell me I can never have that."

"I'm sorry. Forgive me, Gilbert," was all Anne could say. Where, oh, where were all the gracious and graceful speeches wherewith, in imagination, she had been wont to dismiss rejected suitors?

Gilbert released her hand gently.

"There isn't anything to forgive. There have been times when I thought you did care. I've deceived myself, that's all. Good-bye, Anne."

Anne got herself to her room, sat down on her window seat behind the pines, and cried bitterly. She felt as if something incalculably precious had gone out of her life. It was Gilbert's friendship, of course. Oh, why must she lose it after this fashion?

"What is the matter, honey?" asked Phil, coming in through the moonlit gloom.

Anne did not answer. At that moment she wished Phil were a thousand miles away.

"I suppose you've gone and refused Gilbert Blythe. You are an idiot, Anne Shirley!"

"Do you call it idiotic to refuse to marry a man I don't love?" said Anne coldly, goaded to reply.

"You don't know love when you see it. You've tricked something out with your imagination that you think love, and you expect the real thing to look like that. There, that's the first sensible thing I've ever said in my life. I wonder how I managed it?"

"Phil," pleaded Anne, "please go away and leave me alone for a little while. My world has tumbled into pieces. I want to reconstruct it."

"Without any Gilbert in it?" said Phil, going.

A world without any Gilbert in it! Anne repeated the words drearily. Would it not be a very lonely, forlorn place? Well, it was all Gilbert's fault. He had spoiled their beautiful comradeship. She must just learn to live without it.

<h1 id="21">21</h1>

<h2 id="roses-of-yesterday">Roses of Yesterday</h2>

he fortnight Anne spent in Bolingbroke was a very pleasant one, with a little undercurrent of vague pain and dissatisfaction running through it whenever she thought about Gilbert. There was not, however, much time to think about him. "Mount Holly," the beautiful old Gordon homestead, was a very gay place, overrun by Phil's friends of both sexes. There was quite a bewildering succession of drives, dances, picnics, and boating parties, all expressively lumped together by Phil under the head of "jamborees"; Alec and Alonzo were so constantly on hand that Anne wondered if they ever did anything but dance attendance on that will-o'-the-wisp of a Phil. They were both nice, manly fellows, but Anne would not be drawn into any opinion as to which was the nicer.

"And I depended so on you to help me make up my mind which of them I should promise to marry," mourned Phil.

"You must do that for yourself. You are quite expert at making up your mind as to whom other people should marry," retorted Anne, rather caustically.

"Oh, that's a very different thing," said Phil, truly.

But the sweetest incident of Anne's sojourn in Bolingbroke was the visit to her birthplace—the little shabby yellow house in an out-of-the-way street she had so often dreamed about. She looked at it with delighted eyes, as she and Phil turned in at the gate.

"It's almost exactly as I've pictured it," she said. "There is no honeysuckle over the windows, but there is a lilac tree by the gate, and—yes, there are the muslin curtains in the windows. How glad I am it is still painted yellow."

A very tall, very thin woman opened the door.

"Yes, the Shirleys lived here twenty years ago," she said, in answer to Anne's question. "They had it rented. I remember 'em. They both died of fevers at onct. It was turrible sad. They left a baby. I guess it's dead long ago. It was a sickly thing. Old Thomas and his wife took it—as if they hadn't enough of their own."

"It didn't die," said Anne, smiling. "I was that baby."

"You don't say so! Why, you *have* grown," exclaimed the woman, as if she were much surprised that Anne was not still a baby. "Come to look at you, I see the resemblance. You're complected like your pa. He had red hair. But you favor your ma in your eyes and mouth. She was a nice little thing. My darter went to school to her and was nigh crazy about her. They was buried in the one grave and the School Board put up a tombstone to them as a reward for faithful service. Will you come in?"

"Will you let me go all over the house?" asked Anne eagerly.

"Laws, yes, you can if you like. 'Twon't take you long—there ain't much of it. I keep at my man to build a new kitchen, but he ain't one of your hustlers. The parlor's in there and there's two rooms upstairs. Just prowl about yourselves. I've got to see to the baby. The east room was the one you were born in. I remember your ma saying she loved to see the sunrise; and I mind hearing that you was born just as the sun was rising and its light on your face was the first thing your ma saw."

Anne went up the narrow stairs and into that little east room with a full heart. It was as a shrine to her. Here her mother had dreamed the exquisite, happy dreams of anticipated motherhood; here that red sunrise light had fallen over them both in the sacred hour of birth; here her mother had died. Anne looked about her reverently, her eyes dim with tears. It was for her one of the jeweled hours of life that gleam out radiantly forever in memory.

"Just to think of it—mother was younger than I am now when I was born," she whispered.

When Anne went downstairs the lady of the house met her in the hall. She held out a dusty little packet tied with faded blue ribbon.

"Here's a bundle of old letters I found in that closet upstairs when I came here," she said. "I dunno what they are—I never bothered to look in 'em, but the address on the top one is 'Miss Bertha Willis,' and that was your ma's maiden name. You can take 'em if you'd keer to have 'em."

"Oh, thank you—thank you," cried Anne, clasping the packet rapturously.

"That was all that was in the house," said her hostess. "The furniture was all sold to pay the doctor bills, and Mrs. Thomas got your ma's clothes and little things. I reckon they didn't last long among that drove of Thomas youngsters. They was destructive young animals, as I mind 'em."

"I haven't one thing that belonged to my mother," said Anne, chokily. "I—I can never thank you enough for these letters."

"You're quite welcome. Laws, but your eyes is like your ma's. She could just about talk with hers. Your father was sorter homely but awful nice. I mind hearing folks say when they was married that there never was two people more in love with each other—Pore creetures, they didn't live much longer; but they was awful happy while they was alive, and I s'pose that counts for a good deal."

Anne longed to get home to read her precious letters; but she made one little pilgrimage first. She went alone to the green corner of the "old" Bolingbroke cemetery where her father and mother were buried, and left on their grave the white flowers she carried. Then she hastened back to Mount Holly, shut herself up in her room, and read the letters. Some were written by her father, some by her mother. There were not many—only a dozen in all—for Walter and Bertha Shirley had not been often separated during their courtship. The letters were yellow and faded and dim, blurred with the touch of passing years. No profound words of wisdom were traced on the stained and wrinkled pages, but only lines of love and trust. The sweetness of forgotten things clung to them—the far-off, fond imaginings of those long-dead lovers. Bertha Shirley had possessed the gift of writing letters which embodied the charming personality of the writer in words and thoughts that retained their beauty and fragrance after the lapse of time. The letters were tender, intimate, sacred. To Anne, the sweetest of all was the one written after her birth to the father on a brief absence. It was full of a proud young mother's accounts of "baby"—her cleverness, her brightness, her thousand sweetnesses.

"I love her best when she is asleep and better still when she is awake," Bertha Shirley had written in the postscript. Probably it was the last sentence she had ever penned. The end was very near for her.

"This has been the most beautiful day of my life," Anne said to Phil that night. "I've *found* my father and mother. Those letters have made them *real* to me. I'm not an orphan any longer. I feel as if I had opened a book and found roses of yesterday, sweet and beloved, between its leaves."

22

Spring and Anne
Return to Green Gables

he firelight shadows were dancing over the kitchen walls at Green Gables, for the spring evening was chilly; through the open east window drifted in the subtly sweet voices of the night. Marilla was sitting by the fire—at least, in body. In spirit she was roaming olden ways, with feet grown young. Of late Marilla had thus spent many an hour, when she thought she should have been knitting for the twins.

"I suppose I'm growing old," she said.

Yet Marilla had changed but little in the past nine years, save to grow something thinner, and even more angular; there was a little more gray in the hair that was still twisted up in the same hard knot, with two hairpins—*were* they the same hairpins?—still stuck through it. But her expression was very different; the something about the mouth which had hinted at a sense of humor had developed wonderfully; her eyes were gentler and milder, her smile more frequent and tender.

Marilla was thinking of her whole past life, her cramped but not unhappy childhood, the jealously hidden dreams and the blighted hopes of her girlhood, the long, gray, narrow, monotonous years of dull middle life that followed. And the coming of Anne—the vivid, imaginative, impetuous child with her heart of love, and her world of fancy, bringing with her color and warmth and radiance, until the wilderness of existence had blossomed like the rose. Marilla felt that out of her sixty years she had *lived* only the nine that had followed the advent of Anne. And Anne would be home tomorrow night.

The kitchen door opened. Marilla looked up expecting to see Mrs. Lynde. Anne stood before her, tall and starry-eyed, with her hands full of Mayflowers and violets.

"Anne Shirley!" exclaimed Marilla. For once in her life she was surprised out of her reserve; she caught her girl in her arms and crushed her and her flowers against her heart, kissing the bright hair and sweet face warmly. "I never looked for you till tomorrow night. How did you get from Carmody?"

"Walked, dearest of Marillas. Haven't I done it a score of times in the Queen's days? The mailman is to bring my trunk tomorrow; I just got homesick all at once, and came a day earlier. And oh! I've had such a lovely walk in the May twilight; I stopped by the barrens and picked these Mayflowers; I came through Violet-Vale; it's just a big bowlful of violets now—the dear, sky-tinted things. Smell them, Marilla—drink them in."

Marilla sniffed obligingly, but she was more interested in Anne than in drinking violets.

"Sit down, child. You must be real tired. I'm going to get you some supper."

"There's a darling moonrise behind the hills tonight, Marilla, and oh, how the frogs sang me home from Carmody! I do love the music of the frogs. It seems bound up with all my happiest recollections of old spring evenings. And it always reminds me of the night I came here first. Do you remember it, Marilla?"

"Well, yes," said Marilla with emphasis. "I'm not likely to forget it ever."

"They used to sing so madly in the mash and brook that year. I would listen to them at my window in the dusk, and wonder how they could seem so glad and so sad at the same time. Oh, but it's good to be home again! Redmond was splendid and Bolingbroke delightful—but Green Gables is *home*."

"Gilbert isn't coming home this summer, I hear," said Marilla.

"No." Something in Anne's tone made Marilla glance at her sharply, but Anne was apparently absorbed in arranging her violets in a bowl. "See, aren't they sweet?" she went on hurriedly. "The year is a book, isn't it, Marilla? Spring's pages are written in Mayflowers and violets, summer's in roses, autumn's in red maple leaves, and winter in holly and evergreen."

"Did Gilbert do well in his examinations?" persisted Marilla.

"Excellently well. He led his class. But where are the twins and Mrs. Lynde?"

"Rachel and Dora are over at Mr. Harrison's. Davy is down at Boulters'. I think I hear him coming now."

Davy burst in, saw Anne, stopped, and then hurled himself upon her with a joyful yell.

"Oh, Anne, ain't I glad to see you! Say, Anne, I've grown two inches since last fall. Mrs. Lynde measured me with her tape today, and say, Anne, see my front tooth. It's gone. Mrs. Lynde tied one end of a string to it and the other end to the door, and then shut the door. I sold it to Milty for two cents. Milty's collecting teeth."

"What in the world does he want teeth for?" asked Marilla.

"To make a necklace for playing Indian Chief," explained Davy, climbing upon Anne's lap. "He's got fifteen already, and everybody's else's promised, so there's no use in the rest of us stating to collect, too. I tell you the Boulters are great business people."

"Were you a good boy at Mrs. Boulter's?" asked Marilla severely.

"Yes; but say, Marilla. I'm tired of being good."

"You'd get tired of being bad much sooner, Davy-boy," said Anne.

"Well, it'd be fun while it lasted, wouldn't it?" persisted Davy. "I could be sorry for it afterwards, couldn't I?"

"Being sorry wouldn't do away with the consequences of being bad, Davy. Don't you remember the Sunday last summer when you ran away from Sunday School? You told me then that being bad wasn't worth while. What were you and Milty doing today?"

"Oh, we fished and chased the cat, and hunted for eggs, and yelled at the echo. There's a great echo in the bush behind the Boulter barn. Say, what is echo, Anne; I want to know."

"Echo is a beautiful nymph, Davy, living far away in the woods, and laughing at the world from among the hills."

"What does she look like?"

"Her hair and eyes are dark, but her neck and arms are white as snow. No mortal can ever see how fair she is. She is fleeter than a deer, and that mocking voice of hers is all we can know of her. You can hear her calling at night; you can hear her laughing under the stars. But you can never see her. She flies afar if you follow her, and laughs at you always just over the next hill."

"Is that all true, Anne? Or is it a whopper?" demanded Davy staring.

"Davy," said Anne despairingly, "haven't you sense enough to distinguish between a fairytale and a falsehood?"

"Then *what* is it that sasses back from the Boulter bush? I want to know," insisted Davy.

"When you are a little older, Davy, I'll explain it all to you."

The mention of age evidently gave a new turn to Davy's thoughts for after a few moments of reflection, he whispered solemnly:

"Anne, I'm going to be married."

"When?" asked Anne with equal solemnity.

"Oh, not until I'm grown-up, of course."

"Well, that's a relief, Davy. Who is the lady?"

"Stella Fletcher; she's in my class at school. And say, Anne, she's the prettiest girl you ever saw. If I die before I grow up you'll keep an eye on her, won't you?"

"Davy Keith, do stop talking such nonsense," said Marilla severely.

"'Tisn't nonsense," protested Davy in an injured tone. "She's my promised wife, and if I was to die she'd be my promised widow, wouldn't she? And she hasn't got a soul to look after her except her old grandmother."

"Come and have your supper, Anne," said Marilla, "and don't encourage that child in his absurd talk."

23

Paul Cannot Find the Rock People

ife was very pleasant in Avonlea that summer, although Anne, amid all her vacation joys, was haunted by a sense of "something gone which should be there." She would not admit, even in her inmost reflections, that this was caused by Gilbert's absence. But when she had to walk home alone from prayer meetings and A.V.I.S. pow-wows, while Diana and Fred, and many other gay couples, loitered along the dusky, starlit country roads, there was a queer, lonely ache in her heart which she could not explain away. Gilbert did not even write to her, as she thought he might have done. She knew he wrote to Diana occasionally, but she would not inquire about him; and Diana, supposing that Anne heard from him, volunteered no information. Gilbert's mother, who was a gay, frank, light-hearted lady, but not overburdened with tact, had a very embarrassing habit of asking Anne, always in a painfully distinct voice and always in the presence of a crowd, if she had heard from Gilbert lately. Poor Anne could only blush horribly and murmur, "not very lately," which was taken by all, Mrs. Blythe included, to be merely a maidenly evasion.

Apart from this, Anne enjoyed her summer. Priscilla came for a merry visit in June; and, when she had gone, Mr. and Mrs. Irving, Paul and Charlotta the Fourth came "home" for July and August.

Echo Lodge was the scene of gaieties once more, and the echoes over the river were kept busy mimicking the laughter that rang in the old garden behind the spruces.

"Miss Lavendar" had not changed, except to grow even sweeter and prettier. Paul adored her, and the companionship between them was beautiful to see.

"But I don't call her 'mother' just by itself," he explained to Anne. "You see, *that* name belongs just to my own little mother, and I can't give it to any one else. *You* know, teacher. But I call her 'Mother Lavendar' and I love her next best to father. I — I even love her a *little* better than you, teacher."

"Which is just as it ought to be," answered Anne.

Paul was thirteen now and very tall for his years. His face and eyes were as beautiful as ever, and his fancy was still like a prism, separating everything that fell upon it into rainbows. He and Anne had delightful rambles to wood and field and shore. Never were there two more thoroughly "kindred spirits."

Charlotta the Fourth had blossomed out into young ladyhood. She wore her hair now in an enormous pompador and had discarded the blue ribbon bows of auld lang syne, but her face was as freckled, her nose as snubbed, and her mouth and smiles as wide as ever.

"You don't think I talk with a Yankee accent, do you, Miss Shirley, ma'am?" she demanded anxiously.

"I don't notice it, Charlotta."

"I'm real glad of that. They said I did at home, but I thought likely they just wanted to aggravate me. I don't want no Yankee accent. Not that I've a word to say against the Yankees, Miss Shirley, ma'am. They're real civilized. But give me old P.E. Island every time."

Paul spent his first fortnight with his grandmother Irving in Avonlea. Anne was there to meet him when he came, and found him wild with eagerness to get to the shore — Nora and the Golden Lady and the Twin Sailors would be there. He could hardly wait to eat his supper. Could he not see Nora's elfin face peering around the point, watching for him wistfully? But it was a very sober Paul who came back from the shore in the twilight.

"Didn't you find your Rock People?" asked Anne.

Paul shook his chestnut curls sorrowfully.

"The Twin Sailors and the Golden Lady never came at all," he said. "Nora was there — but Nora is not the same, teacher. She is changed."

"Oh, Paul, it is you who are changed," said Anne. "You have grown too old for the Rock People. They like only children for playfellows. I

am afraid the Twin Sailors will never again come to you in the pearly,
enchanted boat with the sail of moonshine; and the Golden Lady will
play no more for you on her golden harp. Even Nora will not meet you
much longer. You must pay the penalty of growing-up, Paul. You must
leave fairyland behind you."

"You two talk as much foolishness as ever you did," said old Mrs.
Irving, half-indulgently, half-reprovingly.

"Oh, no, we don't," said Anne, shaking her head gravely. "We are
getting very, very wise, and it is such a pity. We are never half so interesting when we have leaned that language is given us to enable us to
conceal our thoughts."

"But it isn't—it is given us to exchange our thoughts," said Mrs.
Irving seriously. She had never heard of Tallyrand and did not understand epigrams.

Anne spent a fortnight of halcyon days at Echo Lodge in the
golden prime of August. While there she incidentally contrived to
hurry Ludovic Speed in his leisurely courting of Theodora Dix, as
related duly in another chronicle of her history.[1] Arnold Sherman, an
elderly friend of the Irvings, was there at the same time, and added not
a little to the general pleasantness of life.

"What a nice play-time this has been," said Anne. "I feel like a
giant refreshed. And it's only a fortnight more till I go back to
Kingsport, and Redmond and Patty's Place. Patty's Place is the dearest
spot, Miss Lavendar. I feel as if I had two homes—one at Green Gables
and one at Patty's Place. But where has the summer gone? It doesn't
seem a day since I came home that spring evening with the Mayflowers.
When I was little I couldn't see from one end of the summer to the
other. It stretched before me like an unending season. Now ''tis a
handbreadth, 'tis a tale.'"

"Anne, are you and Gilbert Blythe as good friends as you used to
be?" asked Miss Lavendar quietly.

"I am just as much Gilbert's friend as ever I was, Miss Lavendar."

Miss Lavendar shook her head.

[1] *Chronicles of Avonlea.*

"I see something's gone wrong, Anne. I'm going to be impertinent and ask what. Have you quarrelled?"

"No; it's only that Gilbert wants more than friendship and I can't give him more."

"Are you sure of that, Anne?"

"Perfectly sure."

"I'm very, very sorry."

"I wonder why everybody seems to think I ought to marry Gilbert Blythe," said Anne petulantly.

"Because you were made and meant for each other, Anne—that is why. You needn't toss that young head of yours. It's a fact."

24

Enter Jonas

"Prospect Point,

"August 20th.

"Dear Anne—spelled—with—an—E," wrote Phil, "I must prop my eyelids open long enough to write you. I've neglected you shamefully this summer, honey, but all my other corespondents have been neglected, too. I have a huge pile of letters to answer, so I must gird up the loins of my mind and hoe in. Excuse my mixed metaphors. I'm fearfully sleepy. Last night Cousin Emily and I were calling at a neighbor's. There were several other callers there, and as soon as those unfortunate creatures left, our hostess and her three daughters picked them all to pieces. I knew they would begin on Cousin Emily and me as soon as the door shut behind us. When we came home Mrs. Lilly informed us that the aforesaid neighbor's hired boy was supposed to be down with scarlet fever. You can always trust Mrs. Lilly to tell you cheerful things like that. I have a horror of scarlet fever. I couldn't sleep when I went to bed for thinking of it. I tossed and tumbled about, dreaming fearful dreams when I did snooze for a minute; and at three I wakened up with a high fever, a sore throat, and a raging headache. I knew I had scarlet fever; I got up in a panic and hunted up Cousin Emily's 'doctor book' to read up the symptoms. Anne, I had them all. So I went back to bed, and knowing the worst, slept like a top the rest of the night. Though why a top should sleep sounder than anything else I never could understand. But this morning I was quite well, so it couldn't have been the fever. I suppose if I did catch it last night it couldn't have developed so soon. I can remember that in daytime, but at three o'clock at night I never can be logical.

"I suppose you wonder what I'm doing at Prospect Point. Well, I always like to spend a month of summer at the shore, and father insists that I come to his second-cousin Emily's 'select boardinghouse' at Prospect Point. So a fortnight ago I came as usual. And as usual old 'Uncle Mark Miller' brought me from the station with his ancient buggy and what he calls his 'generous purpose' horse. He is a nice old man and gave me a handful of pink peppermints. Peppermints always seem to me such a religious sort of candy—I suppose because when I was a little girl Grandmother Gordon always gave them to me in church. Once I asked, referring to the smell of peppermints, 'Is that the odor of sanctity?' I didn't like to eat Uncle Mark's peppermints because he just fished them loose out of his pocket, and had to pick some rusty nails and other things from among them before he gave them to me. But I wouldn't hurt his dear old feelings for anything, so I carefully sowed them along the road at intervals. When the last one was gone, Uncle Mark said, a little rebukingly, 'Ye shouldn't a'et all them candies to onct, Miss Phil. You'll likely have the stummick-ache.'

"Cousin Emily has only five boarders besides myself—four old ladies and one young man. My right-hand neighbor is Mrs. Lilly. She is one of those people who seem to take a gruesome pleasure in detailing all their many aches and pains and sicknesses. You cannot mention any ailment but she says, shaking her head, 'Ah, I know too well what that is'—and then you get all the details. Jonas declares he once spoke of locomotor ataxia in hearing and she said she knew too well what that was. She suffered from it for ten years and was finally cured by a traveling doctor.

"Who is Jonas? Just wait, Anne Shirley. You'll hear all about Jonas in the proper time and place. He is not to be mixed up with estimable old ladies.

"My left-hand neighbor at the table is Mrs. Phinney. She always speaks with a wailing, dolorous voice—you are nervously expecting her to burst into tears every moment. She gives you the impression that life to her is indeed a vale of tears, and that a smile, never to speak of a laugh, is a frivolity truly reprehensible. She has a worse opinion of me than Aunt Jamesina, and she doesn't love me hard to atone for it, as Aunty J. does, either.

"Miss Maria Grimsby sits cati-corner from me. The first day I came I remarked to Miss Maria that it looked a little like rain—and Miss Maria laughed. I said the road from the station was very pretty—and Miss Maria laughed. I said there seemed to be a few mosquitoes left yet—and Miss Maria laughed. I said that Prospect Point was as beautiful as ever—and Miss Maria laughed. If I were to say to Miss Maria, 'My father has hanged himself, my mother has taken poison, my brother is in the penitentiary, and I am in the last stages of consumption,' Miss Maria would laugh. She can't help it—she was born so; but is very sad and awful.

"The fifth old lady is Mrs. Grant. She is a sweet old thing; but she never says anything but good of anybody and so she is a very uninteresting conversationalist.

"And now for Jonas, Anne.

"That first day I came I saw a young man sitting opposite me at the table, smiling at me as if he had known me from my cradle. I knew, for Uncle Mark had told me, that his name was Jonas Blake, that he was a Theological Student from St. Columbia, and that he had taken charge of the Point Prospect Mission Church for the summer.

"He is a very ugly young man—really, the ugliest young man I've ever seen. He has a big, loose-jointed figure with absurdly long legs. His hair is tow-color and lank, his eyes are green, and his mouth is big, and his ears—but I never think about his ears if I can help it.

"He has a lovely voice—if you shut your eyes he is adorable—and he certainly has a beautiful soul and disposition.

"We were good chums right way. Of course he is a graduate of Redmond, and that is a link between us. We fished and boated together; and we walked on the sands by moonlight. He didn't look so homely by moonlight and oh, he was nice. Niceness fairly exhaled from him. The old ladies—except Mrs. Grant—don't approve of Jonas, because he laughs and jokes—and because he evidently likes the society of frivolous me better than theirs.

"Somehow, Anne, I don't want him to think me frivolous. This is ridiculous. Why should I care what a tow-haired person called Jonas, whom I never saw before thinks of me?

"Last Sunday Jonas preached in the village church. I went, of course, but I couldn't realize that Jonas was going to preach. The fact that he was a minister—or going to be one—persisted in seeming a huge joke to me.

"Well, Jonas preached. And, by the time he had preached ten minutes, I felt so small and insignificant that I thought I must be invisible to the naked eye. Jonah never said a word about women and he never looked at me. But I realized then and there what a pitiful, frivolous, small-souled little butterfly I was, and how horribly different I must be from Jonas' ideal woman. *She* would be grand and strong and noble. He was so earnest and tender and true. He was everything a minister ought to be. I wondered how I could ever have thought him ugly—but he really *is!*—with those inspired eyes and that intellectual brow which the roughly-falling hair hid on week days.

"It was a splendid sermon and I could have listened to it forever, and it made me feel utterly wretched. Oh, I wish I was like *you*, Anne.

"He caught up with me on the road home, and grinned as cheerfully as usual. But his grin could never deceive me again. I had seen the *real* Jonas. I wondered if he could ever see the *real Phil*—whom *nobody*, not even you, Anne, has ever seen yet.

"'Jonas,' I said—I forgot to call him Mr. Blake. Wasn't it dreadful? But there are times when things like that don't matter—'Jonas, you were born to be a minister. You *couldn't* be anything else.'

"'No, I couldn't,' he said soberly. 'I tried to be something else for a long time—I didn't want to be a minister. But I came to see at last that it was the work given me to do—and God helping me, I shall try to do it.'

"His voice was low and reverent. I thought that he would do his work and do it well and nobly; and happy the woman fitted by nature and training to help him do it. *She* would be no feather, blown about by every fickle wind of fancy. *She* would always know what hat to put on. Probably she would have only one. Ministers never have much money. But she wouldn't mind having one hat or none at all, because she would have Jonas.

"Anne Shirley, don't you dare to say or hint or think that I've fallen in love with Mr. Blake. Could I care for a lank, poor, ugly theologue—named Jonas? As Uncle Mark says, 'It's impossible, and what's more it's improbable.'

"Good night,
           "Phil."

"P.S. It is impossible—but I am horribly afraid it's true. I'm happy and wretched and scared. *He* can *never* care for me, I know. Do you think I could ever develop into a passable minister's wife, Anne? And *would* they expect me to lead in prayer? P.G."

25

Enter Prince Charming

"I'm contrasting the claims of indoors and out," said Anne, looking from the window of Patty's Place to the distant pines of the park.

"I've an afternoon to spend in sweet doing nothing, Aunt Jimsie. Shall I spend it here where there is a cosy fire, a plateful of delicious russets, three purring and harmonious cats, and two impeccable china dogs with green noses? Or shall I go to the park, where there is the lure of gray woods and of gray water lapping on the harbor rocks?"

"If I was as young as you, I'd decide in favor of the park," said Aunt Jamesina, tickling Joseph's yellow ear with a knitting needle.

"I thought that you claimed to be as young as any of us, Aunty," teased Anne.

"Yes, in my soul. But I'll admit my legs aren't as young as yours. You go and get some fresh air, Anne. You look pale lately."

"I think I will go to the park," said Anne restlessly. "I don't feel like tame domestic joys today. I want to feel alone and free and wild. The park will be empty, for every one will be at the football match."

"Why didn't you go to it?"

"'Nobody axed me, sir, she said,'—at least, nobody but that horrid little Dan Ranger. I wouldn't go anywhere with him; but rather than hurt his poor little tender feelings I said I wasn't going to the game at all. I don't mind. I'm not in the mood for football today somehow."

"You go and get some fresh air," repeated Aunt Jamesina, "but take your umbrella, for I believe it's going to rain. I've rheumatism in my leg."

"Only old people should have rheumatism, Aunty."

"Anybody is liable to rheumatism in her legs. Anne. It's only old people who should have rheumatism in their souls, though. Thank goodness, I never have. When you get rheumatism in your soul you might as well go and pick out your coffin."

It was November—the month of crimson sunsets, parting birds, deep, sad hymns of the sea, passionate wind-songs in the pines. Anne roamed through the pineland alleys in the park and, as she said, let that great sweeping wind blow the fogs out of her soul. Anne was not wont to be troubled with soul fog. But, somehow, since her return to Redmond for this third year, life had not mirrored her spirit back to her with its old, perfect, sparkling clearness.

Outwardly, existence at Patty's Place was the same pleasant round of work and study and recreation that it had always been. On Friday evenings the big, fire-lighted living-room was crowded by callers and echoed to endless jest and laughter, while Aunt Jamesina smiled beamingly on them all. The "Jonas" of Phil's letter came often, running up from St. Columba on the early train and departing on the late. He was a general favorite at Patty's Place, though Aunt Jamesina shook her head and opined that divinity students were not what they used to be.

"He's *very* nice, my dear," she told Phil, "but ministers ought to be graver and more dignified."

"Can't a man laugh and laugh and be a Christian still?" demanded Phil.

"Oh, *men*—yes. But I was speaking of *ministers*, my dear," said Aunt Jamesina rebukingly. "And you shouldn't flirt so with Mr. Blake—you really shouldn't."

"I'm not flirting with him," protested Phil.

Nobody believed her, except Anne. The others thought she was amusing herself as usual, and told her roundly that she was behaving very badly.

"Mr. Blake isn't of the Alec-and-Alonzo type, Phil," said Stella severely. "He takes things seriously. You may break his heart."

"Do you really think I could?" asked Phil. "I'd love to think so."

"Philippa Gordon! I never thought you were utterly unfeeling. The idea of you saying you'd love to break a man's heart!"

"I didn't say so, honey. Quote me correctly. I said I'd like to think I *could* break it. I would like to know I had the *power* to do it."

"I don't understand you, Phil. You are leading that man on deliberately—and you know you don't mean anything by it."

"I mean to make him ask me to marry him if I can," said Phil calmly.

"I give you up," said Stella hopelessly.

Gilbert came occasionally on Friday evenings. He seemed always in good spirits, and held his own in the jests and repartee that flew about. He neither sought nor avoided Anne. When circumstances brought them in contact he talked to her pleasantly and courteously, as to any newly-made acquaintance. The old camaraderie was gone entirely. Anne felt it keenly; but she told herself she was very glad and thankful that Gilbert had got so completely over his disappointment in regard to her. She had really been afraid, that April evening in the orchard, that she had hurt him terribly and that the wound would be long in healing. Now she saw that she need not have worried. Men have died and the worms have eaten them but not for love. Gilbert evidently was in no danger of immediate dissolution. He was enjoying life, and he was full of ambition and zest. For him there was to be no wasting in despair because a woman was fair and cold. Anne, as she listened to the ceaseless badinage that went on between him and Phil, wondered if she had only imagined that look in his eyes when she had told him she could never care for him.

There were not lacking those who would gladly have stepped into Gilbert's vacant place. But Anne snubbed them without fear and without reproach. If the real Prince Charming was never to come she would none of a substitute. So she sternly told herself that gray day in the windy park.

Suddenly the rain of Aunt Jamesina's prophecy came with a swish and rush. Anne put up her umbrella and hurried down the slope. As she turned out on the harbor road a savage gust of wind tore along it. Instantly her umbrella turned wrong side out. Anne clutched at it in despair. And then—there came a voice close to her:

"Pardon me—may I offer you the shelter of my umbrella?"

Anne looked up. Tall and handsome and distinguished-looking— dark, melancholy, inscrutable eyes—melting, musical, sympathetic voice—yes, the very hero of her dreams stood before her in the flesh.

He could not have more closely resembled her ideal if he had been made to order.

"Thank you," she said confusedly.

"We'd better hurry over to that little pavilion on the point," suggested the unknown. "We can wait there until this shower is over. It is not likely to rain so heavily very long."

The words were very commonplace, but oh, the tone! And the smile which accompanied them! Anne felt her heart beating strangely.

Together they scurried to the pavilion and sat breathlessly down under its friendly roof. Anne laughingly held up her false umbrella.

"It is when my umbrella turns inside out that I am convinced of the total depravity of inanimate things," she said gaily.

The raindrops sparkled on her shining hair; its loosened rings curled around her neck and forehead. Her cheeks were flushed, her eyes big and starry. Her companion looked down at her admiringly. She felt herself blushing under his gaze. Who could he be? Why, there was a bit of the Redmond white and scarlet pinned to his coat lapel. Yet she had thought she knew, by sight at least, all the Redmond students except the Freshmen. And this courtly youth surely was no Freshman.

"We are schoolmates, I see," he said, smiling at Anne's colors. "That ought to be sufficient introduction. My name is Royal Gardner. And you are the Miss Shirley who read the Tennyson paper at the Philomathic the other evening, aren't you?"

"Yes; but I cannot place you at all," said Anne, frankly. "Please, where *do* you belong?"

"I feel as if I didn't belong anywhere yet. I put in my Freshman and Sophomore years at Redmond two years ago. I've been in Europe ever since. Now I've come back to finish my Arts course."

"This is my Junior year, too," said Anne.

"So we are classmates as well as college-mates. I am reconciled to the loss of the years that the locust has eaten," said her companion, with a world of meaning in those wonderful eyes of his.

The rain came steadily down for the best part of an hour. But the time seemed really very short. When the clouds parted and a burst of pale November sunshine fell athwart the harbor and the pines Anne and her companion walked home together. By the time they had reached the gate of Patty's Place he had asked permission to call, and had received it. Anne went in with cheeks of flame and her heart beating to her fingertips. Rusty, who climbed into her lap and tried to kiss her, found a very absent welcome. Anne, with her soul full of romantic thrills, had no attention to spare just then for a crop-eared pussy cat.

That evening a parcel was left at Patty's Place for Miss Shirley. It was a box containing a dozen magnificent roses. Phil pounced impertinently on the card that fell from it, read the name and the poetical quotation written on the back.

"Royal Gardner!" she exclaimed. "Why, Anne, I didn't know you were acquainted with Roy Gardner!"

"I met him in the park this afternoon in the rain," explained Anne hurriedly. "My umbrella turned inside out and he came to my rescue with his."

"Oh!" Phil peered curiously at Anne. "And is that exceedingly commonplace incident any reason why he should send us long-stemmed roses by the dozen, with a very sentimental rhyme? Or why we should blush divinest rosy-red when we look at his card? Anne, thy face betrayeth thee."

"Don't talk nonsense, Phil. Do you know Mr. Gardner?"

"I've met his two sisters, and I know of him. So does everybody worthwhile in Kingsport. The Gardners are among the richest, bluest, of Bluenoses. Roy is adorably handsome and clever. Two years ago his mother's health failed and he had to leave college and go abroad with her—his father is dead. He must have been greatly disappointed to have to give up his class, but they say he was perfectly sweet about it. Fee—fi—fo—fum, Anne. I smell romance. Almost do I envy you, but not quite. After all, Roy Gardner isn't Jonas."

"You goose!" said Anne loftily. But she lay long awake that night, nor did she wish for sleep. Her waking fancies were more alluring than any vision of dreamland. Had the real Prince come at last? Recalling those glorious dark eyes which had gazed so deeply into her own, Anne was very strongly inclined to think he had.

26

Enter Christine

The girls at Patty's Place were dressing for the reception which the Juniors were giving for the Seniors in February. Anne surveyed herself in the mirror of the blue room with girlish satisfaction. She had a particularly pretty gown on. Originally it had been only a simple little slip of cream silk with a chiffon overdress. But Phil had insisted on taking it home with her in the Christmas holidays and embroidering tiny rosebuds all over the chiffon. Phil's fingers were deft, and the result was a dress which was the envy of every Redmond girl. Even Allie Boone, whose frocks came from Paris, was wont to look with longing eyes on that rosebud concoction as Anne trailed up the main staircase at Redmond in it.

Anne was trying the effect of a white orchid in her hair. Roy Gardner had sent her white orchids for the reception, and she knew no other Redmond girl would have them that night—when Phil came in with admiring gaze.

"Anne, this is certainly your night for looking handsome. Nine nights out of ten I can easily outshine you. The tenth you blossom out suddenly into something that eclipses me altogether. How do you manage it?"

"It's the dress, dear. Fine feathers."

"'Tisn't. The last evening you flamed out into beauty you wore your old blue flannel shirtwaist that Mrs. Lynde made you. If Roy hadn't already lost head and heart about you he certainly would tonight. But I don't like orchids on you, Anne. No; it isn't jealousy. Orchids don't seem to *belong* to you. They're too exotic—too tropical—too insolent. Don't put them in your hair, anyway."

"Well, I won't. I admit I'm not fond of orchids myself. I don't think they're related to me. Roy doesn't often send them—he knows I like flowers I can live with. Orchids are only things you can visit with."

"Jonas sent me some dear pink rosebuds for the evening—but—he isn't coming himself. He said he had to lead a prayer-meeting in the slums! I don't believe he wanted to come. Anne, I'm horribly afraid Jonas doesn't really care anything about me. And I'm trying to decide whether I'll pine away and die, or go on and get my B.A. and be sensible and useful."

"You couldn't possibly be sensible and useful, Phil, so you'd better pine away and die," said Anne cruelly.

"Heartless Anne!"

"Silly Phil! You know quite well that Jonas loves you."

"But—he won't *tell* me so. And I can't *make* him. He *looks* it, I'll admit. But speak-to-me-only-with-thine-eyes isn't a really reliable reason for embroidering doilies and hemstitching tablecloths. I don't want to begin such work until I'm really engaged. It would be tempting Fate."

"Mr. Blake is afraid to ask you to marry him, Phil. He is poor and can't offer you a home such as you've always had. You know that is the only reason he hasn't spoken long ago."

"I suppose so," agreed Phil dolefully. "Well"—brightening up—"if he *won't* ask me to marry him I'll ask him, that's all. So it's bound to come right. I won't worry. By the way, Gilbert Blythe is going about constantly with Christine Stuart. Did you know?"

Anne was trying to fasten a little gold chain about her throat. She suddenly found the clasp difficult to manage. *What* was the matter with it—or with her fingers?

"No," she said carelessly. "Who is Christine Stuart?"

"Ronald Stuart's sister. She's in Kingsport this winter studying music. I haven't seen her, but they say she's very pretty and that Gilbert is quite crazy over her. How angry I was when you refused Gilbert, Anne. But Roy Gardner was foreordained for you. I can see that now. You were right, after all."

Anne did not blush, as she usually did when the girls assumed that her eventual marriage to Roy Gardner was a settled thing. All at once she felt rather dull. Phil's chatter seemed trivial and the reception a bore. She boxed poor Rusty's ears.

"Get off that cushion instantly, you cat, you! Why don't you stay down where you belong?"

Anne picked up her orchids and went downstairs, where Aunt Jamesina was presiding over a row of coats hung before the fire to warm. Roy Gardner was waiting for Anne and teasing the Sarah-cat while he waited. The Sarah-cat did not approve of him. She always turned her back on him. But everybody else at Patty's Place liked him very much. Aunt Jamesina, carried away by his unfailing and deferential courtesy, and the pleading tones of his delightful voice, declared he was the nicest young man she ever knew, and that Anne was a very, fortunate girl. Such remarks made Anne restive. Roy's wooing had certainly been as romantic as girlish heart could desire, but—she wished Aunt Jamesina and the girls would not take things so for granted. When Roy murmured a poetical compliment as he helped her on with her coat, she did not blush and thrill as usual; and he found her rather silent in their brief walk to Redmond. He thought she looked a little pale when she came out of the coeds' dressing room; but as they entered the reception room her color and sparkle suddenly returned to her. She turned to Roy with her gayest expression. He smiled back at her with what Phil called "his deep, black, velvety smile." Yet she really did not see Roy at all. She was acutely conscious that Gilbert was standing under the palms just across the room talking to a girl who must be Christine Stuart.

She was very handsome, in the stately style destined to become rather massive in middle life. A tall girl, with large dark-blue eyes, ivory outlines, and a gloss of darkness on her smooth hair.

"She looks just as I've always wanted to look," thought Anne miserably. "Rose-leaf complexion—starry violet eyes—raven hair—yes, she has them all. It's a wonder her name isn't Cordelia Fitzgerald into the bargain! But I don't believe her figure is as good as mine, and her nose certainly isn't."

Anne felt a little comforted by this conclusion.

27

Mutual Confidences

arch came in that winter like the meekest and mildest of lambs, bringing days that were crisp and golden and tingling, each followed by a frosty pink twilight which gradually lost itself in an elfland of moonshine.

Over the girls at Patty's Place was falling the shadow of April examinations. They were studying hard; even Phil had settled down to text and notebooks with a doggedness not to be expected of her.

"I'm going to take the Johnson Scholarship in Mathematics," she announced calmly. "I could take the one in Greek easily, but I'd rather take the mathematical one because I want to prove to Jonas that I'm really enormously clever."

"Jonas likes you better for your big brown eyes and your crooked smile than for all the brains you carry under your curls," said Anne.

"When I was a girl it wasn't considered lady-like to know anything about Mathematics," said Aunt Jamesina. "But times have changed. I don't know that it's all for the better. Can you cook, Phil?"

"No, I never cooked anything in my life except a gingerbread and it was a failure—flat in the middle and hilly round the edges. You know the kind. But Aunty, when I begin in good earnest to learn to cook don't you think the brains that enable me to win a mathematical scholarship will also enable me to learn cooking just as well?"

"Maybe," said Aunt Jamesina cautiously. "I am not decrying the higher education of women. My daughter is an M.A. She can cook, too. But I taught her to cook *before* I let a college professor teach her Mathematics."

In mid-March came a letter from Miss Patty Spofford, saying that she and Miss Maria had decided to remain abroad for another year.

"So you may have Patty's Place next winter, too," she wrote. "Maria and I are going to run over Egypt. I want to see the Sphinx once before I die."

"Fancy those two dames 'running over Egypt'! I wonder if they'll look up at the Sphinx and knit," laughed Priscilla.

"I'm so glad we can keep Patty's Place for another year," said Stella. "I was afraid they'd come back. And then our jolly little nest here would be broken up—and we poor callow nestlings thrown out on the cruel world of boardinghouses again."

"I'm off for a tramp in the park," announced Phil, tossing her book aside. "I think when I am eighty I'll be glad I went for a walk in the park tonight."

"What do you mean?" asked Anne.

"Come with me and I'll tell you, honey."

They captured in their ramble all the mysteries and magics of a March evening. Very still and mild it was, wrapped in a great, white, brooding silence—a silence which was yet threaded through with many little silvery sounds which you could hear if you hearkened as much with your soul as your ears. The girls wandered down a long pineland aisle that seemed to lead right out into the heart of a deep-red, over-flowing winter sunset.

"I'd go home and write a poem this blessed minute if I only knew how," declared Phil, pausing in an open space where a rosy light was staining the green tips of the pines. "It's all so wonderful here—this great, white stillness, and those dark trees that always seem to be thinking."

"'The woods were God's first temples,'" quoted Anne softly. "One can't help feeling reverent and adoring in such a place. I always feel so near Him when I walk among the pines."

"Anne, I'm the happiest girl in the world," confessed Phil suddenly.

"So Mr. Blake has asked you to marry him at last?" said Anne calmly.

"Yes. And I sneezed three times while he was asking me. Wasn't that horrid? But I said 'yes' almost before he finished—I was so afraid he might change his mind and stop. I'm besottedly happy. I couldn't really believe before that Jonas would ever care for frivolous me."

"Phil, you're not really frivolous," said Anne gravely. "'Way down underneath that frivolous exterior of yours you've got a dear, loyal, womanly little soul. Why do you hide it so?"

"I can't help it, Queen Anne. You are right—I'm not frivolous at heart. But there's a sort of frivolous skin over my soul and I can't take it off. As *Mrs. Poyser* says, I'd have to be hatched over again and hatched different before I could change it. But Jonas knows the real me and loves me, frivolity and all. And I love him. I never was so surprised in my life as I was when I found out I loved him. I'd never thought it possible to fall in love with an ugly man. Fancy me coming down to one solitary beau. And one named Jonas! But I mean to call him Jo. That's such a nice, crisp little name. I couldn't nickname Alonzo."

"What about Alec and Alonzo?"

"Oh, I told them at Christmas that I never could marry either of them. It seems so funny now to remember that I ever thought it possible that I might. They felt so badly I just cried over both of them— howled. But I knew there was only one man in the world I could ever marry. I had made up my own mind for once and it was real easy, too. It's very delightful to feel so sure, and know it's your own sureness and not somebody else's."

"Do you suppose you'll be able to keep it up?"

"Making up my mind, you mean? I don't know, but Jo has given me a splendid rule. He says, when I'm perplexed, just to do what I would wish I had done when I shall be eighty. Anyhow, Jo can make up his mind quickly enough, and it would be uncomfortable to have too much mind in the same house."

"What will your father and mother say?"

"Father won't say much. He thinks everything I do right. But mother *will* talk. Oh, her tongue will be as Byrney as her nose. But in the end it will be all right."

"You'll have to give up a good many things you've always had, when you marry Mr. Blake, Phil."

"But I'll have *him*. I won't miss the other things. We're to be married a year from next June. Jo graduates from St. Columba this spring, you know. Then he's going to take a little mission church down on Patterson Street in the slums. Fancy me in the slums! But I'd go there or to Greenland's icy mountains with him."

"And this is the girl who would *never* marry a man who wasn't rich," commented Anne to a young pine tree.

"Oh, don't cast up the follies of my youth to me. I shall be poor as gaily as I've been rich. You'll see. I'm going to learn how to cook and make over dresses. I've learned how to market since I've lived at Patty's Place; and once I taught a Sunday School class for a whole summer. Aunt Jamesina says I'll ruin Jo's career if I marry him. But I won't. I know I haven't much sense or sobriety, but I've got what is ever so much better—the knack of making people like me. There is a man in Bolingbroke who lisps and always testifies in prayer-meeting. He says, 'If you can't thine like an electric thtar thine like a candlethtick.' I'll be Jo's little candlestick."

"Phil, you're incorrigible. Well, I love you so much that I can't make nice, light, congratulatory little speeches. But I'm heart-glad of your happiness."

"I know. Those big gray eyes of yours are brimming over with real friendship, Anne. Some day I'll look the same way at you. You're going to marry Roy, aren't you, Anne?"

"My dear Philippa, did you ever hear of the famous Betty Baxter, who 'refused a man before he'd axed her'? I am not going to emulate that celebrated lady by either refusing or accepting any one before he axes me."

"All Redmond knows that Roy is crazy about you," said Phil candidly. "And you *do* love him, don't you, Anne?"

"I—I suppose so," said Anne reluctantly. She felt that she ought to be blushing while making such a confession; but she was not; on the other hand, she always blushed hotly when any one said anything about Gilbert Blythe or Christine Stuart in her hearing. Gilbert Blythe and Christine Stuart were nothing to her—absolutely nothing. But Anne had given up trying to analyze the reason of her blushes. As for Roy, of course she was in love with him—madly so. How could she help it? Was he not her ideal? Who could resist those glorious dark eyes, and that pleading voice? Were not half the Redmond girls wildly envious? And what a charming sonnet he had sent her, with a box of violets, on her birthday! Anne knew every word of it by heart. It was very good stuff of its kind, too. Not exactly up to the level of Keats or Shakespeare— even Anne was not so deeply in love as to think that. But it was very tolerable magazine verse. And it was addressed to *her*—not to Laura or Beatrice or the Maid of Athens, but to her, Anne Shirley. To be told in rhythmical cadences that her eyes were stars of the morning—that her cheek had the flush it stole from the sunrise—that her lips were redder than the roses of Paradise, was thrillingly romantic. Gilbert would never have dreamed of writing a sonnet to her eyebrows. But then, Gilbert could see a joke. She had once told Roy a funny story—and he had not seen the point of it. She recalled the chummy laugh she and Gilbert had had together over it, and wondered uneasily if life with a man who had no sense of humor might not be somewhat uninteresting in the long run. But who could expect a melancholy, inscrutable hero to see the humorous side of things? It would be flatly unreasonable.

28

A June Evening

"I wonder what it would be like to live in a world where it was always June," said Anne, as she came through the spice and bloom of the twilit orchard to the front door steps, where Marilla and Mrs. Rachel were sitting, talking over Mrs. Samson Coates' funeral, which they had attended that day. Dora sat between them, diligently studying her lessons; but Davy was sitting tailor-fashion on the grass, looking as gloomy and depressed as his single dimple would let him.

"You'd get tired of it," said Marilla, with a sigh.

"I daresay; but just now I feel that it would take me a long time to get tired of it, if it were all as charming as today. Everything loves June. Davy-boy, why this melancholy November face in blossomtime?"

"I'm just sick and tired of living," said the youthful pessimist.

"At ten years? Dear me, how sad!"

"I'm not making fun," said Davy with dignity. "I'm dis—dis—discouraged"—bringing out the big word with a valiant effort.

"Why and wherefore?" asked Anne, sitting down beside him.

"'Cause the new teacher that come when Mr. Holmes got sick give me ten sums to do for Monday. It'll take me all day tomorrow to do them. It isn't fair to have to work Saturdays. Milty Boulter said he wouldn't do them, but Marilla says I've got to. I don't like Miss Carson a bit."

"Don't talk like that about your teacher, Davy Keith," said Mrs. Rachel severely. "Miss Carson is a very fine girl. There is no nonsense about her."

"That doesn't sound very attractive," laughed Anne. "I like people to have a little nonsense about them. But I'm inclined to have a better opinion of Miss Carson than you have. I saw her in prayer-meeting last night, and she has a pair of eyes that can't always look sensible. Now, Davy-boy, take heart of grace. 'Tomorrow will bring another day' and I'll help you with the sums as far as in me lies. Don't waste this lovely hour 'twixt light and dark worrying over arithmetic."

"Well, I won't," said Davy, brightening up. "If you help me with the sums I'll have 'em done in time to go fishing with Milty. I wish old Aunt Atossa's funeral was tomorrow instead of today. I wanted to go to it 'cause Milty said his mother said Aunt Atossa would be sure to rise up in her coffin and say sarcastic things to the folks that come to see her buried. But Marilla said she didn't."

"Poor Atossa laid in her coffin peaceful enough," said Mrs. Lynde solemnly. "I never saw her look so pleasant before, that's what. Well, there weren't many tears shed over her, poor old soul. The Elisha Wrights are thankful to be rid of her, and I can't say I blame them a mite."

"It seems to me a most dreadful thing to go out of the world and not leave one person behind you who is sorry you are gone," said Anne, shuddering.

"Nobody except her parents ever loved poor Atossa, that's certain, not even her husband," averred Mrs. Lynde. "She was his fourth wife. He'd sort of got into the habit of marrying. He only lived a few years after he married her. The doctor said he died of dyspepsia, but I shall always maintain that he died of Atossa's tongue, that's what. Poor soul, she always knew everything about her neighbors, but she never was very well acquainted with herself. Well, she's gone anyhow; and I suppose the next excitement will be Diana's wedding."

"It seems so funny and horrible to think of Diana's being married," sighed Anne, hugging her knees and looking through the gap in the Haunted Wood to the light that was shining in Diana's room.

"I don't see what's horrible about it, when she's doing so well," said Mrs. Lynde emphatically. "Fred Wright has a fine farm and he is a model young man."

"He certainly isn't the wild, dashing, wicked, young man Diana once wanted to marry," smiled Anne. "Fred is extremely good."

"That's just what he ought to be. Would you want Diana to marry a wicked man? Or marry one yourself?"

"Oh, no. I wouldn't want to marry anybody who was wicked, but I think I'd like it if he *could* be wicked and *wouldn't*. Now, Fred is *hopelessly* good."

"You'll have more sense some day, I hope," said Marilla.

Marilla spoke rather bitterly. She was grievously disappointed. She knew Anne had refused Gilbert Blythe. Avonlea gossip buzzed over the fact, which had leaked out, nobody knew how. Perhaps Charlie Sloane had guessed and told his guesses for truth. Perhaps Diana had betrayed it to Fred and Fred had been indiscreet. At all events it was known; Mrs. Blythe no longer asked Anne, in public or private, if she had heard lately from Gilbert, but passed her by with a frosty bow. Anne, who had always liked Gilbert's merry, young-hearted mother, was grieved in secret over this. Marilla said nothing; but Mrs. Lynde gave Anne many exasperated digs about it, until fresh gossip reached that worthy lady, through the medium of Moody Spurgeon MacPherson's mother, that Anne had another "beau" at college, who was rich and handsome and good all in one. After that Mrs. Rachel held her tongue, though she still wished in her inmost heart that Anne had accepted Gilbert. Riches were all very well; but even Mrs. Rachel, practical soul though she was, did not consider them the one essential. If Anne "liked" the Handsome Unknown better than Gilbert there was nothing more to be said; but Mrs. Rachel was dreadfully afraid that Anne was going to make the mistake of marrying for money. Marilla knew Anne too well to fear this; but she felt that something in the universal scheme of things had gone sadly awry.

"What is to be, will be," said Mrs. Rachel gloomily, "and what isn't to be happens sometimes. I can't help believing it's going to happen in Anne's case, if Providence doesn't interfere, that's what."

Mrs. Rachel sighed. She was afraid Providence wouldn't interfere; and she didn't dare to.

Anne had wandered down to the Dryad's Bubble and was curled up among the ferns at the root of the big white birch where she and Gilbert had so often sat in summers gone by. He had gone into the newspaper office again when college closed, and Avonlea seemed very dull without him. He never wrote to her, and Anne missed the letters that never came. To be sure, Roy wrote twice a week; his letters were exquisite compositions which would have read beautifully in a memoir or biography. Anne felt herself more deeply in love with him than ever when she read them; but her heart never gave the queer, quick, painful bound at sight of his letters which it had given one day when Mrs. Hiram Sloane had handed her out an envelope addressed in Gilbert's black, upright handwriting. Anne had hurried home to the east gable and opened it eagerly—to find a typewritten copy of some college society report—"only that and nothing more." Anne flung the harmless screed across her room and sat down to write an especially nice epistle to Roy.

Diana was to be married in five more days. The gray house at Orchard Slope was in a turmoil of baking and brewing and boiling and stewing, for there was to be a big, old-timey wedding. Anne, of course, was to be bridesmaid, as had been arranged when they were twelve years old, and Gilbert was coming from Kingsport to be best man. Anne was enjoying the excitement of the various preparations, but under it all she carried a little heartache. She was, in a sense, losing her dear old chum; Diana's new home would be two miles from Green Gables, and the old constant companionship could never be theirs again. Anne looked up at Diana's light and thought how it had beaconed to her for many years; but soon it would shine through the summer twilights no more. Two big, painful tears welled up in her gray eyes.

"Oh" she thought, "how horrible it is that people have to grow up—and marry—and *change!*"

29

Diana's Wedding

"fter all, the only real roses are the pink ones," said Anne, as she tied white ribbon around Diana's bouquet in the westward-looking gable at Orchard Slope. "They are the flowers of love and faith."

Diana was standing nervously in the middle of the room, arrayed in her bridal white, her black curls frosted over with the film of her wedding veil. Anne had draped that veil, in accordance with the sentimental compact of years before.

"It's all pretty much as I used to imagine it long ago, when I wept over your inevitable marriage and our consequent parting," she laughed. "You are the bride of my dreams, Diana, with the 'lovely misty veil'; and I am your bridesmaid. But, alas! I haven't the puffed sleeves—though these short lace ones are even prettier. Neither is my heart wholly breaking nor do I exactly hate Fred."

"We are not really parting, Anne," protested Diana. "I'm not going far away. We'll love each other just as much as ever. We've always kept that 'oath' of friendship we swore long ago, haven't we?"

"Yes. We've kept it faithfully. We've had a beautiful friendship. Diana. We've never marred it by one quarrel or coolness or unkind word; and I hope it will always be so. But things can't be quite the same after this. You'll have other interests. I'll just be on the outside. But 'such is life' as Mrs. Rachel says. Mrs. Rachel has given you one of her beloved knitted quilts of the 'tobacco stripe' pattern, and she says when I am married she'll give me one, too."

"The mean thing about your getting married is that I won't be able to be *your* bridesmaid," lamented Diana.

"I'm to be Phil's bridesmaid next June, when she marries Mr.

Blake, and then I must stop, for you know the proverb 'three times a bridesmaid, never a bride,'" said Anne, peeping through the window over the pink and snow of the blossoming orchard beneath. "Here comes the minister, Diana."

"Oh, Anne," gasped Diana, suddenly turning very pale and beginning to tremble. "Oh. Anne—I'm so nervous—I can't go through with it—Anne, I know I'm going to faint."

"If you do I'll drag you down to the rain-water hogshed and drop you in," said Anne unsympathetically. "Cheer up, dearest. Getting married can't be so very terrible when so many people survive the ceremony. See how cool and composed *I* am, and take courage."

"Wait till your turn comes, Miss Anne. Oh, Anne, I hear father coming upstairs. Give me my bouquet. Is my veil right? Am I very pale?"

"You look just lovely. Di, darling, kiss me good-bye for the last time. Diana Barry will never kiss me again."

"Diana Wright will, though. There, mother's calling. Come."

Following the simple, old-fashioned way in vogue then, Anne went down to the parlor on Gilbert's arm. They met at the top of the stairs for the first time since they had left Kingsport, for Gilbert had arrived only that day. Gilbert shook hands courteously. He was looking very well, though, as Anne instantly noted, rather thin. He was not pale; there was a flush on his cheek that had burned into it as Anne came along the dim hall towards him, in her soft, white dress with lilies-of-the-valley in the shining masses of her hair. As they entered the crowded parlor together a little murmur of admiration ran around the room. "What a fine-looking pair they are," whispered the impressible Mrs. Rachel to Marilla.

Fred ambled in alone, with a very red face, and then Diana swept in on her father's arm. She did not faint, and nothing untoward occurred to interrupt the ceremony. Feasting and merry-making followed; then, as the evening waned, Fred and Diana drove away through the moonlight to their new home, and Gilbert walked with Anne to Green Gables.

Something of their old comradeship had returned during the informal mirth of the evening. Oh, it was nice to be walking over that well-known road with Gilbert again!

The night was so very still that one should have been able to hear the whisper of roses in blossom—the laughter of daisies—the piping of grasses—many sweet sounds, all tangled up together. The beauty of moonlight on familiar fields irradiated the world.

"Can't we take a ramble up Lovers' Lane before you go in?" asked Gilbert as they crossed the bridge over the Lake of Shining Waters, in which the moon lay like a great, drowned blossom of gold.

Anne assented readily. Lovers' Lane was a veritable path in a fairyland that night—a shimmering, mysterious place, full of wizardry in the white-woven enchantment of moonlight. There had been a time when such a walk with Gilbert through Lovers' Lane would have been far too dangerous. But Roy and Christine had made it very safe now. Anne found herself thinking a good deal about Christine as she chatted lightly to Gilbert. She had met her several times before leaving Kingsport, and had been charmingly sweet to her. Christine had also been charmingly sweet. Indeed, they were a most cordial pair. But for all that, their acquaintance had not ripened into friendship. Evidently Christine was not a kindred spirit.

"Are you going to be in Avonlea all summer?" asked Gilbert.

"No. I'm going down east to Valley Road next week. Esther Haythorne wants me to teach for her through July and August. They have a summer term in that school, and Esther isn't feeling well. So I'm going to substitute for her. In one way I don't mind. Do you know, I'm beginning to feel a little bit like a stranger in Avonlea now? It makes me sorry—but it's true. It's quite appalling to see the number of children who have shot up into big boys and girls—really young men and women—these past two years. Half of my pupils are grown up. It makes me feel awfully old to see them in the places you and I and our mates used to fill."

Anne laughed and sighed. She felt very old and mature and wise—which showed how young she was. She told herself that she longed greatly to go back to those dear merry days when life was seen through a rosy mist of hope and illusion, and possessed an indefinable something that had passed away forever. Where was it now—the glory and the dream?

"'So wags the world away,'" quoted Gilbert practically, and a trifle absently. Anne wondered if he were thinking of Christine. Oh, Avonlea was going to be so lonely now—with Diana gone!

30

Mrs. Skinner's Romance

nne stepped off the train at Valley Road station and looked about to see if anyone had come to meet her. She was to board with a certain Miss Janet Sweet, but she saw no one who answered in the least to her pre-conception of that lady, as formed from Esther's letter. The only person in sight was an elderly woman, sitting in a wagon with mail bags piled around her. Two hundred would have been a charitable guess at her weight; her face was as round and red as a harvest-moon and almost as featureless. She wore a tight, black, cashmere dress, made in the fashion of ten years ago, a little dusty black straw hat trimmed with bows of yellow ribbon, and faded black lace mits.

"Here, you," she called, waving her whip at Anne. "Are you the new Valley Road schoolma'am?"

"Yes."

"Well, I thought so. Valley Road is noted for its good-looking schoolma'ams, just as Millersville is noted for its humly ones. Janet Sweet asked me this morning if I could bring you out. I said, 'Sartin I kin, if she don't mind being scrunched up some. This rig of mine's kinder small for the mail bags and I'm some heftier than Thomas!' Just wait, miss, till I shift these bags a bit and I'll tuck you in somehow. It's only two miles to Janet's. Her next-door neighbor's hired boy is coming for your trunk tonight. My name is Skinner—Amelia Skinner."

Anne was eventually tucked in, exchanging amused smiles with herself during the process.

"Jog along, black mare," commanded Mrs. Skinner, gathering up the reins in her pudgy hands. "This is my first trip on the mail rowte. Thomas wanted to hoe his turnips today so he asked me to come. So

I jest sot down and took a standing-up snack and started. I sorter like it. O' course it's rather tejus. Part of the time I sits and thinks and the rest I jest sits. Jog along, black mare. I want to git home airly. Thomas is terrible lonesome when I'm away. You see, we haven't been married very long."

"Oh!" said Anne politely.

"Just a month. Thomas courted me for quite a spell, though. It was real romantic."

Anne tried to picture Mrs. Skinner on speaking terms with romance and failed.

"Oh?" she said again.

"Yes. Y'see, there was another man after me. Jog along, black mare. I'd been a widder so long folks had given up expecting me to marry again. But when my darter—she's a schoolma'am like you—went out West to teach I felt real lonesome and wasn't nowise sot against the idea. Bime-by Thomas began to come up and so did the other feller—William Obadiah Seaman, *his* name was. For a long time I couldn't make up my mind which of them to take, and they kep' coming and coming, and I kep' worrying. Y'see, W. O. was rich—he had a fine place and carried considerable style. He was by far the best match. Jog along, black mare."

"Why didn't you marry him?" asked Anne.

"Well, y'see, he didn't love me," answered Mrs. Skinner, solemnly.

Anne opened her eyes widely and looked at Mrs. Skinner. But there was not a glint of humor on that lady's face. Evidently Mrs. Skinner saw nothing amusing in her own case.

"He'd been a widder-man for three yers, and his sister kept house for him. Then she got married and he just wanted some one to look after his house. It was worth looking after, too, mind you that. It's a handsome house. Jog along, black mare. As for Thomas, he was poor, and if his house didn't leak in dry weather it was about all that could be said for it, though it looks kind of pictureaskew. But, y'see, I loved Thomas, and I didn't care one red cent for W. O. So I argued it out with myself. 'Sarah Crowe,' say I—my first was a Crowe—'you can marry your rich man if you like but you won't be happy. Folks can't get along together in this world without a little bit of love. You'd just better tie up to Thomas, for he loves you and you love him and nothing else ain't going to do you.' Jog along, black mare. So I told Thomas I'd take him. All time I was getting ready I never dared drive past W. O.'s place for fear the sight of that fine house of his would put me in the swithers again. But now I never think of it at all, and I'm just that comfortable and happy with Thomas. Jog along, black mare."

"How did William Obadiah take it?" queried Anne.

"Oh, he rumpussed a bit. But he's going to see a skinny old maid in Millersville now, and I guess she'll take him fast enough. She'll make him a better wife than his first did. W. O. never wanted to marry *her*. He just asked her to marry him 'cause his father wanted him to, never dreaming but that she'd say 'no.' But mind you, she said 'yes.' There was a predicament for you. Jog along, black mare. She was a great housekeeper, but most awful mean. She wore the same bonnet for eighteen years. Then she got a new one and W. O. met her on the road and didn't know her. Jog along, black mare. I feel that I'd a narrer escape. I might have married him and been most awful miserable, like my poor cousin, Jane Ann. Jane Ann married a rich man she didn't care anything about, and she hasn't the life of a dog. She come to see me last week and says, says she, 'Sarah Skinner, I envy you. I'd rather live in a little hut on the side of the road with a man I was fond of than in my big house with the one I've got.' Jane Ann's man ain't such a bad sort, nuther, though he's so contrary that he wears his fur coat when the thermometer's at ninety. The only way to git him to do anything is to coax him to do the opposite. But there ain't any love to smooth things down and it's a poor way of living. Jog along, black mare. There's Janet's place in the hollow— 'Wayside,' she calls it. Quite pictureaskew, ain't it? I guess you'll be glad to git out of this, with all them mail bags jamming round you."

"Yes, but I have enjoyed my drive with you very much," said Anne sincerely.

"Git away now!" said Mrs. Skinner, highly flattered. "Wait till I tell Thomas that. He always feels dretful tickled when I git a compliment. Jog along, black mare. Well, here we are. I hope you'll git on well in the school, miss. There's a short cut to it through the ma'sh back of

Janet's. If you take that way be awful keerful. If you once got stuck in that black mud you'd be sucked right down and never seen or heard tell of again till the day of judgment, like Adam Palmer's cow. Jog along, black mare."

31

Anne to Philippa

"Anne Shirley to Philippa Gordon, greeting.

"Well-beloved, it's high time I was writing you. Here am I, installed once more as a country 'school-ma'am' at Valley Road, boarding at 'Wayside,' the home of Miss Janet Sweet. Janet is a dear soul and very nice-looking; tall, but not over-tall; stoutish, yet with a certain restraint of outline suggestive of a thrifty soul who is not going to be over-lavish even in the matter of avoirdupois. She has a knot of soft, crimpy, brown hair with a thread of gray in it, a sunny face with rosy cheeks, and big, kind eyes as blue as forget-me-nots. Moreover, she is one of those delightful, old-fashioned cooks who don't care a bit if they ruin your digestion as long as they can give you feasts of fat things.

"I like her; and she likes me—principally, it seems, because she had a sister named Anne who died young.

"'I'm real glad to see you,' she said briskly, when I landed in her yard. 'My, you don't look a mite like I expected. I was sure you'd be dark—my sister Anne was dark. And here you're redheaded!'

"For a few minutes I thought I wasn't going to like Janet as much as I had expected at first sight. Then I reminded myself that I really must be more sensible than to be prejudiced against any one simply because she called my hair red. Probably the word 'auburn' was not in Janet's vocabulary at all.

"'Wayside' is a dear sort of little spot. The house is small and white, set down in a delightful little hollow that drops away from the road. Between road and house is an orchard and flower-garden all mixed up together. The front door walk is bordered with quahog clam-shells—'cow-hawks,' Janet calls them; there is Virginia Creeper over the porch and moss on the roof. My room is a neat little spot 'off the parlor'—just big enough for the bed and me. Over the head of my bed there is a picture of Robby Burns standing at Highland Mary's grave, shadowed by an enormous weeping willow tree. Robby's face is so lugubrious that it is no wonder I have bad dreams. Why, the first night I was here I dreamed I *couldn't laugh*.

"The parlor is tiny and neat. Its one window is so shaded by a huge willow that the room has a grotto-like effect of emerald gloom. There are wonderful tidies on the chairs, and gay mats on the floor, and books and cards carefully arranged on a round table, and vases of dried grass on the mantel-piece. Between the vases is a cheerful decoration of preserved coffin plates—five in all, pertaining respectively to Janet's father and mother, a brother, her sister Anne, and a hired man who died here once! If I go suddenly insane some of these days 'know all men by these presents' that those coffin-plates have caused it.

"But it's all delightful and I said so. Janet loved me for it, just as she detested poor Esther because Esther had said so much shade was unhygienic and had objected to sleeping on a feather bed. Now, I glory in feather-beds, and the more unhygienic and feathery they are the more I glory. Janet says it is such a comfort to see me eat; she had been so afraid I would be like Miss Haythorne, who wouldn't eat anything but fruit and hot water for breakfast and tried to make Janet give up frying things. Esther is really a dear girl, but she is rather given to fads. The trouble is that she hasn't enough imagination and *has* a tendency to indigestion.

"Janet told me I could have the use of the parlor when any young men called! I don't think there are many to call. I haven't seen a young man in Valley Road yet, except the next-door hired boy—Sam Tolliver, a very tall, lank, tow-haired youth. He came over one evening recently and sat for an hour on the garden fence, near the front porch where Janet and I were doing fancy-work. The only remarks he volunteered in all that time were, 'Hev a peppermint, miss! *Dew* now— fine thing for cat*arrh*, peppermints,' and, 'Powerful lot o' jump-grasses round here ter-night. Yep.'

"But there *is* a love affair going on here. It seems to be my fortune to be mixed up, more or less actively, with elderly love affairs. Mr. and

Mrs. Irving always say that I brought about their marriage. Mrs. Stephen Clark of Carmody persists in being most grateful to me for a suggestion which somebody else would probably have made if I hadn't. I do really think, though, that Ludovic Speed would never have got any further along than placid courtship if I had not helped him and Theodora Dix out.

"In the present affair I am only a passive spectator. I've tried once to help things along and made an awful mess of it. So I shall not meddle again. I'll tell you all about it when we meet."

32

Tea with Mrs. Douglas

O n the first Thursday night of Anne's sojourn in Valley Road Janet asked her to go to prayer-meeting. Janet blossomed out like a rose to attend that prayer-meeting. She wore a pale-blue, pansy-sprinkled muslin dress with more ruffles than one would ever have supposed economical Janet could be guilty of, and a white leghorn hat with pink roses and three ostrich feathers on it. Anne felt quite amazed. Later on she found out Janet's motive in so arraying herself—a motive as old as Eden.

Valley Road prayer-meetings seemed to be essentially feminine. There were thirty-two women present, two half-grown boys, and one solitary man, beside the minister. Anne found herself studying this man. He was not handsome or young or graceful; he had remarkably long legs—so long that he had to keep them coiled up under his chair to dispose of them—and he was stoop-shouldered. His hands were big, his hair wanted barbering, and his moustache was unkempt. But Anne thought she liked his face; it was kind and honest and tender; there was something else in it, too—just what, Anne found it hard to define. She finally concluded that this man had suffered and been strong, and it had been made manifest in his face. There was a sort of patient, humorous endurance in his expression which indicated that he would go to the stake if need be, but would keep on looking pleasant until he really had to begin squirming.

When prayer-meeting was over this man came up to Janet and said, "May I see you home, Janet?"

Janet took his arm—"as primly and shyly as if she were no more than sixteen, having her first escort home," Anne told the girls at Patty's Place later on.

"Miss Shirley, permit me to introduce Mr. Douglas," she said stiffly. Mr. Douglas nodded and said,

"I was looking at you in prayer-meeting, miss, and thinking what a nice little girl you were."

Such a speech from ninety-nine people out of a hundred would have annoyed Anne bitterly; but the way in which Mr. Douglas said it made her feel that she had received a very real and pleasing compliment. She smiled appreciatively at him and dropped obligingly behind on the moonlit road.

So Janet had a beau! Anne was delighted. Janet would make a paragon of a wife—cheery, economical, tolerant, and a very queen of cooks. It would be a flagrant waste on Nature's part to keep her a permanent old maid.

"John Douglas asked me to take you up to see his mother," said Janet the next day. "She's bed-rid a lot of the time and never goes out of the house. But she's powerful fond of company and always wants to see my boarders. Can you go up this evening?"

Anne assented; but later in the day Mr. Douglas called on his mother's behalf to invite them up to tea on Saturday evening.

"Oh, why didn't you put on your pretty pansy dress?" asked Anne, when they left home. It was a hot day, and poor Janet, between her excitement and her heavy black cashmere dress, looked as if she were being broiled alive.

"Old Mrs. Douglas would think it terrible frivolous and unsuitable, I'm afraid. John likes that dress, though," she added wistfully.

The old Douglas homestead was half a mile from "Wayside" cresting a windy hill. The house itself was large and comfortable, old enough to be dignified, and girdled with maple groves and orchards. There were big, trim barns behind it, and everything bespoke prosperity. Whatever the patient endurance in Mr. Douglas' face had meant it hadn't, so Anne reflected, meant debts and duns.

John Douglas met them at the door and took them into the sitting-room, where his mother was enthroned in an armchair.

Anne had expected old Mrs. Douglas to be tall and thin, because Mr. Douglas was. Instead, she was a tiny scrap of a woman, with soft pink cheeks, mild blue eyes, and a mouth like a baby's. Dressed in a beautiful, fashionably-made black silk dress, with a fluffy white shawl over her shoulders, and her snowy hair surmounted by a dainty lace cap, she might have posed as a grandmother doll.

"How do you do, Janet dear?" she said sweetly. "I am *so* glad to see you again, dear." She put up her pretty old face to be kissed. "And this is our new teacher. I'm delighted to meet you. My son has been singing your praises until I'm half jealous, and I'm sure Janet ought to be wholly so."

Poor Janet blushed, Anne said something polite and conventional, and then everybody sat down and made talk. It was hard work, even for Anne, for nobody seemed at ease except old Mrs. Douglas, who certainly did not find any difficulty in talking. She made Janet sit by her and stroked her hand occasionally. Janet sat and smiled, looking horribly uncomfortable in her hideous dress, and John Douglas sat without smiling.

At the tea table Mrs. Douglas gracefully asked Janet to pour the tea. Janet turned redder than ever but did it. Anne wrote a description of that meal to Stella.

"We had cold tongue and chicken and strawberry preserves, lemon pie and tarts and chocolate cake and raisin cookies and pound cake and fruit cake—and a few other things, including more pie—caramel pie, I think it was. After I had eaten twice as much as was good for me, Mrs. Douglas sighed and said she feared she had nothing to tempt my appetite.

"'I'm afraid dear Janet's cooking has spoiled you for any other,' she said sweetly. 'Of course nobody in Valley Road aspires to rival *her*. Won't you have another piece of pie, Miss Shirley? You haven't eaten *anything*.'

"Stella, I had eaten a helping of tongue and one of chicken, three biscuits, a generous allowance of preserves, a piece of pie, a tart, and a square of chocolate cake!"

After tea Mrs. Douglas smiled benevolently and told John to take "dear Janet" out into the garden and get her some roses. "Miss Shirley will keep me company while you are out—won't you?" she said plaintively. She settled down in her armchair with a sigh.

"I am a very frail old woman, Miss Shirley. For over twenty years I've been a great sufferer. For twenty long, weary years I've been dying by inches."

"How painful!" said Anne, trying to be sympathetic and succeeding only in feeling idiotic.

"There have been scores of nights when they've thought I could never live to see the dawn," went on Mrs. Douglas solemnly. "Nobody knows what I've gone through—nobody can know but myself. Well, it can't last very much longer now. My weary pilgrimage will soon be over, Miss Shirley. It is a great comfort to me that John will have such a good wife to look after him when his mother is gone—a great comfort, Miss Shirley."

"Janet is a lovely woman," said Anne warmly.

"Lovely! A beautiful character," assented Mrs. Douglas. "And a perfect housekeeper—something I never was. My health would not permit it, Miss Shirley. I am indeed thankful that John has made such a wise choice. I hope and believe that he will be happy. He is my only son, Miss Shirley, and his happiness lies very near my heart."

"Of course," said Anne stupidly. For the first time in her life she was stupid. Yet she could not imagine why. She seemed to have absolutely nothing to say to this sweet, smiling, angelic old lady who was patting her hand so kindly.

"Come and see me soon again, dear Janet," said Mrs. Douglas lovingly, when they left. "You don't come half often enough. But then I suppose John will be bringing you here to stay all the time one of these days."

Anne, happening to glance at John Douglas, as his mother spoke, gave a positive start of dismay. He looked as a tortured man might look when his tormentors gave the rack the last turn of possible endurance. She felt sure he must be ill and hurried poor blushing Janet away.

"Isn't old Mrs. Douglas a sweet woman?" asked Janet, as they went down the road.

"M—m," answered Anne absently. She was wondering why John Douglas had looked so.

"She's been a terrible sufferer," said Janet feelingly. "She takes terrible spells. It keeps John all worried up. He's scared to leave home for fear his mother will take a spell and nobody there but the hired girl."

33

"He Just Kept Coming and Coming"

hree days later Anne came home from school and found Janet crying. Tears and Janet seemed so incongruous that Anne was honestly alarmed.

"Oh, what is the matter?" she cried anxiously.

"I'm—I'm forty today," sobbed Janet.

"Well, you were nearly that yesterday and it didn't hurt," comforted Anne, trying not to smile.

"But—but," went on Janet with a big gulp, "John Douglas won't ask me to marry him."

"Oh, but he will," said Anne lamely. "You must give him time, Janet."

"Time!" said Janet with indescribable scorn. "He has had twenty years. How much time does he want?"

"Do you mean that John Douglas has been coming to see you for twenty years?"

"He has. And he has never so much as mentioned marriage to me. And I don't believe he ever will now. I've never said a word to a mortal about it, but it seems to me I've just got to talk it out with some one at last or go crazy. John Douglas begun to go with me twenty years ago, before mother died. Well, he kept coming and coming, and after a spell I begun making quilts and things; but he never said anything about getting married, only just kept coming and coming. There wasn't anything I could do. Mother died when we'd been going together for eight years. I thought he maybe would speak out then, seeing as I was left alone in the world. He was real kind and feeling, and did everything he could for me, but he never said marry. And that's the way it has been going on ever since. People blame *me* for it.

They say I won't marry him because his mother is so sickly and I don't want the bother of waiting on her. Why, I'd *love* to wait on John's mother! But I let them think so. I'd rather they'd blame me than pity me! It's so dreadful humiliating that John won't ask me. And *why* won't he? Seems to me if I only knew his reason I wouldn't mind it so much."

"Perhaps his mother doesn't want him to marry anybody," suggested Anne.

"Oh, she does. She's told me time and again that she'd love to see John settled before her time comes. She's always giving him hints—you heard her yourself the other day. I thought I'd ha' gone through the floor."

"It's beyond me," said Anne helplessly. She thought of Ludovic Speed. But the cases were not parallel. John Douglas was not a man of Ludovic's type.

"You should show more spirit, Janet," she went on resolutely. "Why didn't you send him about his business long ago?"

"I couldn't," said poor Janet pathetically. "You see, Anne, I've always been awful fond of John. He might just as well keep coming as not, for there was never anybody else I'd want, so it didn't matter."

"But it might have made him speak out like a man," urged Anne. Janet shook her head.

"No, I guess not. I was afraid to try, anyway, for fear he'd think I meant it and just go. I suppose I'm a poor-spirited creature, but that is how I feel. And I can't help it."

"Oh, you *could* help it, Janet. It isn't too late yet. Take a firm stand. Let that man know you are not going to endure his shilly-shallying any longer. *I'll* back you up."

"I dunno," said Janet hopelessly. "I dunno if I could ever get up enough spunk. Things have drifted so long. But I'll think it over."

Anne felt that she was disappointed in John Douglas. She had liked him so well, and she had not thought him the sort of man who would play fast and loose with a woman's feelings for twenty years. He certainly should be taught a lesson, and Anne felt vindictively that she would enjoy seeing the process. Therefore she was delighted when

Janet told her, as they were going to prayer-meeting the next night, that she meant to show some "sperrit."

"I'll let John Douglas see I'm not going to be trodden on any longer."

"You are perfectly right," said Anne emphatically.

When prayer-meeting was over John Douglas came up with his usual request. Janet looked frightened but resolute.

"No, thank you," she said icily. "I know the road home pretty well alone. I ought to, seeing I've been traveling it for forty years. So you needn't trouble yourself, *Mr.* Douglas."

Anne was looking at John Douglas; and, in that brilliant moon-light, she saw the last twist of the rack again. Without a word he turned and strode down the road.

"Stop! Stop!" Anne called wildly after him, not caring in the least for the other dumbfounded onlookers. "Mr. Douglas, stop! Come back;"

John Douglas stopped but he did not come back. Anne flew down the road, caught his arm and fairly dragged him back to Janet.

"You must come back," she said imploringly. "It's all a mistake, Mr. Douglas—all my fault. I made Janet do it. She didn't want to—but it's all right now, isn't it, Janet?"

Without a word Janet took his arm and walked away. Anne followed them meekly home and slipped in by the back door.

"Well, you are a nice person to back one up," said Janet sarcastically.

"I couldn't help it, Janet," said Anne repentantly. "I just felt as if I had stood by and seen murder done. I *had* to run after him."

"Oh, I'm just as glad you did. When I saw John Douglas making off down that road I just felt as if every little bit of joy and happiness that was left in my life was going with him. It was an awful feeling."

"Did he ask you why you did it?" asked Anne.

"No, he never said a word about it," replied Janet dully.

34

John Douglas Speaks at Last

Anne was not without a feeble hope that something might come of it after all. But nothing did. John Douglas came and took Janet driving, and walked home from prayer-meeting with her, as he had been doing for twenty years, and as he seemed likely to do for twenty years more. The summer waned. Anne taught her school and wrote letters and studied a little. Her walks to and from school were pleasant. She always went by way of the swamp; it was a lovely place—a boggy soil, green with the greenest of mossy hillocks; a silvery brook meandered through it and spruces stood erectly, their boughs a-trail with gray-green mosses, their roots overgrown with all sorts of woodland lovelinesses.

Nevertheless, Anne found life in Valley Road a little monotonous. To be sure, there was one diverting incident.

She had not seen the lank, tow-headed Samuel of the peppermints since the evening of his call, save for chance meetings on the road. But one warm August night he appeared, and solemnly seated himself on the rustic bench by the porch. He wore his usual working habiliments, consisting of vari-patched trousers, a blue jean shirt, out at the elbows, and a ragged straw hat. He was chewing a straw and he kept on chewing it while he looked solemnly at Anne. Anne laid her book aside with a sigh and took up her doily. Conversation with Sam was really out of the question.

After a long silence Sam suddenly spoke.

"I'm leaving over there," he said abruptly, waving his straw in the direction of the neighboring house.

"Oh, are you?" said Anne politely.

"Yep."

"And where are you going now?"

"Wall, I've been thinking some of gitting a place of my own. There's one that'd suit me over at Millersville. But ef I rents it I'll want a woman."

"I suppose so," said Anne vaguely.

"Yep."

There was another long silence. Finally Sam removed his straw again and said,

"Will yeh hev me?"

"Wh—a—t!" gasped Anne.

"Will yeh hev me?"

"Do you mean—*marry* you?" queried poor Anne feebly.

"Yep."

"Why, I'm hardly acquainted with you," cried Anne indignantly.

"But yeh'd git acquainted with me after we was married," said Sam. Anne gathered up her poor dignity.

"Certainly I won't marry you," she said haughtily.

"Wall, yeh might do worse," expostulated Sam. "I'm a good worker and I've got some money in the bank."

"Don't speak of this to me again. Whatever put such an idea into your head?" said Anne, her sense of humor getting the better of her wrath. It was such an absurd situation.

"Yeh're a likely-looking girl and hev a right-smart way o' stepping," said Sam. "I don't want no lazy woman. Think it over. I won't change my mind yit awhile. Wall, I must be gitting. Gotter milk the cows."

Anne's illusions concerning proposals had suffered so much of late years that there were few of them left. So she could laugh wholeheartedly over this one, not feeling any secret sting. She mimicked poor Sam to Janet that night, and both of them laughed immoderately over his plunge into sentiment.

One afternoon, when Anne's sojourn in Valley Road was drawing to a close, Alec Ward came driving down to "Wayside" in hot haste for Janet.

"They want you at the Douglas place quick," he said. "I really believe old Mrs. Douglas is going to die at last, after pretending to do it for twenty years."

Janet ran to get her hat. Anne asked if Mrs. Douglas was worse than usual.

"She's not half as bad," said Alec solemnly, "and that's what makes me think it's serious. Other times she'd be screaming and throwing herself all over the place. This time she's lying still and mum. When Mrs. Douglas is mum she is pretty sick, you bet."

"You don't like old Mrs. Douglas?" said Anne curiously.

"I like cats as *is* cats. I don't like cats as is women," was Alec's cryptic reply.

Janet came home in the twilight.

"Mrs. Douglas is dead," she said wearily. "She died soon after I got there. She just spoke to me once—'I suppose you'll marry John now?' she said. It cut me to the heart, Anne. To think John's own mother thought I wouldn't marry him because of her! I couldn't say a word either—there were other women there. I was thankful John had gone out."

Janet began to cry drearily. But Anne brewed her a hot drink of ginger tea to her comforting. To be sure, Anne discovered later on that she had used white pepper instead of ginger, but Janet never knew the difference.

The evening after the funeral Janet and Anne were sitting on the front porch steps at sunset. The wind had fallen asleep in the pinelands and lurid sheets of heat-lightning flickered across the northern skies. Janet wore her ugly black dress and looked her very worst, her eyes and nose red from crying. They talked little, for Janet seemed faintly to resent Anne's efforts to cheer her up. She plainly preferred to be miserable.

Suddenly the gate-latch clicked and John Douglas strode into the garden. He walked towards them straight over the geranium bed. Janet stood up. So did Anne. Anne was a tall girl and wore a white dress; but John Douglas did not see her.

"Janet," he said, "will you marry me?"

The words burst out as if they had been wanting to be said for twenty years and *must* be uttered now, before anything else.

Janet's face was so red from crying that it couldn't turn any redder, so it turned a most unbecoming purple.

"Why didn't you ask me before?" she said slowly.

"I couldn't. She made me promise not to—mother made me promise not to. Nineteen years ago she took a terrible spell. We thought she couldn't live through it. She implored me to promise not to ask you to marry me while she was alive. I didn't want to promise such a thing, even though we all thought she couldn't live very long—the doctor only gave her six months. But she begged it on her knees, sick and suffering. I had to promise."

"What had your mother against me?" cried Janet.

"Nothing—nothing. She just didn't want another woman—*any* woman—there while she was living. She said if I didn't promise she'd die right there and I'd have killed her. So I promised. And she's held me to that promise ever since, though I've gone on my knees to her in my turn to beg her to let me off."

"Why didn't you tell me this?" asked Janet chokingly. "If I'd only *known!* Why didn't you just tell me?"

"She made me promise I wouldn't tell a soul," said John hoarsely. "She swore me to it on the Bible; Janet, I'd never have done it if I'd dreamed it was to be for so long. Janet, you'll never know what I've suffered these nineteen years. I know I've made you suffer, too, but you'll marry me for all, won't you, Janet? Oh, Janet, won't you? I've come as soon as I could to ask you."

At this moment the stupefied Anne came to her senses and realized that she had no business to be there. She slipped away and did not see Janet until the next morning, when the latter told her the rest of the story.

"That cruel, relentless, deceitful old woman!" cried Anne.

"Hush—she's dead," said Janet solemnly. "If she wasn't—but she *is.* So we mustn't speak evil of her. But I'm happy at last, Anne. And I wouldn't have minded waiting so long a bit if I'd only known why."

"When are you to be married?"

"Next month. Of course it will be very quiet. I suppose people will talk terrible. They'll say I made enough haste to snap John up as soon as his poor mother was out of the way. John wanted to let them know the truth but I said, 'No, John; after all she was your mother, and we'll keep the secret between us, and not cast any shadow on her memory. I don't mind what people say, now that I know the truth myself; It don't matter a mite. Let it all be buried with the dead,' says I to him. So I coaxed him round to agree with me."

"You're much more forgiving than I could ever be," Anne said, rather crossly.

"You'll feel differently about a good many things when you get to be my age," said Janet tolerantly. "That's one of the things we learn as we grow older—how to forgive. It comes easier at forty than it did at twenty."

35

The Last Redmond Year Opens

"Here we are, all back again, nicely sunburned and rejoicing as a strong man to run a race," said Phil, sitting down on a suitcase with a sigh of pleasure. "Isn't it jolly to see this dear old Patty's Place again—and Aunty—and the cats? Rusty has lost another piece of ear, hasn't he?"

"Rusty would be the nicest cat in the world if he had no ears at all," declared Anne loyalty from her trunk, while Rusty writhed about her lap in a frenzy of welcome.

"Aren't you glad to see us back, Aunty?" demanded Phil.

"Yes. But I wish you'd tidy things up," said Aunt Jamesina plaintively, looking at the wilderness of trunks and suitcases by which the four laughing, chattering girls were surrounded. "You can talk just as well later on. Work first and then play used to be my motto when I was a girl."

"Oh, we've just reversed that in this generation, Aunty. *Our* motto is play your play and then dig in. You can do your work so much better if you've had a good bout of play first."

"If you are going to marry a minister," said Aunt Jamesina, picking up Joseph and her knitting and resigning herself to the inevitable with the charming grace that made her the queen of housemothers, "you will have to give up such expressions as 'dig in.'"

"Why?" moaned Phil. "Oh, why must a minister's wife be supposed to utter only prunes and prisms? I shan't. Everybody on Patterson Street uses slang—that is to say, metaphorical language—and if I didn't they would think me insufferably proud and stuck up."

"Have you broken the news to your family?" asked Priscilla, feeding the Sarah-cat bits from her lunchbasket.

Phil nodded.

"How did they take it?"

"Oh, mother rampaged. But I stood rock-firm—even I, Philippa Gordon, who never before could hold fast to anything. Father was calmer. Father's own daddy was a minister, so you see he has a soft spot in his heart for the cloth. I had Jo up to Mount Holly, after mother grew calm, and they both loved him. But mother gave him some frightful hints in every conversation regarding what she had hoped for me. Oh, my vacation pathway hasn't been exactly strewn with roses, girls dear. But—I've won out and I've got Jo. Nothing else matters."

"To you," said Aunt Jamesina darkly.

"Nor to Jo, either," retorted Phil. "You keep on pitying him. Why, pray? I think he's to be envied. He's getting brains, beauty, and a heart of gold in ME."

"It's well we know how to take your speeches," said Aunt Jamesina patiently. "I hope you don't talk like that before strangers. What would they think?"

"Oh, I don't want to know what they think. I don't want to see myself as others see me. I'm sure it would be horribly uncomfortable most of the time. I don't believe Burns was really sincere in that prayer, either."

"Oh, I daresay we all pray for some things that we really don't want, if we were only honest enough to look into our hearts," owned Aunt Jamesina candidly. "I've a notion that such prayers don't rise very far. I used to pray that I might be enabled to forgive a certain person, but I know now I really didn't want to forgive her. When I finally got that I did want to I forgave her without having to pray about it."

"I can't picture you as being unforgiving for long," said Stella.

"Oh, I used to be. But holding spite doesn't seem worth while when you get along in years."

"That reminds me," said Anne, and told the tale of John and Janet.

"And now tell us about that romantic scene you hinted so darkly at in one of your letters," demanded Phil.

Anne acted out Samuel's proposal with great spirit. The girls shrieked with laughter and Aunt Jamesina smiled.

"It isn't in good taste to make fun of your beaux," she said severely; "but," she added calmly, "I always did it myself."

"Tell us about your beaux, Aunty," entreated Phil. "You must have had any number of them."

"They're not in the past tense," retorted Aunt Jamesina. "I've got them yet. There are three old widowers at home who have been casting sheep's eyes at me for some time. You children needn't think you own all the romance in the world."

"Widowers and sheep's eyes don't sound very romantic, Aunty."

"Well, no; but young folks aren't always romantic either. Some of my beaux certainly weren't. I used to laugh at them scandalous, poor boys. There was Jim Elwood—he was always in a sort of day-dream—never seemed to sense what was going on. He didn't wake up to the fact that I'd said 'no' till a year after I'd said it. When he did get married his wife fell out of the sleigh one night when they were driving home from church and he never missed her. Then there was Dan Winston. He knew too much. He knew everything in this world and most of what is in the next. He could give you an answer to any question, even if you asked him when the Judgment Day was to be. Milton Edwards was real nice and I liked him but I didn't marry him. For one thing, he took a week to get a joke through his head, and for another he never asked me. Horatio Reeve was the most interesting beau I ever had. But when he told a story he dressed it up so that you couldn't see it for frills. I never could decide whether he was lying or just letting his imagination run loose."

"And what about the others, Aunty?"

"Go away and unpack," said Aunt Jamesina, waving Joseph at them by mistake for a needle. "The others were too nice to make fun of. I shall respect their memory. There's a box of flowers in your room, Anne. They came about an hour ago."

After the first week the girls of Patty's Place settled down to a steady grind of study; for this was their last year at Redmond and graduation honors must be fought for persistently. Anne devoted herself to English, Priscilla pored over classics, and Philippa pounded away at Mathematics. Sometimes they grew tired, sometimes they felt discouraged, sometimes nothing seemed worth the struggle for it. In one such mood Stella wandered up to the blue room one rainy November evening. Anne sat on the floor in a little circle of light cast by the lamp beside her, amid a surrounding snow of crumpled manuscript.

"What in the world are you doing?"

"Just looking over some old Story Club yarns. I wanted something to cheer *and* inebriate. I'd studied until the world seemed azure. So I came up here and dug these out of my trunk. They are so drenched in tears and tragedy that they are excruciatingly funny."

"I'm blue and discouraged myself," said Stella, throwing herself on the couch. "Nothing seems worthwhile. My very thoughts are old. I've thought them all before. What is the use of living after all, Anne?"

"Honey, it's just brain fog that makes us feel that way, and the weather. A pouring rainy night like this, coming after a hard day's grind, would squelch any one but a *Mark Tapley*. You know it *is* worthwhile to live."

"Oh, I suppose so. But I can't prove it to myself just now."

"Just think of all the great and noble souls who have lived and worked in the world," said Anne dreamily. "Isn't it worthwhile to come after them and inherit what they won and taught? And think of all the great people in the world today! Isn't it worthwhile to think we can share their inspiration? And then, all the great souls that will come in the future? Isn't it worthwhile to work a little and prepare the way for them—make just one step in their path easier?"

"Oh, my mind agrees with you, Anne. But my soul remains doleful and uninspired. I'm always grubby and dingy on rainy nights."

"Some nights I like the rain—I like to lie in bed and hear it pattering on the roof and drifting through the pines."

"I like it when it stays on the roof," said Stella. "It doesn't always. I spent a gruesome night in an old country farmhouse last summer. The roof leaked and the rain came pattering down on my bed. There was no poetry in *that*. I had to get up in the 'mirk midnight' and chivy round to pull the bedstead out of the drip—and it was one of those solid, old-fashioned beds that weigh a ton—more or less. And then that drip-drop, drip-drop kept up all night until my nerves just went to pieces. You've no idea what an eerie noise a great drop of rain falling with a mushy thud on a bare floor makes in the night. It sounds like ghostly footsteps and all that sort of thing. What are you laughing over, Anne?"

"These stories. As Phil would say they are killing—in more senses than one, for everybody died in them. What dazzlingly lovely heroines we had—and how we dressed them! Silks—satins—velvets—jewels—laces—they never wore anything else. Here is one of Jane Andrews' stories depicting her heroine as sleeping in a beautiful white satin nightdress trimmed with seed pearls."

"Go on," said Stella. "I begin to feel that life *is* worth living as long as there's a laugh in it."

"Here's one I wrote. My heroine is disporting herself at a ball 'glittering from head to foot with large diamonds of the first water.' But what booted beauty or rich attire? 'The paths of glory lead but to the grave.' They must either be murdered or die of a broken heart. There was no escape for them."

"Let me read some of your stories."

"Well, here's my masterpiece. Note its cheerful title—'*My Graves.*' I shed quarts of tears while writing it, and the other girls shed gallons while I read it. Jane Andrews' mother scolded her frightfully because she had so many handkerchiefs in the wash that week It's a harrowing tale of the wanderings of a Methodist minister's wife. I made her a Methodist because it was necessary that she should wander. She buried a child every place she lived in. There were nine of them and their graves were severed far apart, ranging from Newfoundland to Vancouver. I described the children, pictured their several death beds, and detailed their tombstones and epitaphs. I had intended to bury the whole nine but when I had disposed of eight my invention of horrors gave out and I permitted the tenth to live as a hopeless cripple."

While Stella read *My Graves*, punctuating its tragic paragraphs with chuckles, and Rusty slept the sleep of a just cat who has been out all night curled up on a Jane Andrews tale of a beautiful maiden of fifteen who went to nurse in a leper colony—of course dying of the loathsome disease finally—Anne glanced over the other manuscripts and recalled the old days at Avonlea school when the members of the Story Club, sitting under the spruce trees or down among the ferns by the brook, had written them. What fun they had had! How the sunshine and mirth of those olden summers returned as she read. Not all the glory that was Greece or the grandeur that was Rome could weave such wizardry as those funny, tearful tales of the Story Club. Among the manuscripts Anne found one written on sheets of wrapping paper. A wave of laughter filled her gray eyes as she recalled the time and place of its genesis. It was the sketch she had written the day she fell through the roof of the Cobb duckhouse on the Tory Road.

Anne glanced over it, then fell to reading it intently. It was a little dialogue between asters and sweet-peas, wild canaries in the lilac bush, and the guardian spirit of the garden. After she had read it, she sat, staring into space; and when Stella had gone she smoothed out the crumpled manuscript.

"I believe I will," she said resolutely.

36

The Gardners' Call

"Here is a letter with an Indian stamp for you, Aunt Jimsie," said Phil. "Here are three for Stella, and two for Pris, and a glorious fat one for me from Joe. There's nothing for you, Anne, except a circular."

Nobody noticed Anne's flush as she took the thin letter Phil tossed her carelessly. But a few minutes later Phil looked up to see a transfigured Anne.

"Honey, what good thing has happened?"

"The *Youth's Friend* has accepted a little sketch I sent them a fortnight ago," said Anne, trying hard to speak as if she were accustomed to having sketches accepted every mail, but not quite succeeding.

"Anne Shirley! How glorious! What was it? When is it to be published? Did they pay you for it?"

"Yes; they've sent a check for ten dollars, and the editor writes that he would like to see more of my work. Dear man, he shall. It was an old sketch I found in my box. I re-wrote it and sent it in—but I never really thought it could be accepted because it had no plot," said Anne, recalling the bitter experience of *Averil's Atonement*.

"What are you going to do with that ten dollars, Anne? Let's all go up town and get drunk," suggested Phil.

"I *am* going to squander it in a wild soulless revel of some sort," declared Anne gaily. "At all events it isn't tainted money—like the check I got for that horrible Reliable Baking Powder story. I spent *it* usefully for clothes and hated them every time I put them on."

"Think of having a real live author at Patty's Place," said Priscilla.

"It's a great responsibility," said Aunt Jamesina solemnly.

"Indeed it is," agreed Pris with equal solemnity. "Authors are kittle cattle. You never know when or how they will break out. Anne may make copy of *us*."

"I meant that the ability to write for the Press was a great responsibility," said Aunt Jamesina severely; "and I hope Anne realizes it. My daughter used to write stories before she went to the foreign field, but now she has turned her attention to higher things. She used to say her motto was 'Never write a line you would be ashamed to read at your own funeral.' You'd better take that for yours, Anne, if you are going to embark in literature. Though, to be sure," added Aunt Jamesina perplexedly, "Elizabeth always used to laugh when she said it. She always laughed so much that I don't know how she ever came to decide on being a missionary. I'm thankful she did—I prayed that she might—but—I wish she hadn't."

Then Aunt Jamesina wondered why those giddy girls all laughed.

Anne's eyes shone all that day; literary ambitions sprouted and budded in her brain; their exhilaration accompanied her to Jennie Cooper's walking party, and not even the sight of Gilbert and Christine, walking just ahead of her and Roy, could quite subdue the sparkle of her starry hopes. Nevertheless, she was not so rapt from things of earth as to be unable to notice that Christine's walk was decidedly ungraceful.

"But I suppose Gilbert looks only at her face. So like a man," thought Anne scornfully.

"Shall you be home Saturday afternoon?" asked Roy.

"Yes."

"My mother and sisters are coming to call on you," said Roy quietly.

Something went over Anne which might be described as a thrill, but it was hardly a pleasant one. She had never met any of Roy's family; she realized the significance of his statement; and it had, somehow, an irrevocableness about it that chilled her.

"I shall be glad to see them," she said flatly; and then wondered if she really would be glad. She ought to be, of course. But would it not be something of an ordeal? Gossip had filtered to Anne regarding the light in which the Gardners viewed the "infatuation" of son and brother. Roy must have brought pressure to bear in the matter of this call. Anne knew she would be weighed in the balance. From the fact that they had consented to call she understood that, willingly or unwillingly, they regarded her as a possible member of their clan.

"I shall just be myself. I shall not *try* to make a good impression," thought Anne loftily. But she was wondering what dress she would better wear Saturday afternoon, and if the new style of high hairdressing would suit her better than the old; and the walking party was rather spoiled for her. By night she had decided that she would wear her brown chiffon on Saturday, but would do her hair low.

Friday afternoon none of the girls had classes at Redmond. Stella took the opportunity to write a paper for the Philomathic Society, and was sitting at the table in the corner of the living-room with an untidy litter of notes and manuscript on the floor around her. Stella always vowed she never could write anything unless she threw each sheet down as she completed it. Anne, in her flannel blouse and serge skirt, with her hair rather blown from her windy walk home, was sitting squarely in the middle of the floor, teasing the Sarah-cat with a wishbone. Joseph and Rusty were both curled up in her lap. A warm plummy odor filled the whole house, for Priscilla was cooking in the kitchen. Presently she came in, enshrouded in a huge work-apron, with a smudge of flour on her nose, to show Aunt Jamesina the chocolate cake she had just iced.

At this auspicious moment the knocker sounded. Nobody paid any attention to it save Phil, who sprang up and opened it, expecting a boy with the hat she had bought that morning. On the doorstep stood Mrs. Gardner and her daughters.

Anne scrambled to her feet somehow, emptying two indignant cats out of her lap as she did so, and mechanically shifting her wishbone from her right hand to her left. Priscilla, who would have had to cross the room to reach the kitchen door, lost her head, wildly plunged the chocolate cake under a cushion on the inglenook sofa, and dashed upstairs. Stella began feverishly gathering up her manuscript. Only Aunt Jamesina and Phil remained normal. Thanks to them, everybody was soon sitting at ease, even Anne. Priscilla came down, apronless and smudgeless, Stella reduced her corner to decency, and Phil saved the situation by a stream of ready small talk.

Mrs. Gardner was tall and thin and handsome, exquisitely gowned, cordial with a cordiality that seemed a trifle forced. Aline Gardner was a younger edition of her mother, lacking the cordiality. She endeavored to be nice, but succeeded only in being haughty and patronizing. Dorothy Gardner was slim and jolly and rather tomboyish. Anne knew she was Roy's favorite sister and warmed to her. She would have looked very much like Roy if she had had dreamy dark eyes instead of roguish hazel ones. Thanks to her and Phil, the call really went off very well, except for a slight sense of strain in the atmosphere and two rather untoward incidents. Rusty and Joseph, left to themselves, began a game of chase, and sprang madly into Mrs. Gardner's silken lap and out of it in their wild career. Mrs. Gardner lifted her lorgnette and gazed after their flying forms as if she had never seen cats before, and Anne, choking back slightly nervous laughter, apologized as best she could.

"You are fond of cats?" said Mrs. Gardner, with a slight intonation of tolerant wonder.

Anne, despite her affection for Rusty, was *not* especially fond of cats, but Mrs. Gardner's tone annoyed her. Inconsequently she remembered that Mrs. John Blythe was so fond of cats that she kept as many as her husband would allow.

"They *are* adorable animals, aren't they?" she said wickedly.

"I have never liked cats," said Mrs. Gardner remotely.

"I love them," said Dorothy. "They are so nice and selfish. Dogs are *too* good and unselfish. They make me feel uncomfortable. But cats are gloriously human."

"You have two delightful old china dogs there. May I look at them closely?" said Aline, crossing the room towards the fireplace and thereby becoming the unconscious cause of the other accident. Picking up Magog, she sat down on the cushion under which was secreted Priscilla's chocolate cake. Priscilla and Anne exchanged agonized glances but could do nothing. The stately Aline continued to sit on the cushion and discuss china dogs until the time of departure.

Dorothy lingered behind a moment to squeeze Anne's hand and whisper impulsively.

"I *know* you and I are going to be chums. Oh, Roy has told me all about you. I'm the only one of the family he tells things to, poor boy— nobody *could* confide in mamma and Aline, you know. What glorious times you girls must have here! Won't you let me come often and have a share in them?"

"Come as often as you like," Anne responded heartily, thankful that one of Roy's sisters was likable. She would never like Aline, so much was certain; and Aline would never like her, though Mrs. Gardner might be won. Altogether, Anne sighed with relief when the ordeal was over.

"'Of all sad words of tongue or pen
The saddest are it might have been,'"

quoted Priscilla tragically, lifting the cushion. "This cake is now what you might call a flat failure. And the cushion is likewise ruined. Never tell me that Friday isn't unlucky."

"People who send word they are coming on Saturday shouldn't come on Friday," said Aunt Jamesina.

"I fancy it was Roy's mistake," said Phil. "That boy isn't really responsible for what he says when he talks to Anne. Where *is* Anne?"

Anne had gone upstairs. She felt oddly like crying. But she made herself laugh instead. Rusty and Joseph had been *too* awful! And Dorothy *was* a dear.

37

Full-fledged B.A.'s

"**I** wish I were dead, or that it were tomorrow night," groaned Phil. "If you live long enough both wishes will come true," said Anne calmly.

"It's easy for you to be serene. You're at home in Philosophy. I'm not—and when I think of that horrible paper tomorrow I quail. If I should fail in it what would Jo say?"

"You won't fail. How did you get on in Greek today?"

"I don't know. Perhaps it was a good paper and perhaps it was bad enough to make Homer turn over in his grave. I've studied and mulled over notebooks until I'm incapable of forming an opinion of anything. How thankful little Phil be when all this examinating is over."

"Examinating? I never heard such a word."

"Well, haven't I as good a right to make a word as any one else?" demanded Phil.

"Words aren't made—they grow," said Anne.

"Never mind—I begin faintly to discern clear water ahead where no examination breakers loom. Girls, do you—can you realize that our Redmond life is almost over?"

"I can't," said Anne, sorrowfully. "It seems just yesterday that Pris and I were alone in that crowd of Freshmen at Redmond. And now we are Seniors in our final examinations."

"'Potent, wise, and reverend Seniors,'" quoted Phil. "Do you suppose we really are any wiser than when we came to Redmond?"

"You don't act as if you were by times," said Aunt Jamesina severely.

"Oh, Aunt Jimsie, haven't we been pretty good girls, take us by and large, these three winters you've mothered us?" pleaded Phil.

"You've been four of the dearest, sweetest, goodest girls that ever went together through college," averred Aunt Jamesina, who never spoiled a compliment by misplaced economy. "But I mistrust you haven't any too much sense yet. It's not to be expected, of course. Experience teaches sense. You can't learn it in a college course. You've been to college four years and I never was, but I know heaps more than you do, young ladies."

> "*There are lots of things that never go by rule,*
> *There's a powerful pile o' knowledge*
> *That you never get at college,*
> *There are heaps of things you never learn at school,*"

quoted Stella.

"Have you learned anything at Redmond except dead languages and geometry and such trash?" queried Aunt Jamesina.

"Oh, yes. I think we have, Aunty," protested Anne.

"We've learned the truth of what Professor Woodleigh told us last Philomathic," said Phil. "He said, 'Humor is the spiciest condiment in the feast of existence. Laugh at your mistakes but learn from them, joke over your troubles but gather strength from them, make a jest of your difficulties but overcome them.' Isn't that worth learning, Aunt Jimsie?"

"Yes, it is, dearie. When you've learned to laugh at the things that should be laughed at, and *not* to laugh at those that shouldn't, you've got wisdom and understanding."

"What have you got out of your Redmond course, Anne?" murmured Priscilla aside.

"I think," said Anne slowly, "that I really have learned to look upon each little hindrance as a jest and each great one as the foreshadowing of victory. Summing up, I think that is what Redmond has given me."

"I shall have to fall back on another Professor Woodleigh quotation to express what it has done for me," said Priscilla. "You remember that he said in his address, 'There is so much in the world for us all if we only have the eyes to see it, and the heart to love it, and the hand to gather it to ourselves—so much in men and women, so much in art and literature, so much everywhere in which to delight, and for which to be thankful.' I think Redmond has taught me that in some measure, Anne."

"Judging from what you all say," remarked Aunt Jamesina, "the sum and substance is that you can learn—if you've got natural gumption enough—in four years at college what it would take about twenty years of living to teach you. Well, that justifies higher education in my opinion. It's a matter I was always dubious about before."

"But what about people who haven't natural gumption, Aunt Jimsie?"

"People who haven't natural gumption *never* learn," retorted Aunt Jamesina, "neither in college nor life. If they live to be a hundred they really don't know anything more than when they were born. It's their misfortune not their fault, poor souls. But those of us who have some gumption should duly thank the Lord for it."

"Will you please define what gumption is, Aunt Jimsie?" asked Phil.

"No, I won't, young woman. Any one who has gumption knows what it is, and any one who hasn't can never know what it is. So there is no need of defining it."

The busy days flew by and examinations were over. Anne took High Honors in English, Priscilla took Honors in Classics, and Phil in Mathematics. Stella obtained a good all-round showing. Then came Convocation.

"This is what I would once have called an epoch in my life," said Anne, as she took Roy's violets out of their box and gazed at them thoughtfully. She meant to carry them, of course, but her eyes wandered to another box on her table. It was filled with lilies-of-the-valley, as fresh and fragrant as those which bloomed in the Green Gables yard when June came to Avonlea. Gilbert Blythe's card lay beside it.

Anne wondered why Gilbert should have sent her flowers for Convocation. She had seen very little of him during the past winter. He had come to Patty's Place only one Friday evening since the Christmas holidays, and they rarely met elsewhere. She knew he was studying very hard, aiming at High Honors and the Cooper Prize, and he took little part in the social doings of Redmond. Anne's own winter had been quite gay socially. She had seen a good deal of the Gardners; she and Dorothy were very intimate; college circles expected the announcement of her engagement to Roy any day. Anne expected it herself. Yet just before she left Patty's Place for Convocation she flung Roy's violets aside and put Gilbert's lilies-of-the-valley in their place. She could not have told why she did it. Somehow, old Avonlea days and dreams and friendships seemed very close to her in this attainment of her long-cherished ambitions. She and Gilbert had once pictured out merrily the day on which they should be capped and gowned graduates in Arts. The wonderful day had come and Roy's violets had no place in it. Only her old friend's flowers seemed to belong to this fruition of old-blossoming hopes which he had once shared.

For years this day had beckoned and allured to her; but when it came the one single, keen, abiding memory it left with her was not that of the breathless moment when the stately president of Redmond gave her cap and diploma and hailed her B.A.; it was not of the flash in Gilbert's eyes when he saw her lilies, nor the puzzled pained glance Roy gave her as he passed her on the platform. It was not of Aline Gardner's condescending congratulations, or Dorothy's ardent, impulsive good wishes. It was of one strange, unaccountable pang that spoiled this long-expected day for her and left in it a certain faint but enduring flavor of bitterness.

The Arts graduates gave a graduation dance that night. When Anne dressed for it she tossed aside the pearl beads she usually wore and took from her trunk the small box that had come to Green Gables on Christmas day. In it was a thread-like gold chain with a tiny pink enamel heart as a pendant. On the accompanying card was written, "With all good wishes from your old chum, Gilbert." Anne, laughing over the memory the enamel heart conjured up the fatal day when Gilbert had called her "Carrots" and vainly tried to make his peace with a pink candy heart, had written him a nice little note of thanks. But she had never worn the trinket. Tonight she fastened it about her white throat with a dreamy smile.

She and Phil walked to Redmond together. Anne walked in silence; Phil chattered of many things. Suddenly she said,

"I heard today that Gilbert Blythe's engagement to Christine Stuart was to be announced as soon as Convocation was over. Did you hear anything of it?"

"No," said Anne.

"I think it's true," said Phil lightly.

Anne did not speak. In the darkness she felt her face burning. She slipped her hand inside her collar and caught at the gold chain. One energetic twist and it gave way. Anne thrust the broken trinket into her pocket. Her hands were trembling and her eyes were smarting.

But she was the gayest of all the gay revellers that night, and told Gilbert unregretfully that her card was full when he came to ask her for a dance. Afterwards, when she sat with the girls before the dying embers at Patty's Place, removing the spring chilliness from their satin skins, none chatted more blithely than she of the day's events.

"Moody Spurgeon MacPherson called here tonight after you left," said Aunt Jamesina, who had sat up to keep the fire on. "He didn't know about the graduation dance. That boy ought to sleep with a rubber band around his head to train his ears not to stick out. I had a beau once who did that and it improved him immensely. It was I who suggested it to him and he took my advice, but he never forgave me for it."

"Moody Spurgeon is a very serious young man," yawned Priscilla. "He is concerned, with graver matters than his ears. He is going to be a minister, you know."

"Well, I suppose the Lord doesn't regard the ears of a man," said Aunt Jamesina gravely, dropping all further criticism of Moody Spurgeon. Aunt Jamesina had a proper respect for the cloth even in the case of an unfledged parson.

38

False Dawn

"Just imagine—this night week I'll be in Avonlea—delightful thought!" said Anne, bending over the box in which she was packing Mrs. Rachel Lynde's quilts. "But just imagine—this night week I'll be gone forever from Patty's Place—horrible thought!"

"I wonder if the ghost of all our laughter will echo through the maiden dreams of Miss Patty and Miss Maria," speculated Phil.

Miss Patty and Miss Maria were coming home, after having trotted over most of the habitable globe.

"We'll be back the second week in May," wrote Miss Patty. "I expect Patty's Place will seem rather small after the Hall of the Kings at Karnak, but I never did like big places to live in. And I'll be glad enough to be home again. When you start traveling late in life you're apt to do too much of it because you know you haven't much time left, and it's a thing that grows on you. I'm afraid Maria will never be contented again."

"I shall leave here my fancies and dreams to bless the next comer," said Anne, looking around the blue room wistfully—her pretty blue room where she had spent three such happy years. She had knelt at its window to pray and had bent from it to watch the sunset behind the pines. She had heard the autumn raindrops beating against it and had welcomed the spring robins at its sill. She wondered if old dreams could haunt rooms—if, when one left forever the room where she had joyed and suffered and laughed and wept, something of her, intangible and invisible, yet nonetheless real, did not remain behind like a voiceful memory.

"I think," said Phil, "that a room where one dreams and grieves and rejoices and *lives* becomes inseparably connected with those processes and acquires a personality of its own. I am sure if I came into this room fifty years from now it would say 'Anne, Anne' to me. What nice times we've had here, honey! What chats and jokes and good chummy jamborees! Oh, dear me! I'm to marry Jo in June and I know I will be rapturously happy. But just now I feel as if I wanted this lovely Redmond life to go on forever."

"I'm unreasonable enough just now to wish that, too," admitted Anne. "No matter what deeper joys may come to us later on we'll never again have just the same delightful, irresponsible existence we've had here. It's over forever, Phil."

"What are you going to do with Rusty?" asked Phil, as that privileged pussy padded into the room.

"*I* am going to take him home with me and Joseph and the Sarah-cat," announced Aunt Jamesina, following Rusty. "It would be a shame to separate those cats now that they have learned to live together. It's a hard lesson for cats and humans to learn."

"I'm sorry to part with Rusty," said Anne regretfully, "but it would be no use to take him to Green Gables. Marilla detests cats, and Davy would tease his life out. Besides, I don't suppose I'll be home very long. I've been offered the principalship of the Summerside High School."

"Are you going to accept it?" asked Phil.

"I—I haven't decided yet," answered Anne, with a confused flush.

Phil nodded understandingly. Naturally Anne's plans could not be settled until Roy had spoken. He would soon—there was no doubt of that. And there was no doubt that Anne would say "yes" when he said "Will you, please?" Anne herself regarded the state of affairs with a seldom-ruffled complacency. She was deeply in love with Roy. True, it was not just what she had imagined love to be. But was anything in life, Anne asked herself wearily, like one's imagination of it? It was the old diamond disillusion of childhood repeated—the same disappointment she had felt when she had first seen the chill sparkle instead of the purple splendor she had anticipated. "That's not my idea of a diamond," she had said. But Roy was a dear fellow and they would be very happy together, even if some indefinable zest was missing out of life. When Roy came down that evening and asked Anne to walk in the park every one at Patty's Place knew what he had come to say; and every one knew, or thought they knew, what Anne's answer would be.

"Anne is a very fortunate girl," said Aunt Jamesina.

"I suppose so," said Stella, shrugging her shoulders. "Roy is a nice fellow and all that. But there's really nothing in him."

"That sounds very like a jealous remark, Stella Maynard," said Aunt Jamesina rebukingly.

"It does—but I am not jealous," said Stella calmly. "I love Anne and I like Roy. Everybody says she is making a brilliant match, and even Mrs. Gardner thinks her charming now. It all sounds as if it were made in heaven, but I have my doubts. Make the most of that, Aunt Jamesina."

Roy asked Anne to marry him in the little pavilion on the harbor shore where they had talked on the rainy day of their first meeting. Anne thought it very romantic that he should have chosen that spot. And his proposal was as beautifully worded as if he had copied it, as one of Ruby Gillis' lovers had done, out of a Deportment of Courtship and Marriage. The whole effect was quite flawless. And it was also sincere. There was no doubt that Roy meant what he said. There was no false note to jar the symphony. Anne felt that she ought to be thrilling from head to foot. But she wasn't; she was horribly cool. When Roy paused for his answer she opened her lips to say her fateful yes.

And then—she found herself trembling as if she were reeling back from a precipice. To her came one of those moments when we realize, as by a blinding flash of illumination, more than all our previous years have taught us. She pulled her hand from Roy's.

"Oh, I can't marry you—I can't—I can't," she cried, wildly.

Roy turned pale—and also looked rather foolish. He had—small blame to him—felt very sure.

"What do you mean?" he stammered.

"I mean that I can't marry you," repeated Anne desperately. "I thought I could—but I can't."

"Why can't you?" Roy asked more calmly.

"Because—I don't care enough for you."

A crimson streak came into Roy's face.

"So you've just been amusing yourself these two years?" he said slowly.

"No, no, I haven't," gasped poor Anne. Oh, how could she explain? She *couldn't* explain. There are some things that cannot be explained. "I did think I cared—truly I did—but I know now I don't."

"You have ruined my life," said Roy bitterly.

"Forgive me," pleaded Anne miserably, with hot cheeks and stinging eyes.

Roy turned away and stood for a few minutes looking out seaward. When he came back to Anne, he was very pale again.

"You can give me no hope?" he said.

Anne shook her head mutely.

"Then—good-bye," said Roy. "I can't understand it—I can't believe you are not the woman I've believed you to be. But reproaches are idle between us. You are the only woman I can ever love. I thank you for your friendship, at least. Good-bye, Anne."

"Good-bye," faltered Anne. When Roy had gone she sat for a long time in the pavilion, watching a white mist creeping subtly and remorselessly landward up the harbor. It was her hour of humiliation and self-contempt and shame. Their waves went over her. And yet, underneath it all, was a queer sense of recovered freedom.

She slipped into Patty's Place in the dusk and escaped to her room. But Phil was there on the window seat.

"Wait," said Anne, flushing to anticipate the scene. "Wait till you hear what I have to say. Phil, Roy asked me to marry him—and I refused."

"You—you *refused* him?" said Phil blankly.

"Yes."

"Anne Shirley, are you in your senses?"

"I think so," said Anne wearily. "Oh, Phil, don't scold me. You don't understand."

"I certainly don't understand. You've encouraged Roy Gardner in every way for two years—and now you tell me you've refused him. Then you've just been flirting scandalously with him. Anne, I couldn't have believed it of *you*."

"I *wasn't* flirting with him—I honestly thought I cared up to the last minute—and then—well, I just knew I *never* could marry him."

"I suppose," said Phil cruelly, "that you intended to marry him for his money, and then your better self rose up and prevented you."

"I *didn't*. I never thought about his money. Oh, I can't explain it to you any more than I could to him."

"Well, I certainly think you have treated Roy shamefully," said Phil in exasperation. "He's handsome and clever and rich and good. What more do you want?"

"I want some one who *belongs* in my life. He doesn't. I was swept off my feet at first by his good looks and knack of paying romantic compliments; and later on I thought I *must* be in love because he was my dark-eyed ideal."

"I am bad enough for not knowing my own mind, but you are worse," said Phil.

"I *do* know my own mind," protested Anne. "The trouble is, my mind changes and then I have to get acquainted with it all over again."

"Well, I suppose there is no use in saying anything to you."

"There is no need, Phil. I'm in the dust. This has spoiled everything backwards. I can never think of Redmond days without recalling the humiliation of this evening. Roy despises me—and you despise me—and I despise myself."

"You poor darling," said Phil, melting. "Just come here and let me comfort you. I've no right to scold you. I'd have married Alec or Alonzo if I hadn't met Jo. Oh, Anne, things are so mixed-up in real life. They aren't clear-cut and trimmed off, as they are in novels."

"I hope that *no* one will ever again ask me to marry him as long as I live," sobbed poor Anne, devoutly believing that she meant it.

39

Deals with Weddings

nne felt that life partook of the nature of an anticlimax during the first few weeks after her return to Green Gables. She missed the merry comradeship of Patty's Place. She had dreamed some brilliant dreams during the past winter and now they lay in the dust around her. In her present mood of self-disgust, she could not immediately begin dreaming again. And she discovered that, while solitude with dreams is glorious, solitude without them has few charms.

She had not seen Roy again after their painful parting in the park pavilion; but Dorothy came to see her before she left Kingsport.

"I'm awfully sorry you won't marry Roy," she said. "I did want you for a sister. But you are quite right. He would bore you to death. I love him, and he is a dear sweet boy, but really he isn't a bit interesting. He looks as if he ought to be, but he isn't."

"This won't spoil *our* friendship, will it, Dorothy?" Anne had asked wistfully.

"No, indeed. You're too good to lose. If I can't have you for a sister I mean to keep, you as a chum anyway. And don't fret over Roy. He *is* feeling terribly just now—I have to listen to his outpourings every day—but he'll get over it. He always does."

"Oh—*always?*" said Anne with a slight change of voice. "So he has 'got over it' before?"

"Dear me, yes," said Dorothy frankly. "Twice before. And he raved to me just the same both times. Not that the others actually refused him—they simply announced their engagements to some one else. Of course, when he met you he vowed to me that he had never really loved before—that the previous affairs had been merely boyish fancies. But

I don't think you need worry."

Anne decided not to worry. Her feelings were a mixture of relief and resentment. Roy had certainly told her she was the only one he had ever loved. No doubt he believed it. But it was a comfort to feel that she had not, in all likelihood, ruined his life. There were other goddesses, and Roy, according to Dorothy, must needs be worshipping at some shrine. Nevertheless, life was stripped of several more illusions, and Anne began to think drearily that it seemed rather bare.

She came down from the porch gable on the evening of her return with a sorrowful face.

"What has happened to the old Snow Queen, Marilla?"

"Oh, I knew you'd feel bad over that," said Marilla. "I felt bad myself. That tree was there ever since I was a young girl. It blew down in the big gale we had in March. It was rotten at the core."

"I'll miss it so," grieved Anne. "The porch gable doesn't seem the same room without it. I'll never look from its window again without a sense of loss. And oh, I never came home to Green Gables before that Diana wasn't here to welcome me."

"Diana has something else to think of just now," said Mrs. Lynde significantly.

"Well, tell me all the Avonlea news," said Anne, sitting down on the porch steps, where the evening sunshine fell over her hair in a fine golden rain.

"There isn't much news except what we've wrote you," said Mrs. Lynde. "I suppose you haven't heard that Simon Fletcher broke his leg last week. It's a great thing for his family. They're getting a hundred things done that they've always wanted to do but couldn't as long as he was about, the old crank."

"He came of an aggravating family," remarked Marilla.

"Aggravating? Well, rather! His mother used to get up in prayer-meeting and tell all her children's shortcomings and ask prayers for them. 'Course it made them mad, and worse than ever."

"You haven't told Anne the news about Jane," suggested Marilla.

"Oh, Jane," sniffed Mrs. Lynde. "Well," she conceded grudgingly, "Jane Andrews is home from the West—came last week—and she's going to be married to a Winnipeg millionaire. You may be sure Mrs. Harmon lost no time in telling it far and wide."

"Dear old Jane—I'm so glad," said Anne heartily. "She deserves the good things of life."

"Oh, I ain't saying anything against Jane. She's a nice enough girl. But she isn't in the millionaire class, and you'll find there's not much to recommend that man but his money, that's what. Mrs. Harmon says he's an Englishman who has made money in mines but *I* believe he'll turn out to be a Yankee. He certainly must have money, for he has just showered Jane with jewelry. Her engagement ring is a diamond cluster so big that it looks like a plaster on Jane's fat paw."

Mrs. Lynde could not keep some bitterness out of her tone. Here was Jane Andrews, that plain little plodder, engaged to a millionaire, while Anne, it seemed, was not yet bespoken by any one, rich or poor. And Mrs. Harmon Andrews did brag insufferably.

"What has Gilbert Blythe been doing to himself at college?" asked Marilla. "I saw him when he came home last week, and he is so pale and thin I hardly knew him."

"He studied very hard last winter," said Anne. "You know he took High Honors in Classics and the Cooper Prize. It hasn't been taken for five years! So I think he's rather run down. We're all a little tired."

"Anyhow, you're a B.A. and Jane Andrews isn't and never will be," said Mrs. Lynde, with gloomy satisfaction.

A few evenings later Anne went down to see Jane, but the latter was away in Charlottetown—"getting sewing done," Mrs. Harmon informed Anne proudly. "Of course an Avonlea dressmaker wouldn't do for Jane under the circumstances."

"I've heard something very nice about Jane," said Anne.

"Yes, Jane has done pretty well, even if she isn't a B.A.," said Mrs. Harmon, with a slight toss of her head. "Mr. Inglis is worth millions, and they're going to Europe on their wedding tour. When they come back they'll live in a perfect mansion of marble in Winnipeg. Jane has only one trouble—she can cook so well and her husband won't let her cook. He is so rich he hires his cooking done. They're going to keep a cook and two other maids and a coachman and a man-of-all-work.

But what about *you*, Anne? I don't hear anything of your being married, after all your college-going."

"Oh," laughed Anne, "I am going to be an old maid. I really can't find any one to suit me."

It was rather wicked of her. She deliberately meant to remind Mrs. Andrews that if she became an old maid it was not because she had not had at least one chance of marriage. But Mrs. Harmon took swift revenge.

"Well, the over-particular girls generally get left, I notice. And what's this I hear about Gilbert Blythe being engaged to a Miss Stuart? Charlie Sloane tells me she is perfectly beautiful. Is it true?"

"I don't know if it is true that he is engaged to Miss Stuart," replied Anne, with Spartan composure, "but it is certainly true that she is very lovely."

"I once thought you and Gilbert would have made a match of it," said Mrs. Harmon. "If you don't take care, Anne, all your beaux will slip through your fingers."

Anne decided not to continue her duel with Mrs. Harmon. You could not fence with an antagonist who met rapier thrust with blow of battle axe.

"Since Jane is away," she said, rising haughtily, "I don't think I can stay longer this morning. I'll come down when she comes home."

"Do," said Mrs. Harmon effusively. "Jane isn't a bit proud. She just means to associate with her old friends the same as ever. She'll be real glad to see you."

Jane's millionaire arrived the last of May and carried her off in a blaze of splendor. Mrs. Lynde was spitefully gratified to find that Mr. Inglis was every day of forty, and short and thin and grayish. Mrs. Lynde did not spare him in her enumeration of his shortcomings, you may be sure.

"It will take all his gold to gild a pill like him, that's what," said Mrs. Rachel solemnly.

"He looks kind and good-hearted," said Anne loyally, "and I'm sure he thinks the world of Jane."

"Humph!" said Mrs. Rachel.

Phil Gordon was married the next week and Anne went over to Bolingbroke to be her bridesmaid. Phil made a dainty fairy of a bride, and the Rev. Jo was so radiant in his happiness that nobody thought him plain.

"We're going for a lovers' saunter through the land of Evangeline," said Phil, "and then we'll settle down on Patterson Street. Mother thinks it is terrible—she thinks Jo might at least take a church in a decent place. But the wilderness of the Patterson slums will blossom like the rose for me if Jo is there. Oh, Anne, I'm so happy my heart aches with it."

Anne was always glad in the happiness of her friends; but it is sometimes a little lonely to be surrounded everywhere by a happiness that is not your own. And it was just the same when she went back to Avonlea. This time it was Diana who was bathed in the wonderful glory that comes to a woman when her first-born is laid beside her. Anne looked at the white young mother with a certain awe that had never entered into her feelings for Diana before. Could this pale woman with the rapture in her eyes be the little black-curled, rosy-cheeked Diana she had played with in vanished schooldays? It gave her a queer desolate feeling that she herself somehow belonged only in those past years and had no business in the present at all.

"Isn't he perfectly beautiful?" said Diana proudly.

The little fat fellow was absurdly like Fred—just as round, just as red. Anne really could not say conscientiously that she thought him beautiful, but she vowed sincerely that he was sweet and kissable and altogether delightful.

"Before he came I wanted a girl, so that I could call her *Anne*," said Diana. "But now that little Fred is here I wouldn't exchange him for a million girls. He just *couldn't* have been anything but his own precious self."

"'Every little baby is the sweetest and the best,'" quoted Mrs. Allan gaily. "If little Anne *had* come you'd have felt just the same about her."

Mrs. Allan was visiting in Avonlea, for the first time since leaving it. She was as gay and sweet and sympathetic as ever. Her old girl friends had welcomed her back rapturously. The reigning minister's wife was an estimable lady, but she was not exactly a kindred spirit.

"I can hardly wait till he gets old enough to talk," sighed Diana. "I just long to hear him say 'mother.' And oh, I'm determined that his first memory of me shall be a nice one. The first memory I have of my mother is of her slapping me for something I had done. I am sure I deserved it, and mother was always a good mother and I love her dearly. But I do wish my first memory of her was nicer."

"I have just one memory of my mother and it is the sweetest of all my memories," said Mrs. Allan. "I was five years old, and I had been allowed to go to school one day with my two older sisters. When school came out my sisters went home in different groups, each supposing I was with the other. Instead I had run off with a little girl I had played with at recess. We went to her home, which was near the school, and began making mud pies. We were having a glorious time when my older sister arrived, breathless and angry.

"'You naughty girl,' she cried, snatching my reluctant hand and dragging me along with her. 'Come home this minute. Oh, you're going to catch it! Mother is awful cross. She is going to give you a good whipping.'

"I had never been whipped. Dread and terror filled my poor little heart. I have never been so miserable in my life as I was on that walk home. I had not meant to be naughty. Phemy Cameron had asked me to go home with her and I had not known it was wrong to go. And now I was to be whipped for it. When we got home my sister dragged me into the kitchen where mother was sitting by the fire in the twilight. My poor wee legs were trembling so that I could hardly stand. And mother—mother just took me up in her arms, without one word of rebuke or harshness, kissed me and held me close to her heart. 'I was so frightened you were lost, darling,' she said tenderly. I could see the love shining in her eyes as she looked down on me. She never scolded or reproached me for what I had done—only told me I must never go away again without asking permission. She died very soon afterwards. That is the only memory I have of her. Isn't it a beautiful one?"

Anne felt lonelier than ever as she walked home, going by way of the Birch Path and Willowmere. She had not walked that way for many moons. It was a darkly-purple bloomy night. The air was heavy with blossom fragrance—almost too heavy. The cloyed senses recoiled from it as from an overfull cup. The birches of the path had grown from the fairy saplings of old to big trees. Everything had changed. Anne felt that she would be glad when the summer was over and she was away at work again. Perhaps life would not seem so empty then.

> "'I've tried the world—it wears no more
> The coloring of romance it wore,'"

sighed Anne—and was straightway much comforted by the romance in the idea of the world being denuded of romance!

40

A Book of Revelation

he Irvings came back to Echo Lodge for the summer, and Anne spent a happy three weeks there in July. Miss Lavendar had not changed; Charlotta the Fourth was a very grown-up young lady now, but still adored Anne sincerely.

"When all's said and done, Miss Shirley, ma'am, I haven't seen any one in Boston that's equal to you," she said frankly.

Paul was almost grown-up, too. He was sixteen, his chestnut curls had given place to close-cropped brown locks, and he was more interested in football than fairies. But the bond between him and his old teacher still held. Kindred spirits alone do not change with changing years.

It was a wet, bleak, cruel evening in July when Anne came back to Green Gables. One of the fierce summer storms which sometimes sweep over the gulf was ravaging the sea. As Anne came in the first raindrops dashed against the panes.

"Was that Paul who brought you home?" asked Marilla. "Why didn't you make him stay all night. It's going to be a wild evening."

"He'll reach Echo Lodge before the rain gets very heavy, I think. Anyway, he wanted to go back tonight. Well, I've had a splendid visit, but I'm glad to see you dear folks again. 'East, west, hame's best.' Davy, have you been growing again lately?"

"I've growed a whole inch since you left," said Davy proudly. "I'm as tall as Milty Boulter now. Ain't I glad. He'll have to stop crowing about being bigger. Say, Anne, did you know that Gilbert Blythe is dying?"

Anne stood quite silent and motionless, looking at Davy. Her face had gone so white that Marilla thought she was going to faint.

"Davy, hold your tongue," said Mrs. Rachel angrily. "Anne, don't look like that—don't *look like that!* We didn't mean to tell you so suddenly."

"Is—it—true?" asked Anne in a voice that was not hers.

"Gilbert is very ill," said Mrs. Lynde gravely. "He took down with typhoid fever just after you left for Echo Lodge. Did you never hear of it?"

"No," said that unknown voice.

"It was a very bad case from the start. The doctor said he'd been terribly run down. They've a trained nurse and everything's been done. *Don't* look like that, Anne. While there's life there's hope."

"Mr. Harrison was here this evening and he said they had no hope of him," reiterated Davy.

Marilla, looking old and worn and tired, got up and marched Davy grimly out of the kitchen.

"Oh, *don't* look so, dear," said Mrs. Rachel, putting her kind old arms about the pallid girl. "I haven't given up hope, indeed I haven't. He's got the Blythe constitution in his favor, that's what."

Anne gently put Mrs. Lynde's arms away from her, walked blindly across the kitchen, through the hall, up the stairs to her old room. At its window she knelt down, staring out unseeingly. It was very dark. The rain was beating down over the shivering fields. The Haunted Wood was full of the groans of mighty trees wrung in the tempest, and the air throbbed with the thunderous crash of billows on the distant shore. And Gilbert was dying!

There is a book of Revelation in every one's life, as there is in the Bible. Anne read hers that bitter night, as she kept her agonized vigil through the hours of storm and darkness. She loved Gilbert—had always loved him! She knew that now. She knew that she could no more cast him out of her life without agony than she could have cut off her right hand and cast it from her. And the knowledge had come too late—too late even for the bitter solace of being with him at the last. If she had not been so blind—so foolish—she would have had the right to go to him now. But he would never know that she loved him—he would go away from this life thinking that she did not care. Oh, the black years of emptiness stretching before her! She could not live through them—she could not! She cowered down by her window and wished, for the first time in her gay young life, that she could die, too. If Gilbert went away from her, without one word or sign or message, she could not live. Nothing was of any value without him. She belonged to him and he to her. In her hour of supreme agony she had no doubt of that. He did not love Christine Stuart—never had loved Christine Stuart. Oh, what a fool she had been not to realize what the bond was that had held her to Gilbert—to think that the flattered fancy she had felt for Roy Gardner had been love. And now she must pay for her folly as for a crime.

Mrs. Lynde and Marilla crept to her door before they went to bed, shook their heads doubtfully at each other over the silence, and went away. The storm raged all night, but when the dawn came it was spent. Anne saw a fairy fringe of light on the skirts of darkness. Soon the eastern hilltops had a fire-shot ruby rim. The clouds rolled themselves away into great, soft, white masses on the horizon; the sky gleamed blue and silvery. A hush fell over the world.

Anne rose from her knees and crept downstairs. The freshness of the rain-wind blew against her white face as she went out into the yard, and cooled her dry, burning eyes. A merry rollicking whistle was lilting up the lane. A moment later Pacifique Buote came in sight.

Anne's physical strength suddenly failed her. If she had not clutched at a low willow bough she would have fallen. Pacifique was George Fletcher's hired man, and George Fletcher lived next door to the Blythes. Mrs. Fletcher was Gilbert's aunt. Pacifique would know if—if—Pacifique would know what there was to be known.

Pacifique strode sturdily on along the red lane, whistling. He did not see Anne. She made three futile attempts to call him. He was almost past before she succeeded in making her quivering lips call, "Pacifique!"

Pacifique turned with a grin and a cheerful good morning.

"Pacifique," said Anne faintly, "did you come from George Fletcher's this morning?"

"Sure," said Pacifique amiably. "I got de word las' night dat my fader, he was seeck. It was so stormy dat I couldn't go den, so I start vair early dis mornin'. I'm goin' troo de woods for short cut."

"Did you hear how Gilbert Blythe was this morning?"

Anne's desperation drove her to the question. Even the worst would be more endurable than this hideous suspense.

"He's better," said Pacifique. "He got de turn las' night. De doctor say he'll be all right now dis soon while. Had close shave, dough! Dat boy, he jus' keel himself at colloge. Well, I mus' hurry. De old man, he'll be in hurry to see me."

Pacifique resumed his walk and his whistle. Anne gazed after him with eyes where joy was driving out the strained anguish of the night. He was a very lank, very ragged, very homely youth. But in her sight he was as beautiful as those who bring good tidings on the mountains. Never, as long as she lived, would Anne see Pacifique's brown, round, black-eyed face without a warm remembrance of the moment when he had given to her the oil of joy for mourning.

Long after Pacifique's gay whistle had faded into the phantom of music and then into silence far up under the maples of Lover's Lane Anne stood under the willows, tasting the poignant sweetness of life when some great dread has been removed from it. The morning was a cup filled with mist and glamor. In the corner near her was a rich surprise of new-blown, crystal-dewed roses. The hills and trickles of song from the birds in the big tree above her seemed in perfect accord with her mood. A sentence from a very old, very true, very wonderful Book came to her lips,

"Weeping may endure for a night but joy cometh in the morning."

41

Love Takes Up the Glass of Time

've come up to ask you to go for one of our old-time rambles through September woods and 'over hills where spices grow,' this afternoon," said Gilbert, coming suddenly around the porch corner. "Suppose we visit Hester Gray's garden."

Anne, sitting on the stone step with her lap full of a pale, filmy, green stuff, looked up rather blankly.

"Oh, I wish I could," she said slowly, "but I really can't, Gilbert. I'm going to Alice Penhallow's wedding this evening, you know. I've got to do something to this dress, and by the time it's finished I'll have to get ready. I'm so sorry. I'd love to go."

"Well, can you go tomorrow afternoon, then?" asked Gilbert, apparently not much disappointed.

"Yes, I think so."

"In that case I shall hie me home at once to do something I should otherwise have to do tomorrow. So Alice Penhallow is to be married tonight. Three weddings for you in one summer, Anne—Phil's, Alice's, and Jane's. I'll never forgive Jane for not inviting me to her wedding."

"You really can't blame her when you think of the tremendous Andrews connection who had to be invited. The house could hardly hold them all. I was only bidden by grace of being Jane's old chum— at least on Jane's part. I think Mrs. Harmon's motive for inviting me was to let me see Jane's surpassing gorgeousness."

"Is it true that she wore so many diamonds that you couldn't tell where the diamonds left off and Jane began?"

Anne laughed.

"She certainly wore a good many. What with all the diamonds and white satin and tulle and lace and roses and orange blossoms, prim little Jane was almost lost to sight. But she was *very* happy, and so was Mr. Inglis—and so was Mrs. Harmon."

"Is that the dress you're going to wear tonight?" asked Gilbert, looking down at the fluffs and frills.

"Yes. Isn't it pretty? And I shall wear starflowers in my hair. The Haunted Wood is full of them this summer."

Gilbert had a sudden vision of Anne, arrayed in a frilly green gown, with the virginal curves of arms and throat slipping out of it, and white stars shining against the coils of her ruddy hair. The vision made him catch his breath. But he turned lightly away.

"Well, I'll be up tomorrow. Hope you'll have a nice time tonight."

Anne looked after him as he strode away, and sighed. Gilbert was friendly—very friendly—far too friendly. He had come quite often to Green Gables after his recovery, and something of their old comradeship had returned. But Anne no longer found it satisfying. The rose of love made the blossom of friendship pale and scentless by contrast. And Anne had again begun to doubt if Gilbert now felt anything for her but friendship. In the common light of common day her radiant certainty of that rapt morning had faded. She was haunted by a miserable fear that her mistake could never be rectified. It was quite likely that it was Christine whom Gilbert loved after all. Perhaps he was even engaged to her. Anne tried to put all unsettling hopes out of her heart, and reconcile herself to a future where work and ambition must take the place of love. She could do good, if not noble, work as a teacher; and the success her little sketches were beginning to meet with in certain editorial sanctums augured well for her budding literary dreams. But—but—Anne picked up her green dress and sighed again.

When Gilbert came the next afternoon he found Anne waiting for him, fresh as the dawn and fair as a star, after all the gaiety of the preceding night. She wore a green dress—not the one she had worn to the wedding, but an old one which Gilbert had told her at a Redmond reception he liked especially. It was just the shade of green that brought out the rich tints of her hair, and the starry gray of her eyes and the iris-like delicacy of her skin. Gilbert, glancing at her sideways as they walked along a shadowy woodpath, thought she had never looked so lovely. Anne, glancing sideways at Gilbert, now and then, thought how much older he looked since his illness. It was as if he had put boyhood behind him forever.

The day was beautiful and the way was beautiful. Anne was almost sorry when they reached Hester Gray's garden, and sat down on the old bench. But it was beautiful there, too—as beautiful as it had been on the far-away day of the Golden Picnic, when Diana and Jane and Priscilla and she had found it. Then it had been lovely with narcissus and violets; now golden rod had kindled its fairy torches in the corners and asters dotted it bluely. The call of the brook came up through the woods from the valley of birches with all its old allurement; the mellow air was full of the purr of the sea; beyond were fields rimmed by fences bleached silvery gray in the suns of many summers, and long hills scarfed with the shadows of autumnal clouds; with the blowing of the west wind old dreams returned.

"I think," said Anne softly, "that 'the land where dreams come true' is in the blue haze yonder, over that little valley."

"Have you any unfulfilled dreams, Anne?" asked Gilbert.

Something in his tone—something she had not heard since that miserable evening in the orchard at Patty's Place—made Anne's heart beat wildly. But she made answer lightly.

"Of course. Everybody has. It wouldn't do for us to have all our dreams fulfilled. We would be as good as dead if we had nothing left to dream about. What a delicious aroma that low-descending sun is extracting from the asters and ferns. I wish we could *see* perfumes as well as smell them. I'm sure they would be very beautiful."

Gilbert was not to be thus sidetracked.

"I have a dream," he said slowly. "I persist in dreaming it, although it has often seemed to me that it could never come true. I dream of a home with a hearth-fire in it, a cat and dog, the footsteps of friends— and *you!*"

Anne wanted to speak but she could find no words. Happiness was breaking over her like a wave. It almost frightened her.

"I asked you a question over two years ago, Anne. If I ask it again today will you give me a different answer?"

Still Anne could not speak. But she lifted her eyes, shining with all the love-rapture of countless generations, and looked into his for a moment. He wanted no other answer.

They lingered in the old garden until twilight, sweet as dusk in Eden must have been, crept over it. There was so much to talk over and recall—things said and done and heard and thought and felt and misunderstood.

"I thought you loved Christine Stuart," Anne told him, as reproachfully as if she had not given him every reason to suppose that she loved Roy Gardner.

Gilbert laughed boyishly.

"Christine was engaged to somebody in her home town. I knew it and she knew I knew it. When her brother graduated he told me his sister was coming to Kingsport the next winter to take music, and asked me if I would look after her a bit, as she knew no one and would be very lonely. So I did. And then I liked Christine for her own sake. She is one of the nicest girls I've ever known. I knew college gossip credited us with being in love with each other. I didn't care. Nothing mattered much to me for a time there, after you told me you could never love me, Anne. There was nobody else—there never could be anybody else for me but you. I've loved you ever since that day you broke your slate over my head in school."

"I don't see how you could keep on loving me when I was such a little fool," said Anne.

"Well, I tried to stop," said Gilbert frankly, "not because I thought you what you call yourself, but because I felt sure there was no chance for me after Gardner came on the scene. But I couldn't—and I can't tell you, either, what it's meant to me these two years to believe you were going to marry him, and be told every week by some busybody that your engagement was on the point of being announced. I believed it until one blessed day when I was sitting up after the fever. I got a letter from Phil Gordon—Phil Blake, rather—in which she told me there was really nothing between you and Roy, and advised me to 'try again.' Well, the doctor was amazed at my rapid recovery after that."

Anne laughed—then shivered.

"I can never forget the night I thought you were dying, Gilbert. Oh, I knew—I *knew* then—and I thought it was too late."

"But it wasn't, sweetheart. Oh, Anne, this makes up for everything, doesn't it? Let's resolve to keep this day sacred to perfect beauty all our lives for the gift it has given us."

"It's the birthday of our happiness," said Anne softly. "I've always loved this old garden of Hester Gray's, and now it will be dearer than ever."

"But I'll have to ask you to wait a long time, Anne," said Gilbert sadly. "It will be three years before I'll finish my medical course. And even then there will be no diamond sunbursts and marble halls."

Anne laughed.

"I don't want sunbursts and marble halls. I just want *you*. You see I'm quite as shameless as Phil about it. Sunbursts and marble halls may be all very well, but there is more 'scope for imagination' without them. And as for the waiting, that doesn't matter. We'll just be happy, waiting and working for each other—and dreaming. Oh, dreams will be very sweet now.

Gilbert drew her close to him and kissed her. Then they walked home together in the dusk, crowned king and queen in the bridal realm of love, along winding paths fringed with the sweetest flowers that ever bloomed, and over haunted meadows where winds of hope and memory blew.

A Note About the Author

Lucy Maud Montgomery (1874–1942), a Canadian national treasure, grew up on Prince Edward Island, where her stories are set. She wrote *Anne of Green Gables* in the evenings while working as a reporter for the *Halifax Daily Echo*. Her manuscript was rejected by four publishers before she revised it and a Boston publisher accepted it for publication in 1908. It has remained in print ever since. *Anne of Avonlea* was first published in 1909 and *Anne of the Island* followed in 1915. In 1911 Lucy Maud Montgomery married Ewan Macdonald and they had two sons. She was made an Officer of the Order of the British Empire in 1935. She died in Toronto in 1942.